WEEKEND
WITH THE RABBI

WEEKEND WITH THE RABBI

Friday the Rabbi Slept Late
•
Saturday the Rabbi Went Hungry
•
Sunday the Rabbi Stayed Home

by Harry Kemelman

NELSON DOUBLEDAY, Inc.   Garden City, New York

FRIDAY
THE RABBI
SLEPT LATE

To My Father and Mother

1

They sat in the chapel and waited. They were still only nine, and they were waiting for the tenth so that they could begin morning prayers. The elderly president of the congregation, Jacob Wasserman, was wearing his phylacteries, and the young rabbi, David Small, who had just arrived, was putting his on. He had withdrawn his left arm from his jacket and rolled up his shirt sleeve to the armpit. Placing the little black box with its quotation from the Scriptures on the upper arm—next to the heart—he bound the attached strap seven times around his forearm, and then thrice around his palm to form the first letter of the Divine Name, and finally around his middle finger as a ring of spiritual betrothal to God. This, together with the headpiece which he now placed on his forehead, was in literal response to the biblical injunction: "Thou shalt bind them [the words of God] for a sign upon thine hand, and they shall be for a frontlet between thine eyes."

The others, who were dressed in silken-fringed prayer shawls and black skullcaps, sat around in small groups talking, glancing idly through their prayer books, occasionally checking their watches against the round clock on the wall.

The rabbi, now prepared for morning service, strolled up and down the center aisle, not impatiently, but like a man who has arrived early at the railroad station. Snatches of conversation reached him: talk about business, about family and children, about vacation plans, about the chances of the Red Sox. It was hardly the proper conversation for men waiting to pray, he thought, and then immediately rebuked himself. Was it not also a sin to be too devout? Was not man expected to enjoy the good things of this life? the pleasures of family? of work—and of resting from work? He was still very young, not quite thirty, and introspective, so that he could not help raising questions, and then questioning the questions.

Mr. Wasserman had left the room and now returned. "I just called Abe Reich. He said he'd be down in about ten minutes."

Ben Schwarz, a short, plumpish, middle-aged man, got up abruptly. "That does it for me," he muttered. "If I have to be beholden to that sonofabitch Reich to make up a minyan, I'll do my praying at home."

Wasserman hurried over and halted him at the end of the aisle. "Surely you're not going now, Ben? That will leave us only nine, even when Reich gets here."

"Sorry, Jacob," said Schwarz stiffly, "I've got an important appointment and I've got to leave."

Wasserman spread his hands. "You have come to say Kaddish for your father, so what kind of appointment can you have that can't wait a few minutes longer so you can pay respects to him?" In his mid-sixties, Wasserman was older than most of the members of the congregation, and he spoke with a faint accent which manifested itself not so much in mispronounced words as in the special care he took to pronounce them correctly. He saw that Schwarz was wavering. "Besides, I have Kaddish myself today, Ben."

"All right, Jacob, stop churning my emotions. I'll stay." He even grinned.

But Wasserman wasn't finished. "And why should you be sore at Abe Reich? I heard what you said. You two used to be such good friends."

Schwarz needed no prompting. "I'll tell you why. Last week—"

Wasserman held up his hand. "The business with the automobile? I heard it already. If you feel he owes you some money, sue him and get it over with."

"A case like this you don't take to court."

"Then settle your differences some other way. But in the temple we shouldn't have two prominent members who they can't even stand to be in the same minyan. It's a shame."

"Look, Jacob—"

"Did you ever think that's the real function of a temple in a community like this? It should be a place where Jews should settle their differences." He beckoned the rabbi over. "I was just saying to Ben here that the temple is a holy place, and all Jews who come here should be at peace with each other. Here they should make up their differences. Maybe that's more important for the temple than just a place to pray. What do you think?"

The young rabbi looked from one to the other uncertainly. He reddened. "I'm afraid I can't agree, Mr. Wasserman," he said. "The temple is not really a holy place. The original one was, of course, but a community synagogue like ours is just a building. It's for prayer and study, and I suppose it is holy in the sense that anywhere a group of men gathers to pray is holy. But settling differences is not traditionally the function of the temple, but of the rabbi."

Schwarz said nothing. He did not consider it good form for the young rabbi to contradict the president of the temple so openly. Wasserman was really his boss, besides being old enough to be his father. But Jacob did not seem to mind. His eyes twinkled and he even seemed pleased.

"So if two members of the temple quarrel, what would you suggest, rabbi?"

The young man smiled faintly. "Well, in the old days I would have suggested a Din Torah."

"What's that?" asked Schwarz.

"A hearing, a judgment," the rabbi answered. "That, incidentally, is one of the rabbi's main functions—to sit in judgment. In the old days, in the ghettos of Europe, the rabbi was hired not by the synagogue but by the town. And he was hired not to lead prayers or to supervise the synagogue, but to sit in judgment on cases that were brought to him, and to pass on questions of law."

"How did he make his decisions?" asked Schwarz, interested in spite of himself.

"Like any judge, he would hear the case, sometimes alone, sometimes in conjunction with a pair of learned men from the village. He would ask questions, examine witnesses if necessary, and then on the basis of the Talmud, he would give his verdict."

"I'm afraid that wouldn't help us much," said Schwarz with a smile. "This is about an automobile. I'm sure the Talmud doesn't deal with automobile cases."

"The Talmud deals with everything," said the rabbi flatly.

"But automobiles?"

"The Talmud doesn't mention automobiles, of course, but it does deal with such things as damages and responsibility. Particular situations differ from age to age, but the general principles remain the same."

"So, Ben," asked Wasserman, "are you ready to submit your case for judgment?"

"It wouldn't bother me any. I don't mind telling my story to anybody. The more the better. I'd just as soon the whole congregation knew what a louse Abe Reich is."

"No, I mean it seriously, Ben. You and Abe are both on the board of directors. You've both given I don't know how many hours of your time to the temple. Why not make use of the traditional Jewish way of settling an argument?"

Schwarz shrugged his shoulders. "As far as I'm concerned . . ."

"How about you, rabbi? Would you be willing—"

"If Mr. Reich and Mr. Schwarz are both willing, I will hold a Din Torah."

"You'll never get Abe Reich to come," Schwarz said.

"I'll guarantee that Reich will be there," said Wasserman.

Schwarz was interested now, even eager. "All right, how do we go about it? When do you have this—this Din Torah, and where do you have it?"

"Is this evening all right? In my study?"

"Fine with me, rabbi. You see, what happened was that Abe Reich—"

"If I am to hear the case," the rabbi asked gently, "don't you think you ought to wait until Mr. Reich is present before you tell your story?"

"Oh sure, rabbi. I didn't mean—"

"Tonight, Mr. Schwarz."

"I'll be there."

The rabbi nodded and strolled away. Schwarz watched his retreating figure and then said, "You know, Jacob, when you come right down to it, this is a kind of silly thing that I've agreed to do."

"Why silly?"

"Because—because here I've agreed to what amounts to a regular trial."

"So?"

"So who is the judge?" He nodded in the direction of the rabbi, moodily, noting the young man's ill-fitting suit, his rumpled hair, his dusty shoes. "Look at him—a boy, like a college kid. I'm practically old enough to be his father, and I should let him try me? You know, Jacob, if that's what a rabbi is supposed to be—I mean, a kind of judge— then maybe Al Becker and some of the others who say we ought to have an older, more mature man, maybe they're right. Do you really think Abe Reich will agree to all this?" A sudden thought occurred to him. "Say, Jacob, if Abe doesn't agree, I mean if he doesn't appear at the what-do-you-call-it, does that mean the case goes to me by default?"

"There's Reich now," said Wasserman. "We'll begin in a moment. And about tonight, don't worry; he'll be there."

The rabbi's study was on the second floor, overlooking the large asphalt parking lot. Mr. Wasserman arrived as the rabbi drove up, and the two men went upstairs together.

"I didn't know you were planning to come," said the rabbi.

"Schwarz began to get cold feet, so I said I would be present. Do you mind?"

"Not at all."

"Tell me, rabbi," Wasserman went on, "have you ever done this before?"

"Held a Din Torah? Of course not. As a Conservative rabbi, how would I have been likely to? For that matter, in Orthodox congregations here in America, who thinks to go to the rabbi for Din Torah these days?"

"But then—"

The rabbi smiled. "It will be all right, I assure you. I am not entirely unaware of what goes on in the community. I have heard rumors. The two men were always good friends and now something has come up to upset their friendship. My guess is that neither one is very happy about this quarrel and both are only too anxious to make up. Under the circumstances, I ought to be able to find some common ground between them."

"I see," said Wasserman, nodding. "I was beginning to be a little worried. As you say, they were friends. And that for a long time. In all probability when the story comes out it will turn out to be the wives that are behind it. Ben's wife, Myra, she's a regular *kochlefel.* She's got a tongue on her."

"I know," said the rabbi sadly. "Only too well."

"Schwarz is a weak man," Wasserman went on, "and in that household it's the wife who wears the pants. They used to be good neighbors, the Schwarzes and the Reichs, and then Ben Schwarz came into some money when his father died a couple of years ago. Come to think of it, it must have been a couple of years ago today, because he came to say Kaddish. They moved out to Grove Point and began to hobnob with the Beckers and the Pearlsteins—that crowd. I suspect that a good part of this is just Myra trying to break away from her old associations."

"Well, we'll know soon enough," said the rabbi. "That must be one of them now."

The front door banged and they heard steps on the stairs. The outer door opened and closed again and in came Ben Schwarz and, a moment later, Abe Reich. It was as though each had waited to see whether the other would show up. The rabbi motioned Schwarz to a seat at one side of the desk and Reich at the other.

Reich was a tall man, quite handsome, with a high forehead and iron-gray hair brushed back. There was a touch of the dandy about him. He wore a black suit with narrow lapels and side pockets aslant in the continental style. His trousers were slim and cuffless. He was the divisional sales manager of a national low-price shoe company and he had an air of dignity and executive decisiveness. He strove to hide his present embarrassment by looking indifferent.

Schwarz, too, was embarrassed, but he tried to pass off the whole matter as a joke, an elaborate gag his good friend Jake Wasserman had cooked up and which he was prepared to go along with, as a good guy.

Schwarz and Reich had not spoken since entering the room; in fact, they avoided looking at each other. Reich began by talking to Wasserman, so Schwarz addressed himself to the rabbi.

"Well," he said with a grin, "what happens now? Do you put on your robe and do we all rise? Is Jacob the clerk of the court or is he the jury?"

The rabbi smiled. Then he hitched up his chair to indicate that he was ready to begin. "I think you both understand what's involved here," he said easily. "There are no formal rules of procedure. Normally it is customary for both sides to acknowledge the jurisdiction of the court and willingness to abide by the rabbi's decision. In this case I won't insist on it, however."

"I don't mind," said Reich. "I'm willing to abide by your decision."

Not to be outdone, Schwarz said, "I certainly don't have anything to fear. I'll go along, too."

"Fine," said the rabbi. "As the aggrieved party, Mr. Schwarz, I suggest that you tell us what happened."

"There isn't very much to tell," said Schwarz. "It's pretty simple. Abe, here, borrowed Myra's car, and through sheer negligence he ruined it. I'll have to pay for a whole new motor. That's it in a nutshell."

"Very few cases are that simple," said the rabbi. "Can you tell me the circumstances under which he took the car? And also, just to keep the record clear, is it your car or your wife's? You refer to it as your wife's, but then you say you will have to pay for the motor."

Schwarz smiled. "It's my car in the sense that I paid for it. And it's her car in the sense that it's the one she normally drives. It's a Ford convertible, a 'sixty-three. The car I drive is a Buick."

"Nineteen sixty-three?" The rabbi's eyebrows shot up. "Then it's practically a new car. Isn't it still within the guarantee period?"

"Are you kidding, rabbi?" Schwarz snorted. "No dealer considers himself bound if the damage is due to the owner's negligence. Becker Motors where I bought the car is as reliable as any dealer in the business, but Al Becker made me feel like a damn fool when I suggested it to him."

"I see," said the rabbi, and indicated that he should proceed.

"Well, there's a group of us who do things together—go on theater parties, auto trips, that sort of thing. It all started as a garden club made up of a few congenial couples who lived near each other, but some of us have moved out of the area. Still, we meet about once a month. This was a skiing party to Belknap in New Hampshire and we took two cars. The Alberts drove up with the Reichs in their sedan. I took the Ford and we had Sarah, Sarah Weinbaum, with us. She's a widow. The Weinbaums were part of the group, and since her husband died we try to include her in everything.

"We went up early Friday afternoon—it's only a three-hour ride— and were able to get some skiing in Friday before nightfall. We went out Saturday—all except Abe here. He had caught a bad cold and was sneezing and coughing. Then, Saturday night, Sarah got a call from her kids—she has two sons, one seventeen and one fifteen—to the effect that they had been in an automobile accident. They assured her it was nothing serious, and that's how it turned out—Bobby had got a scratch, and Myron, that's the oldest boy, had to have a couple of stitches. Still, Sarah was awfully upset and wanted to go home. Well, under the circumstances I couldn't blame her. Since she had come up with us, I offered to let her take our car. But it was late and foggy out, and Myra wouldn't hear of her going alone. So then Abe here volunteered to drive her back."

"Are you in agreement with what has been said so far, Mr. Reich?" asked the rabbi.

"Yes, that's what happened."

"All right, proceed, Mr. Schwarz."

"When we got home Sunday night, the car wasn't in the garage. That didn't disturb me, because obviously Abe wasn't going to leave it at our house and then walk to his. The next morning, I went off in my own car and my wife called him to make arrangements about delivering her car. And then he told her—"

"Just a minute, Mr. Schwarz. I take it that's as far as you can go with the story from your own knowledge. I mean, from here on you would be telling what your wife told you rather than what you yourself experienced."

"I thought you said we weren't going to have any legalistic rules—"

"We're not, but since we want to get the story down first, obviously it would be better to let Mr. Reich continue. I just want the story in chronological order."

"Oh, all right."

"Mr. Reich."

"It's just as Ben told it. I started out with Mrs. Weinbaum. It was foggy and dark of course, but we drove along at a good clip. Then, when we were getting home, the car slowed to a stop. Fortunately, a cruising car came along and the cop asked what the trouble was. I told him we couldn't get started, so he said he'd get us a tow. About five minutes later, a tow truck came from an outlying garage and pulled us to town. It was late then, past midnight I guess, and there was no mechanic in attendance. So I called a cab and took Mrs. Weinbaum home. And wouldn't you know it, when we got there the house was dark and Mrs. Weinbaum had forgotten her key."

"Then how did you get in?" asked the rabbi.

"She said she always left one of the windows unlatched and it could be reached by climbing the porch. The way I was feeling, I couldn't have made it up a steep flight of stairs, and of course she couldn't. The cabby was a young fellow but claimed he had a game leg. Maybe he did and maybe he didn't, and maybe he was afraid we were trying to get him involved in a burglary. But he did tell us that the night patrolman usually stopped for coffee and a cigarette at the milk plant about that time. By now Mrs. Weinbaum was almost frantic, so we sent the cabby after the cop, and just as they came back, who should drive up but the two boys. They'd gone to a movie in town! Well, I guess Mrs. Weinbaum was so relieved to see they were all right she didn't even bother to thank me, just swept into the house with them, leaving me to explain it to the cop."

Schwarz, sensing an implied criticism, said, "Sarah must have been very upset because normally she's very considerate."

Reich made no comment, but continued, "Well, I told the cop what had happened. He didn't say anything, just gave me that suspicious look they have. You can imagine how I felt by that time. My nose was stuffed up so I couldn't breathe, my bones ached, and I guess I was running a fever. I stayed in bed all day Sunday, and when my wife came home from Belknap, I was asleep and I didn't even hear her come in. The next morning, I still felt rotten so I decided not to go to the office. When Myra called, Betsy, my wife, answered. She woke me up and I told her what had happened and gave her the name of the garage, to give to Myra. Next thing I know, maybe ten minutes later, the phone rings again and it's Myra and she insists on talking to me. So I got out of bed and she tells me that she has just called the garage and they say that I ruined her car, that I ran it without oil and that the whole engine is junk and that she's holding me responsible, and so on and so forth. She was pretty rough over the phone, and I wasn't feeling too good, so I told her to do anything she darn pleased, and hung up on her and went back to bed."

The rabbi looked questioningly at Schwarz.

"Well, according to my wife, he said some other things too, but I guess that's about what happened."

The rabbi swiveled around in his chair and slid back the glass door of the bookcase behind him. He studied the books on the shelf for a moment, and then drew one out. Schwarz grinned, and catching Wasserman's eye, winked at him. Reich's mouth twitched as he suppressed a smile. The rabbi, however, was oblivious as he thumbed through the book. Every now and then, he halted at a page and skimmed through it, nodding his head. Occasionally, he massaged his forehead as if to stimulate cerebration. He looked about his desk nearsightedly and finally found a ruler, which he used to mark a place in the book. A moment later he used a paperweight to mark another. Then he drew out a second volume, and here he seemed more certain for he quickly found the passage he was looking for. Finally he pushed both volumes away and looked benignly at the two men before him.

"There are certain aspects of the case that are not entirely clear to me. I notice, for example, that you, Mr. Schwarz, speak of Sarah, whereas you, Mr. Reich, speak of Mrs. Weinbaum. Does this indicate merely a greater informality in Mr. Schwarz, or that the lady is closer to the Schwarzes than she is to the Reichs?"

"She was a member of the group. We were all friends. If any one of us had a party or an affair, they would invite her just as we did."

The rabbi looked at Reich, who said, "I'd say she was closer to them. We met the Weinbaums through Ben and Myra. They were particularly friendly."

"Yes, perhaps that's so," Schwarz admitted. "What of it?"

"And it was in your car that she drove up to the skiing area?" asked the rabbi.

"Yes, although it just worked out that way. What are you driving at?"

"I am suggesting that she was essentially your guest, and that you felt a greater sense of responsibility for her than did Mr. Reich."

Mr. Wasserman leaned forward.

"Yes, I suppose that's so," Schwarz admitted again.

"Then in driving her home, wasn't Mr. Reich in a sense doing you a favor?"

"He was doing himself a favor too. He had a bad cold and wanted to get home."

"Had he made any suggestion to that effect before Mrs. Weinbaum received the call?"

"No, but we all knew he wanted to get home."

"If the call had not come, do you think he would have asked for your car?"

"Probably not."

"Then I think we may leave it that in driving Mrs. Weinbaum home he was doing you a favor, however advantageous it may have been to himself."

"Well, I don't see that it makes any difference. What of it?"

"Just this, that in the one case he would be in the position of a borrower, but in the second case he is in effect your agent, and a different set of rules applies. As a borrower, the responsibility of returning your car in good condition rests squarely on him, and to avoid liability he would have to prove that there was a flaw in the car and also that there was no negligence on his part. Furthermore, it would be his responsibility to make sure that the car was in good condition when he took it. As an agent, on the other hand, he has a right to assume that the car was in good condition and the burden of proof rests with you. It is you who has to prove that he was grossly negligent."

Wasserman smiled.

"I don't see that it makes much difference. I feel that in either case he was grossly negligent. And I can prove it. There wasn't a drop of oil in the car. That's what the garage mechanic said. Now, he let the oil run dry and that is gross negligence."

"How would I know the oil was low?" demanded Reich.

Until now, both men had addressed themselves to the rabbi, talking to each other through him. But now Schwarz swung around and facing Reich directly, said, "You stopped for gas, didn't you?"

Reich also turned in his chair. "Yes, I stopped for gas. When I got into the car I noticed you had less than half a tank, so after we'd been driving for about an hour, I pulled into a station and told him to fill her up."

"But you didn't tell him to check the oil," said Schwarz.

"No, and I didn't tell him to check the water in the radiator or in the battery or the pressure in the tires. I had a nervous, hysterical woman on the seat beside me who could hardly wait until he finished pumping the gas. Why did I have to check everything out? It was practically a new car. It wasn't a jalopy."

"And yet Sarah told Myra that she mentioned the oil to you."

"Sure, after we had driven on about five or ten miles. I asked her why should I, and she said you had on the way up and that you had put in a couple of quarts. So I said, Then certainly we don't need any, and that ended that. She dozed off and didn't wake up until we got stalled and she thought we were home."

"Well, I would say it's customary when taking a long trip to check oil and water every time you stop," insisted Schwarz.

"Just a minute, Mr. Schwarz," said the rabbi, "I am no mechanic, but I don't understand why a new car would need a couple of quarts of oil."

"Because there was a small leak in the seal, but it was nothing serious. I noticed a few drops of oil on the garage floor and spoke to Al Becker about it. He said he'd take care of it but that I could drive all right until I got around to bringing it in."

The rabbi looked at Reich to see if he had anything to say in reply, and then leaned back in his swivel chair and considered. Finally, he straightened up with a jerk of his shoulders. He patted the books on the desk. "These are two of the three volumes of the Talmud that deal with the general subject of what we would call torts. The subject is treated very fully. This first volume treats of the general causes of damages, and the section that concerns an ox that gores, for example, goes on for about forty pages. A general principle is evolved which the rabbis applied broadly to all kinds of cases. It is the basic distinction they made between *tam* and *muad*, that is, between the docile ox and the ox that has already earned a reputation as a vicious beast by virtue of having gored on several occasions in the past. The owner of the latter was felt to be far more responsible in the event of a goring than the former, since he already had had warning and should have taken special precautions." He glanced at Mr. Wasserman, who nodded in corroboration.

The rabbi got up from behind his desk and began to pace the floor. His tone took on the singsong quality traditional with Talmudists as he followed the thread of the argument. "Now in this case, you knew your car leaked oil. And I suggest, that, at least while it was being driven, it leaked more than just a few drops, since you found it necessary to add two full quarts on the trip up. If Mr. Reich had been a borrower—and we come now to this volume which deals with the subject of borrowing as well as the law of agency—if Mr. Reich, for example, had said that he did not feel well and wanted to go home and had asked to borrow your car for the trip, it would have been his responsibility either to ask you if it were in good condition, or himself to check it. And if he failed to do so, even if the circumstances had been precisely the same as they were, then he would have been responsible and liable for the damage done. But we have already agreed that he was not a borrower but essentially your agent, and hence the responsibility was yours to inform him that the car leaked oil and to watch and see that it did not drop below the safe level."

"Just a minute, rabbi," said Schwarz. "I didn't have to warn him personally. The car has a built-in warning device—the oil light. When a man drives a car, he's supposed to watch his instruments, and if he had, the red light would have told him he was getting dangerously low."

The rabbi nodded. "That is a good point. Mr. Reich?"

"As a matter of fact, the light did go on," he said. "But when it did we were on the open road without a station in sight, and before I could find one we'd stalled."

"I see," said the rabbi.

"But according to the mechanic, he should have smelled something burning long before," Schwarz insisted.

"Not if his nose was stuffed up with a bad cold. And Mrs. Weinbaum, you remember, was asleep." The rabbi shook his head. "No, Mr. Schwarz, Mr. Reich did only what the average driver would have done under the existing road conditions. Therefore, he could not be considered negligent, and if not negligent, then not responsible."

The finality in his tone indicated that the hearing was over. Reich was the first to rise. "This has been a revelation to me, rabbi," he said in a low voice. The rabbi acknowledged his thanks.

Reich turned uncertainly to Schwarz, hoping he would make some gesture of reconciliation, but he remained seated, his eyes focused on the floor as he rubbed the palms of his hands together in vexation.

Reich waited an awkward moment, then said, "Well, I'll be going." At the door he paused. "I didn't see your car in the parking lot, Jacob. Can I give you a lift?"

"Yes, I walked," said Wasserman, "but I think I'd like a ride home."

"I'll wait downstairs."

Only when the door closed did Schwarz raise his head. It was obvious he was hurt. "I guess I had the wrong idea of what this hearing was supposed to do, rabbi. Or maybe you had the wrong idea. I told you, or I tried to tell you, that I wasn't planning to bring suit against Abe. After all, I could afford the repairs a lot better than he could. If he had come forward with an offer of some kind I would have refused it, but we would have remained friends. Instead, he was nasty to my wife, and a man has to back up his wife. I suppose she gave him the rough side of her tongue. And I can understand now why he reacted the way he did."

"Well then—"

Schwarz shook his head. "You don't understand, rabbi. I was hoping that this hearing would effect some kind of compromise, that it would sort of bring us together. Instead, you cleared him completely, which means that I must have been entirely in the wrong. But I don't feel I was all wrong. After all, what did I do? A couple of friends of mine wanted to get home in a hurry and I lent them my car. Was that wrong? It seems to me that you were not acting as an impartial judge, but more like his lawyer. All your questions and your arguments were directed towards me. I don't have the legal training to see the flaw in your line of reasoning, but I'm sure that if I had counsel here to represent me, he would. In any case, I'm sure he would have been able to work out some sort of compromise."

"But we did even better than that," said the rabbi.

"How do you mean? You cleared him of negligence and I'm going to be several hundred dollars out of pocket."

The rabbi smiled. "I'm afraid that you do not grasp the full significance of the evidence, Mr. Schwarz. True, Mr. Reich was cleared of all negligence, but that doesn't automatically make you culpable."

"I don't get it."

"Let us consider what we have here. You bought a car with a leaking seal. And when you noticed the damage, you notified the manufacturer through his representative, Mr. Becker. Now, it is true that the fault was a minor one and that neither Mr. Becker nor you had reason to believe it might become more serious in the immediate future. The likelihood that it might become aggravated by a long trip evidently did not occur to him, else he would have warned you against it, in which case I'm sure you would not have used that car to go up to New Hampshire. But the fact is that driving for a long distance at a high rate of speed did result in expanding the leak, which is why you had to put in a couple of quarts of oil on the way up. Now, under these circumstances, the manufacturer can only require of you that you use normal caution. I think you will agree that Mr. Reich did nothing any cautious driver would not have—"

"So it was really their fault, rabbi?" Schwarz's face showed animation and there was excitement in his voice. "Is that what you're saying?"

Mr. Wasserman smiled broadly.

"Precisely, Mr. Schwarz. It is my contention that it was the fault of the manufacturer and that he must make good under his warranty."

"Well gee, rabbi, that's swell. I'm sure Becker will come across. After all, it's no skin off his nose. Then that makes everything all right. Look, rabbi, if I said anything that—"

The rabbi cut him off. "Quite understandable under the circumstances, Mr. Schwarz."

Schwarz was for taking everyone out for a drink, but the rabbi excused himself. "If you don't mind, some other night perhaps. As I was leafing through those books, I came across a couple of points that interested me. Nothing to do with all this, but I'd like to check them over while they're fresh in my mind." He shook hands with the two men and took them to the door.

"Well, what do you think of the rabbi now?" Wasserman could not help asking on the way downstairs.

"He's quite a guy," said Schwarz.

"A gaon, Ben, a regular gaon."

"I don't know what a gaon is, Jacob, but if you say so, I'll take your word for it."

"And what about Abe?"

"Well, Jacob, between me and you, it was mostly Myra. You know how women are about losing a few bucks."

From the window of his study, the rabbi looked down at the parking lot below to see the three men talking in obvious reconciliation. He smiled and turned from the window. The books on his desk caught his eye. Adjusting the reading lamp, he sat down behind the desk and pulled the books toward him.

2

Elspeth Bleech lay on her back and watched the ceiling slowly tilt, first to one side and then the other. She clutched at the bedclothes as though afraid she might fall out of bed. The alarm clock had awakened her as usual, but as she sat up the vertigo struck and she let her head fall back on the pillow.

The sun slanting in through the slats of the venetian blind gave promise of a perfect June day. She shut her eyes tight to blot out the moving walls and ceiling, but she could sense the sun in a sort of red haze, and at the same time she felt as though the bed were rocking sickeningly under her. Although the morning was cool, her forehead was wet with perspiration.

By an effort of will she sat up again, and then without bothering to put on her slippers fled to the tiny bathroom. After a while she felt better, and came back and sat on the edge of the bed and dried her face, wondering dully if she ought not lie down for another half-hour or so. As if in answer there came a pound on the door and the children, Angelina and Johnnie, shouted, "Elspeth, Elspeth, dress us. We want to go out."

"All right, Angie," she called back. "You and Johnnie go back upstairs and play quietly, and Elspeth will be up in a minute. Now remember, play quietly. You don't want to wake your mummy and daddy."

Fortunately they obeyed, and she sighed with relief. Slipping on a robe and slippers, she brewed herself a cup of tea and made some toast. The food made her feel better.

She had been having strange symptoms for a while, but lately they had grown worse. Today was the second day in a row she had been sick. When it happened yesterday morning, she had assumed it was the ravioli Mrs. Serafino had given her for supper the night before; maybe she had eaten more than was good for her. But yesterday she had eaten sparingly—all day—perhaps she had not eaten enough.

She might speak to her friend Celia Saunders. Celia was older and should know something she could take for it. At the same time, she realized it would be unwise to detail the symptoms too precisely. In the back of her mind was the fear that possibly, just possibly, her sickness might be due to something quite different.

The children in the room overhead were getting noisy. She did not want Mrs. Serafino to see her until she was fully dressed and had had a chance to put a touch of color on her cheeks. She was even more anxious lest Mr. Serafino see her that way, and she hurried back to her room to dress. Taking off her robe and nightgown, she surveyed herself in the full-length mirror on the closet door. She was sure she did not look any stouter. Nevertheless, she decided to put on the new girdle that was firmer than her old one and held her in better.

By the time she was dressed, she felt her old self again. Just the sight of herself in the mirror, trim in her white uniform, made her spirits rise. Suppose it was the other thing? It need not necessarily be dreaded; she might even use it to advantage. But of course she'd have to be sure, and that meant a trip to the doctor, perhaps this Thursday on her day off.

"Then why the hell don't you get the rabbi to write the letter to the Ford Company?" demanded Al Becker. He was a short, stocky man with a powerful torso mounted on short, stumpy legs. Nose and chin both protruded combatively and there was a pugnacious twist to his lipless mouth, out of which jutted a thick, black cigar. When he removed it from the corner of his mouth, he held it between the curled first and second fingers of his right hand, so that it seemed like a glowing weapon in a clenched fist. His eyes were dull blue marbles.

Ben Schwarz had come to him full of glad tidings. He thought his good friend would be happy to hear he wouldn't have to stand the considerable expense of mounting a new motor in the car.

But Becker had been far from pleased. True, it would cost Becker Motors nothing, but it did mean a lot of trouble, perhaps extensive correspondence to explain the matter to the company.

"How does the rabbi get into things like this?" he wanted to know. "You're a sensible feller, Ben. Now I ask you, is this the function of a rabbi of a temple?"

"But you don't understand, Al," Schwarz said. "It wasn't the question of repairs on the car at all. It was, of course, but—"

"Well, was it or wasn't it?"

"Well, sure it was, but I mean I didn't go to him about that. He happened to hear I was sore at Abe Reich so he suggested a Din Torah—"

"A Din who?"

"Din Torah," said Schwarz carefully. "It's when two parties to a conflict or an argument go to the rabbi and he hears the case and makes a judgment according to the Talmud. It's a regular thing that rabbis do."

"First I heard of it."

"Well, I admit I didn't know about it before myself. Anyway, I agreed, and Reich and I and Wasserman—as a kind of witness, I suppose— went to the rabbi, and he worked the whole thing out so that it was plain that neither Reich nor I had been negligent. And by God, if I wasn't negligent and the driver of the car wasn't negligent, then the fault was in the car and the company is supposed to make good."

"Well, goddammit, the company won't make good unless I say so, and I can just see myself going to them for a job this big with that kind of cock-and-bull story." Becker's voice was never soft, and when he was angry he shouted.

Schwarz seemed suddenly deflated. "But there was a leak in the seal," he shouted back. "I told you about that."

"Sure, a couple of drops a week. That kind of leak wouldn't burn out a motor."

"A couple of drops when she was standing still. But she must have been gushing when I drove. I put two quarts in on my way to New Hampshire. That's no couple of drops. Now that I know from my own knowledge."

The door of Becker's office opened and his junior partner, Melvin Bronstein, came in. Bronstein was a youngish man of forty, tall and slim with wavy black hair just beginning to gray at the temples; deep, dark eyes, an aquiline nose, and sensitive lips.

"What's going on?" he asked. "Is it a private argument, or can anyone join? I'll bet they could hear you guys down the block."

"What's going on is that in our temple we've got ourselves a rabbi who can be depended on to do everything except what he's supposed to do," said Becker.

Bronstein looked at Schwarz for enlightenment. Happy to have a somewhat less overpowering audience, Schwarz told his story while Becker rustled papers on his desk in elaborate unconcern.

Bronstein beckoned from the doorway of the office, and somewhat reluctantly Becker went over. Schwarz turned away so he would not appear to eavesdrop.

"Ben is a good customer of ours, Al," whispered Bronstein. "I don't think the company would question it."

"Yeah? Well, I've had dealings with the Ford Company since before you got out of high school, Mel," said Becker aloud.

But Bronstein knew his partner. He grinned at him. "Look, Al, if you turn Ben down you'll only have Myra to deal with. Isn't she president of the temple Sisterhood this year?"

"And last year, too," Ben could not help adding.

"It won't do our business any good to have her sore at us," Bronstein said, once again lowering his voice.

"Well, the Sisterhood don't buy cars."

"But the husbands of all the members do."

"Goddammit, Mel, how am I going to explain that I want the company to put a new engine in a car because the rabbi of my temple decided they ought to?"

"You don't have to mention the rabbi at all. You don't even have to explain how it happened. You can just say that the seal let go while the car was being driven."

"And what if the company sends down an investigator?"

"Have they ever done it to you, Al?"

"No, but they have with some other agencies."

"All right," said Bronstein with a grin, "if he comes, you can introduce him to your rabbi."

Suddenly Becker's mood changed. He chuckled deep in his throat and turned to Schwarz. "All right, Ben, I'll write the company and see if they'll go along. I'm only doing it, you understand, because you sold Mel here a bill of goods. He's the original big-hearted kid, the softest touch in town."

"Aw, you're just teed off because the rabbi was involved," said Bronstein. He turned to Schwarz. "Al would have gone along from the beginning, and glad of a chance to help out a customer, too, if you hadn't mentioned the rabbi."

"What have you got against the rabbi, Al?" asked Ben.

"What have I got against the rabbi?" Becker removed the cigar from his mouth. "I'll tell you what I've got against the rabbi. He's not the man for the job; that's what I've got against him. He's supposed to be our representative, yet would you hire him as a salesman for your company, Ben? Come on now, be truthful."

"Sure, I'd hire him," said Schwarz, but his tone did not carry conviction.

"Well, if you were fool enough to hire him, I hope you would be smart enough to fire him the first time he got out of line."

"When has he got out of line?" demanded Schwarz.

"Oh, come on, Ben. How about the time we had the Fathers and Sons breakfast and we brought down Barney Gilligan of the Red Sox to talk to the kids. He gets up to introduce him and what does he say? He gives the kids a long spiel about how our heroes are scholars instead of athletes. I could've gone through the floor."

"Well . . ."

"And how about the time your own wife had him come down to pep up the girls of the Sisterhood to put on a big campaign for a Chanukah gift for the temple, and he tells them that keeping Judaism in their hearts and a kosher home was more important for Jewish women than campaigning for gifts for the temple."

"Just a minute, Al. Naturally I wouldn't say anything against my own wife, but right is right. That was a luncheon meeting, and Myra served shrimp cocktail, which ain't kosher-type food and which you couldn't blame a rabbi for being sore about."

"And with all this in-fighting going on, you keep trying to get me to join the temple," said Bronstein with a wink at Schwarz.

"Sure," said his partner, "because as a Jew and a resident of Barnard's Crossing you owe it to yourself and to your community to become a member. As for the rabbi, he won't be there forever, you know."

3

The board of directors were using one of the empty classrooms to hold their regular Sunday meeting. Jacob Wasserman, as the president of the temple and chairman of the board, sat at the teacher's desk. The rest, fifteen of them, had squeezed themselves into the pupils' seats, their legs stretched out uncomfortably in the aisles. A few in back were sitting on the desks themselves, their feet on the chairs in front. Except for Wasserman, the board was composed of younger men, half still in their thirties and the rest in their forties and early fifties. Wasserman was dressed in a lightweight business suit, but the others wore the conventional costume in Barnard's Crossing for a warm Sunday in June—slacks, sport shirts, and jackets or golf sweaters.

Through the open windows came the roar of a power lawn mower operated by Stanley, the janitor. Through the open door came the shrill chanting of the children in the assembly down the hall. There was little formality to the proceedings, members speaking whenever they felt like it, and more often than not, as now, several at once.

The chairman rapped on the desk with a ruler. "Gentlemen, one at a time. Now what were you saying, Joe?"

"What I was *trying* to say is that I don't see how we can transact business in all this noise. And I don't see why we don't use the small sanctuary for our regular meetings."

"Out of order," called another voice. "That's Good and Welfare."

"Why am I out of order?" demanded Joe belligerently. "All right, I'll make a motion that all meetings be conducted in the small sanctuary from now on. That's New Business."

"Gentlemen, gentlemen. As long as I'm chairman, anyone who has something important to say can say it any time. Our meetings aren't so complicated that we can't go out of order occasionally. The secretary can always set it right in his minutes. The only reason we aren't using the sanctuary, Joe, is that there's no place for the secretary to write on. However, if the members feel that a classroom like this is not a good place for a meeting, we could have Stanley set up a table in the sanctuary."

"That brings up another point, Jacob. How about Stanley? I don't think it looks right to our Gentile neighbors for him to be out working in plain sight on Sunday, especially since he's a Gentile and it's his holiday as much as theirs."

"What do you suppose they do on a Sunday? You walk along Vine Street and you'll see practically every one of them out cutting the lawn, trimming the hedge, or maybe painting their boat."

"Still, Joe has a good point there," said Wasserman. "Of course, if Stanley objected we certainly wouldn't insist. He's got to work here Sundays because of the school, but maybe it would be better if he kept inside. On the other hand, nobody tells him to work outside. In that respect, he's his own boss. He can arrange his work anyway he wants. He's outside now because he wants to be."

"Yeah, but it doesn't look right."

"Well, it's only for a couple more weeks," said Wasserman. "During the summer, he has Sundays off." He hesitated and glanced at the clock at the back of the room. "That brings up a matter I'd like to talk about for a minute. We've got a couple of more meetings before we adjourn for the summer, but I think we ought to consider the rabbi's contract."

"What about it, Jacob? It runs through the High Holidays, doesn't it?"

"That's true, it does. That's the way rabbis' contracts are always written, so that the temple always has a rabbi for the holiday services. Which is why it's customary to consider the new contract at this time of year. Then if the congregation decides they want to make a change, they have a chance to look around for a new rabbi. And if the rabbi wants to make a change, it gives him a chance to line up a new congregation. I think it might be a good idea if we voted right now to extend our rabbi's contract for another year, and send him a letter to that effect."

"Why? Is he looking around for something else, or did he mention it to you?"

Wasserman shook his head. "No, he hasn't spoken about it. I just think it might be a good idea to send him a letter before he does."

"Just a minute, Jacob, how do we know the rabbi wants to continue? Hadn't we ought to get a letter from him first?"

"I think he likes it here and I think he'd be willing to continue," said Wasserman. "As for the letter, it's usually the employer who notifies. Naturally, we'd have to give him a raise. I think an increase of five hundred dollars would be a proper token of appreciation."

"Mr. Chairman." It was the harsh voice of Al Becker. The vicepresident straddled his chair and leaned forward, supporting his heavy torso on clenched fists on the desk in front of him. "Mr. Chairman, it seems to me that with the tough time we're having, with a brand-new temple and all, that five hundred dollars is a pretty expensive token."

"Yeah, five hundred dollars is a lot of money."

"He's only been here a year."

"Well, that's the best time to give it to him, isn't it, right after his first year?"

"You've got to give him some kind of a raise, and five hundred dollars is only a little more than five percent of his salary."

"Gentlemen, gentlemen." Wasserman rapped on the desk with the ruler.

"I move we lay the whole matter on the table for a week or two," said Meyer Goldfarb.

"What's to lay on the table?"

"Meyer always wants to postpone when it comes to spending money."

"It only hurts for a little while."

"Mr. Chairman." It was Al Becker again. "I second Meyer's motion to lay the matter on the table until next week. That's been our rule—whenever something involved spending a lot of money we've always held it over for at least a week. Now, I consider this a large expenditure. Five hundred dollars is a lot of money, and the new salary, ten thousand dollars, is an awful lot of money. All we've got here now is a bare quorum. I think on a matter as important as this, we ought to have a larger turnout. I move that Lennie be instructed to write to all members of the board asking them to be sure to come to next week's meeting to discuss a matter of special importance."

"There's a motion on the floor."

"Well, it's the same idea. All right, I'll make mine an amendment to the motion."

"Any discussion on the amendment?" asked Wasserman.

"Just a minute, Mr. Chairman," called Meyer Goldfarb. "That amendment is to my motion, so if I accept it then we don't have to have any discussion. I just change my motion, see."

"All right, restate your motion then."

"I move that the motion to extend the rabbi's contract—"

"Just a minute, Meyer, there was no such motion."

"Jacob made the motion."

"Jacob didn't make any motion. He just made a suggestion. Besides, he was in the chair—"

"Gentlemen," said Wasserman, banging with his ruler, "what's the sense of all this motion, amendment, amendment to the amendment. I didn't make a motion, I did make a motion? Is it the sense of this meeting that we should put off any action on the rabbi's contract until next week?"

"Yeah."

"Sure, why not? The rabbi won't run away."

"Even out of respect to the rabbi, there ought to be more people here."

"All right," said Wasserman, "so let's hold it over already. If there's no other business"—he waited for a moment—"then this meeting stands adjourned."

4

Tuesday the weather was fine and mild, and Elspeth Bleech and her friend Celia Saunders, who took care of the Hoskins' children a couple of doors away, led their charges to the park, a ragged bit of turf a few blocks beyond the temple. The little procession was essentially a herding operation. The children ran ahead, but because Johnnie Serafino was still very young, Elspeth always took the stroller along. Sometimes he walked with the two women, his little fist tightly clutching the side or the chrome handle of the carriage, and sometimes he would clamber aboard and insist on being pushed.

Elspeth and Celia would walk about fifty feet and then stop to check on the whereabouts of their charges. If they had fallen behind they called to them, or ran back to pull them apart or make them drop something they had found in the gutter or a trash barrel.

Celia tried to persuade her friend to spend Thursday, their day off, together in Salem. "They're having a sale at Adelson's, and I wanted to see about another bathing suit. We could take the one o'clock bus—"

"I was thinking of going to Lynn," said Elspeth.

"Why Lynn?"

"Well, I've been feeling sort of, you know, sicky lately and I thought I ought to have a check-up by a doctor. Maybe he could give me a tonic, or something."

"You don't need no tonic, El. What you need is a little exercise and some relaxation. Now you take my advice. You come into Salem with me and we can do some shopping, and then we can take in a movie in the afternoon. We can have a bite somewhere and after that we can go bowling. There's the nicest bunch of fellows come down the alleys Thursday nights. We have the grandest times just kidding around. No rough stuff and nobody gets fresh. We just have a lot of fun hacking around."

"Hm—I guess it's nice all right, but I just don't feel up to it, Cele. I'm tired most afternoons, and in the mornings I wake up and I feel light-headed, kind of."

"Well, I know the reason for that," said Celia positively.

"You do?"

"You just don't get enough sleep. That's your trouble. Staying up until two or three o'clock every morning, it's a wonder to me you can stand on your feet. And six days a week. I don't know of another girl who doesn't get Sundays off. Them Serafinos are taking advantage of you—they're working you to death."

"Oh, I get enough sleep. I don't have to stay up until they get home." She shrugged. "It's just that alone in the house with only the kids, I kind of don't like to get undressed and into bed. Most of the time, I nap on the couch. And then I nap in the afternoon, too. I get plenty of sleep, Cele."

"But Sundays—"

"Well, it's the only day they have for visiting their friends. I don't mind really. And Mrs. Serafino told me when I first came that any-time I wanted a Sunday off she would arrange for it. They're really quite nice to me. Mr. Serafino said that if I wanted to go downtown to church, he'd drive me—the buses being so bad on Sundays."

Celia halted in her stride and looked at Elspeth. "Tell me, does he ever bother you any?"

"Bother me?"

"You know, does he ever try to get fresh when the missus isn't around?"

"Oh no," said Elspeth quickly. "Where'd you get that idea?"

"I don't trust those nightclub types. And I don't like the way he looks at a girl."

"That's silly. He hardly says two words to me."

"Is it? Well, let me tell you something—Gladys, that's the girl that had your job before you—Mrs. Serafino fired her because she caught her husband fooling around with her. And she didn't have half your looks."

Stanley Doble was a typical Barnard's Crosser. Of a certain segment of Old Town society, he might even be considered the prototype. He was a thick-set man of forty, with sandy, graying hair. His deeply tanned, leathery skin indicated that he spent most of his time outdoors. He could build a boat. He could repair and install the plumbing and electric wiring in a house. He could take care of a lawn, trimming and mowing and raking tirelessly in the hot summer sun. He could repair an automobile, or the engine of a launch as it rose and fell in a heavy sea. At one time or another, he had earned his living doing each of these as well as by fishing and lobstering. At no time did he ever have trouble getting some kind of work; and at no time did he ever work long enough to make much more than he needed, until he came to work for the temple. This job he had held ever since they first acquired an old mansion and renovated it to serve as a combination school, community center, and synagogue. He had been all-important then, for without him the building would have fallen apart. He kept the boiler running, he fixed the plumbing and the wiring, he repaired the roof, and he spent the summer in painting the building inside and out. Since the completion of the new temple, his work had changed, of course. There was little repair work, but he kept the building clean and the lawn trimmed, regulated the heating system in the winter and the air conditioner when it got warm.

And now, on this bright Tuesday morning, he was raking up the temple lawn. He had already gathered several bushel baskets of lawn clippings and leaves. Although there was the other side to do yet, as much again and more, he decided to stop for lunch. Then after lunch, if he felt like it, he could tackle the other side or let it go until the next day. There was no real hurry.

He had a bottle of milk and some sliced cheese in the refrigerator in the kitchen. Certain meats, actually any meats except those bought in particular stores—what he called 7WD stores, which was the way he read כשר, the Hebrew sign for kosher—he wasn't supposed to put in there. But milk and cheese were all right since they involved no slaughter and were ritually clean. Then he wondered if he wouldn't rather have a glass of beer. His car, a disreputable 1947 Ford convertible with no top and painted bright yellow from the remains of his last housepainting job, was in the parking lot in front of the temple. He could drive to the Ship's Cabin and still be back inside of an hour. There was no one he had to report to, but Mrs. Schwarz had said something about perhaps needing him to help decorate the vestry for the Sisterhood meeting, so he thought he had better be around. Besides, if he got involved in one of the interminable arguments in the Ship's Cabin, like whether shingle or clapboard was better for a house that faced the sea, or whether the Celtics would win the championship, there was no telling when he would get back.

He washed up, got his milk and cheese out of the refrigerator and brought them down to his own private corner in the basement where he had a rickety table, a cot, and a wicker armchair that he had retrieved from the town dump on one of his many excursions there, a favorite pastime of some segments of Barnard's Crossing society. He sat at the table and munched the sandwiches he had made, taking deep swallows from the mouth of the milk carton and staring moodily out of the narrow cellar window, watching the legs of passers-by through the bushes, men's legs encased in trousers, and silk-stockinged women's legs, slim and cool. Sometimes he would lean to one side, the better to follow an exceptional pair of women's legs until they passed the basement window. He would nod his grizzled head approvingly and breathe, "Beauty."

He finished the quart of milk and wiped his mouth with the back of a gnarled, hairy hand. Rising from his chair, he stretched lazily, and then sat down again, on the cot this time, and scratched his rib-cage and his grizzled head with strong, stubby fingers. He lay back, wriggling his head against the pillow to form a comfortable hollow. For a moment he stared straight up at the pipes and conductors that ran across the ceiling like veins and arteries in an anatomy chart. Then his eyes wandered to the wall where he had pasted up a gallery of "art photos," pictures of women in various stages of undress. They were all buxom and saucy and inviting, and as his eyes roamed from one to another, his mouth relaxed in a smile of contentment.

From outside, just in front of his window, came the sound of women's voices. He rolled over to see who was talking and made out two pairs of women's legs, both encased in white stockings, and just beyond, the wheels of a stroller or baby carriage. He thought he knew who they were, having seen them pass often enough. It gave him special pleasure to eavesdrop on their conversation, almost as though he were peeping at them through a keyhole.

". . . then when you're through, you could take the bus to Salem and I could meet you and we could eat at the station."

"I kind of thought I'd stay on in Lynn and go to the Elysium."

"But they've got that picture that takes forever. How will you get home?"

"I checked, and it gets out at eleven-thirty. That will give me enough time to make the last bus."

"Aren't you afraid to go home alone that late at night?"

"Oh, there are plenty of people on that bus, and it's only a couple of blocks beyond the bus stop—Angie, you come right here this minute."

There was a scurry of a child's feet and then the women's legs marched out of view.

He rolled over on his back again and studied the pictures on the wall. One was of a dark girl who was naked except for a narrow garter belt and a pair of black stockings. As he concentrated on the picture, her hair became blonde and her stockings white. Presently his mouth dropped open and he began to snore, a steady, rhythmic, guttural throb like a boat engine in a heavy sea.

Myra Schwarz and the two women of the Sisterhood who were decorating the vestry for the box-supper meeting stood back, their heads tilted to one side.

"Can you get it just a little higher, Stanley?" asked Myra. "What do you think, girls?"

Stanley, perched on a stepladder, obediently raised the crepe paper a couple of inches.

"I think it should be a little lower down."

"Perhaps you're right. Can you lower it a hair, Stanley?"

He dropped it to where it had been before.

"Hold it right there, Stanley," called Myra. "That's just right, isn't it, girls?"

Enthusiastically they agreed. They were very much her junior in the organization; Emmy Adler was barely thirty, and Nancy Drettman, though older, had joined the Sisterhood only recently. As the decorating committee, they had come to the temple in slacks, prepared to work, when Myra, all dressed up, dropped in "to see if everything was going all right" and took over. They had no great passion for decorating, but it was one of those jobs given to newer members. Once they had demonstrated their willingness to work, more important jobs would be assigned to them—such as the advertising committee, which required them to badger the local tradespeople and their husbands' business associates for ads for the Program Book; the friendship committee, where they would visit the sick; and finally, having shown they could get things done, which usually meant coaxing other people to do them, they would see their names on the slate of candidates for positions on the executive council—and they would have arrived.

In the meantime, they practiced by ordering Stanley around. When they had first appeared, fully an hour before Mrs. Schwarz, they asked his help even though they knew he would much rather be outside working on the lawn. "Why don't you two ladies go on ahead and get started," he'd said. "I'll come along in a little while."

Mrs. Schwarz, on the other hand, had brooked no nonsense. She had said decisively, "Stanley, I need your help."

"I got this raking to do, Mrs. Schwarz," he had said.

"That can wait."

"Yes'm, I'll be right there," and put aside his rake and went to fetch the ladder.

It was a tiresome, tedious job, and he took no pleasure in it. Nor did he like working under the supervision of women—hard, brassy women like Mrs. Schwarz. He had just finished tacking the decoration in place when the door opened and the rabbi thrust his head in. "Oh, Stanley," he called out, "could I talk to you for a minute?"

Stanley promptly came down from the ladder, causing the crepe paper decoration to sag. The tack pulled out of the wall and there was a collective groan from the three women. The rabbi, aware of them for the first time, nodded half-apologetically for intruding and then turned to Stanley. "I'm expecting some books to be delivered by express," he said. "They should be here in a day or two. They're rare and quite valuable, so when they arrive please put them right in my study. Don't leave them lying around."

"Sure, rabbi. How will I know it's the books?"

"They're being sent from Dropsie College, and you will see that on the label." He nodded at the women and withdrew.

Myra Schwarz waited in martyred patience for Stanley to rejoin them. "It must have been pretty important for the rabbi to call you away," she remarked acidly.

"Oh, I was just coming down to shift the ladder anyway. He wanted me to keep an eye out for some books he's expecting."

"Very important," she said sarcastically. "His Holiness might be in for a little surprise one of these days."

"Oh, I don't think he saw us here when he first came in," said Emmy Adler.

"I don't see how he could help seeing us," said Mrs. Drettman. Addressing herself to Myra, she went on, "You know, about what you were saying. My Morrie is a board of director, and only yesterday he got a call from Mr. Becker to make sure and turn up for this special meeting—"

Mrs. Schwarz gestured in the direction of Mrs. Adler. "That's supposed to be kept quiet," she whispered.

5

Although she was off at noon, Elspeth rarely managed to leave the Serafino household much before one. Mrs. Serafino made such a fuss about feeding the children their lunch—calling from the kitchen: "Oh El, where did you put Angelina's dish, the one with the three bears?" or "El, could you spare a minute before the bus leaves to put Johnnie on the toidy?"—that she usually preferred to do it herself and take the one o'clock bus or even the one-thirty.

Today in particular she didn't care, since her appointment was not until four. The day was hot and humid and she wanted to feel fresh and cool against the intimacy of the doctor's examination. She would have preferred to wait until three before leaving, but then her mistress might ask questions.

She was giving the children their lunch when Mrs. Serafino came downstairs. "Oh, you've started already," she said. "There was no need to. I'll finish and you can get dressed."

"They're almost through, Mrs. Serafino. Why don't you have your breakfast."

"Well, if you don't mind. I'm dying for a cup of coffee."

Mrs. Serafino was not one to turn down a favor, nor was she effusive in her thanks to the girl. It might give her ideas. When Elspeth had finished feeding the children, Mrs. Serafino was still at her coffee and made no move when she took them upstairs.

Preparing the children for their nap was as much of a chore as giving them lunch. When Elspeth finally came downstairs, Mrs. Serafino was in the hallway, talking on the telephone. She paused long enough to cup her hand over the mouthpiece. "Oh El, are the children already in bed? I was just coming up to do it." Just that, and back to her conversation.

Elspeth went to her room off the kitchen, closed the door, and firmly pushed the sliding bolt. She flung herself face down on the bed and automatically turned on the radio on the night table. She listened, only half-hearing, to the cheery voice of the announcer, "—and that was Bert Burns, the latest hillbilly sensation singing, 'Cornliquor Blues.' And now some news about the weather. That low-pressure area we mentioned earlier is moving closer and that means that we'll probably get some clouds and fog in the evening and maybe some showers. Well, I guess into every life some rain must fall, ha-ha. And now, for Mrs. Eisenstadt of 24 West Street, Salem, who is celebrating her eighty-third birthday, the Happy Hooligans in their latest platter, 'Trash Collection Rock.' And a happy birthday to you, Mrs. Eisenstadt."

She half-dozed through the song and then rolled over and stared at the ceiling through the one that followed, rebelling at the idea of having to get dressed in that humid warmth. Finally she got heavily to her feet and wiggled her dress over her head. She reached around behind and unhooked her bra and then unzipped her girdle and worked it down over her hips, not bothering to detach the stockings. She tossed the undergarments into the bottom drawer of her dresser and hung the dress in her closet.

Beyond the door, in the kitchen, she could hear that Mr. Serafino had come downstairs and was heating up the coffee and getting orange juice out of the refrigerator. She glanced at the bolted door and then, reassured, went into the tiny bathroom and adjusted the shower.

When she emerged from her room half an hour later, she was wearing a sleeveless yellow linen dress, white shoes, white gloves, and carrying a white plastic handbag. Her short hair had been combed back severely and was held in place by a white elastic headband. Mr. Serafino had left, but his wife was in the kitchen, still in housecoat and mules, sipping at another cup of coffee.

"You look very nice, El," she said. "Something special tonight?"

"No, just a movie."

"Well, have a good time. You've got your key?"

The girl opened her bag to show the key attached to the zipper-pull of the change purse inside. Returning to her room, she closed the door behind her, went down a short hallway, and let herself out by the back door. She reached the corner just as the bus came along, and took a seat in the rear by an open window. As the bus started moving she removed her gloves and searched in her bag until she found a heavy, old-fashioned gold wedding band. She slid it on her finger and then drew her gloves on again.

When Joe Serafino returned to the kitchen, he was shaved and dressed.

"Has the girl gone yet?" he asked.

"You mean Elspeth? Yeah, she left a few minutes ago. Why?"

"I thought if she were going to Lynn, I could give her a ride in."

"Since when are you going to Lynn?"

"I've got to take the car in to the garage. The gadget that controls the top needs adjusting. The other day it got stuck in a rainstorm and went up only halfway and I got soaked."

"How come you waited until today to have it fixed?"

"I guess the weather has been so good I didn't think of it," he answered easily. "But I just heard the weather report while I was shaving and it said possible showers. Say, why the third degree?"

"No third degree. Can't a person ask a simple question? What time are you coming home, or maybe I shouldn't ask that either."

"Sure, go ahead and ask."

"Well?"

"I don't know—maybe I'll stay in Lynn and just grab a bite at the club." He sounded angry as he flung out of the room.

She heard the front door open and slam closed, and then the sound of the motor starting. She stared at the door of Elspeth's room and thought hard. Why should her husband, who usually acted as though he did not know the girl existed, suddenly want to be so obliging? For that matter, why did he get shaved at this hour? Ordinarily he waited until just before going to the club. His beard was so heavy that if he shaved earlier it showed before the evening was over.

The more she thought about it, the more suspicious the whole business seemed. Why, for example, did the girl hang around today? Her day off started at noon—why did she offer to feed the kids and then put them to bed? Nobody asked her to. No other girl would do it on her day off. She hadn't left until almost half-past two. Had she been waiting for Joe?

And that business of bolting the door. Up to now it had always amused her; whenever they had company and the conversation got around to maids, as it usually did, she would mention it. "Elspeth always bolts her door. I wonder if she thinks my Joe might come in while she's in bed or getting dressed." She always laughed when she said it as though the idea of her husband's being interested in the maid was completely ridiculous. But now she wondered if it was ridiculous. Could Elspeth be bolting it against her rather than against Joe? You could enter that room through the back way. Did Joe occasionally come in from the back, knowing that the door to the kitchen was bolted and they wouldn't be interrupted by his wife?

Another thought occurred to her. Although the girl had been with them over three months, she seemed to have no friends. All the other girls had dates on their days off. Why didn't she? Her only friend was that big horse of a girl, Celia, who worked for the Hoskins. Could the reason Elspeth had no dates be that she was making beautiful music with her Joe?

She laughed at herself for her foolish suspicions. Why, she was with Joe practically all the time. She saw him at the club every night. Every night, that is, except Thursday. And Thursday was Elspeth's day off.

Several times Melvin Bronstein had reached for the telephone, and each time he withdrew his hand without removing the instrument from its cradle. Now it was after six and the staff had all gone home. Al Becker was still there but he was in his own office, and to judge by the books spread out on his desk, he was there to stay for a while.

He could call Rosalie undisturbed now. All week long she did not obtrude on his thoughts, but Thursdays when he was used to seeing her his need for her became overwhelming. In the year he had known her their relationship had settled down to a routine. Every Thursday afternoon she would call him and they would meet at some restaurant for dinner. Then they would drive out into the country and stop at a motel. He always brought her home by midnight, since the baby-sitter who took care of her children objected to staying later.

But recently there had been a change. He had not seen her last Thursday nor the Thursday before, because of her foolish fear that her estranged husband had hired detectives to watch her.

"Don't even call me, Mel," she had begged.

"But there can't be any harm in calling. You don't think they'd go to the trouble of tapping your telephone, do you?"

"No, but if we talk I might weaken. Then it will start all over again."

He had agreed because she had been insistent, and also because some of her fear had communicated itself to him. And now it was Thursday again. Surely he ought to call if only to inquire whether things had changed in any way. If only he could talk to her, he was sure that her need, which was as great as his, would overcome her fears.

Becker came into the room, making a great effort to appear casual, and said: "Say, Mel, I almost forgot; Sally asked me to be sure and bring you home for dinner tonight."

Bronstein smiled to himself. Ever since Al and Sally had seen him with the girl a month ago, they had tried all kinds of stratagems to entice him to spend Thursday evenings with them.

"Gee Al, let me take a rain check, will you? I don't feel up to people tonight."

"Were you planning to eat at home?"

"No-o—Debbie's having her bridge club as usual. I thought I'd just grab a bite somewhere and then drop into a movie."

"Tell you what, kid, why don't you come over a little later, spend the evening with us. Sally just got some new records—highbrow stuff. We could listen to them and then go downstairs and shoot a couple of racks of pool."

"Well, if I drive by, perhaps I'll drop in."

Becker tried again. "Say, I've got a better idea. Why don't I call Sally and tell her I'm going to stay in town, and then the two of us could make a night of it—go some place for dinner, hoist a couple of drinks, and then take in a movie or go bowling?"

Bronstein shook his head. "Knock it off, Al. You go on home and have your dinner and relax. I'll be all right. Maybe I'll be over later."

He came around to the front of his desk and put his arm around the older man's shoulders. "Go on home, beat it. I'll lock up." Gently he led Becker to the door.

Then he picked up the telephone and dialed. He heard the phone ring at the other end, again and again and again. After a while he hung up.

It was late, after six, when the doctor finished his examination. Elspeth thanked the receptionist for the mimeographed diet and the booklet on pregnancy, and carefully folded and put them away in her purse. As she was about to leave, she asked if there was a public telephone in the building.

"There's one downstairs in the lobby, but you can use ours if you like."

Elspeth blushed shyly and shook her head. The receptionist thought she understood, and smiled.

In the phone booth she dialed a number, praying that he would be home. "It's me, dear, Elspeth," she said when she heard the voice at the other end. "I've got to see you tonight. It's terribly important."

She listened, and then said, "But you don't understand. There's something I've got to tell you . . . No, I can't over the phone . . . I'm in Lynn now, but I'm coming back to Barnard's Crossing. We could have dinner together. I thought I'd eat at the Surfside and then take in a movie at the Neptune."

She nodded as he answered, just as if he could see her. "I know you can't go to a movie with me tonight, but you have to eat so why can't we have dinner together? I'll be at the Surfside around seven. . . . Well, please try to make it . . . If you're not there by half-past seven I'll know that you couldn't come, but you will try, won't you?"

She stopped at a cafeteria before going on to the bus station. Sipping her coffee, she opened the booklet on pregnancy and read it through once and then again. When she was sure she understood the few simple rules, she tucked it behind the leather seat pad of the booth. It was too dangerous to keep; Mrs. Serafino might come across it.

6

At half-past seven Jacob Wasserman rang the bell of the rabbi's house. Mrs. Small answered the door. She was tiny and vivacious, with a mass of blonde hair that seemed to overbalance her. She had wide blue eyes and an open frank face that would have seemed ingenuous were they not offset by a firm, determined little chin.

"Come in, Mr. Wasserman, come in. It's so nice to see you."

Hearing the name, the rabbi, who had been engrossed in a book, came into the hall. "Why, Mr. Wasserman. We have just finished supper, but you'll have some tea, won't you? Make some tea, dear."

He led his visitor into the living room, while his wife went to set the water on. The rabbi placed the book he was holding face-down on the table beside him and looked inquiringly at the older man.

Wasserman suddenly realized that the rabbi's gaze, though mild and benign, was also penetrating. He essayed a smile. "You know, rabbi, when you first came to our congregation you suggested that you ought to sit in on the meetings of the board. I was all in favor of it. After all, if you engage a rabbi to help direct the development of a congregation, what's better than to have him sitting in on the meetings where the various activities are planned and discussed? But they voted me down. And do you know what their reason was? They said the rabbi is an employee of the congregation. Suppose we want to talk about his salary or his contract? How can we, if he's sitting right there with us? So what was the result? All year the matter wasn't even mentioned—until this last meeting. Then I suggested that we ought to decide about the contract for next year since there are only a couple of meetings left before we adjourn for the summer."

Mrs. Small came in with a tray. After serving them, she took a cup for herself and sat down.

"And what was decided about the contract?" asked the rabbi.

"We didn't decide anything," said Wasserman. "It was held over for the next meeting—that is, for this coming Sunday."

The rabbi studied his teacup, his brow furrowed in concentration. Then without looking up, as if thinking aloud, he said, "Tonight is Thursday, three days before the meeting. If approval were certain and the vote only a matter of form, you would have waited until Sunday to tell me. If approval were likely but not absolutely certain, you would probably mention it when next you happened to see me, which would be Friday evening at the services. But if it looked as though the vote were uncertain or even likely to go against me, you would not want to mention it Friday evening for fear of spoiling my Sabbath. So your coming tonight can only mean that you have reason to believe I will not be reappointed. That's it, isn't it?"

Wasserman shook his head in admiration. Then he turned to the rabbi's wife and waggled an admonishing forefinger. "Don't ever try to deceive your husband, Mrs. Small. He'll find you out in a minute." He turned back to the rabbi. "No, rabbi, that's not it, at least not exactly. Let me explain. We have forty-five members on the board of directors. Think of it! It's more than they have on the board of General Electric or United States Steel. But you know how it is, you put on the board anyone who is a little of a somebody; anyone who does a little work for the temple, or you think maybe he'll do some work for the temple, you put him on the board. It's an honor. Without meaning to, you usually end up with a board made up of the richer members of the congregation. Other temples and synagogues do the same thing. So of the forty-five, maybe fifteen come to every meeting. Then maybe ten more come every now and then. The rest, you don't see them from one year to the next. If only the fifteen regulars were to show up, we would win by a large majority, maybe as much as four to one. To most of us, it was merely a matter of form. We would have voted the contract right then and there. But we couldn't fight the motion to hold it over for a week. It seemed reasonable and it's what we do in all important decisions. But the opposition, Al Becker and his group, evidently had something else in mind. He doesn't like you, Al Becker. Just yesterday I found out that they went to work and phoned the thirty or so who don't come regular. And from what I can see, they didn't just argue the question with them. They put on whatever pressure they could. When I heard about it yesterday from Ben Schwarz, I began to contact these people myself, but I was too late, I found that most of them were already committed to Becker and his friends. That's how matters stand now. If we have the usual meeting with the usual members present, we'll have no trouble winning. But if he gets the whole board to attend . . ." He spread his hands, palms up, in token of defeat.

"I can't say that this comes as a complete surprise to me," the rabbi said ruefully. "My roots are in traditional Judaism, and when I entered the rabbinate, it was to become a rabbi of the sort my father was and my grandfather before him, to live the life of a scholar, not in seclusion, not in an ivory tower, but as part of the Jewish community, and somehow to influence it. But I'm beginning to think that there is no place for me or my kind in a modern American Jewish community. Congregations seem to want the rabbi to act as a kind of executive secretary, organizing clubs, making speeches, integrating the temple with the churches. Perhaps it's a good thing, perhaps I'm hopelessly out of fashion, but it's not for me. The tendency seems to be to emphasize our likeness to other denominations, whereas the whole weight of our tradition is to emphasize our differences. We are not merely another sect with minor peculiarities; we are a nation of priests, dedicated to God because He chose us."

Wasserman nodded his head impatiently. "But it takes time, rabbi. These people who make up our congregation grew up during the period between the two World Wars. Most of them never went to a cheder or even a Sunday school. How do you think it was when I first tried to organize a temple? We had fifty Jewish families here at the time, and yet when old Mr. Levy died, just to get a minyan so his family could say Kaddish—it was like pulling teeth. When we first started our temple, I went to see each and every Jewish family in Barnard's Crossing. Some of them had arranged car pools to take their kids to Sunday school in Lynn; some had a teacher come out to give their boys instruction for a few months so they could hold a Bar Mitzvah, and they used to phone back and forth to make arrangements to deliver him to the home of his next pupil. My idea was to establish a Hebrew school first, and use the same building for services for the holidays. Some thought it would cost too much money, and others didn't want their children to feel different by having them go to a special school in the afternoon.

"But little by little, I won them over. I got figures on costs, estimates, prices, plans, and then when we finally acquired a building, it was a wonderful thing. In the evenings, and Sundays, they used to come down—the women in slacks, the men in dungarees, everybody working together, cleaning, fixing, painting. There were no cliques then, no parties. Everybody was interested and everybody worked together. They didn't know very much, these young people. Most of them couldn't even say their prayers in Hebrew, but the spirit was there.

"I remember our first High Holiday services. I borrowed a Scroll from the Lynn synagogue, and I was the leader and the reader, and I even gave a little sermon. For the Day of Atonement, I had a little help from the principal of the Hebrew school, but most of it I did myself. It was quite a day's work, and on an empty stomach, too. I'm not a young man and I know my wife worried, but I never felt better in my life. It was a wonderful spirit we had in those years."

"Then what happened?" asked the rabbi's wife.

Wasserman smiled wryly. "Then we grew. Jews really began to come to Barnard's Crossing then. I like to think that our having a school and a temple had something to do with it. When there were only fifty families everybody knew everybody else, differences of opinion could be hammered out in personal discussion. But when you have three hundred or more families, as we have now, it's different. There are separate social groups now who don't even know each other. You take Becker and his group, the Pearlsteins and the Korbs and the Feingolds, those who live on Grove Point, they keep to themselves. Becker is not a bad man, you understand. In fact, he's a very fine man—and all those I mentioned, they're all fine people, but their point of view is different from yours and mine. From their point of view, the bigger, the more influential, the temple organization is, the better."

"But they're the ones that pay the piper, so I suppose that gives them the right to call the tune," the rabbi remarked.

"The temple and the community are bigger than a few large contributors," said Wasserman. "A temple—"

He was interrupted by the doorbell, and the rabbi went to answer it. It was Stanley.

"You been waiting so anxious for those books, rabbi," he said, "that I thought I'd stop on my way home to tell you they came. It was a big wooden box, so I brought it up to your study and pried the lid off for you."

The rabbi thanked him and returned to the living room. But he could barely conceal his excitement. "My books have come, Miriam."

"I'm so glad, David."

"You won't mind if I go over to look through them?" Then he suddenly remembered his guest. "They're some rare books that were sent to me from the Dropsie College Library for a study I'm doing on Maimonides," he explained.

"I was just going, rabbi," said Wasserman, rising from his chair.

"Oh, you can't go now, Mr. Wasserman. You haven't finished your tea. You'll embarrass me if you leave now. Insist that he remain, Miriam."

Wasserman smiled good-naturedly. "I can see, rabbi, that you're anxious to get to your books and I don't want to keep you. Why don't you go on and I'll keep Mrs. Small company for a while."

"You're quite sure you don't mind?" But already he was heading for the garage.

His way was blocked by his wife, her firm little chin held high. "You will not leave this house, David Small," she announced, "unless you put on your topcoat."

"But it's mild out," he protested.

"By the time you get home, it will be quite chilly."

Resigned, the rabbi reached into the closet for his coat, but instead of putting it on he draped it defiantly over his arm.

Mrs. Small came back to the living room. "He's like a boy," she said by way of apology.

"No," said Mr. Wasserman. "I think maybe he wanted to be by himself for a while."

The Surfside was considered a reasonable restaurant: the prices were moderate, the service, though not fancy, was brisk and efficient, and although the decor was plain the food was good and the seafood exceptional. Mel Bronstein had never eaten there but as he approached, a car parked in front of the door pulled away and he took this as a sign. He remembered having heard the place well spoken of, and tooled his big blue Lincoln into the spot just vacated.

There were not too many people in the restaurant, he saw, as he made his way to a booth and ordered a martini. The walls were hung with lengths of fishnet, and other articles suggestive of the sea: a pair of oars, a mahogany ship's wheel, painted wooden lobster-trap floats, and occupying a wall to itself, a truly imposing swordfish mounted on a mahogany panel.

He glanced around and, not surprisingly, saw no one he knew. The Surfside was in the lower part of town, Old Town, and people from his section, Chilton, rarely went there.

Most of the booths were occupied by couples, but diagonally across from him a young girl was, like himself, sitting alone. She was not pretty, but she had a young, fresh look. By the way she kept looking at her wristwatch he assumed she was waiting for someone; she had not ordered, but every now and then she sipped at her water glass, not because she was thirsty but because everyone else was eating.

The waitress came over to ask if he were ready to order, but he motioned to his glass to indicate a refill.

The girl opposite now seemed increasingly disturbed over the failure of her escort to appear. Each time she heard the door open, she turned around on her bench. Then, quite suddenly, her mood changed. She straightened up as if she had come to a decision. She drew off her white gloves and stuffed them into her handbag as though making ready to order. He saw she was wearing a wedding ring. As he watched, she twisted her ring off, opened her bag, and dropped it into the change purse.

She looked up and saw him watching her. Blushing, she turned away. He glanced at his watch. It was quarter to eight.

Hesitating only a moment, he eased out of the booth and went over to her. She looked up, startled.

"I am Melvin Bronstein," he said, "and quite respectable. I hate to eat alone and I imagine you do. Wouldn't you care to join me?"

Her eyes widened like a child's. For a moment she lowered them, and then she looked up at him again and nodded.

"Let me give you some more tea, Mr. Wasserman."

He inclined his head in thanks. "I can't tell you how badly I feel about this business, Mrs. Small. After all, I picked your husband; he was my personal choice."

"Yes, I know, Mr. Wasserman. We wondered about it at the time, David and I. Usually when a congregation wants to hire a rabbi they ask a number of candidates to come down on successive Sabbaths to conduct the services and to meet with the board of directors or with the ritual committee. But you came down to the seminary alone, and on your own responsibility you picked David." She eyed him speculatively and then immediately dropped her eyes to her teacup. "Perhaps if the ritual committee had acted as a whole they would have felt friendlier to him," she said quietly.

"You think perhaps I insisted on making the selection myself? Believe me, Mrs. Small, the responsibility was not of my choosing. I would have preferred to let the decision rest with the ritual committee or with the board, but the building was finished in early summer, and the board was determined to start the New Year in September completely organized. When I suggested that the ritual committee go down to New York in a body—there are only three of us: Mr. Becker, Mr. Reich, and myself—it was Mr. Becker, if you please, who insisted that I go alone. 'What do Reich and I know about rabbis, Jacob?' Those were his exact words. 'You know, so you go down and pick him. Anyone you choose will be all right with us.' Maybe he was busy and couldn't go out of town at the time, or maybe he really meant it. At first, I didn't want to take the whole responsibility. Then, when I thought it over, I decided maybe it would be for the best. After all, Reich and Becker, they really do know nothing. Becker can't even say his prayers in Hebrew, and Reich isn't much better. I had already had one lesson. When it came to awarding the contract for the construction of the temple they hired Christian Sorenson as the architect. A Jewish architect wouldn't do. If I hadn't spoken out, the name Christian Sorenson—Christian, mind you—would have been on a bronze plate on the front of the temple.

The renowned ecclesiastical architect, Christian Sorenson, an exquisite with a black silk artist's bow tie and pince-nez on a black ribbon to gesture with, had prepared a pasteboard model showing a tall, narrow box of a building with long narrow windows alternating with decorative columns of stainless steel. "I have spent the last fortnight in familiarizing myself with the basic tenets of your religion, gentlemen, and my design is intended to express its essential nature." (A gaon, Wasserman had thought, who can understand the essential nature of Judaism in two weeks!) "You will note that the tall narrow lines give a sense of aspiration, calling as they do for an upward movement of the eyes; that the simplicity of the design, stark and unrelieved by any trumpery decoration"—(Was he referring to the traditional Jewish symbols: Star of David, seven-branched candelabrum, Tables of the Law?)—"typifies the practical simplicity, if I may say so, gentlemen, the basic common sense of your religion. The stainless steel columns suggest both the purity of the religion and its resistance to the decay and erosion of time."

The front elevation showed a row of stainless-steel doors from either side of which extended a long wall of glazed white brick that started at the full height of the doors and sloped away in a gentle curve to the extremities of the plot, "serving not only to soften the lines of the central mass, but also to relate it to the terrain. You will note that the effect is like a pair of open, embracing arms, calling upon people to come and worship. As a practical matter, these two walls, one on either side of the entrance, will separate the parking lot in front from the lawn which encircles the rest of the building."

"At least I was able to see that only his first initial is on the plate—and after all, it's not the building that forms the character of the congregation. But the character of the rabbi might. So I agreed to go down to the seminary alone."

"And why did you pick my David, Mr. Wasserman?"

He did not answer immediately. He realized that here was a very shrewd and forceful young woman and he should be careful with his answers. He tried to think just what it was that had attracted him to her husband. For one thing, he showed a considerable background in the study of the Talmud. No doubt the information in his folder, that he was descended from a long line of rabbis and that his wife was the daughter of a rabbi, had had something to do with it. Someone brought up in a rabbinical household could be expected to take the traditional, conservative point of view. But his first meeting had been disappointing: the young rabbi's appearance was not imposing; he looked like a very ordinary young man. However, as they talked, he found himself beguiled by David Small's friendliness, by his common sense. Then there was something about his gestures and tone vaguely reminiscent of the bearded patriarch from whom he himself had learned the Talmud when a lad in the old country; the young man's voice had that gentle, coaxing quality, a certain rhythm that stopped just short of developing into the chant that was traditional with Talmudists.

Almost as soon as Wasserman had settled the matter, however he had had misgivings. Not that he himself was dissatisfied, but he suspected that Rabbi Small was probably not what most of the congregation had in mind. Some expected a tall, austere man with a deep resonant voice, an Episcopal bishop sort of man; Rabbi Small was not tall, and his voice was gentle and mild and matter-of-fact. Some expected a jolly undergraduate sort of young man in gray flannels who would be at home on a golf course or at the tennis courts and be one with the young married set; Rabbi Small was thin and pale and wore eyeglasses, and although in excellent health he was obviously no athlete. Some had an image of the rabbi as a dynamic executive, an organizer, a go-getter who would set up committees, cajole or badger the entire congregation into ever more ambitious programs of service; Rabbi Small was rather absent-minded, had constantly to be reminded of his appointments, and had no idea of time or money. Although seemingly amenable to suggestions, he was also very good at forgetting them, especially if he had no great interest in them in the first place.

Wasserman picked his words carefully. "I'll tell you, Mrs. Small. I chose him partly because I liked him personally. But there was something else. As you know, I interviewed several others at the time. They were all fine boys with good smart Jewish heads on them. But a rabbi of a community has to be something more than just smart. He has to have courage and he has to have conviction. With each of them I sat and talked for a while. We talked about function of the rabbi in the community. And each of them agreed with me. We were feeling each other out—you always do in this kind of an interview—and as soon as they thought they knew the general direction of my Jewishness they would give it to me as their view in much better form than I could put it. I said they were smart. But your husband didn't seem interested in finding out my views. And when I stated them, he disagreed with me, not disrespectfully, but quietly and firmly. An applicant for a job who disagrees with his prospective employer is either a fool or he has convictions, and there was nothing to suggest to me that your husband was a fool.

"And now, Mrs. Small, question for question: Why did your husband apply for the job and accept it when it was offered? I'm sure the placement office at the seminary gave the candidates some idea of the kind of community it was, and in my meeting with your husband I answered all his questions fairly."

"Your idea is that he should have tried for a position with a more settled community," she asked, "one likely to be more traditional in its practices and its attitude toward the rabbi?" She set her empty cup on the table. "We talked about it, and he felt that the future is not with them. Just to go along the established groove, just to mark time, that is not my David, Mr. Wasserman. He does have conviction, and he thought he could give it to your community. The fact that they sent a man like you, alone, to pick the rabbi, instead of a committee with the customary people like Mr. Becker, persuaded him that he had a chance. And now it appears that he was wrong. They definitely are planning to oust him?"

Wasserman shrugged his shoulders. "Twenty-one admit that they are going to vote against him. They're sorry, but they promised Al Becker or Dr. Pearlstein, or somebody else. Twenty say they'll vote for the rabbi. But of these, at least four I'm not so sure about. They might not show up. They promised me, but from the way they talked—'I've got to go out of town Saturday, but if I get back in time you can count on me.' So I can count on they won't come in Sunday morning, and when they see me later on, they'll tell me what a shame it is and how hard they tried to get back in time to come to the meeting."

"That's forty-one. What about the other four?"

"They'll think it over. That means that they've already made up their minds to vote against, but they didn't want me to argue with them. What can you say to someone who promises to think it over?—Don't think?"

"Well, if that's the way they want it—"

Suddenly Wasserman was angry. "How do they know what they want?" he demanded. "When they first began to come here and I tried to get a congregation started—not even a congregation, more like a little club in case anything should happen, God forbid, we could arrange to have a minyan—this one said he didn't think he could spare the time and another one said he wasn't interested in organized religion, and several said they didn't think they could afford it. But I kept after them.

If I had taken a vote and acted accordingly, would we have a temple with a cantor and a rabbi and a school with teachers?"

"But by your own figures, Mr. Wasserman, it's twenty-five, maybe even twenty-nine, out of forty-five."

He smiled wanly. "So maybe I'm figuring with a black pencil. Maybe the ones who want to think it over, maybe they really haven't made up their minds. And Al Becker and Irving Feingold and Dr. Pearlstein, can they be so sure that everyone who promised them will come to the meeting? The outlook, it's not very bright, but a chance there is. And I'll be plain with you, Mrs. Small. Some of it is your husband's fault. There are many in the congregation, and I don't mean only Becker's friends, who feel that above all and most important, the rabbi is their personal representative in the community at large. And these people object to your husband's general attitude. They say it is almost as though he doesn't care. They say he's careless about his appointments, careless in his appearance, even careless in his manner in the pulpit. His clothes, they're apt to be wrinkled. When he gets up to speak in front of the congregation, or at a meeting, it doesn't look right."

She nodded. "I know. And maybe some of these critics blame me. A wife should see to her husband. But what can I do? I see that his clothes are neat when he leaves in the morning, but can I follow him around all day? He's a scholar. When he gets interested in a book, nothing else matters. If he feels like lying down to read he doesn't bother to take off his jacket. When he's concentrating he runs his hands through his hair. So his hair gets mussed and he looks as if he just got up from sleep. When he's studying he makes notes on cards and puts them in his pockets, so that after a while they bulge. He's a scholar, Mr. Wasserman. That's what a rabbi is, a scholar. I know what you mean. I know the sort of man the congregation wants. He gets up in a public meeting to give the invocation. He bows his head as though the Almighty were right there in front of him. He shuts his eyes lest His Radiance should blind him, and then speaks in a low, deep voice—not the voice he uses in talking to his wife, but in a special voice, like an actor. My David is no actor. Do you think God is impressed by a low, deep voice, Mr. Wasserman?"

"Dear Mrs. Small, I'm not disagreeing with you. But we live in the world. This is what the world wants now in a rabbi, so this is what a rabbi has to be."

"David will change the world, Mr. Wasserman, before the world will change my David."

7

When Joe Serafino arrived at the club, he found a new hat-check girl. He strolled over to the headwaiter, who acted as manager in his absence.

"Who's the new broad, Lennie?"

"Oh, I was going to tell you, Joe. Nellie's kid is sick again so I got this girl to stand in for her."

"What's her name?"

"Stella."

Joe looked her over. "She sure fills out that uniform," he admitted. "Okay, when things settle down, send her into the office."

"No funny business, Joe. No passes. She's like a distant cousin of my wife."

"Take it easy, Lennie. I got to get her name and address and Social Security, don't I?" Joe smiled. "You want I should bring the book out here?" He left to make his rounds of the dining room. Normally, he spent a good portion of the evening circulating among the customers, greeting one, waving to another, occasionally sitting down with one of the regulars to chat for a few minutes, after which he would snap his fingers at a passing waiter: "Give these good people a drink, Paul." But Thursday nights, maids' night out, the atmosphere was different. There were always a number of empty tables, and the people nursed their drinks, conversed in low voices, and seemed to lack spirit. Even the service was not the same; the waiters tended to huddle near the kitchen door instead of scurrying around filling orders. When Leonard glared at them or snapped his fingers to attract their attention, they would separate reluctantly, only to group together the moment his back was turned.

Thursdays, Joe spent much of the time in his office working on accounts. This evening he finished early and was trying to catch a brief nap on the couch when there was a knock on the door. He got up and seated himself at the desk with his account books open before him. "Come in," he said, in a gruff, businesslike tone.

He heard the doorknob turn ineffectually and then, smiling, he got up from his chair and turned back the night latch. He motioned the girl to the couch. "Siddown, kid," he said. "I'll be with you in a minute." Casually he pushed the door closed and returned to the swivel chair at the desk and frowned at the books in front of him. For a minute or two he appeared very busy, making little marks on paper and checking against the pages of his ledgers. Then he swung around and looked at her, letting his gaze wander slowly over her. "What's your name?"

"Stella, Stella Mastrangelo."

"How do you spell it? Never mind, here write it down on this piece of paper."

She came to the desk and bent over to write. She was young and fresh, with a smooth olive skin and dark provocative eyes. His hand itched to pat her bottom, so enticingly encased in the black satin shorts of her uniform. But he had to play it cool, so in the same businesslike voice he said, "Put down your address and your Social Security. And you better put down your telephone number too, in case we want to get in touch with you in a hurry."

She finished writing and straightened up, but she did not immediately return to the couch. Instead, she leaned against the edge of the desk, facing him. "Is that all you want, Mr. Serafino?" she asked.

"Yeah." He studied the paper. "You know, we might be able to use you from time to time. Nellie was hinting she'd like an extra night off. It'd give her more time with her kid."

"Oh, Mr. Serafino, I'd appreciate that."

"Yeah, well, we'll see about it. Say, you got your car here?"

"No, I came on the bus."

"Then how were you planning on getting home?"

"Mr. Leonard said I could leave just before midnight. That way I could catch the last bus."

"Aren't you afraid to go home that late at night alone? That's a hell of an arrangement. Tell you what, I'll drive you home tonight, and you can make some better arrangement next time. Pat, in the parking lot, can usually work out something for you with one of the cabbies."

"Oh, I couldn't have you do that, Mr. Serafino."

"Why not?"

"Well, Mr. Leonard said—"

He held up a hand. "Nobody has to know," he said, and his voice was easy and coaxing. "This door here leads right to the parking lot. You leave at quarter of twelve and walk down to the bus stop and wait for me there. I'll get my car and pick you up."

"But Mr. Leonard—"

"Lennie wants to see me, he comes here. He finds the door locked and he knows I'm grabbing a little shut-eye. He knows better than to disturb me when I'm having a little snooze. Okay? Besides, we got business to talk about, ain't we?"

She nodded her head and fluttered her eyelashes at him.

"Okay, run along, kid, and I'll see you later." He patted her in dismissal, in a fatherly sort of way.

The Ship's Cabin served sandwiches, doughnuts, and coffee during the day. In the evening they offered hot dishes—spaghetti and meatballs, fried clams and french fried potatoes, baked beans and frankforts— which were described on greasy, fly-specked cards and inserted in the frame of the bar mirror. Each dish was numbered and regulars like Stanley would order by number, presumably to speed up the operation.

There was no heavy drinking either during the day or in the early evening. The patrons who dropped in at midday usually took ale or beer to wash down their sandwich. Those who came later might have a shot of whiskey before supper. But the regular customers, like Stanley, usually returned around nine. That was when the Ship's Cabin really came alive.

After leaving the rabbi's house, Stanley drove his yellow jalopy to the Ship's Cabin, had his regular evening meal, one of the three specials, together with a few glasses of ale. He sat at the bar eating stolidly, his jaws moving rhythmically like a machine. He focused on his plate just long enough to load his fork and then turned his head to watch the television screen set high in one corner of the room, as he chewed away. Every now and then, he reached for his glass and took a long draught, his eyes remaining fixed on the screen.

Except for exchanging a remark about the weather with the bartender when he first set his plate before him, Stanley spoke to no one. The program ended, and he drained the remains of his second glass, wiped his mouth with the paper napkin that had lain folded all through supper, and ambled over to the cashier to pay his tab.

He left the tavern with a wave to the bartender, and drove the few blocks to Mama Schofield's. No point in hanging around; there would be nothing doing for another hour or two.

Mrs. Schofield was sitting in her parlor when he stuck his head in to say good evening. Upstairs in his room he took off his shoes, his denim work pants, and shirt and lay down on the bed, his hands clasped under his head, staring up at the ceiling. There were no pictures like those he had on the wall in the temple basement; Mama Schofield would not have stood for them. The only decoration was a calendar showing a picture of a little boy and a puppy that was somehow supposed to induce fond feelings for the Barnard's Crossing Coal Company.

Usually he napped for an hour or so, but tonight for some reason he was restless. He realized he was undergoing one of his frequent attacks of loneliness. In his circle of acquaintances, his bachelorhood was regarded as proof that he was too smart to have got himself caught. He wondered uneasily now if he hadn't outsmarted himself. What sort of life did he have? Supper, a greasy meal eaten at a counter stool; then back to a furnished room, with the boozy good fellowship of the Ship's Cabin afterward the only thing to look forward to. If he were married now—and his mind slipped into a pleasant daydream of married life. Soon he dozed off.

When he awoke, it was almost ten o'clock. He got up and dressed in his good clothes and drove to the Ship's Cabin. The dream persisted. He drank more than usual in an effort to drown it, but it only bobbed up whenever the talk lagged or the noise momentarily abated.

Toward midnight the crowd began to thin out and Stanley got up to go. The loneliness was stronger than ever. He realized that it was Thursday and there probably would be some girl getting off the last bus at Oak and Vine. Maybe she would be tired and appreciate the offer of a ride the rest of the way home.

Elspeth sat in the back seat of the car. The rain had let up somewhat, but large drops still bounced on the asphalt, turning it into a sleek black pool. She was at ease now, and to prove it she took slow, graceful puffs at her cigarette, like an actress. When she spoke, she stared straight ahead, only occasionally darting quick looks at her companion to see how he was reacting.

He was sitting bolt upright, his eyes wide and unwinking, his jaw set and his lips tight—in anger? in frustration? in despair? She could not tell. She leaned forward to snuff her cigarette in the ashtray attached to the back of the front seat. Very deliberately, as if to emphasize each word, she tapped her cigarette out against the little metal snuffer.

She sensed, rather than saw, his hand reaching forward. She felt it on her neck and was about to turn to smile at him when his fingers curled around her silver choke collar. She tried to complain he was holding too tight but his hand gave the heavy chain a sudden twist, and it was too late—too late to remonstrate—too late to cry out. The cry was stifled in her throat and she was enveloped in a red mist. And then there was blackness.

He sat with his arm still outstretched, his hand gripping the silver choker as one would to restrain a vicious dog. After a while he relaxed his grip, and as she began to fall forward he caught her by the shoulder and eased her onto the seat again. He waited. Then, cautiously, he opened the door of the car and looked out. Certain that there was no one in sight, he got out, and leaning in, scooped her up in his arms and eased her out of the car. Her head lolled back.

He did not look at her. With a swing of his hip, he slammed the door to. He carried her over to the wall where it was lowest, barely three feet high. Leaning over, he tried to set her down gently on the grass on the other side, but she was heavy and rolled out of his arms. He reached down in the darkness to close her eyes against the rain, but it was her hair that he felt. There seemed to be no point in trying to turn her over.

8

The alarm clock on the night table beside Rabbi Small's bed rang at a quarter to seven. That gave him time to shower, shave, and dress for morning services at the temple at seven-thirty.

He reached and turned off the alarm, but instead of getting up he made happy animal sounds and rolled over again. His wife shook him. "You'll miss services, David."

"This morning I'm going to pass them up."

She thought she understood and did not insist. Besides, she knew he had come in very late the night before, long after she had gone to bed.

Later, in his study, Rabbi Small was reciting the morning prayer, while in the kitchen Miriam was preparing his breakfast. When she heard his voice raised exultantly in the Shema: Hear O Israel, the Lord is our God, the Lord is One, she began heating the water; when she heard the buzz-buzz of the Amidah, she started his eggs, cooking them until she heard him chant the Alenu, when she took them out of the boiling water.

He came out of the study a few minutes later, rolling down the left sleeve of his shirt and buttoning the cuff. As always, he looked with dismay at the table set for him.

"So much?"

"It's good for you, dear. Everybody says that breakfast is the most important meal of the day." Her mother-in-law had been most insistent on it: "You should see that he eats, Miriam. Don't ask him what he wants, because for him, if he has a book propped up in front of him or if he has some idea spinning around in his head, he can gnaw on a crust of bread and be satisfied. You've got to see that he eats regular, a balanced diet with lots of vitamins."

Miriam had already breakfasted—toast and coffee and a cigarette—so she hovered over him, seeing to it that he finished his grapefruit, setting his cereal down before him with an air that indicated she would brook no refusal. As soon as he had finished the last spoonful, she served his eggs, along with his toast already buttered. The trick was to avoid any delay during which his mind could wander and he would lose interest. Not until he had started on his eggs and toast did she pour herself another cup of coffee and permit herself to sit down opposite him.

"Did Mr. Wasserman stay long after I left?" he asked.

"About half an hour. I think he feels I should take better care of you, see that your suits are always pressed and your hair combed."

"I should be more careful of my appearance. Am I all right now? No egg stains on my tie?" he asked anxiously.

"You look fine, David. But you can't seem to stay that way." She regarded him critically. "Maybe if you used one of those collar pins, your tie would stay in place."

"You need a shirt with a special collar for that," he said. "I tried one once. It binds my throat."

"And couldn't you use some of that stuff that keeps your hair in place?"

"You want women to chase me? Would you like that?"

"Don't tell me you're above wanting to be attractive to women."

"You think that would do it?" he asked in mock eagerness. "A shirt with a tab collar and stickum on my hair?"

"Seriously, David, it is important. Mr. Wasserman seemed to think it was very important. Do you think they'll drop your contract?"

He nodded. "Quite probably. I'm sure he wouldn't have come down to see us yesterday if he thought otherwise."

"What will we do?"

He shrugged his shoulders. "Notify the seminary that I am at liberty and have them find me another congregation."

"And if the same thing happens again?"

"We notify them again." He laughed. "You remember Manny Katz, Rabbi Emmanuel Katz, the one with that tomboy wife? He lost three jobs one right after the other because of her. She used to wear shorts around the house during the summer, and when they went to the beach she wore a bikini, which is exactly what the women her age in the congregation would wear. But what they tolerated in their young women they wouldn't tolerate in the rebbitzin. And Manny wouldn't ask his wife to change. He finally got a job with a congregation down in Florida, where I guess everybody dresses that way. He's been there ever since."

"He was lucky," she said. "Do you expect to strike a congregation where the leaders wear sloppy clothes and are absent-minded and don't keep their appointments?"

"Oh, probably not. But when we get tired wandering, I can always get a job teaching. Nobody cares how teachers dress."

"Why don't we do that right away instead of waiting to be kicked out of half a dozen congregations? I'd like to be a teacher's wife. You could get a job at some college in Semitics, maybe even at the seminary. Just think, David, I wouldn't have to worry whether the president of the Sisterhood approved of my housekeeping or if the president of the local Hadassah thought my dress was in good taste."

The rabbi smiled. "Only the dean's wife. And I wouldn't have to attend community breakfasts."

"And I wouldn't have to smile every time a member of the congregation looked in my direction."

"Do you?"

"Of course. Till my face muscles ache. Oh let's do it, David."

He looked at her in surprise. "You're not serious." His face turned sober. "Don't think I don't feel my failure here, Miriam. It bothers me, not merely failing at something that I set out to do, but knowing that the congregation needs me. They don't know it yet, but I know it. Without me, or someone like me, you know what happens to these congregations? As religious institutions, that is, as Jewish religious institutions, they dry up. I don't mean that they're not active. As a matter of fact, they become veritable hives of activity with dozens of different groups and clubs and committees—social groups and art groups and study groups and philanthropy groups and athletic groups, most of them ostensibly Jewish. The dance group works up an interpretive dance they call Spirit of the Israeli Pioneer; the choral group adds 'White Christmas' to its repertoire so they can sing it at Christian churches during Brotherhood Week and the church can respond by having its lead tenor sing 'Eli, Eli.' The rabbi conducts the holiday services with great decorum, and except for an occasional responsive reading he and the cantor perform the entire service between them. You would never know that this is the spiritual home of a people who for three thousand years or more considered themselves a nation of priests sworn to the service of God, because every bit of the energy of the congregation and the rabbi too will be bent on showing that this Jewish church is no different from any other church in the community."

The doorbell rang. Miriam opened the door to a stocky man with a pleasant Irish face and snow-white hair.

"Rabbi David Small?"

"Yes?" The rabbi looked at him inquiringly, then at the card that indicated he was Hugh Lanigan, chief of police of Barnard's Crossing.

"Can I talk to you privately?" he asked.

"Of course." The rabbi led the way to his study. He closed the door, asking his wife as he did so to see that they were not interrupted.

Motioning his visitor to a chair, he sat down himself and looked at his guest expectantly.

"Your car was parked in the temple parking lot all night, rabbi."

"This is not permitted?"

"Of course. The parking lot is private property, and I guess if anyone has a right it would be you. As a matter of fact, we don't usually fuss too much if a car is parked on the street all night unless it's winter and there's a snowstorm and it interferes with the plows."

"So?"

"So we wondered why you left it there instead of in your own garage?"

"Did you think someone might steal it? It's very simple. I left it at the temple because I did not have the keys to drive it off with." He smiled, a little embarrassed. "That's not too clear, I'm afraid. You see, I went to the temple last night and spent the evening in my study. Some books had arrived that I was anxious to look over. Then, when I left, I closed the door of the study, and that locked it. You understand?"

Lanigan nodded. "Spring latch on the door."

"All my keys, including the key to the temple study, were on a key ring on my desk inside. I couldn't open the door of the study to get them, so I had to walk home. Does this explain the mystery?"

Lanigan nodded reflectively. Then, "I understand you people have prayers every morning. This morning you did not go, rabbi."

"That's right. There are some members of my congregation who take it amiss if their rabbi skips a daily service, but I hardly expected them to lodge a complaint with the police."

Lanigan laughed shortly. "Oh, nobody complained. At least, not to me, not in my capacity as police chief—"

"Come, Mr. Lanigan, evidently something has happened, a police matter in which my car is concerned—no, I myself must be concerned or you wouldn't want to know why I didn't go to morning prayers. If you will tell me what happened, perhaps I can tell you what you wish to know, or at least be able to help you more intelligently."

"You're right, rabbi. You understand that we're bound by regulations. My common sense tells me that you as a man of the cloth are in no way implicated, but as a policeman—"

"As a policeman you are not supposed to use your common sense? Is that what you were going to say?"

"That's not far from the truth! And yet there's good reason for it. We are bound to investigate everyone who could be involved, and although I know a rabbi would be no more likely to commit the sort of crime we're investigating than a priest, we've got to check everyone through."

"I would not presume to suggest what a priest would or would not do, chief, but anything that a man might do a rabbi might do. We are no different from ordinary men. We are not even men of the cloth, as you call it. I have no duties or privileges that any member of my congregation does not have. I am only presumed to be learned in the Law by which we are enjoined to live."

"It's kind of you to put it on that footing, rabbi. I'll be candid with you. This morning, the body of a young woman of nineteen or twenty was found on the temple grounds right behind the low wall that divides the parking lot from the lawn. She had evidently been killed sometime during the night. We'll have a pretty good idea of the time when the laboratory gets through checking."

"Killed? An accident?"

"Not an accident, rabbi. She was strangled with a silver chain that she wore around her neck, one of those heavy link chains with a locket. No chance of it being an accident."

"But this is terrible. Was it—was it a member of my congregation? Someone I know?"

"Do you know an Elspeth Bleech?" asked the chief.

The rabbi shook his head. "It's an unusual name, Elspeth."

"It's a variation of Elizabeth, of course. It's English and the girl was from Nova Scotia."

"From Nova Scotia? A tourist?"

Lanigan smiled. "Not a tourist, rabbi, a domestic. You know, during the Revolution a number of the more important and wealthier citizens of the Colonies, especially right here in Massachusetts, ran off to Canada, mostly to Nova Scotia. Loyalists, they were called. And now their descendants come back down here to go into domestic service. Pretty bad guessing on the part of their ancestors. This one worked for the Serafinos. Do you know the Serafinos, rabbi?"

"The name sounds Italian." He smiled. "If I have any Italians in my congregation, I'm not aware of it."

Lanigan grinned back at him. "They're Italians all right, and I know they don't go to your church because they go to mine, the Star of the Sea."

"You're Catholic? That surprises me, by the way. I didn't think of Barnard's Crossing as the sort of town where a Catholic was apt to get to be chief of police."

"There have been a few Catholic families here since the Revolution. Mine was one of them. If you knew the history of the town, you'd know that this is one of the few communities in Puritan Massachusetts where a Catholic could live in peace. The town was started by a group that didn't care too much about Puritanism."

"That's very interesting. I must investigate it someday." He hesitated, then he said, "The girl—had she been attacked or molested?"

Lanigan spread his hands in a gesture of ignorance. "Seemingly not, but the medical examiner might come up with something. There were no signs of struggle, no scratches, no torn clothing. On the other hand, she wasn't wearing a dress—just a slip, with a light topcoat and one of those transparent plastic raincoats over that. From what we have right now, there are no signs of struggle. The poor girl didn't have a chance. This chain she was wearing is what they call a choker, I believe. It closely encircles the neck. The murderer had only to grab it in back and twist."

"Terrible," the rabbi murmured, "terrible. And you think this was done on temple grounds?"

Lanigan pursed his lips. "We're not sure where it happened. For all we know, she could have been killed elsewhere."

"Then why was she brought there?" asked the rabbi, ashamed that his mind automatically reverted to thoughts of a scheme to discredit the Jewish community with some fantastic plot of ritual murder.

"Because, when you come to think of it, it's not a bad place for the purpose. You might think that out here in the suburbs there'd be any number of places where you could dispose of a body, but actually there aren't. Most of the likely places are apt to be under someone's view. Places where there are no houses tend to become lovers' lanes. No, I'd say the temple area would be one of the best spots. It's dark, there are no houses in the immediate vicinity, and there's not likely to be anyone around most nights." He paused and then said, "By the way, between what times were you there?"

"You are wondering if I heard or saw anything?"

"Ye-es."

The rabbi smiled. "And you would also like to know how I was myself engaged during the critical time. Very well. I left my house around half-past seven or eight o'clock. I'm not sure of the time because I don't

have the habit of glancing at my watch. Most of the time I don't bother
to wear one. I had been having tea with my wife and Mr. Wasserman,
the president of our congregation, when Stanley—he's our janitor—
stopped by to tell me that a box of books I had been expecting had
arrived and was now in my study. I excused myself and got into my
car and drove to the temple. I left only minutes after Stanley left, so
between my wife and Mr. Wasserman and Stanley you should be able
to get pretty close to the exact time. I parked my car and let myself into
the temple and went directly to my study on the second floor. I stayed
until after twelve. I know that because I happened to glance at the
clock on my desk and saw that it was midnight and decided I should be
getting back. I was in the middle of a chapter, however, so I didn't leave
immediately." He had a sudden idea. "This might help you to fix the
time with greater precision: just before I arrived home, there was a
sudden cloudburst and I had to sprint the rest of the way. I suppose
somebody, the weather bureau perhaps, keeps an accurate record of
the weather."

"That was at 12:45. We checked that first thing because the girl was
wearing a raincoat."

"I see. Well, normally it takes me twenty minutes to walk from the
temple to my house. I know because we do it every Friday evening and
Saturday. But I think I walked more slowly last night. I was thinking of
the books I had read."

"But on the other hand, you ran part of the way."

"Oh, that was just the last hundred yards or so. Call it twenty-five
minutes and I think that would be fairly accurate. That would mean
that I left the temple at twenty past."

"Did you meet anyone on the way?"

"No, just the police officer. I suppose he knew me because he said
good evening."

"That would be Officer Norman." He smiled. "He wouldn't have to
know you to say good evening. He rings in at one o'clock at the box
on Vine Street just beyond the temple. I'll be able to get the time from
him when I see him."

"You mean he records it?"

"Probably not, but he'll remember. He's a pretty good man. Now,
when you entered the temple, you turned on the light, I suppose."

"No, it wasn't dark yet."

"But you turned on the light in your study of course."

"Of course."

"So that anyone passing by would have seen it."

The rabbi considered. Then he shook his head. "No, I turned on my

desk lamp rather than the overhead light. I opened the window, of
course, but I lowered the venetian blind."

"Why?"

"Frankly, so that I wouldn't be interrupted. A member of the congregation might pass by and see the light and come up to chat."

"So no one approaching the temple would guess anyone was there.
Is that right, rabbi?"

The rabbi thought a moment and then nodded.

The police chief smiled.

"This has some significance for you?"

"Well, it might help to clarify the time element. Suppose the light
could be seen. Then that, in conjunction with your car in the parking
lot, would indicate that someone was still in the building and might
come out at any time. If that were the case, it would be fair to assume
the body had been deposited behind the wall after you left. But with
no light showing, it might be assumed your car had been left for the
night perhaps because you couldn't get it started. Under those circumstances, the body could have been dropped while you were still
upstairs. Now the medical examiner's first estimate was that the girl was
killed around one o'clock. At this point in his examination, that's just
an educated guess. If your light had been visible, it would tend to
corroborate his estimate, but since the light could not be seen the girl
could have been dropped near the wall while you were in your study,
and that could have been anytime from the early evening on."

"I see."

"Now think carefully, rabbi, did you hear or see anything unusual—
a cry? the sound of an automobile driving onto the parking lot?"

The rabbi shook his head.

"And you saw no one either while you were in your study or on your
way home?"

"Only the police officer."

"Now you say you do not know Elspeth Bleech. Is it possible that
you know her but not by name? After all, she lived with the Serafinos
no great distance from the temple."

"It is possible."

"A girl of nineteen or twenty, blonde, about five feet four, a little
on the stocky side but not unattractive. Perhaps later I'll be able to show
you a picture."

The rabbi shook his head. "I don't recognize her from your description. It would fit many girls I may have seen. Nothing comes to mind
at the moment, however."

"Well, let me put it this way: did you give anyone a lift in your car in the last day or two who might answer that description?"

The rabbi smiled and shook his head. "A rabbi, no less than a priest or a minister, finds it necessary to be circumspect about those things. I would be no more likely to offer a lift to a strange young woman than they would. One's congregation might misinterpret it. No, I gave no one a lift."

"Could your wife perhaps?"

"My wife doesn't drive."

Lanigan rose and held out his hand. "You've been very cooperative, rabbi, and I appreciate it."

"Any time."

At the door, Lanigan paused. "I hope you won't be needing your car for a little while. My boys are checking it over."

The rabbi looked his surprise.

"You see, the girl's handbag was found in it."

9

Hugh Lanigan knew Stanley, just as he knew all the Old Towners. He found him working in the vestry, setting up a long table on which the Sisterhood would later serve the little cakes and tea things that constituted the usual collation after the Friday evening service.

"Just checking on this business, Stanley."

"Sure, Hugh, but I told Eban Jennings all I know."

"Well, you might as well give it to me again. You went to the rabbi's house last night to tell him about a box of books. When did the books arrive?"

"Delivered by Robinson's Express around six o'clock. Maybe a little after. It was his last stop."

"And when did you go over to the rabbi's?"

"Seven-thirty or so. I got this box and it's a pretty big wooden case and it's for the rabbi. I don't know that it's books at first—I mean, the rabbi, he told me about a shipment of books he was expecting, but I had no idea it would come in a wooden box. But then I notice it was shipped from Dropsie College. Well, the rabbi had mentioned that the books were coming from Dropsie College. Now that's a funny name for a college, and I remembered it because my Aunt Mattie—you remember her—well, that's what she had, dropsy, I mean. She was all puffed up, you could hardly see her eyes—"

"Never mind, just tell me about the box."

"Oh yeah, so I see the name and I remember that that's where the books were supposed to come from. So I figure it must be the books. Well, you wouldn't believe it, Hugh, but this rabbi—he's a nice feller and all that—but he wouldn't know which end of a hammer you hit with. So no matter what's in that case, I'm going to have to open it for him anyway. Right? So I figured I might as well do it right then. So I toted the whole business, box and all—and it was heavy as a son-ofabitch, Hugh—right up to his study. Then I kind of finished my chores here and I thought I'd let him know that they came, seeing as he was so anxious for them and it was on my way home anyway."

"Where you living now, Stanley?"

"I got a room at Mama Schofield's."

"Didn't you used to live at the temple?"

"Yeah, at the old place. I had me a room up in the attic. Beauty. It was kind of nice, living right at the job, you know. But then they stopped it. They gave me a few bucks more each month to pay for a room, and I've been at Mama Schofield's ever since."

"Why did they stop it?" asked Lanigan.

"I'll tell you the truth, Hugh. They found out I was having some company up there once in a while. No wild parties, you understand, Hugh. I wouldn't do anything like that, and never while the temple was being used. Just a couple of people over for a little talk and a few beers. But I guess they got to thinking I might take it into my head to bring a broad up there, maybe on one of their holy days." He gave a loud chortle and slapped his thigh. "I suppose they were afraid that while they were praying down below, I might be bouncing a broad upstairs, and that would kind of short-circuit their prayers on the way up, see?"

"Go on."

"So they asked me to find myself a room, and I did. There was no hard feelings."

"How about here in the new building? Don't you ever sleep over?"

"Well, in the winter after a heavy snowfall, when I got to get the sidewalks cleared early. I got me a cot down in the boiler room."

"Let's go take a look at it."

"Sure, Hugh." Stanley led the way down a short flight of iron stairs and then stood aside as Lanigan pushed open a steel-clad fire door. The boiler room was immaculate, except for the corner where Stanley had set up his cot. Lanigan pointed out that the blankets were rumpled.

"Been that way since the last snowfall?" he asked.

"I lie down for a nap most afternoons," said Stanley easily. He watched while Lanigan poked idly through the cigarette butts in the ashtray. "I told you I never have anybody down here."

Lanigan sat down in the wicker chair and let his eyes wander over Stanley's art gallery. Stanley grinned sheepishly.

The police chief motioned for him to sit down, and he obediently plumped down on the cot. "Now let's get on with it. Around half-past seven you stopped at the rabbi's house to tell him about the box. Why couldn't you wait until morning? Did you expect the rabbi to leave his house at night?"

Stanley showed surprise at the question. "Why sure, the rabbi is up there reading and studying plenty of nights."

"Then what did you do?"

"I went on home."

"Stop on the way?"

"Sure, I stopped at the Ship's Cabin for a bite of supper and a couple of beers. Then I went on to Mama Schofield's."

"And you stayed there?"

"Yeah, I was there all the early evening."

"And then you went to bed?"

"Well, I went out for a beer just before turning in. At the Ship's Cabin it was."

"And what time did you leave this time?"

"Maybe around midnight. Maybe a little later."

"And you went right home to Schofield's?"

For a moment he hesitated, then, "Uh-huh."

"Anybody see you come in?"

"No, why should they? I got my own key."

"All right. What time did you come to work this morning?"

"Same as always. A little before seven."

"And what did you do?"

"They have a service here at half-past seven in the chapel. So I put on the lights and open a couple of windows to kind of air the place out. Then I set about my regular work, which this time of year it's mostly working on the lawn. I been raking up grass clippings mostly. I started yesterday working on the Maple Street side. So I started where I left off and gradually worked my way around the back of the building and then around to the other side. That's when I saw the girl. They were just coming out of the service and getting in their cars when I spotted her up against the brick wall. I walked over and I could see she was dead. I looked over the wall and Mr. Musinsky—he's a regular, I mean he comes every morning—he hadn't got in his car yet, so I hailed him. He took a look and then went right back into the temple to call you people."

"Did you notice the rabbi's car when you arrived this morning?"

"Oh sure."

"Surprised?"

"Not particularly. I figured he had come for morning prayers and had just got there early. When I saw he wasn't in the chapel, I figured he was in his study."

"You didn't go up to look?"

"No, what would I do that for?"

"All right." Lanigan rose and Stanley did likewise. The police chief strode out into the corridor with Stanley right behind him. He turned his head and said matter-of-factly, "You recognized the girl, of course."

"No," Stanley said quickly.

Lanigan turned around to face him. "You mean you never saw her before?"

"You mean this girl that was—"

"What other girl are we talking about?" asked Lanigan coldly.

"Well, working around the temple here, naturally I see a lot of people. Yes, I seen her around. I mean, I've seen her walking with those two little dago kids she takes care of."

"Did you know her?"

"I just said I seen her." Stanley sounded exasperated.

"Did you ever make a pass at her?"

"Why would I do that?" demanded Stanley.

"Because you're as horny as a mink."

"Well, I didn't."

"Ever talk to her?"

Stanley drew a dirty handkerchief from a pocket of his dungarees and began to mop his forehead.

"What's the matter, feeling warm?"

Stanley exploded. "God damn it, Hugh, you're trying to get me tied up in this. Sure I talked to her. I'm standing around and a young chick comes along with a couple of kids in tow and one of them starts pulling at the shrubbery, naturally I'm going to speak up."

"Naturally."

"But I never went out with her or anything."

"Never showed her that little pigpen you've got down in the basement?"

"Just, Hello or It's a nice morning, isn't it?" said Stanley doggedly. "And half the time, she never even answered."

"I can imagine. All right, how did you know the kids were Italian?"

"Because I seen them with their father, Serafino, and I knew him because I once did some work on his house."

"When was this?"

"When did I see him? A couple or three days ago maybe. He drove up in his convertible and he sees the girl and the kids and he asks do they want their daddy should get them some ice cream. Then they all pile into the front seat, the girl and then the kids fighting about who was going to sit next to the door, and the girl wiggling over to make room and the old man kind of arsing her. Disgusting."

"Disgusting because it wasn't you?"

"Well, at least I'm free and not a married man with a couple of kids."

10

It had been a hectic morning for the Serafinos. Although Mrs. Serafino went to bed early on Thursday nights, she did not usually rise much before ten on Fridays. But this morning she had been awakened by the children, who, having pounded on Elspeth's door to no effect, burst into her bedroom demanding to be dressed.

Angry at the girl for oversleeping, she wrapped a robe about her and went down to wake her up. She pounded on the door and called her name. When the girl failed to respond, it occurred to her that Elspeth might not be in her room, and that could only mean she had not come home at all last night. For a live-in maid, this was a cardinal offense punishable by immediate dismissal. She was about to run outside to peer through the window and confirm her suspicions when the front doorbell rang.

She was so certain it was Elspeth, probably with some cock-and-bull story about having lost her key, that she raced down the hall and flung open the front door. It was a uniformed policeman. Her robe had fallen open, and for a moment she just stood there staring at him stupidly. His blush of embarrassment suddenly made her realize that she was exposed, and she hastily gathered the garment about her.

There followed a nightmare of a morning. Other policemen came, in and out of uniform. The telephone rang incessantly, all police business. She was told to get her husband up and dressed so that he could accompany one of the officers to make formal identification of the body.

"Couldn't I identify her?" she asked. "My husband needs his sleep."

"He's a good man if he can sleep through all this," said the officer, and then not unkindly, "Believe me, lady, you better have him do it. She's not very pretty."

Somehow the children managed to get fed and dressed, and she even prepared a breakfast of sorts for herself. And all the time she was eating, there were questions: formal interrogations with one officer sitting across the table and another taking notes; questions while they were measuring and photographing the girl's room; questions asked abruptly as if to take her by surprise.

After a while they left. The children were out in the backyard for the moment, and she had decided to lie down on the couch for a few minutes of relaxation, when the doorbell rang once again. It was Joe.

She scanned his face anxiously. "Was it the girl?"

"Sure it was the girl. Who else would it be? You think the cops didn't know who it was before I identified her?"

"Then why did they need you?"

"Because it's the law, that's why. It's like a routine you got to go through."

"Did they ask you any questions, Joe?"

"Cops always ask questions."

"Like what? What did they ask you?"

"Like did she have any enemies? What was the name of her boyfriend? Who were her friends? Was she upset lately? When was the last time I saw her?"

"And what did you tell them?"

"What do you think I told them? I told them I didn't know of no boyfriend, that this girl Celia who works for the Hoskins is the only girlfriend she's got I know of, that she looked all right to me and I didn't see no signs of her being upset."

"And did you tell them when was the last time you saw her?"

"Sure, it was around one-two o'clock yesterday. Jesus, what's all this questioning? I get it from the cops and then I come home and get it from you. And all morning, I haven't even had a cup of coffee yet."

"I'll get you some coffee, Joe. Would you like some toast with it? Eggs? Cereal?"

"No, just coffee. I'm all wound up—my stomach it's all tied up in knots."

She went about heating the coffee. Without turning she asked, "Which was it, one or two o'clock, that you last saw her, Joe?"

He canted his head at the ceiling. "Let's see, I came down and had my breakfast—around noon, wasn't it? I saw her then. I guess I did—" uncertainly. "Anyway, I heard her giving the kids their lunch and then getting them ready for their nap. Then I went up to get dressed and by the time I came back she was already gone."

"You didn't see her after that?"

"What do you mean? What the hell are you driving at?"

"Well, you were going to give her a ride in to Lynn, remember?"

"So?"

"So I wondered, did you meet her before she caught the bus? Or maybe, did you bump into her in Lynn?"

A tinge of red crept into his swarthy face. He rose slowly from the kitchen table. "All right, come on. Let's have it. What are you hinting at?"

She was a little frightened now, but she had gone too far to stop. "Don't you think I've seen the looks you've given her? How do I know you weren't seeing her on her day off? Or maybe right here when I wasn't around?"

"So that's it! I look at a babe and that means I'm sleeping with her. And when I get tired of her, I kill her. Is that what you're trying to say? And I suppose, like a good citizen, you're going to tell the cops."

"You know I wouldn't do that, Joe. I'm just thinking maybe somebody saw you, and if they did I could say like she was going on an errand for me, to cover you."

"I ought to break this over your face," he said, picking up the sugar bowl.

"Oh, yes? Well, don't you go acting innocent with me, Joe Serafino," she shouted. "Don't tell me you wouldn't make a pass at a girl living right here in the same house. I've seen you when you gave the girl and the kids a ride and how you'd brush up against her when you were helping her out of the car. How come you never have to help me out of the car? I saw you right here through the kitchen window. And how about the other girl, Gladys? Don't try to tell me there was nothing between you and her, with her walking around practically mother-naked in her room while you were sitting here in the kitchen and the door half open. And how many's the time—"

The doorbell rang. It was Hugh Lanigan.

"Mrs. Serafino? I want to ask you some questions."

11

Alice Hoskins, Bryn Mawr '57, the mother of two children and very obviously soon to have a third, invited the chief of police into her living room. The floor was covered with an oyster-white wall-to-wall figured broadloom. The furniture was Danish modern, odd-shaped pieces of highly polished teak and black sailcloth seemingly curved or sloping the wrong way, yet strangely comfortable to sit in. There was a coffee table, a slab of dark walnut supported by four glass legs. On one wall hung a large abstract painting, vaguely suggestive of a female head; on another, a grotesque ebony mask, the features sharply etched and heightened in white. There were ashtrays scattered about, of sharp-edged crystal, most of them full to overflowing with cigarette butts. It was the sort of room that could be attractive only if kept scrupulously tidy with everything in its rightful place; and the room was a mess. Toys were scattered about the floor; a child's red sweater had been tossed on a chair of wrought iron and white leather; a glass, a quarter full of milk, was on the mantelpiece; a mussed newspaper was on the couch.

Mrs. Hoskins, thin and drawn except for her protuberant belly, waddled over to the couch, swept the newspaper onto the floor, and sat down. She patted the seat beside her in invitation, offered Lanigan a cigarette from a crystal box on the coffee table, and took one for herself. There was a matching table lighter, but as he reached for it she said, "It doesn't work," and struck a match for him.

"Celia is out with the children just now, but she should be back very soon," she said.

"It's just as well," he said. And then getting right to business: "Was she very friendly with Elspeth?"

"Celia is friendly with everybody, Mr Lanigan. She's one of those plain girls who goes in for being friendly. You know, a plain girl has to have something else. Some go in for brains and some go in for causes and some go in for being friendly and good sports. That's Celia. She's jolly and a good sport and frightfully keen on the children. And they're crazy about her. I'm just here to have them; she takes care of them from then on."

"She been with you long?"

"Ever since before the first one arrived. She came to us when I was in my last month."

"So she's a good bit older than Elspeth?"

"Goodness, yes. Celia is twenty-eight or nine."

"Did she talk to you about Elspeth?"

"Oh yes. We talked about all kinds of things. We're quite good pals, you know. I mean, Celia has a lot of common sense even though she hasn't had much schooling. I think she left school about the second year of high, but she's been around and she knows people. She felt sorry for Elspeth. Celia is always feeling sorry for people. In this case, I suppose with some justification, Elspeth being a stranger and all. And the girl *was* shy. She didn't like to go places and do things. Celia bowls regularly and goes to dances and beach parties in the summer and skating in the winter, but she could never get Elspeth to come along. She would take in a movie with her occasionally, and of course they were together most afternoons with the children, but Celia could never get her to go bowling or to dances—you know, places where a girl could meet men."

"Surely you talked about the reason for it."

"Of course we did. Celia thought that part of it was just natural shyness—some girls are, you know—and that maybe she didn't have the clothes for dances. Also, I suspect that Celia's crowd were probably too old for Elspeth."

Lanigan fished in his pocket and brought out a snapshot of the girl and the two Serafino children. "Mrs. Serafino gave me that. It was the only picture she had of the girl. Would you say it was a good likeness?"

"Oh, that's the girl all right."

"I mean, would you call that a characteristic expression, Mrs. Hoskins? We might run it in the papers—"

"You mean with the two children?"

"Oh no, we'd block them out."

"I suppose public curiosity must be satisfied, but I didn't realize the police were so cooperative," she said coldly.

He laughed. "It's the other way around, Mrs. Hoskins. We expect the press to cooperate by printing the picture. It may enable us to trace her movements yesterday."

"Oh, I'm sorry."

"And would you say that the expression is characteristic?" he persisted.

She looked at the snapshot again. "Yes, that's like her. She was really quite an attractive girl. A little on the stocky side, but not fat—what we used to call corn-fed. Perhaps buxom would be a nicer word. Of course, I used to see her around with the children with little or no makeup and her hair just pulled back—but what woman does look nice when she's doing housework or taking care of children? I saw her all dressed up once in high heels and a party dress and her hair curled, and she looked quite lovely. It was just a few days after she came to work for the Serafinos. Oh, I remember—it was in February, Washington's Birthday. We'd bought a couple of tickets to the Policemen and Firemen's Ball. We gave them to Celia, of course—"

"Of course," murmured Lanigan.

"Well—" She hesitated and then blushed. "Oh, I'm sorry," she said.

"Don't apologize, Mrs. Hoskins. Everyone gives them away—usually to the maid."

"Well," she went on, "what I meant to say was that it was just like Celia to invite her instead of one of her men friends. Elspeth came over here because my husband was going to drive them down."

There was a noise at the front door and Mrs. Hoskins said, "That's Celia with the children now."

The door did not open so much as explode inward, and a moment later Hugh Lanigan found himself in the vortex of two children, Mrs. Hoskins, and the tall, plain Celia. The two women tried to divest the children of their sweaters and caps.

"I'll give them their lunch, Celia," said Mrs. Hoskins, "so that you can talk to this gentleman. He's here about poor Elspeth."

"I'm Chief Lanigan of the Barnard's Crossing police department," he began when they were alone in the living room.

"Yes, I know. I saw you at the Policemen and Firemen's Ball last Washington's Birthday. You led the Grand March with your missus. She's a looker."

"Thank you."

"And she looks smart too. I mean you can see that she's got something upstairs."

"Upstairs? Oh yes, I see. You're quite right. I can see that you're quite a judge of character, Celia. Tell me, what were your impressions of Elspeth?"

Celia appeared to give the matter some thought before answering. "Well, most people thought of her as a quiet, mousy type, but you know that could have been just on the surface."

"How do you mean?"

"She was inclined to be stand-offish—not stuck-up, mind you, but sort of reserved. I figured the poor thing was all alone here and friendless, and I was sort of the old-timer in the neighborhood, so I decided it was my duty to kind of bring her out of her shell. Well, I had these two tickets to the Policemen and Firemen's Ball that Mr. Hoskins gave me. So I invited her, and she went and had a very nice time. She danced every dance, and during the intermission she had a fellow with her."

"And she was happy?"

"Well, she wasn't laughing and giggling all night, but you could see she was having a good time in the quiet sort of way that was her style."

"That was a promising beginning."

"That was the end, too. I invited her to any number of dances and double dates after that but she never accepted. I've got lots of gentlemen friends and I could have fixed her up practically every Thursday night, but she always refused."

"Did you ever ask her why?"

"Of course I did, but she'd always say she just didn't feel like it, or she was tired and she wanted to get home early, or she had a headache."

"Perhaps she wasn't well," Lanigan suggested.

Celia shook her head. "Nothing like that. No girl ever gave up a date for a headache. I used to think maybe she didn't have the clothes, and being shy, you know, but then I thought maybe there was another reason." She lowered her voice. "I was waiting in her room once when we were going to a movie together. She was just getting dressed, and I was sort of looking at the things on her bureau while she was fixing her hair, and she had this sort of fancy box like a jewel box with a lot of pins and beads and hairpins, things like that in it. And I was just poking through, looking at her things—not nosy, you understand, but just looking—and I saw this wedding ring in the box. So I said, 'El, you getting ready to get married one of these days?' You know, sort of joking. Well, she got kind of red and closed the box and said something about it being her mother's."

"You think she may have been secretly married?"

"That would explain her not going out with fellows, wouldn't it?"

"Yes, it might. What did Mrs. Hoskins think about it?"

"I didn't tell her. I figured it was El's secret. If I told Mrs. Hoskins, she might mention it to some one and it might get back to the Serafinos and then Elspeth could lose her job. Not that that would have been such a bad idea, and many a time I've told her she ought to get another place."

"Didn't Mrs. Serafino treat her well?"

"I guess she treated her all right. Of course, they weren't pals the way I am with Mrs. Hoskins, but you can't expect that. What bothered me was her having to be in that house all alone night after night with just the kids, and her room right on the first floor."

"She was frightened?"

"I know she was at first, and later I suppose she got used to it. This is a nice, quiet neighborhood and I guess after a while she felt safe enough."

"I see. Now about yesterday. Did you know what her plans were?"

Celia shook her head slowly. "I didn't see her all week, not since Tuesday when we took the children out for a walk." Her face brightened. "She said something then about not feeling well and thinking she might make an appointment with a doctor for a check-up. Then she said she might go to a movie. Come to think of it, she said something about going to the Elysium and I said it was an awfully long picture, and she said she could still make the last bus home and didn't mind walking from the bus stop that late—and here just what I was afraid of and warned her against happens." The tears came to Celia's eyes and she daubed at them with her handkerchief.

The children had returned and stood looking wide-eyed at the two adults. When Celia began to cry, one of them ran up to hug her and the other began punching Lanigan with a tiny fist.

He reached down to hold the child away. "Take it easy, boy," he said, laughing.

Mrs. Hoskins appeared in the doorway. "He thinks you made Celia cry? Isn't that precious? Come here, Stephen. Come to mother."

It took some minutes before the children were mollified and once again led from the room. "Now Celia," said Lanigan when they were alone again, "what was it you were afraid of and what did you warn her against?"

Celia looked at him blankly and then she remembered. "Why, of going home late at night alone. I told her I wouldn't do it. It's so dark, that couple of blocks from the bus stop with the trees and all."

"But wasn't there anything in particular?"

"Well, I think that's something particular."

Again tears came to her eyes. "She was young and real innocent. The girl they had before her, Gladys, wasn't much older than she was, but I was never really friendly with her, for all that we went to a lot of places together. She was a wise kid who knew all the answers, but Elspeth . . ." She left it hanging there and then impulsively, "Tell me, was she all right when they found her? I mean, had she been, you know—mauled? I heard she was all naked when they found her."

He shook his head. "No. There was no sign that she had been sexually attacked. And she was decently dressed."

"I'm glad you told me," she said simply.

"It will be in the evening papers anyway." He got up. "You've been very helpful and I'm sure that if you think of something else, you'll let us know."

"I will, I will," she said and impulsively held out her hand. Lanigan took it and was mildly surprised to find she had the firm grip of a man. He started for the door, and then stopped as though a sudden thought had just occurred to him. "By the way, how did Mr. Serafino treat Elspeth? Was he decent to her?"

She gave him a look of approval, even admiration. "Now you're talking."

"Yes?"

She nodded. "He liked her. He let on that he didn't know she was alive, he hardly ever talked to her, but he was always watching her when he didn't think anyone was noticing. He's the kind that undresses a girl when he looks at her. That's what Gladys used to say, but she thought it was funny and kind of led him on."

"And what happened to her?"

"Oh, Mrs. Serafino got jealous and gave her the sack. I say when a wife is jealous, she usually has reason."

"I should think she would have hired an older woman then."

"And where would she get an older woman to take a job like that, six days a week and baby-sitting until two and three every morning?"

"I see your point."

"Besides, don't you think he had something to do with who got hired?"

12

Lieutenant Eban Jennings of the Barnard's Crossing police force was an angular man in his late fifties with watery blue eyes, and he dabbed at them constantly with a handkerchief.

"Damn eyes start tearing first week in June and keep on clear through September," he remarked as Hugh Lanigan entered the office at the station house.

"Probably an allergy, Eban. You ought to get yourself tested."

"I went through that a couple of years back. They found I was sensitive to a lot of things, but none of them that would hit just at this time. I figure maybe I'm sensitive to summer residents."

"Could be, but they don't usually show up till the end of June."

"Yes, but there's the anticipation. Get anything on the girl?"

Lanigan tossed the snapshot that Mrs. Serafino had given him onto the desk. "We'll give that to the papers. Might start something."

Jennings examined the picture carefully. "She wasn't bad-looking—sure a lot prettier than when I saw her this morning. I like them built that way, kind of stocky. I don't much care for these skinny little dames you see nowadays. I like a girl to be well-cushioned, know what I mean?"

"I know what you mean, Eban."

"And now I've got something for you, Hugh. The medical examiner's report came in." He handed his chief a paper. "Take a look at that last paragraph."

Lanigan emitted a low whistle. "The girl was two months pregnant."

"Yep, how do you like that? Somebody upstumped our little girl."

"It sort of gives a new slant to things, doesn't it? The people who knew her, Mrs. Serafino and her friend Celia and Mrs. Hoskins, are all agreed that she was quite shy and had no men friends at all."

Just then a patrolman walked by the door and he called him in. "Want to see you for a couple of minutes, Bill."

"Yes, sir." Patrolman William Norman was a young man with dark hair and a serious, businesslike demeanor. Although he had known Hugh Lanigan all his life and they had been on a first-name basis, characteristically he stood at attention and addressed the chief formally.

"Sit down, Bill."

Norman took one of the office chairs, managing to give the impression that he was still at attention.

"Sorry I couldn't let you off last night, but I had no one to cover for you. A man shouldn't have to work the night of his engagement party."

"Oh, that's all right, sir. Alice understood."

"She's a wonderful girl, and she'll make a fine wife. And the Ramsays are fine people."

"Yes, sir, thank you."

"I grew up with Bud Ramsay and I can remember Peggy in pigtails. They're conservative and kind of straitlaced, but the salt of the earth. And I tell you they didn't object to your taking your regular tour of duty —quite the contrary."

"Alice told me the party broke up a little after, so I guess I didn't miss much. I guess the Ramsays aren't much for staying up late anyway." He blushed slightly.

Lanigan turned to his desk to consult the duty roster. "Let's see, you came on duty last night at eleven?"

"Yes sir. I left the Ramsays at half-past ten in order to change into my uniform. The cruising car picked me up and dropped me off at Elm Square at a couple of minutes before eleven."

"You were headed up Maple Street to Vine?"

"Yes sir."

"You were supposed to pull the box on Vine Street at 1:00 A.M."

"Yes sir, I did." He reached into his thigh pocket and drew out a small notebook. "At one-three I pulled the box."

"Anything unusual from Maple to Vine?"

"No sir."

"On your route, did you meet anyone?"

"Meet someone?"

"Yes, did you see anyone walking down Maple as you were walking up?"

"No sir."

"Do you know Rabbi Small?"

"He was pointed out to me once and I've seen him around."

"Didn't you see him last night? He said he met you as he was walking home from the temple. That would be sometime after half-past twelve."

"No sir. From the time I finished trying doors in the Gordon block—that would be around a quarter-past twelve—to the time I rang in, I saw no one."

"That's curious. The rabbi says he saw you and you said good evening."

"No sir, not last night. I saw him coming home late from the temple a couple of nights ago and I spoke, but not last night."

"All right, what did you do when you got to the temple?"

"I tried the door to see that it was locked. There was a car in the parking lot and I flashed my light on it. Then I pulled the box."

"And you saw nothing unusual, or heard nothing unusual."

"No sir, just the car in the parking lot, and that wasn't too unusual."

"O.K., Bill. Thanks." Lanigan dismissed him.

"The rabbi told you he had seen Bill?" asked Jennings after Norman had left.

Lanigan nodded.

"So he was fibbing. What's it mean, Hugh? Think he could have done it?"

Lanigan shook his head slowly. "A rabbi? Not too likely."

"Why not? He lied about seeing Bill. That means he wasn't where he said he was, which means he could have been where he shouldn't have been."

"Why would he lie about something we could check on so easily? It doesn't make sense. More likely he was a little confused. He's a scholar. His head's in his books most of the time. You know, the president of the temple was at his house visiting when Stanley came to tell him some books he'd been expecting had arrived. So what does he do but run right out to the temple to look them over and stays in his study poring over them until well after midnight. A man like that, he could be a little confused about a casual meeting with a policeman a couple of days earlier. He could have telescoped the two nights and thought it was last night when it was actually a week ago."

"It seems to me his leaving a guest, especially where the guest is the president of the congregation, is pretty strange by itself. He says he was studying all night. Well, how do we know that he didn't meet the girl up there in his study? Look at the evidence, Hugh. The medical examiner fixes the time of the girl's death at one o'clock. Figure twenty minutes either way. The rabbi admits he was there about that time."

"No, twenty minutes to one is about the time he estimated he got home."

"But suppose he's shading the time a little, even five or ten minutes. Nobody saw him. The girl's handbag was in his car. And one thing more—" Jennings held up a forefinger—"today he didn't go to the services they hold every morning. How come? Was it because he didn't want to be around when the body was discovered?"

"Good Lord, the man is a rabbi, a religious man—"

"So what? He's a man, isn't he? How about that priest over in Salem a couple of years back? Father Damatopoulos? Didn't he get in trouble with a girl?"

Lanigan looked disgusted. "That was an entirely different case. He wasn't fooling around with the girl, in the first place. And in the second place, he's a Greek priest, and they're allowed to marry. They're even expected to, I understand. The trouble was that her folks tried to force a match."

"Well, I don't remember the details," Eban insisted doggedly, "but I remember there was some scandal connected with it."

"The only scandal was that a lot of people assumed that as a priest he wasn't supposed to marry, like the Roman Catholic priests. They thought it was terrible that a priest should be courting a girl. But the point is that as a Greek Orthodox priest, he had every right to."

"My point is that woman trouble can happen to any man," said Jennings. "That's the one thing, to my way of thinking, that his calling wouldn't protect him against. Any other crime in the book, stealing, breaking and entering, forging, assault, you could say a man who was a priest or a minister or a rabbi wouldn't do things like that. They wouldn't care enough about money, or they'd have better control of their tempers, but a woman can happen to any man, even a Roman priest. That's my way of looking at it."

"You've got a point there, Eban."

"And another thing, if not the rabbi, who've you got?"

"As to that, we've just started. But even then if you want to consider possibles there are plenty of them. Take Stanley. He's got a key to the temple. He's got a cot down in the basement. And the wall above the cot is covered with pictures of naked girls."

"He's a horny bastard, Stanley is," Eban agreed.

"And how about the job of carrying her to where she was finally dumped? That girl was no light weight and the rabbi is not a big man. But that wouldn't faze Stanley."

"Uh-huh, but would he then go and put the girl's pocketbook in the rabbi's car?"

"He might. Or they could have been sitting there to get out of the rain. That jalopy he drives has no top to it. Yes, and another thing, suppose the man who murdered the girl had been carrying on with her for some little time, long enough to get her pregnant. Now between the two—the rabbi and the girl in his study, or Stanley and the girl in the basement—which is the more likely to be found out? If the rabbi had been meeting the girl, I'll bet Stanley would have known it inside of a week, especially since he cleans up every morning. Whereas if it were Stanley, the rabbi wouldn't find it out in a year."

"You've got a point there. What did Stanley tell you when you questioned him?"

Lanigan shrugged. "He claims he had a few beers at the Ship's Cabin and then went home. He's living at Mama Schofield's, but he says no one saw him come in. He could have met the girl after he left the Ship's Cabin and no one the wiser."

"It's the same story he gave me," said Jennings. "Why don't we pull him in and ask him a few questions?"

"Because we don't have a damn thing on him. You asked who it could be if not the rabbi, so I gave him as a possible. I'll give you another. How about Joe Serafino? He could have been carrying on with the girl right there in his own house. Mrs. Serafino did the shopping and ran the household. The girl was only a baby-sitter. All right, that means there must have been plenty of times when the missus was out of the house and Joe could have been with the girl. If his wife came home unexpectedly, why there was a bolt on the girl's door. Mrs. Serafino couldn't get in through the kitchen, and Joe could go out quietly through the back way. It could explain why the girl didn't have any boyfriends. She wouldn't need any if she had one right in the house where she lived. What's more, it could explain the way the girl was dressed when we found her. She must have come home, because she took her dress off and it was hanging in the closet. Suppose Joe came into her room just after and persuaded her to go out for a short walk. Since it was raining and she'd be wearing a coat anyway, she wouldn't go to the trouble of putting her dress on again. Besides, if they were that cozy he'd seen her in a lot less than a slip. Mrs. Serafino would be asleep and wouldn't know a thing about it."

"Now that has real possibilities, Hugh," declared Eban enthusiastically. "They could have gone for a walk and got as far as the temple when it really began to come down. Only natural that they'd take shelter in the rabbi's car."

"What's more, both Stanley and Celia, who was Elspeth's particular pal, hinted at some connection between Serafino and the girl. And I got the feeling that Mrs. Serafino was a little afraid her husband might be connected with the case. It's too bad I didn't get a chance to see him first thing in the morning."

"I did. We got him out of bed to identify the body. He was upset, but nothing more than you'd expect under the circumstances."

"What kind of car does he drive?"

"Buick convertible."

"I didn't see it."

"We might ask *him* a few questions," said Jennings.

Lanigan laughed. "And you'll find he was at that club of his from about eight o'clock Thursday evening to two o'clock Friday morning, and probably in plain sight of half a dozen employees and several dozen diners all the time. What I'm trying to tell you, Eban, is that if you're going to consider who could possibly have done it, there's no limit to the number of suspects. Here's another one: Celia. She was supposed to be the only one the dead girl knew. She's a big, strong, strapping young woman."

"You're forgetting that Elspeth was knocked up. Celia couldn't have done that no matter how big and strong and strapping she is."

"No I'm not. You're assuming the one responsible for her pregnancy is the one who killed her. It doesn't necessarily follow. Suppose Celia was in love with some man and Elspeth beat her time with him. Suppose he was responsible for the girl's pregnancy and suppose Celia found out. She admitted to me that she knew Elspeth had said something about going to a doctor for a check-up. Well, suppose she suspected what was really wrong, or suppose Elspeth confided in her. That would be only natural since she was all alone here. She'd want to confide in an older woman, and that could be only Celia. She might even tell her who was responsible, not knowing how Celia felt about the same man."

"But Elspeth didn't know any men."

"That's Celia's story. Mrs. Serafino didn't think she knew any man, but did mention something about some letters Elspeth got regularly, postmarked in Canada. I might also point out that Celia was away for the evening and probably got home late. Mrs. Hoskins would be asleep so she wouldn't know what time Celia got in. Suppose Celia noticed a light in Elspeth's room. She knew the girl had been to see the doctor, so she drops in to find out what happened. The girl had just had her fears confirmed and she wants to talk to someone about it. Celia persuades her to toss a coat on—her attire makes sense if she's with a girlfriend— and they go for a walk. It's raining quite hard by the time they come to the temple, so they get in the rabbi's car. It's then that Elspeth tells her who the man is and Celia, in a rage, chokes her."

"Any more?"

Hugh smiled. "That'll do for a starter."

"I'm still voting for the rabbi," said Eban.

Immediately after Lanigan left, the rabbi went to the temple. He did so out of a sense of fitness, not because he thought he could be of any help. There was nothing, unfortunately, he could do for the poor girl. And he was helpless when it came to police matters. Come to think of it, what more could he do at the temple than he could at home? But since the temple was involved he felt he should be there.

From his study, he watched the police go about busily measuring and photographing and searching. A group of idlers, some women but mostly men, followed the policemen about the parking lot, edging up close whenever they spoke. He wondered how so many managed to be free at that hour, but then he saw that the crowd was constantly changing. A man would stop his car and inquire what happened. When someone told him, he would join the group for a while and then leave. The crowd never varied very much in size.

There was actually little to see, but the rabbi could not tear himself away from the window. He had the venetian blind drawn and adjusted the slats so that he could look out without himself being observed from the parking lot. A uniformed officer was standing guard over his car, telling anyone who came too close to move on. There were reporters and news photographers on the scene now, and he wondered how long it would be before they discovered he was in his study and came up to interview him. He had no idea what to say to them, or whether he ought to talk to them at all. Perhaps the best thing would be to refer them to Mr. Wasserman, who would probably in turn refer them to the attorney who handled the temple legal affairs. But then, would not his refusal to discuss the case be regarded as suspicious?

The knock on the door, when it came, turned out to be not the reporters but the police. A tall, watery-eyed man introduced himself as Lieutenant Jennings. "Stanley told me you were here," he said.

The rabbi motioned him to a seat.

"We'd like to take your car down to the police garage, rabbi. We want to give it a good going-over and we can do it better down there."

"Certainly, lieutenant."

"You got a lawyer representing you, rabbi?"

The rabbi shook his head. "Should I have?"

"Well, maybe I shouldn't be the one to tell you, but we like to do things friendly-like. Maybe if you had a lawyer, he might tell you that you don't have to agree if you don't want to. Of course, if you didn't, we'd get a court order easy enough—"

"It's quite all right, lieutenant. If you think that taking my car downtown will help you in this shocking business, go right ahead."

"If you got your keys handy . . ."

"Of course." The rabbi detached them from the ring that was still lying on the desk. "This one is for the ignition and glove compartment, and this one is for the trunk."

"I'll give you a receipt for the car."

"It's not necessary."

He watched from the window as the lieutenant got into his car and drove off, and was pleased to see a good portion of the crowd leave with him.

Several times during the course of the day the rabbi tried to call his wife, but each time the line was reported busy. He called Mr. Wasserman's office, but was told that he was away and was not expected back.

He opened one of the books on his desk to leaf through it. Presently he made a note on a card. He checked a passage in another book and made another note. Soon he was completely absorbed in his research.

The phone rang. It was Miriam.

"I tried to get you three or four times, but the line was busy," he said.

"I took the receiver off the hook," she explained. "It started just after you left, people calling to ask if we had heard the news, and wanting to know if there was anything they could do. There was even one call to tell me that you had been arrested. That was when I took the receiver off, but then it makes funny little scratchy noises and you start wondering if it might be an important call. Didn't anyone call you?"

"Not a single call." He chuckled. "Guess no one wants to admit he's on speaking terms with Barnard's Crossing's Public Enemy Number One."

"Please don't! It's nothing to joke about." Then: "What are we going to do, David?"

"Do? Why, what is there to do?"

"I thought, what with all this—well, Mrs. Wasserman called up and invited us to stay with them—"

"But that's silly, Miriam. Tonight is the Sabbath and I intend to welcome it in my own house and at my own table. Don't worry, it will be all right. I'll be home in time for dinner, and then we'll go to the services as always."

"And what are you doing now?"

"Why I'm working on my Maimonides paper."

"Do you have to do that now?"

He wondered at the edge in her voice. "What else would I do?" he asked simply.

13

There were four or five times as many people at evening services as usual, much to the consternation of the members of Sisterhood, who had prepared cake and tea for the collation in the vestry afterward.

Considering the reason for the unexpectedly large attendance, the rabbi was none too pleased. He sat on the platform beside the Holy Ark, and grimly made up his mind that he would make no reference whatsoever to the tragedy. Pretending to be studying his prayer book, he glowered under his eyebrows at member after member who had never before attended a Friday evening service, smiling only when one of the few regulars entered, as if to show he knew thay had come to worship rather than out of vulgar curiosity.

With Myra the president of Sisterhood, the Schwarzes were one of the regulars, but they usually sat fairly well back, in the sixth or seventh row. Tonight, however, although Ben slid into his regular seat, Myra continued on down front to the second row where the rabbi's wife was sitting. She sat down beside her, and leaning over, patted her hand and murmured in her ear. Miriam stiffened—then managed a smile.

The rabbi caught the little byplay and was touched by this consideration on the part of the Sisterhood president, all the more because it was unexpected. But as he thought about it, its full significance began to dawn on him. It was a gesture of reassurance, the sympathy one extends to the wife of someone who is under suspicion. It gave him another explanation for the large attendance. Although some may have come in hopes he might speak of the crime, others wanted to see if he would show signs of guilt. To remain silent and not mention the affair might give the wrong impression and imply he was afraid to speak.

He made no mention of the subject in the course of his sermon, but later, near the close of the service, he said: "Before the mourners in the congregation rise to recite the Kaddish, I should like to recall to you the true significance of the prayer."

The congregation sat up and edged forward in their seats. Now he was coming to it.

"There is a belief," the rabbi went on, "that reciting the Kaddish is a duty the mourner owes to the dear departed. If you will read the prayer, or its English translation on the opposite page, you will notice that it contains no mention of death or any suggestion of a plea for the soul of the dead. Rather, it is an affirmation of the belief in God and in His power and glory. What is the significance of the prayer then? Why is it especially reserved for those who mourn? And why, when most of our prayers are whispered, is this one prayer said aloud?

"Perhaps our very manner of delivery will give a clue to its meaning. It is a prayer not for the dead but for the living. It is an open declaration by one who has just suffered the loss of a dear one that he still has faith in God. Nevertheless, our people persist in thinking of the Kaddish as an obligation they owe to the dead, and because in our tradition custom takes on the force of law, I shall recite the Kaddish with the mourners, for one who was not a member of this congregation, nor even of our faith, someone about whom we know little, but whose life happened through tragic accident to touch this congregation. . . ."

The rabbi and his wife said little as they walked home from the temple. Finally he broke the silence. "I noticed Mrs. Schwarz went out of her way to extend her sympathy to you."

"She's a good soul, David, and she meant well." Then, "Oh, David, this can be a nasty business."

"I'm beginning to think so," he said.

As they approached their house, they could hear the telephone ringing inside.

14

The religious revival did not extend to the Saturday morning service; no more than the usual twenty or so turned up. When the rabbi got home, he found Chief Lanigan waiting for him.

"I don't like to intrude on your Sabbath," the chief apologized, "but neither do we like to interrupt our investigations. We police have no holidays."

"It's perfectly all right. In our religion, emergencies always supersede ritual."

"We're about through with your car. I'll have one of the boys drive it up here sometime tomorrow. Or if you're downtown, you can pick it up yourself."

"Fine."

"I'd like to check over with you what we found." From his briefcase he drew several pliofilm bags, each marked in black ink. "Let's see, this first one is stuff found under the front seat." He dumped the contents onto the desk. It consisted of some loose change, a receipt for repairs to the car dated several months back, a wrapper from a five-cent candy bar, a small calendar giving Hebrew and English equivalent dates, and a woman's plastic barrette.

The rabbi gave them a cursory glance. "Those are ours. At least, I recognize the barrette as my wife's. But you can ask her to be sure."

"We already have," said Lanigan.

"I can't vouch for the candy wrapper or the money, but I have eaten that candy. It's kosher. That calendar is the kind that various institutions and business houses distribute on the Jewish New Year. I must get dozens of them each year." He opened his desk drawer. "Here's another."

"All right." Lanigan replaced the contents of the bag and emptied another on the desk. "This is the contents of the trash bag under the dashboard." There were several crumpled tissues with lipstick, a stick from a chocolate-covered Eskimo Pie, and an empty, crumpled cigarette package.

"Those look all right," said the rabbi.

"Does that look like your wife's lipstick?"

The rabbi smiled. "Why don't you check with her?"

"We have," said Lanigan, "and it is." He then offered the contents of the next bag, which was from the glove compartment. There was a crushed box of tissues, a lipstick, several road maps, a prayer book, a pencil, a plastic ball-point pen, half a dozen three-by-five cards, a two-cell flashlight, and a rumpled pack of cigarettes.

"That seems right," said the rabbi. "I think I can even be sure of the lipstick, because I remember when my wife got it I made some remark about its being worth a king's ransom if all that jewelry were real. I think my wife paid a dollar or a dollar and a half, and yet see with what brilliant gems it is encrusted."

"They sell thousands of them, so you would have no way of knowing if this particular one is your wife's."

"No, but surely it would be quite a coincidence if it were not."

"Coincidences happen, rabbi. The girl used the same lipstick. And it isn't such a terribly remarkable coincidence at that, since I gather it's a very popular make and a very popular shade for blondes."

"She was blonde then?"

"Yes, she was blonde. The flashlight, rabbi, shows no fingerprints."

The rabbi thought a moment. "The last time I recall using it was to check the dipstick, after which I wiped it, of course."

"All that's left now is the contents of the ashtrays. The one in the rear had one cigarette, lipstick-stained. There were ten butts in the front ashtray, all the same brand and all lipstick-stained. Your wife's, I take it. You don't smoke."

"If I did, I don't think my cigarette would be lipstick-stained."

"Then that's about it. We're keeping these things for a while."

"Take all the time you need. How is the investigation going?"

"Well, we know quite a bit more than we did when I saw you yesterday. The medical examiner found no signs that she had been sexually attacked, but he did come up with one curious finding: the girl was pregnant."

"Could she have been married?"

"We don't even know that for sure. We found no marriage certificate among her effects at home, but in her purse, the one we found in your car, there was a wedding ring. Mrs. Serafino assumed that she was single, but if the girl had been secretly married, she never would have confided in her employer because it might have meant her job."

"Then that could account for her having the ring in her handbag instead of on her finger," suggested the rabbi. "She would wear it while she was with her husband and then take it off before coming home."

"That's a possibility."

"And have you arrived at any theory as to how the girl's handbag got in my car?"

"It could have been put there by the murderer deliberately to cast suspicion on you. Do you know anyone who might want to do that to you, rabbi?"

The rabbi shook his head. "There are a number of people in my congregation who don't care for me, but none who dislike me so much they would want to see me mixed up in this sort of thing. And I know almost no one here outside of the members of my congregation."

"No, it doesn't seem too likely, does it? But if someone didn't put it there, it can only mean the girl was in your car at some time. Then for some reason—perhaps 'the murderer had noticed the light in your study—she was transferred to where we found her."

"I suppose so."

Lanigan grinned. "There is another theory, rabbi, which we're duty-bound to consider because it fits the facts as we know them."

"I think I know. It is that when Stanley came to tell me my books had arrived I used that as an excuse to get out of the house in order to meet this girl. We had been having an affair and our meeting place was my study. I waited for her until I got tired or decided she was not going to appear, but she turned up just as the study door locked behind me. So we sat in my car and it was there she told me she was pregnant and that she expected me to divorce my wife and marry her to give her baby a name. So I strangled her and carried her body over to the grass plot beyond the wall. Then I coolly strolled home."

"It does sound silly, rabbi, but it's also possible as far as time and place are concerned. If I were asked to make book on it, I'd put it at a million to one. Nevertheless, if you told me you were planning a long trip someplace I'd have to tell you I'd rather you didn't."

"I understand," said the rabbi.

Lanigan opened the door to leave, then stopped. "Oh, there's another thing, rabbi. Patrolman Norman has no recollection of meeting you or anyone else that night." He grinned at the look of astonishment on the rabbi's face.

15

Elspeth Bleech's picture appeared in the Saturday papers, and by six that evening Hugh Lanigan was getting results. Nor was he altogether surprised. The girl had left the Serafino household early in the afternoon and had been gone all day. Surely a number of people must have seen her. Some would call almost immediately, but some might want to think over getting involved with the police.

The first call was from a doctor in Lynn who said he believed he had seen the young woman in question Thursday afternoon under the name of Mrs. Elizabeth Brown. She had given an address and telephone number. The street was the Serafinos', but the house number was reversed. The telephone number was that of the Hoskins.

The doctor reported that he had examined her and found her in excellent health and in the first stages of pregnancy. Had she appeared upset or nervous? No more than many of his patients in similar circumstances. Many were delighted when they discovered they were pregnant, but there were also any number who found the news upsetting, even though they were legitimately married.

Had she mentioned her plans for the rest of the afternoon or evening? He was sure she had not. Perhaps she had spoken to his secretary, who had now already left for the day. If the police thought it important he would get in touch with her and inquire. They did, and he said he would.

Almost immediately there came another call, this time from the secretary, who had seen the girl's picture in the paper and was sure she had been in the office Thursday afternoon. No, she had noticed nothing unusual. No, the girl had not mentioned what her plans were for the afternoon or evening. Oh yes, just before leaving, she had asked where she could make a call. The secretary had offered the office phone, but she preferred the privacy of a pay station.

Then came a rash of telephone calls from people who were sure they had seen her, some in stores in Lynn, where she could have been, and others from nearby towns, where the likelihood was less. A gasoline station attendant called in to say she had been on the back seat of a motorcycle that had stopped for directions. There was even a call from an operator of an amusement part in New Hampshire who insisted the girl had been there around three o'clock to ask for a job in one of the concessions.

Lanigan remained at his desk until seven and then went home for his dinner, leaving strict orders that any call concerning Elspeth Bleech should be transferred to him at home. Fortunately, none came in and he was able to eat in peace. He had no sooner finished, however, than his doorbell rang; he opened the door to Mrs. Agnes Gresham, who owned and operated the Surfside Restaurant.

Mrs. Gresham was a fine-looking woman of sixty with beautifully coiffed snow-white hair. She carried herself with the dignity becoming to one of the town's leading businesswomen.

"I called the police station and they told me you had gone home, Hugh." Her tone carried a faint air of disapproval.

"Come right in, Aggie. Can I get you a cup of coffee?"

"This is business," she said.

"There's no law that says we can't be comfortable while talking business. Can I fix you a drink?"

This time she refused more graciously, and took the seat he indicated.

"Okay, Aggie, is it my business or your business?"

"It's your business, Hugh Lanigan. That girl whose picture was in the paper—she was in my restaurant having dinner Thursday night."

"Around what time?"

"From before half-past seven when I took over the cashier's cage so that Mary Trumbull could get her dinner, to around eight o'clock."

"This for sure, Aggie?"

"I am quite sure. I took particular notice of the girl."

"Why?"

"Because of the man she was with."

"Oh? Can you describe him?"

"He was about forty years old, dark, good-looking. When they finished eating, they left the restaurant and got into a big blue Lincoln that was parked in front of the door."

"What made you pay such particular attention to him? Were they arguing or quarreling?"

She shook her head impatiently. "I noticed them because I knew him."

"Who was it?"

"I don't know his name, but I know where he works. I bought my car at the Becker Ford Agency and I saw him there once behind a desk when I went there on business."

"You've been very helpful, Aggie, and I appreciate it."

"I do my duty."

"I'm sure you do."

As soon as she was gone, he telephoned the Becker home.

"Mr. Becker is not in. This is Mrs. Becker. Can I help you?"

"Perhaps you can, Mrs. Becker." Lanigan introduced himself. "Can you tell me the name of the person in your husband's employ who drives a blue Lincoln?"

"Well, my husband drives a black Lincoln."

"No, this is blue."

"Oh, you must mean my husband's partner, Melvin Bronstein. He has a blue Lincoln. Is anything wrong?"

"No, nothing at all, ma'am."

Then he called Lieutenant Jennings. "Any luck at the Serafinos'?"

"Not much, but I did get something. The Simpsons across the way saw a car parked in front of the Serafino house very late Thursday night, midnight or even later."

"A blue Lincoln?"

"How'd you know?"

"Never mind, Eban. Meet me at the station right away. We've got work to do."

Eban Jennings was already there when he arrived. Hugh filled him in on what Aggie Gresham had said. "Now Eban, I want a picture of this Melvin Bronstein. Go down to the offices of the *Lynn Examiner*."

"What makes you so sure they'll have one?"

"Because this Bronstein lives in Grove Point and owns a car agency. That makes him important, and anyone who's important gets put on a committee of some kind or is made an officer of some organization, and the first thing they do is have their picture taken and printed in the *Examiner*. Look through everything they have on him and get a nice clear picture that shows his features plainly and have about half a dozen of them printed up."

"We going to give these to the papers?"

"No. As soon as you have the prints, you and maybe Smith and Henderson—I'll look through the roster and line up a couple or three men—will drive along Routes 14, 69, and 119. You'll stop at every motel and show Bronstein's picture, and see if he's stayed there any time in the last few months. You can't go by their registers because chances are that he didn't sign under his right name."

"I don't get it."

"What don't you get? If you had a girl you wanted to shack up with, where would you take her?"

"Up in back of Chisholm's barn."

"Tcha. You'd drive up country and stop at a motel. That girl was pregnant. She may have got that way in the back seat of a car, but she also may have got that way in some motel not too far from here."

16

Sunday morning was bright and sunny; the sky was cloudless and there was a gentle breeze off the water. It was perfect weather for golf, and as the board of directors of the temple dribbled in to the meeting room their clothes indicated that many of them would be off to the links the moment the meeting was adjourned.

Jacob Wasserman watched them come in by twos and threes and knew he was beaten. He knew it by the number who finally appeared, almost the full complement of forty-five. He knew it by the friendly way they greeted Al Becker and the way he was avoided by the few who had told him they were still undecided. He knew it by a sudden realization that the great majority were all of the same type: sleek, successful professional men and businessmen who belonged to the temple primarily as a social obligation, who were used to and expected the best of everything, who could be expected to have the same attitude toward a casual, unfashionable rabbi as they might toward an inefficient junior executive in their employ. He saw all this in their ill-concealed impatience to get on with the unpleasant business at hand and go about their pleasures, and he blamed himself for having permitted so many men like this to be nominated for the board. He had yielded to the needs of the building committee, who had recommended each candidate on the grounds that he was doing all right for himself. "If we put him on the board, there's a good chance he'll kick in with a sizable contribution."

He called the meeting to order, and proceeded through the reading of minutes and the reports of committees. There was an audible sigh when Wasserman completed Old Business and began to explain the issues involved in the rabbi's contract. "Before I call for discussion," he concluded, "I should like to point out that Rabbi Small is willing to remain, although I imagine he could probably better himself by going elsewhere." (He knew no such thing, of course.) "I have been in closer touch with the rabbi than has anyone else in the congregation. That is only natural in my capacity as chairman of the ritual committee. I would like to say at this point that I am more than satisfied with the way he has carried on his duties.

"Most of you see the rabbi only in his public capacity, when he is conducting services on the holidays, or when he is addressing a meeting. But there is a great deal of work of a more private nature that is part of his job. Take weddings for example. One of the marriages this year involved a girl who was not Jewish. There were lengthy discussions with both sets of parents, and when the girl decided to accept Judaism the rabbi gave her a course of instruction in our religion. He meets with every one of the Bar Mitzvah boys individually. As chairman of the ritual committee, I can tell you that we go over every service together. He is in constant touch with the principal of the religious school. And then there are dozens—dozens? hundreds—of calls from outsiders, both from Jews and from Gentiles, from individuals and from organizations, some having nothing to do with the temple, all with questions, requests, plans, that have to be considered and discussed. I could go on all morning, but then you would never get to the golf course."

There was appreciative laughter.

"To most of you," he went on seriously, "these and countless other phases of the rabbi's work are unknown. But they are known to me. And I want to say that the rabbi has done his work even better than I had hoped when we first hired him."

Al Becker raised his hand and was recognized. "I'm not so sure that I care for the idea of the rabbi we employ and whose salary we pay, busying himself with matters that have no connection with this temple. But maybe our good president is stretching things a little." He leaned forward, and supporting himself on the table with his two clenched fists, looked around at each of the members and went on in a loud voice. "Now, there is no one here who has a greater respect for our president, Jake Wasserman, than I have. I respect him as a man, and I respect the work he has done for the temple. I respect his integrity and I respect his judgment. Normally, if he said to me, this fellow is a good man, I'd be willing to gamble that he was. And when he says that the rabbi is a good man, I'm sure he is." His jaw protruded aggressively. "But I say he is not a good man for this particular job. He may be an excellent rabbi, but not for this congregation. I understand he's a fine scholar, but right now that's not what we need. We are part of a community. In the eyes of our non-Jewish neighbors and friends we are one religious organization of the several in the community. We need someone who will represent us properly to our Gentile neighbors and friends. We need someone who can make an impressive appearance on a public platform, who can carry on the public relations job that the position requires. The headmaster of the high school confided in me that next year he plans to offer the honor of making the graduation address to the spiritual leader of our temple. Frankly, friends, the sight of our present rabbi up on the stage in baggy pants and unpressed jacket, his hair uncombed, his tie twisted, speaking as he usually does with little stories from the Talmud and his usual hair-splitting logic— well, frankly, I would be embarrassed."

Abe Reich was recognized. "I just want to say this: I know exactly what Mr. Wasserman means when he says the rabbi is involved in a lot of other activities that most of us don't realize. I myself had the privilege of seeing this side of the rabbi, and let me tell you it was an important matter to me and I have been full of admiration for the rabbi ever since. Maybe he's no Fourth of July orator, but when he talks to us from the pulpit, he talks sense and he reaches me. I'd rather have that than someone who puts on an act and uses a bunch of ten-dollar words. When he talks I feel he's sincere, and that's more than I can say about a lot of high-powered rabbis I've heard."

Dr. Pearlstein rose to support his friend, Al Becker. "A dozen times a week when I prescribe for a patient I am asked if they can use the same medicine I prescribed for them last year, or that I prescribed for someone they know who had the same symptoms. I have to explain that an ethical doctor prescribes for a particular person for a particular condition—"

"Nothing like getting a plug in, Doc," someone shouted, and the doctor joined in the laughter.

"What I mean to say is that it's like Al Becker said. No one claims that the rabbi is incapable or insincere. The question is, is he the rabbi that this congregation needs at this time? Is he what the doctor ordered for this particular patient in this particular condition?"

"Yeah, but maybe there s more than one doctor."

Several were shouting at the same time, and Wasserman banged on the desk for order.

One of those who had never attended a board meeting before raised his hand and was recognized. "Look fellows," he said, "what's the sense of our discussing this? When you talk about an idea or about some project, okay, so the more you talk, the clearer it gets. But when you talk about a person, you don't get anywhere. You just get a lot of bad feeling. Now all of us know the rabbi and we know whether we want him or not. I say, let's not discuss the matter any further and let's vote."

"That's right!"

"Move the previous question!"

"Let's vote."

"Just a minute." It was the roar that everyone recognized as belonging to Abe Casson, who had developed its raucousness and its volume at a thousand political meetings. "Before you move the previous question, I'd like to say a few words on the situation in general." He left his seat and walked down the aisle to the front of the room to face them. "I'm not going to argue whether the rabbi is doing a good job or not. But I am going to say a few words on public relations, which my good friend Al Becker has brought up. As you all know, when a Catholic priest is assigned to a parish by his bishop, he stays there until the bishop reassigns him. And if any member of the parish doesn't like him, he is free—to move out of the parish. It's different with the different Protestant churches. They all have different ways of hiring a minister and of dropping him, but in general, they don't fire a minister unless there's something definite that he's done, and it has to be something pretty God-awful definite."

He lowered his voice to a more conversational tone. "Now I've been chairman of the Republican committee of the county for almost ten years now, so I guess I can lay claim to knowing about the way our non-Jewish friends and neighbors think. They don't understand our method of engaging a rabbi or of firing him. They don't understand that twenty minutes after a rabbi lands in town, there's a pro-rabbi and an anti-rabbi party. They can't understand how some members of the congregation can become anti-rabbi just because they don't like the kind of hats his wife wears. It's routine with us. As a man in politics all my life, I know all the goings-on in all the temples and synagogues in Lynn and Salem, yes and in most of the Boston ones too. When a rabbi takes over a new pulpit, there is a group made up of friends of the last rabbi that is automatically opposed to him. That's the way it is with us Jews. Now the Gentiles don't understand this, as I say. So when we fire the rabbi, the first thing they'll think is that there must have been some big reason. Now what reason is bound to occur to them? Let's think about it. Just a few days ago, a young girl was found murdered in our backyard. As you know, at the time our rabbi was alone in the temple, in his study. His car was in the parking lot, and the girl's handbag was found in his car. Now you and I know, and the police know too, that the rabbi could not have done it—"

"Why couldn't the rabbi have done it?" asked a member.

There was dead silence at this open expression of what had not been entirely absent from the minds of many of them.

But Casson turned on them. "Whoever said that ought to be ashamed of himself. I know the men in this room and I'm sure that no one here really thinks the rabbi could have done this terrible thing. As the campaign manager of the present district attorney, I can tell you that I have some idea of what his thinking is and what the thinking of the police is. I tell you that they don't for a minute think that the rabbi did this. But"—he leveled a forefinger at them for emphasis—"he has to be considered. If he weren't a rabbi, he would be the A-number-one suspect." He held up his hand and ticked off on his fingers the points as he made them. "Her bag was found in his car. He was there at the time. He is the only one we know for sure was there. We have only his word that he was in his study all the time. There is no other suspect."

He looked around impressively. "And now, two days after the event you want to fire him. How's that for public relations, Al? What are your Gentile friends going to think when they find out that two days after the rabbi becomes a suspect in a murder case, his congregation fired him? What are you going to say to them, Al? 'Oh, we didn't fire him for that. We fired him because his pants weren't pressed.' "

Al Becker rose. He was no longer quite so sure of himself. "Look, I have nothing against the rabbi personally. I want that distinctly understood. I am only thinking of what is best for the temple. Now if I thought that what our friend Abe Casson just told us might turn the scales against the rabbi, that as a result of our firing him he might get mixed up in this murder—more mixed up than he is right now, that is—I'd say, no. But you know and I know that the police can't seriously connect him with this crime. You know that they're not going to try to pin it on him because we drop him. And if we don't, then we have him for all of next year."

"Just a minute, Al." It was Casson again. "I don't think you get the point. I'm not concerned with the reaction to the rabbi. I'm concerned with the reaction to the temple, to the congregation. Some are going to say that we dropped him because we suspected he was guilty. And they'll say we must have a fine bunch of men in the rabbinate if one of them could be so quickly suspected of murder. And there'll be others who'll think it absurd that the rabbi could be suspected. And all they'll think is that we Jews don't trust each other and are willing to fire our spiritual leader just on suspicion. In this country where a man is considered innocent until he's proved guilty, that won't sit so well. Do you get it, Al? It's us I'm concerned about."

"Well, I'm not voting another contract to the rabbi," said Becker, and sat back with arms folded as if to show he wanted no further part in the proceedings.

"What are we fighting for?" It was another member whom Becker had induced to come vote against the rabbi. "I can see Abe Casson's point of view, and I can see Al Becker's point of view. But I can't see why we have to make up our minds today. There's another meeting next week. The police work fast these days. By the next meeting the whole thing may be all settled. I say, let's lay the matter on the table until then. And if worst comes to worst, we can still have another meeting."

"If the worst comes, you won't have to bother about another meeting," said Abe Casson grimly.

17

Wasserman had been so sure the rabbi would lose that his face could not help show his relief.

"Believe me, rabbi," he said, "the future looks brighter. Who can tell what will happen in the next week or two? Suppose the police don't come up with the guilty man, then do you think we will permit another postponement? No, I'll put my foot down. I'll tell them that it isn't fair to you to keep you waiting this way when you could be looking for another position. I'm sure they'll see the justice of that. But even if the police do find the man, do you think Al Becker will be able to rally the same number of people at the next meeting? Believe me, I know these people. I have tried to get them to come to meetings. Maybe he could turn the trick once, but he won't be able to a second time. And if we have the usual people present, I'm sure we'll win."

The rabbi was troubled. "I feel as if I'm forcing myself on them. Maybe what I ought to do is to resign. It's not pleasant to hold a pulpit on sufferance. It's not dignified."

"Rabbi, rabbi. We've got over three hundred members. If it came to a vote of the entire membership, believe me you'd get a majority. I tell you, the great majority of the membership is with you. These board members—it's not as if they were the representatives of the congregation. They were appointed. I appointed them, or at least I appointed the nominating committee that appointed the slate, and you know what happens—the membership endorse the slate as a whole. These board members, they're people that we hoped would do some work for the temple, or they're people who are a little richer than the rest. But they represent only themselves. Becker reached them first so they voted his way. But if he asks them to come to the next meeting, he'll find that they all have previous appointments."

The rabbi laughed. "You know, Mr. Wasserman, at the seminary one of the favorite subjects of discussion in student bull sessions was what a rabbi could do to ensure his job. The best way is to marry a very rich girl. Then the congregation feels that it doesn't make any difference to you whether you stay or leave. This gives you a tremendous psychological advantage. Then too, if she is indeed very rich, that gives her social position in the congregation, and this counts for a great deal with the wives of the members. Another way is to write and publish a popular book. The congregation then takes on prestige vicariously. Their rabbi is a famous author. A third way is to get into local politics so that the Gentiles speak well of you. If you develop a reputation in the community of being a 'rabbi with guts,' it's practically impossible to fire you. But now I could offer still another way: become a suspect in a murder case. This is a fine way for a rabbi to ensure his position."

But the rabbi returned from seeing Wasserman to his car much less light-heartedly. He watched gloomily as Miriam went through her usual ministrations after Sunday dinner, arranging the fruit bowl on the coffee table in the living room, puffing up the cushions on the couch and the easy chairs, giving a last-minute dusting to the tables and the lamps.

"Expecting someone?" he asked.

"No one in particular, but people always drop in Sunday afternoon, especially when it's so nice out. Don't you think you had better put on your jacket?"

"Frankly, right now I'm a little fed up with my congregation and my pastoral duties. Do you realize, Miriam, that we've been here in Barnard's Crossing almost a year and we've never really explored the town? Let's take a holiday. Suppose you change into some comfortable shoes and we'll take a bus downtown and just wander around."

"Doing what?"

"Nothing, I hope. If you feel we really need an excuse, we can stop at the police station and recover the car. But I would just like to meander like a tourist through the narrow, crooked streets of Old Town. It's a fascinating place, and has quite a history. Did you know that Barnard's Crossing was originally settled by a bunch of roughnecks, sailors and fishermen for the most part, who didn't care to live under the repression of the Puritan theocracy. Ever since Hugh Lanigan told me that I have done a little checking on my own. They didn't observe the Sabbath too carefully here, or even have a church or a minister for years after the place was settled. And we thought it was a staid, stuffy, ultra-conservative community. Barnard's Crossing breeds a special kind of independence that you don't find in the average New England town.

Most New England towns have a tradition of independence, but all it means is that they took an active part in the Revolution. Here there is also a tradition of independence against the rest of New England. It's land's end, so they tend to be suspicious of the rest of the world. Why don't we look it over."

They left the bus near the edge of Old Town and sauntered along, stopping whenever they saw anything of interest. They went into the town hall and gawked at the old battle flags that were mounted in glass cases along the walls. They read the bronze plaques that had been set up on the historic buildings. At one point they found themselves part of a crowd of sightseers who were being lectured by a guide, and they went along until the party returned to their bus. Then they walked along the main street looking at the windows of the antique shops, the gift shops, and the wonderful window of a ship chandler with its coils of rope, its brass ship fittings, compasses, and anchors. They found a little park that overlooked the harbor, and sat on one of the benches and just looked down at the water with its boats, some sailing along gracefully, others, motor-powered, scooting along the surface like water bugs. They did not talk but just drank in the peaceful scene.

Finally they set out to find the police garage to reclaim their car, and promptly got lost. For an hour or so, they wandered in and out of little blind alleys with sidewalks so narrow two could not walk abreast. They were flanked on either side by frame houses, often less than a foot apart, but they looked down these narrow slits to see, in back, tiny old-fashioned gardens with rock flowers and hollyhocks and sunflowers and little arbors covered with vines. They retraced their steps and wandered into another little private street where the few houses were of painted brick and had gardens enclosed by white picket fences; beyond, they could glimpse the water with a boat bobbing up and down beside a rickety landing that lurched under every movement of the waves. Occasionally, they caught sight of someone in a bathing suit lying on the landing, taking the sun, and they quickly averted their eyes as though they were intruding; unconsciously they found themselves lowering their voices.

The sun was hot and they were beginning to grow tired. There was no one about to ask the way back to the main street. The front porches they passed usually were set back from the street and sealed off by the inevitable white picket fence. To push back the gate and walk up fifty feet of flagstone path and knock on the door of the screened-in porch seemed an invasion of privacy. The entire atmosphere seemed designed to keep one's neighbor at arm's length, not from unfriendliness but rather as though each householder were content to cultivate his own garden.

Then, quite suddenly, they found themselves on a street that skirted the waterfront, and a block ahead they saw the main street with its many shops. They quickened their pace to make sure they wouldn't lose sight of it again, but just as they were about to turn in, they were hailed by Hugh Lanigan, relaxing on his front porch.

"Come on up and sit for a while," he called. They needed no second invitation.

"I thought you'd be working," said the rabbi with a grin. "Or is the case solved?"

Lanigan smiled back. "Just taking a breather, rabbi—just like you. But I'm no further away from my work than the telephone."

It was a large, comfortable porch with wicker armchairs. No sooner were they seated than Mrs. Lanigan, a slim gray-haired woman in sweater and slacks, came out to join them.

"You can have a drink, can't you, rabbi?" asked Lanigan anxiously. "I mean, it's not against your religion?"

"No, we're not Prohibitionists. I take it you're offering me one like yours."

"Right, and no one makes a Tom Collins like Amy here."

"How is the investigation going?" the rabbi asked when Mrs. Lanigan had returned with a tray.

"We're making progress," said the chief cheerfully. "How is your congregation?"

"Making progress," said the rabbi with a smile.

"I understand you're having your troubles with them."

The rabbi looked at him questioningly, but said nothing.

Lanigan laughed. "Look, rabbi, let me teach you something about police work. In a big city there's what might be called a stable criminal population that accounts for most of the crime the police have to contend with. And how do they control it? Largely through informers. In a town like this, we don't have a criminal population. We do have a few chronic troublemakers, but the way we control the situation is the same way, through informers. Only they're not regular informers. It's just a lot of gossip that we hear, that we listen to carefully. I know what's happening in your temple almost as well as you. At the meeting today there were about forty people present. And when they got home, they all told their wives. Now do you think that eighty people can keep a secret in a town like this, especially when it's not supposed to be a secret in the first place? Ah, rabbi, we do these things so much better in our church. With us, what the priest says, goes."

"Is he so much a better man than the rest of you?" asked the rabbi.

"He's a good man usually," said Lanigan, "because the process of selection screens out most of the incompetents. Of course, we have some damn fools in the clergy, but that's not the point. The point is that if you're going to have discipline, you have to have someone whose authority is not subject to question."

"I suppose that's the difference between the two systems," said the rabbi. "We encourage the questioning of everything."

"Even matters of faith?"

"There is very little in the way of faith that is demanded of us. And that little, such as the existence of a single All-Powerful, All-Knowing, Ever-Present God, we do not forbid to be questioned. We merely recognize that it leads nowhere. But we have no articles of faith which must be subscribed to. For example, when I got my S'michah—you call it ordination—I was not questioned on my beliefs and I took no oath of any sort."

"You mean you are not dedicated in any way?"

"Only as I feel myself dedicated."

"Then what makes you different from the members of your flock?"

The rabbi laughed. "They are not my flock in the first place, at least not in the sense that they are in my care and that I am responsible to God for their safety and their behavior. Actually, I have no responsibility, or for that matter no privilege, that every male member of my congregation over the age of thirteen does not have. I presumably differ from the average member of my congregation only in that I am supposed to have a greater knowledge of the Law and of our tradition. That is all."

"But you lead them in prayer—" He stopped when he saw his guest shaking his head.

"Any adult male can do that. At our daily service it is customary to offer the honor of leading the prayers to any stranger who happens to come in, or to anyone who is not usually there."

"But you bless them and you visit the sick and you marry them and you bury them—"

"I marry them because the civil authorities have empowered me to; I visit the sick because it is a blessing that is enjoined on everyone; I do it as a matter of routine, largely because of the example set by your priests and ministers. Even the blessing of the congregation is officially the function of those members of the congregation who happen to be descendants of Aaron, which is the custom in Orthodox congregations. In Conservative temples like ours, it is really a usurpation on the part of the rabbi."

"I see now what you mean when you say you are not a man of the cloth," said Lanigan slowly. Then a thought occurred to him. "But how do you keep your congregation in line?"

The rabbi smiled ruefully. "I don't seem to be doing a very good job of it, do I?"

"That's not what I meant. I wasn't thinking of your present difficulties. I mean, how do you keep them from sinning?"

"You mean how does the system work? I suppose by making everyone feel responsible for his own acts."

"Free will? We have that."

"Of course, but ours is a little different. You give your people free will, but you also give them a helping hand if their foot slips. You have a priest who can hear confession and forgive. You have a hierarchy of saints who can intercede for the sinner, and finally you have a Purgatory, which is in the nature of a second chance. I might add that you have a Heaven and a Hell that help to right any wrongs in life on this earth. Our people have only the one chance. Our good deeds must be done on this earth in this life. And since there is no one to share the burden with them or to intercede for them they must do it on their own."

"Don't you people believe in Heaven, or in life after death?"

"Not really," said the rabbi. "Our beliefs have been influenced by those around us, of course, as have yours. At times in our history concepts of a life after death have cropped up, but even then we saw them our own way. Life after death means for us that part of our life that lives on in our children, in the influence that survives us after death, and the memories people have of us."

"Then if someone is evil in this life, and yet is prosperous and happy and healthy, he gets away with it?" It was Mrs. Lanigan who asked the question.

The rabbi turned to face her. He wondered if her question had perhaps been prompted by some personal experience. "It's questionable," he said slowly, "whether a thinking organism like man can ever 'get away with' something he's done. Nevertheless, it is a problem, and all the religions have wrestled with it: how does the good man who suffers get recompense and the evil man who prospers get punished? The Eastern religions explain it by reincarnation. The wicked man who is prosperous merited his prosperity by his virtue in a previous reincarnation and his wickedness will be punished in his next reincarnation. The Christian church answers the question by offering Heaven and Hell." He appeared to consider, and then he nodded his head briskly. "They're both good solutions, if you can believe them. We can't. Our view is given in the Book of Job, which is why it is included in the Bible.

Job is made to suffer undeservedly, but there is no suggestion that he will be recompensed in the next life. The suffering of the virtuous is one of the penalties of living. The fire burns the good man just as severely and painfully as it does the wicked."

"Then why bother to be good?" asked Mrs. Lanigan.

"Because virtue really does carry its own reward and evil its own punishment. Because evil is always essentially small and petty and mean and depraved, and in a limited life it represents a portion wasted, misused, and that can never be regained."

His tone while he was talking to Hugh Lanigan had been conversational and matter-of-fact, but as he spoke to Mrs. Lanigan it grew solemn and portentous, almost as though he were delivering a sermon. Miriam coughed warningly to him. "We should be getting back, David," she said.

The rabbi looked at his watch. "Why, it is getting late. I didn't mean to run on this way. I suspect it was the Tom Collins."

"I'm glad you did, rabbi," said Lanigan. "You might not think it, but I'm very interested in religion. I read books on the subject whenever I can. I don't get a chance to discuss it very often though. People are reluctant to talk about religion."

"Maybe it's no longer very important to them," he suggested.

"Well now, that might very well be, rabbi. But I enjoyed this afternoon, and I'd like to repeat it sometime."

The telephone rang. Mrs. Lanigan went inside to answer it and returned almost immediately. "It's Eban on the phone, Hugh."

Her husband, in the midst of explaining the shortest way to the police garage, said, "Tell him I'll call him back."

"He's not at home," she said. "He's calling from a pay station."

"Oh, all right, I'll talk to him."

"We'll find our way," said the rabbi. Lanigan nodded absently and hurried inside. As he walked down the porch steps, the rabbi was vaguely disturbed.

18

The next morning Melvin Bronstein was arrested. Shortly after seven, while the Bronsteins were still at breakfast, Eban Jennings and a sergeant, both in plain clothes, appeared at the Bronstein home.

"Melvin Bronstein?" asked Jennings when a man answered the door.

"That's right."

The policeman showed his badge. "I'm Lieutenant Jennings of the Barnard's Crossing police department. I have a warrant for your arrest."

"What for?"

"You're wanted for questioning in the matter of the murder of Elspeth Bleech."

"Are you charging me with murder?"

"My instructions are to bring you in for questioning," said Jennings.

Mrs. Bronstein called from the dining room, "Who is it, Mel?"

"Just a minute, dear," he called back.

"You're going to have to tell her," said Jennings, not unkindly.

"Will you come with me?" Bronstein asked in a low voice, and led the way to the dining room.

Mrs. Bronstein looked up, startled.

"These gentlemen are from the police department, dear," he said. "They want me to come to the police station to give them some information and to answer some questions." He swallowed hard. "It's about that poor girl who was found in the temple yard."

A spot of color appeared in Mrs. Bronstein's naturally pale face, but she did not lose her composure. "Do you know anything about the girl's death, Mel?" she asked.

"Nothing about her death," said Bronstein with great earnestness, "but I know something about the girl and these gentlemen think it might help them in their investigation."

"Will you be home for lunch?" asked his wife.

Bronstein looked at the policemen for an answer.

Jennings cleared his throat. "I don't think I'd count on it, ma'am."

Mrs. Bronstein placed her hands against the edge of the table and gave a slight push. She rolled back a few inches, and the policemen realized for the first time that she was in a wheelchair.

"If you can be of any help to the police in their investigation of this terrible business, Mel, then of course you must do everything you can."

He nodded. "You better call Al and ask him to get in touch with Nate Greenspan."

"Of course."

"Do you want me to help you back to bed," he asked, "or will you sit up?"

"I think I'd better go back to bed."

He bent down and scooped her up in his arms. For a moment he just stood there, holding her. She looked deep into his eyes.

"It's all right, sweetheart," he whispered.

"Of course," she murmured.

He carried her out of the room.

The news spread like wildfire. The rabbi had just returned from a busy morning at the temple and was about to sit down to lunch when Ben Schwarz called to tell him.

"Are you sure?" asked the rabbi.

"Oh, it's on the level, rabbi. It will probably be on the next radio news broadcast."

"Do you have any details?"

"No, just that he was taken into custody for questioning." He hesitated and then said, "Er—rabbi, I don't know how it will affect anything you might be planning to do, but I think you ought to know that he's not a member of our temple."

"I see. Well, thank you."

He reported the conversation to Miriam. "Mr. Schwarz seemed to think I could ignore the matter if I liked. At least, I assume that's what he meant by telling me Mr. Bronstein was not a member of the temple."

"Are you planning to?"

"Miriam!"

"Well, what are you going to do?"

"I'm not sure. I'll see him in any case. I suppose that will involve getting clearance from the authorities and probably from his lawyer as well. Perhaps it's even more important that I see Mrs. Bronstein."

"How about talking to Chief Lanigan?"

The rabbi shook his head. "What can I say to him? I know nothing about the case they have; I hardly know the Bronsteins. No, I'll call Mrs. Bronstein right now."

A woman answered and said that Mrs. Bronstein could not come to the telephone.

"This is Rabbi Small speaking. Would you ask her if it would be convenient for her to see me sometime today?"

"Will you hold the line a minute, please?" A moment later she returned to say that Mrs. Bronstein appreciated his calling, and would he make it sometime early in the afternoon?

"Tell her I'll be there at three o'clock."

He had no sooner hung up than the doorbell rang. It was Hugh Lanigan.

"I was just on my way back from the temple," he explained. "We've got something definite to check now. You heard about Bronstein?"

"I did, and the idea that he could have done this is utterly fantastic."

"You know him well, rabbi?"

"No, I don't."

"Well, before you go jumping to conclusions, let me tell you something: Mr. Bronstein was with the girl the night she was killed. That's not one of those fantastic mistakes the police make every now and then. He admits he was with her. He had dinner with her and he was with her all evening. He admits that, rabbi."

"Freely?"

Lanigan smiled. "You're thinking of a third degree, something in the nature of a rubber hose? I assure you we don't do that sort of thing here."

"No, I was thinking of questioning that might go on for hours on end, and little tongue slips being magnified until they are interpreted as admissions of guilt."

"You've got it all wrong, rabbi. As soon as he came to the station he made a statement. He could have refused to talk until he'd conferred with his lawyer, but he didn't. He said he had gone to the Surfside Restaurant and that he'd picked up the girl there. He claims he'd never seen her before. After dinner, they went to a movie in Boston and then had a bite. Afterwards, he drove her home and left her. That all seems pretty clear and straightforward, doesn't it? But the girl's body was found on Friday morning. Today is Monday. Four days later. If he was not involved, why didn't he come forward and give the police the information he had?"

"Because he's a married man. He was guilty of an indiscretion which suddenly ballooned up to monster proportions. It was very wrong of him not to go to the police, it was cowardly, it was unwise, but it still doesn't make him guilty of murder."

"That's just point number one, rabbi, but you'll admit it's enough to justify our picking him up for questioning. Here's point number two. The girl was pregnant. Mrs. Serafino, whom the girl worked for, was truly surprised to hear that; first, because she was a quiet girl who didn't run around, and secondly, because she never went out with men. In all the time she was with them, not once to Mrs. Serafino's knowledge did a man call for her, not once did she intimate or hint that she had been out with a man. On her evenings off, Thursdays, she would usually go to a movie, either alone or with a girlfriend who worked a few houses down. We questioned the girl, Celia, and she said that several times she had offered to fix Elspeth up with a man but each time she was refused. When Elspeth first came to town, Celia persuaded her to go to the Policemen and Firemen's Ball. All the housemaids go. That was the only time they went to a dance. Celia thought Elspeth might have a boyfriend back home in Canada—she got letters from time to time—that was the only way she could explain it. Celia was her only friend here and she certainly didn't get pregnant from Celia. So we did a little hunting and we found that your friend Mr. Bronstein had registered at least half a dozen times at various motels all along Route 14 and Route 69. He usually signed in under the name of Brown, and he was always with someone he registered as his wife. And as near as we can ascertain, it was always on a Thursday. We got positive identification on him by means of his picture and in one place by means of a penciled notation of his car license number. And a couple of the motelkeepers were pretty certain that his 'wife' was a blonde and that she resembled the picture we showed them of the murdered girl. That's point number two, rabbi."

"Did you tell him this about the motels?"

"Of course, or I wouldn't have told it to you."

"And what did he say?"

"He admits he was at those motels, but insists he wasn't there with this girl, that it was somebody else whose name he refuses to divulge."

"Well, if it's true—and it could be—that's rather admirable of him."

"Yes, if it's true. But we've got more. There is point three, which is not of too much significance but might be indicative. The girl went to see an obstetrician Thursday afternoon. She probably wore that wedding ring we found in her purse—for fairly obvious reasons. It was her first visit, so although she may have suspected her condition, she wasn't sure until Thursday. She gave her name as Mrs. Elizabeth Brown. And remember that Bronstein always registered as Mr. and Mrs. Brown."

"It's about as common as Smith," the rabbi observed.

"True."

"And nothing that you've said ties in with the fact the girl had only a slip under her coat and raincoat. Quite the contrary. He must have taken her home as he said, because that is where she left her dress. I suppose there's no doubt that the coat and raincoat are hers, or that the dress she wore was found in her room."

"That's right, and that brings us to point four. You've got to know the layout in the Serafino establishment in order to understand it. You don't know the Serafinos. I think I asked you once. Mr. Serafino operates a sort of nightclub. It's a small place where people sit around postage-stamp tables and drink watered-down liquor while Mr. Serafino sometimes plays the piano and his wife sings songs, risqué songs, bawdy songs, downright obscene songs. Not very nice people, you might say, but at home they're like any other young couple. They have two young children, and the family never misses a Sunday at church. The club doesn't close until two in the morning, so they need someone to take care of the children every night in the week, except Thursday, when Mrs. Serafino stays home and only her husband goes to the club. That's because Thursday is a slow night. It's maid's day off, so people, the kind that are apt to go to the Club Serafino, stay home. Anyway, the Serafinos need a live-in baby-sitter, which is not easy to come by for people in moderate circumstances. And in spite of what you might think of nightclub owners the Serafinos are people in moderate circumstances, and their house is arranged to meet their particular needs. It's two-story, and the Serafinos, Mr. and Mrs. and the two children, all sleep on the second floor. Off the kitchen on the first floor there's what amounts to a suite for the maid. She has a bedroom, a small lavatory, a stall shower, and, most important, a private entrance. Do you get the picture?"

The rabbi nodded.

"Here we have an apartment that's almost completely separated from the rest of the house. Now what was to prevent our friend Mr. Bronstein from coming into the house with the girl—"

"And she took off her dress while he was in the room?"

"Why not? If our theory is right, she'd taken off more than her dress on previous occasions."

"And then why did she go out again?"

Lanigan shrugged his shoulders. "I'll admit that here we're in the realm of pure conjecture. It's even possible that he strangled her right there in the room and then carried her out. A neighbor across the street who was beginning to get ready for bed looked out the window and saw Bronstein's blue Lincoln drive up to the Serafino house. That was shortly after twelve. Half an hour later he saw the Lincoln was still there. That's our fourth point."

"Did he see them get out of the car or get back in it?"

Lanigan shook his head.

"I know very little about these things," said the rabbi, "but as a Talmudist I am not entirely without legal training. Your theory has a thousand loopholes."

"Such as?"

"Such as the business of the coat and the raincoat. If he had murdered her in her room, why did he then dress her up in a topcoat and then a raincoat? And why did he take her to the temple? And how did her handbag get into my car?"

"I've thought of all those objections, rabbi, and some others that you haven't mentioned, but I have more than enough to justify picking him up and holding him until we can check out a good many things. It's always that way. Do you think a case is ever presented to you with all the facts neatly explained? No, sir. You get a lead and you go to work on it. There are objections and you're aware of them, but as you keep digging you get answers to them, quite simple answers usually."

"And if you don't get the answers, after a while you release the man and his life is ruined," said the rabbi bitterly.

"True, rabbi. It's one of the penalties of living in organized society."

19

Nathan Greenspan was a scholarly man, slow of thought and speech. He sat behind his desk, and after poking at his pipe with a spoonlike device, he blew through it once or twice to make sure it was drawing properly and then set about filling it very deliberately and methodically, while Becker, the inevitable cigar in his fist, strode up and down the room and told what had happened, what he suspected, and what he expected Greenspan to do. This last was something on the order of storming the police department and demanding that they release Bronstein immediately or face a suit for false arrest.

The lawyer put a match to his pipe, puffed at it until the entire surface was lit, and then firmly tamped down the burning tobacco that had risen in the bowl. He leaned back in his chair and spoke between puffs. "I can get a writ—of habeas corpus—if it seems that—he is being held unjustifiably—"

"Of course it's unjustifiable. He had nothing to do with it."

"How do you know?"

"Because he says so, and because I know him. You know the kind of man Bronstein is. Does he look like a murderer to you?"

"According to what you've told me the police didn't arrest him for murder. They just took him in for questioning. He had information that they had a right to know—he said he had been out with her the night she was killed. Even if he hadn't, even if he only knew her or had ever gone out with her, the police would want to question him."

"But they sent a couple of cops down to arrest him."

"That's because he didn't come in of his own accord—as he should have, by the way."

"All right, so he should have, but you know what that would have meant. I suppose he thought he could stay out of it entirely. So he was wrong, but that's no reason why he should be arrested and disgraced this way—cops coming to his house and hauling him off right in front of his wife."

"It's common practice, Al. Anyway, it's done."

"Well, what do you propose to do?"

"I'll go to see him, of course. They'll probably keep him overnight, but if they want to keep him any longer they're supposed to bring him before a judge and show probable cause. My guess is that they've got enough to hold him if they should want to. So my best bet, I imagine, would be to see the district attorney and see if I can find out just exactly what they have got on him."

"Why can't you force them to release him if they can't prove he did it?"

Greenspan emitted a faint sigh. He put his pipe down on an ashtray and took off his glasses. "Look here, Al, a girl has been murdered. Right now, everybody is anxious to find the person who killed her. That means that every agency of the law is in sympathy with the police and that all laws and regulations will be stretched in their favor. Now if I start pulling legal tricks to get him off, everybody—and that includes the newspapers—is going to resent it. Mel wouldn't have a good press and that won't do him any good no matter what happens. On the other hand, if we seem to be cooperative, the district attorney will give us whatever breaks he can."

"And what do I do?"

"You don't do a darn thing, Al. You just practice being patient."

Patience, however, was one thing Al Becker did not have. He reasoned that if the conduct of the investigation depended on the attitude of the district attorney, he could get quicker action by pressure from his friend Abe Casson, who had put the district attorney in office.

"What do you expect me to do, Al?" asked Casson. "I can tell you they've got a pretty good case against Mel right now. In fact, they could go to the grand jury with what they've got, but they're making it airtight."

"But he didn't do it, Abe."

"How do you know?"

"Because he told me. And because I know him."

Casson remained silent.

"Jesus, man, you know Mel Bronstein. Is he the kind of guy would do a thing like that? He's gentle as a girl. It doesn't make sense."

"These cases never make sense until they're over. Then they make lots of sense."

"Sure," said Becker bitterly. "If there's any little bit of evidence missing, they supply it. If there's a loophole, they plug it. Dammit, Abe, you know how these things work. They've got a lead, so they start chasing it down. They put every man on it. They know what they're trying to prove so they go ahead and prove it, until they get the poor bastard sewed up tight. And the real murderer goes free."

"What can I do, Al?"

"You're buddy-buddy with the D.A., to hear you tell it. You ought to be able to get him to keep his eyes open, to keep hunting for other possibilities."

Abe Casson shook his head. "The immediate investigation is in the hands of Chief Lanigan. You want to help your friend? Go see the rabbi."

"What in hell for? So that he can recite a prayer for him?"

"You know, Al, you've got an awfully big yap. Sometimes I think it's the only part of your head that works. Now listen to me. For some reason Hugh Lanigan has a great deal of respect for our rabbi. They're friendly. The other day, the rabbi and his wife spent the whole afternoon on Lanigan's porch. They were sitting there, the Lanigans and the Smalls, sipping drinks and talking."

"The rabbi never sat on my porch drinking and talking."

"Maybe you never invited him."

"All right, so let's say the chief likes him. What can the rabbi do for me?"

"He might do for you what you wanted me to do for you with the D.A."

"You think he would, knowing I'm the guy that's been working to get him out of here?"

"You believe he'd hold that against you in a matter of this sort? You don't know the rabbi. But if you want my advice—and really want to help your friend—that's what I suggest you do."

Miriam could scarcely pretend she was glad to see him. The rabbi greeted him formally. But Al Becker, if he was aware of the coolness of his reception, did not let it deter him. He fixed the rabbi with his most challenging glare and said, "Rabbi, Mel Bronstein could not possibly have done this terrible thing and you've got to do something about it."

"Anybody could possibly have done it," said the rabbi mildly.

"Yeah, I know," said Becker impatiently. "What I mean is that he's the last man in the world who would have done it. He's a sweet guy, rabbi. He's in love with his wife. They don't have any children. There are just the two of them and he's absolutely devoted to her."

"Do you know the nature of the evidence against him?" asked the rabbi.

"You mean he'd been playing around. So what? Do you know his wife has been in a wheelchair with multiple sclerosis for the last ten years of her life? For ten years they haven't had any—uh—relations."

"No, I didn't know that."

"A healthy man needs a woman. You being a rabbi wouldn't understand—"

"Rabbis aren't castrated."

"All right, I'm sorry. Then you know what I'm talking about. The girls he went out with didn't mean that to Mel." He snapped his fingers. "They were somebody he went to bed with, like he might go to a gym for a workout."

"Well, I'm not sure they're precisely analogous, but that's beside the point. What do you want me to do?"

"I don't know. You were in your study all evening. Maybe you could say you happened to look out the window and saw a man drive out of the parking lot, and you can swear that it wasn't a blue Lincoln—"

"Are you asking me to perjure myself?"

"Jesus, pardon me, rabbi. I'm so upset I don't know what I'm saying. I'm going nuts with this business. This morning I lose a sale to a customer who's been buying Continentals from me every other year, regular like a calendar, for the last ten years. We come to terms Saturday and he's supposed to come in at noon to sign the contract. When he doesn't show, I call him and he tells me he's thinking of holding the old car for a little while longer and maybe he might go into a smaller car. You think business was bad for him this year? He had his biggest year. You know why he suddenly got cold on the deal? Fifteen years Mel and I have worked to build up this business, and now, overnight, it's going to pot."

"Is it your business you are concerned about, or your friend?" asked the rabbi coldly.

"It's everything. It's all mixed up in my mind. Mel wasn't only a partner or a friend—he was like a kid brother to me. And when you've spent fifteen years building up something, it isn't just another way of making a living. It's part of me. It's my life. It's to me what your profession is to you. And now my whole world has suddenly gone sour."

"I can understand your position, Mr. Becker," said the rabbi, not unkindly, "and I wish I could help. But you haven't come here to ask me to give your friend spiritual consolation. What you ask is utterly impossible.

I'm afraid this business has warped your judgment, or you would realize that even if I were willing to do what you suggest, it would not be believed."

"I know, I know. It's just that I'm desperate, rabbi. But something you should be able to do. You're his rabbi, aren't you?"

"I have been led to believe I have been criticized for devoting my time to noncongregational matters," he observed quietly. "I understand that Mr. Bronstein is not a member of the congregation."

Becker was angry now. "All right, so what? Does that mean you can't help him? He's a Jew, isn't he? He's a member of the Jewish community here in Barnard's Crossing and you're the only rabbi here. You can at least go to see him, can't you? You can at least see his wife. They're not members, you say. All right, so I am. Help me."

"As a matter of fact," said the rabbi, "I already have an appointment to see Mrs. Bronstein and I was making arrangements to see Mr. Bronstein when you rang the bell."

Becker was not stupid. He even managed a grin. "All right, rabbi, maybe I had that coming to me. What do you have in mind?"

"Chief Lanigan was here earlier and outlined the case against Mr. Bronstein. At the time, I thought the evidence admitted of another interpretation. But I don't really know the Bronsteins. So I thought I first ought to try to know them."

"You'll never meet two nicer people, rabbi."

"You realize how organizations work, Mr. Becker, and the police, I should imagine, are no different. They look everywhere until they find a suspect, but then they're likely to concentrate on him from then on. I thought I might be able to persuade Chief Lanigan not to stop looking elsewhere."

"That's just what I had in mind, rabbi," said Becker ecstatically. "It's just what I said to Abe Casson. Ask him. I feel better already."

20

The jail consisted of four small steel-barred cells on the first floor of the Barnard's Crossing police station. Each cell had a narrow iron cot, a toilet, and a washbasin; a bulb in a porcelain socket dangled from the ceiling, suspended by a length of BX cable. A dim lamp burned day and night in the corridor, at one end of which was a barred window and at the other the wardroom. Beyond that was Lanigan's office.

From the wardroom, Hugh Lanigan showed the rabbi the cells and then led the way back to his office. "It isn't much of a jail," he said, "but fortunately it's all we need. I suppose it's one of the oldest jails in the country. This building goes back to Colonial times, and was originally used as the town hall. It's been fixed up of course, and renovated from time to time, but the foundation and most of the supporting beams are the original ones. And the cells have been modernized with electricity and flush toilets and running water, but they're still the original cells and they date back to before the Civil War."

"Where do the prisoners eat?" asked the rabbi.

Lanigan laughed. "We don't usually have them in the plural, except perhaps on a Saturday night when we sometimes pick up a few drunk and disorderlies and let them sleep it off overnight. When we do have somebody in during mealtimes, one of the restaurants nearby, Barney Blake's usually, puts up a box lunch. In the old days, the police chief used to make a pretty good thing out of prisoners. The town allowed him a certain amount for each one kept overnight, plus a certain amount for each meal served. When I first joined the force, the chief was constantly after us patrolmen to bring in drunks. Anyone who stumbled on the street was apt to find himself locked up for the night. But some time ago, long before I took over, the town upped the chief's salary and provided a regular allowance for feeding the prisoners, and I guess chiefs haven't been so anxious to make arrests since."

"And your prisoners are confined to those little cells until they come up for trial?"

"Oh no. If we decide to charge your friend, we'll bring him up before a judge sometime tomorrow, and if he tells us to hold him the prisoner will be transferred to the jail in Salem or Lynn."

"And are you planning to charge him?"

"That's pretty much up to the district attorney. We'll show him what we've got and maybe he'll ask some questions and then he'll make up his mind. He could decide not to charge him with the murder but to hold him as a material witness."

"When will I be able to see him?"

"Right now, if you like. You can visit with him in his cell or see him right here in my office."

"I think I'd rather see him alone, if you don't mind."

"Oh, that's all right, rabbi. I'll have him brought in here and leave you two together." He laughed. "You're not carrying any weapons concealed about your person, are you? No files or hacksaws?"

The rabbi smiled and patted his jacket pockets. Lanigan went to the door that opened into the wardroom and shouted to one of the policemen to bring the prisoner into his office. Then he closed the door and left the rabbi alone. A moment later, Bronstein came in.

He seemed much younger than his wife, but the rabbi put that down to a difference in health rather than age. He was embarrassed.

"I sure appreciate your coming to see me, rabbi, but I'd give anything to have this meeting someplace else."

"Of course."

"You know, I found myself thinking that I was glad my parents were both dead—yes, and that I had no children. Because I wouldn't be able to face them, even when the police finally find the guilty person and let me go."

"I understand, but you must realize that misfortune can happen to anyone. Only the dead are safe from it."

"But this is so ugly . . ."

"All misfortune is ugly. You mustn't keep thinking about it. Tell me about the girl."

Bronstein did not answer immediately. He got up from his chair and paced the floor as if to gather his thoughts or to control his emotions. Then he stopped suddenly and faced the rabbi. He spoke in a rush:

"I never saw her before in my life. I'll swear that on my mother's grave. I've played around. I admit it. I suppose some people might say that if I loved my wife, I'd be completely faithful to her, even under the circumstances. Maybe I would have been if we'd had children, or maybe I could have if I were stronger. But what I have done, I'm willing to admit. I've had affairs with women, but there's never been anything serious or intense about them. And I've played fair with them. I never tried to hide the fact that I was married. I never handed a woman this line about my wife not understanding me. I never suggested that there was a possibility that I might divorce my wife. It was always straightforward and aboveboard. I had certain needs—my body had certain needs. Well, there are plenty of women who are in the same position and who use the same remedy. This woman that I shacked up with in motels a couple of times—it wasn't this kid. It's a married woman whose husband deserted her and she's suing for divorce."

"If you gave the police her name—"

Bronstein shook his head violently. "If I did that, it would interfere with her divorce. They might even take her children away. Don't worry, if it ever gets to the point where I'm actually put on trial, and it hinges on this, she'll come forward."

"You saw her every Thursday?"

"No, not last Thursday, and not for a couple of Thursdays before that. To tell the truth, she was getting edgy about our meeting. She got the idea that her husband might be having detectives trailing her."

"So that's how you came to pick up this girl—as a substitute?"

"I'll level with you, rabbi. When I picked her up, I wasn't planning any platonic friendship. I picked her up in a restaurant, the Surfside. If the police were really interested in getting the truth, rather than on pinning it on me, they'd inquire around among people who were there, the waitresses and the customers, and some of them would be sure to remember how I was sitting at one table and she at another, and how I went over to her and introduced myself. Anybody could see that it was a pick-up. But what I was going to say, was that after we had eaten together and talked for a while, I saw that the poor kid was frightened—frightened stiff, and trying awfully hard to be gay and not show it. Wouldn't that show she was expecting trouble?"

"Possibly. In any case, it's something worth looking into."

"I felt sorry for her. I just forgot about making a pass at her. I stopped being interested in her in that way. All I had in mind was a pleasant evening. We drove to Boston and went to a movie." He hesitated and then came to a quick decision. Leaning forward, he lowered his voice as though he were afraid of being overheard. "I'll tell you something I haven't told the police, rabbi. The silver chain that she wore, the one she was strangled with—God forgive me—I bought it for her just before we went into the show."

"You say you haven't told this to the police?"

"That's right. I'm not handing them anything they can use on me that I don't have to. The way they questioned me, they'd latch onto that as proof I was planning all evening to kill her. I'm telling you so you can see I'm leveling with you."

"All right. Then where did you go?"

"After the movie we dropped into a restaurant for pancakes and coffee and then I drove her home. I drove right up to her house, parking right in front, all open and aboveboard."

"Did you go inside?"

"Of course not. We sat outside in the car for quite a while just talking. I didn't even put my arm around her. We just sat there and talked. Then she thanked me and got out of the car and went into the house."

"Did you make arrangements to meet her again?"

Bronstein shook his head. "I had a pleasant evening and I think she did too. She seemed a lot more relaxed by the time I took her home than she had at dinner. But there was no reason for me to repeat it."

"Then you went right home from there?"

"That's right."

"And your wife was asleep at the time?"

"I guess so. I sometimes think she only pretends to be asleep when I come home late. But anyway, she was in bed and the light was off."

The rabbi smiled. "That's the way she described it to me."

Bronstein looked up quickly. "You mean you've seen her? How is she? How is she taking all this?"

"Yes, I've seen her." In his mind's eye he could still visualize a thin, pale woman in a wheelchair, her hair just beginning to gray, brushed back from a high, unlined forehead; a nice-looking woman with finely carved features and gray eyes that were quick and bright.

"Her attitude was quite cheerful," said the rabbi.

"Cheerful?"

"I suppose she was making an effort, but I got the feeling that she was absolutely certain of your innocence. She said that if you had done this thing, she would have known it at a single glance."

"I don't suppose evidence like that would be of any use in court, rabbi, but it's true that we're very close to each other. In most marriages women get involved with their children, more or less to the exclusion of their husbands. But my wife got sick about ten years ago, and so we were together more than most couples. We can practically read each other. Do you understand, rabbi?"

The rabbi nodded.

"Of course, if she were only pretending to be asleep—"

"She said she always waited up for you, except on Thursdays. I thought perhaps it was because she was tired out from the excitement of entertaining her bridge club, but she assured me it wasn't that. It was because she knew you had been out with some woman and she didn't want to embarrass you."

"Oh my God." He covered his face with his hands.

The rabbi looked at him with pity and decided it was no time for preaching. "She was not hurt, she said. She understood."

"She said that? She said she understood?"

"Yes." The rabbi, uncomfortable at the turn of the conversation, tried to change it: "Tell me, Mr. Bronstein, does your wife ever leave the house?"

His face softened. "Oh yes, when the weather is nice and she feels up to it I take her for a ride. I like to drive, and I like to have her beside me. It's a little like old times then. You see, she's sitting there beside me just as she would be if she were well. There's no wheelchair to remind me that she's sick, although I have one, a collapsible one, in the trunk and sometimes on a warm night we drive over to the boulevard and I put her in it and walk her along the water."

"How does she get into the car?"

"I just pick her up and slide her onto the front seat."

The rabbi rose. "There are one or two points I think might be worth calling to the attention of the police. Maybe they can check into them if they haven't already done so."

Bronstein also rose. Hesitantly he offered his hand. "Believe me rabbi, I appreciate your coming here."

"Do they treat you all right?"

"Oh yes." He nodded in the direction of the cells. "After I finished answering their questions they left the door of the cell unlocked so I could walk up and down the corridor if I wanted to. Some of the policemen have been in to chat and they gave me some magazines to read. I wonder—"

"Yes?"

"I wonder if you could get word to my wife that I'm all right. I wouldn't want her to worry."

The rabbi smiled. "I'll be in touch with her, Mr. Bronstein."

21

As he left Bronstein, the rabbi reflected sadly that his first attempts to help had succeeded only in uncovering two points, both minor and both detrimental to the unfortunate man. In his interview with Mrs. Bronstein he had learned that on this one night of the week she had not been up to greet her husband. Of course even if she could say he had not seemed upset, it would not help much; as his wife she would not be given full credence, and in any case it was only negative evidence. And what stuck in his mind from his interview with the husband was the picture of him scooping his wife up in his arms and depositing her on the car seat. He had always thought it might be difficult and awkward for the murderer to carry the body from one car to the other, but now Mel Bronstein had demonstrated it would be no trick at all, that he was a practiced hand at it.

Bronstein's car was a big Lincoln, whereas his was a compact, which could make a difference. When he got home, he drove into the garage, got out, and studied the car, a frown on his thin, scholarly face. Then he called into the house for Miriam to come out for a minute.

She did so, standing beside him and following the direction of his stare. "Did someone scratch it?"

Instead of answering, he put his arm around her waist absently. She smiled affectionately at him, but he did not appear to notice. He reached out and swung open the car door.

"What is it, David?"

He pulled at his lower lip as he surveyed the interior of the car. Then, without a word, he bent down and picked her up in his arms.

"David!"

He staggered with his burden over to the open car door.

She began to giggle.

He tried to ease her onto the seat. "Let your head hang back," he ordered.

Instead, still giggling, she wrapped her arms around his neck and put her face against his.

"Please, Miriam."

She pecked at his ear.

"I'm trying to—"

She swung her legs provocatively. "What would Mr. Wasserman say if he saw us now?"

"Having fun?"

They turned to see Chief Lanigan in the doorway, a broad smile on his face.

The rabbi hastily set his wife down. He felt foolish. "I was just experimenting," he explained. "It's not easy to maneuver a body onto a car seat."

Lanigan nodded. "No, but although the girl probably weighed more than Mrs. Small, Bronstein's a good bit bigger than you."

"I suppose that makes a difference," the rabbi said, as he led the way into the house and to his study.

When they were seated, Lanigan asked how he had made out with Bronstein.

"I got to know him this afternoon," said the rabbi. "He's not the sort of person who would be likely to do a thing like this—"

"Rabbi, rabbi," the chief interrupted impatiently, "when you've seen as many criminals as I have you'll know that appearances are meaningless. Do you suppose a thief has a furtive look? Or that a confidence man is shifty-eyed? Why, his stock in trade is an open, frank appearance and an ability to look you straight in the eye. You people are called the People of the Book, and I suppose a rabbi is a particularly bookish sort of person. I have a great deal of respect for books and for bookish people, rabbi, but in matters such as this it's experience that counts."

"But if appearances and manner are deceptive, then all appearances are neutralized," said the rabbi mildly, "and it's hard to see how a jury system could possibly function. What do you base your convictions on?"

"Evidence, rabbi. On mathematically certain evidence, if it's available, or on the weight of probabilities if it isn't."

The rabbi nodded slowly. Then he said with seeming irrelevance, "Do you know about our Talmud?"

"That's your book of laws, isn't it? Does it have anything to do with this?"

"Well, it's not really our book of laws. The Books of Moses are that. It's the commentaries on the Law. I don't suppose it has any direct connection with the case at hand, but you can't be too sure of that either since all kinds of things can be found in the Talmud. I wasn't thinking at the moment of its contents, however, but rather of the method of its study. When I began to study in the religious school as a youngster, all subjects—Hebrew, grammar, literature, the Scriptures—all were taught in the ordinary way, just as subjects are taught in the public school. That is to say, we sat at desks while the teacher sat at a larger desk on a platform. He wrote on the board, he asked questions, he gave out home lessons and heard us recite. But when I began Talmud, instruction was different. Imagine a large table with a group of students around it. At the head of the table was the teacher, a man with a long, patriarchal beard in this case. We read a passage, a short statement of the Law. Then followed the objections, the explanations, the arguments of the rabbis of old on the proper interpretation of the passage. Before we quite knew what we were doing, we were adding our own arguments, our own objections, our own hair-splitting distinctions and twists of logic, the so-called pilpul. Sometimes the teacher took it on himself to defend a given position and then we peppered him with questions and objections. I imagine a bear-baiting must have been like that—a shaggy bear surrounded by a pack of yelping dogs, and the moment he manages to toss off one another is ready to charge. As you begin to argue, new ideas keep presenting themselves. I remember an early passage I studied, which considered how damages should be assessed in the case of a fire resulting from a spark that flew out from under the blacksmith's hammer. We spent two whole weeks on that one passage, and when we finally reluctantly left it, it was with the feeling that we had barely begun. The study of the Talmud has exercised a tremendous influence over us. Our great scholars spent their lives studying the Talmud, not because the exact interpretation of the Law happened to be germane to their problems at the time—in many cases the particular laws had become dead letters—but because as a mental exercise it had a tremendous fascination for them. It encouraged them to dredge up from their minds all kinds of ideas—"

"And you propose to use this method on our present problem?"

"Why not? Let's examine the weight of probabilities in your theory and see if it stands up."

"All right, go ahead."

The rabbi got up from his chair and began to stride about the room. "We will start not with the body, but with the handbag."

"Why?"

"Why not?"

Lanigan shrugged his shoulders. "Okay, you're the teacher."

"Actually, the handbag is a more fertile field of investigation if only because it touches on three people. The body lying behind the wall concerns only two people: the girl and her murderer. The handbag involves those two and me, because it was in my car that the handbag was found."

"Good enough."

"Now, what are the possibilities by which the handbag could have been left where it was found? It could have been left by the girl or by the man who killed her, or by a third party, unknown, unsuspected, and until now unconsidered."

"You got something new up your sleeve, rabbi?" asked Lanigan suspiciously.

"No, I'm merely considering all the possibilities."

There was a knock on the study door and Miriam came in with a tray.

"I thought you'd like some coffee," she said.

"Thank you," said Lanigan. "Aren't you going to join us?" he said when he noticed there were only two cups on the tray.

"May I?"

"Certainly. There's nothing very confidential about this. The rabbi is just giving me my first lesson in the Talmud."

When she returned with a coffee cup, he said, "All right, rabbi, we've listed all the people who could have left the handbag. Where does that take us?"

"Of course the first question that comes to mind is why she had the bag with her at all. I suppose it's automatic with some women."

"A lot of women attach their house key to the inside of the bag by a chain," suggested Mrs. Small.

Lanigan nodded to her. "Good guess. That's how she had her key, attached by a short chain to the ring that's the zipper-pull for an inside pocket."

"So she took the bag rather than go to the trouble of detaching the key," the rabbi went on. "Now let's consider one by one the people who could possibly have left it in my car. First, to clear him out of the way, the third party, the unsuspected stranger. He would be someone who happened to be walking along and saw the bag, presumably because it was lying on the ground somewhere near my car. He would certainly open it, if only to find out if there was any identification so he could return it to its proper owner. But, more likely, he would open it out of common curiosity. If he were dishonest, he would have taken whatever of value it contained. But he did not do this."

"How do you know that, rabbi?" asked Lanigan, suddenly alert.

"Because you said you found a heavy gold wedding ring. If the man were dishonest, he would have taken it. That he did not, suggests to me that any other thing of value—money, for instance—was left undisturbed."

"There was some money in the purse," Lanigan admitted. "About what you'd expect, a couple of bills and some loose change."

"Very good. So we can assume it is not the case of someone finding the purse, taking out whatever was of value, and then tossing away the bag itself, now valueless, so that it would not be found on him."

"All right, where does that get you?"

"It merely clears the ground. Now suppose he were honest and wanted only to return it to its rightful owner, and he put it in my car because he had found it nearby and assumed it belonged there, or because he thought the driver, finding it in his car, would take the trouble to return it to the rightful party. If that were his sole connection with the bag, why did he put it on the floor in back instead of on the front seat, where the driver would be sure to find it? I could have driven around for days without seeing it."

"All right, so a hitherto unsuspected stranger did not leave the bag in the car, neither an honest one nor a dishonest one. I never said one did."

"So we'll go on to the next. We'll take the girl."

"The girl is out. She was dead at the time."

"How can you be so sure? It would seem that the most likely explanation for the handbag is that the girl herself left it in the car."

"Look here, it was a warm night and you must have had the window of your study open. Right?"

"Yes. The window was up, but the venetian blinds were down."

"How far do you think you were from your car? I'll tell you. The car was twenty feet away from the building. Your study is on the second floor, say eleven feet above ground level. Add another four feet to give you the height of the windowsill. Now if you remember your high-school geometry, the line from the car to you is the hypotenuse of a right triangle. And if you work it out, you'll find that the sill was about twenty-five feet away from the car. Add ten feet to give you your position at your desk. That means you were thirty-five feet from the car. And if someone had got into that car, let alone quarreled and got murdered in it, you'd have heard it no matter how engrossed you were in your studies."

"But it could have happened after I left the temple," the rabbi objected.

Lanigan shook his head. "Not too easily. You said you left sometime after twelve. You figured out it was about twenty past. But Patrolman Norman was walking up Maple Street towards the temple, and about that time or very shortly thereafter he was within sight of the temple. The parking lot was under his observation from that time up to three minutes past one when he pulled the box on the corner. Then he headed down Vine Street, which is the street the Serafinos live on and was therefore the street the girl must have come down."

"All right, then after that?" suggested the rabbi.

Lanigan shook his head again. "Nothing doing. The medical examiner first reported that the girl was killed around one o'clock, with a twenty-minute leeway either side. But that was on the basis of body temperature, rigidity, and so forth. When we questioned Bronstein we discovered they'd eaten after the movie, and that enabled the M.E. to make a determination of the time on the basis of stomach content, which is a good deal more accurate. He gave us a supplementary report that fixes one o'clock at the outside."

"Then in that case we have to consider the possibility that in spite of my proximity to the car I was so engrossed that I heard nothing. Remember, the car windows were up, and if they were careful in opening and closing the car door and if they conversed in low tones I wouldn't have heard them. Also, the way she was killed, by strangulation, would have prevented her from crying out."

Lanigan pointed at the rabbi's head. "What do you call that thing you're wearing?"

The rabbi touched his black silk skullcap. "This? A *kipoh.*"

"Then forgive me, rabbi," he said, grinning, "but you're talking through your *kipoh.* Why would they be careful about opening and closing the car doors and keeping their voices down to a whisper when they had no reason to assume anyone was within earshot? If they were there before it began to rain, they would have lowered the windows. It was warm, remember. And if it was during the rain, Norman surely would have seen them. What's more, there was no indication the girl had been in your car. Look here." He opened his dispatch case and took out some papers, which he spread on the rabbi's desk, and they all drew near to look. "These are the total contents of your car—a list of what was in every receptacle. Here's a diagram of the interior of the car showing where each item was found. Here's where the handbag was found, on the floor under the seat. Here in the plastic trash pocket were lipstick-stained tissues, but it was your wife's lipstick. On the floor in the rear, right behind the front seats, there was a bobby pin but it was your wife's. There were a number of cigarette butts in the front ashtray and one in the rear ashtray, and all were lipstick-stained with your wife's lipstick, and it was the brand she smokes because they're the same as the partially filled pack we found in the glove compartment."

"Just a minute," said Miriam, "that one in the rear ashtray can't be mine. I've never sat in the back seat since we got the car."

"What's that? Never sat in the back seat? That's impossible."

"Is it?" asked the rabbi mildly. "I have never sat in any seat but the driver's seat. Actually, the back seat has never been used, come to think of it. Since we got the car, less than a year ago, I have never had occasion to transport anyone. When I am in the car, I am in the driver's seat, and when Miriam comes along she sits beside me. What is so strange about that? How often do you sit in the back seat of your car?"

"But it must have got there somehow. The lipstick is your wife's, the brand of cigarette is hers. Look here, here's a list of what was in the girl's handbag. No cigarettes, you notice."

The rabbi studied the list. Then he pointed. "But there's a cigarette lighter, and that would indicate that she smoked. As far as the lipstick goes, you said it was the same brand and shade as Miriam's. After all, they're both blondes."

"Just a minute," said Lanigan. "The bobby pin was found in the back of the car, so you must have—"

Miriam shook her head. "Sitting in the front seat, it would be in the back that the pin would fall."

"Yes, I suppose so," said Lanigan, "but it still doesn't give us what you'd call a clear picture. She had no cigarettes—at least there were none in her purse, right?"

"Right, but she was not alone. There was someone with her—the murderer—and he probably had cigarettes."

"Are you saying that the girl was murdered in your car, rabbi?"

"Precisely. The lipstick-stained cigarette in the rear ashtray proves that a woman was in the rear seat of my car. The handbag on the floor in the rear shows that it was Elspeth Bleech."

"All right, let's say she was there. Let's even grant she was killed in your car. How does that help Bronstein?"

"I'd say it clears him."

"You mean because he had a car of his own?"

"Yes. Why would he drive into the parking lot with the girl, park alongside my car, and then change cars?"

"He might have killed her in his own car and then transferred the body to your car."

"You're forgetting the cigarette in the rear ashtray. She was alive in my car."

"Suppose he forced her into your car."

"For what reason?"

Lanigan shrugged. "Perhaps to avoid having any signs of struggle in his own car."

"You're not giving that cigarette its full weight as evidence. If she smoked that cigarette in the rear seat of my car, then she was at ease. No one had his hand at her throat—no one was threatening her. For that matter, if after taking off her dress she had to go back to Bronstein's car for some reason, why would she have put on the raincoat?"

"Because it was raining, of course."

The rabbi shook his head impatiently. "The car was right in front of the house. How far? Fifty feet? She had put on a topcoat to cover her slip, and that certainly was protection enough against the rain for such a short run."

Lanigan rose and began to pace the floor. The rabbi watched him, unwilling to interrupt his train of thought. But when he continued silent, the rabbi said, "Bronstein should have come to the police as soon as he found out what happened, admitted. For that matter, he shouldn't have picked up the girl in the first place. But even if you can't condone it, it is understandable in the light of the situation at home. And again you can't condone his withholding information from the police, but you can understand it. Arresting him for questioning, with its attendant publicity, is more than enough punishment, don't you agree? Chief Lanigan, take my advice and let him go."

"But that would leave me without a suspect."

"That's not like you."

"What do you mean?" The chief's face reddened.

"I can't imagine you holding a man just so that you can report progress to the press. Besides, it will only hamper your investigation. You'll find yourself thinking about Bronstein, trying to evolve theories that put him in the picture, checking his past, interpreting whatever new evidence comes up, from the point of view of his possible involvement. And that's obviously the wrong direction for your investigation to take."

"Well . . ."

"Don't you see, you've got nothing on him other than his failure to come forward."

"But the D.A. is coming down in the morning to question him."

"Then tell him he'll turn up voluntarily. I'll go bond for him. I'll guarantee his appearance when you want him."

Lanigan picked up his dispatch case. "All right, I'll let him go." He went to the door, and with his hand on the knob he paused. "Of course, rabbi, you realize that you haven't exactly improved your own position."

22

Al Becker was not one to forget a favor. The morning after his partner was released, he went to see Abe Casson to thank him personally for his good offices in the matter.

"Yeah, I spoke to the district attorney but I didn't get far. As I told you, this case is being handled pretty much by the local police, at least so far."

"Is that customary?"

"Well, it is and it isn't. The lines of authority aren't clearly drawn. The state detectives usually come in on murders. The district attorney in whose county a major crime is committed and whose office will have to prosecute, he's in on it. Then the local police, because they know local conditions, they have a hand in it. It depends a lot on the character of the local police chief and on the character of the D.A. and what men are available and what special issues are at stake. You take in a big city like Boston, it would be the Boston police who'd be running the show because they have the men and they're equipped for it. Now down here, the investigation is being run pretty much by Hugh Lanigan. Mel was picked up on his orders and he was released on his orders. And I'll tell you something else: Lanigan released him as a result of some new angle or some new interpretation of the evidence that the rabbi showed him. That's not customary, if you like—I mean, a cop giving someone else the credit for some clever detective work—but then Hugh Lanigan is no ordinary cop."

Al Becker did not take Abe Casson's remarks at face value. He did not doubt that the rabbi had spoken to Lanigan about the matter—conceivably, in the course of the conversation, some chance remark of the rabbi's may have given the police chief a different slant—but he did not believe the rabbi had been able to work out a convincing defense of his friend. Still, he supposed he ought to see the rabbi and thank him.

Once again, their meeting was not without its awkwardness. Becker came straight to the point. "I understand that you had a lot to do with Mel Bronstein's being released, rabbi."

It would have been easier had the rabbi made the expected modest disclaimer, but instead he said, "Yes, I suppose I did."

"Well, you know how I feel about Mel. He's like a kid brother to me. So you can understand how grateful I am. I haven't exactly been one of your most active supporters—"

The rabbi smiled. "And now you are somewhat embarrassed. There's no need to be, Mr. Becker. I'm sure your objection was in no way personal. You feel that I'm not the right man for the position I hold. You have every right to go on feeling that way. I helped your friend as I would help you or anyone else who needed it, just as I'm sure you would in like circumstances."

Becker phoned Abe Casson to report on his conversation with the rabbi, ending with, "He's a hard man to like. I went there to thank him for helping Mel and to more or less apologize for having worked against him on the contract business, and he as much as told me he didn't need my friendship and didn't care if I continued to oppose him."

"That's not the impression I got from your story. You know, Al, maybe you're too smart to understand a man like the rabbi. You're used to reading between the lines and guessing what people really mean. Has it ever occurred to you that the rabbi might not talk between the lines, that he says pretty much exactly what he means?"

"Well, I know you and Jake Wasserman and Abe Reich are sold on him. The rabbi can do no wrong as far as you people are concerned, but—"

"He seems to have done all right for you too, Al."

"Oh, I'm not saying that he didn't do me and Mel a favor, and I'm grateful. But you know very well that Mel would have got off anyway, maybe in another day or two, because they didn't have a thing on him."

"Don't be so sure. You don't know how they play the game. In an ordinary case where a man is tried for some ordinary crime—sure, the chances are that if he's innocent he'll go free. But in a case of this kind there's another element. It's no longer just a case at law. Politics enters into it, and then they're not so concerned about whether a man is guilty or not. They start thinking in different terms: have we got enough to go before a jury with? If the man is innocent, let his lawyer take care of him and if he doesn't, it's just too bad. It becomes a sort of game, like football, with the D.A. on one side and the defendant's lawyer on the other, and the judge the referee. And the defendant? He's the football."

"Yes, but—"

"And another thing, Al, if you really want to see this in its proper perspective, just ask yourself what happens now? Who's the chief suspect? I'll tell you—it's the rabbi. Now whatever your opinion of the rabbi, you can't call him stupid. So you can be sure he knows that in getting Bronstein off the hook he was putting himself squarely on. Think about that for a while, Al, and then ask yourself again if the rabbi is such a hard man to like."

23

Sunday it rained. The rain had started early in the morning, and the corridor and classrooms of the Sunday school were pervaded with the smell of wet raincoats and rubbers. Mr. Wasserman and Abe Casson, standing just inside the outer door, stared moodily at the parking lot, watching raindrops bounce against the shiny asphalt.

"It's a quarter-past ten, Jacob," said Casson. "It doesn't look as though we're going to have a meeting today."

"A little bit of rain, and they're afraid to go out."

They were joined by Al Becker. "Abe Reich and Meyer Goldfarb are here, but I don't think you'll be getting many more."

"We'll wait another fifteen minutes," said Wasserman.

"If they're not here now, they won't be here," said Casson flatly.

"Maybe we should make a few telephone calls," Wasserman suggested.

"If they're afraid of a little rain," said Becker, "your calling them won't change their minds."

Casson snorted derisively. "You think that's what's keeping them away?"

"What else?"

"I think the boys are playing it cozy. Don't you understand, Al? They don't any of them want to get mixed up in this."

"Mixed up in what?" demanded Becker. "What the hell are you talking about?"

"I'm talking about a girl who was murdered. And about the rabbi's possible connection with her. We were supposed to vote today on the rabbi's new contract, remember? And I imagine some of the boys started to think about the possibilities. Suppose they vote for keeping the rabbi, and then it turns out he's guilty. What would their friends say, especially their Gentile friends? What would be the effect on their business? Now do you get it?"

"It never occurred to me," Becker began slowly.

"That's because it probably never occurred to you that the rabbi could have done it," said Casson. He looked at Becker curiously. "Tell me, Al, didn't you get any phone calls?"

Becker looked blank, but Wasserman's face began to color.

"Ah, I see you got some, Jacob," Casson went on.

"What kind of calls?" asked Becker.

"Tell him, Jacob."

Wasserman shrugged his shoulders. "Who pays attention? Cranks, fools, bigots, am I going to listen to them? I hang up on them."

"And you've been getting them, too?" Becker demanded of Casson.

"Yeah. I imagine they called Jacob because he's president. And they called me because I'm in politics and so I'm known."

"And what have you done about it?" demanded Becker.

Casson shrugged his shoulders. "Same as Jacob—nothing. What can you do about it? When the murderer is found, it'll stop."

"Well, something ought to be done about it. At least we ought to tell the police or the Selectmen or—"

"And what can they do? Now if I were to recognize a voice, that would be something else again."

"Yeah."

"It's new to you, eh? And it's probably new to Jacob. But it's not new to me. I've had this type of call in every political campaign. The world is full of nuts—bitter, disappointed, disturbed men and women. Individually, they're mostly harmless. Collectively, they're kind of unpleasant to think about. They write nasty obscene letters to the newspapers or to people whose names are mentioned in the news, and if it happens to be someone local, they telephone."

Wasserman looked at his watch. "Well, gentlemen, a meeting I'm afraid we won't have today."

"It wouldn't be the first time we didn't get a quorum," said Becker.

"And what do I tell the rabbi? That he should wait another week? And next week, we are sure we'll get a quorum?" He looked quizzically at Becker.

Becker colored. Then suddenly he was angry. "So if we don't get a quorum, it'll be next week, or the following week, or the week after that. You've got the votes. Does he need it in writing?"

"There's also the little matter of the opposition votes that you mustered," Casson reminded him.

"You don't have to worry about them now," said Becker stiffly. "I told my friends I was in favor of renewing the rabbi's contract."

Hugh Lanigan dropped by that evening to see the rabbi.

"I thought I'd congratulate you on your reprieve. According to my source of information, the opposition to you has collapsed."

The rabbi smiled noncommittally.

"You don't seem very happy about it," said Lanigan.

"It's a little like getting in through the back door."

"So that's it. You think you're getting this reappointment or election, or whatever it is, because of what you were able to do for Bronstein. Well, here, I am in a position to teach you, rabbi. You Jews are skeptical, critical, and logical."

"I always thought we were supposed to be highly emotional," said the rabbi.

"And so you are, but only about emotional things. You Jews have no political sense whatsoever, and we Irish have a genius for it. When you argue or campaign for office, you fight on the issues. And when you lose, you console yourselves with the thought that you fought on the issues and argued reasonably and logically. It must have been a Jew who said he'd rather be right than President. An Irishman knows better; he knows that you can do nothing unless you're elected. So the first principle of politics is to get elected. And the second great principle is that a candidate is not elected because he's the logical choice, but because of the way he has his hair cut, or the hat he wears, or his accent. That's the way we pick even the President of the United States, and for that matter, that's the way a man picks his wife. Now wherever you have a political situation, political principles apply. So don't you worry as to why or how you were chosen. You just be happy that you were chosen."

"Mr. Lanigan is right, David," said Miriam. "We know that if your contract had not been renewed you could have got another position as good or better than this, but you like it here in Barnard's Crossing. Besides, Mr. Wasserman is sure the raise will be granted, and we can find some use for that."

"That's already spoken for, my dear," said the rabbi hurriedly.

She made a face. "More books?"

He shook his head. "Not this time. When this business is finally over, I'm going to apply the extra money toward a new car. The thought of that poor girl . . . Every time I get into the car I almost shudder. I find myself thinking up excuses for walking instead of riding."

"Understandable," said Lanigan, "but maybe you'll feel differently once we find the murderer."

"Oh? How does it look?"

"We're getting new material all the time. We're working around the clock. Right now, we've got some promising leads."

"Or to put it another way," said the rabbi, "you're at a dead end."

Lanigan's answer was a shrug and a wry grin.

"If you want my advice," said Miriam, "you'll put it out of your mind and have a cup of tea."

"That's sound advice," said Lanigan.

They sipped their tea and talked about the town, politics, the weather —the aimless, idle conversation of people who had nothing weighing on their minds. Lanigan finally rose with obvious reluctance.

"It's been very pleasant just sitting here and talking, rabbi, Mrs. Small, but I've got to get back now."

Just as he was leaving, the telephone rang, and although the rabbi was nearest his wife ran to answer. She said hello, and then listened for a moment, the receiver pressed firmly against her ear. "I'm sorry, you have the wrong number," she said firmly and hung up.

"We seem to be getting quite a few wrong numbers the last couple of days," observed the rabbi.

Lanigan, his hand on the doorknob, looked from the rabbi, his face innocent and bland, to his wife, her cheeks pink with embarrassment? with annoyance? with anger? In response to his questioning look he thought he detected an almost imperceptible shake of her head, so with a smile and a wave of his hand he let himself out.

Night after night pretty much the same group sat in the circular booth down front at the Ship's Cabin. Sometimes there were as many as six, most nights only three or four. They called themselves the Knights of the Round Table and were inclined to be noisy and boisterous. Although Alf Cantwell, the proprietor of the tavern, was strict and prided himself on running an orderly establishment, he was likely to be lenient with them because they were regular customers, and if they did occasionally get quarrelsome they kept it within the confines of their own circle. Even then, on the two or three occasions he had had to order his barman to stop serving them and had in fact told them to leave, they had taken it in good part and had come back the following evening without rancor and a little repentant: "Guess we were a little high last night, Alf. Sorry, won't happen again."

There were four of them at the table when Stanley came in at half-past nine Monday. Buzz Applebury, a tall, lean man with a long nose, hailed him as he entered. He was a painter-contractor who had his own shop, and Stanley had worked for him on occasion.

"Hi, Stan'l," he called, "come on over and have a drink."

"Well . . ." Stanley temporized. They were a cut above him socially. In addition to Applebury, there was Harry Cleeves who had an appliance repair shop, Don Winters who operated a small grocery store, and Malcolm Larch who had a real estate and insurance office. These men were all merchants, whereas he was a laborer.

"Sure, come on and sit down, Stan'l," Larch urged and moved over on the circular bench to make room for him. "What'll you have to drink?"

They were drinking whiskey, but his customary drink was ale and he did not want them to think he was taking advantage of their hospitality.

"I'll have ale," he said.

"Attaboy, Stan'l, you keep sober because maybe we'll need you to take us home."

"Beauty," said Stanley in appreciation.

Harry Cleeves, a blond giant with a round baby face, had been staring moodily at his glass all this time and had paid no attention to Stanley. Now he turned around and addressed him with an air of great seriousness. "You still work up at the Jew church?"

"At the temple? Yeah, I still work there."

"You been there a long time now," Applebury observed.

"Couple—three years," said Stanley.

"You wear one of them dinky little hats they wear when they pray?"

"Sure, when they're having a service and I'm on duty."

Applebury turned to the others. "When they're having a service and he's on duty, he says."

"How do you know that don't make you a Jew?" asked Winters.

Stanley looked quickly from one to the other. Deciding they were joking, he laughed and said, "Jeez, Don, that don't make you no Jew."

"Of course not, Don," said Applebury, looking down his long nose reprovingly at his friend. "Everybody knows they got to cut off your whatsis to make you a Jew. They cut you off, Stan'l?"

Stanley was sure this was intended as a joke and laughed accordingly. "Beauty," he added to indicate his full appreciation of the jest.

"You want to watch out, Stan'l," Winters went on, "you might get so smart associating with them Jews you'll just naturally stop working."

"Oh, they ain't so smart," said Applebury. "I did a job of work for one of them up on the Point. They ask me for an estimate, so I give them a figure maybe a third higher than the job is worth, calculating on coming down in the dicker. But this Jew fellow just says, Go ahead but do a good job. At that, what with his wife wanting the colors just so, and Would you make this wall just a shade darker than the other, Mr. Applebury? and Could you make the woodwork perfectly flat, Mr. Applebury?—why, maybe it was worth the difference at that. She was a real nice little woman," he added reminiscently. "She wore those tight black pants—toreador pants, I guess they call them—and her little arse wiggled so when she walked I couldn't keep my mind on my work."

"I heard that Hugh Lanigan was setting up to become one," said Harry Cleeves. The others laughed, but he seemed not to notice. Suddenly he turned to Stanley. "How about that, Stan'l? You hear anything about any preparations they were making down there to swear Hugh Lanigan in?"

"Naw."

"Now Harry, I heard something about that," said Malcolm Larch. "It ain't that Hugh's planning to join them. It's just this business about the girl. I figure Hugh is working with this rabbi of theirs to make sure no evidence gets out that would show that the rabbi did it."

"How could he do that?" asked Cleeves. "If the rabbi did it, how's Hugh going to cover up for him?"

"Well, the way I heard it, he tried to pin it onto this Bronstein fellow instead, on account Bronstein wasn't a member of their outfit. But then it turns out that he's connected with one of their high officers so they had to let him go. Those in the know figure they'll try to pin it on some outsider next. Hugh been bothering you any, Stan'l?" He turned to him innocently.

Stanley knew they were pulling his leg now, but instead of finding it amusing he felt uneasy. He forced a grin. "No, Hugh don't pay me no mind."

"What I don't understand," said Cleeves reflectively, "is what this rabbi would want to kill that little girl for."

"Somebody was saying, but it didn't seem too likely, that it's part of the religion," explained Winters.

"I don't figure there's much in that," said Larch, "at least not around these parts. Maybe in Europe, or in some big city like New York where they're powerful and could get away with it, but not around here."

"Then what would he want with a young girl like that?" demanded Winters.

"She was pregnant, wasn't she?" Cleeves turned suddenly to Stanley. "Isn't that what he wanted her for, Stan'l?"

"Aw, you guys are nuts," said Stanley.

They laughed, but Stanley did not feel the atmosphere lighten. He felt uncomfortable.

Larch said, "Hey Harry, didn't you have to make a telephone call?"

Cleeves glanced at his wristwatch. "It's a little late, isn't it?"

"The later the better, Harry." He winked at his friends, and said, "Ain't that right, Stan'l?"

"Guess so."

This caused renewed laughter. Stanley kept a fixed grin on his face. He wanted to leave but did not know how. They all watched, not talking now, as Cleeves dialed a number and then talked on the phone. A few minutes later he came out and made an O with his thumb and forefinger to indicate that the call had been successful.

Stanley got up so that Cleeves could regain his seat. Standing, he realized that this was the time to break away. "Got to go now," he said.

"Aw, c'mon, Stan'l, have another."

"The night's young, Stan'l."

"Shank of the evening—"

Applebury grabbed his arm, but Stanley shook him off and made for the door.

24

Carl Macomber, chairman of the Board of Selectmen of Barnard's Crossing, was by nature a worrier. A tall, spare man with gray hair, he had been in town politics for forty years, and on the Board of Selectmen for almost half that time. The two hundred and fifty dollars per year that he received, fifty dollars more than the other members, for being chairman was certainly inadequate compensation for the three or more hours a week he spent in attending Board meetings all through the year, the dozens of hours he spent on town business, and the hectic weeks of campaigning every other year if he wanted to be re-elected.

There was no doubt that his business—he operated a small haberdashery—had suffered from his devotion to politics. Every election he and his wife had extensive debates about whether he should run again, and convincing her, he often said, was the biggest hurdle of the campaign.

"But, Martha, I've simply got to remain on the Board now that the question of taking over the Dollop Estate by eminent domain is coming up. There just isn't anyone else who knows the ins and outs of that business except me. If Johnny Wright would run, I could stay out. But he's going to Florida for the winter. He was the only one besides me who was in on the negotiations with the heirs back in '52. And if I should drop out now, I'd hate to think how much it would cost the town."

Before that it had been the new school, and before that the new sanitation and health department, and before that the wage survey of town employees, and before that something else. Sometimes he wondered about it himself. The unbending Yankee in him would not permit him to admit to himself anything so sentimental as love for the town. Instead, he told himself that he liked to be in the middle of things and know what was going on, and that it was his duty since he could do the job better than any of the other candidates.

Running the town wasn't just a matter of dealing with questions as they came up, he always said; by that time it was too late. Rather, it involved sensing a crisis in the making and forestalling it. Such was the situation right now with respect to Rabbi Small and the Temple Murder, as the newspapers had labeled the case. It wasn't anything he cared to discuss at the regular meeting of the Board. Even the five members were too many when all he needed was a majority of three to railroad anything they decided through an official meeting with a minimum of discussion.

He had called Heber Nute and George Collins, the two older members of the Board, and next to himself the oldest in length of service. They were sitting now in his living room sipping at the iced tea and munching at the gingerbread cookies that Martha Macomber had brought in on a tray. They discussed the weather, the state of business, and the national political situation. Now Carl Macomber spoke up.

"I called you together about this business of the temple down in the Chilton area. It's got me worried. I was in the Ship's Cabin the other night and heard some talk down there that I didn't like. I was sitting in one of the booths, so I wasn't seen, but there were the usual loafers that you find around there, nursing a beer and talking to hear themselves, mostly. They were saying that this rabbi must have done it, and that nothing was being done because the police were being paid off by the Jews; that Hugh Lanigan and the rabbi were great friends and were always at each other's houses."

"Was it Buzz Applebury who was doing most of the talking?" asked George Collins, an expansive, smiling man. "I had him out to the house a couple days ago to give me a figure on painting the trim and he was talking that way. Of course, I laughed at him and called him a damn fool."

"It was Buzz Applebury," admitted Macomber, "but there were three or four others there and they seemed to be in pretty general agreement."

"Is that what's troubling you, Carl?" asked Heber Nute. He was a fidgety, irascible man who always appeared to be angry about something. The skin on his bald head seemed stretched tight and a large vein quivered with his annoyance. "Goddam, you can't pay any attention to that kind of character." He sounded indignant that he should have been called to discuss so unimportant a matter.

"You're wrong, Heber, this wasn't just one crank like Applebury.

The others seemed to think it was reasonable. This kind of talk has been going around, and it can be dangerous."

"I don't see that you can do very much about it, Carl," observed Collins judiciously, "short of just telling him he's a damn fool the way I did."

"Doesn't seem to have done any good," observed Nute sourly. "Something else is bothering you, Carl. You're not one to get worked up by the likes of Applebury. What is it?"

"It's not just Applebury. I've had remarks passed by other people, customers in my store. I don't like it. I've heard it all along, ever since the case broke. It quieted down a little when they picked up Bronstein, but it's got worse ever since he's been released. The general tone is that if it isn't Bronstein, then it has to be the rabbi, and that the case against him is not being prosecuted because he and Hugh Lanigan are friends."

"Hugh is all cop," asserted Nute. "He'd arrest his own son if he were guilty."

"Wasn't it the rabbi who got Bronstein off?" asked Collins.

"That's right, but people don't know that."

"Well, as soon as they find the real killer, it'll all quiet down," said Collins.

"How do you know it won't be the rabbi?" demanded Nute.

"For that matter, how do we know they'll find the killer?" asked Macomber. "An awful lot of cases of this type don't ever get solved. And in the meantime, a lot of damage can be done."

"What kind of damage?" asked Collins.

"A lot of nastiness can be stirred up. Jews tend to be sensitive and edgy, and this is their rabbi."

"That's just too damn bad," said Nute, "but I don't see that we have to use kid gloves just because they're sensitive."

"There are over three hundred Jewish families in Barnard's Crossing," said Macomber. "Since most of them live in the Chilton area, you can figure present market value on their houses at around twenty thousand dollars apiece. Many didn't pay that, but that's what they're worth in today's market on average. Our assessments run fifty percent of market evaluation. That's three hundred times ten thousand, which is three million dollars. Taxes on three million dollars is a lot of taxes."

"Well, if the Jews should move out, then Christians would move in," said Nute. "That wouldn't bother me."

"You don't cotton to Jews, do you, Heber?" asked Macomber.

"No, I can't say that I do."

"How about Catholics and colored people?"

"Can't say as I'm overpartial to them either."

"How about Yankees?" asked Collins with a grin.

"He don't care for them either," said Macomber, also grinning. "That's because he's one himself. We Yankees don't like anybody, including each other, but we tolerate everybody."

Even Heber chuckled.

"Well," Macomber went on, "that's why I asked you to come tonight. I was thinking about Barnard's Crossing and what a change there's been in the last fifteen or twenty years. Our schools today are as good as any in the state. We've got a library that's supposed to be one of the best in towns of this size. We've built a new hospital. We've built miles of sewers and paved miles of streets. It's not only a bigger town than it was fifteen years ago—it's a better town. And it was these Chilton people that did it—Jews *and* Christians. Don't kid yourself. These people in the Chilton area, the Christians I'm talking about now, they're not like us here in Old Town. They're a lot more like their Jewish neighbors. They're young executives and scientists and engineers and professional people generally. They're all college graduates and their wives are college people, and they expect their kids to go to college. And you know what brought them—"

"What brought them," said Nute flatly, "is being half an hour from Boston and near the ocean for the summer."

"There are other towns that are on the ocean, and none of them have done half the things we've done and every one has a higher tax rate," said Macomber quietly. "No, it's something else, maybe the spirit that Jean Pierre Bérnard, that old reprobate, brought with him and left for us. When they were hunting witches in Salem, several of them came here and we hid them out. We've never had a witch-hunt here and I don't want one now."

"Something has happened," said Collins, "something definite that's bothering you, and I don't think it's Buzz Applebury shooting off his mouth, or remarks by your customers either. I never knew you to take any sass from customers. Now what is it, Carl?"

Macomber nodded. "There've been telephone calls, crank calls, sometimes late at night. Becker who has the Lincoln-Ford agency was in to see me about making a bid on the new police cruising car. That's what he said he came for, but during the conversation he managed to mention that the president of their temple, Wasserman, and Abe Casson—you know him—they've been getting calls. I spoke to Hugh about it and he said he hadn't heard, but he wouldn't be a bit surprised if the rabbi wasn't getting a lot of them too."

"There's nothing we can do about that, Carl," said Nute.

"I'm not so sure. If we could give everybody in town the idea that we, the Selectmen, were dead set against this kind of thing, it might help. And since most of it seems to be centered on the rabbi—although if you ask me he's just a handy excuse so Buzz Applebury can make himself a big shot—I was thinking we might use this nonsense the Chamber of Commerce instituted two or three years back, the business of blessing the fleet at the beginning of Race Week, to show we don't approve of what's going on. Now Monsignor O'Brien did it one year and Dr. Skinner did it one year—"

"Pastor Mueller did it last year," said Collins.

"All right, that's two Protestants and one Catholic. Suppose we announce that Rabbi Small is going to do it this year."

"Dammit, Carl, you can't do that. The Jews don't even have a boat club. The Argonauts have a lot of Catholic members and that's why they asked Monsignor O'Brien. As for the Northern and the Atlantic, they don't have any Catholic members, much less Jews. They wouldn't stand for it. They even kicked about having the monsignor."

"The town does a lot for the yacht clubs," said Macomber, "and if they were told that the Selectmen were unanimous about this, they'd damn well have to stand for it."

"But dammit," said Nute, "you can't ask the yacht clubs to let a Jew rabbi bless their boats, no more than you could ask them to let him christen one of their kids."

"Why not? Who blessed them before the Chamber of Commerce dreamed this up?"

"Nobody."

"Then the boats don't require any blessing. And I haven't noticed that they've been making any faster time since we started blessing them. So the worst anyone could say was that the rabbi's blessing wouldn't do any good. I don't think it would either, not any more than the pastor's or the monsignor's. But I don't suppose anyone would argue that it would hurt."

"All right, all right," said Nute. "What do you want us to do?"

"Not a damn thing, Heber. I'll go see the rabbi and extend the invitation. Just back me up if we run into trouble with the rest of the Board."

Joe Serafino stood at the entrance to the dining room and checked the house. "Good business, Lennie," he remarked.

"Yeah, it's a nice crowd." Then without moving his lips, the headwaiter added, "Note the fuzz—third table from the window."

"How do you know?"

"I can smell a cop, I know that one anyway. He's a state detective."

"Did he speak to you?"

Leonard shrugged his shoulders. "They've been around, you know, ever since that business with the girl. But this is the first time one of them came in and ordered a drink."

"Who's the woman with him?"

"Must be his wife."

"So maybe he wants a little relaxation." Suddenly he stiffened. "What's the kid doing here, that Stella?"

"Oh, I meant to tell you. She wanted to see you. I told her I'd let her know when you came in."

"What's she want?"

"I suppose she wants to talk to you about a regular job. I can give her the brush-off, if you like. Tell her you're too busy to see her tonight and that you'll call her."

"Why don't you do that. No, hold it. I'll talk to her."

He left the doorway and began to meander among the tables, stopping every now and then to greet an old customer. Unhurriedly, without looking in her direction, he maneuvered to the table where she was sitting. He said, "What's the score, kid? You come to ask me about a job, you don't sit at a table."

"Mr. Leonard said I should. He said it would look better than waiting in the foyer."

"All right, what do you want?"

"I've got to speak to you—in private."

He thought he detected a threatening note in her voice, so he said, "All right. Where's your coat?"

"In the checkroom."

"Get your coat. Do you know where my car is?"

"In the same place you always keep it?"

"Yeah. You go there and wait for me. I'll follow along."

He continued his rounds of the tables until he reached the kitchen door. He drifted on through and a minute later was hurrying through the parking lot.

Easing in behind the wheel, he said, "All right, what's on your mind? I haven't got much time."

"The police came to see me this morning, Mr. Serafino."

"What you tell them?" he said quickly. Then he realized his mistake and, almost casually, asked what they wanted.

"I don't know. I wasn't home. The woman I live with, they spoke to her. They left a name and a phone number I was supposed to call, but I told her if they should call back, to say I hadn't been home all day. I wanted to talk to you first. I'm scared."

"What are you scared about? You don't know what they want you for."

In the darkness he could see her nodding her head. "I got an idea, because they asked her if she knew what time I got home, you know, that night."

He shrugged his shoulders in an elaborate gesture of unconcern. "You were working here that night, so they got to question you. They questioned everybody in the place. Just routine. If they come back again, tell them the truth. You were afraid to go home alone that late at night, it being your first time here, so I drove you home and left you off about a quarter-past one."

"Oh, no, it was earlier, Mr. Serafino."

"Yeah? One o'clock?"

"I looked at the clock when I came in, Mr. Serafino. It was only half-past twelve."

Now he was angry—angry and a little frightened. "You trying to pull something, sister? You trying to put me in the middle of a murder rap?"

"I'm not trying to do anything, Mr. Serafino," she said stubbornly. "I know it was half-past twelve when you dropped me off at my house, a little earlier even, because it was half-past when I got in. I'm not very good at lying, Mr. Serafino, so I thought maybe if I were to go to New York—I got a married sister there—and try to get a job, like in a show, if this was just a routine checkup like you say, they might not bother with me if I wasn't around."

"Well, you got a point there."

"I'd need a little expense money, Mr. Serafino. There'd be my fare, and even if I could live with my sister—and I think maybe it would be better if I didn't, at least at first—I'd still have to pay her board and room rent."

"What'd you have in mind?"

"If I got a job right away, it wouldn't have to be so much, but I ought to have maybe five hundred dollars to be safe."

"A shakedown, eh?" He leaned toward her. "Listen here. You know I had nothing to do with that girl."

"I don't know what to think, Mr. Serafino."

"Yes, you do." He waited for her to speak, but she remained silent. He changed his tone. "This business of going to New York—that's no good. If you were to disappear, the cops would get suspicious right away. And they'd find you, believe me. And five hundred bucks—forget about it. I don't have that kind of money." He drew out his wallet and took out five ten-dollar bills. "I don't mind giving you a stake. And if you need it, you can count on a ten-spot now and then—but nothing big, you understand. And if you behave yourself, I can maybe work you in on a regular job at my club. But that's all. And when the cops ask you what time you got in that night, you'll say you don't remember, but it was late, probably after one. Don't worry about not being a good liar. The cops will expect you to be flustered."

She was shaking her head.

"What's the matter?"

In the dim glow from the club's electric sign he saw a smug little smile on her face.

"If you didn't have anything to do with it, Mr. Serafino, I don't figure you'd give me anything. And if you did, then what you're offering is not enough."

"Look, I had nothing to do with that girl. Get that through your head. Why am I doing this? I'll tell you. Any guy who operates a night club, he's fair game for the police. They can raise hell with him, see? If they start bearing down on me, my business goes to pot. That Bronstein guy that they picked up and then let go, he sells cars. So if he finds it hurt his business, he drops his prices or gives better trade-ins for a little while, and that's all. But if the same thing happened to me, I'd have to close up for good. And I'm a married man with a couple of kids. So it's worth a few bucks to me to avoid trouble. But that's all."

She shook her head.

He sat very still, his fingers drumming lightly on the steering wheel. Then he turned away from her, as if talking to someone else. "In this business, you run up against all kinds of characters. You need, like a kind of insurance, if you're to have any peace of mind. A character starts pushing you, so you try to make a deal. If you can't you get in touch with your—uh—insurance agent. You'd be surprised what kind of service you can get for five hundred bucks. Now where the job's a nice-looking girl like you, there are agents would give me a special rate—maybe not even charge me at all. Some of those guys like to play, especially it's a nice-looking young girl. They do it for kicks." He glanced at her from the corner of his eye and knew he was getting through to her. "Like I said, I want to be friendly. I don't mind helping a friend out now and then. A friend needs a job bad, I can usually arrange it. A friend needs a few bucks, say for a new outfit, I can be touched."

He held out the money again.

This time she took it.

25

Macomber had phoned ahead to make sure the rabbi would be in when he arrived.

"Macomber? Do we know a Macomber?" the rabbi asked when Miriam told him about the call.

"He said it was something about town business."

"Do you suppose it's the Selectman? Macomber is the name of the chairman, I believe."

"Why don't you ask him when he gets here?" she said shortly. And then added, as if she realized she had been abrupt, "He said seven o'clock."

The rabbi looked at his wife questioningly but said nothing. She had been moody for several days now, but he did not like to question her.

The rabbi recognized Macomber immediately and started to lead him into his study, assuming he had come on some matter concerning the temple or the Jewish community. But he seemed content to remain in the living room.

"I won't be but a minute, rabbi. I stopped by to ask if you would care to take part in the opening ceremonies of Boat Race Week."

"What sort of part?" asked the rabbi.

"Well, in the last few years we've made quite a thing of it. We get boats from all over, you know, from all the yacht clubs along the North Shore, and quite a few from the South Shore and even further. Before the first race, we have a ceremony on the judge's dock—a band concert, flag-raising and finally the blessing of the fleet. Last couple of years we've had Protestant ministers and before that we've had a Catholic priest. So this year, we thought it would be only fair to have a rabbi, now that we have one in town."

"I'm not sure just what it is that you want me to bless," said the rabbi. "These are pleasure craft of one sort or another that are coming down here to race. Is there any danger involved?"

"Not really. Of course, you can always get hit by a spar when coming about and get thrown into the water, but that doesn't happen very often."

The rabbi was puzzled and uncertain. "Then you want me to pray for victory?"

"Well, naturally we'd like our folks to win, but we're not competing as a town, if that's what you mean."

"Then I'm not quite sure that I understand. You mean that you just want the boats themselves blessed?"

"That's the idea, rabbi. Your job would be to bless the boats, not only ours, but all those that are in the harbor at the time."

"I don't know," said the rabbi doubtfully. "I haven't had much experience in that sort of thing. You see, our prayers are rarely petitionary. We don't so much ask for things that we don't have as give thanks for what we have received."

"I don't understand."

The rabbi smiled. "It's something like this. You Christians say, 'Our Father who art in Heaven, give us this day our daily bread.' Our comparable prayer is, 'Blessed art Thou, O Lord, who bringest forth bread from the earth.' That's rather oversimplified, but in general our prayers tend to be prayers of thanksgiving for what has been given to us. Of course, I could offer thanks for the boats which provide us with the pleasures of sailing. It's a little farfetched; I'd have to think about it. I'm not really in the blessing business, you know."

Macomber laughed. "That's a curious way of putting it. I don't suppose Monsignor O'Brien who did it a couple of years ago, or Dr. Skinner who took a turn at it one year, think of themselves as being in the blessing business either. But they did it."

"It's at least more appropriate to their respective professions than it is to mine."

"Aren't you all in the same profession?"

"Oh no, we stem from different traditions, all three of us. Monsignor O'Brien is a priest in the tradition of the priests of the Bible, the sons of Aaron. He has certain powers, magical powers, that he exercises in the celebration of the Mass, for example, where the bread and wine are magically changed to the body and blood of Christ. Dr. Skinner as a Protestant minister is in the tradition of the prophets. He has received a call to preach the word of God. I, a rabbi, am essentially a secular figure, having neither the *mana* of the priest nor the 'call' of the minister. If anything, I suppose we come closest to the judges of the Bible."

"Well," said Macomber slowly, "I think I see what you mean, but nobody really— What I mean to say is that we're primarily interested in the ceremony."

"Were you about to say nobody listens to the prayer anyway?"

Macomber laughed shortly. "I'm afraid, rabbi, that I was going to say just that. And now I've offended you."

"Not at all. As a rabbi I am just as aware that people do not listen to my prayers as you are that they don't listen to your most serious arguments. I am not concerned with whether those standing on the dock will be in a mood of proper devotion so much as whether the purpose of the prayer might not be frivolous."

Macomber seemed disappointed.

"Why are you so anxious to have my husband give the prayer?" asked Miriam.

Macomber glanced from one to the other and saw in her even look and in the determined set of her chin that it was futile to temporize. He decided to gamble on the truth.

"It's the bad reaction to this unfortunate business at the temple. Especially the last few days, there's been talk—not nice talk. We've never had anything of this sort and we don't like it. We had the idea it might help matters if we could announce that the Board of Selectmen had invited you to bless the fleet. I agree with you, it's pretty silly—a brainstorm the Chamber of Commerce dreamed up a few years back. Oh, it's done in some Catholic countries in the small fishing villages, but there ships are serious business and their success affects the whole economy. And there's considerable danger, too. It's even reasonable in Gloucester, where the big fleets sail from. Here it's just meaningless ceremony, but as far as you're concerned, rabbi, it will serve to underscore the fact that the Selectmen—and therefore the responsible people in town—will have no part of these shameful acts."

"That's very kind of you, Mr. Macomber," the rabbi said, "but aren't you perhaps exaggerating the situation?"

"No, believe me. You personally may not have suffered any annoyance or embarrassment, or if you have you may have shrugged it off as the work of a crackpot or two that will stop when the real culprit is caught. But this kind of case is the hardest to solve and frequently doesn't get solved at all. In the meantime, some very decent people can be hurt. I don't say that this scheme will solve the situation, but I'm sure it'll help a little."

"I appreciate what you are trying to do and the spirit that prompts it—"

"Then you agree?"

The rabbi shook his head slowly.

"Why not? Is it against your religion?"

"As a matter of fact, it is. It's specifically mentioned: Thou shalt not take the name of the Lord thy God in vain."

Macomber rose. "I guess there's nothing more to be said but I wish you'd think about it. It's not just you, you understand, it's the whole Jewish community."

When he left, Miriam exclaimed, "Oh David, these are good people."

He nodded but said nothing.

The telephone rang and he picked up the receiver. "Rabbi Small," he said, and then listened. She watched him, alarmed as she saw the color rise in his face. He put the instrument back on its rest and turned to his wife. "Is that the kind of wrong number you've been getting?" he said quietly.

She nodded.

"The same person each time?"

"Sometimes it's a man's voice and sometimes a woman's. It has never seemed like the same voice twice. Several times it has been just a string of obscenities, but most of the time they say terrible things."

"This person, quite a nice voice by the way, wanted to know if human sacrifice was required for our approaching festival—I suppose he was referring to Pesach."

"Oh no!"

"Oh yes."

"It's terrible. This lovely town has such nice people like Hugh Lanigan and Mr. Macomber, and then those people on the phone . . ."

"Crackpots," he said in contemptuous dismissal. "Just a few nasty crackpots."

"It's not only the phone calls, David."

"No? What else?"

"When I go into the stores, the clerks used to be so warm. Now they're polite. And the other customers, those I know, they try to avoid me."

"You're sure you're not imagining it?" But he sounded less certain of himself.

"Quite sure, David. Isn't there something you can do?"

"Such as what?"

"I don't know. You're the rabbi; you're supposed to know. Maybe you ought to tell Hugh Lanigan what's been happening. Maybe you ought to consult a lawyer. Maybe you ought to consider Macomber's offer."

He made no answer but returned to the living room. She looked in to find him sitting in his armchair, his eyes staring fixedly at the wall opposite. When she offered to make him some tea, he shook his head with annoyance. Later she ventured to look in again, and he was still in his chair, his eyes staring straight ahead.

"Will you unzip me, please?" she asked.

Without rising and quite automatically, he pulled at the zipper on the back of her dress. He seemed to come to, for he asked, "Why are you taking off your dress?"

"Because I'm exhausted and I want to go to bed."

He laughed. "Why, of course. How stupid of me. You can't very well go to bed with your dress on. If you don't mind, I'll stay up a little while longer."

Just then they heard a car drive up and stop at the door. "Someone is coming," he said. "Who could it be at this hour?"

They waited, and after a while the doorbell rang. Miriam, who had quickly zipped herself up, went to answer, but even as she approached there was the sound of a roaring motor and wheels spinning against gravel. She opened the door and looked out. She saw the taillight of a car speeding down the street in the darkness.

Behind her, she heard her husband exclaim, "Oh my God!" She turned and then saw it too: a swastika on the door, the red paint still fresh and dripping like blood.

He put out a tentative forefinger and stared dumbly at the red spot on his finger. All at once Miriam burst into tears.

"I'm sorry, David," she sobbed.

He held her close until he felt she had regained her composure. Then, his voice harsh, he said: "Get me some of that household cleaning stuff and a rag."

She pressed her face against his shoulder. "I'm afraid, David, I'm afraid."

26

Although the rabbi's picture had been in the papers as one of those connected with the case, Mrs. Serafino did not recognize him when he rang her bell.

"I am Rabbi Small," he said. "I should like to talk to you for a few minutes."

She was not sure she ought to, and would have liked to ask her husband, but he was still asleep.

"Is it about the case? Because if it is, I don't think I should."

"I came to see her room." There was something so positive and assured in his tone that to refuse seemed almost impertinent.

She hesitated and then said, "I guess it will be all right. It's back here beyond the kitchen," and she led the way.

The telephone rang on their way into the kitchen and she raced over to pick it up at the first ring. She talked for a moment and then hung up. "Excuse me," she said to the rabbi. "We have an extension beside our bed, and I didn't want to wake Joe."

"I understand."

She opened a door from the kitchen and stood aside so he could enter. He looked around the room—at the bed, at the night table beside it, at the bureau, at the small armchair. He went to the night table and read the titles of the few books on its shelf; he glanced at the small plastic radio on top of the table. He studied it for a moment and then turned the knob and waited until he heard a voice announce, "This is Station WSAM, Salem's own station, bringing you music—"

"I don't think you're supposed to touch anything," she said.

He turned it off and smiled apologetically. "She play it much?"

"All the time—this crazy rock and roll music."

The door of the closet stood open. He asked her permission and then looked inside. Mrs. Serafino herself opened the door to the bathroom.

"Thank you," he said. "I've seen enough."

She led the way back to the living room. "Did you find anything special?"

"I didn't expect to. I just wanted to get some idea about the girl. Tell me, was she pretty?"

"She was no beauty, for all the newspapers kept calling her 'an attractive blonde.' I guess they call any girl that. She was sort of attractive in a corn-fed farm-girl sort of way, you know, thick waist, thick legs and ankles—oh, I'm sorry."

"It's all right, Mrs. Serafino," he reassured her, "I know about ankles and legs. Tell me, did she seem happy?"

"I guess so."

"And yet I understood she had no friends."

"Well, she and this Celia who works for the Hoskins a couple of houses down sometimes went to a movie together."

"Any men friends, or wouldn't you have known?"

"I think she would have told me if she had a date. You know how it is, two women in a house together, they talk. But I'm sure there were no men friends. When she went to a movie Thursday nights, she'd either go alone or with Celia. Yet in the papers it said she was pregnant, so I guess she must have known at least one man."

"That Thursday, was there anything unusual about her behavior?"

"No, it was about like any other Thursday. I was busy, so she took care of the children's lunch, but she left right after. Usually she would go out before."

"But it was not unusual for her to leave when she did?"

"I wouldn't say so."

"Well thank you, Mrs. Serafino, you have been very kind."

She went to the door with him and watched him walk down the path. Then she called after him, "Rabbi Small—there's Celia now if you want to talk to her, the girl with the two children." She watched him hasten down the street and accost the girl.

Rabbi Small spoke to Celia for a few minutes and then walked to the corner of the street and glanced at the mailbox. He got into his car and drove to Salem, where he spent some time before driving back home.

Mr. Serafino got up shortly after noon. He washed, rubbed his hand against his blue-black beard stubble and decided not to shave until evening, and went down to the kitchen. Outside in the backyard he saw his wife playing with the children and he waved. She came in to serve him his breakfast and he sat at the kitchen table reading the comics in the morning newspaper while she puttered at the stove.

Not until he finished breakfast did a word pass between them. Then she said, "I'll bet you'll never guess who was here this morning."

He made no reply.

"It was that Rabbi Small from the Jewish temple," she went on. "You know, the one whose car they found the bag in."

"What'd he want?"

"He wanted to ask me about the girl."

"He's got a nerve. You didn't say anything?"

"I talked to him. Why not?"

He looked at her in astonishment. "Because he's a party to the case and what you know is evidence, that's why not."

"But he seemed like such a nice sort of young man, not like what you'd expect a rabbi to be. I mean, he didn't have a beard or anything."

"None of them do these days. Don't you remember the Gold's wedding we went to last year. That rabbi didn't have a beard either."

"He wasn't even like that, you know, dignified. He was just an ordinary young fellow, like he might be an insurance salesman or a car salesman, but not a fast-talker, just nice and polite. He wanted to see the girl's room."

"And you showed it to him?"

"Sure I did."

"The police told you to keep the door shut. How do you know he wasn't planning to take something or rub out a fingerprint or even leave something behind?"

"Because I was with him all the time. He only stayed a couple of seconds altogether."

"Well, I'll tell you what I'm going to do. I'm going to call the police and report it." He rose.

"But why?"

"Because this is a murder case, and what's in that room is evidence, and he's a party to the case, and he might have been tampering with the evidence. And hereafter, don't you go talking about this case to anybody, you understand?"

"All right."

"Anybody, get it?"

"All right."

"I don't want you should say one single, solitary word, you understand."

"All right, all right. What are you so excited for? You're all red in the face."

"A guy has a right to have some peace and quiet in his own house," he raged.

She smiled at him. "You're just edgy, Joe. C'mon, sit down, baby, and let me get you another cup of coffee."

He sat down and ducked behind his newspaper. She got a fresh cup and saucer and poured his coffee. She was puzzled and uncertain and worried.

27

The rabbi was not altogether surprised when Hugh Lanigan dropped in that evening.

"I understand you went calling on the Serafinos this morning," he said.

The young man reddened and nodded.

"You were sleuthing, weren't you, rabbi?" Lanigan's lips twitched in an effort to be stern, although he obviously thought the situation amusing. "Don't do it, rabbi. You could muddy the trail, and Lord knows it's obscure enough as it is. I might also mention that it could excite suspicion. Mr. Serafino, who called to tell us about it, thought you might have come there to remove something, presumably something incriminating, from the girl's room."

"I had no idea," he said contritely. "I'm sorry." He hesitated, and then went on timidly, "I had an idea I wanted to check."

Lanigan shot him a quick glance. "Yes?"

The rabbi nodded and went on hurriedly, "In any sequence of events there's a beginning and a middle and an end. The last time we discussed this case, I'm afraid we started at the end, with the handbag. I suggest you would get further if you started at the beginning."

"And what do you call the beginning? The girl's getting pregnant?"

"That could be the beginning, but we have no real certainty that was connected with the girl's death."

"Then where would you start?"

"If I were conducting the investigation," said the rabbi, "I would first want to know why she left the house after Bronstein brought her home."

Lanigan considered the suggestion and then shrugged his shoulders.

"She could have left for any number of reasons, to mail a letter perhaps."

"Then why take off her dress?"

"It was raining at the time," Lanigan observed. "Maybe she didn't want to get the dress wet."

"Then she would simply have slipped on a coat or raincoat—as she did. Besides, mail is not collected until nine-thirty the next morning. I looked at the box."

"All right, then she didn't go out to mail a letter. Maybe she just wanted to take a short walk, to get some air."

"In the rain? After she had been out all afternoon and evening? Besides, the same objection holds—why would she take off her dress? That's really the basic question: why did she take off her dress?"

"All right, why did she?"

"Why, to go to bed," announced the rabbi.

Lanigan stared at the triumphant look on his face. Finally he said, "I don't get it. What are you driving at?"

The rabbi could not help showing some impatience. "The girl comes home from a night out. It's late and she has to get up early the next morning. So she starts to prepare for bed. She takes off her dress and hangs it up carefully in the closet. Normally she would have gone on to take off the rest of the things, but something interrupted her in the process. I suggest it could only have been a message of some sort."

"You mean she got a telephone call?"

Rabbi Small shook his head. "She couldn't have because there is an extension upstairs and Mrs. Serafino would have heard the phone ring."

"Then how?"

"The radio. According to Mrs. Serafino she had it on all the time. With girls of that age, turning on the radio is a conditioned reflex. As automatic as breathing. I suggest she turned it on as soon as she came in."

"All right, so she turned on the radio. What sort of message could she have received?"

"There's a news round-up from WSAM, the Salem station, at 12:35. The last few minutes are devoted to local news."

"And you think she heard a bit of local news that sent her scurrying out into the rain? Why?"

"Because she had to meet someone."

"At that hour? How could she know where to meet this someone. I know that program—it doesn't run personals. And if she was meeting someone, why didn't she put on a dress first? Really, rabbi—"

"She didn't have time to put on a dress because she had to get there by one o'clock," said the rabbi quietly. "And she knew he would be there because that was the time he was supposed to ring in at the police box."

Lanigan stared at him. "You mean—Bill Norman?"

The rabbi nodded.

"But that's impossible. He just became engaged to Bud Ramsay's girl. I went to the engagement party. It was that very night. I was one of the guests of honor."

"Yes, I know. That was the announcement over the radio. I called the station today and checked. Think about it for a minute, and keep in mind the fact that the girl was pregnant. According to all those who knew her, the only time she was ever in the company of men—socially, that is—was her one excursion to Old Town, the Policemen's Ball. I suggest she met Norman there."

"You're not suggesting the keel for her little ship was laid at the Policemen's Ball?"

"Hardly. That was back in February. But that's where she first made Norman's acquaintance. I'm not sure just how it was renewed, but I can imagine. Like most laymen, I know that the patrolman on his beat is required to call in at regular intervals. I had always assumed that like a night watchman in a factory, the time between calls depended on the length of time it took him to walk from one box to the next."

"Well, not exactly," Lanigan began. "He's given a certain leeway."

"So I discovered some weeks ago when I was called on to settle a dispute between two members of our congregation. One of them had to get into a house late at night without a key, and the cab driver rounded up the patrolman on duty who made it a practice to stop off nearby for an unofficial coffee break."

"It's an eight-hour tour of duty. You can't expect a man to be on his feet all that time without a rest," said Lanigan defensively. "And in the winter a man has to warm up every now and then."

"Of course," the rabbi agreed, "and thinking it over, I realized that it was only common sense to allow him considerable leeway, if only because of the investigating he might have to do along the way. I spoke to Officer Johnson, who patrols this same beat during the day, and he explained that the night patrolman usually makes his own arrangements. On this route, for example, he stops with the night watchman for a while at the Gordon block. Then there is the milk plant, and when Stanley was staying overnight at the temple that was another stop. Now here is the Serafino house, and except for the children who are asleep upstairs Elspeth is all alone until two o'clock or later every morning. Along comes a dashing young policeman, a bachelor moreover, who has to ring in a box on the corner of Maple and Vine streets at one o'clock and whose beat then takes him down Vine Street right near the Serafino house. So on cold, bitter nights, what better arrangement than to drop in on the girl for a hot cup of coffee and a pleasant chat for half an hour before going out into the night again."

"But how about Thursdays? Wouldn't she expect him to take her out on her night off?"

"Why should he? She was seeing him every other night in the week. And he was on night duty, so he needed his sleep during the day. I imagine she loved him and presumed that he loved her. She probably expected to marry him. There is nothing to indicate she was a loose girl. On the contrary, that's probably why she did not go out with other men and refused to double-date with Celia. She considered herself engaged."

"It's ingenious," admitted Lanigan, "but it's all conjectural."

"Granted, but it all adds up. And it enables us to reconstruct the events of that fatal Thursday in the only way that makes sense. She suspects she's pregnant, so she goes to an obstetrician on her day off. She gets dressed up nicely, not forgetting to wear a wedding ring. Was it her mother's, or did she buy it in the fond hope that she would be wearing it legitimately shortly? At the doctor's office, she gives her name as Mrs. Elizabeth Brown, not because of Bronstein whom she hadn't met as yet but because it is a common name like Smith and because it is natural to retain the same initials. She is examined and the doctor tells her she is pregnant.

"Now Bronstein said that when he first saw her in the restaurant, she kept glancing at the clock as if she were waiting for someone. I imagine you have since verified with the waitresses that she didn't order when she first came into the restaurant. My guess is that since they normally didn't see each other on Thursdays, she had phoned her lover and made a special appointment with him."

"The doctor's secretary said she asked if there was a pay station in the building," Lanigan remarked.

The rabbi nodded. "Norman must have agreed, or at least said he would try to make it, so she went to the Surfside to wait."

"Yet she went out with Bronstein."

"She probably felt hurt when he didn't show up—hurt and perhaps apprehensive. Bronstein said that he went over only when he decided she had been, er—stood up, and then all he did was ask her to join him because he did not like to eat alone. He was a much older man and she probably saw no danger in it. After all, she was in a restaurant, a public place. During the course of the meal, she evidently concluded that he was a decent sort, so she consented to spend the evening with him.

She probably wanted company badly—she must have been feeling pretty blue at the time. He brought her home and she got ready for bed. She had taken off her dress when she heard the announcement of Norman's engagement."

"So knowing that Norman was due to ring in at Maple and Vine at one o'clock and it was then, say, five of, she had to dash. She threw on her coat and because it was raining and she had several blocks to go, her raincoat over that, and went to meet him. Is that it, rabbi?"

"I would say so."

"And then what do you think happened?"

"Well, it was raining, and quite hard. He had seen my car parked outside the temple and I suppose he suggested they get in and talk it over. They got in the back seat and he offered her a cigarette. They talked for a while. Perhaps they quarreled. Perhaps she threatened to go to his fiancée. So he seized the chain she was wearing and twisted. He could not leave the body in the car, of course, since I suppose he was expected to give at least a cursory inspection to any vehicle parked outside all night. If the body had been found in the car, he'd have had some explaining to do. So he carried it out to the grass plot and hid it behind the wall. The handbag had slid to the floor and he just didn't notice it."

"Of course you realize, rabbi, that we don't have an iota of proof for any of this."

The rabbi nodded.

"But it certainly does all hang together," Lanigan went on reflectively. "If she had gone to the Ramsays with her story, that would have ended his engagement to Alice. I know the Ramsays. Decent people—but proud. I also thought I knew him." He raised an inquisitive eyebrow at the rabbi. "You had this all figured out and then went to the Serafinos to check your theory?"

"Not really. I had a vague notion, but it was not until I had seen the radio in the girl's room that the explanation began to form. Of course, I had an advantage over you because I had reason to be suspicious of Officer Norman from the beginning."

"What do you mean?"

"He denied that he saw me, but I knew that he had. What reason could he have? Since he did not know me, it could not be a personal dislike. If he had admitted seeing me, it would not have helped his position in any way—only mine. It would have established the fact that I had already left the temple well before the murder had been committed. But if he were guilty or in some way involved, wouldn't it be to his advantage to have suspicion point at someone else?"

"Why didn't you tell me this before, rabbi?"

"Because it was only a suspicion, and besides, it is not easy for a rabbi to point a finger at a man and say he is a murderer."

Lanigan was silent.

"Of course we still have no real proof," the rabbi ventured.

"I'm not worried about getting it."

"What do you propose to do?"

"Well, at the moment," said Lanigan, "I'm not sure whether to ask Norman what Elspeth Bleech said to him on the phone Thursday afternoon, or why he didn't keep his appointment with her at the Surfside Restaurant. In the meantime, I'll arrange for that girl Celia to have a look at him. She said Elspeth was with one man most of the evening at the Policemen's Ball. If your theory's right, I figure that would be Norman. And we'll question the Simpsons who live across the street from the Serafinos. If he saw her as often as you think he did, they may have noticed him going in there late at night." His lips relaxed in a tight little smile. "When we know what we're looking for, rabbi, we don't have too much trouble finding it."

28

The board meeting was unusual in that the rabbi was present. When Jacob Wasserman had come to him and asked if he would be willing to sit with the board at their regular meeting, he was pleased and grateful.

"You don't have to, you know. I mean, we won't hold it against you if you don't come to a meeting, or to any of them for that matter. I just want you to know that any time you choose to come, we'll be happy to have you."

And now he was present at his first meeting. He listened carefully to the secretary read the minutes of the previous meeting. He was most attentive during the reports of the chairmen of various committees. The principal piece of Old Business was a motion to floodlight the parking lot at night.

The original motion had been made by Al Becker and he now rose to speak. "I've done a little checking around. We've got this electrical contractor that does a lot of work for us and I had him come out and look the place over and give us a very rough figure as to the cost. According to him, we can do it in one of two ways. Either put up three towers, which would come to about twelve hundred apiece, or we could put up six special floodlights mounted on the temple itself. Mounting them would be cheaper, but it would spoil the outline of the building. We could get those for five hundred apiece, so it's three thousand against thirty-six hundred. Then we'd have to have a clock arrangement to turn the lights on and off automatically. That wouldn't cost much, but we'd have to figure in the cost of electricity. All told, the job could be done for five thousand bucks at the outside."

Becker was nettled at the groan from those around the table. "I know it's a lot of money, but this is necessary. I'm glad our rabbi is here today because no one knows better than he how important it is to have our parking lot lit up at night."

"But think what it will cost us year after year, Al. You can't put sixty-watt bulbs in those babies. In the winter, that can be about fourteen hours."

"Would you rather have the place become a lovers' lane, or maybe have another little business like the one we had?" Becker shot back.

"In the summer, those lights will attract a zillion mosquitoes."

"So—they'll be up around near the light, won't they? If anything, it will keep the grounds free of them."

"That's not the way it works up at the driving range. When they have those lights on, the mosquitoes are all over the place."

"And how do you think the people that live nearby are going to like having a place the size of the parking lot lit up all night?"

The rabbi murmured something.

"What is it, rabbi?" Mr. Wasserman asked. "Did you want to say something on this matter?"

"I was just thinking," said the rabbi diffidently, "there's only one car entrance to the parking lot. Why can't you just put up a gate?"

There was sudden silence. Then they all started to explain it to each other.

"Sure, it's asphalt so nobody would come there except in a car."

"There are bushes and shrubs all around the front. All we'd have to block off is the driveway."

"Stanley could close it every night and open it first thing in the morning."

"Even if Stanley weren't around some night and a committee wanted to hold a meeting, so they could park their cars in the street."

As suddenly as they had begun, they stopped and looked at their young rabbi with respect and admiration.

The rabbi was at home, a large volume on the desk in front of him, when his wife came to the door of the study. "Chief Lanigan is here, dear."

The rabbi started to rise, but Lanigan said, "Don't get up, rabbi." Then he noticed the volume on the desk. "Am I interrupting?"

"Not at all."

"Nothing special," Lanigan went on. "Ever since we solved the case I've missed our little chats. But I was in the neighborhood, so out of habit I thought I'd drop in and say hello."

The rabbi smiled his pleasure.

"I just came up against a little bit of pedantry that might amuse you,"

Lanigan said. "You know, every two weeks I have to submit the salary schedule for the department to the town comptroller for audit and approval. I list the regular hours worked by each man, overtime if any, special assignments, and then total it up for each man. You understand?"

The rabbi nodded.

"Well, I had the whole thing turned back to me"—Lanigan could not keep the exasperation from showing in his voice—"because Patrolman Norman was included for his full tour of duty. The comptroller claimed he should have been docked for all the time after he killed the girl because, as a criminal, he was no longer entitled to be on the police payroll. How do you like that? I don't know whether to fight him on it, or just drop the item and forget about it."

The rabbi pursed his lips and then glanced at the big book on his desk. He smiled. "Shall we see what the Talmud says?"

SATURDAY
THE RABBI
WENT HUNGRY

To Anne

1

*. . . On the tenth day of this seventh month is the day of atone-
ment, a holy convocation shall it be unto you, and ye shall fast . . .
and no manner of work shall ye do on this day . . . it shall be a statute
forever throughout your generations in all your dwellings. A sabbath of
rest it shall be unto you, and ye shall fast: on the ninth day of the
month at evening shall ye begin, from evening unto evening shall ye
celebrate your sabbath.*

This year the Day of Atonement coincided with the weekly Sabbath,
so that the ninth day of the month in the Hebrew calendar fell on a
Friday and the tenth on Saturday. It did not make the day any holier—
that was impossible—but it enabled most Jews to observe the holiday
without interrupting their normal work week. Late Friday afternoon
the Jewish community of Barnard's Crossing, like Jews everywhere,
was making ready for this most holy day of the year. The women were
preparing the evening meal, which traditionally was more elaborate
than usual not only to set off more sharply the twenty-four-hour fast
that followed but to give the sustenance needed to endure it. The men
had left work early to give them time to bathe, change into holiday
clothes, dine, and still get to the synagogue before sundown when the
chanting of Kol Nidre ushered in the Holy Day.

David Small, the young rabbi of the community, had finished dressing and now stood for inspection in front of the critical eye of his wife,
Miriam. He was of medium height, but although in excellent health he
was thin and pale, and behind his glasses his eyes were dark, deep-set,
and brooding. He carried his head slightly forward as though peering at
a book; his shoulders had a scholarly stoop.

His wife was tiny and vivacious with a mass of blonde hair that seemed to overbalance her. She had wide blue eyes and an open, trusting countenance that would have seemed ingenuous were it not offset by a determined little chin. There was a certain childlike quality about her that not even the protuberant belly marking her final month of pregnancy could dispel.

"Your suit, David—the jacket doesn't hang right somehow. Stand up straight and throw your shoulders back."

He made the effort.

"It's that top button. It's a good half inch off and pulls the lapel askew."

"It fell off and I sewed it on myself. You were at a Hadassah meeting."

"Well, give it to me and I'll resew it." She examined the button critically. "Why did you use blue thread when the suit is gray?"

"Actually it's white thread. I colored it with my fountain pen. Besides, my kittel will cover it during services."

"And what about on the way to the temple? And talking to the members afterward? And your shoes are dusty."

He started to rub his shoe against the calf of his trouser leg.

"David!"

"They'll only get dusty again when we walk to the temple," he said apologetically.

"Use the shoe brush."

He uttered a faint sigh of protest but went to the back hallway, and presently she heard sharp staccato whisks.

When he returned she helped him on with his jacket, adjusting the set on his shoulders like a tailor, and then buttoned it. She patted the front of the jacket. "There, that looks better."

"Am I all right now? Do I pass muster?"

"You're handsome, David."

"Then we'd better get on with it." From his wallet he extracted two one-dollar bills and gave her one and kept one for himself. Automatically he started to return the wallet to his back pocket, then thought better of it and went inside and put it away in his bureau drawer. He did not carry money on the Sabbath.

He came back with a prayer book in hand. Flipping the pages with index and second fingers, he found the place and handed her the open book. He pointed. "There's the prayer."

She read the Hebrew passage that explained that this money was for charity in partial atonement for her sins. Then she folded the bill and inserted it in the opening of the blue tin charity box that she kept on a shelf in the kitchen.

"Is a dollar enough, David?"

"It's just a token." He slipped in his own folded bill. "You know, my grandfather who lived with us a few years before he died, used for his offering a live rooster, which, I understood, was given to the poor. According to the custom, a man would use a rooster and a woman a hen. You now, in your condition, would be expected to use a hen and an egg."

"You're joking."

"No, seriously."

"And what would happen to the egg?"

"Oh, I suppose we'd eat it."

"It sounds cannibalistic."

"Now that you mention it. My folks used money, of course, usually in some multiple of eighteen. My father would accumulate coins for the purpose, dimes, as I recall, and he and my mother each would use eighteen. As a youngster I was given eighteen pennies."

"Why eighteen?"

"Because in Hebrew the two letters in the alphabet that represent the numerals eight and ten spell *chai*, which means life—a bit of cabalistic nonsense really. Come to think of it, today is the eighteenth of September, which gives it even added significance. I should have arranged to get some coins."

"I've got a bunch of pennies, David—"

"I think the poor would appreciate a dollar more than eighteen cents. We'll let it go this time and try to remember next year. But now if we don't want to be late we'd better eat."

They sat down and he pronounced the blessing. The telephone rang. The rabbi, who was nearer, picked up the instrument.

From the receiver came a loud voice. "Rabbi? Rabbi Small? This is Stanley. You know, Stanley Doble from the temple."

Stanley was the temple janitor and general maintenance man, and although he saw the rabbi almost every day he still found it necessary to identify himself as Stanley Doble from the temple—like some heraldic title—whenever he phoned. Although he had an instinctive knowledge of all things electrical and mechanical, apparently he considered the phone wire a hollow tube through which he had to shout to be heard.

"I'm sorry to bother you, Rabbi, but the public-address system is on the blink."

"What's the matter with it?"

"It don't work right. It don't work right at all. It howls."

"Maybe by tonight it will straighten itself out," suggested the rabbi, who regarded all mechanical devices as a mystery; they got out of order owing to some perversity and might right themselves if let alone. Then hopefully, "Maybe a minor adjustment?"

"I checked the wiring. I couldn't find anything. I think it's the microphone. I think maybe it's broken."

"Is there anyone you can call for service? How about the company that installed it?"

"It's a Boston outfit."

The rabbi glanced at his watch. "Then there's no sense in calling at this hour. What about someone in Lynn or Salem?"

"It's pretty late, Rabbi. Most places are closed by now."

"Well, I'll just have to talk a little louder then. Perhaps you had better call the cantor and tell him."

"Okay, Rabbi. Sorry to bother you, but I thought you'd like to know."

The rabbi returned to his soup which his wife had set before him. He just started on it when the phone rang again. It was Mrs. Robinson, president of the Sisterhood. "Oh, Rabbi, Sue Robinson." Her voice had a breathless quality as though she had sighted him at a distance and caught up with him only at the corner. "Forgive me for interrupting your pre-Holy Day meditations, but it's frightfully important. You *were* going to make an announcement on the floral decorations, weren't you?" She sounded accusing.

"Of course. Just a minute." He opened his prayer book to a sheet of paper he had inserted. "I have it right here—Floral decorations, courtesy of the Sisterhood."

"Well, there's a change. Do you have a pencil and paper handy? I'll hold on."

"All right."

"Rose Bloom—no, you had better make that Mr. and Mrs. Ira Bloom, in memory of her father David Isaac Lavin—"

"Lavin?"

"That's right, she pronounces it Lavin, L-a-v-i-n, with a long A. She insists that's nearer the original Hebrew than if she spelled it the usual way with an E. Is that right, Rabbi?"

"Yes, I suppose it is."

"Well, of course if you say so, but it still sounds affected to me. Anyway, Floral decorations, courtesy of Mr. and Mrs. Ira Bloom. You don't want to make a mistake on the names, Rabbi," she said sharply. "I would have called earlier, but she called me only half an hour ago."

"I won't forget." He read the announcement back to her from his scribbled notes.

"Splendid. Oh, and Rabbi, you might tell Miriam. She'll want to know."

"Of course. I'll tell her."

He carefully copied over the hastily penciled note, printing the names neatly so he would make no mistake when making his announcements from the pulpit. Back at the table, he took a few spoonfuls of soup and shook his head. "I don't think I care for any more," he said apologetically.

"It's probably cold by now." She removed the plate.

The phone rang again. It was a Mrs. Rosoff. "Tell me, Rabbi," she said, and tried to keep her voice calm, "I don't like to disturb you at this time, but how much does the Torah weigh? You know, the Scroll?"

"Why, I don't know, Mrs. Rosoff. The Scrolls are of different sizes, so I suppose they would vary quite a bit in weight. Is it important? I imagine most of ours would be about thirty pounds apiece, but that would be only a guess."

"Well, I think it's important, Rabbi. My husband got a notice last week that he was to have an honor for Yom Kippur. They said he would be *hagboh*. And I just found out what it means. It means, Rabbi, that he is supposed to lift the Scroll up by the handles way over his head. Is this the kind of honor you give to a man who had a heart attack not three years ago, and who to this day wouldn't think of going out into the street without his little bottle of nitroglycerine pills? Is this how you give out honors, Rabbi? You'd like to see my husband have a heart attack right there on the altar?"

He tried to explain that the honors were distributed by the Ritual Committee and that he was sure they had no knowledge of Mr. Rosoff's condition. "But it's really nothing serious, Mrs. Rosoff, because *hagboh* is one of a pair. There's *hagboh* and *glilloh*. *Hagboh* lifts the Scroll, and *glilloh* rolls it up and ties it. Your husband has only to say he would prefer the honor of rolling up the Scroll instead of lifting it, and the other man can do the lifting."

"You don't know my husband. You think he'll admit he can't lift the Scroll after you have announced he will? My big hero would rather take a chance on a heart attack."

He assured her he would take care of it, and rather than rely on his memory immediately dialed Mortimer Schwarz, president of the congregation, who announced the honors from the pulpit.

"I'm glad you called, Rabbi," he said after he had taken the message. "I wanted to phone but I hated to disturb you at this time. You heard about the public-address system?"

"Yes, Stanley told me."

"It isn't as bad as he probably said it was. When you talk right into it there's a low hum, but you can pretty much tune it out by turning down the volume. It's only when you don't talk into it directly that you get a kind of howl. So if you can remember to talk into it directly—"

"I doubt if I could, Mr. Schwarz, but on the other hand I don't think I really need it."

"I was thinking about tomorrow. The going will be a lot tougher. That's a full day's service and on an empty stomach."

"I'm sure we can manage. The hall has good natural acoustics."

"Suppose I could get hold of a mechanic to work on it right after our service tonight—"

"Oh, I'm afraid that's out of the question," said the rabbi quickly.

"Well, perhaps you're right. It would cost us an arm and a leg, and people might notice that there was a light on in the temple. You're sure you don't mind?"

He returned to the table. "Mortimer Schwarz being solicitous," he remarked. "The effect of the Yom Kippur spirit, no doubt."

He was halfway through his roast chicken when the phone rang again. Miriam started for it purposefully, but her husband waved her aside. "It's probably for me," he said. "It seems as though I've been on the phone all evening talking to people who don't want to disturb me."

He lifted the receiver: "Rabbi Small."

"Oh, Rabbi, how fortunate to find you in. This is Mrs. Drury Linscott. I am not of your faith, but both my husband and I have the highest opinion of your people. As a matter of fact, my husband's principal assistant, a man in whom he has the highest confidence, is a full-blooded Jew." She waited for him to be duly grateful.

"I see," he murmured.

"Now my husband reports that Morton—that's my husband's assistant, Morton Zoll—do you know him?"

"I—I don't think so."

"A very fine man, and really quite dependable. Well, my husband claims that Morton told him that starting at sundown tonight he is not supposed to eat or drink, not even water, until sunset tomorrow. Now I find that hard to believe, and I am sure that Mr. Linscott must have misunderstood."

"No, it's quite true, Mrs. Linscott. We fast from sunset to sunset."

"Indeed? And he must not do work of any kind during that time?"

"Quite true."

"Oh!"

The rabbi waited.

"Very well then." And she hung up.

The rabbi looked quizzically at the instrument and then gently replaced it on its cradle.

"What was that all about?" asked Miriam.

He reported the conversation.

"I'll answer the phone from now on," she said. Almost immediately it rang again.

She waved him away and picked up the receiver. She cupped her hand over the mouthpiece. "It's Cantor Zimbler," she whispered.

"I better take it."

The cantor sounded frantic. "Rabbi, have you heard about the public-address system? Stanley called me and I came right over to the temple. I'm calling from there now. I just tested it and it's terrible. I started singing my *Hineni heoni memaas* and it sounded like an old-fashioned phonograph with a dull needle. If I turned my head the least bit, it went awooh, awooh, like a fire alarm. What are we going to do, Rabbi?"

The rabbi smiled. He wondered if the cantor had put on his robes and tall white yarmulka to make the test. He was a short fat man with a little black moustache and goatee, who looked like the chef in a spaghetti advertisement. They shared the same enrobing room, and the cantor insisted on affixing a full-length mirror to the door. Only the year before last he had served in an Orthodox congregation, and in applying for his present job he sent along with his résumé one of the posters he used in advertising special concerts. There he had referred to himself as Yossele Zimbler. Since then, he had had new ones printed up in which he called himself the Reverend Joseph Zimbler.

"With a voice like yours, Cantor, I shouldn't think you'd need a public-address system."

"You think not, Rabbi?"

"No question of it. Besides, you are Orthodox in outlook, aren't you?"

"So?"

"So I shouldn't think you would want to use a public-address system at all. As I understand it, it's an electric system where the circuit is made and broken by the inflections of your voice."

"So?"

"So it's like turning the electric light on and off all through the service."

"We-el . . ." the cantor obviously was not convinced.

"That's why many of the Orthodox congregations don't use it at all during the Sabbath, and of course Yom Kippur is the Sabbath of Sabbaths."

"That's true, Rabbi," said the cantor slowly. Then, "But we used it last Yom Kippur."

"That's because we are a Conservative congregation and the Conservative synagogue permits it. But this year the Holy Day comes on the Sabbath, so this year it is the Sabbath of Sabbaths of Sabbaths," and he rotated his free hand in slow circles, Talmudic fashion, to indicate the ever-increasing sanctity of Sabbath piled on Sabbath. "You could argue that if the rule applies for the Sabbath for the Orthodox synagogue, then it should apply for us Conservatives on Yom Kippur, and on a third-degree Sabbath such as we're having this year, it ought to apply even to Reform congregations."

The cantor's chuckle told him he was won over. The rabbi returned to the table. His wife shook her head with a smile. "That was a terrible pilpul."

"You're probably right," the rabbi said wryly. "However, since pilpul is a fine, hairline distinction the rabbi has used for a couple of thousand years to prove a point his common sense has already told him is right, this serves the purpose—and in the present case I have converted into a blessing something that has to be tolerated anyway. It made him feel pious and devout instead of aggrieved." He laughed. "They're like children—so many of these cantors. Maybe that's why they always call themselves by their diminutives—Yossele, Mottele, Itzekel."

"Maybe if I call you Dovidel, I can exercise enough authority to keep you at the table until you finish your meal. Remember, there's a long fast ahead."

The telephone did not ring again and he was able to drink his coffee in peace. Miriam cleared away and washed the dishes and got dressed. "You're sure you don't mind the walk?" he asked solicitously.

"Of course not. The doctor wants me to get plenty of exercise. But let's start now to avoid any more idiot calls."

It was half-past six, and although the sun was not due to set for another hour the service started fifteen minutes earlier. It was only a twenty-minute walk to the temple, but tonight it was well to get there early. They were on their way out the door when the telephone rang.

"Let it ring, David."

"And wonder all evening who it was? Don't worry, I'll cut it short."

"Rabbi?" The voice was low and hoarse and urgent. "This is Ben Goralsky. I've got a favor to ask of you. Could you stop at my house before going to the temple? It's awfully important. It's my father. He's very sick."

"But we're just leaving to walk to temple and haven't much time. And your house is not en route."

"Rabbi, you've got to come. It's a matter of life and death. I'm sending a car for you, and I can drive you to the temple afterwards. It's all right to ride over, isn't it? It's only after services that you don't want to ride. Don't worry, you'll get there the same time you would if you walked."

"Well . . ."

"He's already started out. He'll be over your place in minutes."

2

Hugh Lanigan, chief of police of Barnard's Crossing, pulled back his chair and, plumping himself down on its leather seat, swiveled around to face his visitor. He was a stocky man with a pleasant Irish face and snow-white hair. "What can I do for you, Padre?" he said genially.

The man in the visitor's chair was young—not more than thirty-five. He was tall with broad shoulders and a deep chest. A pillar of neck supported a handsome, craggy face surmounted by blond, curly hair that was just beginning to thin out in two peaks above the forehead. In spite of the clerical collar and black silk rabat, he looked more like a football player than an Anglican minister. And indeed, Peter Dodge had been an All-American guard on the Wabash varsity and played professionally for several seasons before the call to enter the ministry.

"I am Peter Dodge, assistant to Dr. Sturgis at St. Andrew's," he said in a deep baritone.

Lanigan nodded.

"I've come to lodge a complaint against a couple of your men."

"Oh? Who are they?"

"I don't know their names—"

"Badge numbers?"

"I don't know those either, but they were the two men riding the patrol car Wednesday night."

Lanigan glanced at a chart on the wall. "That would be Loomis and Derry. They're both good men. What did they do?"

"There was a fracas of some sort at Bill's Cafe over near the Salem line—"

"I know where it is."

"Of course. Well, there was some sort of trouble and Bill, er—the proprietor—asked some of the participants to leave. They did so without argument, but I gather they hung around outside and when customers drove up urged them not to go in. They made nuisances of themselves, but I'm sure there was nothing vicious in it. It was all quite good-natured, without animosity."

"Even though they were urging customers to stay away?"

"I spoke to the proprietor and he assured me he did not take the matter seriously—"

"Oh, then you weren't there at the time."

"No, I came along some time afterward."

"In the course of your regular evening walk?"

The younger man showed his surprise. "You know that I take a walk every evening? Don't tell me I'm under police surveillance?"

The chief smiled. "This is a small town, Padre, but we've got a lot of territory to cover and not enough men to do a thorough job. Other towns are the same way. If you want to cover the area with foot patrol-men, you need a lot more men than the town is willing to pay for. And cruising cars or motorcycles miss a lot. So we use a combination of the two, and take up the slack by trying to know things before they happen. You're new here—couple of months?"

Dodge nodded.

"And I suppose you come from a big city—" he hesitated, "from the Midwest judging by your accent—"

"South Bend."

"Well, that's a pretty big city. People who live in cities usually aren't aware of their police until they actually need them. The police are a service they expect will function when they need them the same way they expect water when they turn on the tap or electricity when they flip a switch. But in small towns like this, police are still people. They're neighbors and friends and you know them the way you do any other neighbor. It's part of our job to know what's going on. We see a man walking along the street after dark, and the patrolman on the beat will make a point of speaking to him." He looked at the young min-ister quizzically. "Weren't you ever approached by a policeman?"

"Oh, shortly after I came, but he only asked if he could help me. I suppose he thought I was looking for a street number."

"And you explained that you always take a walk after dinner?"

"Oh—"

"You start out from Mrs. Oliphant's where you board, and you go up Oak Street just beyond Colonial Village, and then you swing down

Main Street over to the Salem line, and then along the waterfront and home."

"So that's how it's done?"

"That's how it's done."

"And if instead of this collar, I had been wearing—well, ordinary clothes?"

"Then he would have been just as polite, but probably he would have asked a few more questions. And maybe if you had explained you were just walking to the bus station, he might have suggested you wait for the cruising car to give you a lift."

"I see."

"Now my guess is that you came by Bill's place about half-past eight and found the boys standing around, full of indignation, and asked them—"

"One of them goes to our church. And according to him, and the others agreed, your two policemen were abusive and unnecessarily rough. There were two Negro lads in the group. Your men were especially abusive to them."

It crossed Lanigan's mind idly that his own pastor, Father O'Shaughnessy, would have referred to them as "colored boys" but doubted Dodge would understand no offense was intended. "Your complaint then is that my men were unnecessarily rough? Did they hit them? Did they use their clubs?"

"I want to make it clear, first of all, that the cruising car was not called; it just happened by."

"Yeah, we check Bill's place two or three times a night."

"Which would indicate that nothing very serious had happened there."

"All right."

"I'm mostly concerned about the particular abuse that was meted out to the Negro lads. This isn't Alabama, I hope."

"So that's it. You're connected with the Civil Rights movement, aren't you?"

"I certainly am."

"All right. Now what happened to the colored boys that upset you?"

"Well, for one thing, I protest their having been singled out. They were pushed and one of them fell. Your men were vituperative, and as public servants I don't think—"

"Maybe that's the point, Padre, I mean that they are public servants. But they think of themselves as servants of the Barnard's Crossing public rather than the public in general, and those two boys were not from our town."

"How do you know?"

"Because we have no colored families in Barnard's Crossing. And before you go jumping to conclusions, let me assure you that it isn't because we don't want them or because we have some sort of gentlemen's agreement to keep them out. It's just that real estate prices around here are high and most Negroes can't afford it."

He wondered whether it was worthwhile trying to explain to this outlander how things were in Barnard's Crossing. "You've got to understand the situation here, Padre. Ed Loomis, and I guess it must have been Ed, has no prejudice against blacks, or against any other ethnic group. We don't have much of that kind of thing in this town. The spirit of the town is live and let live, and after you've been here a while, you'll realize it. It was settled by people who left Salem because they didn't want the theocracy there telling them what they could do and couldn't do. And for a long time we had neither church nor minister here. They were a rough lot, but they were tolerant, and I'm inclined to believe that both traditions have carried down some to the present. The fact that my people, Irish Catholic, could settle here during colonial times will give you some idea of the spirit of tolerance that prevailed. Those two boys were from Salem, and I suppose there is a kind of prejudice against outsiders, and that would include anyone not born here. They call them foreigners. But I assure you that Ed Loomis meant nothing personal. If it's wrong for Barnard's Crossing police to shoo out-of-towners a little more forcefully than they would local youngsters, at least it's understandable."

"So you condone it?"

"I don't condone it, but I understand it."

"I don't think it's enough. Mr. Braddock, the chairman of the Board of Selectmen, is a member of our church and I intend to speak to him about it."

Lanigan pursed his lips. Then he glanced at the clock on the wall and leaned back in his swivel chair far enough to see down the connecting corridor to the sergeant's desk. "Will you contact the patrol car, Joe?" he called out. "See that they get right down to the temple to help with the traffic. I spoke to the rabbi, and he said they'd start arriving around half-past six and that traffic would be heaviest between a quarter of and a quarter past seven. They can leave after that and Lem'l can stay on for another half hour. Then they can circle back and pick him up."

He straightened up in his chair and smiled at his visitor. "You go right ahead and talk to Alf Braddock about Ed, Padre. He knows Ed Loomis pretty well. Ed crews for him during Race Week."

3

Colonial Village was the first real-estate development in the Chilton area of Barnard's Crossing. The usual jokes about developments did not apply to Colonial Village; no danger here of the husband returning home and blundering into the wrong house. Although all floor plans were identical, Colonial Village had three different exteriors and no two adjoining houses were built in the same style. There was no confusing the Moderne with its flush door and three small diagonal panes of glass with the Cape Cod, which had a white paneled door flanked by two long narrow windows—or either with the Renaissance, which had a massive-looking door hung on two wrought-iron hinges generously studded with hammered iron nails and a small square window set in a black iron frame. In each case the porch light and railing leading to the front door carried out the motif. And inside too, as the agent went to pains to point out, light fixtures and hardware matched perfectly. The Cape Cod had glass doorknobs and crystal chandeliers; the Renaissance, hammered copper hardware and square lanterns of pebbled stained glass set in frames of hammered iron; and the Moderne featured polished brass doorknobs and light fixtures composed of a shallow curve of polished brass.

And though the house lots were modest—five thousand square feet for the most part—they afforded privacy while offering the added advantage of a closer relationship between neighbors. Shared barbecue meals were common in Colonial Village during summer, and several times a season there were block parties on Saturday nights.

The older inhabitants of the town tended to be supercilious toward Colonial Village. They came from a background of ugly but solid and spacious Victorian houses, and referred to Colonial Village as "cracker boxes" and joked about their indoor swimming pools in sneering reference to flooded cellars after a rainstorm. This was unfair. Not all Colonial Village cellars were subject to flooding—only those at the lower end of the development.

Nor was it true that only Jews lived in the village. Almost as many non-Jews lived there. Bradford Lane, where Isaac and Patricia Hirsh lived, for example, may have been solidly Jewish at their end of the street, but the other end had a Venuti, an O'Hearne, and Stan Padefsky who was Polish.

Right now, on the eve of Yom Kippur, there was a bustle of activity in many Colonial Village households as families got ready for temple. The Hirsh home, however, was relatively quiet. Patricia Hirsh, a tall, statuesque woman in her thirties, with red hair and freckles and bright blue eyes, had already had her supper and cleared away the dishes. She frequently ate alone since there was no telling when her husband would get home from the lab. Normally she did not mind, but tonight she had promised to baby-sit across the street for Liz Marcus so she could go to the Kol Nidre service. Her husband's tardiness was annoying, especially since Pat had told him to be sure to get home early. His place was laid in the tiny dining area, set off from the rest of the living room by a two-tier painted bookcase. (Renaissance had a wrought-iron railing, and Moderne a low wall of glass brick.) She glanced at the clock and was considering calling the lab to see if he'd started out when she heard his key in the lock.

In contrast to his attractive young wife, Isaac Hirsh was short, fat, and fifty. He had a fringe of grizzled iron-gray hair around a bald head, and a short bristly moustache under his bulbous, red-veined nose. She bent forward to kiss him perfunctorily, then said, "I told you I was going to baby-sit for Liz Marcus. I promised to be over early."

"You have plenty of time, baby. They don't start services until after seven, maybe not till quarter past, just before sundown."

"How would you know?" she said. "You haven't gone in years."

"Some things you don't forget, baby."

"Well, if you can't forget it, why don't you go?"

He shrugged his shoulders and sat down at the table.

"I mean it's like Christmas, isn't it? I don't go to church and we never did much back home, but I always feel I've got to celebrate Christmas. When Ma and Pa were alive, I always made a point of trying to get back to South Bend." She began serving his dinner. "It's like that, isn't it?"

He considered. "Yes, for some it's like that. But for most, it's like anything religious—a kind of superstition. And I just don't happen to be superstitious."

She sat down opposite him and watched him eat. He spoke between mouthfuls. "There are some Jews who let on to be awfully proud of being Jews, although they had nothing to do with it and it certainly wasn't of their own choosing. . . . And there are some that are sorry they were born Jews. It's the same feeling really, just turned inside out." He waved his spoon at her. "Nothing so much resembles a hollow as a swelling. So they do what they can to change it—poor buggers."

She took the plate away and brought him another.

"If they go out of town, they change their names," he went on. "If they remain in their hometown, it's not so easy but they work at it. I'm a Jew, and I'm not proud of it and I'm not sorry for it. I don't try to hide it, but I don't glory in it either. It's what I am because it's what I was born. It's just a pigeonhole, a category, and you can make categories any way you like—shift them up or down, one side or the other."

"I don't understand."

"Well, you come from South Bend. Are you proud of it? Do you regret it? You're a female—"

"There have been times when I've been sorry for that, I can tell you."

He nodded. "All right, maybe I've been sorry a couple of times. It's only human." He grew reflective. "At that, I guess I've been lucky. In science it doesn't matter so much. If I had gone into business or one of the professions like medicine where a lot of doors are closed to you if you're Jewish, maybe I would have regretted it more and then I might have tried to do something about it—hide it, or gone the other way. But in my field, in math research, it's no particular liability. In fact, some people even think we've got a special knack; it gives us an edge like an Italian looking for a job with an opera company."

"My, aren't we getting philosophical."

"Maybe. Fact is I'm bushed. That can make a man philosophical—just being tired."

"Has Sykes been bearing down on you?" she asked, at once sympathetic. "He called you, by the way."

"Sykes? When did he call?"

"About ten or fifteen minutes before you got home. He wanted you to call him back."

"All right."

"Aren't you going to call him?"

"No, I'll run up later and see him at the lab. That's probably what he wanted."

"But you're tired," she protested, "and it's your holiday too."

"Oh, Sykes knows I don't go to the synagogue. The old man has been chewing him out so naturally he's on my tail."

"Is something wrong, Ike?" she asked anxiously.

He shrugged his shoulders. "The usual headaches. You get an idea and it looks good. So you work on it and work on it, and then it turns out sour."

"That happens all the time in research, doesn't it?"

"Sure, and for the boys in pure research at the universities, it doesn't make any difference. But with us, where we're working for industry, and you've got to charge the customer, it can become a little sticky. This job was for Goraltronics, and they're not easy people to work for at any time. Right now, for some reason, they seem jumpier than ever, and it rubs off on everyone else down the line. Well, let the big boys worry, I'm just one of the peasants. I do my work and draw my pay."

"Then you'll be working late?"

"Maybe a couple of hours. Why?"

"Peter Dodge called earlier to say he might drop by."

"To see me or to see you?"

She colored. "Oh, Ike—"

He laughed at her embarrassment. "I'm just kidding, baby. C'mere."

She came over and he put his arm around her and nuzzled her thigh while massaging her buttock with his hand.

"He's just friendly because we're from the same hometown," she said defensively.

The phone rang and she left him to answer it, saying over her shoulder, "That's probably Sykes again wondering why you didn't call back."

But it was the petulant, metallic voice of Liz Marcus: "Hey, Pat, I thought you promised to get here early." Turning to her husband, she said, "Got to go, dear. Try not to let him keep you there too late."

"Right, baby."

From the door, she pursed her lips in a token kiss.

4

To native Barnard's Crossers the sprawling Goralsky showplace was always referred to as "the old Northcliffe estate." It had passed to the Goralskys three years before, and Myron Landis, the local realtor who had negotiated the sale, never tired of telling how the purchase was made. "Cinny Northcliffe—that's the young one, although she was the last one and was a good sixty or sixty-five at the time—gave me an exclusive in this area on the estate, and I ran an ad in the Boston papers. A hundred-twenty-thousand-dollar proposition, I figured it was worth a fifty-dollar ad. So the next day, in come these two characters: an old geezer with a beard, and this feller, his son, maybe fifty years old or so. And the old guy says—he does the talking, and he's got an accent you can hardly understand him—'You the agent the Nortcliff place?'

"So I says, 'Yes, sir.'

"So then he says, 'So how much they asking?'

"And I say, 'One hundred and twenty thousand dollars.'

"So then he gives his son a nod and they go over to the corner of the room and they argue a little. I could hear what they're saying, but it's not in English so it don't do me any good. So then they come back to the desk and the young man writes out a check and he gives it to the old man to sign. And the old man he takes off his glasses and he puts on another pair. And he reads over the check, his head moving from side to side and his lips moving like he's spelling it out. Then he takes out a fountain pen, one of those old-fashioned kind that you fill, and he shakes it a couple of times and then writes his name like he has to draw each letter. Then he hands it to me and it's a check for a hundred thousand dollars signed by a Moses Goralsky.

"So I say, 'This is for a hundred thousand. The price is a hundred and twenty thousand.' Which is a kind of crazy thing to say, because of course you don't buy property that way. Without even showing the place or answering questions. To say nothing of arranging financing, a mortgage, a second mortgage. I mean I never sold property like that before. A check for five thousand, or even a thousand as a binder, or even an option—that would be normal, you understand. So he says, 'You get in touch with your seller. Say you got it a check for a hundred thousand dollars. I can have certify if you want.' So naturally I got in touch with Miss Northcliffe and she says to go ahead. I told her, 'Miss Northcliffe, where they offer a hundred I'm sure they'll go the other twenty.' And you know what she says? She says, 'Landis, you're a damn fool, and you don't know the first thing about business. Take his offer.' And that's how it went."

It was a large gray stone mansion, set well back from the street by a few acres of lawn, and encircled by a high iron fence. The rear of the house faced the sea, in fact was part of the sea wall, and as the car approached the front gate Rabbi Small and Miriam could hear the pounding of the surf against the wall and feel the chill ocean air.

The car circled the driveway and stopped at the front door. The chauffeur jumped out and opened the door for them. Almost immediately they were joined by Ben Goralsky, a tall, heavy man, swarthy, with bluish jowls and heavy black eyebrows.

He grasped the rabbi's hand and wrung it gratefully. "Thank you, Rabbi, thank you. I would have come for you myself but I didn't like to leave my father." He turned to the chauffeur. "You can go now, but leave the car here. I'll drive them back." To his guests he explained, "All the servants except the housekeeper have tonight and tomorrow off. My father's idea that they mustn't work because they are of our household. But I'll drive you to the temple myself. Don't worry, you'll get there in time."

"How is he?" asked the rabbi.

"Not good. The doctor just left about half an hour ago. We had Hamilton Jones. You've heard of him, I'm sure. The biggest man in the field—professor at Harvard."

"Your father's conscious?"

"Oh, sure. Sometimes he dozes off for a little but he's conscious all right."

"Was this something sudden? It seems to me I saw him only recently at the minyan."

"That's right, Tuesday—Tuesday he went to the minyan. Then Wednesday he's a little out of sorts, and Thursday he runs a little fever and he's coughing, and then today when it keeps up I figure I better bring in somebody. It's a strep infection, the doctor says. And you know how it is, he's an old man—at his age, any little cold it can become serious."

They paused in the ornate foyer. "Do you mind waiting here, Mrs. Small?" asked Goralsky. "The housekeeper is upstairs—"

"Certainly, Mr. Goralsky. I'll be all right. Don't mind me."

"This way, Rabbi." He led him to the wide marble staircase, which had a thick-piled red carpet running down the middle.

"When did he ask for me?" the rabbi asked.

"Oh, he didn't ask for you, Rabbi. It was my idea." Suddenly Goralsky seemed embarrassed. "You see, he won't take his medicine."

The rabbi stopped and looked at him incredulously.

Goralsky too stopped. "You don't understand. The doctor said he had to take his medicine every four hours—all through the night. We even have to wake him up to give it to him. I told the doctor I didn't like to wake him up, and he said if I wanted my father to live I'd wake him. They have no heart, these doctors. To him, my father is just a case. This is what I tell you to do—do it or don't do it, that's your business."

"And you want me to give him his medicine?"

Goralsky seemed desperate to make the rabbi understand. "The medicine I can give him, or the housekeeper. But he won't take it because it's Yom Kippur and it will mean breaking his fast."

"But that's nonsense. The rule doesn't apply to the sick."

"I know, but he's stubborn. I thought maybe you could convince him. Maybe he'll take it from you."

They had come to the first-floor landing, and now Goralsky led him down a short corridor. "Right here," he said, and pushed open the door.

The housekeeper rose when they entered, and Goralsky motioned her to wait outside. The room was in marked contrast to the rest of the house, or that portion the rabbi had been able to see as they went up the stairs. In the center of the room was a large, old-fashioned brass bed, in which, propped up by pillows, the old man lay. A large roll-topped oak desk, scratched and scarred and piled high with papers, stood against the wall, and in front was a mahogany swivel chair of the same vintage; on top of its cracked leatherette cushion was another of well-worn tapestry, long removed from some ancient sofa. There were a couple of straight-backed chairs covered in green plush that the rabbi assumed probably had been part of the Goralsky dining-room furniture.

"The rabbi has come to see you, Papa," said Goralsky.

"I thank him," said the old man. He was small with a pale, waxen face, and a straggly beard. His dark eyes, sunk deep in bony sockets, were bright with fever. One thin hand picked nervously at the coverlet.

"How do you feel, Mr. Goralsky?" asked the rabbi.

"Nasser should feel like this." He smiled in self-deprecation.

The rabbi smiled back at him. "So why don't you take your medicine?"

The old man shook his head slowly. "On Yom Kippur, Rabbi, I fast."

"But the regulation to fast doesn't apply to medicine. It's an exception, a special rule."

"About special rules, exceptions, Rabbi, I don't know. What I do, I learned from my father, may he rest in peace. He was not a learned man, but there wasn't another one in the village in the old country who could touch him for praying. He believed in God like in a father. He didn't ask questions and he didn't make exceptions. Once, when I was maybe thirteen or fourteen years old, he was in the house saying his morning prayers when some peasants pushed open the door. They had been drinking and they were looking for trouble. They shouted to my father he should give them some *bromphen*, brandy. My mother and I, we were frightened, and she hugged me, but my father didn't look at them and he didn't even skip a word in his prayer. One of them came up to him, and my mother screamed, but my father went on praying. Then the others, they must have got nervous, because they pulled their friend back, and then they left the house."

His son obviously had heard the story many times for he made a grimace of impatience, but his father did not notice and went on. "My father worked hard, and he always managed to feed us and clothe us. And with me, it's the same way. I always obeyed the rules, and God always took care of me. Sometimes I worked harder and sometimes there was trouble, but looking back it was more good than bad. So what I'm told to do, I do, and this must be what God wants because He gave me a good wife who lived till she was full of years, and good sons, and in my old age He even made me rich."

"Do you think that the regulations—to pray, to keep the Sabbath, to fast on Yom Kippur—do you think these are good-luck charms?" the rabbi said. "God also gave you a mind to reason with and to use to protect the life He entrusted to your care."

The old man shrugged his shoulders.

"In fact, if you are sick, the regulation specifically states that you must not fast. And it's not an exception either. It's a general principle that is basic to our religion."

"So who says I'm sick? A doctor says I'm sick, that makes me sick?"

"All day he goes on like that," said Ben admiringly. "A mind like a steel trap." To his father he said, "Look, Papa, I asked Dr. Bloom who we should get and he tells me Dr. Hamilton Jones is the best there is.

So we get Hamilton Jones. He's not just any doctor; he's a professor, from Harvard College."

"Mr. Goralsky," said the rabbi earnestly, "man was created in God's image. So to disregard the health of the body that was entrusted to our care, God's image, Mr. Goralsky, this is a serious sin. It is *chillul ha-Shem*, an affront to the Almighty."

"Look, Rabbi, I'm an old man. For seventy-five years at least— seventy-five years I can give you a guarantee—I fasted on Yom Kippur. So this Yom Kippur you think I'm going to eat?"

"But medicine is not eating, Mr. Goralsky."

"When I take in my mouth and I swallow, by me this is eating."

"You can't beat him," Ben Goralsky murmured in the rabbi's ear.

"Do you realize, Mr. Goralsky," said the rabbi seriously, "that if, God forbid, you should die because you refused medication, it could be considered suicide."

The old man grinned.

The rabbi realized that the old man was enjoying this, that he was deriving a perverse sort of pleasure from debating with a young rabbi. David Small wanted to smile, but he made one last effort and managed to sound somber and portentous. "Think, Mr. Goralsky. If I should judge you a suicide, you would not receive formal burial. There would be no eulogy over your grave. There would be no public mourning. No Kaddish would be recited in your memory. According to strict interpretation of the Law, you might be buried in a corner off to one side of the cemetery—you couldn't even be placed beside your dear wife—and your children and grandchildren would be shamed—"

The old man held up a thin, blue-veined hand. "Look, Rabbi, in all my life I never did anybody any harm. I never cheated; I never bore false witness. Fifty years I'm in business for myself and show me one person who can say I took from him a penny. So I'm sure God will take care of me and not let me die tonight."

The rabbi couldn't resist the gambit. "If you are on such good terms with the Almighty, Mr. Goralsky, then why did He let you get sick in the first place?"

The old man smiled as though his opponent had fallen into the trap he had set. "Such a question! If He didn't let me get sick, so how could He make me well?"

"He can stop you like that every time," said the son.

"Don't worry, Rabbi," said the old man. "I'm not going to die tonight. Benjamin, send in the woman. You better go now; you'll be late for Kol Nidre." He closed his eyes in dismissal.

As the two men walked down the stairs, the rabbi said, "I'm afraid

I wasn't of much help." He looked at his host curiously. "But I would have thought he would listen to you—"

"When does a parent ever listen to a child, Rabbi?" asked Goralsky bitterly. "To him, I'm just a boy. He's proud when other people say nice things about me. Last year, I was written up in *Time* magazine and he carried the clipping in his wallet and pulled it out and showed it to people whenever my name was mentioned. And if it wasn't mentioned, he'd bring it up himself: 'Did you read about my son, Benjamin?' But when it comes to taking my advice, that's another story. In matters of business, at least, he listens; but when it's his own personal health—talk to the wall."

"Has he been well all along?"

"He's never sick. He doesn't see a doctor from one year to the next. That's the trouble: he thinks he's indestructible and when something like this happens, he won't do anything about it."

"He must be pretty old."

"Eighty-four," said Goralsky proudly.

"Then maybe he's right," suggested the rabbi. "After all, you can't argue with success. If, at his age, he is well and never sees a doctor, then he's probably learned instinctively how to take care of himself."

"Maybe, Rabbi, maybe. Well, thanks anyway for trying. I'll drive you and Mrs. Small to the temple now."

"Aren't you coming to services?"

"No, I think tonight to be on the safe side I better hang around here."

5

A light panel truck bearing the sign Jackson's Liquor Mart drove up to the Levensons across the street from the Hirsh house. The driver got out and stood at the front door with a small parcel under his arm. He pushed the doorbell and waited. He rang again, his fingers drumming a nervous tattoo on the aluminum cover of his voucher book. Just then he saw Isaac Hirsh leave his house and start for his car. He hailed him and walked over.

"You live in that house, Mister?"

"That's right."

"You know"—he peered at the name on the package—"Charles Levenson?"

"Sure. That's his house right there."

"Yeah, I know." Suddenly the driver was exasperated. "Look, this is my last delivery today and I'm running late. And tomorrow all my deliveries are on the other side of town. There's no one home, and I hate to leave this where anyone can get at it, if you know what I mean. Would you mind taking this and give it to Mr. Levenson when you see him tomorrow?"

"Why not?"

"Fine. Sign here."

Tweaking the belly of the toy troll suspended from the rearview mirror, Hirsh set it dancing on its elastic. "Wasn't that a gurgle we heard, Herr Einstein?" The little figure with its wild mop of hair seemed to nod in agreement. "This needs looking into, I should say," and suiting the action to the word, he carefully opened the package and extracted a bottle. "A fifth of vodka no less, and of the right brand."

He held the enclosed card under the dashboard light and read, "To Charlie Levenson for a Happy Birthday." "Very touching, don't you think, Einstein, old friend? I am strongly tempted to drink a toast to our friend and neighbor Charlie Levenson. But first let us consider. It's been six months since we've had a drink. What's that you say? Nearer eight months? Well, perhaps you're right. Either way, it's a long time between drinks. On the one hand, it's a shame to spoil the record, but on the other hand, only a lout would refuse to drink good old Charlie's health. Did I hear you say something? You say I don't know when to stop once I begin? You've got a point there, old friend, but how do we know unless we test ourselves every now and then? After all, we didn't ask for this; we didn't go looking for it. We were just minding our business, setting out for the lab, and this comes along, out of the blue, you might say. Now I'd call that an omen. And on this night, particularly. And suppose we do overdo it a little, what's the harm? Tomorrow is Saturday and we can sleep as late as we like. You say Levenson will miss his bottle? Why, that's the beauty of the thing, old friend. Charlie's off to temple and won't be home till late. Being it's Yom Kippur he won't or he shouldn't—feel like taking a drink. Then tomorrow before he gets back from services all we have to do is buy another bottle and he'll never know. I say, we should vote on it. All in favor say Aye. All opposed Nay—The Ayes have it."

He unscrewed the cap and took an experimental nip. "Just as I said, Einstein, old friend, it's the right brand." He took another drink and then recapped the bottle. "Yes, sir, it seems to be clearing the cobwebs out of the brain. And tonight of all nights we need a clear head." He set the car in motion.

Several times along the way he stopped to toast Charlie's good health. Behind him, he heard the loud blare of an automobile horn. He swung his car to the right; the wheel grated against the road divider and he swung left. Once again there was the blare of a horn, and a car swept around him and hung alongside for a moment as the driver cursed at him.

"You know what, Einstein? Traffic here on Route 128 is moving just a little too fast for us. The old brain is clear as a bell, but the reflexes are a bit slow. What say we stop for a while? There's a turnout ahead just a couple of hundred yards before we get to the lab where we can let things kind of catch up."

He pulled to a stop. He fumbled clumsily with the wrapper of the bottle. Then, in annoyance, he ripped off the wrapping paper and cardboard box and with a lordly gesture threw them out the window. "The big trick is to time yourself. You time yourself, and there's no problem." He turned off the motor and headlights. "Better wait half an hour or so, grab a little shut-eye maybe, and then go on to the lab. You mark my words, Einstein, old friend, if past experience is any guide, when I wake up the old brain will be ticking like a regular computer."

6

The Smalls arrived at the temple just in time. The rabbi left Miriam to make her way through the front door where stragglers were still coming in, and hurried to a side door that led to the vestry and the narrow staircase to the enrobing room adjoining the altar. The room had become something of a catchall for old prayer books, florists' baskets used to decorate the altar, piles of cantorial music, and two coils of BX cable left by the electricians when the building was constructed some three years before. The rabbi hung up his topcoat and hat and put on his skullcap and the white robe which was the conservative compromise on the orthodox kittel or grave vestment. Then bracing against his locker—there was no chair—he changed from street shoes to white rubber-soled canvas shoes, a modern compromise on the ancient Mishnah ban against wearing shoes during the day of prayer. Lastly he draped his silk prayer shawl over his shoulders, and after a glance in the mirror opened the door that led to the altar.

On either side of the Ark were two high-backed red velvet chairs. The two on the far side were occupied by the vice-president and cantor; the two nearest the anteroom were reserved for himself and the president of the congregation, Mortimer Schwarz. He came forward and shook hands with the president, then crossed in front of the Ark to shake hands with the cantor and Ely Kahn, the vice-president. He returned to his chair and looked around at the congregation, nodding to members who happened to catch his eye.

"You cut it rather fine, Rabbi," said Schwarz. He was a tall, youngish-looking man of fifty, with thin gray-black hair slicked back as if to emphasize his high forehead. He had a long thin face and a thin, high-bridged nose. His mouth was small and the lips full and round, almost as though pursed for kissing. He was an architect; and something about his dress, the long points of his shirt collar, the thickly knotted tie, suggested some connection with the arts. He was good-looking, even handsome; and his posture and general movements—not studied, but controlled—suggested he knew it. With the rabbi he maintained an armed truce which manifested itself in a kind of jocose teasing that occasionally developed an unpleasant edge.

"For a Hadassah meeting, or a Sisterhood committee meeting," he went on, "understandable. Ethel tells me that they don't even expect you to remember. They have an unofficial Rabbi Delivering Committee whose job it is to keep reminding you of the meeting date, and if necessary to go fetch you. She thinks it adds spice to the meeting: will the rabbi turn up in time or not? It's a convenient trait, since I suppose it enables you to miss an occasional meeting. But Kol Nidre, Rabbi! I wonder you were able to find a parking place."

"Oh, Miriam and I plan to walk home. I'm a little old-fashioned about these things."

"You walked? Why didn't you tell me and I would have arranged to get you a ride?"

"I did ride. As a matter of fact, I rode in style, in a Lincoln Continental, I believe. Just as I was leaving the house, Ben Goralsky called and insisted I had to see his father. A matter of life and death, he said. So I couldn't very well refuse. Ben drove me down afterward."

Schwarz sounded suddenly concerned. "Something's the matter with the old man? It sounds serious if they sent for you."

The rabbi grinned. "He wouldn't take his medicine."

Schwarz frowned his disapproval of the rabbi's levity. In his relation with the rabbi, humor was a one-way street. "This is serious business. Tell me, is something really wrong?"

"Any time a man that age gets sick, it's serious, I suppose. But I think he'll be all right." He went on briefly to describe his visit.

The frown did not lift from the president's handsome face; if anything, it grew more pronounced. "You mean to say you threatened old man Goralsky with a suicide's grave, Rabbi? You must have offended him."

"I don't think so. I think he rather enjoyed fencing with me. He could see that I was more than half fooling."

"I certainly hope so."

"Why this tremendous interest in Mr. Goralsky? He's a member, to be sure, but a relatively new one and rather a cantankerous one at that."

"Yes, they're new. When was it they joined? About a year ago, wasn't it, when the old lady died and they bought the big center lot in the cemetery? But with their kind of money, they're important. Surely I don't have to tell you, Rabbi, that when you're running an organization like this, you need money. And if you don't have money—and what synagogue does?—the next best thing is to have members who do."

"I've heard something to that effect. But surely it must be the son, Ben, who has the money."

Schwarz's face brightened and he looked straight out at the congregation. Then he leaned toward the rabbi and said, "You'd think so, wouldn't you? But actually the father is everything, and the son, at least while the father is alive, is just a messenger boy."

"And the father is willing to give and the son is not?"

"You don't get the picture, Rabbi." He gestured with his hands spread as if to frame the picture. "The money, they're both prepared to give. When you accumulate the kind of money thay have, you're prepared to give some of it away. It's expected of you. It goes with your status like Continentals and a uniformed chauffeur. Now the old man has been a pious Jew all his life. As you know, he comes to the minyan almost every day when the weather permits. So a man like that, his idea of giving away money is to give it to a temple.

"But Ben? Ben is a businessman through and through. When a businessman decides that the time has come to give charity, he views it as a business proposition. He is buying *kovod,* honor. And naturally he wants to get the most for his *kovod* dollar. If he uses the money to build a chapel—say the Goralsky Memorial Chapel—who will see it? Who will know about it except the folks here in Barnard's Crossing? But," he lowered his voice, "suppose he were to donate a laboratory to Brandeis or even to Harvard? The Goralsky Chemical Research Laboratory? Eh? Scientists and scholars from all over the world would get to hear of it."

The congregation had quieted as people began to settle down, their eyes now on the altar in anticipation. The rabbi glanced at the clock and said he thought they had better begin.

The two men rose and beckoned the cantor and the vice-president on the other side of the Ark with a nod. The cantor pulled the cord that parted the white velvet curtains in front of the Ark. As he slid back the wooden doors of the Ark to expose the precious Scrolls of the Law, the congregation rose.

The president, reading from a slip of paper, called the names of half a dozen of the more important members of the congregation to come forward, and they ascended the steps to the altar and the cantor handed each of them a Scroll. When all the Scrolls were received, the men clustered around the reading desk facing the congregation and the rabbi recited first in Hebrew and then in English the ancient formula that traditionally introduces the Yom Kippur service: "By the authority of the Court on high, and by the authority of the Court below, by permission of God and by permission of this holy congregation, we hold it lawful to pray with the transgressors."

Then the cantor began the mournful yet uplifting chant of the Kol Nidre. Three times he would chant the prayer, and by the time he had finished the sun would have gone down and the Day of Atonement, the Sabbath of Sabbaths, would have begun.

"How did the public-address system work out?" asked Miriam as they walked home from the service. "Did it put much of a strain on your voice?"

"Not a bit. I just spoke a little slower." He chuckled. "But our president was quite upset. Every time he got up to announce the names of those who had honors, they had difficulty hearing him. The Ritual Committee sends out notices indicating the approximate time a man will be called, but we were running a little late and there was some confusion. A Mr. Goldman, who sits well back, didn't hear his name, so Mr. Schwarz took the next name on the list and that upset the whole schedule. Did you get that bit at the end? When Marvin Brown was called?"

"Yes, what happened?"

"Well, I guess he didn't hear his name, but instead of calling up a substitute as he had been doing all evening, Schwarz kept repeating the name. I suppose because Marvin is a special friend of his and he didn't want him to miss his honor, even though it was just to open the Ark. Finally, after he called Mr. Brown, Mr. Marvin Brown, two or three times, the vice-president came over and opened the Ark himself. Our president was a little annoyed with him for it."

"It seems a small thing to make a fuss about."

"Mr. Schwarz evidently didn't consider it so. As a matter of fact, he kept grousing a good part of the evening about the acoustics. At first I thought it was professional jealousy, but then I got the feeling he had something else in mind. Especially when he said something about expecting us at his house tomorrow after we broke our fast. Did Mrs. Schwarz call you?"

"This morning. Ethel invited us for dessert and coffee. Isn't it the usual custom? Don't we always go to the president's house for coffee after Yom Kippur?"

"I guess we do at that. But somehow, when Mr. Wasserman and even Mr. Becker were president, I didn't think of it as a custom. I felt they asked us over, as they did on other occasions, because they wanted to see us. But I don't feel it's quite the same with Mortimer Schwarz. You know, in your present condition, we could easily duck it."

"There'll be a lot of other people there, David; we won't have to stay long. Ethel seemed particularly anxious for us to come. Maybe they're just trying to be nice and show they want to let bygones be bygones."

The rabbi looked doubtful.

"You both seemed quite friendly up there on the platform."

"Naturally, we're not going to sit there and glare at each other. On the surface everything is fine. We even joke with each other, although it's apt to be rather patronizing on his part—the way I would imagine he jokes with his junior draftsmen. When I answer in kind, I get the feeling he regards it as an impertinence, although of course he wouldn't say so."

She was troubled. "Aren't you perhaps imagining a lot of this because he opposed renewing your contract when it came up before the Board?"

"I don't think so. There were others who opposed me, and when I was voted my five-year contract they came up to congratulate me. When my five years are up they may oppose me again, but in the meantime, they will remain neutral and work with me. With Schwarz, on the other hand, I have the feeling that if he could get me out tomorrow, he would."

"But that's just the point, David, he can't. You have a five-year contract that has four more years to go. And his term of office is only one year. You'll outlast him."

"It really isn't much of a contract, you know," he said.

"I don't understand."

"It's a service contract, which means they can't drop me as long as I behave myself. What constitutes proper behavior is up to them to decide, while nothing is said about *their* behavior. They can do all kinds of things against which I have no recourse. Suppose they decide to make some change in the ritual that I couldn't possibly live with. What happens then? The only thing I could do would be to resign."

"And you think Schwarz might do something like that?"

"Just to get me out? No. But we could disagree about something, and he might use that as an excuse. And to give him his due, he'd probably feel it was for the good of the congregation."

7

Just before midnight the call came in. "Barnard's Crossing Police Department," the man at the desk said. "Sergeant Jeffers. Yes, I see . . . Do you want to give me the name again? . . . H-I-R-S-H, no C . . . Mrs. Isaac Hirsh." He repeated as he wrote, "Bradford Lane . . . that's in Colonial Village, isn't it? . . . Now what time did he leave? . . . Well then, what time did you call the lab? . . . I see . . . Can you give me a description of the car and the license number? . . . Any marks on the car? . . . All right, ma'am, I'll notify State Police and local police departments to be on the lookout. And I'll have the cruising car stop by at your house. . . . In a few minutes. Will you put your porch light on, please . . . We'll do everything we can, ma'am."

The patrol car answered his signal right away. "Take this down, Joe. Chevrolet, four-door sedan, light blue, rusty dent on left rear fender. License number 438,972, repeat, 438,972. Isaac Hirsh, 4 Bradford Lane. It's next to the corner. The porch light will be on. His wife just called in. He works at the Goddard Lab on Route 128. She was out baby-sitting for a neighbor, and when she got back he had gone. Nothing unusual, he's apt to run down to the lab and work at night. But she called the lab a little while ago and he wasn't there and hadn't been there. Stop over and talk to her. See if she's got a picture of him we can broadcast."

"Okay, Sarge. Say—Isaac Hirsh—isn't that the guy who went on a toot some months back and we finally located him in a dive in the South End in Boston?"

"Yeah, come to think of it. I'll notify Boston police to keep an eye out for him. That's probably what happened—got thirsty again. When you go over, kind of suggest that she look around and see if anything is missing, like the cooking sherry or his aftershave bay rum. Those guys will drink anything when it hits them."

"Got it, Sarge." He turned to his partner. "Let's go, Tommy boy."

"What is it, a missing drunk? Why don't we stop at a couple of places downtown first, The Foc'sle and the Sea and Sand, and see if he's there."

"Not that kind of drunk, Tommy. He's some hot-shot scientist. He don't drink, except every now and then he goes on a big toot that lasts for days, even weeks. Last time, at least last time we know about on account of the missus calling in, he was missing three days. It must have been all of eight months ago, maybe more. The Boston police finally found him holed up in a filthy little dive of a hotel in the South End. He was lying in bed fully dressed with a pile of dead soldiers on the floor. I don't think he had eaten in all that time. Mark my words, when we turn him up, it'll probably be another such place. Ah, here we are, the house with the porch light. I recognize it now, we took him home in the ambulance last time. You wait here in case the sergeant calls in."

Patricia Hirsh opened the door before he had a chance to ring. "Thank you for coming so quickly, Officer." Although she was obviously agitated, her voice was controlled.

"Just as soon as we got the message, ma'am." He took out his notebook and pencil from the thigh pocket of his uniform. "Now, can you tell me what your husband was wearing?"

"Oh." She went to the hall closet. "A light topcoat—it's gray, dark gray herringbone. And—no, his hat is here. Underneath he had on a regular business suit—dark brown."

"And can you give me a description of him, height, weight, and so on."

"He's quite plump. He weighs about a hundred and ninety pounds and is about five three." As he looked up involuntarily, she said, "Yes, he's shorter than I am. He's also quite a bit older. He's fifty-one, and bald," she added defiantly, "with a moustache."

"You got a picture of him, ma'am?"

"Yes, upstairs in the bedroom. Would you like me to get it?"

"If you please." As she started for the stairs, he called after her, "I'll just give this information to my partner outside so he can call it in right away."

At the car he asked Tommy if there had been any calls. His partner shook his head, then said: "Better check out the house, Joe. The garage door, I notice it's down. When we first came on duty about eight o'clock a number of them were up. Probably because so many people were over at the temple."

"Okay, I'll check it. Meantime, call in this description." And after repeating what Mrs. Hirsh had told him, he went back to the house. She was waiting for him with the picture. He took it, studied it for a moment, then said gently, "You haven't noticed anything missing, have you?"

"I haven't looked. Like what?"

"Well, like whiskey—"

"We don't have it in the house."

"Cooking sherry?"

"I don't use it."

"Maybe bay rum or rubbing alcohol?"

"No, nothing like that."

"All right, ma'am. We'll get right on to it. Why don't you just go to bed. I'll let myself out through the back."

"That only leads to the garage."

"Never hurts to look around, ma'am."

"You'll call me—no matter what time, won't you?"

"Sure will." Making his way through the kitchen to the garage, he opened the back door, and then quickly closed it behind him. The car was in the garage, and on the front seat, on the passenger side, was Isaac Hirsh.

Even slim as he was, it was a tight squeeze for Joe between the wall of the garage and the car, but he managed. He opened the front door and leaned across the driver's seat to touch the man. By the light of his flashlight he noted the position of the key in the ignition switch. He noted the half-empty vodka bottle. Then he withdrew and closed the car door. Squeezing his way to the front of the garage he raised the overhead door just enough to duck under, and pulled it down after him.

He got into the cruising car, but as the driver started to shift into gear he held onto his hand. "No, Tommy, we're not going anywhere. I've found him. He's in the garage."

"Dead to the world?"

"Yeah, only this time it's for good."

8

The daylong Yom Kippur services began at nine with the recital of
morning prayers. Only a handful of people were in the temple, mostly
the older men, and on the platform only the rabbi was in his seat. Even
the cantor had not yet arrived, since it was customary to have someone
else lead the morning service to give him a measure of relief. The honor
usually went to Jacob Wasserman, the first president of the temple and
the man who more than anyone else had organized the congregation.
His voice made up in genuine fervor what it lacked in volume, and the
rabbi enjoyed his chanting with its traditional quavers and trills more
than the studied effects of the cantor who surreptitiously would stoop
and tap his tuning fork and hum the pitch before beginning a chant.

The congregation kept drifting in all morning. Shortly after the
cantor took his seat, Mortimer Schwarz appeared. He shook hands ceremoniously with the rabbi, and then crossed over to shake hands with the
cantor. He returned to his seat and whispered that, just as he had expected, Marvin Brown called last night.

"You mean about the honor he missed?"

"Well, Rabbi, he didn't come right out and say so, but I know that's
what it was."

"I wouldn't have thought it meant so much to him."

"Oh, I don't think he's particularly religious. But he's a salesman
first, last, and always. And, something like that, he builds it up in
his mind as kind of good luck. And if he should somehow miss out, it
could throw him off stride. Do you understand?"

"I can understand how he might feel that way," said the rabbi.

"Well, I don't mind saying I felt Ely Kahn kind of jumped the gun
by going ahead and opening the Ark when Marvin didn't come down

right away. Nothing terrible would have happened if we'd waited a few minutes. Anyway, today I'm going to be extra careful. I'll call out these names good and loud, and we'll wait until we're sure the person is not in the temple before picking a substitute."

By a quarter past ten, when the Scrolls were removed from the Ark for the Reading, the sanctuary was full. Some chose to regard this point in the service as a recess; and while a few left, most remained. For the Memorial Service for the Dead that followed, the Yizkor service, the sanctuary filled up again. Many came just for this portion out of a sense of respect for departed members of their immediate family. Traditionally it was considered bad luck for anyone whose parents were alive to be present, but the rabbi, like most Conservative rabbis, felt this to be idle superstition. He began by explaining that it was proper for all to attend, that since those who had died in the Nazi holocaust were going to be memorialized, everyone could consider himself bereaved; but here and there he could see some of the older congregants brought up in Orthodoxy urge their children to leave.

However, after Yizkor he could not help feeling pleased to note a large portion of the young people return, presumably to hear his sermon. One portion of the Holy Day service described the way the High Priest of ancient times purified himself and his family before making the sacrifice to atone for the sins of his people. The sermon discussed this portion of the service, comparing this with the attempted sacrifice of Isaac by Abraham—a reference to the New Year Reading on Rosh Hashanah, the beginning of the ten Days of Awe. With many a rabbinic allusion, he explained that the sacrifice of Isaac was a stern injunction *against* the human sacrifice that was universally practiced at the time, and then went on to show how the whole concept of sacrifice and atonement had gradually changed from sacrificing a live scapegoat to the modern attitude toward prayer, which meant begging forgiveness—from the Lord for sins committed against Him as well as from individuals for sins committed against them.

As in all his sermons, the tone and style was instructional and informal, like a college lecture. He himself thought of his sermons as theses in which he attempted to explain seeming contradictions in the Law, rather than as exhortations. He knew some members of the congregation, including the president, grew restive during his discourse, and would have preferred a more oratorical, hortative style, but he felt his type of sermon was more in keeping with his basic function of teacher, implicit in the word "rabbi."

The service continued, the day wore on; people came and left, some to go home for a nap or perhaps even a hurried snack, while outside, boys and girls stood about in their new clothes, laughing and flirting. The very young played on the temple grounds, their high shrill voices sometimes disturbing the decorum inside, requiring one of the ushers to go out and lecture them for making noise while the service was in progress.

At four o'clock, it became apparent that they were proceeding too rapidly and the service was in danger of ending before sunset. The rabbi approached the reading desk, "We're running ahead of time, Cantor Zimbler. Can you slow it down?"

The cantor shrugged his shoulders. "What do you want me to do, Rabbi, hold the notes longer?"

The rabbi smiled. Then: "I guess we'd better have a recess." He announced that the congregation was praying with such fervor that they were outrunning the sun. "So we'll have a half-hour break."

There was a murmur of grateful laughter from the congregation but only a few left since those present at that hour represented the hard core of worshipers who came with the intention of remaining through the day. But they appreciated the respite and engaged their neighbors in a few minutes' conversation before returning to the concluding portion which ended with the blowing of the shofar.

The president stretched on his thronelike chair and turned to the rabbi. "You know, apropos of your sermon, it occurs to me I made a sacrifice of my own. This is the first year in a long time that I have fasted, and I feel fine, just fine. Other years, I didn't exactly eat, I mean, I didn't have a regular meal. I'd have some juice in the morning, and then around noon I might go home for a cup of coffee and a sandwich, but this year I felt, being president, I ought to go the distance. And though I feel a little weak, otherwise I'm just fine."

"Mr. Goralsky told me he had been doing it for seventy-five years, and it doesn't appear to have hurt him any."

"Gosh, I forgot all about the old man. Have you heard how he is? I haven't seen Ben around."

"I'm sure he hasn't been here or I would have seen him."

"That sounds bad, Rabbi. The old man must be very sick—Ben would have come for Yizkor at least, with his mother dead only recently, within the year."

"Not necessarily. They're quite Orthodox and according to custom those recently bereaved, who are still in the year of mourning, do not attend the Yizkor service."

"That so? Then, maybe that's it. I certainly hope so."

The rabbi regarded him curiously. "Are you really so sure of getting a large contribution from Mr. Goralsky?"

"I've talked to the old man—informally, you know," Schwarz said smugly. "No definite promise, of course, but I can tell he's receptive to the idea."

"And how big a contribution do you hope for?"

Schwarz looked at him in some surprise. "I told you about it last night, Rabbi. A memorial chapel."

"You mentioned it, but I thought it was just by way of example. You mean he really is interested in building a Goralsky Memorial Chapel? What kind of money would be involved?"

"Oh, a hundred thousand dollars—to a hundred and a half."

The rabbi pursed his lips in a soundless whistle. "They're in electronics?"

"That's right, electronics and transistors. They've got a big new plant on Route 128. They're loaded. Right now, I understand, they're planning to merge with some big outfit out West, and their stock has been going up like a skyrocket. It's doubled in the last couple of weeks. And they started in the poultry business."

"The poultry business?"

"The absolute truth. My grandmother used to buy fresh-killed chickens from their store in Chelsea, and the old man himself used to wait on her in a blood-smeared white apron and a straw hat. Then they got a little ahead of themselves and began to gamble in futures and made quite a bit of money. So they had spare money when a chance came to invest in a transistor company and they were on their way. They bought out their partner, the man who started the business, and after that they really began to expand. They were lucky enough to go public right at the boom, and the rest is financial history. Maybe you saw the write-up on Ben Goralsky in *Time* magazine?"

The rabbi shook his head.

"A column and a half plus picture. I tried to put him on the Board, but he said he was too busy." He sounded gloomy.

"And do you think if you got him on the Board he might be inclined to favor a chapel over a chemistry lab?"

"At least it would get him interested in our organization and its problems."

"But do we need a chapel? It seems to me we have plenty of room right now—"

Schwarz looked at him. "Rabbi, a growing organization *never* has plenty of room. If it's enough for today, then it's not enough for tomorrow. Besides, next to the high school, our sanctuary is the biggest auditorium in town. Once or twice in the past we've been asked for the loan of our facilities by outside organizations. Now, how does it sit with you to have a secular organization like Kiwanis, say, transacting their business right here in front of the Holy Ark?"

"Well—"

"But suppose we had a small chapel built right onto the wall behind us, a small jewel of a chapel that you could tell was a chapel and not a barracks or a light and power company office building?"

"You don't like this building?"

Schwarz smiled condescendingly. "Remember, Rabbi, I'm an architect by profession. Look, are you and Miriam coming over tonight after you break your fast? Ethel is expecting you."

"If Miriam is up to it."

"Good. I'll show you something that will knock your eye out."

From where she was sitting, Miriam signaled her husband with a nod. He left the pulpit and joined her as she made her way out of the sanctuary.

"Something wrong, dear?"

"I feel a little done in. I guess I've got used to napping in the afternoon. Alice Fine is going home, and I thought I'd get a ride with her."

"You'll make yourself some tea, won't you? Or perhaps a glass of warm milk would be even better. I think you should eat something. You sure you're all right?"

"Believe me, David, I feel fine."

"Anything wrong?" asked Schwarz when the rabbi returned to the pulpit. He told him Miriam felt a little tired.

"Well, it's understandable. I hope she's not fasting."

"She was, but she promised to eat something."

The sun began to set, and many of those who had left earlier returned to take part in the final congregational confession of sins, "We have trespassed, we have been faithless . . ." and to ask once again for forgiveness, "Our God and God of our fathers, pardon our iniquities on this Day of Atonement. . . . Accept, O Lord our God, thy people Israel and their prayer. . . ."

The sun set as they began to read responsively the *Ovenu Malkenu,* "Our Father, our King." Then in a voice of fervor and exultation, they declaimed, "Hear, O Israel: the Lord our God, the Lord is One," followed by "Blessed be His Name, whose glorious Kingdom is forever and ever," recited three times. Then seven times, the cantor and the congregation exclaimed, "The Lord, He is God," each time louder and more passionately, the last time climaxed by a long blast—eerie, piercing, and exultant—of the shofar, the ram's horn, signifying the end of the long Day of Atonement and the ten Days of Awe.

The Mourner's Kaddish remained to be said, and a benediction by the rabbi, but the members of the congregation were already folding their prayer shawls and shaking hands with their neighbors and wishing them a healthy and happy New Year.

The rabbi shook hands with Mortimer Schwarz, with the cantor, and with the vice-president.

"See you tonight, Rabbi?" asked Schwarz.

"If Miriam feels well enough."

9

Reluctantly Jordan Marcus went to the telephone, but before picking up the instrument he made one more appeal. "I tell you, Liz, I still don't think we ought to get mixed up in this. We're new members, for one thing."

"So?" his wife said. "You paid your dues, didn't you?"

"You know damn well I did, and don't think that hundred bucks didn't hurt plenty, plus fifty bucks on top of that for two tickets—"

"So? So what did you want to do on the High Holidays? Go to the movies?"

"You didn't even have to show your tickets. We could have just walked in—"

"And when you got in you'd be invisible? The Levensons, the Baylisses—they wouldn't see you? And wouldn't know you're not a member?"

"We could have gone to my folks' place in Chelsea. It would have cost me ten bucks apiece for the tickets, and I would have saved myself a hundred and thirty bucks."

"And next year, when Monte has to start religious school, you'd take him to Chelsea three days a week, I suppose."

"So we could have joined next year. And that's a sweet little racket, by the way, making you join the temple so your kids can go to the religious school."

"They all do it, all the new temples. I guess they got to. Besides what's the difference if we join this year or next year?"

"A hundred and thirty bucks' difference."

"You want everybody to know you only joined at the last minute because you had to? You want everybody to think we're cheap?"

"Well, by God, I'd just as soon. I'm getting sick and tired of worrying about whether people think I'm cheap. I put in wall-to-wall broadloom for almost a thousand bucks so people wouldn't think I was cheap; I swapped the Chevy for a Pontiac so people wouldn't think I was cheap; and when Henry Bayliss suggests going to the Checkerboard for a bite after the movie, I got to say, Fine—swell idea, because if I mention someplace where you can get a hamburg and coffee for under a buck, that means I'm cheap."

"So? That's gracious living. You're in Barnard's Crossing now. When in Rome you got to do like the Romans. We got a responsibility to the kids, and that's why you joined the temple. But now that you're a member in good standing, you got rights like anybody else. So stop stalling and call the rabbi."

"But, Liz, he's just got back from the temple. He's probably at dinner and must be starved. Besides, there's more involved than you realize. The bylaws say you got to be a bona fide member to be buried in the cemetery. Now you want me to ask the rabbi to forget the bylaws and make an exception for a friend of mine whose wife isn't even Jewish. That's what I mean I'm a new member. To ask a favor like this, you got to be one of the big shots. If it were a relative of mine, that's one thing. But this guy Hirsh, I hardly knew him. Maybe all the time we've been living here I've said Hello to him three times. I say we shouldn't get involved."

"But we are involved. Patricia Hirsh was right here in this house taking care of your kids while her husband was dying in his garage not a hundred feet away. Besides, didn't we tell her to have him buried by Jewish law?"

"You did; I didn't. As a matter of fact, seems to me she was already planning to anyway before we even got there. You just said, the way I remember, you thought it was a wonderful idea and we could talk to the rabbi. And she said that this Dr. Sykes, her husband's boss, was going to make all the arrangements, he planned to call the rabbi himself. If he's going to, why do we have to?"

"You keep forgetting I am practically her best friend around here and she was baby-sitting for us. It was all I could do to get you to go over to see her when we heard."

He had indeed been reluctant. He dreaded the weeping, the depressing conversation he associated with a house of mourning. But it turned out to be not so bad. Except for the Levensons across the street, the others present had all been Gentiles. Dr. Sykes, Hirsh's section head, seemed to be in charge. At least, he had come to the door and introduced them around. There was someone in a gray suit and Roman collar, the Reverend Peter Dodge, who seemed to know the family because he and Hirsh were both active in the Civil Rights movement. The MacCarthys who lived down the street were just going when they came in. Liz ran over and threw her arms around Mrs. Hirsh, and both of them had been teary for a minute, but then Mrs. Hirsh got control of herself. When the question of a Jewish ceremony came up, Dodge had even got her to smile when after saying he knew Rabbi Small well, they were both in the Ministers' Association, he added: "But I don't think it would be proper for me to ask him to officiate at the burial, Pat, not where we're business competitors, so to speak." And that's when Dr. Sykes said he was going to arrange everything.

Once outside, Jordan told his wife he had to hand it to her. "I was afraid we'd be stuck there all morning."

"When I saw what the situation was, I wasn't going to hang around," she answered primly. "This Dodge fellow, Pat knew him from South Bend where she came from. You notice he called her by her first name? He's not married. You notice how he was looking at her?"

"How was he looking at her?"

"You know, kind of hungry."

"Oh, Jesus. You dames, all you got on your minds. The guy isn't even buried yet, and you're already trying to marry her off."

As he dialed he rehearsed in his mind what he would say to the rabbi. "Rabbi Small? . . . Oh, Mrs. Small? Am I disturbing your dinner?"

"Is that the rabbi's wife?" Liz took the instrument from him. "Mrs. Small? This is Liz Marcus. I sat right behind you at the Hadassah meeting, and you asked me about taking off your hat when the film began? . . . Well, a very good friend of ours—she's not Jewish, but she's got a real Jewish heart. . . ."

"The Marcuses," Miriam explained as she returned to the table. "They're recent members—"

"Yes, I know. Joe, no, Jordan Marcus?"

"That's right. They called about an Isaac Hirsh who died last night. As a matter of fact, that's the second call. A Dr. Sykes called just after I got back from the temple. He wanted to see you about this same Isaac Hirsh. I made an appointment for him for tomorrow. Do we know an Isaac Hirsh?"

"He's not a member of the congregation. I don't think we even have an Isaac." He smiled. "Too bad, because around here, it's an old Yankee name. Isn't the Town Clerk Isaac Broadhurst?" He nodded at her middle. "How about Isaac for the coming Small?"

"You know we decided on Jonathan," she said with determination.

"I know, but it has been bothering me. It suggests David. Now I'm David, and it might give the young man the idea that we were pals, friends, contemporaries—David and Jonathan. I'm afraid the young man might presume."

"Well, Isaac is out of the question," she said again. "Your uncle is named Isaac, and your family would never agree to another Isaac Small while he is still living."

"I suppose not. I'm inclined to believe the Christians are a little smarter than we in the matter of names. When they can't decide what to call a child, they can always use Junior. And then Second and Third. David Small the Third. Now there's a name for you!"

"It could be a girl, you know."

The rabbi appeared to consider. Then he shook his head. "I'm afraid not. My mother is a strong-minded woman. She has decided that the first one will be a boy. I don't think she'd countenance the change."

"I'm kind of strong-minded myself, and recently I've been thinking that perhaps I'd prefer a girl. I think you'd like a girl, David. Girls are gentle and kind and—"

"Strong-minded."

"Of course, if it were a girl," she went on, "I'd have to name her after my Aunt Hetty. I'd *have* to. Uncle Zachary would never forgive me if I didn't."

"And I'd never forgive you if you did. It's too big a handicap for a girl, and it's asking too much of a new father. Perhaps if the fifth or sixth child should be a girl— By then I'd be an old hand as a parent and more able to take the name in stride."

"But Aunt Hetty has been dead barely a year, and there's no one else who can name a child for her. Certainly Dot is not likely to have any more children. Even if it's a boy, and we name him Jonathan, I'll have a hard time explaining to my uncle why we didn't call him something like Harry or Henry or Herbert."

"And how would that constitute naming him after your Aunt Hetty?"

"Well, it's the same initial."

"Talk about silly superstitions. When we name a child, the father is called up for the Reading of the Torah, and then a blessing is made in the Hebrew name of the child. The Hebrew name is always a combination of the given name and the name of the father. Your aunt's name was what? Hepzibah? So she was Hepzibah *bas* Joshua. She was your father's sister, wasn't she?"

"His oldest sister."

"Fine. Now if we named our boy after her, he would have to be something like Hillel—Hillel *ben* David. Now does Hillel *ben* David in any way match Hepzibah *bas* Joshua?"

She was troubled. "But if the baby should be a girl, we could name it after my aunt and call her Harriet or Helen—"

"Or we could call her Sally and say that we were matching the last letter of the name rather than the first."

She glanced at him doubtfully. "Would that be quite the same?"

"It would certainly be just as sensible." His face softened. "As you know, every Jewish child has two names: a Hebrew name which is used in the temple and is primarily for religious purposes, such as for naming or being called up to the Reading, or Bar Mitzvah, or marriage; and an English name which is normally the English equivalent, such as Moses for Mosheh. When we go beyond that simple rule, we are apt to do something silly, as when we give children the name Harold or Henry from Zevi because Zevi means deer and the Yiddish-German word for deer is Hirsh. Harold, however, means something entirely different. It means champion. So we call a child a champion when we intended to call him a deer because the Yiddish word for deer begins with an H. Or take this name, Ytschak. The normal English equivalent is Isaac, but a lot of Jews, feeling Isaac sounded too Jewish, used Isidore instead because it had the same initial, not realizing that the only Isidore of any historic significance was the Archbishop of Seville. That's almost like naming a child Adolph instead of Aaron from the Hebrew Aharon.

"The English name is the one that the child will use for ninety-nine percent of his life. So the obviously intelligent thing to do is to select a name you like that will not be a burden to the child and will be fairly euphonious in conjunction with his surname. Then pick a Hebrew name on the same principle and don't worry whether the two match or not. So if it's a girl, you could call her Hepzibah, which is a very pretty name in Hebrew, and that would take care of your Aunt Hetty. And you could use precisely the same name for her English name, or you could call her Ruth or Naomi or any other name you happened to like."

"Minna Robinson suggested we ought to use a Hebrew name for both—I mean, give the English name the Hebrew pronunciation instead of translating it. It's rather fashionable now."

"You mean call him Yonason instead of Jonathan? And how about the surname, Small? In Hebrew that's *koton*. There's an idea—Yonason Cotton, or even Jonathan Cotton. Now there's a real New England name for you. Say, I wonder if Cotton Mather was originally Little Mather."

"Look, if you don't finish so we can get over to the Schwarzes, your name will be neither Small nor Cotton, but Mud. We were due there ten minutes ago."

10

"And now," said Schwarz, "I want to show you two something."

There had been a great crush of people when they arrived, but the crowd thinned out until around midnight just the two of them were left. Ethel Schwarz served tea and cookies as they sat around the dining-room table and held a general post-mortem on the High Holy Day services: on the rabbi's sermons, on the cantor's singing, on the faulty public-address system, on the disorder during the Reading. And through it all, much to the rabbi's surprise, Schwarz had been pleasant and cordial; but now, he felt, they had come to the real reason the president insisted they remain after the others had gone.

"This is my study," Schwarz called over his shoulder as he led them down a hall. "I do a lot of work here." He stood aside to let his guests enter. The room had no books but against one wall there were a large tilt drafting table and a broad cabinet with drawers for storing blue-prints. But what attracted their attention was the table in the center of the room—on which was a pasteboard replica of the temple done to scale. Even the landscaping had been reproduced, the grass made of green fuzzy material, the shrubbery of twigs and wrapped wire, the wall setting off the parking lot a piece of cardboard painted to repre-sent rough fieldstone. There were even a few plaster of Paris manikins to give some idea of the size of the structure.

"It's lovely," exclaimed Miriam.

"Seventy hours of work," said Schwarz. "But you haven't seen the best part." He led them around the table. Abutting the rear wall of the temple was a small structure which the rabbi guessed was the chapel Schwarz had mentioned. Slightly lower than the parent build-ing, it had a parabolic dome suggesting the architecture in the Holy

Land. A portico in front was supported by a row of columns—twin cylinders, obviously intended to represent Torah Scrolls.

"How do you like it?" asked Schwarz. And without waiting for an answer, he went on, "It's rich; it's classic. It's simple and it's elegant. How about using the Scrolls as supporting columns? Could anything be more natural, more right? You've seen Jewish temples and synagogues using Greek columns, and Byzantine temples and Colonial temples. And all the time we've had the Scroll, which couldn't be more suitable—and beautiful. The cylinder, of course, gives the greatest support with the greatest economy of material. It is naturally graceful. So why do we have to borrow from the Greeks when we have in the Scroll a double cylinder, if you please—the greatest symbol of our religion?

"Next, look at the portico. Have you ever thought of the significance of the portico, Rabbi? In our present building we have a door—that's all." His voice was contemptuous. "You're either in or you're out. How does that jibe with our services and prayer habits? On the High Holy Days, for example, we're in and out all day long. And on Friday nights or Saturdays, don't we stand around after the services and *schmoos* a while? Now do you see the significance of the portico? It's in *and* out. It's a stopping-off place, a lingering place. It expresses our reluctance to leave the temple when the service is over."

"It certainly is an—interesting concept," the rabbi said. "But doesn't it—well, change the general effect of the original building?"

"You bet it does," said Schwarz. "But it doesn't clash, it blends with it. That was part of the problem. If I had a free hand, if I didn't have to take into account Christian Sorenson's phony modernism—" he broke off abruptly. "You know, when the temple was first organized and they selected committees I was a little surprised not to be put on the Building Committee. Surprised, and frankly a little annoyed. After all, I was the only member of the congregation who was a practicing architect. Once I even mentioned it casually to Jake Wasserman, and he said he suggested my name but the committee said we'd be putting up a permanent building in the not too distant future, and since I would probably be called on to submit a design, how would it look if I were on the committee that made the final selection? Fair enough. So then they decide to build. I couldn't very well submit a design, out of the blue, so to speak. After all, I'm not a youngster just out of college—I'm an established architect; I expect to be invited to submit. You'll hear around that Mort Schwarz is only interested in the buck, but I assure you I didn't care about this commission for the money in it. I wouldn't have charged them one red cent beyond my out-of-pocket expenses.

But not a whisper, not a murmur. After a while, I swallowed my pride and made a few inquiries and was told the project was still a long way off—they were holding things close to their chests, the gang that was in power the first year. And the next thing I knew, they had engaged Christian Sorenson, a Gentile if you please, to build the temple. You get it? I can't serve on the Building Committee because I'm an architect and would naturally be called on to submit a design, and then I'm kept from submitting a design."

Miriam shook her head sympathetically.

"I'm not blaming Jake Wasserman. He's all right, threw me a bone, as a matter of fact, and put me on the Board because of all the work I'd done for the temple—but that runaway Building Committee . . . Did you ever stop to think, Rabbi, what it means to a Jewish architect? The anti-Semitism that was common, at least up until recently, in medicine, or in banking, or in big business—it was nothing compared to my field, architecture. It's a little better now, I understand, but do you know what chance a Jew had of getting placed with one of the big firms of architects? Just exactly zero, and it wouldn't make any difference if he were top man in his class, yes, and was willing to start as a draftsman."

"I had no idea it was that bad," said Miriam.

"You bet, and it was the time of the Depression, too, which didn't help any. But you struggle and somehow or other you serve your apprenticeship and you get your experience, and you finally take the plunge and open up your own office. You're full of ideas and artistic ideals. You want to build something worthwhile, that people will see, that might be written up and pictured in architectural journals. You're trying to make a reputation. And what do you get? A block of stores, a job of redesigning standard plans for a bunch of cracker boxes in a cheap real-estate development like Colonial Village, a factory, a warehouse. And it can't be experimental because then your client starts to worry whether the bank will advance the mortgage money, or whether it won't detract from the price if he should want to sell."

"But isn't that true of many people?" the rabbi asked gently. "They have to compromise to make a living."

"Right, Rabbi. It's a living and you're not hungry anymore, but suddenly you're fifty years old. You're not a youngster anymore and you've drawn a lot of plans in your time, and you're not satisfied. And then your chance comes along. Your own community is going to build a temple. In the trade journals you've seen pictures of big new projects, some of them designed by people you went to school with and didn't think much of. Now at last you've got a chance to show what you can do. And what happens? They bring in a phony, and because he's associated with a well-known firm that has built a couple of churches he gets the job."

"Well—"

"But now I'm president of the temple, and that makes me chairman ex officio of the Building Committee and I will not be denied." And he slammed his hand down on the table.

The rabbi was embarrassed by the president's emotion. "But a building like that, I would imagine would cost a lot of money."

"Old man Goralsky will provide it. I'm sure of it. I've spoken to him; I've described and explained my design, and he likes the idea."

"And do we really need it?"

"How can you talk that way, Rabbi? It isn't a matter of mere need. This is a thing of the spirit. For a community to build an edifice like this is an act of religious dedication. Visit the great cathedrals of Europe and ask yourself how many were actually needed. Ethel and I went to Europe last summer with the Wolffs. Took the grand tour, and believe you me it was an eye-opener. And you know what really got me—me a believing Jew and president of a temple, at that? The churches, the cathedrals! And not just because of the architecture, although naturally that interested me. It was something else. You'd come into some church like Santa Croce in Firenze—that's Florence—and on the walls there are Giotto frescoes, and the ceilings are painted beams, and the walls are lined with tombs of famous artists and scientists— Michelangelo, Rossini, Galileo—Charlie Wolff said to me, and he's only a dress manufacturer, 'Mort, that was to me a religious experience.' And I felt the same way. And Ethel did too, didn't you?"

"Oh, I did, Rabbi. I felt—how shall I put it—spiritually uplifted."

"So I thought, why them and not us? Why can't we—why can't I— build a temple that will give our people some of that same feeling, that same uplift, as Ethel says? That's something that's been missing in our temples. The old ones are nothing and the new ones are like Sorenson's phony designs."

"Sometimes," the rabbi said slowly, "we tend to confuse aesthetic with religious experiences."

"I'm afraid, Ethel," said Schwarz with a bitter smile, "our rabbi is not too enthusiastic about our project."

The rabbi colored. "It would be hypocritical of me if I were to say I had no interest in the appearance and size of the synagogue where I was serving. The physical plant is a rough indication of the size and importance of the community, and naturally as a young man not without ambition I prefer to be associated with a large, growing, vigorous community rather than one on the decline. When friends of mine, former classmates at the seminary, come to visit me, I am not unmindful of their appreciation of our synagogue with all that implies. But size for the sake of size? When there is no need? Not even in the foreseeable future? Barnard's Crossing is a small community, and even at Kol Nidre, when temples and synagogues are traditionally crowded, we have empty seats. And that is only one night in the year.

"That you want to perform an act of spiritual dedication does you great credit, Mr. Schwarz, but it is only fair to point out that what you propose is not in the general direction of our tradition. Those churches, full of marvelous statues and paintings—to the worshipers they are holy. The buildings themselves are holy. The ground on which they stand is hallowed ground. But this is not our way. We are subject to the commandment, Thou shalt not make unto thyself any graven image. Our synagogues and temples—the piles of masonry, I mean— are not in themselves holy, only the words that are said there. For a long time, we got along very well housing the Ark of the Lord in only a tent."

"I'm not interested in sermons, Rabbi," said Schwarz coldly. "Are you trying to tell me that you plan to tout Goralsky off the project?"

"I certainly have no intention of seeking him out, but if he were to ask my opinion I would have to be candid with him."

"You'd say you were opposed to it?"

The rabbi temporized. "It would depend on what he asked."

"And what do you mean by that?"

"If he were to ask if I had any objection to the new chapel I would tell him, of course, that adding it to the main structure is not contrary to either our doctrine or our tradition." He shrugged. "If, however, he were to ask if I thought it necessary, I could not in all conscience say I did. And if he were to ask if I thought it was a worthy project, a worthy use of the money, I would have to tell him that I could think of dozens of uses to which the money could be better put."

"Of all the smug, sanctimonious!—" Schwarz shook his head angrily. "You know, that's what comes of giving a man too much security. When they first proposed giving him a five-year contract, I opposed it, and by God I knew what I was doing."

"He doesn't mince words, our rabbi," said Ethel as she loaded the dishwasher. "What I don't understand is that it's all meant for him. I mean, that sanctuary would really be his—I'd think he'd like his own chapel instead of the public auditorium."

"That's just the point. In a sense I *was* doing it for him. At least, he's the one who will benefit most from it. Why wouldn't he want it? I'll tell you why—it's just to defy me. There can't be any other reason."

"Well, I don't know what he had in mind, but it seems pretty bad manners on his part. I mean, as our guest, the least he could have done was say it was nice. Even if he didn't like it, he could have been sort of noncommittal."

"That's what I'm telling you. That's just my point. He went out of his way to be unnecessarily unpleasant. And that can only mean that he was opposing me on personal grounds. Maybe he's sore about my voting against him on the new contract, and is trying to get back at me."

"Do you think he'll talk to Goralsky about it?"

"He'd better not, that's all I can say. He'd better not. Because if he does, then contract or no contract, this place will be too hot to hold him."

"It wouldn't have hurt to show some enthusiasm, David. He was trying so hard to be nice and friendly, the least you could have done was to compliment him on the design."

"Honestly, Miriam, I tried, but the words stuck in my throat. I kept thinking how ridiculous the temple would look with that what did he call it? rich, simple, elegant, classic monstrosity along with his *schmoosing* gallery, and the words wouldn't come out. Sorenson's design may not be much, but it is simple and it has an austere grace that Schwarz wants to spoil just so he can show he can build something besides a supermarket. We need a chapel about as much as we need a bowling alley. We don't need the extra space. And when the sanctuary is used for secular purposes, there's no reason we can't put a simple screen in front of the Ark as they do in other synagogues. Don't you see, he wasn't interested in improving the temple—only in advertising himself."

"All I see is that he was trying to be friendly, and you turned him down."

"I couldn't buy his friendship on that basis. I don't think for a moment that Goralsky would ask my opinion, but if he did I couldn't give him a false impression just to curry favor with Schwarz." He could see she was still unconvinced. "Look, Miriam, as the rabbi of the congregation, a sort of public figure, I have to be nice to all kinds of people. I have to pretend an interest in things that truthfully don't interest me at all. I have to busy myself with matters that aren't worth the time I spend on them. And I do it. No matter how much I resent it, I do it. I do it because in some small way, they help the congregation or the community. But if I gushed all over Schwarz about how wonderful his design was, and how wonderful it would be for the congregation to have a little jewel of a chapel which could never be profaned by anything mundane or secular, and if I assured him that I would back him to the hilt in dealing with Goralsky, then I'd be doing it just to get in good with him, to make my job more secure, and that I couldn't do."

"I don't think the design is really so bad," she said tentatively.

"By itself, no. It's a little fancy for my taste, but well within the range of acceptability if it stood alone. But when you slap it up against the wall of our present structure, don't you see what the effect would be? The two buildings don't blend. They clash. And because our present structure is simple with clean lines, and the proposed building is ornate and fancy, he's hoping that people will make the comparison. What he's saying in effect is, 'See what you would have got if you had engaged me originally.'"

Still she did not answer. Her silence made him uncomfortable. "What is it, Miriam? What's troubling you? Are you worried about what Schwarz can do?"

"Oh, David, you know I've gone along with you in every important decision. After you got your degree, when you turned down that job in Chicago that paid so much money because you didn't like the kind of congregation it seemed to be, I didn't say a word although we were living on my salary as a typist—that and whatever occasional fees you got as a fill-in rabbi for the High Holy Days in small towns. And then there was the job at a good salary down in Louisiana that was the right kind of congregation but which you refused because you felt you couldn't serve effectively in the South. Then there was the job as assistant rabbi in that Cleveland temple that paid more than most full rabbi jobs, but you said you didn't want to serve under someone else and have to subordinate your own thinking to his. It was near the end of the hiring season, and you yourself felt that Hanslick was getting tired of offering you jobs you kept turning down. And it was I who urged you to turn it down; I told you I didn't mind continuing my job and that I loved our little one-room basement apartment that was so cold in the winter and hot in the summer, and doing all the shopping and the cooking—"

"I did some of the shopping and the cooking," he protested.

"But when you did it, the clerks always gave you the worst—the vegetables that were just starting to rot—and the butcher, that kosher butcher on the corner—I'll bet his eyes lit up when he saw you come in—all the fat and bones and gristle, and you couldn't even remember to take off the roast until it started to burn—" She began to laugh.

"Do you remember that time when you started to cut away the burnt part and I said I liked meat well done, and you said you could eat any kind of meat but you couldn't stand a liar, and you went out and bought some delicatessen?"

"Yes"—and he, too, started laughing—"and remember the time—" He broke off. "But what are you getting at?"

"Just that in those days it didn't make any difference."

"And now is it different? Since living in Barnard's Crossing, have I been buying two-hundred-dollar suits and alligator shoes?"

"You need a new suit, and the collars on half your shirts are frayed—"

"Stick to the point, woman," he cried in exasperation.

"The point is, that was all right when there were just two of us. But I'm carrying a child and I feel responsible for it."

"For *him,* and I'm responsible. Are you worried that I might lose my job and not be able to make a living for my wife and child? Don't worry. As long as we haven't developed a taste for luxury, then if not this job, another. And if not another pulpit, then a teaching job. And if I can't get that, then a job as a bookkeeper in an office, or a clerk in a store. These days there's always some job for a man who is willing to work. Remember, a rabbi doesn't have to have a pulpit to be a rabbi. Traditionally, we don't even approve of being paid for one's learning. 'One should not use the Torah as a spade to dig with.' But don't think that I haven't thought about it.

"I'm aware of my responsibilities. And I'm aware of the added burden that will fall on our child as a rabbi's son. I am a rabbi's son and I know what it means. Because your father is a public figure, everyone expects more of you, and you feel guilty when you don't come up to expectations. As a youngster, you can't imagine how often I wished my father owned a shoe store or went to work in an office like the fathers of the other boys. Believe me, I envied the boys whose fathers earned a living in the ordinary way. But there were compensations, and much of it was fun. When I went to the synagogue on a Friday night with my mother, and I saw my father in the pulpit conducting the service, delivering his sermons, I always felt that the synagogue was ours, that I was being taken there as other boys were occasionally taken to their father's offices on Saturday.

"But when I got a little older and would overhear, and partly understand, the talk of men such as Schwarz—and don't think my father didn't have his Schwarzes—every rabbi does—then it wasn't so pleasant. A rabbi is a public servant, and anyone who has many masters can't expect to please them all. Once I asked my father about something I overheard—some controversy he was having with the members of his synagogue at the time—and he smiled at me and said, 'In this life you sometimes have to choose between pleasing God and pleasing man. And in the long run, it's better to please God—He's more apt to remember.' After that, I wasn't bothered so much. Whenever I heard an uncomplimentary remark about my father, I figured he had chosen to please God again."

"Oh, David, I don't want you to do anything you think is wrong. Only—" she looked up at him—"please couldn't we please God *after* the baby is born?"

II

Precisely at noon the next day a cab pulled up to the door and out stepped a slim, boyish-looking man in his early forties. Dr. Ronald Sykes had a long narrow face with thinning dark hair; it was an intelligent face with shrewd knowing eyes and a ready smile. He was wearing stout English boots, gray flannels, and a tweed jacket. If the hair had been a little thicker, the face a little fuller, and the eyes somewhat less knowing, he could have passed for an undergraduate.

"I came to see you in behalf of my late friend and colleague, Isaac Hirsh," he said when they were seated in the rabbi's study, "You heard of his death of course."

"I don't believe I knew an Isaac Hirsh," the rabbi said with a tinge of embarrassment. "He wasn't a member of my congregation, was he?"

"No, Rabbi, but he did live here and was part of the Jewish community, so I thought you might know him."

The rabbi shook his head slowly.

"Well, he died Friday night, and his wife, or rather his widow, would like to arrange for him to have a Jewish funeral. Is that possible—I mean where he was not a member of your congregation?"

"Oh, yes. Although our cemetery is reserved for members of the congregation, we make provision for Jews in the community who are not members. Upon paying a small fee they are accorded nominal membership, which of course is exclusive of the price of a lot. However, as a resident of Barnard's Crossing, Mr. Hirsh can be buried in the town cemetery, Grove Hill, which is nonsectarian. I don't know what fees would be involved, but I could give him Jewish burial there just as well."

The doctor shook his head. "No, I think Mrs. Hirsh would want him buried among his own kind. Mrs. Hirsh is not Jewish."

"Oh."

"Does that make a difference?" Sykes asked quickly.

"It might." The rabbi hesitated. "In that case, I'd have to be sure that the deceased had in fact been a Jew—that is, had remained a Jew."

"I'm not sure I understand. His wife considers him a Jew. As long as I knew him, which is only this past year, to be sure, he never pretended to be anything else."

The rabbi smiled. "It's a religious rather than an ethnic distinction. Anyone born of a Jewish mother, not father if you please, is automatically considered Jewish, provided"—he paused to emphasize the point— "that he has not repudiated his religion by conversion to another religion or by public disclaimer."

"To the best of my knowledge he belonged to no other church."

"But you said Mrs. Hirsh was not Jewish. Was she Catholic or Protestant?"

"I don't know. Anglican, I think, originally. At least the Anglican minister came to pay his respects while I was there."

"Well, you see how it is. If they had come to me and asked me to marry them, I would have refused unless she converted. So perhaps the late Mr. Hirsh was converted when they were married. Tell me, why didn't Mrs. Hirsh come, or send for me herself?"

"The shock of her husband's death, Rabbi. As a matter of fact, she's been kept under mild sedation. So as his section head, his boss you might say, she naturally turned to me to make the arrangements. And as for his religious status, I can only say I very much doubt if he would have undergone even nominal conversion to marry. He never cared much for all this mumbo jumbo—" he checked himself. "I'm sorry, Rabbi, but those were his words; I was quoting him." He had a sudden thought. "His name, Isaac, is essentially Jewish. He didn't change that, so wouldn't that indicate how he felt?"

The rabbi smiled. "You must have noticed when Mrs. Small opened the door that we are expecting a child. So our interest in names is more than just academic. We were just talking about that and decided the name Isaac, these days, is as likely to be pure Yankee."

Sykes spread his hands in token of defeat. "Well, all I can say is that I feel he had no religious affiliations. Poor devil, he would have been better off if he had. He might have been alive today if he like the rest of the Jews had gone to temple Friday night."

"Then his death was unexpected?"

"He was found dead in his garage Friday night. Patricia Hirsh notified me the next day, and I came right over."

"Heart attack?"

"Carbon monoxide poisoning."

"Oh." The rabbi, who had been lounging back in his chair, now leaned forward. His face became thoughtful and his fingers drummed a soft tattoo on the desk.

"You're thinking of suicide, Rabbi? Would that make a difference?"

"It might."

"I suppose it could be suicide," said Sykes slowly, "although there was no note, and if he were going to take his own life, you'd think he'd have left some word for his wife. He was very fond of her. The police officially called it accidental death. You see, he had been drinking heavily—"

"You mean he was drunk?"

"Must have been. He had gone through half a bottle of vodka, about a pint, in a pretty short time. He probably blacked out, and the motor kept running."

"He was a heavy drinker?"

"He was an alcoholic, Rabbi, but as long as he had been with us he was all right. It's not that they drink much—only that when they start, they can't stop."

"And this did not interfere with his work? By the way, what was his work?"

"He was a mathematician in my unit at the Goddard Research and Development Laboratory."

The rabbi nodded thoughtfully. "Our people don't run to alcoholism. I am rather surprised that considering this—this affliction, that you hired him."

"Well, there aren't too many mathematicians kicking around, at least not of the stature of Isaac Hirsh. It may help to explain our attitude, and perhaps his problem, when I tell you that he was on the original Manhattan Project and worked with Fermi. When we dropped the bomb on Hiroshima, it raised hell with a lot of men there."

"In that case, he must have been well along in years."

"Early fifties, I should say. He got his Ph.D. from M.I.T. in 1935. I got mine same place in '43, in case you are wondering."

"And yet you are the head of the unit and he was your subordinate?"

"Just that I got there first. I went to Goddard as soon as I got my degree."

"Tell me, what did you call him?"

"Eh? Oh, you mean how did I address him?" He flushed. "Mostly, I'd call him Doctor. You see, he was quite a bit older than I. But sometimes when we were just sitting around talking—what was the expression he used? *schmoosing*, that's Yiddish, I guess. He used a lot of Yiddish words from time to time—well, then he would sometimes call me Ronald or Ron, and I'd call him Ike. Most of the time it was Doctor, though, because there are always technicians around and you use first names indiscriminately and after a while the technicians start calling you by your first name and there goes the discipline. At least, that's our director's idea. He's an old army man."

"I see." He thought for a moment. "It would help if I could visit Mrs. Hirsh. Would it be all right if I dropped over this afternoon?"

"I'm sure that will be fine."

"Then perhaps you had better make your arrangements for the cemetery plot. You will have to see the chairman of our Cemetery Committee. If you like, I'll call Mr. Brown. Do you know him, Marvin Brown, insurance business?"

Sykes shook his head. "If he can see me now I'd go right over there. Would you mind calling me a cab?"

"Of course." The rabbi started out the door and then hesitated. "Oh, and by the way, if money is a consideration to the widow, and I suppose it is, a plain undecorated pine box is most correct according to our traditions."

Marvin Brown was a live wire, a go-getter. He was a wiry terrier of a man who knew that time was money and that there were a hundred cents to every dollar. He had long ago learned the supreme lesson of salesmanship, that if you made one sale for every ten calls you could make two sales by making twenty calls. This doctrine he not only preached, he practiced. Over the years, his wife had learned to adjust to his pace. She planned her evening meal for six o'clock, knowing that Marve might not get to it until nine and then he might tell her he had grabbed a bite somewhere and wasn't hungry.

"How do you stand it, Mitzi?" her friends would ask. "It would drive me up a wall if my husband didn't get home at a regular time for his meals. And how does he stand it? Marvin's no youngster, you know. He ought to begin taking it easy."

And it worried Mitzi every now and then, because Marve was almost forty and it seemed to her he was working harder than ever. He had been a member of the Million Dollar Club for four years running now, and although nearly every year his sales earned him a trip to Florida or Mexico or Puerto Rico, even on his vacations he wouldn't relax. Every day he played golf and went for a swim, and then he would see people around the hotel and talk business.

But, as Mitzi reflected, when Marve was out, or when he called to say that he would be home late, she was always sure it was insurance business, not monkey business. As a matter of fact, not only insurance business kept him busy; there were also the temple, and the Parent-Teacher Association of which he was vice-president, and the Community Fund of which he was a district leader. When she protested that with all his own work it was foolish of him to take on more, he pointed out it was really all insurance business. It meant that many more contacts, and the insurance business was all a matter of contacts. But she knew better—she knew he did these things because he liked to be active, he liked to race around. And she had to admit it seemed to be good for him.

"Honest," she would say to her friends, "the children hardly know their father. The only time they can count on seeing him is Sunday morning when he takes them to Sunday school. The rest of the time, they're usually in bed asleep when he gets home." But secretly she was pleased. He was her man and he was working night and day to make a good living for her—just how good was attested by the winter trips, her mink stole, and the shiny black Lincoln they had finally worked up to.

Marvin Brown's success was not due simply to his many contacts. He never went to see a prospective client cold. As he never tired of saying to the salesmen in his office, "Before you go to see your prospect, find out all you can about him." So when his wife told him that a Dr. Sykes would be calling on him, and that the appointment had been arranged by the rabbi, he immediately phoned to find out what it was all about.

"He's acting for the widow of Isaac Hirsh who died Friday night," said the rabbi.

"Did you say Isaac Hirsh? My God, I sold him a policy less than a year ago."

"Really? A life insurance policy? Do you remember for how much?"

"Not offhand. I think it was about twenty-five thousand dollars, but I could look it up. Why?"

"Tell me, Mr. Brown, did he have any difficulty passing the physical?"

"Not that I know of. That doesn't mean anything, though. Some of these doctors don't even touch the patient with a stethoscope. They ask him a few questions and if he looks all right and has a pulse, they pass him. What's it all about, Rabbi? Was it a heart attack?"

"I think the police ruled it accidental death."

"Uh-oh—there's a double indemnity clause for accidental death on most of our policies. It's only a small additional fee, so we usually write them. I guess the widow is mighty happy—I mean, it's a lucky thing for her that he decided to take out the policy, although, as I remember it, I didn't have to do much selling."

"Well, Dr. Sykes is acting for the widow. Mr. Hirsh was not a member of our temple, but his wife would like him buried in a Jewish cemetery according to Jewish rites. She herself is not Jewish."

"I get the picture, Rabbi. Don't worry about a thing. Just leave everything to me."

12

Nothing Sykes said had prepared the rabbi for Mrs. Hirsh. He found her surprisingly young, in her early thirties, for a man in his fifties. And she was tall. Even though her blue eyes were swollen from weeping he found them attractive, and her red hair was striking. At first he thought she looked flashy. Although she was dressed in black, her silk dress had flounces and lawn sleeves hardly appropriate for mourning—but then he realized she probably had not bought it for the occasion and must be wearing it because she had nothing more suitable. Normally of a gay and happy temperament, this would be reflected in her wardrobe.

He introduced himself.

"Oh, come in, Rabbi. Dr. Sykes phoned to say you were going to drop over. Peter Dodge was here earlier, he said he knows you. And the Lutheran minister, Pastor Kal—Kalt—"

"Pastor Kaltfuess."

"That's it, and then there was the Methodist minister and the Unitarian minister, I guess. I sure got a lot of spiritual comfort today."

"They came to console you."

"Oh, I know. And are you, too, going to tell me that Ike's soul is in Heaven or in a better world?"

Because he was aware that grief can take many forms the rabbi was not offended by her bitter flippancy. "I'm afraid we don't peddle that kind of merchandise," he said.

"You mean you don't believe in life after death, in a Hereafter?"

"We believe that his soul lives on in your memory and in the remembrance of his friends and in his influence on their lives. Of course, if he had children, he would live on in them, too."

"Well, that's pretty obvious."

"It doesn't make it any the less true." He paused, reluctant to broach the real reason for his visit. No matter how much experience he had with death, he still had not acquired the professional touch.

But she helped him out. "Dr. Sykes said you wanted to ask me some questions about my husband."

He nodded gratefully. "Burial is a ritual, Mrs. Hirsh, and I must be sure that your husband was a Jew according to our Law. And since he married out of the faith—"

"Does that make him any less a Jew?"

"Not that in itself, but the circumstances might. Tell me, who officiated at your wedding?"

"We were married by a justice of the peace. Do you want to see the license?"

He smiled. "I'll take your word for it."

Impulsively she said, "Forgive me, Rabbi. I've been bitchy, haven't I?"

"A little, and now you're trying to shock me."

She smiled. "All right, let's start again. Ask me any questions at all."

He settled back in his chair. "All right, why do you want to give him a Jewish burial?"

"Because Ike was a Jew. He never thought of himself as anything else."

"And yet he never practiced our religion, I understand."

"Well, he always said there were two ways of being a Jew. You could be one by practicing the religion or just by being born and thinking of yourself as a Jew. Was he wrong?"

"No," said the rabbi cautiously, "but a Jewish funeral is a religious ceremony. Would he have wanted that?"

"I know it can be done by a funeral director, but what connection would he have with Ike? No, this is what he would have wanted. We never discussed it, of course. For himself, he probably wouldn't have cared. But out of respect for my feelings, I think he would have wanted some kind of ceremony. And what could have any meaning for him except a Jewish ceremony?"

"I see. All right, I'll perform the service. It's customary to say a few words at the grave. But I didn't know your husband. So you'll have to tell me about him. He was quite a bit older, wasn't he? Were you happy together?"

"Twenty years, but we were happy." She thought a moment. "He was good to me. And I was good for him. As for his being so much older—

well, I had had enough of the other before I met him. He needed me and I needed him. Yes, I think we had a good marriage."

The rabbi hesitated and then took the plunge. "I understand his death was due indirectly to his—to his drinking. Didn't it bother you—his drinking, I mean?"

"That really bugs you people, doesn't it? Well, it bothered Ike a lot, too. Oh, of course it made things hard sometimes. He lost jobs because of it, and sometimes we had to move and that's not easy, making new arrangements and finding a new place to live. But it didn't frighten me the way it might some. He was never ugly when he was drunk, and that's what counts—more weak and silly like, and would cry like a child. But never ugly and never nasty to me. And it didn't really bother me. My father was a heavy drinker, and my mother was no teetotaler. So I was kind of used to it. Later on, when he got worse and began to black out—that was frightening, but I was frightened *for* him because there was no knowing what might happen to him."

"And did that happen often?"

She shook her head. "The last couple or three years he never touched a drop, except once or twice when he got started and couldn't stop. I mean, he didn't drink regularly. He was on the wagon, but whenever he fell off it was all the way. The last time was months and months ago."

"Except for Friday night."

"Yes, I forgot about that." She closed her eyes, and the rabbi was afraid she was going to break down. But she opened her eyes and even managed a smile.

He rose, as if to signify he had finished. Then he thought of something. "Could you tell when one of these spells was coming on?"

She shook her head.

"Can you account for his suddenly starting to drink? Was something bothering him?"

Again she shook her head. "I guess he was always bothered about something. That's why people drink, I suppose. I would try to comfort him—you know, make him feel I was always there and would always understand."

"Perhaps you were better for him than he was for you," suggested the rabbi gently.

"We were good for each other," she said emphatically. "I told you he was always kind to me. Look, Rabbi, I was no innocent when I met Ike. I had been around. He was the first man I had known who was nice to me with no strings attached. And I was good to him; I took care of him like a mother."

"And yet he drank."

"That started before I met him. And I'm not sorry," she added defiantly, "because that's how I met him."

"So?"

"He had holed up at this little hotel where I was working on the cigar counter in the lobby. If he hadn't been on a bender, how could the likes of me have met a man like him?"

"And you feel you got the best of the bargain?"

"It was the best kind of bargain there is, Rabbi, where both parties feel they've got the best of it."

13

"Yeah, this is Ben Goralsky talking. All right, I'll hold on . . . Hello, hello . . ." At the other end he could hear someone talking, and then he realized the voice was not talking to him but to someone else in the other room at the other end.

"Mr. Goralsky? Ted Stevenson speaking."

"Oh, hello Ted, nice to hear your voice. Where you calling from?"

"From our offices."

"On Sunday? Don't you guys ever stop working?"

"There are no regular hours and no days off for top management in this company, Mr. Goralsky, not when there's important business to be done. And if you join us, you'll work the same way."

Goralsky had an inkling of the purpose of the call, and the implication of the "if" was not lost on him.

"We were going to call you yesterday, as a matter of fact," Stevenson went on, "but we knew it was your holiday and assumed you would be at your synagogue."

"Well, as a matter of fact, I didn't go. I was right here all the time. My father took sick, and with a man that age—"

"Oh, I'm sorry to hear that. How is he?"

"He's all right now, but for a while it was kind of like touch and go."

"Well, I'm delighted to hear he's on the mend. Give the old gentleman our regards and best wishes for his recovery."

"Thanks. He'll be pleased."

The voice at the other end shifted gears abruptly. "We have been somewhat disturbed over here, Mr. Goralsky, over the action of your stock in the last week or so."

"Yeah, well, Ted, you know how it is. Rumors of a merger get out.

We tried to keep it mum at this end, and as far as I know no one here has leaked. But when your crew came down, someone may have recognized somebody in your party—I tell you, when it first got back to me, you could have knocked me over with a feather. But I guess that's the way it is in these things—"

"No, Mr. Goralsky, that's not the way it is. We know that there always are rumors preceding a merger, and that can affect your stock. But your stock has climbed so precipitously, we did a little investigating. We inquired among some of our good friends in the market down in Boston, and we learned that the reason for the climb was not the rumor of a merger with us but some new process."

"Well, that turned out to be a dud, I guess," said Ben unhappily.

"So we discovered on further inquiry. Of course these things happen from time to time in any R and D program, but if we thought that it was deliberately engineered for the purpose of increasing the value of your stock preliminary to the merger, we would regard that as—er—sharp practice, and would be forced to reconsider the entire proposition."

"And I wouldn't blame you Mr. Stevenson, but I give you my word—"

The other cut him off unceremoniously. "We're not interested in explanations or excuses. What we want from you is . . ."

When Ben finally hung up, he was dripping with perspiration. For a long time thereafter he sat staring at the telephone.

14

The rabbi had intended to go right home after seeing Mrs. Hirsh, but once outside and behind the wheel of his car he found himself driving in the opposite direction, downtown, and presently he was caught in the maze of narrow crooked streets of Old Town. After two turns he got lost and turned up one street and down another in the hope of finding himself on familiar ground; but each time he thought he spotted a house he knew, the road curved another way. Perched on a hill tantalizingly close he could see the town hall which was on familiar territory, yet none of the streets seemed to lead toward it. All the while, he caught kaleidoscopic glimpses of lovely old-fashioned gardens hidden behind charming weather-beaten houses, most of them with a golden eagle over the door lintel, interesting shops of handcrafters and artists, and most fascinating of all, the ship chandler's shop with its windows stuffed with fascinating gear—brass compasses, coils of nylon rope, bells, curiously shaped nautical fittings of mysterious function, and, incongruously, a pair of stout rubber boots.

Suddenly he found himself on an extremely narrow street which had cars parked on both sides and traffic going in both directions. He slowed down to worm his way through and his car stalled. Horns blared behind him as he twisted the key viciously; the only response was the high-pitched whine of the starting motor. As he pumped the gas pedal in vexation, a voice at his side said, "You've probably flooded it, Rabbi."

He looked up and was tremendously relieved to see Hugh Lanigan. The local chief of police was wearing a sport shirt and chinos, and under his arm he had the Sunday paper.

"Here, let me try it."

The rabbi set the brake and moved over so that the other could get in. Whether because those behind recognized the chief or they realized the offending driver was in genuine difficulty, the blaring horns stopped. The chief pressed the accelerator all the way to the floor, turned the key, and miraculously the motor caught.

He grinned at the rabbi. "How about a drink at our place?"

"I'd love one. You drive."

"All right." Effortlessly Lanigan threaded the maze between oncoming and parked cars, and when he reached his house he ran the right wheels up on the sidewalk to obstruct as little of the road as possible. Opening the gate of his white picket fence he marched the rabbi up the walk and short flight of steps that led to the verandah. He shouted through the screen door, "We got some company, Gladys."

"Coming," his wife shouted back from inside, and a moment later appeared at the door. She was dressed in slacks and sweater and looked as though she had just finished helping her husband with the lawn. But her white hair was carefully combed and her makeup was fresh. "Well, this is a pleasant surprise, Rabbi Small," she said and held out her hand. "You'll join us in a drink? I was just fixing Manhattans."

"That will do very nicely," said the rabbi with a grin.

"I can't help thinking," said the rabbi, as she left to prepare them, "that on the few occasions I have called on you it always starts with a drink—"

"Spirits for the spiritual, Rabbi."

"Yes, but when you dropped in on me, I always offered you tea."

"At the rate I was coming around it was just as well," said Lanigan. "Besides, I was usually on business, and I don't drink during business hours."

"Tell me, were you ever drunk?"

The chief stared at him. "Why, of course. Haven't you ever been?"

The rabbi shook his head. "And didn't Mrs. Lanigan mind?"

Chief Lanigan laughed. "Gladys has been kind of high herself on occasion. No, why would she mind? It isn't as though I've ever been really blind drunk. Always it's been on some special occasion where it's kind of expected. Why? What are you getting at?"

"I have just been to see Mrs. Hirsh—"

"Ah-hah."

"And I'm just trying to understand. Her husband was an alcoholic, and that's something I haven't had much experience with. We Jews don't run to alcoholism."

"That's true, you don't. I wonder why."

The rabbi shrugged his shoulders. "I don't know. The Chinese and the Italians also have low incidences of alcoholism, yet none of us are teetotalers. As far as Jews are concerned, all our holidays and celebrations involve drinking. At the Passover feast, everyone is expected to drink at least four glasses of wine. Even the young children partake. It's sweet, but the alcoholic content is there nonetheless. You can get drunk on it, but I can't remember any Passover when anyone did. Maybe the very fact that we do not forbid it enables us to enjoy it in moderation. For us, it doesn't carry the joys of forbidden fruits."

"In France, I understand, they drink wine as freely as water, but they have a lot of alcoholism there."

"That's true. I don't suppose there's any single explanation. There are certain similarities among the three groups that do encourage speculation. All have a strong family tradition that might provide a sense of security other people may look for in alcohol. The Chinese, especially, feel about their elders somewhat as we do. You know, we have a saying that other people boast of the beauty of their women; we boast of our old men."

"Well, that might apply to the Italians, too—respect for elders, I mean, although they seem to lean more toward the mother than the father. But how does that help?"

"Simply that the embarrassment of being seen drunk might act as a deterrent in societies where elders are greatly revered."

"Possible," Lanigan said judiciously.

"But there's another explanation—and here we share a similarity with the Chinese. Their religion, like ours, emphasizes ethics, morals, and good behavior; and like us they attach less importance to faith than you Christians. This helps to keep us from being guilt-ridden."

"What's faith got to do with it?"

"In Christianity, it's the key to salvation. And faith is not easy to maintain at all times. To believe is to question. The very act of affirming implies a doubt."

"I don't get it."

"We don't have that much control of our minds. Thoughts come unbidden—unpleasant thoughts, awful thoughts—and if you believed that doubt could lead to damnation, you'd be apt to feel guilty a good part of the time. And one place you might find solace would be in alcohol."

Lanigan smiled easily. "Yes, but any mature, intelligent person knows how the mind works and discounts it."

"Any intelligent, mature person, yes. But how about the immature?"

"I see, so you think one reason Jews don't become alcoholics is because they don't have guilt feelings?"

"It's a theory. I'm just speculating idly while waiting for a drink."

"Gladys," Lanigan bawled. "What are you doing in there? The rabbi is dying of thirst."

"Coming."

She appeared with a tray of glasses and a pitcher. "You can replenish your glass whenever you've a mind to, Rabbi."

"And how about Isaac Hirsh?" asked Lanigan as he raised his glass in silent toast to his guest. "As I understand it, he didn't have any interest in the Jewish religion, let alone the Christian."

"But he may have felt guilt. At least so thinks his superior, a Dr. Sykes. He suggested he may have become an alcoholic because of the work he did on the bomb dropped on Hiroshima."

"That so? And how are you involved? Was Hirsh a member of your congregation?"

"No, but his widow thought he should be buried in our cemetery."

"I think I'm beginning to see. You're wondering if it really was an accident, or if it was suicide. You people have the same attitude toward suicide that we have—I mean as far as burial is concerned?"

"Not quite. In a sense, our practice is similar to yours. The suicide is not publicly mourned, no eulogy is said, and he is supposed to be buried off to one side rather than in the main part of the cemetery. But your church is a large authoritarian organization—"

"And what difference would that make?"

"Just that there's a sort of hierarchy, a chain of command that tends to keep the rules of the church uniform."

"And you are your own boss. Is that it?"

"Something like that. At least no religious body passes on my decision."

"So if the rabbi is easygoing and soft-hearted—"

"He still has his own integrity to live up to," said the rabbi firmly. "But apart from that, the philosophical basis for our disapproval of suicide is somewhat different from yours, and that in itself permits greater flexibility."

"How so?"

"Well, the attitude of your church is that each and every one of us was put on this earth to fulfill some divine purpose, and life is essentially a test to determine an individual's eventual destination—Heaven or Hell or Purgatory. So the man who takes his own life is in a sense dodging the test and flouting God's will. For us, on the other hand, life on this earth is the sum total of man's destiny. But we hold that man was created in God's image, and hence to destroy himself is to commit a sort of sacrilege by destroying God's image.

"At the same time, we do not condemn the man who is driven to suicide by reason of insanity or by great pain, grief, or mental anguish. In the Old Testament, there are several suicides whose memories we still honor. Samson for one. He pulled down the pillars of the Philistine temple, you remember. That could be defended on the grounds that it not only killed him but large numbers of Philistines who were the enemy. In a sense, then, his could be regarded as death on the battle-field. King Saul is another example, a more clear-cut case perhaps. After the death of his sons in battle and realizing he was likely to be captured by the enemy, he asked his armor-bearer to run him through with his sword. When he refused, Saul thrust the sword into his bosom with his own hand. Here it has been argued that the suicide was justified on the ground that if he had been captured, the enemy would have made a mockery of him which would have brought great shame and dishonor to the Jewish nation. Then too, there was the certainty his men would have tried to recapture him and that many would have died as a result. So his death could be regarded as a sacrifice to save the lives of his people.

"Martyrdom is really a form of suicide even though the actual blow is not dealt by one's own hand. And starting with Hannah and her seven sons, all of whom died rather than bow down to Greek idols as recorded in Maccabees of the Apocrypha, we have had a long record of martyrdom. It is referred to, in fact, as *kiddush ha-Shem,* the sanctification of the Name. Not all the rabbis were in agreement on the matter. Maimonides, for example, held that it was justifiable to pay lip service to false gods to save one's life. But the general consensus was that there were worse things than suicide; that where a man had to choose between killing himself and killing another, suicide was preferable. So, too, with the woman forced to transgress the commandment 'Thou shalt not commit adultery'; rather than permit herself to be ravished, a woman should commit suicide.

"These attitudes still prevail today. Look at the enormous pride the modern State of Israel, an Orthodox theocracy if you please, takes in the reconstructed fortress of Masada, where, according to Josephus, some nine hundred Jewish defenders were besieged and withstood the might of the Roman armies for several years and then committed suicide en masse rather than be captured and enslaved."

"But if you condone suicide when a man is not in his right mind or when driven to it, what's left?" Lanigan asked. "It seems to me that that would include just about every suicide."

"Well, it certainly gives us a lot of leeway," the rabbi admitted. "But I don't think you'd find many rabbis who would approve of the Japanese practice of hara-kiri, where it is considered proper to take one's life because of some fancied dishonor to one's house or loss of face. Nor would we condone the old Indian practice of suttee where a wife to show her loyalty throws herself on her husband's funeral pyre."

"How about those Buddhist monks who set fire to themselves in Viet Nam? We've even had a couple such cases here."

The rabbi nodded thoughtfully. "That *would* pose quite a problem. My guess is that most modern rabbis would dodge the issue by considering it a form of insanity; on the other hand, a stickler for the rules might treat it as a bona fide suicide on the grounds that it presumed a sound mind and was being done knowingly, out of philosophical conviction."

"Still, there are plenty of loopholes—enough certainly to include Hirsh."

"Then you *do* think it was suicide: Why did you call it accidental death?"

"To answer your second question first, Rabbi, because we couldn't prove it either way. So naturally we called it accidental death, which is kinder to his widow. Remember, suicide is a crime and we can't go labeling a man a criminal with no definite or positive proof."

"And my first question?"

"What was that?"

"I asked whether you thought it was suicide, setting proof aside."

"No, Rabbi, I don't. You tell someone that a man was found dead of carbon monoxide in his garage and the first thing that comes to mind is suicide. But actually, there are plenty of accidental deaths from carbon monoxide. It's pretty tricky stuff. A few years back, a couple of kids parked their car, a leaky old rattrap of a jalopy, right up here near Highland Park. They were just planning on a little fancy necking, but it was midwinter and cold so they kept the motor running to stay warm. The stuff seeped through the car and we found them both dead. It happens all the time. A man goes into the garage to tinker with his car. It's cold, so he keeps the garage closed and passes out. If he's not found in time, he's dead.

"Another thing. You wouldn't think so in a town of this size, but in my time I have seen quite a few suicides. Most of them, curiously enough, are apt to be young people. But there have been grown-ups too. The grown-ups almost always leave a note of some kind. The kids don't for some reason. Maybe they're just trying to make their folks feel sorry. You know that poem by Edwin Arlington Robinson, Rabbi? 'Richard Cory'? About this young fellow who had everything and then for some reason put a bullet through his brain? A bachelor might do that, but somebody who has a family, they usually leave a note."

"Is that your only reason? That Hirsh left no note?"

"There's another reason, although it wouldn't be much good in a court of law. This is a heavy drinking town. We've got a lot of pretty rich people with idle time on their hands, and they drink. Then we've got a lot of high-strung executive types who are busy raising ulcers— and they tend to drink more than is good for them. And finally, we have a bunch of fishermen, and they know what to do with a bottle. Well, I've never known a heavy drinker, what is apt to be called an alcoholic these days, I've never known one of them to commit suicide. I once asked a psychiatrist who was down here for the summer why that was. And do you know what he said? He said they don't commit suicide because they're already doing it. According to him, these alcoholics are really suicides who are doing it the long way. Does that make sense to you, Rabbi?"

"Why, yes, I can understand that. But how about legal proof? Anything?"

"Well, except for the absence of the note and the fact Hirsh was drunk, there's nothing definite. It's the drinking that tips the scales with me. A man taking his life usually does so with a clear head. My experience is that in that last final step he's not thinking about chickening out, because he has thought it through and made up his mind that this is the logical—the only—thing to do.

"Now you look at the facts leading up to his drunk, and they certainly don't seem the pattern of a man determined to commit suicide. In fact, it seems all a grotesque accident.

"When Mrs. Hirsh called in that her husband was missing, we notified the State Police as well as various police departments hereabouts to be on the lookout. A State Police cruising car remembered seeing a car matching the description parked on Route 128 at one of the turnouts not far from the Goddard Lab. So they drove over, and the car was gone. But they found a ball of rumpled paper and cardboard— the wrapper from a vodka bottle. It had a gift card enclosed and was addressed to a party who lives right across the street from Hirsh. A little routine police work showed that the bottle had been delivered after the Levensons—that was the party—had gone off to the temple. The driver asked Hirsh if he would sign for it and give it to the Levensons, and Hirsh agreed."

"I see."

"Now, he wouldn't have taken the wrapper off just to look at the bottle. He must have taken an experimental drink or two. In fact, why else would he have pulled up at the turnoff? He must have started for the lab, and stopped at the turnoff for a drink, then decided to go home and do a good job of it. As a matter of fact, it might explain his drinking in the first place. He wouldn't go out and buy a bottle—he was trying to keep off the stuff. But receiving a bottle out of the blue, you might say—getting it on the eve of the Holy Day, too—well, I can see where he might regard it as almost foreordained."

"I doubt if even a devout believer, and I don't suppose Hirsh was, would think of a bottle of vodka as having been sent by the Almighty," said the rabbi with a smile. "But, in any case, in your view, the weight of the evidence is on the side of accidental death."

"Well, that's the way it seemed to us. But keep in mind we naturally preferred that finding to suicide. Of course the insurance company is likely to look at the picture a little differently."

"Oh? Have they made inquiries?"

"No, not yet," Lanigan said, "but they will, they will."

15

Pat Hirsh, accompanied by Liz Marcus, arrived home in the undertaker's limousine to find Dr. Sykes parked in the driveway. His small foreign roadster had made the trip from the cemetery much faster than the big limousine.

"Come in, Liz," said Pat. "I'll make some tea."

"Thanks, but I don't think I'd better. Joe is taking care of the kids, and he'll be wanting to get back to the office." Liz kissed her impulsively —she had been more emotional than Pat during the entire proceedings —and left, saying she'd try to get over that evening after putting the kids to bed.

Dr. Sykes held open the door for Mrs. Hirsh. "You didn't need to go to the expense of renting the limousine, Mrs. Hirsh. I could have driven you out and back."

"I know, but somehow it didn't seem right to go to the funeral in a sports car. Can I fix you something to drink?"

"No thanks, I've got to be getting back to the lab. I just stopped for a minute to see that everything was all right."

"Oh." She took off her coat. "It was a nice funeral, wasn't it?"

"I guess so. I couldn't tell much since it was all in Hebrew. I guess it was Hebrew—or Yiddish. No, Hebrew. Yiddish is a kind of German, and with all the scientific reading I do I would have caught a word here and there."

She fished in her purse. "The rabbi gave me this little booklet. It has the prayers with the English translation on the opposite page. So I could follow the service, you know. But I was kind of upset and just put it in my purse."

He looked over her shoulder as she leafed through the pages.

"It doesn't say much about death," she remarked, "Just praises God. Oh, here's a section—'O God, who art full of compassion . . . grant perfect rest beneath the shelter of Thy divine Presence. . . . We beseech thee . . . shelter him evermore under the cover of Thy wings. . . .' It says *El Moley Rachamim*. What do you suppose it means?"

"That's just a transliteration of the Hebrew. That must have been what the cantor chanted. You remember in the middle he said Ike's name. Here, you see there's a dash where you supply the name of the deceased."

"Oh, yes. Didn't he have a lovely voice?"

"It was kind of eerie, all that twisting and turning—in a minor key."

"Yes, but it reminded me of Ike somehow. You know, he used to sing like that sometimes. Not sing exactly, but kind of hum. Sometimes when he was trying to work something out in his head, he would walk up and down the room and hum that way to himself. Poor Ike. He was alone so much of the time. He had no family, no friends. He had cut himself off from his own kind—"

He was afraid she was going to break down. "There were a lot more people there than I expected would be," he said to change the subject.

She brightened. "Yes, weren't there? Of course, I knew Liz Marcus was going to come. But the Levensons, and Aaron and Molly Drake, I wasn't sure they could make it. They've been good friends. That little thin man was Mr. Brown the insurance agent. I was surprised he came."

"He's also chairman of the Cemetery Committee. I guess he wanted to make sure everything went off all right."

"Who were those three people standing together behind the rabbi?"

"They were from Goddard. One is a general handyman we have and the other two were technicians. They were all friends of your husband."

"It was nice of them to come. And did you see Peter Dodge?"

He grinned. "I noticed he wasn't wearing his collar."

"Well, under the circumstances I think that's only natural," she said defensively. "Who was that tall, heavy man who kept pretty much to himself?"

He looked at her in surprise. "Didn't you know?"

She shook her head.

"That's the great Mr. Goralsky, Mr. Benjamin Goralsky, financial genius, president of Goraltronics."

"What a shame I didn't know," she said. "I would have thanked him for coming today, a busy man like that. He left right after it was over, though."

"Yes. His mother is buried there and I guess he wanted to visit her grave."

"It's a very nice cemetery, don't you think? Ike would have liked it, a big field on a hill out in the country and all."

"There were only about two or three graves."

"Well, I suppose that's because it's new. Probably in time they'll have to put in a road and replace that broken wire fence, but I like the way it is right now. And Ike's grave, right there near the entrance. Everyone will have to pass by—"

He sat down on the arm of the sofa.

"I meant to ask you, Dr. Sykes. Who was the little red-faced man?"

"No one I ever saw."

"He kept eyeing me all through the service. Every time I'd look up, he was looking at me."

"That's only natural. You were the principal mourner."

"No, everyone else looked at the rabbi or the cantor."

"Maybe it was a friend of Dodge's; they were standing next to each other. Here he comes now. We can ask him."

He opened the door for Peter Dodge and the two men shook hands ceremoniously. "You did a wonderful job," Dodge said. "Everything went off splendidly. I would have offered to help, but it might have proved a bit awkward, you understand—"

"Of course. And I really didn't have to do much, the people at the temple took care of most everything. Well, now that you're here and Mrs. Hirsh is in good hands I'd better be getting back to the lab."

"Oh, do you have to go now, Dr. Sykes?" She held out her hand. "I haven't really thanked you for all you've done. You've been just wonderful."

"Glad I could help. Your husband was a friend, a real friend. He'll be deeply missed. Oh, by the way," he said to Dodge, "who was the short little man standing beside you?"

The minister shook his head. "Don't know. Why?"

"We thought perhaps he was a friend of yours. Well, he must have been someone from the temple."

"You think so? He didn't look Jewish."

"How can you tell these days?"

Both men laughed. Dodge watched through the open door until Sykes had climbed into his car, then shut the door and turned to Pat. He took her hands in his, and holding them wide apart looked at her, his eyes shining with admiration. "You were magnificent, Pat," he said. "A couple of times, I thought you were going to break down, but you rallied splendidly. I can't tell you how proud I was of you."

16

The Goraltronics plant, set back from Route 128 by half an acre of carefully tended lawn, was a one-story building covering two and a half acres with a parking space in the rear for four hundred cars. Seated in his modern office with discreet gray carpeting, the president of the corporation, Mr. Benjamin Goralsky, glanced at the calling card and snapped the corner of it with his thumb. " 'Investigator,' " he read aloud. "That's a detective. I saw you at the funeral. You don't look much like a detective, Mr. Beam."

The figure in the visitor's chair on the other side of the curved slab of teak that comprised Goralsky's desk was short and fat with a round red face like an Edam cheese. His dark eyes all but disappeared when he laughed. He laughed easily.

"I don't suppose any detective that looked like one would be worth much," he said and smiled. "But I'm not a detective—at least, not the kind you read about. I don't carry a gun and go around rescuing beautiful blondes. I just ask questions."

"And you want to ask me some questions about Isaac Hirsh. Why me?"

"Well, for one thing, Mr. Goralsky, you were at the funeral. Everybody else I could account for: they were friends of the widow, or associates of the deceased, or officials of the temple. But I couldn't understand why a big, important businessman like you would be there. And in the middle of a working day too."

"It's what we call a *mitzvah*, a blessing or a good deed, to go to a funeral. The rabbi announced it at the minyan—that's our regular service —this morning. He asked as many as could to go. Strictly speaking, it's a service so you're supposed to have ten men there. The others couldn't get away—they've got jobs. I'm my own boss, so I went. Besides, my mother is buried there and it gave me a chance to visit her grave."

"I see."

"But what's all this about? Does your company always make this kind of investigation before settling a claim?"

"Only where there's a question, Mr. Goralsky."

"What sort of question?"

"Well, when a man drives into his garage, turns off the headlights, closes the garage door behind him, and then is found dead of carbon monoxide poisoning there's always a question."

"Suicide?"

"Isaac Hirsh took out an insurance policy of twenty-five thousand dollars less than a year ago. There's a two-year suicide clause on all our policies and double indemnity for accidental death. If his death was an accident, the company forks out fifty thousand dollars. If it was suicide, we don't pay a red cent. The company feels that fifty thousand dollars is worth a little investigation."

"Yeah, I guess it is. And now that you've done a little investigating, what do you think?"

Beam smiled, and his eyes seemed to vanish. "I'm not the front office, but I'm guessing that when they get my report they won't pay without the beneficiary going to court and making us. Look, this is a little narrow garage he's got. There's a trash barrel on the right. To get the car in far enough to close the door, Hirsh has to drive all the way to the back wall and in between the barrel on one side and the garage wall on the other. It's a tight squeeze—I measured it myself. As it was, he left himself just over a foot on the driver's side and about the same on the other. Get the picture?

"Now that's pretty good driving for a drunk. Then he douses the lights but leaves the motor running. He slides out from under the wheel on the passenger side. It's too tight a squeeze on the driver's side because he's kind of a fat little guy like me—and he pulls down the garage door. Then he comes back and gets in the front seat again, on the passenger side, where he was found.

"Now when you consider that most people shut off the motor almost automatically when they get into the garage, and that he didn't forget to turn off the car lights or shut the garage door, that's kind of hard to see as an accident. If he was so boozed up that he didn't remember to shut off the motor, how come he was able to drive so straight and true, and how come he was able to remember to turn off the car lights and pull down the garage door behind him?"

"So why did the police call it accidental death?"

"The police! The guy is a citizen. He's got an important job with the Goddard Lab, which is kind of a big outfit around here. What are they going to do? Make trouble? I figure before they'd call it suicide they'd practically expect him to make out a written statement stating his intentions and then have it witnessed by a notary."

"I see. So what do you want from me?"

"Anything at all, Mr. Goralsky. Anything you can tell me."

The interoffice communicator buzzed. Goralsky pressed a button. "Yeah?"

"Mr. Stevenson of Halvordsen Enterprises is here to see you," came from the box on the desk.

"I'll be right out." He turned to Beam, visibly agitated. "Sorry, Mr. Beam, this is important. There's nothing I can tell you, nothing at all."

17

"Is something wrong?" Mrs. Hirsh asked Dr. Sykes. He had phoned from the lab to say he had important news she ought to know about at once. She led him into the living room, still unstraightened from the afternoon visitors.

"I wouldn't call it wrong, exactly, Mrs. Hirsh, but I thought you ought to know. That fat little red-faced man who was at the funeral—you remember you said he was eyeing you all through the ceremony."

"Yes, I remember."

"Well, his name is Beam, Charles Beam. He was at the lab when I got back. He's an investigator for the insurance company that sold your husband his policy."

"What was he doing at the funeral?"

"Good question. I guess he was investigating."

"What are you trying to tell me, Dr. Sykes? What is there to investigate?"

"That policy your husband took out, like all policies written these days, had a suicide clause. It also had an accidental death clause."

"I knew that."

"Very well. If it was suicide they pay nothing; if it was an accident they pay fifty thousand dollars. That's a lot of money, and naturally they want to make sure it wasn't suicide."

"Well, sure, I don't blame them, but it wasn't. The police did some investigating, too, and they decided officially it was accidental. I should think that would settle it."

"I'm afraid it isn't as easy as that. The police don't have to pay out any hard cash. They just have to come up with a cause of death for their records. Naturally, unless they have positive proof, they'll put down accidental death. It's kinder to the family."

"But why would Ike commit suicide? He'd have no reason. He liked living here. We were getting along fine."

Sykes said nothing.

"They've got to prove that it was suicide, don't they? They can't just say they think it was suicide and refuse to pay, can they?"

"No, of course not."

"Well?"

"Look, Mrs. Hirsh, the custom in such cases is to investigate and should they decide it's suicide they refuse to pay and it's up to you to bring suit to collect. If they don't have positive proof, they're apt to offer a settlement—seventy-five percent of the claim, say, or fifty percent—depending on how strong they feel their case is."

"But I don't have to take it."

"No, of course not, but you should have all the facts before you make up your mind one way or the other."

"What do you mean by that?"

"That's why I came over." Choosing his words carefully, he said, "I never was going to tell you this, Mrs. Hirsh, and I wouldn't now if you didn't need to know to help decide a very important question. But the fact is your husband was going to be fired and he knew it."

"Fired? But why? I thought he was doing well."

Sykes obviously was embarrassed. "I wish that were so," he said gently. "Especially since from all I've heard, your husband was quite a man when younger. When he was on the Manhattan Project his work was very well thought of by some mighty important people. But since coming to Goddard, and probably for a while before that, he just didn't have it. He made half a dozen mistakes in the—what is it, less than a year?—he'd been with us. I covered for him each time with the boss, but this last time he made a mistake that was pretty serious. It was on a job for one of our most important clients, and I did what I could but the boss was stubborn. Ike had an appointment with him for Monday morning."

"But what did he do?"

"I don't think I could explain it unless you were a mathematician. But in general, his research seemed to prove that a whole new process was possible, a much cheaper way of doing the thing—sorry but I can't be any more explicit—and doing it better. The story leaked out and the company's stock went up. And then we found that your husband had made a mistake. Naturally the client was angry. What made it bad is that the company is involved in a merger, so it makes them look as though they were manipulating their stock."

"And Ike knew it?"

Dr. Sykes remained silent.

"Oh, Ike, you poor dear. He must have known and wanted to keep it from me. He was probably afraid we'd have to pick up and move along. We had moved so many times—because of the drinking, you know—and he knew I was beginning to think we had it pretty much licked and we'd be able to stay. He knew I liked it here—"

She broke off as a sudden thought occurred to her. "You don't think it was because he was afraid he didn't have it anymore, Dr. Sykes? I mean, you say he made mistakes—he never used to make mistakes. If he thought his mind wasn't as sharp—from the drinking perhaps— But I wouldn't have cared. He must have known that. No matter what happened, he'd still be plenty smart for me."

"I'm sure he did know, Mrs. Hirsh," Sykes said.

She sat up and squared her shoulders. "All right, then, what do I do now?"

"Nothing. You don't have to do anything. When you hear from the insurance company, you can decide then. If I can help—" He got up. "If there is anything I can do, Pat—anything at all—you have only to call."

She nodded. "Yes, I know. You've been a good friend to us."

18

"*Possel?* What do you mean *possel?*"

"It's like tref, not kosher, it's unclean."

"What are you saying, Mr. Goralsky? How can our cemetery be unclean?"

"It's unclean because there's a suicide buried there. A suicide is supposed to be buried in a corner, near the wall, off to one side. You buried a suicide right in front and that makes the whole place *possel.*"

"We didn't bury any suicide, Ben. Who are you talking about?"

"Look, Mr. Schwarz, don't pull that with me. Yesterday you people buried Isaac Hirsh in your cemetery. I was there. I saw it. Today, the insurance investigator comes to see me, and there's no doubt the guy committed suicide. So I mention it to my father and he gets terribly upset."

"Why should he be upset?"

"Why? Because, in case it's slipped your mind, my mother is also buried there. All her life, she was a good, pious woman. She kept a kosher house and observed every rule and regulation, and now she lies in ground that's been contaminated. And I shouldn't be concerned? And my father shouldn't be upset?"

"Look, Ben, Mr. Goralsky, I don't know anything about Isaac Hirsh. First I've heard of the name. This is a matter the Cemetery Committee takes care of. I'm sure there's some explanation. Did the rabbi officiate at the burial?"

"Of course he did. And he made a eulogy, and he made the blessings. Yet only a few days ago—on the eve of Yom Kippur—with my own ears I heard him threaten my father that if he didn't take his medicine and died, he would consider him a suicide and bury him in a corner without blessings or eulogy. Then along comes this Isaac Hirsh, who isn't even a member of the temple—and this is supposed to be a private cemetery for members only—and his wife isn't even Jewish, and the rabbi buries him with all the trimmings. You say there's an explanation. I guess there is. The explanation is that you guys wanted to sell a cemetery lot, and for the couple of hundred bucks or whatever it runs, you didn't care what happened to anybody else who was buried there."

"I assure you, Ben, it was nothing like that. Marvin Brown, the chairman of our committee, would never do a thing like that. And our rabbi wouldn't either. There must be some mistake."

"You think my father doesn't know what's kosher and what ain't?"

"Of course not, but that insurance investigator could be mistaken."

"How could he be mistaken? He laid it out for me plain as day. This Hirsh goes into his garage and closes the door. Then he sits in his car swigging booze with the motor running. So is it suicide, or isn't it?"

"Well, it certainly sounds that way, but— Look, if anything can be done—"

"If?"

"Well, tell me, what do you want us to do?"

"You can get him out of there."

"You mean exhume the body? Ben, we couldn't do that. You wouldn't want us to do that. It would create a scandal. We'd need the consent of the widow. The town would—"

"Look, Schwarz"—Goralsky's tone was cold and dispassionate—"you've been sweet-talking my father about building a chapel, and he's half committed himself to you. Personally, I think the congregation needs a new chapel about as much as they need a pogrom, but if the old man wants it it's all right by me. But I'm telling you right here and now that if you don't take care of this cemetery business, any money you get out of us wouldn't even build a pup tent."

"Mort, I'm not one of the rabbi's most ardent admirers any more than you are, but you've got to admit he knows his stuff. I mean, if he buried Hirsh then it must be okay."

"You don't understand, Marvin. You still don't get it," said Schwarz wearily. "The rabbi probably didn't go into the question of suicide at all. Maybe he suspected and maybe he didn't. Suppose he did, what would he do? He'd call his friend the police chief who would naturally give him the official finding, death by accident. So he went ahead. In his place I wouldn't have done any different. And if we ask him, I'm sure he'll say everything is right and kosher. He's not going to come right out and say he made a mistake."

"So what can we do about it now? We can't take the body out."

"Well— You know, if the widow wouldn't object—"

"Forget it, Mort. Even if she were willing, and if I'm any judge of character she wouldn't be, we'd have to get the approval of the Board of Health of Darbury where our cemetery is, and of the Board of Health of the place where he would be reburied. There'd be so much red tape and so much publicity—"

"Actually, it was Ben Goralsky's idea, Marve. I told him all that."

"So have you got any other ideas?"

"Well," Schwarz began cautiously, "it stands to reason this must happen fairly often, especially where we bury them as soon as we can. Then a couple of days later they find a note, and what they thought was a normal death now is a suicide. So I figure there must be some machinery for taking care of this kind of thing. Some ceremony of purification, say, that the rabbi can perform that would make the cemetery kosher again. The rabbi could dress it up, put on a real show— What's the matter?" as Marvin shook his head slowly.

"I don't think the rabbi would do it."

"Dammit, if the Board orders him to, he'll have to."

"I don't know. I'm not sure that's something the Board can order. It seems to me it would be up to the rabbi to decide. And I'll tell you something else: I'm not so sure I like the idea myself."

"Why not?"

"Because I don't think it would do the cemetery any good."

"Now what's that supposed to mean?"

"Look, Mort, you're an architect so maybe you don't understand the psychology of selling. It's hard enough to sell someone a cemetery lot— it's what we call an intangible, like insurance. The people in our congregation are all pretty young. Their minds aren't running to things like cemetery lots. But a good salesman can convince them. Sometimes, he appeals to their sense of loyalty to the temple; sometimes to their sense of responsibility to their wives and families. Sometimes you just shame them into it. But whatever your approach, you've got to make sure your product is perfect, without a flaw. The minute there's something wrong with your product and your prospect knows it, he grabs onto it and uses it against you. If we let on there is something wrong with the cemetery, that maybe it isn't a hundred percent kosher, I figure three quarters of those people I've got lined up right now I can kiss them goodby."

"So they'll buy a little later—"

"Mort, you talk as though you didn't realize what the cemetery can do for a congregation. Remember, the temple bought the land last year when Becker was president. And whatever you say against Becker, remember he was a businessman. He made me chairman of the committee because he figured that a guy who could sell insurance could sell cemetery lots. Like I say, they're both intangibles. He used to kid me about it. 'Marve,' he used to say, 'you sell them insurance which is like betting them that they're going to live, and they're betting they won't. So when you sell them a lot, you're hedging your bets. Son of a gun, you got them coming and going.' And I've used that on some of my prospects—it kind of makes a joke of it."

"I'll admit you're good, Marve. That's why I kept you on as chairman when I was making up my committees. So what are you getting at?"

"All I'm saying," said Marvin doggedly, "is you should appreciate what the cemetery can mean to the congregation."

"But if we don't do something right now, we stand to lose the Goralskys."

Marvin was not impressed. "I'll admit it's nice to have a first-class tycoon type like Ben Goralsky associated with the temple, but not if we have to kowtow to him every time he—"

"Look Marvin, if I tell you something, can you keep it under your hat? Suppose I said I practically have an ironclad promise from the old man, Ben's father, that he will ante up the money for a new chapel—not just a big donation, but the whole cost, maybe a hundred and fifty thousand dollars."

Marvin whistled. "A hundred and fifty grand!"

"Maybe more."

Marvin drew a pencil from his pocket. "Then in that case, I may just have an idea," he said. He fished around and brought forth from an inside pocket an advertising folder, which he discarded in annoyance.

"What are you looking for? Paper?" Schwarz slid a pad over to him.

"Thanks." He drew a rough square and in the bottom righthand corner made a small x. "This is the cemetery and here is where Hirsh is buried. All right. According to Goralsky, a suicide is supposed to be buried in a corner off to one side. So we make a corner." He drew an oval inside the perimeter of the square. It enclosed the entire area except for the four corners. "By building a circular road inside the cemetery, that leaves Hirsh's grave *outside*—and in a corner. What do you think?"

Schwarz looked at the drawing in amazement. "Marvin, you're a genius! You just thought that up?"

"Well, I've been playing with the idea in another connection. You remember a couple of Board meetings ago I said we had to have a road through the cemetery. The Board turned it down because they didn't want to go into that kind of money at the time. But I thought about it a lot, trying to figure out a pattern that would give access to all parts of the cemetery and still eat up the least possible land. This seemed to fill the bill."

"But isn't a circular road apt to be more expensive?"

"We don't have to do the whole road. Even keeping to our present budget—the money already voted that I have in hand—we can lay it out and do just one corner, Hirsh's corner to start with. We'll finish the rest when the Board votes more money."

"By God, Marve, I think that'll do it. I still say you're a genius."

Marvin looked dubious. "How about the rabbi?"

"What about him?"

"Do we tell him?"

Schwarz considered. "I guess we better, if only to make sure this will do the trick."

19

"Surely you must be joking," exclaimed the rabbi. "You're harking back to the Dark Ages. During the Nazi Terror, there must have been hundreds of suicides. Would you have denied them ritual burial?"

"But you yourself threatened old man Goralsky with just that, according to his son," said Schwarz.

"Threatened him? I was scaring an adult with the bogeyman. He could tell I wasn't really serious. I was just trying to get him to take his medicine. I told you all about it at the temple."

"Yes, but Ben Goralsky evidently took it seriously," said Schwarz.

"I doubt if he did at the time," said the rabbi. "But in any case, on what grounds can you assume Hirsh was a suicide? The police verdict was accidental death. And I went to the trouble of discussing it personally with the chief of police, and he feels the evidence overwhelmingly favors that finding. Are we to be more callous in our dealings with the dead and bereaved than the civil authorities?"

"Suppose it finally was decided that he was a suicide?" asked Marvin.

"Decided by whom?"

"Well, by a court of law."

"Even then, the chances are that he was either temporarily insane or suffering from a compulsion so extreme he was powerless to withstand it. So he wouldn't be accounted a suicide in the eyes of Jewish Law."

"Yes, but if he *was* a suicide, just suppose he was," Marvin persisted. "Then wouldn't it be up to us or to you to do something about it?"

"Why would anything have to be done about it? He was buried—that in itself is a cleansing action. 'The earth is the Lord's and the fullness thereof.' Burial itself cleanses. When a utensil becomes tref, the way you cleanse it is to bury it in the earth. Are you suggesting that the presence of this man's body pollutes God's earth? And if so, where does it stop? At the boundary of our cemetery, which is an artificial line recorded in the Registry of Deeds, or does it go on indefinitely until it reaches the ocean?"

"Well, maybe there's some prayer—"

"Some bit of hocus-pocus? That I can make a few magician's passes over the grave? Is that what you had in mind, Mr. Brown?"

"Now look here, Rabbi," said Schwarz. "We are all practical men, I hope, and we are up against a practical matter. I'm not worried about the cemetery being polluted and Marvin here isn't either. But this is something that Ben Goralsky, and evidently his father, take seriously. Call it superstition, if you will. Call it ignorance, but it bothers them.

"Now we're practical men, Rabbi, Marvin and I. As chairman of the Cemetery Committee, Marvin is concerned with the effect on sales of cemetery lots if this story gets around, and I am concerned with keeping the Goralskys in the temple organization. We've worked out what I consider a practical solution to a sticky little problem, and what we want from you is just some information. What we have in mind is to build a circular road inside the cemetery. Like this—" And he took out the sketch. "Now here is where Hirsh is buried. If we keep him outside the road and from now on sell lots only on the inside, will that satisfy the regulations? Actually, Hirsh stands to gain. Since we can't use the corner land naturally we'd want to beautify it—put in some shrubbery, trees. What we want to know is whether that would do it?"

The rabbi rose from his chair. He looked at each of them in turn, as though unable to believe they were serious. "Is a man a dog?" he demanded, his fury all the more intense because he kept it controlled, "that you presume to toss his body from one place to another as suits you? Is the service I conducted at his grave just a bit of mumbo jumbo of no significance and no meaning? Last week I joined with other rabbis in submitting a petition to our State Department asking them to protest the Russian government's desecration of Jewish graves. And now you would have me party to a plan to desecrate a grave in our own cemetery to satisfy the superstitions of a foolish and ignorant old man and his equally foolish and ignorant son? Are our ceremonies to have a price to be sold to the highest bidder?"

"Just a minute, Rabbi, we're not desecrating any grave. We have no intention of molesting Hirsh's grave."

The rabbi lowered his voice even further. "A woman not of our faith comes to us and asks us to bury her dead husband in our cemetery because he was Jewish. She regards it as her last act of loyalty and love to lay him to rest among his own people, and you propose to differentiate his grave from all the rest? And you don't consider this desecration? In good faith, she paid her money—three or four times the price of a lot in the public cemetery, mind you—only to have her husband separated, markedly separated from the rest of the cemetery, as—as a thing unclean?"

"I'll bet I could get her to agree," said Marvin.

"It's purely an administrative matter," said Schwarz.

"You are a salesman, Mr. Brown, and a successful one," said the rabbi. "It's quite possible you could persuade a widow in her bereavement to consent to your plan. But you can't persuade me. And I consider it something more than just an administrative matter, Mr. Schwarz. I will not be a party to it."

"Well, I'm sorry you feel this way, Rabbi," said Schwarz. "I consider it a practical solution to a practical problem. I am concerned with the living rather than the dead. I am concerned with the effect on our congregation of having the Goralskys as members rather than whether the grave of Isaac Hirsh who was not even a member of our organization is on one side of a road or another."

"I cannot approve and I will so tell the Board when the matter comes up."

Schwarz smiled. "I'm sorry we don't have your approval, Rabbi, but I'm afraid we'll have to go ahead without it. And it won't come up before the Board. This is a matter in which the Cemetery Committee has full authority."

"Of course, we'll take a vote of the committee," Marvin observed.

"Vote or no vote, I forbid it."

"Look, Rabbi, we didn't have to come to you in the first place. We just wanted everything aboveboard."

"But you did come, and I forbid it."

Schwarz shrugged his shoulders. He rose and the two men left. The rabbi stood by his desk, angry and baffled.

"What did he mean he forbids it?" asked Marvin. "Can he do something?"

"Like what?"

"I don't know, call some board of rabbis—"

"Don't be silly. Our temple is a completely autonomous body, and the rabbi is just an employee. He's told us that often enough himself. The only thing he can do if he doesn't like it is resign."

"After what I just heard, that might not be such a bad idea," said Marvin.

"You don't like him?"

"I think we can do better," said Marvin evenly.

"Yeah? How do you mean?"

"Well, I'm a businessman. Over the past few years I've had a lot of people working for me—salesmen and office help. I've got a rule about help. I don't care how good they are, I don't care how much of a world-beater a salesman is; if he can't take orders, he goes."

"That's the way I feel, Marve. Say, who's on your committee?"

"Sumner Pomeranz, Bucky Lefkowitz, and Ira Dorfman. Why? Not one of them has done a damn thing, but they're on the committee."

"That's three and you make four. Didn't I appoint another so as to have an odd number?"

"You're on it ex officio. That makes five."

"Good. So all we need is one more for a majority. Look, Marve, why don't you get hold of them. Tell them as much as you think they have to know and get their vote for this new road. Just in case the rabbi gets cute."

"No sweat. They know I do all the work, and they don't ever go against my decisions."

"Right. When you get it nailed down, why don't you call the rabbi and tell him you've taken a vote, and your committee is one hundred percent in favor of the new road."

"That is a good idea, Mort. It will keep him from getting any fancy ideas."

"Let me know how you make out. But act fast. I don't want to give the rabbi a chance to block us."

20

Marvin was elated when he called Schwarz Friday morning. "I just got through talking to the rabbi. I didn't crow, but told him I thought he'd like to know that the committee vote was unanimous."

"What did he say?"

"He didn't say anything."

"Dammit, Marvin, he must have said something."

"I'm telling you he didn't say anything. Just, 'I see,' or something like that. No, come to think of it, that's all he said, 'I see.'"

"Was he sore?"

"I couldn't tell, but since he didn't say anything, I figure he knows he's beaten. So the thing for us to do is go ahead full steam."

"I'm not so sure, Marve. I've had some second thoughts on the matter."

"How do you mean?"

"A thing like this—it could backfire on us. If he were to bring the matter before the Board Sunday—"

"And Wasserman and maybe Becker side with him and between them they'd pull over a few more—yeah, you got a point there. What do you think we ought to do?"

"What we need, Marve, is a consensus. Maybe I ought to talk to some of the members before the Board meeting. What are you doing tomorrow night?"

"Well, Mitzi suggested we take in this foreign film at the Strand—"

"Strictly a dud. Ethel and I saw it last week in town. Why don't you come over, and I'll contact some of the boys—"

"I get it. You're going to show them the model."

"Right."

The group returned from the study to the living room where Ethel Schwarz had prepared coffee and ice cream and delicious little French cookies. "You know, Mort," Hal Berkowitz said, "what I can't get through my noggin is why the rabbi, of all people, should want to do anything to keep that building of yours from going up. I mean, your chapel has class, and what's more, it's his—"

"That's right," chimed in Abner Sussman. "It's his place of business, you might say. I was visiting my brother in Richmond Friday night and the rabbi was over. Most of the time we were talking business, and I had been telling them how I remodeled my store. After dinner we all started out for services, and when we got to the temple the rabbi says, 'How do you like *my* store?'"

"What gets me," Berkowitz said, "our rabbi is supposed to be so traditional and the building we got now looks like anything but a synagogue. Now Mort's scheme here makes it look like a real synagogue—"

"Seems to me you're both missing the point," said Nelson Bloomberg. "Here we've got a chance to make a giant step forward. We can make our temple a real showplace on the North Shore. I don't claim to have any great aesthetic appreciation—although in the dress business, let me tell you, you better develop a sense of style or you're in trouble—but to me, Mort's is the kind of building that would get talked about. The kind of building you might expect to see pictured in some magazine. To me, it represents progress. And what's standing in the way? A ghost. No, not even a ghost, a corpse—the dead body of this guy Hirsh who wasn't even a member of the congregation. Here we have something that means progress for an entire community—something wholesome and alive—and the rabbi throws in a monkey wrench with a lot of ghoulish technicalities about graves and burials and death. It's just plain gruesome, when you come right down to it."

"Nel's put the whole thing in a nutshell," said Nate Shatz. "We had a pretty awkward situation here. This idea of having the driveway so everybody is satisfied, Goralsky, the widow, the temple—that's the kind of thing the rabbi is supposed to dope out. And what happens? Marve and Mort figure it out, and the rabbi instead of being grateful says he forbids it. Either we like it or lump it. Well, I say the fat's in the fire and we go ahead with the road. He can resign, for all I care."

"What's he ever done to you?" asked Jerry Feldman. "You sound angry."

"I am. He acts as though he's too good for the likes of us. I see him at the Board meetings and sometimes he says hello and sometimes he doesn't. My wife gave a bridge and invited his wife, but when she got there all she would take was tea. If he's too good to eat with us, he's too good to rabbi for us."

"Well, I wouldn't condemn a man because he sticks to his principles," said Feldman. "If a man wants to eat kosher, especially if he's a rabbi, I see no harm in it. My mother always kept a kosher house with two sets of dishes and everything. When she'd come to my house, she wouldn't eat with us either. At the same time—I say maybe we can do better. Personally I'd like to see a man who was a leader and looked like a leader. A man who would take hold and build this place up."

"A lot of people come into your store, Abner, and you must have heard them talking," said Schwarz. "How do you think people feel about him?"

Sussman rotated his hand. *"Comme ci, comme ça.* Some people say he keeps to himself a lot and they don't like a rabbi to be so standoffish. Some say when they go to the temple on a Friday night they like to hear a sermon—not just a casual talk like he thought it up on his way over. But don't think he hasn't friends; he has. A lot of people like the way he talks—common sense and no bull. Like Jerry here, some object to the way he dresses—more like a bookkeeper making seventy-five a week. But that works for him too—brings out the motherly instincts, if you know what I mean.

"Of course, I see mostly women in my place, and they're always complaining about something. He's not interested in their work. Half the time when he's supposed to go to a Sisterhood meeting, they're not even sure he'll show up. But you know women; if he were a big handsome guy he could do anything he liked and they'd love it. On the other hand, there's no doubt they've got a lot of influence with their menfolk."

"How about those who are strong for him?"

"Well, like I say, he's got his friends but they're scattered, so I wouldn't say he has what you might call a following. I mean he's not the kind of guy that goes out of his way to get a group behind him. And he hasn't exactly got what you'd call a magnetic personality like some of these glad-handers. You know, my father was president of one temple and a big shot in another, so I know a little about rabbis. You take a smart rabbi, the first thing he does when he comes to a new place he sort of gets the lay of the land—who's important and who isn't. Then he develops a party, a clique. Everybody knows they're the rabbi's friends, see? Then any time the rabbi wants something, he doesn't ask the Board of Directors himself personally. He whispers to one of his buddies who is damn important, some guy with plenty of dough who has kicked in to the building fund or who can be tapped for a big contribution when you need it. Then this guy, he talks to the other friends of the rabbi and when one of them gets up in the Board meeting and says, I think we should do thus and so, why somebody else seconds it quick as a wink and before you can say *Gut Shabbes* it's passed. A rabbi like that, he runs the organization."

"I see."

"Now our rabbi—he don't have any organization behind him."

"How about Wasserman and Becker and Doc Carter?"

Sussman shook his head. "They're not an organization. Wasserman backs him because he picked him, and Becker because he helped out his partner when he got into that trouble a couple of years ago so he feels obligated. You know how a rabbi goes about setting up an organization? He visits with them, he invites them to his house. He's nice to their wives and he's helpful to their kids. One I knew who used to help his friends' kids with their school lessons when he'd come to visit—not their Hebrew school lessons but their public school lessons. Another one would play baseball with some of the kids, and this one even had a beard. Can you imagine our rabbi playing ball?"

Everyone laughed.

"All right," said Schwarz, "so the consensus of the meeting is. . . ."

Marvin Brown held back after the others left. "You know, Mort, if this doesn't go through we'll be left with egg all over our faces."

"Marve, old boy, it's in the bag. Nel Bloomberg gave it to us when he said the rabbi was fighting progress. That's our new theme song— the rabbi is against progress."

"I didn't mean the rabbi, I was thinking of Goralsky. How much of a commitment do you have from the old man?"

"It's pretty firm. Ben was the stumbling block, but now with this, he's sure to be on our side."

"How do you mean?"

"Well, when he called to tell me about the cemetery, he mentioned his father's interest in the chapel and said we wouldn't get it if the situation wasn't taken care of. Well, if we do clean it up, and we point out that to do it we had a regular hassle with the rabbi, will he have the nerve to say he changed his mind?"

"Maybe, but you know how these things work. Goralsky can stall. The old man can say he put it in his will—why not?" as Schwarz shook his head.

"Because, Marve old boy, I just decided this is going to be called the Hannah Goralsky Memorial Chapel. Get it? We'll make this a memorial to his wife, Ben's mother. So isn't the old man going to want to see it? Isn't he going to want to be there to lay the cornerstone, and be at the ceremony when it's completed, and to be the first one called up for the Reading on the first service that's held there?"

Marvin Brown began to chuckle. "You know, Mort, you're pretty cute yourself. I think we pulled a fast one on the rabbi."

21

Saturday morning at morning services the rabbi's throat felt dry and scratchy. When he got home he was tired and had little appetite for lunch. He intended to return and spend the afternoon in the temple study, but his bones ached so he lay down on the living-room couch and dozed off. After his nap he felt better and went to the temple for the evening service, and by the time he got home he had a chill; his head felt warm.

The rush of warm air as Miriam opened the door struck him like a blow. His nose twitched and he exploded in a loud sneeze.

"Are you catching cold, David?"

"I don't think so," he said, but she stood on tiptoe and kissed him on the forehead. "You're warm. You've probably got a temperature."

"Oh, I'm all right." But he sneezed again. Paying no attention she marched into the bathroom and appeared a moment later shaking the thermometer with a professional snap of the wrist, inserting it over his mumbled protest.

"101.4. You've got a fever," she announced. "You get undressed right now, David Small, and get into bed."

"You're making too much of it," he said. "I caught cold. I'll be fine in the morning."

"Not if you don't take care of yourself." She forced water and orange juice on him and aspirin, but when she took his temperature later on in the evening it had risen to 102.

"I'm calling Dr. Sigman," she said.

"Oh, what's the sense. It's just a cold, there's nothing he can do about it. I'd rather you wouldn't call."

"Why not?"

"Because he won't charge me but he'll feel it necessary to come out anyway."

"I can ask him if he wants to see you." From her tone of voice he knew it was useless to argue.

"He had it himself last week," she said when she returned to the bedroom. "He says there's a lot of it going around. It's a virus infection but doesn't last long, a couple of days. Just as I said, you are to stay in bed, take aspirin and liquids, and you're not to venture out until you've had a normal temperature for twenty-four hours."

"A couple of days! But I've got a Board meeting tomorrow."

"Not any longer. You're staying in bed, at least until Monday. The Board will manage for once without the wisdom of your counsel, I'm sure."

"But tomorrow is particularly important. I've just *got* to be there."

"We'll talk about it tomorrow. And don't count on it."

The Board meeting began at ten; but a number of members arrived earlier, since they had children in the religious school which began at nine. Before that, at eight-thirty, was the morning minyan when the rabbi normally arrived on Sundays. After the service, he would go visit the classrooms, and at ten join the Board of Directors at their meeting. Since it was a special privilege, he tried to attend as often as possible; of all the rabbis in the area, he alone was permitted at Board meetings.

But this Sunday he did not appear at the minyan or at religious school classes. Instead he was at his own breakfast table in bathrobe and slippers having eggs and toast, the diet Miriam considered proper for a sick man.

At the temple, no one commented particularly on his absence; several times before he had been unable to attend. But Mortimer Schwarz and Marvin Brown felt it had special significance.

"It's obvious, isn't it?" said Schwarz. "He's thought it over and found he hasn't a leg to stand on. If he were to make a fight of it—and he'd have to—and were beaten, he'd either have to resign or back down. He doesn't want to do either one so he just stayed away."

"So what do we do now?"

"Well, you know, Marve, I think this kind of changes things. With the rabbi not here, maybe you should give a committee report. This might be a good time to ask for an increase in your budget. You don't have to mention Hirsh. You could just talk of the need to build a road."

Just then Arnold Green, the corresponding secretary, signaled Schwarz to come over.

"What's up, Arnie?"

Green drew the president to a corner and held out a letter. "Read this. It was in the Board mailbox when I came in. According to the postmark, we must have got it Saturday. It's from the rabbi. I thought I better speak to you before I read it to the Board."

Schwarz read the letter quickly, then folded it and put it back in the envelope. When he spoke his voice was intense. "Look, Arnie, I don't want this read at the meeting today. I want you to forget you ever received it, understand?"

"But I'm supposed to read all communications received."

"Well, you weren't supposed to receive this one. It was addressed to me, and I want you to promise you won't say a word about it."

"What's it all about?"

"I don't know a hell of a lot more than you do, but unless I get a chance to find out, this organization can be split wide open. You remember what happened when his contract came up for renewal. You wouldn't want that again, would you?"

"Of course not. But when the rabbi sends a letter to the Board, he's going to wonder why it wasn't read."

"But he's not here today. Don't worry—it'll get read. But it'll keep for a week."

"If that's the way you want it."

"That's the way I want it. Now let's get the meeting going."

"The rabbi's got a touch of the grippe," Dr. Sigman explained when the Board members had settled into their places. "Had it myself last week. He should be up and around by the middle of the week."

"I just got over it a couple of days ago," remarked Bob Fine. "And I was going to call you, Doc, but when your Shirley told Myra you'd had it, too, I figured you wouldn't have anything to prescribe so why not save myself a few bucks?"

Dr. Sigman laughed. "I'll have to talk to Shirley about giving away my secrets."

Sitting well to the back in the room, Marvin Brown managed to catch the president's eye. Schwarz nodded briefly and called the meeting to order. The secretary read the minutes, then he called for the reports of the committee. Marvin Brown did not offer a report, but when the New Business was announced he raised his hand and was recognized.

"I don't know if I should have given this during committee reports, but I'm planning to make a motion so I thought I'd hold it until now. Before I make my motion, I'd like to give a few words of explanation."

"You're supposed to make your motion, then if it's seconded and the president calls for discussion you can make your explanation." Al Becker, last year's president, was a stickler for parliamentary rules.

"Well, that's all right, Al, but suppose nobody seconds my motion. Then I don't get a chance to explain."

"So it means the explanation isn't necessary."

"Yeah, well then if I quit as chairman of the Cemetery Committee, and you ask me why, I'll tell you the reason was in the explanation you didn't let me give."

"Look, fellows, there's no sense getting sore about this," Schwarz interposed. "You're absolutely right about the correct procedure, Al, but it sounds as though Marve has a beef and I think we ought to hear it. I can rule him out of order if in my opinion he's not talking to the point."

"That's just the point," Becker objected. "How can you tell if he's talking to the point when he hasn't made a point yet."

"Aw, let him talk."

"I'm not trying to keep him from talking. I just say we ought to operate according to the rules. But you guys want to do it this way, go ahead."

"All right, Marvin."

"Well, it's like this. I'm damn sick and tired of trying to sell what can't be sold. It's a thankless job. Now I'm a salesman by profession and a salesman depends on his confidence. And this assignment of the Cemetery Committee—I tell you, fellows, I'm losing my confidence. It seems to me that most of you don't have the slightest idea of how important the cemetery is to the congregation. Most of you take the attitude that it's some kind of joke. Oh, I don't mind you whistling a funeral march when I get up to give my report. I can take a joke as well as the next guy, but what bothers me is that you're not serious about the thing itself. All these wisecracks about my getting you coming and going, insurance while you're living, and a plot in the cemetery when you're not—that's well and good; but sometime we've got to look at this realistically, and as far as I'm concerned the sometime is now."

"So what do you want, Marve?"

"I want you to think about what this cemetery can mean for a progressive organization like ours. This community is growing. Someday, and it's not far off, there's going to be another temple in Barnard's Crossing, maybe a couple of them. And their membership won't be made up entirely of newcomers to the area. Maybe one of the temples will be Reform and I'll bet there'll be a lot of our members who will feel like switching. But if they own a family plot with us, or if a member of their family is buried there—a husband, a wife, a father, a child— wouldn't that make them think twice before they leave us? And then think of the money. A cemetery can be a gold mine. We charge about four times what the town charges for a lot in the public cemetery. In ten or fifteen years, it could cut our dues, or if it's operated right enable us to expand.

"Now, what are the problems I'm faced with? First off, most of our members are young people. They haven't even started to think about maybe God forbid they'll need a plot someday. And let's face it, when you ask someone to plank down a hundred and fifty-odd bucks for a lot which he doesn't think he's going to need—and I for one hope he doesn't—it's a lot of dough. What's more, a lot of our members work for some of the big corporations and they don't know when they might be transferred to another city. So are they going to come back here to be buried? Well, I got some ideas on the subject. I think we ought to sell lots on the installment plan. I'd like to see members pay as little as ten bucks a year, which could be billed with their membership dues. And I'm in favor of having a clause in the contract to the effect that they can sell the lot back to us anytime they want without losing money. In that way, if they're transferred, they can always get their money back. I'm even toying with the idea of maybe selling lots like a kind of insurance policy, where if the member dies before he has paid in full the widow doesn't have to pay any more."

"Is this the motion you're making, Marve?"

"No, that isn't my motion. I just mentioned all this to show that your committee is thinking about their job all the time. I've had prospects make the kind of objections I've mentioned. But," and here he looked around to make sure he had their attention, "the biggest argument my prospects give me is, 'See me when you get a cemetery. All you've got now is an abandoned hayfield.' And that's the truth. That's all we've got there right now. A hayfield with a saggy wire fence running along the main road and a tumbled-down stone fence running along one side. We don't have a chapel. We don't have flowers and shrubbery to make the place look halfway decent. We don't have the place properly fenced off. We don't have a road to give us full access to the cemetery, the back plots especially. That's the main trouble right now."

"We're planning all those things, but wasn't it decided we would make all the improvements out of income?"

"Sure, but you've got to spend a little money to make some money. Remember, it's the packaging that sells the product."

"Well, you've got a budget of two thousand dollars."

"Yeah, and how far will that take you? Just keeping the grass cut and paying for a part-time caretaker eats that up."

"So what do you want, twenty-five thousand dollars for a regular

Forest Lawn so you can sell a couple of lots for a hundred and fifty bucks?"

"I don't think that's fair to Marve," said Schwarz.

"I'll tell you what I want: I want enough money to build a decent road. Then I can sell lots in any part of the cemetery, not just near the corner where there's a hole in the fence. To take care of that we've worked out a scheme that's both practical and economical. What we're planning is a circular road. That will give us access to all parts of the cemetery. What I want is for our budget to be increased to at least five thousand dollars so we can go ahead. We could lay out the whole road and get bids on what it would cost to pave it. Then if the low bid goes above the five grand, and I don't think it will, I'd expect the Board to pick up the tab. And that's my motion."

The secretary looked up from hastily scribbled notes. "A motion was made—did anybody second it?"

"Second the motion."

"Sure, I'll second it."

"All right. A motion was made and seconded that the Cemetery Committee budget be increased to five thousand dollars for the purpose of building a road—"

"Make that a circular road."

"All right—a circular road within the boundaries of the cemetery, any excess monies that are necessary to be . . ."

Mortimer Schwarz sought out Marvin Brown after the meeting. "I've got to hand it to you, Marve, you certainly put that over. I thought you were all set to hand in your resignation."

Marve grinned. "It's just a selling job as I see it."

"Well, you certainly got the technique. And you sure worked in our theme song." He chuckled. "I'd like to see the rabbi buck this setup."

22

As the founder and first president of the congregation, Jacob Wasserman was considered the elder statesman of the temple. In his sixties, he was quite a bit older than most of the members. He had worked almost single-handed to get the organization started, spending his evenings going to see each of the fifty or so Jewish families that comprised the Jewish community in Barnard's Crossing shortly after the end of World War II. The first High Holy Day services had been held in the basement of his house with a Torah Scroll borrowed from one of the Lynn synagogues, and he had led the prayers and chanted the portions from the Torah.

Al Becker, who succeeded him as president, accompanied him on his visit to the rabbi. Becker was a short, stocky man with a deep gravelly voice and a belligerent way of using it. Although he had none of Wasserman's learning, to say nothing of his understanding of Jewish tradition, he followed him faithfully and usually voted with him on most Board matters.

"It's lucky Becker and I decided to drop in on you, Rabbi, to see how you were getting along," said Wasserman. "I knew old man Goralsky was an ignoramus, but that his son, a boy born and brought up in America, should be such a superstitious idiot, too—this I wouldn't have believed."

"Just a minute, Jacob," said Becker. "Right is right. How can you say the old man is an ignoramus? A man like that with a beard—he says the prayers faster than anyone in the congregation and most of the time he doesn't even bother to look at the book."

"Please, Becker, stick to things you know about. Goralsky may pray faster than anybody in the congregation and he knows the prayers by heart. Why not? He's been saying them every day morning and night for almost eighty years. But he doesn't know the meaning of them."

"You mean he doesn't understand what he's saying?"

"Do you, when you recite the prayers in Hebrew?"

"To tell the truth, most of the time I use the English side."

"So that's an advantage that you have over him. But the question is what are we going to do now?"

Becker shook his head dolefully. "Too bad you had to get sick, Rabbi. If you had been at the meeting yesterday when the discussion came up, you could have explained what the real issue was—"

"I'm not sure I could have, from the way you report it," said Rabbi Small. "As I gather, the motion was a general one—to give the Cemetery Committee a budget to improve the grounds. In general I think that's a good idea, so under the circumstances I'd be unlikely to rise and accuse Marvin Brown and your president of ulterior motives."

"Of course not," said Wasserman. "It would have been unseemly for the rabbi. It would be like calling Schwarz a liar. And even if he had, and the whole business had come out into the open, what good would it have done? After Schwarz got through explaining, do you doubt that the majority of the Board would have voted with him? Building a road which might affect the grave of an outsider against a building worth a hundred thousand dollars or more?"

"I cannot permit the desecration of the grave of a Jew by fellow Jews," said the rabbi quietly.

"But what can you do about it, Rabbi?" said Becker. "You've got to be reasonable. The road has already been voted, so it's no longer a simple question of being fair to this guy Hirsh. Now it's a question of who is to set policy for the congregation, you or the Board."

"Not quite, Mr. Becker," said the rabbi. "In this matter, my authority is supreme."

"I'm afraid I don't follow you there, Rabbi."

"It's simple enough. Although it is customary to speak of the rabbi as an employee of the congregation, it is a mistake to equate him with other employees. My position here is more like that of the CPA who is engaged to audit the books than that of Stanley Doble who is hired to maintain the building and grounds. I am not a tool of the congregation to be used any way they see fit. I cannot be asked to do something that runs counter to the principles of my profession any more than you can ask a CPA to cover up some discrepancy in the books. The CPA has loyalties to the entire business community that transcend his loyalties to the person who engages him. In the same manner my loyalties cannot be commanded completely. Transcending my loyalties to this congregation are my loyalties to the Jewish tradition, to the Jews of the past, and to Jews as yet unborn. In certain areas, and this is one, my authority is supreme and not subject to question by the congregation."

"But—"

"A widow comes to me," the rabbi went on impatiently, "and asks to have her late husband buried in a Jewish cemetery according to Jewish custom. It is for me to determine if he is a Jew, and I decided he was. Again, it is for me, and only for me, to determine if his manner of death warrants burial according to Jewish rites. If there is the suspicion of suicide, it is for me, and only for me, to decide how much weight to give the evidence, how much to allow for mitigating circumstances, and then to decide how rigidly to apply the regulations that govern burial of a suicide. These are not congregational matters; these are purely rabbinic."

"Well, if you put it that way—"

"Now, having made my decision, I referred the widow, or her representative, to the chairman of the Cemetery Committee. Mr. Brown, as the voice of the congregation in this matter, sold the widow a lot in good faith and accepted her money. If the congregation had a regulation limiting the cemetery only to members, and on those grounds had refused to bury Hirsh, I might have considered the regulation harsh or ill-advised but there I would have no authority—only what influence I could bring to bear. But the regulations made special provisions for a case like this. It called for the payment of a fee which conferred nomial membership. And this fee was paid and accepted."

"No question."

"Once having made Hirsh a nominal member of the congregation in accordance with the regulations they themselves made up, they then have to treat his burial exactly as they would any other member's."

"That's not only in the bylaws, but it's in accordance with our tradition," said Wasserman.

"Now, suppose sometime later evidence is adduced, incontrovertible evidence, that Hirsh had actually committed suicide—and such is not the case—then once again it becomes a decision entirely for me, and me alone, whether his presence compromises the cemetery. And if I were to decide that it did, it would be up to me, and me alone, to decide what measures of purification were necessary. But the Board chooses to follow Mr. Goralsky in this matter. Why? Is his *smicha* greater than mine? Did he perhaps receive his from the Vilna Gaon?"

The rabbi's voice had risen, and his normally pale face showed the heat of his indignation. He sat back in his chair and smiled, a small, deprecatory smile. "I told Mr. Schwarz and Mr. Brown that I would forbid this desecration of Hirsh's grave. Of course, in the present congregation-rabbi relationship, my ban has no force behind it. So when Mr. Brown called to say that the committee was going ahead anyway, I did the only thing I could do: I sent in my resignation."

"You resigned!" Wasserman was aghast.

"You mean already, you've already sent it in?" said Becker.

The rabbi nodded. "When Brown hung up, I wrote out my resignation and dropped it in the mailbox."

"But why, Rabbi, why?" Becker pleaded.

"I've just explained that."

Wasserman was upset. "You could have called me. You could have discussed it with me, explained your position. I could have talked to Schwarz. I could have brought the matter up before the Board. I could—"

"How could I do that? This was between Brown and Schwarz and me. Could I come running to you to help me exercise my authority? Besides, what good would it have done? You would have split the congregation, and in the end the Board would have voted with Schwarz. As you yourself said, given the choice between an unknown's corpse and a hundred-thousand-dollar building, is there any question which way the Board would vote?"

"And how does Mrs. Small feel about this?" asked Wasserman.

"Just a minute, Jacob," interrupted Becker. "You say you sent this letter out Friday morning? So it must have been received no later than Saturday. If it was addressed to the president of the temple it would have been put in with the rest of the temple mail, and the corresponding secretary would have got it and showed it to Mort Schwarz. So why didn't Schwarz have it read at the meeting?"

"That's a good question, Becker."

"It must mean that Schwarz just isn't accepting it."

"That could be," said Wasserman slowly, "but I don't think so."

"You think he wanted to discuss it with the rabbi first?"

"That could also be, but I doubt it."

"So how do you figure it?"

"I think he wants to talk it over with his group on the Board first, and get them all to agree. Then when he brings up the matter in the meeting, they'll railroad it through just like that." He snapped his fingers.

"But why, Jacob? You think he wants the rabbi out?"

"I don't think he'll let anything interfere with his new building."

"Why is the building so important to him? We don't really need it."

"Because it's a building, that's why. It's that progress they were talking about. It's something he can point to, something solid and substantial. It's a hundred- to a hundred-and-fifty-thousand-dollar property.

It's a value that he can say he brought into the temple organization. Now the present building came in during my administration."

"I didn't put up any buildings," said Becker.

"The cemetery—that you bought. When they put up the central gate, your name will be on it. Schwarz wants something he can say, 'This is what I did.' What do you say, Rabbi?"

The rabbi, who had promised to say nothing about Schwarz's personal involvement, nodded slowly. "Yes, I think it might be something like that."

"Well, Rabbi," said Wasserman, "it's not going to be easy, but we'll try our best."

Outside, Becker said, "What really gets me is why he didn't get in touch with us. We're his friends, and we're not the only ones. And he sure went out of his way to help me that time my partner Mel Bronstein was in all that bad trouble. So I, for one, sure owe him one mighty big favor.

"You know, the rabbi has changed in the few years he's been here. I remember when he first came, he was so shy you could hardly hear him when he spoke. Now he lays it on the line like he's in complete control of the situation."

"That's because he's grown; he's matured," Wasserman said. "When he came here, he was fresh out of the seminary, a boy. He had ideas, and he was firm about them, but he said them so quietly no one really paid attention. But in these few years he's got confidence, and he doesn't mind asserting himself. I tell you, Becker, he's got like a radar beam in his head."

"What do you mean, radar beam?"

"It's like the way an airplane flies at night. He's got an instrument, the pilot, and it's as if he's flying an invisible line. The minute he goes off to one side or the other, the instrument gives out a beep. It's like that with the rabbi. He's got in his head the principles of the Jewish tradition. When the congregation goes off to one side or the other, the rabbi gets a warning, like a beep, and he knows we're making a mistake."

"Yeah, well, this time that beep may cause a crash landing."

"Why?"

"Because the poor bugger is apt to lose his job. And his wife's going to have a baby soon."

"You might at least have told me," said Miriam. "It was all I could do to restrain myself from coming in when I heard you tell Mr.

Wasserman and Mr. Becker. I noticed when one of them asked how I felt about it, you were careful not to answer. Evidently they thought it was my concern."

"I'm sorry, Miriam dear. It was foolish of me; I was wrong, but I didn't want to distress you at this time. I thought that by today, by this morning, the whole affair would have been properly settled. It didn't occur to me that Schwarz would suppress my letter."

"And suppose he had read your letter and the Board had gone along with him?"

"I didn't think they would have—not with me there to explain it." He had been talking apologetically, but now his tone changed. "If they did, then I would have no choice but to resign. I could not remain here. The issue, as far as I'm concerned, is basic and fundamental. Either we are a religious group, a congregation, or we are nothing and I have no job here."

"So what are you going to do now?"

He shrugged. "What can I do now? The matter is out of my hands. We can only hope that Wasserman and Becker can rally enough support—"

"You mean you're going to sit with your hands folded and wait until the matter is resolved one way or the other?"

"What do you suggest?" He was nettled.

"You called this desecrating a grave. Very well, then you can appeal to the town authorities. You could talk to Mrs. Hirsh."

He shook his head. "I could never do that. I am still an employee of the congregation, and if their elected representatives want to do something I disapprove of, I can't protest to authorities outside."

"It seems to me," she said tartly, "that you're a lot more concerned with your struggle with the Board than you are with Hirsh. You've dissociated yourself from their action, but if as you say it's the desecration that really concerns you, what are you doing to prevent it?"

"Well—"

"The least you could do is prove what really happened."

"Yes? And how would I go about that?"

"Well, if you found a note, that would prove that it was a suicide, wouldn't it?"

"Yes, but not finding it proves nothing. It's negative evidence."

"It seems to me that if you can prove something took place, you ought to be able to prove it didn't."

He realized that her fine scorn for logic was because she was hurt he had not confided in her. "But don't you see," he said patiently, "that simply because you can prove one thing doesn't mean—"

"All I know is that if someone has done something, someone else ought to be able to find out what it was. Besides, there's the widow to think of. There's been a man around town, an investigator for the insurance company, and Mrs. Marcus—you remember she called—was saying that her friend Mrs. Hirsh was worried about losing the insurance money if he proves it's suicide."

"He can't prove it's suicide any more than we can prove it was an accident."

"Yes, but he could make her a lot of trouble—hold up the money indefinitely. David, you've *got* to do something."

"But how, woman, how?"

"I don't know. You're the rabbi. That's your department. At least, you could try."

He looked at her for a moment. Her face was intense. "All right, Miriam, I'll try. I'll call Lanigan and see if he'll go over the facts with me. It's just possible we can come up with something."

"I'll do better than that," said the police chief when the rabbi got him on the phone. "I hear you've been under the weather, so instead of your coming down to my office tomorrow, I'll get the files on the case and bring them over to your house tonight."

"Oh, I don't want to put you to that bother."

"Look, Rabbi, you'll be doing me a favor. Gladys is having some friends over, and I don't want to be caught in a hen party."

"Well, if you put it that way—"

"I do. Say, I've got another idea: has Charlie Beam got around to talking to you yet?"

"Beam?"

"He's the man who's been investigating for the insurance company. How about if I bring him along?"

"Fine."

"Beauty," said Lanigan. He chuckled. "You know, I'm really going to enjoy this little get-together."

"How do you mean?"

"Well, you're hoping to prove that it's a case of death by accident, and Beam naturally would like to prove that it's suicide so his company won't have to pay. And here I am, in the middle, and for once in the clear. I'll just let you boys fight it out and I'll sit back and enjoy it."

23

Out of respect for his guests, the rabbi had shed his bathrobe and was dressed in slacks and a sport shirt. After the introductions, Miriam, feeling this was not part of her husband's official function and that she had a stake in the proceedings, remained in the room.

"Maybe I'd better run through the facts as we know them," said Lanigan, "and then we can talk about it afterward." He opened a Manila folder. "All right. Isaac Hirsh, 4 Bradford Lane, married, white, fifty-one years old. He was five foot three or four and weighed one hundred and ninety pounds. Did you know him, Rabbi? Had you ever met him?"

The rabbi shook his head.

"He was built along the lines of Charlie here. Maybe a little shorter—"

"I'm five feet five," said Beam.

"I would have said so. I make a point of this because it's important, as you'll see. All right, it's Friday evening, September 18, the eve of your Yom Kippur. Hirsh gets home from the Goddard Lab where he works, his regular time—a little after six. In this case, that's unusual because all other Jewish employees left a bit early. But although Hirsh was Jewish he did not attend services, so he worked a full day. He got home and left his car in front of the house instead of putting it in the garage—"

"He didn't want to trouble himself getting out to open the garage door, is that it?" remarked Beam.

"No, the garage door was up. It's common around here; we don't have much pilfering. A man will leave the door up all day and close it only when he locks up for the night."

"You know this in the Hirsh case?" asked Beam.

"Yeah. It also figures in the story, as you'll see. Now there are a number of Jewish families in this section of Colonial Village; in fact, all his immediate neighbors are Jewish. I understand it's sometimes called the Ghetto." He smiled apologetically at the rabbi. "That's a little joke among them."

"I understand."

"Patricia Hirsh, that's Isaac Hirsh's wife, was going to baby-sit for the Marcuses who live across the street. She agreed to be there early, so she served Hirsh his dinner and left at six-thirty. Hirsh finished and left around seven."

"You're sure of the time?" asked the rabbi.

"Pretty sure. We got that from the deliveryman I told you about. Anyway, after the deliveryman left, Hirsh headed for the laboratory. He was next sighted by the State Police at a siding on Route 128 about four hundred yards from the lab. You remember, they went back and found the wrapper from the bottle."

"Did they indicate when they saw him?"

The chief shook his head. "They had no reason to note the time. They just remembered having seen the car during the evening; they didn't even remember the exact place. They had to check each of the sidings along the section they patrol until they found the right one. All we know is that Hirsh was there sometime during the evening. And that was the last time he was seen alive."

"But you yourself said they didn't really see him. They just saw the car. Isn't that right?" asked the rabbi.

"Well, they saw a figure in the car. We assume it was Hirsh. Is it important?"

"Probably not. Go on."

"Mrs. Hirsh came home around eleven or a little after."

"As late as that?" asked the rabbi. "Our services ended at a quarter past ten."

"The Marcuses didn't return directly. They stopped off to visit some friends," explained Beam. "I got that from Mrs. Marcus."

"And I suppose they talked with Mrs. Hirsh for a few minutes when they did get back," said Lanigan. "Around midnight, she called the lab to find out when her husband was coming home."

"How did she know he was there?" asked the rabbi.

"He frequently returns at night, and at supper he mentioned he was going. But the janitor–night watchman reported he never signed in that evening, which is when she called us." He went on to explain how they put out an alert, and how when the cruising car stopped by to get more information, the patrolman noticed the garage door was down and remembered it had been up when he passed earlier.

"So he investigated and found the car inside, right close to the side of the garage, about a foot and a half. He squeezed by, opened the front door on the driver's side, and found Hirsh dead on the passenger side. About half the bottle was gone. The ignition was on but the motor was not running—out of gas. He radioed in to the station and we sent down the doctor and a photographer—the usual."

He opened the folder and took out a large glossy photograph. "This picture shows the situation best. It was taken from the driveway when the garage door was first raised. You'll notice how close the car is to the side of the garage on the driver's side, about a foot and a half. And on the other side, you'll notice this trash barrel about a foot from the car. That's important to Charlie's case. The picture doesn't show it, of course, but the bumper of the car was just touching the rear wall of the garage. Since the car had no gas, we took out the body and left the car where it was. The following morning, we poured some gas into the tank and drove it down to the station where we've had it ever since. Mrs. Hirsh doesn't drive, at least she doesn't have a license, so we haven't got around to bringing it back yet. And that's about all.

"Oh, yes, we did an autopsy on the body that confirmed the presence of alcohol in quantity commensurate with the amount missing from the bottle. It also gave us the time of death, roughly eight-thirty, give or take twenty minutes. That would be pretty accurate since it was based on stomach content."

All four were silent for a moment as if out of respect for the deceased. Then the rabbi said, "There was much that you didn't mention, Chief, I suppose because you assumed we knew it. One was that the man was an alcoholic, and you yourself indicated that alcoholics don't generally commit suicide."

Beam smiled. "That's one of those generalizations, Rabbi, that are used to bolster a pet theory. And since there are almost as many theories about alcoholism as there are doctors studying the subject, it's easy to theorize. There's one to the effect that all alcoholics are sexually deficient. If something runs counter to your theory, you just say it proves the man wasn't a true alcoholic. It's arguing in circles."

"All right. How about this? From all I can gather, Hirsh was very fond of his wife. He took out a sizable insurance policy—that alone indicates he cared about her welfare and well-being. Would he take his own life without leaving a note of explanation?"

"They do it all the time. Sometimes the note turns up later, sometimes it's found and suppressed by the interested parties, if you know what I mean. Sometimes, too, they purposely don't leave one in hopes it won't be thought suicide, and the beneficiary can collect."

"But nothing in his general attitude would indicate that he might commit suicide."

"How do we know? How do we know what sets a man off? Maybe the fact it was your Yom Kippur, the Day of Judgment as I understand it, had something to do with it."

"What is that supposed to mean?" asked the rabbi.

"Merely that he may have been thinking about suicide for a long time, and the bottle of vodka coming on the Day of Judgment the way it did—well, it could be kind of an omen."

"More likely it served as an excuse to satisfy the thirst that was always with him," the rabbi retorted. "We know he discarded the wrapper on the siding, and if he started drinking then, he must have been pretty far gone by the time he got home."

"And yet was able to drive a car for some distance, a good ten miles, and steer it into the garage so nice and true that he doesn't hit the wall on the one side or the trash barrel on the other?"

"That's your case, is it?" asked the rabbi. "That he was able to drive into the garage without bumping into anything?"

"That," said Beam, "and the fact that he had sufficient command of his reasoning faculties to shut off the car lights but not shut off the motor, get out of the car and pull down the garage door, and then get back into the front seat. If he were drunk and didn't know what he was doing, why would he have gone back to the car? Why wouldn't he go directly into his own house? He knew he'd be alone and alone for some time. He may not have gone to the temple regularly, but I guess he'd know that on your Yom Kippur the services wouldn't be over much before ten."

"Alcoholics frequently have special feelings about where they can drink and where they can't," interposed Lanigan mildly. "I suppose his house was one place he considered off limits. For that matter, after he pulled down the garage door, why get into the front seat at all? If you say he was planning to commit suicide—and may have wanted to anesthetize himself with alcohol, since carbon monoxide takes a little time—why not get into the back seat, which is not only more comfortable but nearer the garage door?"

Beam shrugged. "Matter of habit, probably. The important thing is that he was sober enough to do all these things: to steer within the narrow space between the trash barrel and the garage wall—"

"Just a minute. What kind of trash barrel is that, Chief? It looks like one of those new plastic types."

"That's right, Rabbi. It's a red plastic twenty-gallon barrel with a cover."

"Full or empty?"

"Oh, it must have been empty, David," said his wife. "It was Friday." She explained to Beam that the trash on even-numbered houses is collected Friday morning. "The husbands usually put out the barrels Thursday night and the wives bring in the empties the next morning."

"The lady is right," said Lanigan. "The barrel was empty."

"So what?"

"So there is a difference," the rabbi began, his voice taking on the impersonal tone of a lecturer. "There is a difference between a full barrel and an empty one, and an even greater difference between a galvanized iron barrel and one made of plastic."

"Are you going to pull one of those Talmudic tricks of yours, Rabbi? What do you call it, a pil—something?"

"You mean a pilpul? And why not, if it helps us to get at the truth."

Lanigan grinned. "The Talmud," he said to Beam, "is the Jewish book of Law. They have a special way of arguing that the rabbi has used on me on occasion. This pilpul, it's a kind of hair-splitting that—"

"Rather it's the tracing of a fine distinction," said the rabbi reprovingly.

"Well, I don't mind fine distinctions," said Beam patronizingly. "But what difference does it make whether the barrel is full or empty, or made of galvanized iron or plastic or anything else for that matter?"

"Actually, there are four possibilities." The rabbi rose from his chair and, thrusting his hands deep in his trouser pockets, began to pace the floor. "The barrel can be of iron and full or empty, and it can be of plastic and full or empty. The first point to consider is the difference between the full one and the empty one. The full barrel is normally heavy and relatively immovable. The empty barrel is light. That is, of course, why men usually take it out onto the sidewalk; while bringing it back empty is something a woman can do because it does not tax her strength. Now, if the barrel were full, then it could indeed be considered a fixed obstruction. A sober man would no more think of driving his car into it than of driving into the wall. But what if the barrel were empty? Then it is comparatively light, and if he struck it with his car no great damage would be done beyond a scratch or two. And the barrel? Even if it were toppled over nothing would spill out. But—" and he held up an admonishing forefinger, "the sober driver would have no problem in either case. He has more than a foot on either side—plenty of room, even for a driver of my caliber. How about the drunken driver, though? Let us admit that he would have trouble"—he paused "*if* it were a full barrel. But he knows it is empty—"

"Just a minute," Beam interrupted, "how does he know that the barrel is empty?"

"Because it was inside the garage, of course. If it were full, it would be outside on the sidewalk where he'd left it the night before. So here we have a man parking his car in a narrow garage. He knows he has to be careful on one side, but on the other there's only an empty barrel. Even half sober he'd know that subconsciously, and know it really would not constitute an obstruction. Still, he would probably try to avoid it, and his capacity to steer between the two might be some indication of his relative sobriety. But"—and again he held up a forefinger—"this is not a galvanized iron barrel that could be dented if struck by the car fender and that in turn could damage the car. It is a plastic barrel, an empty plastic barrel. When struck, it yields or skitters away."

Then, as his voice took on a Talmudic singsong, his forefinger made circles in the air in time to the rhythm of his discourse. "Now if a man would not mind hitting a galvanized barrel because he knew it was empty, then *al achas cammo v'cammo*"—he broke off and smiled. "I'm sorry, I got carried away. That Hebrew phrase, a common one in Talmudic argument means—er—'how much more.' How much more, then, would he be likely to disregard an empty plastic barrel." Turning to Lanigan, he said, "Because you have expressed an interest, that line of reasoning is very common in the Talmud. It is called *cal v'chomar*, which means 'light and heavy,' and consists of showing that if one argument applies, then a stronger argument of the same sort is even more applicable and can be considered proof. Now from our point of view, the empty plastic barrel is no more obstruction than a beach ball. Hirsh could in fact have struck it, and it could very well have caromed off the fender and come to rest in its present position."

The chief shook his head in admiration. "He's got you fair and square, Charlie. The fact that it is an empty plastic barrel just about kills your case."

"Well, I'm a city boy myself and I don't know about plastic barrels. But that's not all there is to my argument by a long shot. How about bringing the car right up against the rear wall of the garage? That's a mighty neat trick for a guy too soused to know enough not to turn off the ignition."

The chief looked at the rabbi for an answer but he seemed not to have heard. In fact, he seemed to have forgot they were there, for he was leaning back in his chair, his eyes focused on the ceiling.

"What do you say to that, Rabbi?" asked Beam.

The rabbi disregarded the question.

"There is another facet of Talmudic reasoning," he said, and his voice was withdrawn as though he were talking to himself. "It is the *im kain* argument. The words mean 'if so,' and it is essentially a sort of *reductio ad absurdum*. In the present case, it would go like this: if the car was so near the side of the garage, how could he get out on the driver's side? And if it were so near the barrel, how could he get out on the other side?"

Lanigan looked at the rabbi in surprise. "But you've already answered that. You proved that the barrel was no obstruction."

"It was no obstruction to the car, but it was an obstruction to Hirsh."

Lanigan was exasperated. "Dammit, Rabbi, you can't have it both ways. You pointed out that an empty plastic barrel was no obstruction, and now you say it is."

The rabbi nodded. "Precisely. It was no obstruction to a man driving a car, but it was an obstruction to Hirsh going to lower the garage door."

"Why? He had only to nudge it aside with his foot."

"But he didn't, because it was still there when you found him and took your picture."

"I'm not sure I understand what you're driving at," said Lanigan.

"Include me," said Beam.

"Very well. Hirsh brings the car to a stop. He can't get out on the driver's side. No room. So he gets out on the passenger side. He nudges the barrel out of the way, walks to the front of the garage and pulls the door down. Very good! Now he comes back to the front seat of the car. He passes the barrel. What does he do? Pull it back in position again? Why would he do that?"

"Why—why he must have," exclaimed Lanigan. "Or maybe when he pushed it away the first time, he pushed it so hard he sent it spinning and—no, that doesn't make sense either." He glared at the rabbi. "Dammit, we know he couldn't get out on the driver's side. We know that. It was physically impossible. And now it seems he didn't get out on the other side. But those are the only two ways of getting out of the car, so—"

"Go on, say it. If he didn't get out on either side, then he didn't get out of the car. But the garage door was down, so it must have been pulled down by someone else. And that person, in all likelihood, was the driver. And Hirsh was sitting on the passenger side, because he was indeed the passenger. And that in turn could explain how a man could consume a pint of liquor and yet travel by automobile ten miles or more and park his car in his garage. There was no problem because he was not driving; he was being driven. And when they got to the garage, the driver, a much thinner person than Hirsh, got out of the car on the driver's side, pulled down the garage door and walked away. And Hirsh did nothing about it because he was either too drunk to know what was happening, or more likely, had passed out completely."

Lanigan stared at the rabbi. "But that's murder!"

The rabbi nodded. . . .

An hour later, they were still at it.

"It's crazy, Rabbi."

"But it fits all the facts. There are obvious objections to suicide, and similar strong arguments against accidental death, but there are no logical arguments against murder. On the contrary, murder explains everything."

"And I thought I was in the clear," said Lanigan ruefully.

"Are you going to report it to the district attorney?" asked the rabbi.

"I can't right now. First I've got to check it out."

"Check it out how?"

"I've got to talk to my boys. Maybe they didn't shoot that picture as soon as they raised the garage door. Maybe they circled the car first, I don't know, but I've got a lot of questions."

The chief was unhappy. "Hell, I'll need some kind of legal proof. I can't go to the D.A. and he can't go to a jury with this—this chop logic of yours, Rabbi. I'm not even sure I could repeat it. I need something definite. I've got to be able to prove beyond a doubt that the barrel wasn't moved. I've got to prove beyond a doubt that Hirsh couldn't have got by that barrel. I've got to have accurate measurements."

"You said Hirsh was short, five feet three. The chances are the driver was taller," said the rabbi. "Wouldn't the position of the car seat—if it were pushed back, that is—indicate that someone else was driving?"

"You would bring that up," said Lanigan morosely. "Trouble is, the police officer who found the body could have changed the position. If not, we probably would have done so to get the body out. In any case, Sergeant Jeffers, who is close to six feet, would have pushed it back to drive the car to the station, and even if he remembered doing it I couldn't accept that as evidence. No, we flubbed it all right." He threw up his hands. "But how could we know it was anything except a straightforward case of suicide or accident?"

"Fingerprints?" suggested Beam.

Lanigan shook his head dolefully. "We didn't take any. Why should we? The patrolman who found him opened the car door, and later we were all over the car getting him out. Any fingerprints would be on the door handles, the steering wheel, and the gear shift, and they would be obliterated."

"How about the light control?" asked the rabbi.

"You mean for the headlights?"

"Someone turned them off that night."

"So?"

"Well, if the car was driven to the police garage by day, there'd be no need to put them on again."

"By God, you're right, Rabbi! They would have no reason to touch the button. It's a chance. The car has been under seal ever since."

He reached for the phone and dialed. "I'll get Lieutenant Jennings —he's our fingerprint expert." Then into the phone, he said, "Eban, Lanigan. Meet me at the station house in five minutes. No, I'm not there yet but I'll be there by the time you are. Come along, Rabbi?"

"I think he'd better stay right here," said Miriam.

"Maybe you're right. I'll call you."

"Mind if I go along, Chief?" asked Beam.

"Come on, if you're sure you're all through here."

Beam's eyes all but vanished as he smiled. "The rabbi has convinced me it's murder. But I'll be staying in town a little while. There are a few points I want to clear up. When I talked to Mrs. Marcus, she said they called home to say they'd be late and there was no answer. They tried again when they arrived at their friends' house, and the phone rang for the longest time before Mrs. Hirsh answered. She said she'd been napping."

"So?"

"So maybe the reason she didn't answer was not because she was asleep but because she wasn't there."

"Mrs. Hirsh?" Lanigan exclaimed. "But how could she be involved? She doesn't know how to drive."

"She doesn't have to—only how to pull down the garage door."

"You mean she might have done it? Mrs. Hirsh?"

"Done it, or helped to do it."

"Why do you want to pin it on her?"

Beam smiled. "Because the law says a murderer can't benefit from his crime."

"Rabbi?" It was Chief Lanigan calling from the station.

"Yes?" He had been pacing the floor impatiently, waiting for the call. The moment the phone rang he snatched it up.

"There were no prints on the light button."

"No prints? But there had to be. The car was driven at night, so somebody had to turn them off."

"Wiped clean," said Lanigan grimly. "You know what that means?"

"I—I think so."

"No chance of the driver saying he walked away and forgot to turn off the motor. He knew what he was doing, all right. Which makes it first-degree murder."

24

The Reverend Peter Dodge stood framed in the doorway, one hand resting on either doorjamb like Samson about to collapse the temple.

"Why, look who's here, David," Miriam said. "Come in."

His handsome head instinctively lowered to enter. "I heard you were a bit under the weather, David, and decided to include you in my pastoral calls."

"That was thoughtful of you, but it was just a touch of the virus. I'll be going to services tomorrow."

"Your trouble, David, is you don't get enough exercise. I wouldn't recommend anything strenuous, but you ought at least to arrange time for a nice long walk every day. It will firm up your muscle tone. Now every evening without fail I take a regular walk over a regular route. It's exactly four and six-tenths miles, and I do it in just over an hour, depending on whether I meet anyone. And most afternoons when I can manage it I get in a couple of sets of tennis."

"Where do you play?"

"We have a court back of the Parish House. Any time you want, just give me a ring and we can volley for a while. It would do you good."

The rabbi laughed. "How do you think my congregation would feel if their rabbi went to the Episcopal Church to play tennis?"

"About the same way my people would feel if I came down to your temple." He hesitated. "I hear you have been having a spot of trouble with them lately."

The rabbi and his wife both showed their surprise. Dodge chuckled. "You're from New York, aren't you? And I'm from South Bend. We're city folks, so I don't suppose we'll ever get used to how fast news travels in a small town like Barnard's Crossing. I was chaplain in a federal prison for a little while, and the grapevine there is the only thing comparable—"

"What did you hear, Peter?" asked Miriam.

Dodge became vague. "Oh, something to the effect that poor Ike Hirsh had committed suicide and you weren't supposed to have buried him. It didn't seem to make much sense to me, because how could David know he was a suicide, especially when the official police finding was death by accident? Surely your congregation can't expect you to play detective every time someone passes away."

"You knew Hirsh?" asked the rabbi. "Of course you did—you were at the funeral, weren't you?"

"Hirsh? Oh, yes. He was in the movement."

"What movement?"

"The Civil Rights movement. He made a small contribution and I went to see him. I try to make a personal visit to anyone like that— you'd be surprised how often they kick in with more. Besides, I pass by the Hirshes' street on my regular walk, so I took a chance and just rang the bell. Well, talk about a small world, who should come to the door but Mrs. Hirsh who turns out to be Pat Maguire. We went to school together in South Bend. After that, I made it a habit to pop in from time to time, and had dinner there once."

"What sort of man was Hirsh?"

"Oh, a very decent sort. I thought at first he was motivated more by his dislike of the South and Southerners—he had lived there for a while. But later, when I got to know him better, I felt he had a genuine sympathy for the oppressed. Once he even said something about going down to Alabama to join the demonstrators, but I don't think he was really serious. It's the sort of thing well-intentioned people say."

"Were you recruiting demonstrators for Alabama?" asked Miriam.

"Oh, that goes on all the time. But right now, Miriam, I'm really involved. I am in charge of MOGRE for the entire North Shore."

"Mogah?"

"M-O-G-R-E, Rabbi—Men of God for Racial Equality. It's made up of ministers of all faiths. Although mostly Protestant, there's a Greek Orthodox priest, and we're negotiating with the Archdiocese for a contingent of Catholic priests and we've got several rabbis." He said casually, "Interested, David?"

The rabbi smiled.

"Think it over." He hitched his chair closer. "I'll bet it might even solve your little problem here with your congregation."

"How would it do that?"

"Well, as I heard it, you have forbidden them to build a special road, and they're going ahead anyway. If you stand by and do nothing it's going to be pretty embarrassing. But if you're down there, obviously you can't do anything. Then when you come back, you'll have got a lot of prestige which ought to give you more bargaining power with your congregation."

"*If* he comes back."

"What's that, Mrs. Small? Oh, I see what you mean. You're thinking of the danger. Actually, there's less than you might think, for our group at least. All of us will be clearly identified as ministers, men of God, my bunch and the Catholics and the Lutherans—we'll have our clerical collars, and, as I understand it, the rabbis are planning to wear the skullcap—what do you call it?"

"Kipoh."

"That's right, the rabbis will be wearing the kipoh and, I believe, the prayer shawl."

"The tallis?"

"That's it. Even if they don't recognize the regalia they'll sense it has something to do with religion. Oh, there'll be incidents, I suppose. But compared to the opportunity to demonstrate for the sake of the Lord—"

"I thought it was for the sake of the Negro."

He smiled to show he was aware that he was being twitted and that he could take a joke. "Same thing, David. For the glory of God manifested in man, in all men, black as well as white. What do you say?"

The rabbi shook his head.

"You're not feeling up to it yet? The group is not leaving for a couple of days."

Again the rabbi declined.

"Oh, you're thinking of Miriam. It should be pretty soon now, shouldn't it?"

"It's not so much that either," said the rabbi. "You see, Peter, I'm not really a man of God, at least no more so than any other man. And what would I say? We don't go in much for petitionary prayer. If I prayed in Hebrew, who would understand? And if I recited any of our regular prayers in English, the Shema or the Kaddish or the Shimonesra, they don't really apply. No, I'm afraid I couldn't go down there as a rabbi. I could as an individual, of course, like the college students; but you don't want that."

"Well, of course we want you as a rabbi. There are rabbis who are coming down with us, and many have already been down and borne witness."

The rabbi shrugged. "We have no hierarchy to promulgate belief. This is my view of the situation; other rabbis see it differently, I suppose. Some feel it their duty as spiritual leaders of their congregations —a habit of mind they picked up from you people, incidentally, or perhaps it was the congregations who then forced it on them. And others are so moved by the plight of the Negro that they don't care to balance their attitudes as men and citizens against their attitudes as rabbis. Frankly, that may be just as well."

"Now you've lost me completely."

"People differ: there are the quiet ones and those who storm barricades. I'm afraid I'm one of the quiet ones, but I must admit that the others, the aggressive ones, are probably the ones who bring about changes in the world. I respect you for what you are doing, Peter, and I respect the others; but I don't feel an urgency to thrust myself personally and physically into the battle any more than I feel an urgency to go to South Africa to help the Negro there. So if I did, it would be for some secondary reason like the one you suggested—to give me prestige in the eyes of my congregation—and that would be hypocritical."

"But this is more than just helping the southern Negro, David. It's a new feeling, a new spirit that's developing in the church, your church as well as mine, and we mustn't let it die out. The church is coming out of its traditional shell. It's burgeoning with new life. It's giving up its self-satisfied praying and smug psalm singing to go out into the highways and byways of men to serve them, to help them to fulfill themselves. The Civil Rights movement is not for the Negro alone; it's also for the church itself. And that's why her ministers, priest and rabbi and pastor, are all involved."

"It's not new to us, Peter," the rabbi said softly. "We've been doing that for several thousand years, in fact, ever since we accepted Deuteronomy and the commandment, 'Six days shalt thou labor . . . but the seventh day is the Sabbath in honor of the Lord; on it thou shalt not do any work, neither thou, nor thy son, nor servant, nor thy ox, nor thy ass, nor any of thy cattle, nor the stranger that is within thy gates; in order that thy man-servant and thy maid-servant may rest as well as thou.' You people parted company with us a couple of thousand years ago when you fixed your eyes on Heaven. A little suffering here on this earth didn't matter much to you, because compared to the infinite time in the next world, life here was a snap of the fingers, a blink of the eye. But we've always been involved with life on this earth and its many injustices. So I suppose you could say that we've been in the Civil Rights movement from the beginning."

"But haven't you missed something in the process, David?"

"Such as?"

"Such as the inspiration of the blessed saints. Such as the inspiration of lives devoted to Heaven and God. Such as the handful of people who by their example brought mankind a little closer to the angels."

"Yes, I suppose we have, but we thought it was worth it. And now, it seems as though you people are beginning to think so, too."

25

"The district attorney is not happy with me," said Lanigan. He had stopped by the Smalls on his way home. "And I don't think he's happy with you either, Rabbi."

"What have I done?"

"A district attorney doesn't mind going into court with a clear case and winning it. Just as a ballplayer doesn't mind hitting a home run. But to dump a murder case in his lap, with no suspects and a good chance that the murderer may never be found, that he doesn't like. And that's why he's not happy with you. And he's not happy with me because he thinks I bungled it. It never occurred to me that it might be murder, so I didn't take the normal precautions on fingerprints and—"

"But the fingerprints were wiped off."

"On the light button, yes, but what about the steering wheel and door handles and handles on the garage door? You might assume that if the murderer took the trouble to wipe the light button he'd wipe off the rest, but it doesn't necessarily follow. You'd be amazed how often they slip up. And they can slip up on the most obvious thing while being scrupulously careful on the least likely. If I had thought there was a possibility of murder, I would have handled it differently. And I should have considered the possibility. No, I'm afraid I don't look good in this case so far."

"That will make you look all the better when you find the culprit," said Miriam.

"That's not going to be easy. This isn't like any other case."

"How do you mean?" asked the rabbi.

"Well, in any crime there are three basic questions, three lines of investigation you might say, and where they meet, that's your answer. There's opportunity, there's weapon, and there's motive." The chief ticked them off on his fingers. "Here, what was the weapon? The car. That means that anyone who can drive can be said to have access to the weapon. If you wanted to stretch it, he wouldn't even have to know how to drive a car."

"I'm afraid I don't follow you there."

"Well, say Hirsh had made it back to the garage and then passed out. Anyone passing, seeing him, could just pull down the garage door and that would do it."

"But then Hirsh would have been behind the wheel—not on the passenger seat," the rabbi objected.

"Yeah, that's right. All right, so the murderer—or at least an accomplice—is anyone who can drive a car. That still leaves an awful lot of people. So we come to opportunity. Well, considering how accessible or available the weapon was, it means it could be anyone who might have been at the Hirsh house or was passing by sometime around eight o'clock in the evening." He grinned. "That kind of eliminates your people, Rabbi. Just their luck it was Yom Kippur and they were all in temple. It gives them a collective alibi."

The rabbi smiled faintly.

"And so we come to motive. And that's what makes the case particularly hard, because you see you don't need much of a motive for this killing."

"Why is that?"

"Because it doesn't involve much doing—not much planning and not much nerve either. Look here, suppose you see a man drowning and although you're a good swimmer and could easily reach him you just turn away. See what I mean? Deliberately to plan on drowning a man takes resolution and nerve; you wouldn't do it unless you hated him or had good reason for wishing him dead. But to just turn away—that you might do if you happened only to dislike him. Why should I go to the trouble, you'd say, especially if life would be easier with him gone.

"Take me, for example. I'm considered a pretty decent, law-abiding citizen. I'm considered a good husband and a good father, and even the people I deal with professionally—criminals and lawbreakers—speak of me as fair and honest. But every now and then thoughts go through my head—"

"This is common to all men."

"Of course. It isn't what you think but what you do that matters. But what if the opportunity came to do one of these things just when it happened to occur to me, and it involved no great risk on my part, no real action—just a turning away—failing to do something rather than doing it. Do you see what I mean, Rabbi?"

"All right, I see the point you're trying to make. You mean that in this kind of killing, almost accidental and so easy, no great animus is required."

"That's it."

"So where does that leave you?"

The chief shrugged. "With damn little to go on."

"Suppose you ran the story in the newspapers. That might turn up something."

Lanigan shook his head. "It will have to wait for a few days, I'm afraid. The D.A. thinks we may be able to come up with an answer if the story is kept secret."

"Then you do have a lead."

"Not really," the chief said. "Beam's idea, but the D.A. thinks it's worth checking. And, mind you, from a straight, logical basis, it's possible. He's got it in his head that the widow did it. Why? Because then his company won't have to pay off. His argument is that as far as we know she's the only one who profits. She becomes richer by fifty thousand dollars for one thing, and for another she gets rid of a husband who was not only old enough to be her father but was no bargain in a lot of other respects, too."

"She married him when he was an alcoholic. Does Beam think that now that he at least partially reformed, he was a less desirable husband?"

"I'm just giving you his idea, Rabbi. There's a little more to it. He feels that business about having him buried in a Jewish cemetery with the Jewish rites was just a big act to show how devoted she was, like another woman might pretend to faint or weep whenever she thought someone was watching. That if all this had been on the up and up, she wouldn't have bothered to bury him in the Jewish cemetery since he had no feelings about it when he was alive."

"Such involved psychological analysis," said the rabbi. "I wouldn't have thought our friend Beam capable of it."

"Well, of course, he's seen a lot of this kind of thing," said Lanigan apologetically. "I can understand where he might be suspicious of any unusual manifestation of grief on the part of the widow. And when you add the fact that she didn't answer the phone when the Marcuses rang—"

"But that happened after ten o'clock, and according to the autopsy Hirsh was already dead sometime before nine."

"According to Beam, the fact that she didn't answer shows she left the house. If she left then, she could have left earlier. Suppose she sees him drive into the garage but doesn't see him get out. So she goes across the street. Maybe she tries to rouse him. Maybe she gets a kind of revulsion and says, all right, stay there. It crosses her mind that it might be easier without him. Then later after ten, just before the Marcuses called, she runs out to see what the situation is. Is the motor still running? Is he still alive? She finds him dead and runs back in time to get the second call. Then she plans what she's got to do after that. She goes home, makes believe she hasn't noticed the garage door is down, and calls the police so that they can discover the body for her."

"You keep referring to Beam. How do you like it?"

"Mrs. Hirsh doesn't seem that kind of person to me, but I've had enough experience to know my feelings about people don't mean a darn thing. On the other hand, what else have I got? It's a logical starting point—she's the only one we know who profits from his death."

"I see."

"So we're keeping it quiet for a few days—at least until we can check Mrs. Hirsh out."

"And if it's not Mrs. Hirsh, do you have any other leads?"

"We're checking into anyone who might have had any contact with Hirsh. It's all we can do. I went over to the Goddard Laboratories yesterday to see the big boss himself."

"Goddard?"

"No, Lemuel Goddard has been dead for several years. He was local —a Crosser in fact. He started the lab when he retired from G.E. They retire them at sixty-five there, whether they're ready or not. Lem Goddard wasn't ready, so he started a lab of his own. He had a place—an old warehouse in Lynn. Then he went public and sold stock. They expanded and built this place on Route 128. When he died, the Board of Directors decided that the man they wanted to head up the organization was not a scientist but an administrative expert, so they got this army general, Amos Quint. One of these desk generals from the Quartermaster Corps. Iron-arse Quint, I understand he used to be called in Washington." He glanced at Miriam. "I'm sorry, Mrs. Small, that just came out."

She smiled faintly. "I've heard the word."

"There's nothing so army as one of those desk generals," the chief went on. "His secretary who brought me into his office didn't actually salute but she kind of stood at attention." He laughed. "When I asked him how well he knew Hirsh, the general says, 'I make it a point not to know my men well.' How do you like that?"

"Wasn't it Caesar, or Napoleon, who knew every man in his army by his first name?"

"I guess that's old-fashioned. Quint explained to me that if you're going to run an efficient organization and not get bogged down in a mass of trivia—that's the word he used and with a flick of the hand as though brushing something away—you've got to operate strictly through channels. 'I see them when I hire them and when I fire them and that's all.' From then on, everything goes through channels. He tells them that when he hires them, and when he fires them, he tells them why. So as far as Hirsh was concerned, anything he wanted to bring to the notice of old Iron—of Quint—had to go through his superior, Dr. Sykes."

"I see. The Lowells talk only to Cabots and the Cabots talk only to God."

"That's about it, Rabbi. But, of course, Quint had a dossier on Hirsh and knew quite a bit about him. I gather that Hirsh was not too hot lately. Maybe he was at one time, but certainly not while he was at Goddard. In fact, I gathered he made a number of rather bad mistakes—the last one, just a few days before his death."

"Why didn't they fire him?"

"I asked the same question. I gather Quint was going to this last time because this time it was real serious, or perhaps the general had come to the end of his patience. You know, Rabbi, that could have been another argument in favor of suicide, if I had known about it at the time."

"I wonder why Quint didn't fire him earlier. From what you say, he doesn't sound like the type to stand for more than one error on the part of an employee, especially one so far down the ladder as I gather Hirsh was."

"That was Sykes. I asked the same question, and Quint said Dr. Sykes went to bat for him each time and so he played along. Even the time Hirsh got drunk Sykes managed to get him off. It started right there in the lab as a matter of fact. They were working on a special method for aging whiskey quickly by shooting an electric current through it somehow. The chemist who was working on the project mixed up a batch and brought it around for the boys to sample and give their opinions. Hirsh was one of those offered a taste and it set him off. The chemist, by the way, was fired."

"Why?"

Lanigan laughed. "That's another thing about this lab. You'd think they'd all be working together, sketching diagrams and circuits and formulae and whatnot on the tablecloths at lunch. Nothing like it. You see, most of their work is done for industry, and if news leaks out their clients' stocks can be affected. I gather that in the past some of the scientists weren't above taking a little flyer on this inside information. So the rule was laid down that everyone is to keep his nose firmly set against his own little grindstone. The men in any given section will confer with each other but they don't contact the other sections except when absolutely necessary—and then it's done through the department heads."

"Interesting. So you didn't get much from Quint. Did you question any of the other employees?"

"I did, but I got nothing that helped. As I said, everyone there tends to keep to himself. And Hirsh was a quiet sort, even withdrawn."

"It doesn't leave you with much."

"No, it doesn't." He looked eagerly at the rabbi. "Any ideas, Rabbi? Anything strike you?"

The rabbi shook his head slowly.

"Well, it helps just to talk it over, I suppose." But it was obvious that he was disappointed. He looked directly at the rabbi. "By the way, did you know that Ben Goralsky knew Hirsh?"

"No, I didn't, although I saw him at the funeral."

"S'truth. In fact, it was Goralsky who got Hirsh the job at Goddard."

The door was opened by a maid in uniform. She escorted him into the library and said she would tell Mr. Goralsky he was here.

Ben Goralsky appeared almost immediately, and showed him to a chair. "I'm glad you could come, Rabbi. My father was pleased when I told him you said you'd be over to see how he was."

"I would have made it earlier, but I was laid up myself for a few days."

"Yes, I know." He hesitated. "I heard some rumors—I may have made a little trouble for you about this business with Hirsh."

"There has been a little trouble," the rabbi admitted.

"Well, I just want you to know I'm sorry."

The rabbi was curious. "Your father feels strongly about the matter?"

"I haven't talked about it with him—except that once. When this fellow Beam told me it was probably suicide, I mentioned it to my father and he was awfully upset. It was a day when he wasn't feeling so good. I guess he thought it was near the end. He said it wasn't according to the regulations, and he started to worry maybe you folks weren't going to keep the cemetery on a strict Orthodox basis. You know, this being a Conservative temple, instead of Orthodox like we're used to, you're apt to take a lot of shortcuts and make a lot of changes. So he was worried about being buried there."

"I see."

"According to him, Hirsh should have been buried on the side somewhere with no ceremony or anything. He told me about one that he had seen in the old country when he was a young man. There was this girl who took her own life. She was going to have a baby, and she was still a girl—I mean, she was unmarried. They just put her in the ground, and the next day her father went to work as though nothing happened. I mean, they didn't even mourn her for the seven days. It must have made a terrible impression on him, because he was terribly upset about Hirsh getting a regular funeral. He said if she was buried that way then Hirsh should be, too. Of course, he was confused because there's no connection."

The rabbi made to rise, now that the amenities were over, but Ben Goralsky waved him back. "My father's dozing right now. I told the nurse to let me know when he wakes up. Are you in a hurry?"

"No. As a matter of fact, I wanted an opportunity to talk to you. I understand you knew Isaac Hirsh."

"Yeah, I knew him. I knew his whole family. They lived next door to us in Chelsea, years ago. I knew his father and mother, and I knew him."

"And that's why you recommended him for that job at Goddard's?"

His thick lips parted and his heavy face relaxed in a grin. He shook his head slowly. "I recommended him for that job, and I put enough muscle behind it to make sure he got it. We're good customers of Goddard Lab, and I can talk turkey to Quint who runs the place. I got Hirsh that job because I hated his guts." He laughed aloud at the look of surprise on the rabbi's face.

"Like I said, they lived next door to us, the Hirshes. Both our families were mighty poor. We had this chicken business, his father had a little tailor shop. Mrs. Hirsh was all right. She was a good woman, and when she died I went to the funeral. We all did. My father closed the store so we could all go. Mr. Hirsh, he was something else again. A lazy good-for-nothing, always bragging about his precious son. We were four kids. I got two brothers and a sister, and every one of us worked in the store, after school, Sundays, nights. You had to in those days to make a living. I didn't even finish high school. I quit at the end of my first year and went to work in the store full time. But Ike Hirsh, he finished high and then went on to college and then went on after that to become a doctor—not a regular doctor, a doctor of philosophy. He didn't play with the other kids in the street. He was a little fat, roly-poly kid, the kind the other kids make fun of. So most of the time, he stayed inside reading books. And his father would come over to our house and brag about him. You know how Jews feel about education, so you can imagine how my father felt about us, especially in comparison with him. And old man Hirsh never let him forget it. But let me tell you something, Rabbi, my father never threw it up to us.

"Then Mrs. Hirsh died, and Mr. Hirsh waited just one year, practically to the day, to remarry. Now you know, you don't meet a woman

and ask her to marry you and get married in a day or two. Not at that
age, you don't. That means he was making arrangements during the
year of mourning, while his wife was hardly cold in her grave. Ike had
got himself a government job—big deal, after all that build-up—and
didn't even come to the wedding. And he didn't go to his father's funeral a year later. My father went. He wanted me to go, but I wouldn't.

"Well, things had been getting better for us right along. The war
helped. We had gone on living in the same little old house in Chelsea,
in the same old neighborhood even though at that time we could have
afforded a lot better. By the time the war was over, we were pretty
comfortable. My father had done a little speculating in real estate. He
had bought some good stocks. And still he went to work every morning
in the store. We had expanded there too, doing a big wholesale business, but my father was down there every morning in his apron and
straw hat. That's the kind of man my father is."

"And in all this time, I take it you hadn't heard from Hirsh?"

"That's right. Then one day he comes to visit us. He's got an idea
for manufacturing transistors. Nothing revolutionary, you understand,
but it can cut costs anywhere from ten to twenty percent. I hardly
knew what a transistor was, let alone my father, but he was convincing and my father had great faith in him. I guess without realizing it,
my father had been sort of sold on the idea that he was a genius. Hirsh
had it all worked out, and it looked good. He had contacts with all
kinds of government agencies and we'd be sure to get government contracts. Well, to make a long story short, my father agreed to invest ten
thousand dollars. Hirsh didn't have to put up a dime and he was a full
fifty percent partner.

"We got a warehouse and we set up our plant and started to operate.
He was the big idea man, and I was the dumb slob that knew just
enough to check in supplies, check shipments, see that the employees
worked. And in a year we had lost ten thousand dollars on top of our
original investment. Then we got a contract. It wouldn't show us much
of a profit, but it would carry us for a while. I went out and bought a
bottle to celebrate. We had a couple of drinks, drank each other's health
and success to the business. In the middle I got called away and had to
be gone the whole afternoon. When I got back, I found Hirsh still in
the office—dead drunk."

His face portrayed his shock of the memory. "Imagine, Rabbi, an
educated Jewish boy—a drunkard. I didn't tell my father. I was afraid
to. I was afraid to admit it to myself. I kept telling myself it was an
accident, that he had got a little high and didn't realize how much he
was taking. The next day he didn't come in. But the day after, he was

there right on time as if nothing happened. And the next day, he was drunk again. I stood it for a couple of weeks, and then I told my father. 'Get rid of him'—that's what my father said. 'Get rid of him before he ruins us.'"

"I take it you did."

Goralsky nodded his head in grim satisfaction. "I put it up to him to buy us out or let us buy him out. Of course he couldn't raise the money, and it wouldn't have done him any good if he could. Could a man like that run a business? We paid him fifteen thousand in cold cash, and said goodby. And you know, Rabbi, it was like pulling up an anchor. A couple of months later we got a really good government contract and we were on our way."

"Did you know about the contract when you made him the proposition?"

"As God's my witness, Rabbi. We had filed our bid months before, but we hadn't heard a word about it."

"All right. Then when did you see him next?"

"I never saw him again. We went public and sold stock and we got to be a big operation. We moved to this house. And then one day I get a letter from Hirsh telling me he's applied for a job at Goddard Lab and figures that perhaps I can help him because they must know me. So I called Quint and put it to him as strong as I could, and made sure that in his letter to Hirsh he'd say they were giving him the job largely on my say-so."

"But I don't understand. You say you did it because you hated him."

"That's right. There he was with his Ph.D. from Tech and I hadn't gone beyond the first year high. I wanted him to know that with all his education, he had to come to me for a job, and that I could deliver."

"But didn't you see him after he came?"

Goralsky shook his head. "He called a couple of times, and each time I told the girl to say I was out. I'm like superstitious, Rabbi. You have trouble with some hard-luck guy, I'm afraid it can rub off. And you want to know something: I was right. Twenty years ago, this Hirsh almost ruined us. He comes back to town and, sure enough, the son of a bitch almost ruins me again."

"How do you mean?"

"We had a little problem here and I gave it to Goddard to chew on to see what they can come up with. So after a while, we get a preliminary report and it says they think they've found a way to lick it and then some—a kind of breakthrough. At this time we're sort of playing with the idea of merging with another outfit—on a stock transfer basis. You understand?"

The rabbi nodded.

"This is confidential, Rabbi."

"Of course."

He laughed. "Confidential! Every brokerage house in Boston knows about it, but all they've got is rumors. You can't keep this sort of thing secret. Still, I wouldn't want it known that it came straight from me. See?"

The rabbi nodded again.

"So our stock starts going up. It's normal whenever there's news of a merger. It goes up for a couple of days and then slides back, sometimes even below where it was originally. But it doesn't work that way with us. It keeps climbing, and after a couple of weeks it's almost double. And I know damn well it isn't the rumor of the merger that did it. It was something else—a rumor that we had something special in the works. I guess you can't keep that kind of secret either. Maybe I'm a little sore about it. Maybe I got some idea that those double-domes over at the lab are playing the market, but I'm not hurting. After all, I'm in a merger situation on a stock transfer basis. Where I planned to give two of my shares for one of theirs, it looks now that I'll be swapping even, so what harm is done? And it's perfectly legit, you understand, because if I've got a new process coming through then my stock is worth that much more. Get it?"

"Yes."

"And then I get a call from Quint at Goddard Friday afternoon, just as I was leaving. It was Kol Nidre night, and I was leaving early. And he tells me he's very sorry, the preliminary report was premature—premature, hell, they'd flubbed the dub. You understand?"

"I think so," said the rabbi doubtfully. "They had made a mistake."

"That's right. So where does it leave me? Here I am involved in a merger with a high-class outfit, and it looks like I've been manipulating my stock to get a better deal."

"I see."

"What can I do? It's Yom Kippur, and when I get home I find my father is really sick. And the next day, he's no better—maybe even a little worse. And the next day, Sunday, I get a call from these people, and they're sore—and suspicious. Well, Monday I went down to Goddard to have it out with Quint. Maybe you never had any experience with these army types. He used to be a general, very dignified, very efficient, very businesslike. Bip, bip, bip. But I can see he's uncomfortable, and he's squirming. And finally, you know what he says? 'Well, it's your man who was at fault, Mr. Goralsky. You put him here. You practically forced us to take him—Isaac Hirsh!' How do you like that? The first time I ever did business with him, he almost ruins me. Then for twenty years I don't see or hear from him. When he comes here I'm careful to have nothing to do with him. And again he almost ruins me. See what I mean when I say you've got to keep away from guys like that? You want to know something, Rabbi? I'll bet you're wondering why I went to his funeral."

"Well, to go to a funeral is traditionally considered a blessing, a mitzvah."

"Mitzvah nothing! I wanted to make damn sure he got buried. . . ."

The maid put her head in the door. "Your father is awake now, Mr. Goralsky."

As they started up the staircase, Goralsky said, "Not a word about the cemetery business, Rabbi. I don't want my father upset."

"Of course not."

The old man was out of bed and sitting in a chair when his son and the rabbi entered. He extended a thin, blue-veined hand in greeting.

"See, Rabbi, I fasted and now I'm getting better."

The rabbi smiled at him. "I'm happy to see you looking so well, Mr. Goralsky."

"So well, I'm not yet." He glared at his son. "Benjamin, are you going to let the rabbi stand? Get him a chair."

"Oh, really you don't have to trouble." But Ben had already left the room. He came back carrying a chair, and set it down for the rabbi. He himself sat on the edge of the bed.

"I missed Kol Nidre," the old man went on, "for the first time in my life. Not once, since I was maybe five years old, did I stay away from the Kol Nidre service. My Ben tells me you gave a fine sermon."

The rabbi glanced covertly at Ben, who pursed his lips in a mute plea not to give him away. The rabbi grinned. "You know how it is, Mr. Goralsky, for Yom Kippur one tries a little harder. Next year, you'll be able to judge for yourself."

"Who knows if there'll be a next year. I'm an old man and I've worked hard all my life."

"Well, that's what gives you your vitality. Hard work—"

"He's been saying that for as long as I can remember," said Ben.

The old man looked at his son reproachfully. "Benjamin, you interrupted the rabbi."

"I was only going to say that hard work never hurt anyone, Mr. Goralsky. But you mustn't worry about what will happen a year from now. You must concentrate on getting well."

"That's true. One never knows whose turn will come next. Once, a few years ago, I had a sore on my face like a wart. I read the Jewish papers, Rabbi, and they have there every day a column from a doctor. Once it said that a sore like this could become, God forbid, a cancer. So I went to the hospital. The young doctor who examined me thought maybe I was worried the sore would spoil my looks. Maybe he thought I was an actor and wanted to look pretty. He asked me how old I was. Then I was maybe seventy-five. So when I told him, he laughed. He said if you were younger maybe we'd operate, like with a man my age it was a waste of time. So he gave me a salve, I should put it on and come back the next week. The next week when I come back, is already a different doctor. So I asked where's the doctor from last week, and they told me he had been killed in an automobile accident."

"Serves him right," said Ben.

"Idiot! You think I was complaining he was making fun of me? He was a fine young man, a doctor. What I mean is you can't tell who God will pick first. I understand the Hirsh boy died, right on the night of Kol Nidre. He was a good boy, too, and educated."

"He was a drunkard," said Ben.

The old man shrugged his shoulders. "Used to be, Rabbi, a drunkard was a terrible thing. But only a couple days ago I was reading in the Jewish paper, in this same column from the doctor, how a drunkard he's like a sick person—it's not his fault."

"He took his own life, Papa."

The old man nodded sadly. "That's a terrible thing. He must have suffered a lot. Maybe he couldn't stand it to be a drunkard. He was an educated boy. So maybe for him to be a drunkard was like for another person to have a cancer."

"You knew him well?" asked the rabbi.

"Isaac Hirsh? Sure, I knew him when he was born. I knew his father and mother. She was a fine woman, but the husband, the father, he was a nothing." He canted his head on one side in reflection. "It's hard to know what to do, what's right. Here was Hirsh who never did an honest day's work in his life. Even while his wife was alive, he used to be interested in the ladies. They used to say that a decent woman didn't want to go into his shop for a fitting. He made with the hands—you know what I mean. And when she died, he could hardly wait to get married again. Yet his son was an educated boy who went through college on scholarships and even became a doctor, a Ph.D. doctor. And I, what I worked hard all my life and I observed all the regulations, not one of my four children went to college."

"Well—"

"And yet, Rabbi, on the other side, all my children, they're in good health, they're well off, and they're all good to me. And Isaac Hirsh didn't even come to his father's funeral, and now he too is dead. So you can't tell."

"Then you feel differently now about Hirsh's burial," suggested the rabbi.

The old man's mouth set in a hard line. "No, Rabbi," he said. "A rule is a rule."

27

No formal announcement was made by the district attorney; only a short notice appeared in the inside pages of the *Lynn Examiner* stating that the district attorney's office was looking into the circumstances surrounding the death September 18 of Isaac Hirsh of 4 Bradford Lane, Barnard's Crossing, and that a petition might be filed for an order to exhume the body.

Marvin Brown caught the item as he glanced through the paper during his morning coffee break and called Mortimer Schwarz immediately.

"I'll bet the rabbi had something to do with that, Mort. It's a trick —it's one of the rabbi's little tricks, I tell you." He sounded excited.

"But how could the rabbi get to the district attorney? And what does he gain by it?"

"He's thick as thieves with Chief Lanigan and Lanigan goes to the D.A. As for what he stands to gain—why, he stops us from going ahead."

"You mean with the road? What's that got to do with the D.A.'s investigation?"

"Well, wouldn't it look kind of funny if we start building a road to set off the very grave they're interested in? The paper said they were going to exhume the body. Wouldn't that look nice while they're digging up the body for us to be laying out the road? You don't think there'd be questions?"

"I still don't see anything for us to get excited about, Marve. Obviously there's no connection between our work and theirs. And frankly, I can't imagine the rabbi going to all that trouble, especially where it doesn't change things the least bit. You know what I think? This guy Beam, the investigator for the insurance company, he must have got the ball rolling on this. After all, he represents a big insurance company that has a lot at stake. My guess is that they'd have a lot more influence with the district attorney than the rabbi would."

"Well, as far as I'm concerned, Mort, I'm not going ahead with the road business until after the district attorney is out of there."

"Personally, I don't see it. But if you feel that way, okay, so we'll wait a week."

"But what about the Board meeting Sunday? It's not safe to go ahead with the rabbi's resignation while this business with Hirsh is still hanging fire."

"Yeah, you've got a point there, Marve. You sure you don't want to go ahead with our plans—"

"No."

"All right, I'll tell you what we'll do: we'll call off the Board meeting."

"Isn't that kind of high-handed?"

"I don't think so. As president I can call a special meeting, can't I?"

"Sure, but—"

"So why can't I call off a meeting? Matter of fact, I could just call up our friends and tell them not to show. Then we wouldn't have a quorum."

"Maybe that would be better."

"Well, I'll see. In the meantime, keep your eye on the situation."

Brown was aware that the door of his office had opened and that his secretary was standing on the threshold. He wondered uneasily how much she had heard. He looked up at her inquiringly.

"There are two men to see you, Mr. Brown—from the police."

Since the death of her husband, Patricia Hirsh had not been left alone for a single evening by her friends and neighbors. She had been invited to dinner, and even when she was too tired and had to beg off, someone would drop in to spend part of the long evening with her. So she was not surprised one evening, when Peter Dodge dropped in on her, although she had not seen him since the funeral.

"I'm afraid I've been neglecting you, Pat. But I've been so busy with details of the MOGRE trip."

"Oh, I understand," she said. "And you've had to give up your walks, I suppose."

He seemed embarrassed. "No, I've passed here several times and thought of stopping, but there always seemed to be company—"

"They were just neighbors, friends from around here."

"I suppose it was foolish of me. I—I didn't want them to think I might be calling for—well, for professional reasons."

"Professional reasons?"

"Well, you see your friends and neighbors are mostly Jewish, and I was afraid they might think I was trying to win you back, now that your husband was gone."

"But I was never converted," she said. "Ike and I were married by a justice of the peace."

"I know, I know. It was silly of me. Please forgive me."

"There's nothing to forgive, Peter."

"Oh, but there is. You were all alone, and I should have been by your side, as your oldest friend here, as someone from your hometown—"

She smiled. "Well, all right, Peter, I forgive you."

She patted his hand, and immediately he capped it with his own. "Tell me, how are you really? I know it was a terrible shock, but are you all right now?"

Gently she withdrew her hand. "Yes, Peter. It's lonely, of course, but everyone has been very nice."

"And what are you planning to do? Go back to South Bend?"

"Oh, I don't think so, not to South Bend. I left there some time before I met Ike, and I have no one there, or anywhere else, for that matter. I haven't thought about it much, but I suppose I will stay on here for a while and try to get a job of some sort. I'd like to keep this house as long as I can, but I might have to give it up and take a small flat in Lynn or Salem—"

"A job is a good idea; it will keep your mind occupied."

"I suppose it will do that too, but it will mean I can eat regularly." She smiled. "I sort of got into the habit."

He was shocked. "I didn't realize. Didn't Ike—"

"Leave me provided? There's a small checking account, less than three hundred dollars, and a savings account of a little over a thousand. We paid down four thousand dollars on the house, and I'm sure I won't have any trouble selling the house for what we paid for it. And there's the car which I plan to sell. After what happened I never want to see it again."

"But wasn't there insurance?"

"Yes, there was insurance. But there also was a suicide clause, and there's a man around, a Mr. Beam, who is working for the insurance company, an investigator. If the insurance company decides it was suicide, then they'll just return the premiums we paid in and that's all."

"But they have to prove it, Pat. They can't just decide on their own."

"That's true, they can't. But they can refuse to pay, and then I would have to sue them for the money. It could drag on for years. Dr. Sykes said they might offer me a settlement, but it would be a lot less than the policy calls for. Still I think I'd probably take it if it were anything within reason."

"But why? You don't think he committed suicide, do you?"

She nodded slowly. "I think perhaps he may have." And she told him what happened at Goddard, how he was going downhill. When she finished, Dodge was silent a moment. Then: "I can't believe it. I didn't know your husband for long, and I didn't know him very well, but his mind—well, he was still one of the smartest men I ever met." He rose. "Look, Pat, I've got to go now. I've got to pack. I'm taking a plane south on this Civil Rights business tonight and just came to say goodby. I'll be gone a week or two—three at the most. You can't tell what's likely to happen once you get down there."

She held out her hand and he took it in both of his. "Promise me you won't do anything—you won't come to any decision on the insurance or anything else—until I get back. There are people in my parish, important people, businessmen, and I will consult with them. If you should need a job, I'm sure one of them will help. I want you to stay on here."

She smiled at him. "All right, Peter. I'm not likely to do anything for the next few weeks." She went to the door with him.

"Good. Believe me, dear, we'll work something out."

"Look here, Rabbi, we're on opposite sides of this cemetery business. Maybe I'm wrong and maybe I'm right. To me, it's a matter of what's best for the temple. I don't like the idea of selling a man something and then taking it back from him, even if he pulled a fast one on me in the transaction. If someone puts something over on me, all right, I'll know better the next time. Let the buyer beware—that's law, isn't it? And even though I sold Mrs. Hirsh that lot for her husband and it turns out maybe I shouldn't have, his death not being strictly kosher, I'd be the last one to crybaby on it, even though you're supposed to come to a deal with clean hands. But Mort Schwarz tells me that it isn't kosher, and that it might lose the temple a lot of money, enough to build a whole new chapel. So I come up with this idea, and it was all for the good of the temple. All right, maybe you don't agree with us, and maybe you're right, but what I say is fight fair."

"Would you mind telling me what you're talking about, Mr. Brown?"

"Oh, come on, Rabbi. Everybody in town knows that the chief of police and you are buddy-buddy."

"So?"

"So, I don't think an outsider, who isn't even a member of our faith, should interfere in a matter that is strictly a temple matter."

"Are you trying to tell me that Chief Lanigan came and tried to get you to change your stand on Hirsh?"

"He didn't come himself. But he sent a Lieutenant Jennings down with another officer. They're both in plain clothes and they come in and ask to see me. So my secretary—secretary?—she's the bookkeeper, general office worker, errand girl—she tells them I'm busy and can she help. So they say, no, they got to see me personal. So she says I'm busy and can't be disturbed. And then they flash their badges and say they guess I got to be disturbed. Now you know what that can mean in an office. There were a couple of my salesmen around, and they were talking to some customers. And the girl herself."

"Anyone is subject to police inquiry, I suppose, Mr. Brown. Are you suggesting that I sent them?"

"Well, they came to talk about Hirsh. They wanted to know what connection I had with him. What connection would I have with him? I hardly knew the man. When he first moved into town, I sent him an announcement. I send them out to all new residents, that's business. A little later, I sent him another announcement. It's a special kind of letter that offers a special free premium if you fill out the enclosed card. I think at that time we were using a kind of wallet that you carry in your breast pocket and it has a little pad of paper and a ballpoint pen, twenty-eight fifty a gross. So when he or his wife signed the card and sent it in, I called him on the phone and made an appointment, just like I would with anyone else. Maybe you got one when you first came to town. Then I went over there and I sold him some insurance. And that's all there was to it. I didn't even deliver the policy. I was busy at the time and sent one of my salesmen down. I never saw him again. I'm not even sure if I would remember him if I did see him again. That was my connection with Hirsh."

"But the way they acted and the questions they asked, like I had done something criminal. Why was I so interested in changing the layout of the road? Didn't I realize that it would cut Hirsh's grave off from the others? What did I have against Hirsh? I couldn't tell them about the Goralsky business. That's all hush-hush, and as far as I know Ben Goralsky hasn't even agreed to give the chapel. So I told them about our law against burying suicides. And then they tell me that they understand according to you it isn't against the law, and couldn't it be I had some other reason. Then they begin asking me what I was doing the night Hirsh died."

"Well, that should have been easy. It was Kol Nidre."

"None of it was hard. They were just giving me the business. And don't tell me, Rabbi, that they can't touch me if I haven't done anything wrong. Aside from taking up my time, they can do me lots of harm just by coming to see me. A man in business, especially the insurance business, has to be above suspicion. What if word gets around that the police are coming down to the office to question me? Do you think that would improve my business?"

The rabbi was spared the necessity of answering by the ringing phone. It was Lanigan.

He sounded jubilant. "Rabbi, remember I told you that Goralsky, Mr. Ben Goralsky, was the one who recommended Hirsh for the job at Goddard?"

"Yes."

"Well, did you know that Hirsh and Goralsky were originally partners, and that the process the Goralskys now use, by which they made a fortune, I might add, was Hirsh's idea? They backed him with money and then bought him out."

"Yes, I knew that."

There was a pause, then—and the voice was cold, "You never mentioned it to me."

"I didn't think it was significant."

"I think you and I should have a little talk, Rabbi. Maybe tonight?"

"That will be all right. Right now, Mr. Marvin Brown is here with me. He tells me that a couple of your men were down to see him."

"And I might say that he wasn't what I would call overly cooperative."

"That may be, but what I'm concerned with right now is that he seems to think it was done at my instigation. Did your men say anything to give him that idea?"

"You know better than that, Rabbi."

"Of course. But then how can you possibly be interested in him?"

"Well now, Rabbi, on that point I received a bit of intelligence not twenty minutes ago. Since he's there with you, you might just ask him a question for me. Ask him, why did he leave the temple before the service was over?"

"Are you sure?"

"I'm sure, Rabbi." With a laugh Lanigan hung up.

The rabbi turned to Marvin Brown. "That was Chief Lanigan." Brown's smirk seemed to say, I told you so.

"Tell me, Mr. Brown, Friday night, the Kol Nidre service, did you leave the temple early?"

Marvin Brown reddened.

"So that was why you did not respond when you were called for your honor. Why, Mr. Brown, why?"

"I—I don't think I have to answer. I—I don't care to—that is, I'm not on any witness stand, and I don't have to answer as to my whereabouts to anyone."

28

"I'm a cop first and foremost, Rabbi," said Lanigan, "and I don't take kindly to your withholding information that might be of value to our investigation."

"I don't see how the fact that Goralsky recommended Hirsh for a job should make me think he wanted to kill him," said the rabbi. He was matching the chief's reserve and his tone was coldly polite.

"Rabbi, Rabbi, I explained all that. We've got a weapon that practically anybody could have used, and a motive that can be almost anything. The only line we can take is to check opportunity. I told you the Jews of Barnard's Crossing had practically a communal alibi because they were all in the temple at the time, so for that very reason anyone who wasn't has some explaining to do. Now who wasn't? Your friend Marvin Brown, for one. I understand he's some kind of big shot in your temple, a vestryman or something like that."

"He's on the Board of Directors."

"Okay, so if anyone should have been there, he should. And we know he was at the temple but left early—why, he wouldn't say. Now on top of that, we find he sold Hirsh his insurance. It isn't much, but for a guy like Hirsh who kept to himself pretty much, it's a connection. So we question him. If it upsets him, that's too bad. It's one of the burdens of citizenship."

"Aren't you supposed to tell a man what he's being questioned for? And in a murder case, aren't you supposed to warn him that what he says may be used against him?"

"We haven't accused him of anything. We were just looking for information. Maybe when we go see him again, I'll take just that line. Right now, I'm letting him stew a little. And remember, no one is supposed to know that Hirsh was murdered."

"How long are you going to keep that up?"

The chief grinned, for the first time since he arrived. "It's actually not much of a secret right now. Once I reported the matter to the D.A., it was bound to get around town. You can't keep those things dark. The chances are that your friend Brown has already figured out that we wouldn't send two men to question him at his office and check on his whereabouts unless something like murder was involved. In tonight's *Examiner* there was a little item in Fred Stahl's Roundabout column. Didn't you see it?"

"I don't read gossip columns."

"Well, sometimes it pays. The Roundabout asks: Are the police hiding something? Why should the office of the District Attorney be investigating the death of a well-known scientist in a town not many miles from here? Could the death possibly be more mysterious than it appeared? Did the police goof and are they covering up?"

"And this is how the most important business of the community is conducted?" asked the rabbi sadly. "Hints in gossip columns, rumor, speculation? And if Marvin Brown's secretary and the other people in the office see that item and jump to the conclusion that he's a suspect in a murder case, that's just one of the burdens of citizenship, is it? And all because he sold the dead man an insurance policy."

"It wasn't just the insurance policy. There was also the matter of selling the widow a grave site. And trying to shunt the body aside in the cemetery. And in this crazy case where we have so little to go on, we check any two facts that happen to coincide."

"And Ben Goralsky—he is suspect because he got Hirsh a job and because years ago they were partners for a short time?"

"And because he wasn't at the synagogue either. And according to what I hear, the Goralskys are very Orthodox and very devout. It seems funny that he shouldn't have gone."

"You also heard, I suppose, that his father was very sick and that he was afraid he might die?"

"Not from you, Rabbi." And once again, the atmosphere which had warmed somewhat, cooled.

"You said you were first and foremost a policeman. Well, first and foremost I am a rabbi. Mr. Goralsky is a member of my congregation, and I cannot see myself inviting his confidence in order to transmit it to the police."

"You mean that if you found a member of your congregation had committed murder, you would not inform the police?"

"I am bound by the duties of citizenship just as is everyone else," said the rabbi stiffly.

"But you won't help us find him."

"I will not cast suspicion on innocent people so that the police can harass them—"

"Harass them? Do you think we grill them for the pleasure of seeing them squirm?"

"The effect is the same. Marvin Brown was upset—even frightened. I'm sure it wasn't because he had committed murder and was afraid he might be discovered. He was afraid of the effect on his business and his friends, on his wife and children."

"But he did leave the temple early and he wouldn't tell you why."

"What of it? There were probably lots of people who left the temple at one time or another. It's a long service, and people get tired. They go out for a breath of air, or to stretch their legs—"

"And would they be ashamed to say so?"

"Of course not. But Marvin Brown might have left for any number of reasons he would hesitate to admit to me. Maybe he went home for a bite, and he wouldn't like it known that he had broken his fast."

"And he might have gone to kill Hirsh."

"Why? Because he sold him an insurance policy? You might as well question anyone else who had the slightest contact with Hirsh—the baker who sold him bread, the butcher who sold him meat, the mechanic who fixed his car, a hundred others. And since most of them probably are not Jews, they would not have been in the temple and a good many probably would be unable to prove their whereabouts."

"I'm not saying Brown's guilty of murder because he left the synagogue early. I'm just saying that in a case like this where the weapon was so accessible, and the motive could be almost anything—"

"Aren't you, perhaps, riding that idea a little too hard?"

"How do you mean?"

"Because there was ample opportunity for the killing you have proceeded on the theory that no strong motive was involved. That may very well be true, but it doesn't have to be. The killer may have been planning to kill Hirsh for months, but either didn't quite have the nerve or the opportunity never arose. Perhaps he may have planned to kill him in some conventional manner and taken advantage of this situation merely because it presented itself."

"I don't see how that gets us any further."

"It suggests other lines of investigation."

"Such as?"

The rabbi shrugged his shoulders. "We know Hirsh worked on the Manhattan Project. Perhaps his background there might be worth investigation. I don't want to sound melodramatic, but conceivably he had information someone might want, or even might *not* want him to tell."

"But that was almost twenty years ago. It's unlikely such information would have much significance today. Besides, why wait all this time before acting?"

"There may be nothing to it, but can you rule it out for certain? Up till now, he's been in another part of the country. Now he comes back East—where there is the greatest concentration of scientists. Who's to say he didn't run into someone—maybe at Goddard?"

"I suppose we could check the personnel files to see if anyone else there worked on the Manhattan Project," the chief said doubtfully.

"What about the fact that Mrs. Hirsh is a rather attractive young woman?"

Lanigan looked at the rabbi. "As a rabbi, I wouldn't think you'd notice such things."

"Even your priests who are celibate can, I'm sure, distinguish between an attractive woman and a plain one."

Lanigan smiled reminiscently. "Yeah, I guess Father O'Keefe could, although I have my doubts about Father Chisholm. Are you suggesting that the widow might have a lover—"

"From what I have seen of her I would doubt it, but it's not impossible. Rather I was thinking that some man, a man younger than her husband, might have been attracted to her and think he'd have a better chance with Hirsh out of the way."

"It's worth checking into, I suppose." He turned to his host with sudden suspicion. "You wouldn't be trying to tout me off Marvin Brown and Goralsky, would you now, Rabbi?"

"I am merely suggesting that there are other lines of investigation than members of my congregation who happened for one reason or another to have missed the Kol Nidre service."

"Yeah? Well, that's as may be. But we're going to continue to check into the movements and whereabouts of your friends that Friday night regardless of whatever other approaches we make. I'll bid you good night now, Rabbi, but I don't mind saying I'm a little disappointed. I don't suppose I have to warn you that if you tip off Goralsky or anyone else I've mentioned, I could consider you an accessory after the fact."

29

In a small town there are no secrets; a secret is not something unknown, only something not talked about openly. By Thursday, when the district attorney finally met with the press, it was generally known that there was some mystery connected with the death of Hirsh. Nor did the district attorney clarify matters much in his press conference. In spite of sharp questioning he would admit only that evidence had come to the attention of the police of Barnard's Crossing that suggested Isaac Hirsh had not met with death by accident.

"Are you suggesting that his death was suicide?"

"That's certainly one of the possibilities."

"Are you perhaps suggesting that he might have been murdered?" asked another reporter.

"We are not ruling out that possibility."

"Can you give us some idea of the nature of the new evidence that was brought to your attention?"

"I do not think it would be in the public interest at this time."

"Isaac Hirsh was at one time connected with the Manhattan Project. Is there any connection between his death and his government work on the atom bomb?"

"We are not ruling out that possibility."

"Can you tell us what steps you plan to take—"

"The investigation is at present being conducted largely by the Barnard's Crossing police in cooperation with state detectives."

"If there is any connection with the federal government, or for that matter if it is murder, isn't it unusual to leave this to a small town police force?"

"We have every confidence in Chief Lanigan, and since he is intimately acquainted with the people of the town we feel he is the best man to work on the case at this stage. Of course—through this office—he can call on every facility of the commonwealth, or of the federal government if it should turn out to be involved."

"Are you planning to exhume the body of Isaac Hirsh?"

"That is a distinct possibility."

And that was as far as he would go. To all other questions he answered, "I don't think I care to go into that at this time."

Lieutenant Eban Jennings was a tall, thin man with sparse grayish hair. He had watery blue eyes which he dabbed frequently with a folded handkerchief, and his Adam's apple bobbed in his scrawny neck as he talked.

"I went over to see the widow like you said. You know, Hugh. She's really something."

"How do you mean?"

"Well, she's a big woman and right handsome, with a head of flaming red hair, white skin, and tits like a pair of silver cups—"

"My, aren't we getting poetic!"

"It's just that she's a fine figure of a woman with a lovely round arse your hands just itch to pat—"

"You're a horny bastard."

"I'm just telling you how she struck me," said Jennings reproachfully. "My point is, there she is—a woman like that, not more than thirty-five I'll bet, and she's married to a little shrimp of a guy old enough to be her father. And what a guy. Bald, pot-bellied, a rummy, and a Jew at that. So why would a woman like her want to marry somebody like him? All right, maybe she'd had tough times and wanted someone who'd treat her decent. But, dammit, it couldn't last. After a while, she'd stop feeling grateful and start looking around, and there'd be plenty of men willing to start making up to her."

"Hear anything—rumors, gossip, to that effect?"

"No-o, but then I haven't really asked around. I just questioned the widow about whether anything unusual had happened that day. You know: any unusual letters, phone calls, visits. She couldn't think of anything but did happen to mention that the young curate, whatsis-name, Peter Dodge over at St. Andrews, had said he might drop in on Hirsh that evening."

"The Reverend Peter Dodge?" Suddenly Lanigan had a thought. "Say, that's right. That time he came down to complain about some fracas at Bill's Cafe he mentioned he was from South Bend. And that's where she's from."

"Yeah? Then listen to this. After what she told me, I figured maybe he did drop in that night. Maybe Hirsh said something that could help. So I went on over to this place where Dodge boards, with Milly Oliphant—just routine follow-up—and he was gone."

"Gone?"

"Not for good. According to Milly, Dodge packed a bag and flew to Alabama. He's head of some bunch of clergymen who are going down there to picket. But now, get this—the group isn't supposed to leave for a couple of days. I got that from Dr. Sturgis, the rector, who is his boss. He said Dodge decided to go down a little earlier to take care of some administrative details."

"Peter Dodge. A clergyman."

"Well, that's where we don't agree, Hugh. You can't think of a clergyman in connection with a woman, but to me, they're men just like anyone else. I don't care whether he's a priest or a minister or a rabbi. The right kind of woman comes along, and he's going to feel his pants tighten. And this Dodge fellow—he's pretty new at the game. Before this, I understand he was a professional football player. And he's a big man—which would appeal to a woman her size. And he's young, her age. And he's not married. And he left town."

"Are you trying to suggest that he ran away?"

"All I'm saying is look at the facts, Hugh. This group he's connected with, they aren't scheduled to leave for a couple of days yet. He had planned to go with them but instead he went early."

"So what do you have in mind?"

"Isn't it funny that he left right after that item appeared in the *Examiner*? The one that hinted at new developments about Hirsh's death?"

30

On Friday there were two evening services at the temple: the regular minyan at sunset primarily for mourners that lasted about fifteen minutes; and a more comprehensive family service that began at eight, ran for about an hour, and was followed by a collation in the vestry. Miriam always attended the later service, not only because it was expected of her as the rabbi's wife, but because she felt he appreciated the encouragement of her presence as he delivered his sermon.

But this Friday had been one of her few bad days during a comparatively easy and uneventful pregnancy. She was tired and her feet were swollen from the extra housework required to prepare the house for the Sabbath. Rather than upset him by suggesting she stay home, she asked if he'd mind if she rode to temple.

Immediately he was solicitous. "Aren't you well, dear? It isn't—"

"No, it isn't time yet." She smiled. "It's just that I've been on my feet all day and I'm not up to walking. I'll call the Margolises to pick me up."

"Nonsense, I'll drive you."

"But David, you don't ride on the Sabbath—"

"It's not really a religious scruple, Miriam. That would be hypocritical of me as rabbi of a Conservative congregation where the whole congregation rides. No, it's just a matter of habit really; I'll take you."

"But when they see you drive up, won't they possibly connect it with the rumors of your resignation—"

He laughed. "You mean they'll think I've been a hypocrite all along, and now that I'm resigning I'm showing my true colors? Well, if they want to think that, let them. Come on." He took her by the arm and marched her out to the car. Flinging open the car door, he waved her in.

It would have been a grand gesture if the car had started immediately. But five minutes later, he was still jabbing his toe at the starter—and producing nothing more than an angry whir. He muttered under his breath, and she had just about decided to remark brightly that she was no longer tired and would now like to walk when the motor caught.

He drove to the end of the street and slowed down to make the turn.

"Turn left," Miriam said.

"But the temple is right," he protested.

"We're driving, so we've got plenty of time."

He shrugged as if to say, who can argue with a pregnant woman, but did as he was told.

They went a couple of blocks and she said, "Pull up here." He realized he was abreast of the office of the local cab company, and at last understood.

"My husband has been having some trouble with his car," she said when the proprietor came over, "and one of these days he may have to get me to the hospital in a hurry. Are you available all the time?"

"Twenty-four hours a day, Mrs. Small."

"What happens if all your cabs are busy?" the rabbi asked.

"Don't worry, Rabbi. We've got four cabs, and in the last couple of months the only time I've had them all out at one time was that Friday night you had your important holiday. They were shuttling back and forth to your temple until half-past seven or quarter to eight. And then we didn't have another call until around midnight. Guess everyone drove home with friends." He seemed somewhat aggrieved.

"Then we can depend on you if my husband can't get his car started?"

"Nothing to worry about, believe me, Mrs. Small. With business the way it is these days, I could guarantee to get you there if you was to have twins." He laughed uproariously at his own joke.

When once again the rabbi had difficulty in starting, the taxi man showed professional interest. "Sounds like the carburetor," he said. "Better attend to it right away."

Just then the motor caught and the rabbi raced it for the sheer pleasure of hearing the motor roar. "I'll do that," he called out as he drove off.

"I'm glad you thought to ask about the cab service. It's extra insurance."

"It isn't because you don't want to be indebted to Chief Lanigan, is it?"

"Of course not."

The temple parking lot seemed fuller than usual for a Friday night service.

"Do you think it's because they've heard of your resignation?" asked Miriam. "And they want to show they're behind you?"

"More likely it's curiosity. They may want to find out what's happening with me, and they've probably heard conflicting stories about Hirsh's death."

"You're being bitter and cynical, David."

He looked at her in surprise. "Not at all. Actually, it's an indication that the temple is fulfilling one of its principal and traditional functions—as a center for the community. In the ghettos of Europe, or for that matter in the voluntary ghettos of America, the moment something happened news traveled with the speed of a telegram from house to house. But here, where there is no real Jewish section, where every Jew has Gentiles on either side, if something happens that is of particular interest to Jews they come to the temple to get the lowdown. I don't feel hurt. Quite the contrary, I'm pleased."

But those who thought the rabbi might speak of his rumored resignation and the reasons for it were disappointed; by no word did he suggest that this Friday evening was different from any other. After the service, when he joined the congregation in the vestry for the tea and cake the Sisterhood regularly provided, his ear caught snatches of conversation; for the most part it seemed concerned with the death of Isaac Hirsh. Once he heard someone say, "I'll bet the rabbi knows what it's all about. I wouldn't be surprised if his resignation had something to do with it."

"But how?"

"Don't ask me, but happening at the same time the way they both did—"

Yet to those few who came up and asked him what he thought about the Hirsh business, in each case he replied, "I don't know. I didn't know the man."

He was pleased to see that Miriam, who would normally have remained standing at his side, had shown sense enough to take one of the folding chairs against the wall. A small group of women had gathered around her and were being solicitous.

"Above all, my dear, you mustn't worry. That's the worst thing you can do. When I was having my third, my Alvin, the doctor said to me, 'Whatever you do, don't worry; it tightens the muscles.' I shouldn't worry when my Joe was being transferred here from Schenectady, and we didn't know if we were going to be able to get a house or have to live in a hotel, and what would I do with Marjorie and Elaine, with their school in the meantime. But I made up my mind that the baby comes first, and I told Joe to go ahead and make any arrangements he wanted and I'd live with them."

"That's right," said Mrs. Green. "Mental attitude is important. I know it's old-fashioned to think that you have to think beautiful thoughts during your pregnancy, but when I was having Pat I had the phonograph going all day long, and didn't she get to be the first drum majorette of the high school band? The instructor said she had an innate sense of rhythm, whereas Fred who had trumpet lessons for years could never even keep in step, let alone keep time to the music."

"It didn't work with me," said Gladys Moreland flippantly. "My mother went to the museum every Sunday right up to her seventh month, and I can't draw a straight line."

"Oh, but you've got artistic temperament," insisted Mrs. Green. "Anyone who sets foot in your living room can see that you've got exquisite taste."

"Well, I am interested in interior decorating."

Mrs. Wasserman, wife of the first president of the temple, pulled up a chair alongside Miriam. She was a motherly woman of sixty and had been friendly from the day the Smalls first arrived in Barnard's Crossing.

"You feel tired these days, huh?"—her way of noting that Miriam was sitting down instead of standing by her husband's side.

"A little," Miriam admitted.

She patted her hand. "Pretty soon now. Nothing to worry about. And I'll bet it will be a boy."

"David and his mother, especially his mother, won't accept anything else."

Mrs. Wasserman laughed. "If it's a girl, they'll accept. And after two or three days, you couldn't get them to swap for a boy. He's nervous, the rabbi?"

"Who can tell?"

"Oh, they all try to be like that, like it's not important, but you can tell. Before my first one was born, Jacob, he was so cool and calm. But he had the whole steam system checked over, he thought maybe the house was a little chilly. He had a carpenter come in and make a chute from the baby's room to the laundry in the basement. In those days we didn't have a diaper service. He hired a man to shovel the snow off the steps and the walk for the whole season. He took out extra insurance, God forbid anything should happen to him there would be plenty for me and the baby. I'll bet your husband is the same way."

Miriam smiled faintly. "You don't know my David."

"Well, he's so busy—"

"It was all I could do to make him stop at the taxicab office to arrange

for transportation in case our car wouldn't start. But for the rest"
—she smiled—"he thinks it's enough to examine his conscience and make
sure he isn't doing anything he thinks wrong."

"Maybe that's the best way," suggested Mrs. Wasserman gently.

"Maybe. Though sometimes—"

"You'd like him to be a little more—excited?"

Miriam nodded.

"It doesn't mean anything, my dear. Some men, they keep their tender-
ness all inside. My father, may he rest in peace, he was like that. When
I was born—my mother used to tell about it, it was like a family joke—
she felt the pains coming so she sent a neighbor's boy for my father
who was in the House of Study. It was in the old country, you understand. He was in the middle of a discussion, and maybe being a young
man he was a little embarrassed before the older men, so he told the
boy to go back and tell her to cover herself up good and that it would
probably pass. But a minute later, he excused himself and ran so fast
that he reached home the same time as the neighbor's boy."

Miriam laughed. "My David wouldn't be embarrassed, but if he were
really involved in a discussion he might forget to come. . . ."

Morris Goldman who owned a garage drifted toward where the rabbi
was standing, talking loudly: "—a little shrimp of a guy, bald-headed
with a potbelly, and he turns out to be married to a big gorgeous red-
head, a shicksa yet, who is half his age. Oh, *Gut Shabbes*, Rabbi. I was
talking about this guy Hirsh."

"You knew him?"

"I knew him like I know any customer. You know how it is, they're
waiting around for their car, you pass the time of day. Him I guess I
knew a little better than most because he had an old car so he brought
it in more often—brakes, flat tire. Once I put a new muffler on."

"How'd he come to go to you?" asked one of the bystanders. "Your
garage is way out of town."

"He worked at the Goddard Lab and I get all the cars from there.
My place is off Route 128, maybe five hundred yards from the Lab.
You know, right at the foot of the cutoff just before you get to the Lab.
They leave their cars with me for a lube job, a tune-up, and then walk
to work from there."

"You do all kinds of work?" asked the rabbi.

"You bet, and if I say so myself I've got as good a crew of mechanics
as any place on the North Shore. I've got one man, an ignition specialist,
I've had people come from as far away as Gloucester just so he can service them. Why, your car acting up on you, Rabbi?"

"I've been having a bit of trouble," he said. "She's hard starting. And sometimes when I come to a stop, she dies."

"Well, it could be almost anything, Rabbi. Why don't you ride out someday and let me take a look at it?"

"Maybe I will." He thought he saw Miriam sending out distress signals, and excused himself. "Are you tired, dear? Would you like to go home now?"

"I think I should," she said. "I'll get my coat."

He was waiting for her to find her things in the cloakroom when he saw a jubilant Jacob Wasserman and Al Becker bearing down on him.

"Well, Rabbi! Things certainly look a lot different now, don't they?"

"How do you mean?"

"This announcement by the police, by the district attorney," exclaimed Becker. "Of course, the D.A. was pussyfooting. He's a politician and all politicians have to double-talk, but there's no doubt in anyone's mind that Hirsh was murdered. He as much as admitted it. So you're vindicated! He got you off the hook. You're in the clear."

"If you're referring to the burial service I conducted, Mr. Becker, I needed no vindication from the district attorney. And if I had, I would hardly consider it good news to be let off the hook as you put it, at the cost of a man's murder."

"Sure, sure, nobody likes to hear someone has been murdered. I'm sorry about it. Who wouldn't be? But don't you see—it knocks the pins out from under Mort Schwarz and his gang. You heard that he called off the regular Board meeting Sunday?"

"No, I didn't."

"You'll probably get a card in the mail tomorrow."

"And what significance do you attach to the cancellation?"

Wasserman rubbed his hands gleefully. "We think perhaps under the circumstances they want to see how the Hirsh business comes out before they bring up the matter of your resignation. I have it from a very reliable source that Marvin Brown refused to go ahead with laying out the road."

"Refused? Why?"

"Because the district attorney may exhume the body."

The rabbi gave a wan smile. "It comes to the same thing in the end, doesn't it, Mr. Wasserman?"

"Oh, but Rabbi, there's a difference. This is the civil authority, engaged in bringing a criminal to justice."

"Of course."

"What we've got to think about now is what steps to take. As far as Hirsh is concerned—" He shrugged his shoulders. "Well, it makes no difference to him what caused his death. He's dead; we've got to concern ourselves about the living. Now, the business about your resignation. You don't really want to resign, do you?"

"I wouldn't have if this matter hadn't come up."

"Good. So we have to figure out a way to keep Schwarz from reading your letter to the Board. I've discussed it with Becker here, and we both decided the easiest and best way would be if you wrote Schwarz recalling your resignation." As the rabbi was about to interpose, he hurried on. "You could say that in the light of recent events there is no longer any difference between you and the administration, and for that reason you are revoking your previous letter."

"No."

"But don't you see, Rabbi, without that there's just your letter of resignation. All he has to do is to read it and call for a vote. Strictly speaking, he doesn't even have to call for a vote. He just announces it. But if there are two letters, he's bound to read them both and then he'll have to explain the issue between you. Even then, you're not out of the woods but at least we'll have the advantage."

The rabbi shook his head. "I'm sorry, gentlemen, but—"

"Now look here, Rabbi," said Becker sternly. "Jake and I have gone all out for you. We're trying to help you the best way we can, but there's a certain amount you've got to do for yourself. You can't expect us to work our heads off, calling up people, going to see them, explaining, when you won't do your part."

"I expect nothing." He turned to Miriam, who was emerging from the cloakroom. "You'll have to excuse me. My wife is very tired."

Becker watched his retreating figure, then turned to Wasserman. "That's what you get for trying to help a guy."

Wasserman shook his head. "He's been hurt, Becker. He's a young man, practically a boy. And he's been hurt. . . ."

As they walked through the parking lot to their car, Miriam said, "Mr. Becker and even Mr. Wasserman seemed rather cool, David. Was it something you said to them?"

He reported the conversation, and she smiled wistfully. "So now you have no one behind you—not Mr. Wasserman, not Chief Lanigan, not Mr. Schwarz. Do you have to quarrel with everyone, David?"

"I didn't quarrel with them. I just refused to ask Schwarz to disregard my letter. In effect, it's begging him to keep me on."

"But you do want to stay, don't you?"

"Of course, but I can't ask. Don't you see I can't ask? The relationship between the rabbi and the Board of Directors requires maintaining a delicate balance. If I have to beg them to let me stay when I'm only doing my job, how can I ever have any influence on them? How can I guide them? I would be just a rubber stamp for anything they wanted to do. Once they realized they made me knuckle under while exercising my official function as rabbi, what could I do? And what could they not do?"

"I suppose so," she said softly. "And I know you're right, but—"

"But what?"

"But I'm just a young married woman, a couple of hundred miles from my mother and my family, and I'm going to have a baby any day now."

"So?"

"So I wish I were sure my husband had a job."

31

"I never interfere, Hugh. You know that. I'm no policeman and I'd be the last one to try to tell you your job, but the police department does come under the administrative supervision of the selectmen, and it's the broader aspects"—he made a wide sweep with his arm—"that I think it's our duty to go into."

Alford Braddock was not the typical Barnard's Crossing selectman. He was a native, to be sure—it was unthinkable that anyone not a Crosser born would be elected to the Board—but whereas the rest of the members were small businessmen with a taste for town politics, he was a man of considerable wealth, inherited wealth, which included a stock brokerage firm in Boston. Where others had to campaign personally, calling on voters, appearing at meetings of fraternal orders, speaking before the League of Women Voters, he blitzed the electorate with campaign posters and door-to-door house calls by a group of paid "volunteers." He outpolled all the other candidates easily and consequently was elected chairman of the board. He was tall and distinguished with snow-white hair and the ruddy complexion of the yachtsman. His clear blue eyes were candid and without guile and yet could look hurt—hurt, but determined to bear up and not show it—when you disagreed with him.

"What is it that's bothering you, Alford?" asked Lanigan quietly.

"Bothering me? Bothering me? Well, yes, I suppose you could put it that way. Something Dr. Sturgis mentioned. Said you were inquiring about Peter Dodge. Now he got it into his head that it had something to do with this Hirsh business. Of course, I assured him it was unlikely, most unlikely. After all, what connection would Peter Dodge have with Isaac Hirsh?"

"He might have been trying to convert him," suggested Lanigan with a smile.

"Think so? Yes, it's possible. A very enthusiastic fellow, this Dodge, from the Midwest I believe," he added as though that explained everything.

"As a matter of fact, we know he was planning to see Hirsh the night he was killed," said Lanigan. "About this Civil Rights business, perhaps."

"Yes, that must be it. That must be the connection. He was terribly enthusiastic about Civil Rights. Now I know that for a fact, Hugh. I mean I know that personally."

"There's another connection, Alford. He happens to know Mrs. Hirsh. They come from the same hometown—South Bend."

"Whatsat? Knew Mrs. Hirsh? What are you trying to say, Hugh?"

"Not a thing. I'm not suggesting anything. It's just that we'd like to ask Mr. Dodge a few questions. We sent him a wire down in Alabama asking him to get in touch with us. But he didn't. We called the hotel in Birmingham where he was supposed to be staying, and he wasn't there. I don't mean that he checked out, I mean he wasn't there. In fact, he hadn't been there since checking in a couple of days ago. I spoke to the hotel people and they said it wasn't unusual, not too unusual where these Civil Rights people are concerned. They register at a hotel, but then they contact the local headquarters of their organization down there and that's usually the last the hotel sees of them. Usually, they check out though. So we called the Alabama authorities to contact him for us, but so far we haven't heard."

"You're trying to say something, Hugh. Dammit, why don't you come right out with it? You're trying to say that this man Dodge, an Anglican priest, got involved with the wife of this Jew, and as a result became mixed up in this murder business and ran off—flew the coop, beat it."

Lanigan grinned. "You mean, he took a powder?"

"Dammit, Hugh, it's no laughing matter. That what you're trying to say?"

"It's possible."

"But dammit, a man of the cloth, and from my own church."

"But he's young, unmarried, and—to use your own word—enthusiastic."

"Hugh, do you realize what this could mean?"

"Yeah, but I honestly don't think it will. We don't really have anything on him, we just want to question him. Find out if he saw Hirsh, and if he did, what time he left him."

Braddock was obviously relieved. "You'll probably find there's nothing to his absence from the hotel. I mean, as far as I can gather from news stories, these people who go down to march and picket and whatnot make a point of living with the—er—with the people. You'll probably find he has been staying in some colored sharecropper's shack out of reach of a telephone." Braddock smiled broadly. "You know, Hugh, you really had me going there for a minute."

Lanigan grinned.

"You've got a real suspect, now haven't you? This insurance fellow?"

"Brown? Marvin Brown? We're interested in him. At least we'd like to know where he was at the time."

"No alibi, eh?"

"We haven't asked him yet."

"Why not?"

"Well, there's no hurry. We have nothing on him except a couple of points of contact with Hirsh. He'll keep. It won't do any harm to let him stew for a while. These quick, nervy types—they get bothered and start worrying if you leave them alone, and after a while they're apt to do something just a little foolish."

Braddock rubbed his hands. Police business was fascinating, and as chairman of the Board of Selectmen he was in on the ground floor. "I get it, I get it," he said.

"Actually, we find Mr. Benjamin Goralsky a lot more interesting."

Braddock sat up straight. "Goralsky? Ben Goralsky of Goraltronics? Hold on a minute, Hugh, now you're barking up the wrong tree. I know the man. He's one of the finest specimens of his race. His plant employs over a thousand people from around here. When they went public, our firm helped float the initial stock issue, and we've been close to them ever since. No, nothing there, I assure you."

"Well, maybe not, but we plan to have Ben Goralsky down and ask him a lot of questions."

"I won't have it, Hugh. You're planning some kind of psychological third degree and I won't permit it. You haven't got anything on him, and you're just going on a fishing expedition. Well, I won't allow it. There are things in the wind that you don't know about and this could have repercussions that would affect the whole community."

"You mean the merger?"

"Who said anything about a merger? What do you know about a merger?"

"Oh, come now, Alf, everybody knows there's talk of Goraltronics being involved in a merger."

"Well, maybe, maybe. I suppose there are rumors floating around. Well, I'll admit it, but you keep this under your hat, understand? It's true—there is a merger in the offing. And it could be a tremendous thing for this whole area. I don't mind admitting that my firm is a little interested, and right now things are very touchy. Understand? So I'm telling you to keep your hands off Ben Goralsky."

"And let him get away with murder?"

"Dammit, he's not getting away with murder. You prove that he did it, and he's all yours. But until you have something definite on him, you leave him alone. And that's an order, Hugh. Because if you badger him and come up with nothing, I'll personally have your head."

32

Sergeant Whitaker was a young man, and ambitious. Three nights a week he went into Boston to attend law school. If all went well, he would be able to stand for his bar examination in another four years. It would be a tough grind, but at least Chief Lanigan was understanding and tried not to schedule him for night duty on those evenings when he had school. Tonight he was working late, but since it was Friday and his class did not meet, he did not mind. True, he hadn't had dinner and Aggie was always upset when he couldn't eat with her and the children, but Lieutenant Jennings had made it plain he wanted all his assignments covered before he went off duty, no matter what time that was. Whitaker's sergeant's stripes were quite new, and he had no intention of letting the lieutenant down.

He was seated now in the Goralsky kitchen across the table from Mrs. Chambers, the housekeeper. His notebook was spread out before him, and though he tried hard to be the dignified, impersonal police officer conducting an important investigation, it was difficult. Mrs. Chambers was from the Old Town and knew him from the time he was a grubby little school urchin.

"Now what is it you want to know? You're not planning to cause Mr. Goralsky any trouble, I hope. Because if you are, I'll have no part of it. Mr. Ben is a fine, decent gentleman, and his father is an old dear, for all he's a foreigner and talks funny."

"As I explained, Mrs. Chambers, this is just a routine investigation that I'm conducting—"

"Well, aren't we grand, conducting investigations. And what is it you're investigating?"

"We're just checking anyone and everyone who had any connection whatsoever with the late Isaac Hirsh, the man whose picture I showed you. It's just routine." He flipped the pages of his notebook. "I've been at it all day and I must have questioned twenty people or more."

"Well, I never laid eyes on the man."

"Did he never come here at any time? Think now."

"Who you telling to think, Henry Whitaker? I told you I never laid eyes on him, didn't I?"

"Well, did Mr. Goralsky, Mr. Ben Goralsky, did he ever mention the name Hirsh?"

"Not to me, he didn't."

"And the old man?"

"Not that I remember."

"Well now, think back to the evening of September 18. That was a Friday night. It was the night of the big Jewish holiday—"

"That was the night the old gentleman took sick."

"And Mr. Ben got home early I suppose. At least, all the rest of them, the Jews, I mean, worked a short day, so I suppose he did too."

"That's right. And all the servants were dismissed early too, so it wasn't that they were taking any special privileges that they weren't passing on to others."

"But you stayed on."

"Well of course. Who else was there to take care of the old gentleman, and him burning up with fever?"

"So Mr. Ben got home around three? four?"

"Around four it was, as near as I can remember."

"And he remained here at home until it was time to go to the temple, I suppose."

"He didn't go to the temple. At least he didn't go to pray. He just drove the rabbi and his wife there and came right back."

"So while he was gone, you were here alone with the old man."

"That's right. I was right up there in his room sitting by his bed."

"And when Mr. Ben got back from driving the rabbi to the temple, he came up to the room to see how his father was getting along, I suppose."

"No." She shook her head decisively. "He didn't come up because he didn't want his father to see him. You see, his father assumed that he had gone to the temple and would have been upset if he knew he hadn't. So Mr. Ben stayed out of sight."

"Then how do you know he came right back?"

"Because he told me, of course."

"The next morning, you mean?"

"Oh, no, I saw him later in the evening. The old gentleman dozed off and I came down here to the kitchen to get a bite. That's when I saw Mr. Ben in the living room."

"And that was what time?"

"Nine, half-past."

"So you didn't see him from around seven when he took the rabbi to the temple until about nine." He frowned at his notebook. "But I suppose you heard him moving around downstairs earlier."

"No, can't say that I did," she said tartly. "The door of Mr. Goralsky's room—I kept it closed because there's a draft from the hallway. And the living room is on the other side of the house."

"But you heard the car coming up the driveway?" he persisted.

"I did not."

"No? That's a little funny—"

"It's not funny at all, Henry Whitaker. Do you think Mr. Goralsky drives one of those jalopies that you can hear through the walls of a building like this over the sound of the surf, and me watching the old man and worrying every minute of the time?"

"No, I guess you wouldn't," he said meekly.

"Well now, if you have no more questions, I'll be getting about my work. Mr. Ben will be coming back from the temple soon and will be wanting a late snack."

33

"Got it all wrapped up, have you?" asked Lanigan. "Know exactly how she did it? Why don't you stick around till we get a confession from her, and then we might give you a copy to frame and stick up on the wall of your office?"

But Beam refused to be drawn. "Look, Chief, I've got a job to do same as you. It isn't up to me to solve crimes. I just inquire around and then make a report to the home office. I spoke to them yesterday, and they decided there was sufficient question here to withhold payment to the widow for the present. If it turns out that she's guilty, she wouldn't collect anyway. As a matter of fact, without any other beneficiary the whole amount may escheat to the State. Of course, you may come up with someone else, in which case we'll be happy to pay her."

"And if we don't come up with someone else, your company sits tight and tells the widow to sue if she wants her money. And God help her if she does, because you'll dredge up every bit of scandal, any little tidbit of gossip, so that even if she wins she'll be unable to go on living in the community."

"No, Hugh," said Jennings, "they just threaten to do that and then offer her ten cents on the dollar to settle."

"That's normal business procedure," said Beam.

"I suppose next you'll be off for South Bend to start smelling around."

"Cops are always sore at private investigators," said Beam philosophically. "And everybody has it in for the insurance company. We're the big bad wolf when we come up before a jury, especially if there's a good-looking dame involved. But I didn't come here to fight with you boys. I just came to tell you I was being called back and to say goodby."

"All right, goodby." Morosely, Lanigan watched him leave the room.

"What do you think?" asked Jennings.

"I think he'd accuse his mother if he thought it would help the company."

"It's nice business. The widow practically has to prove she didn't do it."

"That's right. And about the only way she can do so is for us to prove someone else did. And right now, we don't have a thing."

"Well, my money's on Peter Dodge. I think it's funny he left right after Fred Stahl's Roundabout column. His landlady was under the impression he wasn't planning to leave till the end of the week."

"That could be coincidence. I'd be very much surprised if he read Stahl's column."

"Yeah? Then why hasn't he been heard from since?"

"The chances are he's been so involved with the Civil Rights business, running around attending meetings, that the police haven't been able to locate him. Besides, I can't see the police down there exactly knocking themselves out to find some Northern agitator for us. They've probably got their hands so full breaking up picket lines they haven't the time to do their regular work."

"A man like Dodge," Jennings ruminated. "A big, tall, powerful, good-looking guy like that, you wouldn't think he'd be too hard to spot."

"For some reason, Eban, you're always trying to tie in the clergy with some scandal. But the fact is, we don't have a damn thing on him—"

"Except that he had the opportunity—he comes around that way every night at about the right time. He knew Mrs. Hirsh from way back, and she's a nice-looking woman. He's single and her age. You know, Hugh, the trouble with you Catholics is that your priests got you buffaloed so, you can't even imagine a clergyman doing something wrong."

"All right, all right. I didn't say I wasn't considering him. But I haven't got him, and all I can do is wait until the Alabama police pick him up. When we get hold of him we can shake him up and turn him inside out to see what makes him tick, but I can't just sit and twiddle my thumbs until he shows up."

"So there's this Marvin Brown."

"We don't really have anything on him."

"Except that he was pretty damn uncooperative and evasive when I questioned him."

"Yes—"

"And he has no alibi, and he refused to tell the rabbi why he left the services before the rest—"

"Sure, but that's nothing I could go to the D.A. with."

"All right, then how about Goralsky?"

"Now *he* interests me."

"Why? You haven't got any more on him than you do on Brown."

"No? How about this?" He ticked the points off on his fingers. "One, he was not at the temple. Two, he had some special interest in getting Hirsh out of the cemetery. Three, he knew Hirsh from way back, and he's the only man in town who did. Four, he was also in business with him and got rich from him. Finally, he got him the job at Goddard."

"Yeah, but he never saw him after he got here."

"That's what he says."

"It's also what Mrs. Hirsh says."

"He might have been in touch with him by phone—or secretly so she wouldn't know."

"Yeah, but that's just a lot of maybes—he might have, he could've—"

"All right, let's stick with what we do know. Goralsky and Hirsh were partners. Goralsky forced him out, and then right afterward built up the business to a multimillion-dollar concern. There at least we have a motive for the killing."

"But godammit, Hugh, you've got it arse-backwards. In the business dealings between Hirsh and Goralsky, it wasn't Goralsky that got screwed. It was the other way around. You'd have a motive for Hirsh killing Goralsky, but not—"

"How do we know what the relations were between them? Look, way back there was some trouble between them on a business deal. Right?"

"Right."

"Then twenty years later, Hirsh asks Goralsky to recommend him for a job at the Goddard Lab, and he not only gives him an excellent recommendation he practically rams him down their throats."

"Right."

"But then he refuses to see him after he gets here. Now those three things don't jibe. If there was trouble between them, he wouldn't have given him the recommendation and Hirsh wouldn't have asked him for it. If he gave it and got him the job, he wouldn't have refused to see him afterward. Now all that suggests just one thing to me."

"Blackmail!"

"Right. And if you want to let your mind play a little, doesn't it seem mighty funny that it was Hirsh who was responsible for throwing a monkey wrench into this merger business?"

"Hey—and that could be a good reason for Goralsky wanting to kill him."

Lanigan considered. "That's a little weak. For one thing, it isn't a killing matter. And beside, the deal hasn't fallen through—not yet. And since Hirsh was going to be fired anyway he wouldn't be in a position to do any more damage."

"But that's just the point, Hugh." Jennings was excited. "It's like you've been saying all along—that this is the kind of killing where the motive could be weak."

"Yeah," said Lanigan, "and there's nobody I'd rather pin it on."

"I didn't know you knew Goralsky."

"I don't."

"Then why him?"

"Because I'm only human. The rabbi tried to tout me off, and Alf Braddock warned me that if I touched him he'd have my head. Well, I'd like to show the whole lot of them. Besides, if it should be the way we've figured—a weak motive—I'd get a lot of personal satisfaction telling it to the rabbi."

"So let's pick him up."

Lanigan shook his head. "What's the use? He's got an alibi. His pa and the housekeeper would swear he was there all evening. And the rabbi and his wife could account for what little time he wasn't at home."

"We've been able to break alibis before, Hugh. I say, let's pick him up."

"Yeah, but your head isn't on the block. Mine is."

The desk sergeant thrust his head through the door. "There's a guy here, Chief, a Marvin Brown. He wants to make a statement."

Lanigan shuffled the freshly typed pages. "Who's your lawyer, Mr. Brown?"

"Oscar Kahn of Kahn, Kahn, Channing, and Spirofsky. Why?"

"I want to be completely fair. This is a serious matter. It's a murder case, and I'd like everything to be correct. I'm going to ask you to sign this. I told you that when we started. Well, I think it would be a good idea if you had your lawyer look it over before you swear to it."

"I don't get it," said Marvin. He was trying very hard to be jaunty and at ease. "You send a couple of guys to my office to ask me all kinds of questions. You don't bother to hide the fact that you're from the police. So I get to thinking maybe you'll come down again; maybe you'll come to the house and question my wife; maybe you'll shadow me." He laughed nervously. "I guess that's what you guys call using psychology. So I decide to save you the trouble and come down myself and make a statement. And now you say I should get a lawyer."

"I'm merely interested in protecting your rights, Mr. Brown. All I'm suggesting—"

There was a knock on the door and Lanigan shouted, "Come in."

Sergeant Whitaker opened the door. "Can I talk to you for a minute, Chief?"

34

The rabbi watched the car drive into the parking lot and pull up to a stop near the temple door. A uniformed chauffeur opened the rear door and helped out the elderly Goralsky. Although it was early in October, the morning was unseasonably warm, Indian summer. Nevertheless, Mr. Goralsky wore a coat and muffler. He leaned on the arm of the chauffeur. The rabbi hurried over.

"Why, Mr. Goralsky, how nice to see you up and about—and to have you join us at services. But is it wise? Does the doctor approve?"

"Thank you, Rabbi, but when I know what I have to do I don't ask the doctor. Today, I decided I had to come to pray. They came this morning and took my Benjamin." There was a quaver in his voice and his eyes filled with tears.

"Who came? What do you mean they took him? What happened?"

"This morning. We had just barely finished breakfast. I was not even dressed. These days, since I been sick, I wear my pajamas and a bathrobe all day long. I am in and out of bed. The police came. They were very nice, very polite. They were dressed like me and you, without uniforms. One shows his badge. He keeps it in his pocket. The other one shows a card, a business card, like a salesman. He's the chief of police. 'What do you want, gentlemen?' my Benjamin asks them. I thought maybe something happened at the plant, or maybe Gamison, the gardener, got drunk again. He likes to drink, but he's a good worker and always when he has too much he goes to his room and stays there till it's over. No trouble, no loud talk. He hides, I shouldn't see him. But then he works twice as hard afterwards. And he has troubles with a daughter with a couple of children yet and her husband can never hold a job. So I keep him. It's a pity. So I thought maybe this time he didn't hide and the police arrested him. But no, it's my Benjamin they wanted. They want to ask him some questions about this Isaac Hirsh who everybody thought committed suicide, but now it seems it's not suicide.

"So you want to ask questions, so ask. Sit down, have a cup of coffee; make yourselves comfortable and ask your questions. But no, in my house they can't ask my son questions. It isn't big enough? Somebody will maybe disturb them? They got to have my Benjamin should come to the station house with them. There, they'll ask him the questions. What kind of questions can they ask him there that they can't ask him in the house? And they're in a hurry yet. My Benjamin likes to sit with me, especially these last few days when I could come down to breakfast, he likes to sit with me and have another cup of coffee. And we talk— about the business, about problems, what we should do about this customer or that customer. After all, we worked so hard all our lives and there never seemed to be enough time to sit down and have a decent meal, always a bite here and a bite there when there was a minute. And now, when things are better and we can take it easy and Benjamin can go to work a little later, is it wrong, Rabbi? But no, they couldn't wait. They could barely wait until my Benjamin put on his tie and his coat, so much they were in a hurry."

"Do you mean that they arrested him? On what charge?"

"The same question I asked them, and my Benjamin too. And they said they weren't arresting—they were just taking him in for questioning. So if they weren't arresting why did they make him go? What would they do different if they were arresting? Carry him maybe? I said to them, 'Gentlemen, you want to ask my son some questions, ask. You don't want to ask here, only in the station house? All right, he'll come to the station house. But does it have to be now? It's Saturday which it is by us the Sabbath. Let him go now to the temple, and later he'll come to the station house. I'll guarantee it.' But no, it had to be right away. So they took him away. So what could I do? I dressed myself and I came here."

The rabbi took his arm. To the chauffeur he said, "I'll take him from here." Then turning to the old man, "Do you feel strong enough to lead the prayers, Mr. Goralsky?"

"If you want me to, I've got the strength."

"Good," said the rabbi. "Later we can talk."

The dozen or so men who had come to the service were impatient to begin, but when Goralsky entered on the arm of the rabbi those who knew him shook his hand and congratulated him on his recovery. The rabbi helped him off with his coat and scarf and then, draping a prayer shawl around his thin shoulders, led him to the table before the Ark. The old man prayed in a high, quavery voice which cracked occasionally on the higher notes of the chant; but he made no effort to hurry the service along, waiting each time for the rest to finish their recitations before chanting the line or two preceding the next prayer. At the Reading, the rabbi called him up for one of the portions. He seemed to gain strength as he prayed, and when he began the final prayer, the *Olenu*, his voice was strong and the thin little old man seemed to the rabbi to be standing straight and tall. He was as proud of him as though he were his own father.

At the end of the service all came up to wish him a *Gut Shabbes*, and then leisurely strolled out of the temple, as was proper on the Sabbath. But the rabbi detained the old man. "Sit down, Mr. Goralsky. Now we can talk."

To one of the men who asked if everything was all right, he said: "Perhaps you'll be good enough to tell Mr. Goralsky's chauffeur that we're going to sit here and talk for a little while."

"You know, Rabbi, I'm a little bothered," Goralsky said when the man left. "This is the first time that I ever rode on the Sabbath, and yet I led the prayers and you even called me up for a Reading."

"It's all right, Mr. Goralsky, believe me. Now tell me, have you notified your lawyer?"

The old man shook his head. "For a lawyer there'll be plenty time. My Benjamin he also says I should call the lawyer. In the old country, in the *shtetl*, we didn't know about lawyers. When we got into trouble —and what kind of trouble? Like opening your store a little too early on Sunday—did we get a lawyer? We went to see people who could help us: somebody who knew somebody or knew a relative of somebody should do a favor. Now, I'm sure the police don't come down and take my Benjamin to the station house just to ask him he should help them. No, they got it in their minds that my Benjamin had something to do with this Hirsh dying. They must have on him a suspicion." He gave the rabbi a searching look to see if he would deny it.

"Yes, I think you're right, Mr. Goralsky."

"But this is impossible, Rabbi. I know my son. He's a good boy. He's big and he's strong, but a heart he's got like a girl—so gentle. When we were in the chicken business, he would never do the slaughtering, on the nonkosher part of the business, I mean. For the kosher part, naturally we had it a shochet. I know him, I tell you. Years ago when I was younger, I used to be disappointed in him. A father always wants his children should go to school and become educated. He left school early. Sure, it was hard times and I could use his help, but believe me, Rabbi, if he had a head on him and been good in school, somehow I would have kept him there. But he didn't want to study. It came hard for him. And this was a big disappointment to me. And next door, Hirsh had a son, this Isaac, who was a regular gaon and won all kinds scholarships. But later on, I used to think, maybe I didn't do so bad with my Benjamin. This Isaac Hirsh never set foot in a synagogue after he grew up. Then he became a drunkard. Then he married a Gentile. Then they even said that he took his own life."

The rabbi shook his head.

"I know that wasn't true now. I'm only telling you what I was thinking. And my son, who didn't even finish high school, he grew up a fine, kosher young man, and it turned out he even had a head for business. There was even an article they wrote on him in *Time* magazine how he was such a wonderful businessman. Believe me, they're making a mistake, the police. My Benjamin, what interest would he have with this Isaac Hirsh, and after so many years?"

"Well, you've got to understand the situation," the rabbi said. "This Hirsh is comparatively new here and kept to himself. He didn't have any friends to speak of, and no business dealings with anyone who had any connection with him. They found out about your son having known him when they were boys together and about the partnership later on. And then when he made such a point about not wanting Hirsh's body in the cemetery—"

The old man clasped his thin hands together. "God forgive me—that was my fault, Rabbi. He knew nothing about these things. It was from what he heard me say."

"Yes, I know, but there was also the matter of his getting Hirsh the job at the Goddard Lab. He wrote a strong letter of recommendation—"

"See, doesn't that show you what kind of heart he's got, my Benjamin? Never was he friendly with Isaac Hirsh, even when they were boys. I don't blame him. Maybe he got it from seeing my disappointment in him. Maybe I was harsh with him. Even when I realized that he was such a good son, could I tell him to his face? A girl, a daughter, you can pat her on the head and pay her compliments, but a son?—"

"Yes, I understand. But you see, because of all this, it's only natural for the police to want to make sure there wasn't some recent connection between your son and Isaac Hirsh. I would earnestly advise you to consult with a lawyer so he can take care of your son's interests."

"No." The old man shook his head. "With a lawyer it's already official. He goes to a judge; he makes a motion; he gets a paper. Right away, it's public and it's in the newspapers. My son is not just anybody. He's an important man. The newspapers would make a big tumult about the police questioning him."

"Then what are you going to do?"

"That's why I come to you, Rabbi. I understand that you and the chief are good friends."

"I'm afraid we haven't been lately," said the rabbi ruefully. "But even if we were, what could I do?"

"You could talk to him. You could find out what they are looking for. You could explain to them. Please, Rabbi. Try."

And Rabbi Small did not have the heart to refuse. "All right, I'll talk to the chief, but don't expect anything. Please take my advice and get your lawyer."

"The lawyer I can get later, but first I want you should talk to him. I don't mean you should work today, Rabbi. It's the Sabbath, but maybe tonight?"

"A man's reputation is at stake. If you can ride on the Sabbath I can work on the Sabbath." He smiled. "Besides, for a rabbi, the Sabbath is his regular workday."

35

The rabbi's call came just as he was leaving. "I've got to see you about Goralsky."

"Sorry, Rabbi," said Lanigan. "I was just on my way out."

"But it's extremely important."

"I'm afraid it can't be done. I have an appointment with Amos Quint and Ronald Sykes at the Goddard Lab in about twenty minutes. I'm hoping we can come up with something that will wind this thing up."

"I'm sure you're making a terrible mistake, Chief. You've got your mind fixed on Goralsky, and you're going to do him a great injustice."

"Look, Rabbi, I've got to run along. I'll try to get over to you later."

"But later could be too late."

"I can't imagine anything that won't keep."

"Rumor won't keep. You've got Goralsky down at the station house. Before long everyone in town will know."

"All right. But the best I can do is meet you at the lab. You can sit in on the discussion if you want. I guess I owe it to you. That is, if you don't mind riding on the Sabbath."

"For this I would make an exception. But I don't like to leave Miriam alone at this time."

"Bring her along."

"Well, if you don't mind—we'll be there."

He hung up and called to Miriam to get ready. "We're going to meet Lanigan at the Goddard Lab."

As they drove along Route 128, Miriam said, "Do you think Chief Lanigan really has a case against Mr. Goralsky?"

"Who knows? I haven't spoken to him for a week or more, until just now. They may have found something I don't know about, but then they probably would have arrested him outright instead of just taking him in for questioning. I'm sure they can work up a plausible motive. The trouble is, the way Lanigan views this case, they could work up a plausible motive against almost anyone."

"How do you mean?"

"Well, he's decided that it wasn't the result of elaborate planning, that since it involved just walking away no great motive is necessary. Anyone could have that kind of motive—his neighbor who doesn't like the way he keeps his lawn—anyone. It's much the same with the rest—weapon, opportunity. Goralsky could have been there because he wasn't at the temple. Well, a lot of other people weren't at the temple. And of course Goralsky drives a car. Yes, Lanigan could make up a case that would justify holding him."

"But he'd be sure of being acquitted, wouldn't he?"

He shrugged his shoulders. "Suppose he were, would that be the end of it for him? Suppose they don't even bring him to trial but release him, everyone will know he has been arrested. Even if they issue some sort of statement, what can they say? Mr. Goralsky has been released because of insufficient evidence? That wouldn't signify he was innocent, only that they'd been unable to find the evidence they needed to connect him with the murder. And if he went to trial and was acquitted, it would be the same. No, he can be cleared completely only if they find the actual murderer. Well, more often than not, they never do."

The car slowed down.

"Why are you stopping here?"

"I hadn't intended to." He pressed down hard on the accelerator, but instead of responding the car slowed down still more. He shifted into second, went a few feet and stopped altogether. He tried the motor, but it did not catch.

"What's the matter, David?"

He grinned foolishly. "I don't know."

"Well, there's a how-d'ye-do. What do we do now?"

"There was a cutoff back there about a hundred yards. Probably the one that leads to Morris Goldman's garage. We're on an incline. Maybe I can coast back—"

"On 128? With cars zipping along at sixty miles an hour! You'll do no such thing."

"I'm not keen on it myself. I suppose I better ease her back onto the shoulder of the road and raise the hood. That's a sign that you're in trouble. The state troopers will be along in a minute, they patrol this road constantly. . . . What's the matter?"

Her fists were clenched and she was biting her upper lip. Her fore-head suddenly was bathed in perspiration. After a moment, she smiled weakly. "You might look at your watch and time the next one. I think you're about to become a father, David."

"Are you sure? That's all we need right now. Look, don't worry and don't get excited. Just sit tight and I'll flag down a car."

"Be careful, David," she called as he got out.

A moment ago the highway had been filled with cars, but now not a car was to be seen. He drew out his handkerchief and took up a posi-tion in the middle of the road. Presently he saw a car in the distance and began to wave his handkerchief. To his tremendous relief, the car slowed down. It passed, swung over to the side of the road, and then backed up to within a few feet of his car. When the driver got out, the rabbi saw it was Dr. Sykes.

"Why it's Rabbi Small, isn't it? You in trouble?"

"My car stopped."

"Out of gas?"

"I don't think so. No, I'm sure it isn't that. I've been having some trouble—"

"All right, I'll call a garage just as soon as I get to the lab. I'm sup-posed to meet the police chief there. Conked out right in the middle of driving, eh? Could be that your—"

"Look, my wife is in labor."

"Oh, boy, that's bad—" He eyed her in consternation. "Maybe, I— Say wait a minute! Why don't you take my car and I can hoof it to the lab. It's only a few hundred yards up the road."

"It's very kind of you, Dr. Sykes." The rabbi climbed into the bucket seat of the little sports car and grasped the wheel. He looked uncer-tainly at the array of dials on the dashboard and then at the grinning face of Sykes leaning on the open door.

"Stick shift with four speeds forward. She'll do a hundred easily. I had her gone over not long ago and she's tuned like a fine watch."

The rabbi nodded at the sticker on the doorjamb. "Yes, I see. *Chai.*"

"What's that?"

"It's a Hebrew word. It means life."

Sykes looked at him doubtfully, and then over at Mrs. Small and seemed to understand. "Right. You both have it on your mind. Well, let me help your lady out."

"No."

"What's the matter?"

The rabbi had stepped out. "No, I couldn't. I wouldn't dare drive it. I—I wouldn't know how. We'd end up in a ditch. Look, I've got a better idea. Why don't you drive on to the lab and tell Lanigan about our situation here. He'll come and get us. Oh, and you could also have someone call the doctor—Dr. Morton Selig. He's in the book, and tell him what happened and that I'm on my way to the hospital."

"All right if you're sure you'd rather."

He climbed into the car and gunned the motor with a deafening roar. "Good luck and my best to your lady."

"Nothing to be worried about, you two," Lanigan remarked over his shoulder to the couple in the back seat. "When I first joined the force, I was on the ambulance trick and I wouldn't care to venture a guess at the number of women I drove to the hospital. We used to take them over to Salem in those days—didn't have a hospital of our own in the town. I don't claim to be an obstetrician, but in my experience the first child always took a long time."

"The pains are coming every ten minutes now."

"Plenty of time. It's when they start coming fast, every couple of minutes or every minute. It's when it's a second or third child they're apt to pop. And don't think I haven't delivered babies either, or helped to. So you couldn't be in better hands."

He was obviously talking to distract them, and the rabbi recognized it and was grateful. He sat with one arm around his wife and gave her his hand to clutch whenever the pains came. Every so often he would wipe her forehead with his handkerchief.

They reached the outskirts of the city and Lanigan glanced back at them. "You know, if you like I could pick up a motorcycle escort. That way we could get through a little quicker."

Miriam answered before the rabbi could speak. "I don't think it will be necessary." She blushed. "The pains appear to have stopped."

"Doesn't mean a thing," said Lanigan. But he slowed down and proceeded at a more moderate pace until they reached the hospital. "I'll stick around, until you know what's what, Rabbi."

Thanking him the rabbi helped Miriam out of the car and supported her up the steps. Though she needed no assistance, she enjoyed his solicitude. With some embarrassment they explained to the reception clerk that the pains had stopped.

The nurse at the desk informed them it was not uncommon and arranged for Mrs. Small to be escorted to her room. The rabbi remained in the waiting room, where after some ten minutes he was joined by Dr. Selig, a pleasant young man of his own age, who seemed to exude both assurance and reassurance.

"The pains have stopped for the time being. It's quite common. Sometimes the girls get a little lazy, or maybe they just change their minds. If they didn't, they wouldn't be women, ha-ha. Well, we'll keep her here for the night anyway. Even if the pains start in again it will be hours, so there's no sense in your waiting around."

"But she's all right?"

"Oh, perfectly. Nothing for you to worry about. You know, Rabbi, in all my practice I've—"

"I know, you've never lost a father."

"Rabbi," the doctor was reproachful, "that was my line."

"Sorry. Can I see her now?"

"I'd rather you wouldn't. She's being prepared and we've given her some sedation. Why don't you just go home. I'll call you just as soon as anything begins to happen."

36

The rabbi climbed into the front seat beside Lanigan. "The doctor says it will be hours."

"I thought as much. I'll drop you on my way back to the lab."

"It was very decent of you to come and get us, Chief," said the rabbi. "Things were pretty rough there for a few minutes until Sykes came along."

"I understand he offered you his car and you refused. Those little foreign jobs are actually no different from ours, except you have to shift a little more often and they respond to the wheel a little quicker than you're used to. But you would have got the hang of it before you'd driven a quarter of a mile."

"Oh, I had no doubt I could drive it. I just didn't want to be indebted to a murderer for the birth of my child."

"Murderer? Sykes?"

The rabbi nodded soberly.

Lanigan stepped on the brake and brought the car to a halt at the side of the road. "Now. Let's hear it."

The rabbi settled back in his seat. "The man who drove Hirsh home had to be on foot. That's basic. If he'd been driving, and stopped to take the wheel of Hirsh's car, he would have had to leave his own. You had alerted the state troopers, so they were patrolling the road. An empty car would have been spotted. Chances are that it wasn't a hitchhiker, because they're expressly forbidden on Route 128. There are signs posted at each entrance, and the state troopers would pick up anyone they saw."

"So."

"But the people at Goddard regularly leave their cars to be serviced or repaired at Morris Goldman's garage because it's just a few hundred yards from the lab. They drop off their cars in the morning and walk along the embankment of 128 to get to work. At night—and Goldman's, like most garages, stays open late—they walk back, pick up their cars, and drive home."

"Everyone knows that."

"Well, to get to the lab from the garage, you have to pass the turnoff where Hirsh was parked. It's just about halfway."

"Yes, you can see the turnoff from the lab."

"Right. Well, now I know that Sykes had his car serviced at Morris Goldman's garage that Friday, because when I got behind the wheel I saw one of his lube stickers on the doorjamb. It was dated the eighteenth. That was Friday."

"It still doesn't place him on foot. After all, he could have picked up his car after work—before Hirsh returned to the lab after his dinner."

The rabbi shook his head.

"Why not? You yourself said Goldman's stays open late."

"But not that Friday night. It was Kol Nidre. He would have closed well before six. And we know Sykes was at the lab that late because he phoned Mrs. Hirsh and left word that her husband was to call him when he got in."

"That doesn't mean he couldn't get home. He could have called a cab —why not?" as the rabbi shook his head vigorously.

"You can ask Miriam if you wish. The nearest cab company, the only one for practical purposes, is the one in Barnard's Crossing. And when Miriam had me stop off there the proprietor told us the only calls he got that evening were to take people to the temple."

"All right!" Lanigan sounded exasperated. "But it's all conjecture."

"No, Sykes had no car all weekend."

"How do we know that?"

"He didn't pick up his car Friday. And he couldn't pick it up on Saturday, because that was Yom Kippur and Goldman was closed. And I know for a fact he had no car on Sunday."

"Oh?"

"You see, when he came to my house to arrange for Hirsh's funeral, he arrived and departed by cab. Why would he do that if he had his car? Yet we know he had it on Monday, because he drove it to the funeral."

Lanigan was silent for a minute. "So your theory—and it's no more than a theory," he said finally, "is that Sykes sat around waiting for Hirsh to call back. When he didn't, he started out on foot to get his car, saw Hirsh parked in the turnoff on 128, and offered or Hirsh asked him, to drive him home and—"

"And Hirsh passed out on the way."

"But why would he want to kill him? Sykes was probably his closest friend here in Barnard's Crossing. He went to bat and covered up for him half a dozen times. I got that from Amos Quint who admitted he would have fired Hirsh long before if Sykes had not interceded for him."

"And why would Sykes have to intercede for him?" the rabbi demanded.

"I don't understand."

"Quint never spoke to Hirsh except on the day he hired him. Everything there went through channels. Whatever communication there was between Hirsh and Quint passed through Sykes. Now if Sykes didn't want Hirsh fired—if he was such a good friend—why mention his mistakes to Quint in the first place? Why go to bat for him? Quint is no scientist, he's an administrator. If Sykes wanted to cover for Hirsh, all he had to do was refrain from mentioning his name and Quint never would have known. But evidently there were errors—at least half a dozen, according to you. Now suppose they were the fault not of Hirsh but of Sykes? It would be mighty convenient to have Hirsh there to take the blame."

"All the more reason for not wanting to kill him. Why give up a good thing? In any case, Quint was going to fire him Monday, so Sykes would be off the hook."

"Then there's your answer!" said the rabbi triumphantly. "This time apparently there was an important mistake—one Quint couldn't overlook. We know he always made a point of seeing a man he was going to fire. He saw him, told him just why he was firing him, and that ended it. Isn't that the way you reported it? So he tells Hirsh the reason for his dismissal, and Hirsh says, 'Oh, no, sir, it was Ron Sykes that did that; I discovered the error.' There's a confrontation, Hirsh shows his work notes. . . ."

The chief folded his hands behind his head and leaned against the car seat, absorbed in thought. Then he shook his head. "It hangs together, Rabbi, and it sounds plausible, but you're just guessing. It's all surmise and conjecture. We don't have a bit of proof."

When the rabbi spoke, his tone denoted both certainty and finality. "Just ask Sykes how he got home from the lab Friday night. Just ask him that."

"Yeah, I'll do that." He smiled. "You know, Rabbi, somehow or other, you do manage to take care of your flock."

"You mean Goralsky and Brown?"

"Oh, we didn't really have anything on Brown. We were just floundering, looking for some line we could follow. You know why he left the temple early? He was ashamed to tell you, but he made a statement to us. He had a business deal on—a big policy, and the customer insisted on getting the papers signed that night."

"I suspected it might be something like that."

"I guess from your point of view it was a pretty terrible thing for him to do."

The rabbi thought for a moment. "No, I don't think it was terrible. In a way I'm rather pleased."

"Pleased that he ran out on your Yom Kippur service to consummate a business deal?"

"No—pleased that he was ashamed of it."

37

Sunday morning, the Schwarz forces were standing around unhappily in the corridor just outside the Board meeting room.

"Do you think the rabbi will show up today?" asked Marvin Brown.

"I doubt it," said the president. "Stands to reason as an expectant father he'll be at the hospital."

Herman Fine came up and joined them. "I understand the rebbitzin went to the hospital yesterday. Maybe we should hold off on the rabbi's letter of resignation at least for today. I know I for one would feel funny—"

"Are you kidding?" demanded Schwarz. "The resignation is definitely out. I guess you didn't hear what I just told the boys. I ran into Ben Goralsky after the minyan this morning, and for about twenty minutes all he could talk about was how wonderful 'the little rabbi'—that's what he called him—how wonderful he was. You'd think the rabbi saved his life."

"Maybe he did," said Marvin Brown. "You hear about how if a man is innocent he won't be convicted, but every now and then some guy will confess to a crime some other guy has done twenty years in prison for." He ran his hand under his collar. "Don't think I wasn't plenty worried about the same thing. Besides, even if he got off, how about his old man? A thing like that could kill him."

"All right, the resignation is out," said Fine. "And it's okay by me. So what do we do now? I say we ought to go the whole way and do it up handsome. Mort should read the letter, explain it was due to a misunderstanding, and call for a vote from the Board refusing to accept it."

"Like hell."

"What d'you mean, Mort?"

"I mean I'm certainly glad Ben Goralsky got off, and I'm willing to give the rabbi some credit. Still it's one thing to forget about the resignation, because then we could kiss the Goralskys goodby. But I'm damned if I go begging to the rabbi. There'd be no living with him after that. If we ever disagreed on anything again— Watch it, here come Wasserman and Becker."

"Good morning, gentlemen, I got good news. I just called the hospital and they told me the rebbitzen had a boy."

"Hey, that's all right."

"That *is* good news."

"How's the rebbitzin feeling?"

They all gathered around, asking questions.

"Look, fellows," said Schwarz, "are we going to stand out here and *schmoos* all day? Let's get the meeting started."

"Yeah, let's go."

"What do you plan to do about the rabbi's letter?" asked Wasserman as they moved toward the door.

Schwarz looked at him in surprise. The group halted to listen.

"What letter, Jacob? What letter are you talking about?"

The men looked at each other and some smiled.

But Becker's face got red. "What are you trying to pull, Mort? You know damn well what letter Jake is talking about. You planning some—"

Wasserman put a restraining hand on his friend's arm. "Becker, Becker, if Mort doesn't know about the letter, that means he never received it."

"Why, was it something important?" asked Schwarz.

Wasserman shrugged his shoulders. "I guess not. Probably something routine—just routine."

38

"The missus home yet?" asked Lanigan.

"Tomorrow," said the rabbi happily. "I take them home tomorrow."

"I was hoping I'd have a chance to see the boy."

"He looks like a little old man, so wrinkled."

"They all do for a few days. Then they begin to round out and get fat."

"I suppose so. The doctor said it was a fine healthy child, but you couldn't tell by looking at him. He looked like a plucked chicken."

"They're just like puppies. They've got to grow into their skins."

"Well, you've made me feel better already," said the rabbi. "Say, why don't you and Gladys drop around tomorrow? You'll be able to see him then."

"Oh, we intend to. But I was passing and thought I'd be able to sneak a preview. I've just come from the D.A.'s office. He made a deal with Sykes's lawyer for second-degree murder."

"Second-degree? But that's unpremeditated—"

"I know, I know. But the D.A. still thought it best."

"But you had a confession."

"We had a confession but not for premeditated murder. When he confronted Sykes, we carefully refrained from mentioning the wiped fingerprint. We told him we knew he was without his car over the weekend; we told him what we'd uncovered about the work in his department at the lab. And I guess we sort of hinted Hirsh's death was probably accidental, and that if he cooperated fully with us it would go a lot easier for him."

He reddened and looked away from the rabbi's direct glance. "It's common procedure. It's done by lawyers regularly right in the court-

room. If you can trap your man into admitting his guilt—what's wrong
with it? It wasn't as though he was innocent."

"I'm not quarreling with you."

"Well, he admitted that he'd come across Hirsh as you suggested and
drove him home. Also that Hirsh passed out within minutes after they'd
started. He claimed he tried to wake him up when they got to Hirsh's
house, but he couldn't budge him. So he decided to leave him there to
sleep it off. Only after he'd got home did it occur to him that perhaps
he'd forgotten to turn off the motor. By then he was afraid to walk back
and see."

"And what about the way he used Hirsh to cover up his own mistakes?"

"He admitted that. As a matter of fact, he gave us a complete picture
of what happened at the lab. I guess he was smart enough to realize
that we'd find it out eventually, and it would look better for him if he
were completely candid with us. It's only a fool who tries to cover up
and then finds he has to keep retreating as we learn more and more. It
appears that the original brainstorm was Hirsh's. He issued the preliminary report in both their names, but then Sykes assigned Hirsh to
other work and carried this on by himself. He claims he wasn't trying
to steal the credit; that Hirsh just was not as enthusiastic about his own
idea as he was. But he discussed it with Hirsh off and on, and sometimes had Hirsh check his figures.

"Then Hirsh discovered an error. Sykes told him not to say anything
yet, with an idea that he'd admit it gradually in a series of progress reports. One would say that unexpected difficulties had cropped up.
Then he'd issue another to the effect that a great deal more work and
time were needed. And finally, he'd put one out that would make it
clear it was a dud. I guess Hirsh might have gone along, except that
his name was on the first report and that the research was being done
for Goraltronics."

"Hm—that's interesting. Is that your idea, or did Sykes say Hirsh was
concerned about Goraltronics?"

"No, I got that from Sykes. Evidently, Hirsh felt some sort of obligation to Goralsky for having got him the job. He even hinted that
if Sykes didn't tell the truth he was going to speak to Goralsky himself.
Maybe he was just bluffing, but Sykes didn't know. Goralsky had got
him the job, so naturally he had every reason for taking the hint seriously. So late Friday afternoon he went to Quint and told him the truth.
He claims he was going to admit he was to blame, but Quint was so
upset that he lost his nerve. When Quint assumed it was Hirsh's fault,

he did not correct him. You can understand how Quint felt because he knew about the merger and the stock going up and all that. He wanted to call Hirsh in and fire him right then and there, but Sykes lied and said Hirsh had gone home early because of the holiday. That's kind of ironic, isn't it?"

"It's even more ironic than you think," said the rabbi. "Sykes, when he came to visit me that Sunday, remarked that Hirsh would have been alive if he had been a normal practicing Jew."

"That's no lie. Anyway, we typed up his confession and he signed it," Lanigan went on. "Then we sprung the wiped fingerprint on him. We thought that would break him. You see, if we had mentioned it at the beginning he would have realized it was first-degree murder and probably would have refused to talk. This way, at least we had a confession for the major part and if he broke we'd have it all. He clammed up. Refused to say another word until he conferred with a lawyer."

"But you had your case anyway."

Lanigan shook his head gloomily. "After his lawyer got through talking to the D.A., we didn't have much of anything. The fingerprint—or rather the missing fingerprint—would have been peppered by defense counsel. He would have shown that we had men all over that car. He would have argued that one of us could have wiped it accidentally with his sleeve. And the confession? They could say it was obtained under duress."

"And getting home from the lab—how could that be explained away?"

"Easy. He started out to walk to the garage and someone gave him a lift. He doesn't remember the make of car and the driver didn't give him his name. After all, no one saw him near the Hirsh house."

"Peter Dodge did."

"Peter—the minister? When did you see him?"

"He dropped in this morning. He got home from Alabama yesterday."

"And he saw Sykes?"

The rabbi nodded. "He takes a walk every evening, and it leads him past Bradford Lane. He had planned to drop in on Hirsh for a talk, but as he came to the corner he saw the house was dark so he went right past. But he did see Sykes—he's sure that's who it was—walking down Bradford Lane in the other direction toward his home, of course. At the time he had never met the man and just assumed it was someone taking a walk like himself."

"Why didn't he come forward and tell us?"

"Why should he? He didn't know that there was murder involved."

Lanigan began to laugh. "Well, there you have it, Rabbi. We've mismanaged this case from the beginning. We just had bad luck all the way. When we were unable to get in touch with Dodge down in Alabama, we asked the police to pick him up for us so we could question him. The minute they found the police were looking for him, the Negroes hid him, of course—one place to another, I don't suppose he even knew why. Then when he finally returned to his hotel, the Birmingham police did pick him up and called to ask if they should hold him and we told them no, to let him go. After all, we had our man by that time."

"Well, I don't suppose it makes any difference really. But it just shows how much luck counts in solving a case. We had bad luck all the way, and then when we finally hit on the right solution it was still a matter of luck. I mean, Sykes happening to stop and offer you a lift so you were able to see that lube sticker—that was a tremendous stroke of luck."

"Well, we believe in luck, you know."

"I suppose everyone does to some degree."

"No, I mean we believe in a way you Christians don't. Your various doctrines—that God observes the fall of every sparrow, that you can change your misfortune by prayer—it all implies that when someone has bad luck he deserves it. But we believe in luck. That is, we believe it is possible for the truly good man to be unlucky, and vice versa. That's one of the lessons we are taught by the Book of Job."

"Still, I'm not so sure it was all luck. The whole case was permeated with the feeling of our holy day. Subconsciously, I imagine, I thought a great deal about the relations between Hirsh and Sykes, and why Sykes would want to cover up for him. And that's why the explanation occurred to me so readily when I saw the date on the lube sticker. You see, the whole pattern of the crime was laid out before me in our Yom Kippur service."

"How do you mean?"

"Well, part of that service deals with the ceremony of the selection and sacrifice of the scapegoat by the High Priest in ancient Israel. It was even the subject of my sermon. In it I referred to the sacrifice of Abraham, which is the portion of the Scroll read on the day of the New Year, the beginning of the Ten Days of Awe which culminates in Yom Kippur. And that was the whole point of the situation there at the Goddard Lab. In spite of his disassociation from the Jewish community, Hirsh nevertheless played what in the past too often has been the traditional role of the Jew."

"You mean—"

"I mean he was the scapegoat. His very name should have suggested it to me."

Lanigan was puzzled. "Hirsh?"

The rabbi smiled sadly. "No, Isaac."

39

Rabbi Small paced back and forth in the living room. He was practicing the delivery of his Chanukah sermon, and now and again he would glance at his audience—his infant son, firmly wedged into a corner of the divan. Once he interrupted his discourse to call to Miriam in the kitchen, "You know, dear, he follows me. He's actually focusing on me."

"Of course, he's been doing it for days."

"'. . . so we must consider the miracle of the lights not only as an example of the intervention of the Divine power—'"

The infant began to pout.

"You don't like that? I don't care for it too much myself. Suppose I say, 'We are too much inclined to respond to the miraculous—'"

A whimper.

"How about, 'The real miracle of Chanukah is not the burning of the cruse of oil for eight days rather than for the expected one; it is that a tiny nation could challenge the power of mighty Greece—'"

A cry.

"No?"

The infant took breath and then, his face red and contorted, emitted another wail at full volume.

"That bad, eh?"

Miriam appeared in the doorway. "He's hungry. I'd better feed him."

"Perhaps you'd better," said the rabbi. "I'll try it on him again after he's eaten. Maybe he'll be more receptive on a full stomach."

"You'll do no such thing. After he's fed, he's going to bed. Aren't you, Jonathan?" She nuzzled him, and the cries died down to an uncertain whimper and then stopped. "Besides, I think you've got a visitor."

It was Moses Goralsky. Through the window, the rabbi saw the old man being helped out of the car by the chauffeur but then refuse further assistance with a shake of the head. Clinging to the handrailing he mounted the steps to the door.

"Come in, Mr. Goralsky. This is a pleasant surprise."

"I have a question, a *sheileh*. To whom should I come if not to the rabbi?"

He helped the old man off with his coat and showed him into his study. "I'll do the best I can, Mr. Goralsky."

"You know, when my Ben was in trouble I came to the temple to pray."

"I remember."

"So you know when I recite the prayers, they're in Hebrew. I can say the Hebrew, but what I'm saying, this I don't know, because when did I have a chance to learn? We were a poor family. My father—he worked plenty hard in the old country just to feed us. So after I learned the prayers, he took me out of the cheder, you know, the school, and already I was helping him in his work. That's how it was with most people those days."

"Yes, I know."

"So because I don't understand what the words mean, that means I'm not praying? I have thoughts in my head, while my lips are moving, and by me this is praying. Am I right or wrong, Rabbi?"

"I suppose it depends on what the thoughts are."

"Ah-hah. Now that Saturday, what would my thoughts be? They would be about Ben. I asked God He should help him. He should make the police they should find out the truth so they should let my Ben go."

"I would say that was praying, Mr. Goralsky."

"So while I was praying, I made a promise. If my Ben goes free, I thought, then I would do something."

"You don't have to bribe God, and you don't have to make bargains with Him."

"Not a bribe. Not even a bargain. I made with myself a promise—a —a vow."

"All right."

"Now here's my question, Rabbi. Do I have to keep my promise?"

The rabbi did not smile. Hands in his pockets, he strode up and down the room, his forehead creased in thought. Finally he turned and faced the old man. "It depends on what the promise was. If it was something impossible, then obviously you're not bound. If it was something wrong or illegal, again you're not bound. In any case, where you made the promise to yourself it's up to you to decide how committed you are."

"Let me tell you, Rabbi. Months ago, I was talking to Mortimer Schwarz, the president of the temple, and I said I wanted a remembrance for my Hannah, which she had died a few months before that. After all, I'm a rich man now, and my son is rich. And my Hannah was with me all the time we were poor. Even when I got rich, she couldn't enjoy it because already she was sick, in bed most of the time, on a diet so she couldn't even eat good. So this Mortimer Schwarz he asks me what I had in mind. The temple could use an air-condition system, maybe a new organ." The old man shrugged his shoulders. "I'm going to make an air-condition system in remembrance of my wife? Where will her name be? On the pipes? And an organ is better? I had to fight with myself a long time before I went to your temple because there was an organ there. So should I give the temple an organ in my wife's memory? So I said, 'Mr. Schwarz, I don't want a piece of machinery, and I don't want any organs. I had it in mind something like a building.' Nu, that's all I had to say, and that's all he had to hear. He tells me he had it in mind to build like an addition to the temple, a special sanctuary which it would be used only for praying, not for meetings or regular business. I told him I was interested."

"Did he tell you how much it was likely to cost?"

"The cost I didn't care. The money, I can take it with me? Or I got to provide for Ben? Schwarz says more than a hundred thousand; I said even two hundred thousand."

"Well—"

"So then later he shows me a drawing, and he explains how there will be like a gallery so you can stand there and talk when you want to leave the service for a little rest, or after the service, a place you can linger." He hunched his shoulders and spread his hands. "Believe me, Rabbi, at my age, you're interested in lingering. You're not in and you're not out—sort of halfway."

"And then did he show you the model?"

"He showed me."

"And?"

"And the model—" he grimaced, "already I wasn't so crazy over. The building by itself—nice, but attached to the temple, it was already not here not there. The temple—it's plain, it's straight; and the new building, it's fancy. But I'm an architect? What do I know about buildings? So I wasn't sure, but that day when I was praying for my Ben, I made it a promise that if they let Ben go I would give the building."

"And your question is whether you're bound by your promise?"

"That's the question."

"And your objection is that the two, the new and the old, don't go together?"

"Not only that, Rabbi. This I could stand already. But all my life, I'm a businessman. Do you know what is a businessman, Rabbi? A businessman, when he spends a dollar he got to get for a dollar merchandise. Makes no difference for what he spends. If he spends for charity, he got to get for a dollar charity. You understand?"

"I think so."

"So to me it seems like this building is mostly wasted. Do we need an extra building for the temple? To put up a building just to put up a building, just to spend the money, it's not in my nature."

"Suppose the building were separate from the main building. Would you feel better about it?"

"So what would you use it for?"

"It could be a school," the rabbi suggested slowly. "Or even a community center."

"You need a separate building for a school? If you took the school out of the temple and put it in a separate building, for when would you use the temple? For a couple of days a year? It would be a waste. And a center? Here in Barnard's Crossing you need a center for the boys to play basketball? In the city, where nobody had a yard and was lots of kids and was dangerous to play in the street—all right. But here, you need a place for kids to play?"

"Perhaps you're right—"

"Remember, Rabbi, just to put up a building, should be a building—this is foolish. Better in this place should be God's grass and flowers."

Then it came to the rabbi. "You're right, Mr. Goralsky. But there is one building that we do need." He looked at the old man and spoke carefully. "We could use a chapel for our cemetery. Oh, it wouldn't be as big as the plan calls for, but it could be the same general design. And it would be especially fitting since your wife was one of the first to be buried there—"

Goralsky's lined face broke into an old man's smile. "Rabbi, Rabbi, this time you got it. The same design, maybe a little smaller, this would be a nice building for the cemetery. And even a fence, I would be willing to put it in, and flowers and maybe trees. The Hannah Goralsky Memorial Cemetery. It could be like a garden." Then his face fell. "But my vow, Rabbi. I made a promise for an addition to the temple here in Barnard's Crossing. In my own mind, I even saw Mortimer Schwarz's building—"

"But did your vow concern this particular arrangement of buildings?

You made a vow to donate a building to the temple, a memorial to your wife—" He stopped as the old man shook his head.

"Look, Rabbi, you think I made a vow like I was swearing before a notary? I, Moses Goralsky, do hereby promise. . . . No. Was going through my mind all kinds of pictures, feelings, ideas—not so much words, you understand. But I know what I promised," he added stubbornly.

The rabbi nodded thoughtfully. Of course the old man did not verbalize his vow. And he was old enough and rich enough to hold himself to its strict observance, even though he was also shrewd enough to realize that the alternate plan, the cemetery chapel, would be much more useful and appropriate. The rabbi rose from his chair and began to stride up and down the room, while Goralsky waited with the patience of the very old.

The more the rabbi thought of it, the better the plan seemed. No less than Marvin Brown, he realized the importance of the cemetery to the congregation. And it would give Mortimer Schwarz his building —not exactly as he had planned it, but near enough. And it would permit the old man to set up a lasting memorial to his wife's memory. The problem was, how to permit Mr. Goralsky to do what he actually wanted to do.

He paused in front of the bookcase and his eyes wandered over the large leather-bound tomes that comprised his copy of the Talmud. He selected a volume and took it over to his desk. He leafed through the pages until he found the passage he wanted and swiveled around to face Goralsky.

"I told you at the beginning that if your vow involved doing something wrong, that you were absolved. Do you remember?"

"Of course. Nu, so is putting up Schwarz's building a sin?"

The rabbi smiled. "For this one particular case, Mr. Goralsky, I shall rule that the law of *shatnes* applies."

"*Shatnes?* But isn't that about clothing—that you shouldn't mix linen and wool?"

"That's the way it's usually construed. But the regulation is mentioned in two places in the Bible, in Leviticus and in Deuteronomy. Why in two places? When the Bible says the same thing twice, it can mean either that the regulation is very important or that it can have another significance. In Leviticus the regulation is joined with an injunction against letting cattle of different kinds breed together and also an injunction against sowing with mingled seeds. In Deuteronomy the regulation is joined with an injunction against sowing a vineyard with different seeds and an injunction against plowing with an ox and an ass together."

His voice took on the Talmudic chanting intonation. "Now if the two passages were exactly the same, you could argue that what is intended is that the regulation is important and should be strictly applied. But where the rule is given, and in each case accompanied by two other rules, and the two from Leviticus are not the same as the two from Deuteronomy, we can interpret this to mean that the precept is intended to forbid various mixtures of two things of different kinds."

He leaned back in his chair. "So you will say, where does it stop? We use many mixtures of diverse things: shoes made of leather and rubber, houses of wood and stone. If we go beyond the specific regulations, then we must have some kind of a test. What then would be a logical test? Why, obviously, if it seems wrong to you. For what other purpose did God give us our intelligence if not to use it? Your initial objection to Schwarz's design was that the two buildings were of two different orders, and it seemed wrong to join them together. It bothered you from the very first. So my ruling is that this is an example of *shatnes,* and hence forbidden."

The old man scratched his head. Then his wrinkled old face cracked into a smile and he beamed in fond admiration at the young rabbi. "And in the cemetery would be all right—it's separate. It's a pilpul, but you know something, Rabbi? Suddenly, I'm feeling all right."

SUNDAY
THE RABBI
STAYED HOME

To My Children—
Ruth and George, Arthur,
Diane and Stanley

I

"Now, that's what I call praying, Rabbi," said Harvey Andelman. "We finished five minutes"—a glance at his watch—"no, seven minutes ahead of schedule."

The rabbi, Rabbi David Small, smiled as he continued to roll up his phylacteries. He was young, in his mid-thirties; although in good health, he was pale and thin and carried his head slightly forward, as though peering nearsightedly at a book. He had indeed gone through the service at breakneck speed and felt a little sheepish about it. "You see, I'm going on a trip—"

"Sure, and you want to make an early start—naturally." It seemed perfectly reasonable to Andelman, who had a market in Salem and was always trying to speed up the morning prayers so that he could get to his place of business in good time. He was in torment on those days when they had to wait around to secure the ten men needed for the minyan; and as soon as he spotted the tenth man, he would wave him on as he might a runner nearing the tape, calling, "C'mon, c'mon, let's get going." But now, luxuriating in his unexpected five, no, seven minutes of grace, he waited for the rabbi to put away his phylacteries and prayer shawl. "When Wasserman leads, or the cantor, you'd think it was Yom Kippur, that they got all day. And come to think of it, I guess they have. But the rest of us, we got jobs and businesses to go to. Well, be seeing you, Rabbi," he said, loping off to his car.

Because he felt guilty about having hurried the prayers, Rabbi Small slowed down his pace to a stroll as he went along the corridor that led to his study. For the first time in a long while he noted the bare white cinder-block outer wall divided halfway up to no purpose by a strip of black plastic; the similarly divided yellow-glazed brick inner wall; the rubber tile floor, gleaming from a recent waxing, on which only the circled imprint of the floor polisher gave some semblance of design. It had the sterile feel of a hospital corridor.

When he had first come to Barnard's Crossing six years ago, the temple had been brand-spanking-new, and its modernity had a gay sparkle. But now it was beginning to show signs of age. There were scuff marks along the wall, and at one point near the ceiling there was a yellow stain where a pipe joint had let go. The rabbi could not help feeling that the older temples, with their carved paneling in mahogany or walnut, tended to age more gracefully.

As he neared his study he heard his phone ringing and hurried to answer it. He assumed it was Miriam with a last-minute request to pick up something—a bottle of milk, some rolls—at the grocery, but it was a man's voice, the tone accusing.

"Rabbi? Ben Gorfinkle. I called your house, and your wife said you were at the temple."

"The morning services—"

"Of course," said the temple president, as though conceding it was a legitimate excuse. "You know, Rabbi, the damnedest thing happened this morning. We were chewing the fat over a second cup of coffee, and Sarah mentioned that you were going to Binkerton."

"I told you several weeks ago that I was going," the rabbi remarked.

"Oh, I knew you were going to hold Sabbath services for some Hillel group, but I didn't realize you were going to Mass State at Binkerton. It just goes to show you what a small world it is. My Stuart is there."

"Oh, really? I didn't know that."

"Look, I thought maybe you'd say hello for us and—"

"But of course, Mr. Gorfinkle."

"I'm sure he'll come to your service, but just in case he gets tied up, maybe if you took his phone number—"

"Of course. Just a minute—let me get a piece of paper." He jotted down the number.

"It's a dormitory, so if he's not there, you can leave a message."

"I understand."

"If you call him when you get in, maybe he could show you around the campus."

"That's an idea." He was aware of a voice in the background, and Gorfinkle said, "Just a minute, Rabbi." Then after an interval of muffled sounds through the covered receiver, "Of course, he may have a class in the afternoon or have some studying to do."

The rabbi smiled to himself. Mrs. Gorfinkle must have pointed out that their son might not like the idea of being saddled with the rabbi and his family for the afternoon. "That's all right. We'll probably be pretty tired after our trip and will want to rest up."

"Well, it's a thought, anyway. When are you coming back, Rabbi?"

"Saturday night, right after Havdalah."

"Really?" Gorfinkle sounded surprised. "I thought Stuart said—" He sounded his hearty self again. "Well, anyway, it just occurred to me—"

"Yes?" The rabbi felt sure that he was now to hear the real reason for the call.

"If you've got room in your car, if it's not crowding you or inconveniencing you in any way—you see, Stuart will be coming home for Passover, and they've got a week's vacation—"

"That I could give him a lift back?"

"Only if it wouldn't be any trouble to you."

"I'd be very happy to, Mr. Gorfinkle."

He had no sooner hung up when there was a rap on the door, and without waiting to be invited, in came Morton Brooks, the principal of the religious school. He was a bouncy, youngish man of forty, with a kind of theatrical flamboyance about him.

"Thank God I caught you before you left. When I got the call, I came right over."

"What happened?"

"Arlene Feldberg broke out with measles! The doctor was over last night, but Mrs. Feldberg didn't think to notify me until this morning." He sounded betrayed.

"Arlene Feldberg?"

Brooks nervously fingered the long strands of hair that he had carefully combed to cover an incipient bald spot. "You know Arlene Feldberg, the little girl from the first grade who's supposed to say the Four Questions in English at the seder."

"Oh, Harry Feldberg's child. Well, that's all right." The rabbi was considerably relieved. For a moment he had thought the principal was concerned about a possible epidemic. "The Haggadahs we're using have the English translation on the opposite page. Or I suppose the little boy—what's his name?"

"Geoffrey Blumenthal."

"I'm sure Geoffrey can give the translation after he reads it in the Hebrew."

"Impossible, Rabbi."

"You mean he doesn't know what the Hebrew means?"

"Of course he knows," said Brooks indignantly, "but there's a big difference between reading and being able to recite it without adequate rehearsal. But even if there were time to coach him properly, it's still impossible. In fact, it would be adding insult to injury to let him have both parts. The Feldbergs would never forgive me, and they'd talk about it to their friends, and they include the Paffs and the Edelsteins. I assure you, Rabbi, we'd never hear the end of it."

"I see. And Geoffrey is a—"

"Blumenthal, of course—friends of the Gorfinkles, the Epsteins, and the Brennermans. They're cousins of the Brennermans, in fact."

"Oh, come, Morton. Isn't that rather silly?"

"Not at all," said the principal gravely. "Believe me, Rabbi, this is my third school, and I know how these things work. If you don't mind my saying so, I think you would be wise to pay a little more attention to the politics in the congregation. Oh, you attend the board meetings regularly, but the important developments take place in the school. That's where it really shows up."

"In the religious school?" The rabbi made no attempt to hide his amusement.

"Of course. The High Holidays are once a year. And the lesser holidays, if they fall during the middle of the week, we don't get more than seventy-five attending services, like on Friday nights. But the school—the kids go three times a week, and they report anything that happens the minute they get home. You know how we Jews feel about our kids. Any little slight or fancied unfairness, you'd think from the way the parents carry on it was a pogrom."

The rabbi smiled. "So what do you want to do about the present—er, crisis?"

"Well, it's a problem. Most of the members, as you know, hold their own seders at home, so we don't have too many children from the first grade who are coming to the temple seder. And the Paff group, who tend to be a little older, have fewer children in the first grade, anyway. But they have better representation in the upper grades. So I thought about that bit about the four kinds of sons. You know, the wise, the foolish, the simple, the wicked son."

"I know," said the rabbi dryly.

"Yes, of course, Rabbi. Well, I was thinking how would it be if we could act it out, see. You'd say the introductory paragraph, and then the lights would go dark, and we'd have a spotlight focused right in front on the head table." With tiny steps, he approached the rabbi's desk, his hands moving to outline the cone of light from the spot. "Then we could have the sons come on one at a time, see. The wise son, say, might come in wearing glasses and reading a book or maybe fiddling with a slide rule. Then he'd suddenly look up and ask his question. Only, the way I see it, we'd modernize it and have him say something like, 'Golly, this is groovy, Dad. How come the Lord our God asked us to do all these things?' And the way I visualized the wicked son, he'd be dressed in a black leather jacket and one of those peaked caps and sun goggles, or maybe we could have him dressed as a hippie—you know, barefoot with beads and long hair and faded blue jeans." He slouched, his head lolling to one side, and he spoke out of one side of his mouth, as though there were a cigarette dangling there. "'Hey, how come you cats snazzied up your pad like this? Crazy, man, crazy.' Do you get the idea?"

"And how would this help your particular situation?"

"Well, we have a wider choice among the older children. I had the Edelstein boy tabbed for the part of the wicked son. And being all dressed up, the only one in costume, you might say, it would go a long way—"

"Have you thought of a rock and roll band for the chants?"

Brooks looked at him. "Now there's an idea, Rabbi."

"No, Morton. No," he said firmly. "We'll stick to a traditional seder if you don't mind. And let the Blumenthals and Feldbergs just make the best of it." He rose and edged to the door. "I really have to run now."

"Well, think about it over the weekend, won't you, Rabbi?" Brooks pleaded.

"I'll give it all my free time," said the rabbi with unwonted sarcasm.

But Brooks was not to be put off. "No, seriously, Rabbi, what's wrong with livening up the ceremony so's to capture the interest of the kids? Everybody's doing it now—the Catholics, everybody. They've even held jazz masses. After all, the seder's a celebration. Why shouldn't they have a good time?"

The rabbi stopped at the door. "Because, Morton, the Passover seder is something more than a celebration. It's a ritual in which every step is spelled out—and for a purpose. The whole point of a ritual is that it should be repeated exactly every time it is performed for it to have the proper effect. And now if you don't mind, I really am in something of a hurry."

Outside, he stopped for a moment to make sure the windows of his study were closed in case it should rain over the weekend. The exterior of the building was also showing signs of wear, he saw. The stainless steel columns, which Christian Sorenson, the architect, had said were intended to suggest "the purity of the religion and its resistance to the decay and erosion of time," had taken on a dull yellowish tinge—the effect of the salt air, no doubt. And the long walls of glazed white brick that jutted out from either side of the tall boxlike building and sloped away in gentle curves—"like a pair of open and embracing arms calling on people to come and worship"—were chipped here and there and showed black spaces like missing teeth.

In the parking lot the rabbi was delayed once again. Mr. Wasserman, the first president of the congregation, hailed him as he was getting into his car. Wasserman, now in his seventies, was thin and frail after his recent illness, and the hand he put on the rabbi's arm showed blue veins through transparent skin. He spoke softly, his speech not so much accented as showing special care to be correct.

"You'll be back for the board meeting Sunday, won't you, Rabbi?"

"Oh, certainly. We're planning to start back Saturday right after Havdalah, say six o'clock, and we should be home by nine—ten at the latest."

"That's good."

The rabbi paused in the act of getting in behind the wheel. "Are you expecting something important to come up at the meeting?"

"Expecting? I'm always expecting, almost any day, but especially on Sundays when the board meets. This Sunday it could be something serious."

"Why this Sunday?"

Wasserman held up a finger. "Because next Sunday is the first seder, so there won't be a meeting." He held up a second finger. "The next Sunday is again the holiday, so again won't be a meeting. So if Gorfinkle is planning something serious, this Sunday would be a good day, because there wouldn't be another meeting for three weeks." He held up three fingers.

"And if he decides to do something serious, as you put it, how could I stop it?"

"You're the rabbi. That means you're not on one side or the other. You're like neutral, so you can say things that the rest of us can't."

"You're thinking of the committee changes that the president will make?" He settled into the car. "He'll make them sooner or later, anyway."

Wasserman shook his head. "But it will cause trouble, and better later than sooner. You're a rabbi, but I'm an old man. A lot that I've seen, maybe you only know from reading about it. It's like in a marriage. If an open break doesn't develop, it can be cured. After all, there are couples who quarrel almost from the day they get married. If one of them doesn't pack up and move out and go see a lawyer yet, there's a good chance the marriage will last."

"Isn't that being a little—" He looked at the old man; he was obviously troubled, so he changed his tack. "After all, Mr. Wasserman, it's only a board meeting."

Mr. Wasserman looked at him steadily. "Try to be there, Rabbi."

As he drove home to pick up Miriam and Jonathan, he found himself resenting the role he was expected to play. He was a rabbi—by tradition a scholar and a teacher; why should he be mixed up with matters of faction and politics? Even Jacob Wasserman, whom he respected and regarded as one of his few real friends in the Jewish community—the one man who should have an understanding of the traditional role of the rabbi—even he was involving him in the tawdry politics of the temple. It was almost as though they resented his taking a couple of days off.

It had all started a month ago when Rabbi Robert Dorfman, Hillel director and religious advisor to the Jewish students of Mass State, Western Division, at Binkerton, and his wife, Nancy, had driven east to visit her folks in Lynn. They had dropped in on the Smalls in Barnard's Crossing, because it was close by and the two men had been at the seminary together. In the course of conversation Bob Dorfman mentioned that he had applied for a pulpit in New Jersey.

"They've invited me to come down and conduct Friday and Saturday services."

"Sounds encouraging."

"It is, but I wish they had chosen some other date. That's the weekend before our spring vacation."

"And the Hillel people won't let you off for that weekend?" Rabbi Small sounded surprised.

"Oh, there's no trouble that way. It's just that with the Passover coming during the vacation, I feel that I ought to conduct that going-away service."

"Why not ask the New Jersey people for a postponement or an alternate date?"

Rabbi Dorfman shook his head. "You know how it is. They may be having a bunch of candidates for a whole series of Sabbaths."

"You're pretty keen on this?"

"Oh, yes," said Dorfman. "Hillel work is all right, and working with college kids is important, but I'd like to get a regular congregation." He laughed self-consciously. "I'd like to make a speech of benediction at a Bar Mitzvah once in a while. I suppose it's the messianic delusion that we all suffer from a little or we wouldn't get into this business in the first place, but I have the feeling that what I can say at that time might strike the youngster just right. I'd like to be present at a *brith*—"

"And give a eulogy at a grave?"

"Yes, even that, if it could give comfort to the family." Bob Dorfman was stout and round-faced, and as he looked eagerly at his friend he seemed much younger, like a rosy-cheeked schoolboy hoping for his teacher's approval.

"Believe me," said Rabbi Small, "like most things, it doesn't come up to expectation. In a Hillel job, on the other hand, you have lots of time to yourself; you're in an academic atmosphere; you can study."

"But you're not involved in the real world."

"Maybe you're lucky. At least with a Hillel job you get security. In a congregation—in this real world of yours—you never can tell when you're going to step on the toes of somebody important and find you don't have a job."

The other grinned. "I know. I've heard that you've had your troubles, but that's all past, and you're all set now. You're on a long-term contract—"

Rabbi Small shook his head slowly. "Our contracts are service contracts, which means that legally—that is, as something you can sue for in a court of law—they're about useless. Even if you could, if you did sue, you'd merely insure your never getting another pulpit. As you know, I was given a five-year contract, and when it expires at the end of this year, I suppose I will be offered another, probably at an increase in salary."

"So," said Dorfman, "you're all set."

"There are other drawbacks, though. For one thing, it's a full-time job. You're involved with the congregation twenty-four hours a day. Your time is not your own." He smiled. "You might find it a little wearing, even if it did give you a chance to officiate at a *brith* or a Bar Mitzvah."

"Oh, it's not only that," said Dorfman. "It's not only that I want to get into congregational work; I also want to get out of Hillel work. There's the matter of money; with a growing family, I've got to think of the future. But also I don't feel effective with these college kids. They're the wrong age for me. I don't feel that I'm getting across to them. They know everything, and they're cynical about it."

"Sometimes they're affected more than they show," said David Small. "I don't get to see too many of them, of course, only those who come under my hands here in Barnard's Crossing—kids I've had in post-confirmation classes. They usually drop in on me when they're home on vacation. To me they seem keen and vital. When they're cynical, it's because they're basically idealistic and they've been disappointed."

"Yes, but if kids were all you saw—"

"I suppose. Look, would it help if I came down to sub for you that weekend?"

Dorfman's face lit up. "Gosh, David, that would be wonderful." Then immediately it clouded. "But could you arrange it at your end?"

"I don't see why not. The Brotherhood conducts one service each year. This year I think it's the week before the one you're interested in. I'll check my calendar. But it shouldn't be too hard to change it to the following week, and I could then come down to Binkerton."

Miriam and Jonathan were all dressed and waiting for him when he drove up to the door. Tiny and vivacious-looking, Miriam had wide blue eyes, an open countenance, and a firm, determined little chin.

"Does he have to be bundled up like that?" her husband asked. "He'll roast."

"The weather is so changeable. I can always unzip his snowsuit if it gets too warm."

"All right. Get in. Let's get started."

Miriam started to close the door and then stopped as she heard the phone ring inside. "Just a second," she called out. "The phone."

"Don't answer it," he shouted.

She stopped. "Why not?"

"Because I want to get away. I'm tired."

She looked at him doubtfully and then closed the door, while inside the phone continued to ring.

Silently she strapped Jonathan into his harness in the front seat and then took her place beside him. As they drove off he repeated by way of apology, "I'm tired—just plain tired." And then, "I hurried through the prayers this morning, just saying the words, and I was short with Morton Brooks and annoyed with Mr. Wasserman and—"

She patted his hand on the wheel. "That's all right, David. Everybody needs a little change once in a while."

2

The store was large as stores in Barnard's Crossing go, fully twenty feet wide and more than twice as deep. The windows were grimy and the display ledges behind them dusty. A long time ago they had been decorated with crepe paper, with flutings and rosettes and streamers of a poisonous green and saccharine pink—originally an elaborate Coca-Cola display. But the colors had faded and in places were badly water-spotted. The curvaceous cardboard models in one-piece bathing suits, probably quite daring at the time but now sadly old-fashioned, were still sitting, legs drawn up under them to emphasize the curve of the thigh, backs straight, and breasts firm and high with the suggestion of the nipple under the bathing suit, eyes half-closed, bottles of Coca-Cola held to lips parted in anticipatory pleasure. Scattered around among the folds of crepe paper were dusty bottles of Coca-Cola, one of which had leaked open long ago, oozing its contents along the window ledge in a narrow, viscous streak.

Up against the window cases and blocking them off from easy access, which perhaps explained why the leaking Coke bottle had never been removed, were a cigarette vending machine, a jukebox, two pinball machines, and a steel tub of bottled soda embedded in crushed ice.

Along one wall was a large ornate marble soda fountain, behind which, lettered in black crayon across the flyspecked mirror, was a sign: FOUNTAIN OUT OF ORDER. Boxes of packaged cookies, doughnuts, and bags of peanuts were set on the marble counter top. On the opposite wall there were racks of magazines, paperback books, and greeting cards; and across the back of the store were shelves with notebooks, boxes of pencils, blocks of paper, boxes of rulers, erasers, compasses, pencil sharpeners, tubes of mucilage, rolls of tape, balls of twine, key rings, combs, hand mirrors, and other paraphernalia that school youngsters might want.

In the rear of the store was an old-fashioned rolltop desk and an antique swivel chair, its feet held together by several loops of baling wire, which also served as a footrest. In the center there were half a dozen round tables and chairs, where teen-agers would congregate.

The sign in front said: BOOKS AND STATIONERY, JOSEPH BEGG, ESQUIRE, PROP. Mr. Begg was a vigorous, muscular man of fifty, with a large bald head which was seldom seen, since he wore a hat all the time, who presided over his store from his rolltop desk in the rear. He was an unfriendly, crusty man, gruff and cantankerous, yet the store was a popular spot with the youngsters. They waited on themselves, picking up a package of cookies at the counter, a bottle of soda from the cooler, and then reported to the rear to show their purchases and pay up. They always called him Mr. Begg, although some of the older boys ventured to call him Squire because of the sign outside. It was the nearest they ever came to joking with him. "Coke and doughnut. Twenty cents, Mr. Begg," they'd say and hand over money, which he tossed into an old cigar box on his desk. Or sometimes, "Change for the pinball machine, Mr. Begg, please," and he would examine the bill or coin suspiciously before grudgingly handing over the change. When they finished their drink, they were expected to put the empty bottle in the rack, and if they forgot, he called out sharply, "You there, put that bottle away," and they meekly complied.

Years ago Mr. Begg had taught at the high school and even had tenure, but he had left. No one, certainly none of his young patrons, knew why. He had served a term as selectman, but he no longer attended the annual town meetings and did not bother with town politics except to fire off an occasional letter of violent protest to the weekly newspaper—usually directed against some proposed plan to benefit the young, such as taking over land by eminent domain to build a playground.

"He can't stand kids," was the usual explanation. "That's why he gave up teaching."

"But that place of his—only kids go there."

"Well, you know how it is: He started it as a bookstore, and then he added some greeting cards and some stationery items. Then when he found that mostly kids came, he put in other stuff for them. After all, the guy's got to make a living."

Friday morning Begg came in late. He had not been back at his desk more than a few minutes when the door opened and Moose Carter loafed in. "Hey, where you been, Squire?" He was a large muscular boy with the square shoulders and thick neck of a football player. He had blue eyes and a short, tilted nose and an eager grin. "I was down half an hour ago, and the place was shut tight." Begg did not deign to reply but turned to one side and spat in a cuspidor down by his left leg.

The young man did not take offense. "You going to be fixing up your place for the summer?"

"I'll be taking off the storm doors and windows and putting up the screens," the other admitted.

"Won't you be wanting some help?"

"I can use some," he said grudgingly. "Dollar and a half an hour."

"That's not much. I get two bucks an hour at the bowling alley and sometimes tips."

"I'm paying a dollar and a half."

Moose shrugged. "Oh, all right. When do you want me?"

"Sunday morning, first thing."

A thought came to Moose. "Hey, Sunday—it ought to be more for Sunday."

"Why?" Begg looked up humorlessly. "Because you'll miss going to church with your family?"

Moose laughed. "All right, I'll be there." He looked around and then dropped his voice. "Say, Squire, I got a date for tonight. How about some safes?"

"Three for a dollar."

"Look, I'm a little short right now. How about cuffing it against my pay for Sunday?"

Begg studied the face of the young man, then pulled open a desk drawer and reached inside. He handed Moose a small tin container. The young man slipped it into his trouser pocket. "Thanks, Squire." And then with a grin, "And my girl thanks you, too."

3

The key was under the mat. While the rabbi, hampered by a suitcase and an armful of coats, struggled with the lock, Miriam kept a tight hold on Jonathan, arms and legs spread like a starfish as he tried to make for the jungle gym he had spied in the backyard. "No, Jonathan, later," she said automatically. "You've got to have your lunch first and then your nap, and *then* you can go out and play."

They trooped into the reception hall and stood there for a moment, looking left and right at the dining room and facing living room. As Miriam stooped to extricate her young son from his snowsuit, the rabbi wandered into the living room toward a bookcase to inspect the titles. He selected a book and began to thumb through it. Then he sat down on the couch; and a moment later, his eyes still focused on the book, he had unlaced his shoes and kicked them off and stretched out on the couch, his head propped against the arm and the book held high to catch the light from the window.

Miriam found a coat hanger in the hall closet and hung up the snowsuit. She had put away the coats that her husband had left draped over the valise when she noticed the envelope on the hall table with her name printed across it in large block letters. She drew out a couple of sheets of paper typed single-space.

"Dear Miriam," she read aloud. "Welcome to Binkerton and Mass State, Western Division. I hope you followed instructions and didn't bring food. Everything is prepared—a complete Sabbath meal and enough for the weekend. It's all in the refrigerator, and all you have to do is heat it up. Pilot light doesn't work on left front burner. Use matches (in cupboard over stove) . . . Kiddush wine in dining room sideboard . . . meat dishes—blue edging—in cupboard on the right as you face kitchen windows . . . meat silver also on right—floral pattern . . . meat pots and pans in right cupboard . . . dairy utensils all on left . . . when washing dishes, watch out for kitchen faucet—squirts sideways when turned on full . . . arranged for baby-sitter—Kathy (15 and very reliable) next door, No. 47, daughter of Prof. Carson, Math, and very nice . . . feel free to call them if you need help of any kind. Extra blankets—top shelf bedroom closet . . . Bob attached side rail to Rachel's bed for Jonathan . . . No automatic switch for lights on Friday night. Bob and I are not that Orthodox. If you are, leave them on all night . . . Our good friend, Prof. Bill Richardson, Philosophy Department, was much taken with David's paper on Maimonides. He is holding open house in David's honor Saturday night. Did Bob mention it to David?"

Miriam poked her head in the living room and viewed her husband lying on the couch with affectionate annoyance. "David!" she called sharply. "Sit up."

"I took my shoes off," he protested.

"And how about your jacket? It will be all wrinkled for tonight."

"I'm wearing my black suit tonight. This will smooth out when I hang it up."

She sighed. "Did Bob say anything about a party Saturday night?"

"No, I don't think so."

"Well, there's going to be one in your honor. A Professor Richardson is having open house."

This time the rabbi swung his legs over and sat up. "I don't think I care for that. Besides, I was planning to drive back to Barnard's Crossing. I all but promised Mr. Wasserman."

"But it's for you, Nancy says. We'll have to go."

4

At the Malden bowling alley the manager reported a cracked plate-glass window. "It must have happened during the night, Mr. Paff. Everything was all right when I closed up. Then when I came to open this morning—"

"How come you opened this morning? Where's Hank?"

"Oh, yeah, I was going to tell you. Hank called me at the house and asked me to open for him. He wasn't feeling so good."

"Was he drunk?" Paff asked quickly.

"Gee, Mr. Paff, I wouldn't know about that. He just called and asked could I open and take the day shift. So I said all right. You know, he took my shift one night last week when I had that twenty-four-hour bug."

"All right. Get a wide piece of adhesive tape and tape that window up on both sides so there won't be any chance of it shattering. I'll notify the insurance company. Maybe they'll want to come out and take a look at it before I fix it."

"Sure, Mr. Paff. I'll do that right away," the manager assured him. "And can you get someone for the evening shift? I'll stay on if I have to, but it's a long day."

"Did you call the office?"

"I called, but there was no answer."

"Oh yeah, I forgot. I let the girl have the day off. All right, I'll swing by there and get the list and see what I can do."

At the Melrose alley Paff noticed that the gold leaf on the window sign was chipped and peeling near the corner. It made the golden bowling ball, which was the company's trademark, look like a reproving eye.

"When did that happen?" he asked the manager, pointing to the sign.

"What? The sign? It's always been like that, Mr. Paff."

"I never noticed."

"The pinsetting machines in the last two alleys got stuck again, Mr. Paff."

"Did you call the mechanic? You got the number."

"Yeah, I called him yesterday and again today. He says he'll be right over, but he said that yesterday."

"When did you call him today?" Paff asked.

"This morning, first thing when I came in."

"So call him again."

"Oh, I'll call him, but in the meantime we can't use the alleys."

"Those mechanics!" Paff shook his head. "Say, would you like to work an evening shift tonight—over in Malden?"

"Gee, Mr. Paff, I'd like to help you out, but the missus got something planned for tonight."

Business was off at the Medford alley. "It's this new billiard parlor that opened up in the shopping center," the manager explained. "Everybody's suddenly gone crazy over billiards. Even the dames. They come there and knit—can you imagine, knit?—waiting their turn to shoot."

Paff asked if he was free to work the evening shift over in Malden.

"You mean instead of working here? You planning to close this place down? Just because business is off for a couple of days?"

"No, I mean just for tonight, to sub."

"Oh, sure, anytime at all. Glad to help you out. Of course, Fridays I can't. I got this job Friday nights . . ."

He swung over to Chelsea, where his office was located, and only after he had finally found a place to park did he realize that he didn't have his office key.

The janitor was a new man and didn't know him.

"Look, here's my car license. See, I'm Meyer Paff. What more do you want?"

"Yeah, but you're asking me to open the office of the Golden Ball Enterprises. There's nothing on your license, mister, that shows you're connected with them."

Paff bit his lip in annoyance, although strict justice forced him to admit that the janitor was right. "I'm just going to make a couple of phone calls," he said. "You can stand right there while I do it."

"Sorry, mister, I got orders. The management is mighty strict about it. There's been a lot of breaks."

Paff tried to keep his voice calm. "Look, is Dr. Northcott still in his office, or has he gone to lunch? You know, the dentist on the third floor."

"I didn't see him go out."

"All right, take me up to him. He'll tell you who I am."

The dentist showed his annoyance at being called away from his patient, but he identified him.

It sure has been one of those days, Paff thought as he riffled through the card file. He dialed a number and sat with the instrument pressed to his ear as the phone rang and rang. Finally, he hung up and dialed another number. Again, the phone rang without eliciting a response. The third call, the phone was answered immediately. It was a woman. "No, Marty ain't home. Who shall I say called?" He didn't bother to explain.

With the next call, he was lucky. "I figured I'd be hearing from you, Mr. Paff. Hank called me on account I subbed for him a couple of weeks ago, and I said okay."

"Fine. Now look, there's a broken window, and I had Ted tape it with adhesive tape for the time being. I want you to check it before you close to make sure that tape is nice and secure. Okay?"

On his way out he stopped to thank the janitor and commend him for his caution. He pressed a couple of cigars on him.

"Thanks, Mr.—er—"

"Paff."

"Oh, yeah. Well thanks, Mr. Paff. I won't forget next time."

When he got back to his car, it was jammed in between two others. By the time he had extricated himself, he was bathed in perspiration. I'm getting too old for this, he thought. Then he remembered he hadn't had lunch. Glumly, he passed a nearby restaurant, noting the lot was full. He decided to eat on the road and stopped at a diner, where the only stool vacant was in front of the grill. Morosely watching the short order cook in a dirty apron, he managed to consume a dry hamburger and a cup of bad coffee.

5

In the Officers' Cafeteria of Hexatronics, Inc., on Route 128, there was a long middle table where the executives usually ate family-style, while on the sides there were a number of booths available for those who had guests and wished to talk in private. In a booth, Ted Brenner-man studied the menu and said to his host, Ben Gorfinkle, "Hey, you guys do all right for yourselves." He gave his order, and as soon as the waitress left, he leaned across the table. "As I was saying, Ben, there's thirty-seven guys with nameplates on their seats in the sanctuary; there's another fifty or sixty get the same seats all the time—figure a hundred altogether. The rest of us—the peasants—sometimes we get a seat up front, and the next year we're way out in left field someplace. Last year I sat in the last row. So what difference did it make? With the public address system, I could hear just as good. But there are plenty others who don't feel like I do. They want to sit up front." He was a tall, good-looking young man, eager and with a ready, infectious smile.

"But they paid a special price for those seats. At least those with the nameplates did," Gorfinkle pointed out.

"Don't you believe it. I checked into it. I went back to the minutes of the general meeting of five years ago. What happened was they were putting on a drive for the Building Fund and getting all kinds of pledges. Then Becker, who was president that year, said that anyone who would donate a grand could have his seat reserved from year to year. Now, that wasn't anything the board had decided on and voted on. It was during the meeting and came out on the spur of the moment, if you see what I mean. Then"—he pressed Gorfinkle's arm for emphasis—"the board at their next meeting had to make some ruling to get Becker out of the jam he'd got himself into. So they said that those who had come forward with their thousand-buck donation would have their seats held until the last day of the ticket sale each year. But then the very next year they stopped selling seats anyway and made it part of the annual membership dues, so it seems to me that those guys don't have any kind of a claim on those cushy seats that they get year after year. And I'll tell you another thing: Not all of those guys who had nameplates put on their seats gave their thousand bucks."

Gorfinkle, a stocky, square-faced man in his mid-forties, said, "One of these days, we'll be putting in theater-type seats. Maybe we ought to wait till then."

"Nussbaum's project?" Brennerman laughed. "He came to see me right after I was elected president of the Brotherhood, I should have the Brotherhood start a drive for the additional money to put in new seats. And he spoke to me again only last week. He's bugged each of the Brotherhood presidents for the last four years, and the Sisterhood, too. I told him it wasn't anything I thought you could work up any enthusiasm for."

"I don't know, they're mighty uncomfortable. And we've got the money for about half the job."

"Yeah, it's a shame to think of that money lying there, and we can't touch it. Boy, if we could use that for the Social Action Fund! Say, maybe Mrs. Oppenheimer's will could be interpreted so at least we could use the money to buy upholstered pads for the present seats," Brennerman suggested.

Gorfinkle shook his head. "That wouldn't do any good. It would just make the seats higher, and they're too high as it is. It's not so much the seat part as the back. It's so straight or something. The only one who likes it is Doc Klein, the osteopath. He gets more leg cramp and sacroiliac business after Yom Kippur than he gets all year round."

Brennerman laughed. "Who picked that type seat in the first place?"

"Nobody picked it. They were so overwhelmed—most of them, those same people with the seat plates—by the reputation of that architect that they let him do whatever he wanted. Those were copied from some old English church, I understand. What did he care? He was just interested in how it looked; he wasn't going to have to sit in them. It's funny about this seat business. In the *shul* that my father used to go to, where you sat was a big deal. By tradition, the big shots, the guys with *yicchus*, status, always sat down front. The nearer you were to the ark, the more important you were. In that *shul* they even had a row of seats up against the wall where the ark was, facing the rest of the congregation. I remember the guys that sat there, most of them old guys with long beards, wearing these long woolen prayer shawls. My father called them *p'nai*. Gosh, I haven't thought of that word in years. It's a Hebrew word, and it means faces. My father used to explain to me that they were the faces of the congregation, the most pious and the most learned."

"Well, I don't suppose we have any of those in our congregation unless maybe old man Goralsky and Wasserman."

"I think maybe Meyer Paff thinks he's one."

Both men chuckled.

"One thing bothers me, though," Gorfinkle went on. "I still think that this kind of thing—announcing a whole new social action program for the temple—ought to be presented at the general meeting of the congregation. When you come right down to it, we haven't even formally presented it to the board."

"Hell, we campaigned on it, Ben. So it's no secret. And since we've a majority, we've got a right to run things our way."

"Still—"

"And don't you see," said the other eagerly, "presenting it at the Brotherhood service—that's the beauty of it. For one thing, we'll have more people there than we ever get at a general meeting. The last meeting we only got a little over a hundred. We get close to three times that at the Brotherhood service. And with the rabbi away, we won't have to worry about anything he might say afterward."

Gorfinkle chuckled. "And he doesn't know it yet, but he won't be there for the meeting Sunday either."

"No? How come?"

"Well, he expected to drive home right after the evening service Saturday, but they're having a kind of party for him Saturday night at the college, according to Stu. He won't be able to leave until Sunday morning. After all, they've got the kid with them."

"Good thinking."

"But it's not the rabbi I'm worried about; it's Paff."

The younger man grinned. "Well, don't worry about Paff. I've got an idea how to take care of him."

6

There were no customers present, and Meyer Paff looked around uncertainly for a moment and then made his way to the rear of the store, where Mr. Begg sat glowering at him.

"I'm Meyer Paff," he said. "Mr. Morehead said you had the key to the Hillson place, that you were like a caretaker—"

"I live in the carriage house. I keep an eye on the place," said Begg evenly.

Meyer Paff was a big, slow-moving man. Everything about him was big: his large round head surmounted by a tuft of blondish-gray hair, his fleshy nose, the square, chalky teeth, the big red hands with sausage-like fingers, the feet encased in badly turned shoes, as though the leather was not strong enough to contain them. When he spoke, it was in a deep bass burble, with the large red lips scarcely moving, so that the sound seemed to come not so much from the mouth as from the belly. Nevertheless, he felt ill at ease before the stare of the other man.

"Morehead said he called you—"

"I spoke to him on the phone this morning."

"So if I can have the key—"

Begg did not answer but leaned forward and from somewhere under the kneehole of the desk brought out a cardboard on which was a crayoned message: BACK IN ONE HOUR.

"Oh, there's no need for you to leave your store. If you just give me—"

"The house is furnished, and I don't give the key out to strangers," he said flatly. When he saw Paff redden, he added, "No business this time of day, anyway. You got a car? Then you follow me."

Hillson House and the carriage house nearby were built on the promontory known as Tarlow's Point and were set back about forty feet from the street line, the only two houses on the street for some distance. A high, thick hedge all but concealed the front lawn and then continued along the side of the lot to merge with a stand of straggly pines leading to the beach and the water.

Paff pointed beyond the hedge to a narrow path leading down to the water. "Is that part of the estate?" he asked.

"Well, it is and it isn't. It's part of the lot, but it's a public right-of-way. The Hillsons have been fighting with the town about it off and on for a number of years."

"Then it's not a private beach?"

"Well, the Hillsons claim it is. The town says that this vacant lot across the street"—he motioned with his chin—"has access rights to the beach. But then the Hillsons went and bought that lot some years ago, so it would seem that the whole of Tarlow's Point is theirs. But the town council says no, because they could sell that lot separately and the new owner would have access rights."

"I see."

Begg led the way to the front door. "They selling the whole business?" he asked.

"That's what I understand."

The door opened into a short vestibule, beyond which was a large living room. There were three windows, two facing the front lawn and the third on the side facing the carriage house, all hung with lace curtains and heavy, old-fashioned red velvet drapes with valances at the top and drawn back halfway down by a loop of the same material. The furniture was covered with large sheets of heavy plastic, but from what could be seen through them, it seemed of a piece with the velvet drapes —heavy, overstuffed sofas, chairs upholstered in damask, and heavy, clumsy mahogany tables.

"This was used as a summer home? The furniture isn't what you'd expect—"

"I guess they had it originally in their house in Cambridge. Folks didn't throw out good furniture in those days."

Begg led Paff down a hall that ran toward the back of the house, opening doors on either side on the way. The first door revealed a small study with a couch, shelves of books, a couple of chairs, and a flat-topped desk. Like the furniture in the living room, the couch and desk were covered with plastic throws. The other rooms were bedrooms, and in each case the bed at least was covered with a plastic sheet. Paff rapped on the wall. "Is this a supporting wall?" he asked.

"I don't think so."

There was a large inkblot on one of the walls of the far bedroom. Paff pointed at it. "One of the Hillsons have a bad temper?"

"Vandals," replied Begg shortly. "A couple of years back the high school kids took to breaking into some of these summer homes, pinching things, raising hell generally. That's how I happened to get this job. You want to see the upstairs?"

"I don't think so."

They were in the kitchen now, and from the windows through the stand of pines they could see the ocean. "The tide is out now," Begg said, "but when it's in, the water comes right up to the sea wall and cuts the Point off from the rest of the beach."

"Comes up pretty high, does it?"

"Oh, at least a couple or three feet."

From the front of the house the ground sloped away to the beach so that there was a flight of a dozen or more steps leading down from the back door. "Can we look at the place from in back?"

"Look, mister, I got a business back in town."

"Oh, sure," said Paff. "Well, you can just go on ahead. I'll look around by myself."

"Suit yourself." He opened the door, and Paff started down the stairs. Begg locked the door behind him and went out the front to his car.

Paff got as far as the trees and then turned around to face the house. I'll have to come back with a tape and take some measurements, he thought. Maybe bring an architect along. Take out those inside walls. Might have to put beams up, though. I could have a kitchen to one side or upstairs and use a dumbwaiter, and the rest of the place could be tables and booths. I could put up a Quonset hut against the rear for the alleys. It would mean going down a flight of stairs to the alley, but it would make it quieter in the dining area. With windows all around, you could see the ocean, and it would be nice and cool all through the summer. I could blacktop the lot across the street . . .

He returned to his car and debated whether to go to Lynn or Gloucester. Lynn was nearer, but Gloucester involved a long, pleasant drive along the shore road, and he felt he could use the relaxation. The manager of the Gloucester alley had nothing unusual to report; everything was going along smoothly.

"You sure nothing's wrong?"

"What's the matter, Mr. Paff? Don't you think I can run the place? Let me tell you—"

"No, that's all right, Jim. It's just that I've had one of those days when everyplace I went— Know what I mean?"

"Oh, sure. You through now?"

"Just Lynn, and then I'll go on home. I covered some of the places yesterday."

"Well, have a nice weekend, Mr. Paff. And don't worry."

The Lynn alley was empty when he arrived, save for the manager, who was leaning on the counter, puffing on a cigar.

"Slow day, Henry?"

"This time just before supper is always slow, Mr. Paff. You usually get here earlier."

"I did Gloucester first. Everything all right? Those ashtrays look pretty full—"

"I'm just taking a breather for five or ten minutes. We'll get a rush in about half an hour."

"You go off in an hour."

"Yeah, if Moose gets here on time. So far, he's been late every night this week."

He stiffened as a car drove up and a couple of men got out and headed for the door. "Fuzz," he whispered.

"Here? What do they want? What's the matter?"

"H'lo boys," Henry greeted the plainclothesmen. "You want to bowl a couple of strings?"

"Not today, Henry. We just want to look over the joint." One strode purposefully toward the little ell where the toilets were situated. Henry came from behind the counter to watch him. He stopped in front of the door marked LADIES.

"Anybody in here?" he asked.

"No, but you can't go in there," said Henry indignantly.

"Why not?"

"Can't you read? That's the ladies' john."

"So I'm feeling girlish." He opened the door and went inside.

The other man had dumped one of the ashtrays onto the floor and squatted down to inspect the contents. Paff came over. "Look here," he said. "What's all this about?"

"Who're you, mister?"

"I'm Meyer Paff. I own the place."

"Do you mind standing back; you're in my light." He straightened up and went to the next lane to inspect the ashtrays there. "Police business," he said. "We got a tip, so we're checking it. You around here much?"

"Well, I—I come in a couple of times a week maybe. Sometimes only once."

"You don't mind how you mess up a place," said Henry. "You going to leave that stuff there?"

"Sure, we'll leave it for the sweeper."

"You guys got a search warrant?" demanded Henry.

"No, no," said Paff. "Never mind, Henry—"

The policeman looked at the manager in surprise. "What do we need a search warrant for? It's a public place, and my partner had to go to the john."

"Not to the ladies' john."

"Please, Henry." Paff turned to the policeman. "Look, do you mind telling me what you're looking for?"

"We're looking for pot, mister."

"But why here?"

The other policeman joined them, shaking his head in response to his partner's look of inquiry.

"Well, we got a tip, so we checked it through. You ever see any kids acting high?" he demanded of Henry.

"The little bastards all act high," said Henry indignantly. "That still don't give you no call to come down here—"

"Without a search warrant? Look, Buster, we come down here *with* a warrant, we take the place apart."

"No need to get excited, Officer," said Paff. "We're always happy to cooperate with the police."

"Yeah? Well, tell your man."

When he got home, Mrs. Paff greeted him at the door with, "Where were you? It's so late I was beginning to worry. Hurry and wash up. Dinner has been ready for half an hour."

"I don't feel like eating now, Laura. I'm tired. I'll eat later."

"But we've got to go to the temple, Meyer. It's Friday night."

"I think I'll pass it up tonight. I'm tired."

"Come on, Meyer, sit down and eat something, and you'll feel better. And then we'll go to the temple, and you can relax. It's the Brotherhood service. You always enjoy that."

7

As Ted Brennerman strode to the pulpit the congregation settled back expectantly. He had a reputation as a "hot-shot" and a "character." ("That Brennerman, he doesn't care what he says; he gets away with murder.") Leaning against the lectern in a manner obviously reminiscent of Rabbi Small, he announced, "Good evening, this is your friendly Rabbi Brennerman." There was a titter of appreciation, and he went on, "Seriously, folks, I've done a lot of public talking in my time, but this is the first time I've had to give a sermon. Let me tell you, it sobers a fellow up." There was another appreciative chuckle, for among the Brotherhood members Brennerman was reputed to know what to do with a bottle.

"So when I found that the program called for me to give the sermon, I asked our rabbi if I could borrow his sermon book. (Laughter.) Well, he claimed he didn't have one, that he made them up himself. So I thought to myself, I know what to get *you* for your birthday. (Laughter.) Actually, no one here has a greater appreciation of our rabbi than I have. I consider him one of the wisest and most intelligent men I've met. And I guess he proved it when he arranged to play hookey tonight. (Laughter.)

"So since I didn't get any help from our rabbi, I went over his head and consulted his boss, Moses himself. Always deal with the top man is my motto. I took down the family Bible and began to read in Exodus. I read it in English, because I didn't happen to have my Hebrew glasses around. (Laughter.) Well, it was a revelation. And there's no pun intended. We all know the story of the exodus from Egypt, the ten plagues, and all the rest of it from way back in Sunday school. But when you read it in the Bible, you really get an idea of what clowns Pharaoh and the Egyptians were. And I guess recent events in the Middle East tend to prove that they haven't wised up very much in three thousand years. (Appreciative laughter.) Except that *then* they wanted us to stay, and *now* they want us to get out. Can't they make up their minds what they want? (Laughter.)

"But then as I continued reading I discovered that our own folks weren't an awful lot brighter. Get the picture: They had just been treated to as classy a demonstration of God's power as had ever been displayed to mankind. Again and again, God had demonstrated that He regarded the children of Israel with special favor. He had plagued the land with flies and with locusts, with darkness and with death, and in each case the Israelites got off scot-free. Did they need any more proof positive? He gave it to them: He parted the waters of the Red Sea to let them pass. How did the Israelites react? You'd think that after all that they'd be four-square behind Moses. But no, as soon as they realized the Egyptians were after them, some of them—I'm sure it wasn't all of them—began to crack wise at his expense. 'Did you take us out here to die in the wilderness because they didn't have any graves in Egypt?' And to the other Israelites they said, 'Don't you remember? I told you we ought to stay in Egypt and serve the Egyptians. It's better than dying in the wilderness.' Now you all know God's answer to that. When the Egyptians came along, He rolled the waters of the sea back again and drowned the lot of them.

"Did that end the griping? Did that end the doubt? Not by a long shot. It happened again and again. Anytime the situation wasn't a hundred percent kosher, this bunch—and I'm sure it was the same bunch all the time—would begin acting up. It happened when they got to Marah and the available water was bitter. And again later on when rations were low and they yearned for the fleshpots of Egypt. That was when God sent down manna from the heavens. And later on when they ran out of water and they thought God was going to let them die of thirst. That was the time that Moses struck the rock with his rod and produced water. And then it happened again when Moses went up on the mount to receive the tables of the Law. When he didn't come down right away, they were sure they had been abandoned, and they forced Aaron to make them an image of a golden calf so they could worship it."

Brennerman's tone had changed, and the congregation was giving him its full attention. "Now Moses had given them a set of laws. These weren't laws of ritual and prayer; they were laws to live by, the laws necessary to maintain a workable society. It was a primitive society they had in those days, and they needed some pretty elementary ethical rules to make it work, laws like 'Thou shalt not kill' and 'Thou shalt not steal' and 'Thou shalt not bear false witness.' We all know that you can't have a society where murder and stealing and bearing false witness are permitted or condoned. It would disintegrate overnight. Those laws were necessary for the society of that time to maintain itself and to grow and prosper. And isn't that what our religion is essentially—a set of rules that men can live by?

"But now we live in a more complex society, and that calls for different rules, or perhaps for a new interpretation of the old rules. We know now that when large segments of our population have inadequate food and clothing and shelter—that is a form of murder. When we prevent the Negro from stating his case and protesting his true predicament, that is a form of bearing false witness. That when our young men are not permitted to listen to the voices of their own conscience and we force them to do the will of the majority, then you are setting up another god, the god of the Establishment. What I'm saying is that the true function of a temple—or a church, for that matter—is to see that the society of its time is workable, and in these days that means taking the lead in matters like civil rights and social justice and international peace."

Brennerman adjusted his yarmulke on his head. "I would like to see our temple take a positive stand on all these matters and make our voice heard. I would like to see our temple pass resolutions on these matters and then notify the daily press of our stand and send copies to the state legislature and to our representatives in Congress.

"And I would have us do more. When our Negro brothers picket for social justice, I would like to see a team from this temple right there with them. And when there are hearings held on various social matters, I would like to see a group from this temple down at the hearing room making it plain that we regard these as religious matters.

"What's more, I would like us to appropriate monies to be set aside in a special Social Action Fund so that we could make contributions— as a temple—to various worthy causes, like the Poverty March on Washington, legal aid for political prisoners in the South, and yes, even on occasion to support candidates for public office who represent our views and who are running against opponents who are known reactionaries and bigots.

"My attitude on this is no secret and comes as no surprise to you, because it is the platform on which I campaigned for the presidency of the Brotherhood, and it is the platform on which the present administration of the temple campaigned. And the fact of our election indicates that the majority of the congregation agrees with us and has given us a mandate to go ahead. And our platform can be stated in a few words: The job of the temple is to help make democracy work.

"As I said, none of this is a surprise to you, because we have been urging it all along. But it is one thing to urge and another thing to implement. So tonight I would like to announce the first step in our new temple program. We feel that democracy should start at home. So instead of the old system of reserved seats where the best ones always went to the same few individuals, we are going to institute a system of no reservations in the sanctuary, with seating on a first-come, first-served basis. Our president, Ben Gorfinkle, felt it only fitting that I should make the announcement, since the Brotherhood furnishes the ushers for the High Holidays."

There was an excited buzzing in the congregation. But Brennerman went on. "Now, I know that not every member of the congregation or of the Brotherhood, for that matter, agrees with us on our idea of the function of a temple. I know that there are those who feel that a temple should be just a place where you go to recite prayers and go through ritual motions. I think they are the same kind of people who were worried when Moses went up on the mountain and insisted that Aaron make the golden calf. They are the people who are not interested in a real commitment, who are afraid of getting involved in controversy. What they want is a religion where you go through a bunch of religious motions. I consider that akin to the worship of the golden Paff—I mean calf. (Loud sniggers.) And I consider that golden"—he paused, as if to make sure that this time he got it right—"calf religion." He went on for some minutes longer, comparing what he called real religion and calf religion. And each time he was exaggeratedly careful of his pronunciation. He ended up with a call for unity "so we can make this the best religious organization on the North Shore."

He returned to his seat beside Gorfinkle, who rose and gravely offered him the customary congratulatory handshake. But after they were seated again, behind the concealment of his prayer book, Gorfinkle touched the tip of his forefinger to his thumb to form an O to indicate his unqualified approval.

8

"Hello there, Hughie m'boy. 'Tis your old friend Kevin O'Connor."

"Uh-huh." Hugh Lanigan, chief of the Barnard's Crossing police force, did not like to be called Hughie, and he did not particularly like Kevin O'Connor, chief of the neighboring Lynn force. He regarded him as a professional Irishman, even a stage Irishman, since he was American-born and the brogue obviously was put on. The most he would allow was that it might have political advantages in Lynn.

"You'll be going to the Police Chiefs' spring dance, won't you, Hughie?"

"Haven't made up my mind yet."

"Well, I wish you'd let me put your name down now. I'm on the committee, and I'd like to make a good showing."

"I'll let you know, Kevin."

"You don't have to send in the form." Lanigan was amused to note all traces of brogue had vanished. "Just give me a call, and I'll be happy to put your name down, and you can send me the money anytime you think of it."

"Okay, Kevin."

But the other was not yet finished. "Oh, and by the by, would you happen to be knowing an individual name of Paff, a resident of your lovely town, a kind of a Jew type?"

"Meyer Paff?"

"That's the one."

"Yes, I know him," said Lanigan cautiously. "What do you want to know about him?"

"Oh, just the usual. Is he a respectable citizen? Have you ever had any dealings with him—in the way of business, you might say."

"He's well thought of here in town. No police record of any kind, if that's what you mean. What's he done?" But already Lanigan had scribbled the name on a memorandum pad.

"Well now, I don't know that he's done anything. But he owns a bowling alley here."

"He owns half a dozen in cities and towns along the North Shore," said Lanigan.

"I know, but none in Barnard's Crossing." It sounded like an accusation.

"We don't have one here, but the one in Salem is near enough. What's wrong with the bowling alley in Lynn?"

"Well," said O'Connor, "some of the kids who have been smoking pot and have given us a little trouble, that's one of their regular hangouts."

"And you think he might be pushing the stuff?" Lanigan scratched out the name on the pad. "I can't picture him in the part. He's one of the big shots in the local temple, for one thing."

"Well now, Hughie, did you ever think that might be a kind of cover-up?"

"No, I haven't, but I'll think about it—when I've nothing better to do."

"You'll have your little joke, won't you. And down there, aren't you troubled with it?"

"With pot? We've had some," said Lanigan cautiously. "As near as we can make out, it seems to be coming in from Boston."

"Well, if anything comes to you, any bit of gossip about this Paff, I'd appreciate your letting me know."

"Ye can bank on it, Kevin m'boy." Lanigan banged the receiver down and glared at the instrument for a moment. Then he chuckled.

9

"Nice sermon, Ted," said Meyer Paff. Most of the congregation had already filed out of the sanctuary to go down to the vestry, where a collation had been prepared. Paff, standing athwart the middle aisle, had waited for Brennerman and Gorfinkle, who were making their way from the pulpit.

"Did you really like it?" asked Brennerman eagerly, too eagerly.

"Sure, I liked it fine," Paff said in his deep rumble. "All through it I was thinking—here we're paying the rabbi a big salary. For what? To give sermons mostly. The rest of his job—making little speeches to the Bar Mitzvahs, marrying people, visiting the sick—we could have the cantor do it or the president. The one thing was the sermons. And now you prove that any fresh young punk can do just as well."

"Now look here—"

"This is no place to pick a fight, Meyer," said Gorfinkle quietly.

"Who's fighting?" Several tailenders of the congregation filing out stopped to listen. "Would I fight in the sanctuary? Believe me, I wasn't brought up that way. I'd as soon get up in the pulpit and insult one of the members."

"Insult? Who was insulted?" asked Gorfinkle.

"I don't know. Maybe Doc Edelstein. He doesn't favor the temple getting into politics. I doubt he cared much for being called an idol worshiper. Or maybe he doesn't know any better. He always thought he was a good Jew. He helped start this place and gave a lot of money to get it going. My friend Irving Kallen, he wasn't here tonight, but he gave a lot of money, too, for this temple. And maybe you don't know it but the Kallen Family Fund has made a contribution to the NAACP for years. But Irv Kallen never suggested that because he wanted to, I had to.

"You were talking about some of the seats that have little nameplates on them. I don't suppose you happened to notice, but on that stand you were talking from and on the reader's desk behind you and on the very chair you were sitting on, there was a little brass plate telling that it was contributed by the Kallen Family Fund, all the pulpit furniture, including the ark and the public address system you were talking through. Maybe he wouldn't have been in such a hurry to give it if he had known some young wise guy was going to use it to call him a worshiper of the golden calf."

"Money isn't everything," said Gorfinkle, "and it doesn't give you the right—"

"Sure, I know money isn't everything. Some people can talk and make speeches instead. I didn't go to college like you boys. I grew up in the streets, but I learned a couple of things there. One was talk is cheap. And when some wise guy would sound off about something he claimed to know for sure, we would say, 'Put your money where your mouth is.'"

"Well, let me tell you—"

"I just want to ask you one question, Ted. It's about your sermon. I'm not going to ask you what the purpose of it was. That was pretty clear: The temple is growing; it's getting too big for both of us. Maybe you think it would be better for all concerned if you cut it down some in size."

"I didn't—"

"No, what I want to ask you is, in your sermon, in laying down the law the way you did, did you think of yourself as Moses? Or God?"

10

There were less than twenty-five present Friday evening in the tiny Hillel House chapel, and Rabbi Small suspected that some of them were Gentiles. One who sat well in back certainly was not Jewish, since he was dressed in black and wore a Roman collar. The rabbi assumed he was the director of the Newman Club at the college, and so it turned out when he approached him at the end of the service and introduced himself. Father Bennett was a youngish-looking man of thirty, slim and boyish, and he laughed easily.

"Scouting the opposition, Father?" the rabbi teased.

The priest laughed. "For a while, I thought you might need me to round our your minyan. Is that the word?"

"That's the word. The attendance was rather disappointing."

"Actually, I'm surprised you got as many as you did. The great majority of students left this afternoon or earlier—right after their last class. Not that Rabbi Dorfman draws crowds, you understand. For that matter, I figure I am getting only about a quarter of the students I should," he added hastily, as if to avoid any disparagement of Rabbi Dorfman. "In our case, it's understandable: The church is in a state of flux; we're trying to modernize. But so many of our young people are holding back, as though waiting to see which road the church will take. They don't accept blindly; they question and discuss and argue."

"And you find this disturbing?"

"Not at all," said the priest quickly. "But much that they question we are not in a position to answer. Take the matter of birth control. So many of our Catholic students come from large families. In most cases, they are the first of their families to go to college. Well, you know from hearing them talk that they aren't planning to have six or seven children; two or three at the most, and that means birth control."

"Well?"

"Of course, upper-income Catholics have been doing it for years. In the higher social levels the large family is the exception, rather than the rule. But these young people are frightfully sincere. If the church establishes a regulation that runs counter to their common sense, they won't just disregard it, as other generations have done. They're more apt to disassociate themselves from the church completely."

"Young people grow wiser or at least more tolerant as they grow older," said the rabbi.

"Perhaps," said Father Bennett, "although frankly, I'm hoping the church will grow more tolerant, too. On this matter of birth control, for instance, the committee the Pope set up to study the question, opinion was overwhelmingly in favor of permitting the use of the pill."

"But the Pope has come out against the pill."

"For the present, yes. But there's a good chance one of these days he may change the doctrine."

The rabbi shook his head. "He can't. He really can't."

The priest smiled. "It's not a dogma, you know, and the church is a very human institution."

"It's also a very logical institution, and the question of birth control impinges on the sanctity of marriage, which *is* a dogma."

"And what is your position?"

"Well, we regard monogamous marriage as a highly artificial institution which is nevertheless the best system we have for organizing society. It is like a legal contract, which can be broken by divorce in the event that it becomes impossible for the two principals to continue. But with you, marriage is a sacrament and marriages are made in heaven. You can't permit divorce, because that would suggest that heaven had erred, and that is unthinkable. The best you can afford is annulment—a kind of legal fiction that it never happened."

They had left Hillel House and were strolling along the neat campus walk. Now they had arrived in front of the Dorfman home. "And how do you see birth control affecting our teaching on marriage?" asked Father Bennett.

"It becomes a question of what the function of marriage is," said the rabbi. "If it is procreation, then I suppose it makes sense to consider it the business of heaven. But it is hard to imagine heaven being greatly concerned with an institution that is largely intended for recreation. And that would be the effect if the use of the pill were condoned."

When Father Bennett had left them and the baby-sitter had departed and they were alone together, Miriam asked, "What got into you tonight, David? Were you deliberately baiting that nice Father Bennett?"

He looked at her in surprise and then grinned. "I suppose it's hardly the sort of discussion I would be likely to hold with Father Burke in Barnard's Crossing. Somehow I feel freer here. Perhaps it's the academic atmosphere. Do you think he was annoyed?"

"I don't know," she answered. "If he was, he took it well."

Professor Richardson lived in an old Victorian house. A large, square vestibule was separated by sliding doors from the living room, at the other end of which was another pair of sliding doors, which led to the dining room. Both pairs of doors had been pushed back to form one huge L-shaped room. By nine Saturday night the party was in full swing. People were standing around in small groups sipping their drinks. At one end of the room several chairs were clustered around a small table where the rabbi and Mrs. Small were sitting with their host, Professor Richardson, a youngish-looking, athletic man who kept interrupting his conversation with the rabbi to jump up to greet some new arrival, whom he would bring over to present. Mrs. Richardson circulated among her guests with occasional hasty forays into the kitchen to replenish the supply of food and drinks.

Invariably there were questions: "Why do you people wear that shawl thing with the fringed edges at your services?" "Do you have to have ten men in order to pray?" "Those dietary laws you people have—they were a health measure, weren't they? Why do you need them now that we have modern methods of refrigeration?" "What's being done to bring the synagogue up to date?"

Most of the older people, faculty members, made a point of coming over; and they, too, asked questions, meaningless, polite questions, intended only to make conversation: "You from around here, Rabbi?" "How do you like our school?" "You taking Bob Dorfman's place?"

On the other hand, the majority of the young people, he soon saw, had come not to meet him, but one another. They stood around in small groups; in one corner six or eight were sitting on the floor, one of them lying on his belly, his feet in worn moccasins waving in the air. From their intent expressions punctuated by explosive laughter, he gathered they were telling jokes, off-color jokes probably. Some of those who did approach him apologized for having missed the service the night before. When the student president of Hillel slid into the chair beside him, the rabbi remarked on it. The youth nodded. "You know how it is, Rabbi. No matter how you dress it up in your publicity, it's still a religious service. But an open house like this is a party. You can take a girl to something like this, and it constitutes a date. Understand?"

A tall, ungainly student with blondish hair approached. "H'lo, Rabbi, Mrs. Small." It was Stuart Gorfinkle.

"Oh, Stu, we've been trying to get you," said the rabbi.

"Yes, we phoned a couple of times," said Miriam, "and left a message."

"Yeah, I got it. Sorry I couldn't make it to the Hillel service last night. I had a date."

"That's all right," said the rabbi. "Are you driving home with us? We plan to leave about nine tomorrow morning."

"Well, it's like this, Rabbi. A couple of guys who live in Gloucester are leaving tonight, and they offered me a lift—"

He seemed embarrassed, so the rabbi said quickly, "Of course, Stuart."

"Well—say, I thought I'd drop in to see you some time tomorrow afternoon if you're going to be home." The young man sat down.

"By all means. We're expecting the students who are back from school."

Father Bennett came up and took a vacant chair beside the rabbi. He glanced at Stuart and half nodded, as though not sure whether he knew him or not. He smiled at Miriam.

"Do I have to apologize to you, Father?" asked the rabbi. "My wife thought I was baiting you last night."

"Oh, really?" He laughed. "Of course, you realize, Mrs. Small, that your husband is a Jesuit. Myself, I'm not very strong in the hairsplittings of theological argument. You have a name for that sort of reasoning, don't you, Rabbi?"

"Pilpul," said the rabbi, "although I think you will find it somewhat different from Jesuitical disciplines."

"Perhaps not," said Father Bennett. "But, as my young people say, each person must do his thing, and mine is essentially counseling. I try to instill in my people a simple faith, and I leave all the subtleties to the big guns of the church. My feeling is that once a person has faith, then everything else falls into line. Since we're all pretty much in agreement on that, I consider it my contribution to the ecumenical spirit."

The rabbi coughed apologetically. "Well, not quite. There's a difference in orientation. You Catholics are heaven-oriented, while we Jews are content with this world. There was a saint in the Middle Ages who never laughed—"

The priest nodded. " 'My Savior is crucified, and shall I laugh?' "

"That's the one. And it's actually a logical attitude in the light of your theology. You aspire to sainthood. We are content with the human level. Of course," he added, "it isn't because we lack fervor or aspiration. Rather, we believe that if you aspire to something above the human level, there is grave danger of falling below it."

"But faith, Rabbi. If you have faith in the majesty and glory of God—"

"Ah, but we don't—"

"No faith?" The priest was shocked.

"None that is enjoined upon us. It is not a requirement of our religion, as it is of yours. I suspect it's a kind of special talent that some have to a greater degree than others. Basically, our thinking is in line with the passage from Micah: 'What doth the Lord require of thee but to walk in His way?'"

"Isn't that the same thing?"

"Not really. You can walk in His way and still have doubts of His existence. After all, you can't always control your thoughts. When you affirm your belief, doesn't that imply that just prior to your affirmation you doubted? Our doubts are not accompanied by feelings of guilt and terror that afflict your people. Psychologically, I suppose, it's healthier."

"And you, Rabbi, do you believe?"

The rabbi smiled. "I suspect that like you or anyone else for that matter, sometimes I do and sometimes I don't."

Stuart rose. "I got to split now, Rabbi. We'll be starting out pretty soon. See you tomorrow maybe?" He nodded uncertainly at the priest.

"Sure, Stuart."

"Drive carefully," said Miriam.

The rabbi looked around him and remarked that almost all the young people had gone. He turned to Miriam and then said to Father Bennett, "I think maybe—"

Just then Professor Richardson came over. "Oh, you can't go now, Rabbi. We're expecting Lucius Rathbone—oh, there he is now." He hurried off to greet the newcomer.

"Lucius Rathbone?"

"The poet," Father Bennett explained. "*Songs of the Ghetto. Blue Notes.* He's our poet in residence. Bill Richardson said he might be coming over."

The rabbi looked curiously toward the door and saw a tall, light-skinned Negro of forty, resplendent in a white turtle-neck jersey and a black silk Nehru jacket. From his neck hung a silver chain and medallion, which he fingered. Beneath his pencil-line moustache, and above his little goatee he flashed strong white teeth in momentary smiles of greeting as Richardson, with one hand on his elbow, steered him across the room. His head held back, he looked down his aquiline nose from under lidded eyes as Richardson talked.

They came over. "Rabbi Small filled in for Bob Dorfman this week, Lucius. Mrs. Small, Rabbi, Lucius Rathbone."

The poet extended a hand and permitted the rabbi to press it. Still clutching the Negro, Richardson put an arm around the rabbi's shoulder. "Now that the youngsters are gone, Rabbi, we can all have a quiet cup of coffee around the table."

"We really ought to go, professor. We have a baby-sitter—"

"Surely you've got time for a cup of coffee."

The rabbi allowed himself to be persuaded. There were around a dozen seated at the table, and the talk was addressed largely to the poet.

"You working on something special right now, Lucius?"

"What about Prex's statement on the Student Afro-American League?"

"You hear anything about a new department of urban sociology, Lucius?"

It was obvious to the rabbi that they had come not to greet him, but in the hope and expectation of meeting the poet. And it was just as obvious that he enjoyed their attention. He fielded their questions sometimes sarcastically, sometimes even caustically, but always with peremptory authority. And when on occasion his answer embarrassed the questioner, he tossed his head back and laughed hugely, as if to make it clear that no real animus was intended. It was a kind of game he was playing with them. When he noticed the rabbi glancing at his watch, he called across the table, "You're not planning on leaving now, are you, Rabbi?" as though resenting the idea.

"I'm afraid we have to—"

The poet's face took on a cunning look. "You know, my uncle was a rabbi."

"Is that so?" said the rabbi, although he knew he was being drawn.

Rathbone's voice shifted suddenly to a higher pitch, almost a falsetto, and he spoke in the street dialect of the Negro ghetto. "Leastways, that's what we called him. He was a preacher and had a storefront church he called Temple of Zion. Reverend Lucius Harper. I was named after him. We always called him Rabbi Harper. My old daddy said it was a religion he made up so's he could grease up to the Jew landlord who owned the building and maybe get free rent. But Rabbi Harper claimed as how he did it under conviction and that us poor colored folk would be better off if we stuck with the Old Testament. What do you think of that?"

"Naturally, I think you would," said the rabbi.

"Yeah? Then how come all the stores down in our neighborhood that were profiteering on us were owned by Jews?"

"Now, Lucius—" Professor Richardson was distressed.

A spot of color appeared in the rabbi's normally pale cheek. He said quietly, "I know only one Jewish merchant who had a store in the Negro area in the town where I grew up. His father had started it long before your people moved to the neighborhood. He was certainly not a rich man. He couldn't sell the store, and he never had the money to close up and start another in a different location. Finally the decision was made for him when there was a riot in the area. They broke his windows and cleaned out his shelves for him."

The Negro was not abashed; on the contrary, he glared at the rabbi, and when he spoke, it was once again in his normal cultured baritone, and his tone was accusing. "And am I supposed to feel shocked because my people finally kicked over the traces and got a little of their own back? For four hundred years you have oppressed us and brutalized us and enslaved us, robbed us of our heritage and our manhood—"

The rabbi rose, and Miriam, too, got up. "We really have to go, Mrs. Richardson." He turned to the Negro poet. "Those four hundred years you speak of, Mr. Rathbone, my people lived in the ghettos of Europe—Poland, Russia, Germany—and there were no Negroes there. My grandfather, who came to this country from a small town in Russia at the turn of the century, like the rest of my ancestors, had never even seen a Negro, much less enslaved and brutalized and robbed him of his manhood." Miriam had come over to stand beside her husband, and he took her arm. Now he stared directly into the angry eyes of the handsome, light-skinned Negro. "Can you say the same of your ancestors, Mr. Rathbone?"

II

"You whipsawed me," said Irving Kallen ruefully. "You and the Doc between you."

Meyer Paff grinned. "Nothing to it, Irving," he said. "It was the last hand, so we were just trying to make a pot."

"Don't you believe him, Irving," said Dr. Edelstein. He was a round man with a perpetual smile ("A natural bedside manner," his patients would say). "Normal tactics—drive out the buttonhole makers."

"You ended up ahead, didn't you?" demanded Paff.

Kallen evened off the little columns of chips in front of him. "Nope. Let's see, I'm down thirty-two, no, thirty-seven cents. You're the big winner tonight—as usual."

Paff gathered in the chips to put away in the box.

"Luck," said Kallen.

"Don't you believe it, Irv. You've got to know how to play," said Paff.

"Maybe you're right, Meyer. My game is bridge."

"If you got card sense," Kermit Arons offered, "you can play any card game."

"Well, last night, I was playing bridge over at Nelson Shaffer's house—"

"That explains it," said Paff with finality. "You go playing cards on the Sabbath instead of going to the temple, and the next time you play, you're going to lose."

"Well, for thirty-two, no thirty-seven cents, I figure I wasn't punished too bad. Taking the two nights together, I'm still wa-ay ahead of the game. And from what I heard," he added maliciously, "I'll bet you wish you hadn't gone last night."

Paff shrugged his shoulders.

"What Brennerman pulled on Meyer was pretty raw," said Arons, "but actually it was directed against all of us here."

"You mean the business of the seating?" asked Dr. Edelstein. "As far as I'm concerned, I'd just as soon sit in the back row. With the public address system, you can hear just as good, and to tell the truth I kind of like the idea of being near the door so I can go out for a breather every now and then without everybody noticing."

"How about if you find yourself downstairs in the vestry?"

"What do you mean?"

"Last year we had to have two services, one in the vestry. Right?"

"Yes, but the new members were assigned seats downstairs; the old members—"

"Sure, but the whole idea now is to make the seating democratic. If there are no reserved seats, it means that if you come in a little late, you go down to the vestry because all the seats in the sanctuary are full."

"I don't think I'd care for that."

"Well," said Kallen, "I don't like to sit in the back. What's more, my old man considers our seats in the first row a kind of honor."

"And how about the money we paid for those seats?" demanded Arons. "I plunked down a thousand bucks to the Building Fund—not a pledge, but hard cash—back when Becker was president. And it was supposed to reserve my seat for me each year, the same seat, mind you, until the last day of the ticket selling. Well now, I regard that as a contract that I entered into with the temple, and if anybody should live up to their contract, it seems to me it should be an organization like a temple."

"You're one hundred percent right, Kerm," said Kallen. "That's how I feel. If you can't trust the word of a temple, who can you trust?"

"All right, what can you do about it?"

"I'll tell you what I can do about it, Meyer," said Kallen, his tone determined. "I'm still a member of the board of directors. I could place it before the board and demand that they take action."

"So what would that get you? They'd take action, all right. They'd put it to a vote, and they'd vote Gorfinkle's way. Remember, they've got a clear majority."

"Well, if the board should repudiate their solemn promises, I'd pick up my marbles and get out."

"And where would you go, Irv? To Lynn? To Salem? Where nobody knows you?"

"I'll tell you what I would do," Edelstein asserted. "I'd stay, but they'd whistle before they got a dime out of me."

Paff shook his head. "It wouldn't work, Doc. It might work in a church, but not in a temple. Our people don't ask for it; they demand it. It's part of the tradition. You know the old joke: The only thing two Jews can agree on is what a third should contribute to the support of the temple. No, if you were to give less than you gave last year, at the best everybody would think you had a bad year, that your practice was off. As for not giving at all—forget it. They just wouldn't let you get away with it; they'd bother you and pester you until you came across."

"Meyer's right," said Arons. "And you know what it means? It means that from here on in, we'll be putting up the big money, we and our friends, and Gorfinkle and his gang will be spending it. They won't even do us the courtesy of consulting us about it."

"That's right," said Paff. "You don't think this new seating plan was brought up before the board, do you?"

"You mean it was just Ted Brennerman's idea? Dammit, they can't do that. A change like that has to be brought up before the board," said Kallen.

Paff shrugged his shoulders. "Oh, they'll bring it up at the meeting, just to make it legal, and they'll let us talk on it for a while, and then one of them will move the previous question and—zip—it'll go through like that." He snapped his fingers. "And that's how it's going to be from here on in. Make up your mind to it."

"And that's how they'll work this Social Action Fund. They'll appropriate all kinds of money, and they'll disburse it any way they want to. We'll give it, and they'll spend it."

"Aw, come on," said Kallen. "How much of a fund will they set up? Five hundred? A grand? So what? I remember my old man told me that years ago, in all the *shuls*, they had a fund that the president used to control and to disburse when, say, some poor guy would come to town and didn't have a place to sleep or needed a meal—"

"But that was charity," said Paff. "This money is to be used for politics. And it isn't the amount; it's the principle of the thing."

"All right, they won this election, and they're in power. So next year we work a little harder, and we take it away from them."

"Don't kid yourself," said Paff. "They're in, and they're in to stay. They got a different attitude toward this whole business than we have. They look at the temple organization as a corporation—which it is, of course, legally. When Wasserman was president and Becker and even Mort Schwarz, they put men on the board because they were either doing a lot of work for the temple or they hoped they would. The idea was to get the best men. But Gorfinkle's crowd—most of them work for large corporations, administrators, executives—and they look at it like a business corporation where if you get the majority of the stock, you take over all the top jobs and you fill the board of directors with your own men. So from here on in, their nominating committee won't nominate anyone unless they're sure he'll see things their way."

"Well, I think the least we could do is make the most God-awful stink tomorrow at the board meeting," said Arons, "and hope that we'll rouse enough people to rally to our support—"

"We can't," said Paff in his deep bass rumble.

"Why not?"

"Because we don't have anything for people to rally to. What are we going to do? Ask them to support our right to retain our front seats? Be practical."

"Well—"

"Then maybe what'll happen tomorrow *will* give us a better reason," said Kallen.

"And what's going to happen tomorrow?" asked Paff.

"Well, like I said, I was over at Nel Shaffer's last night. Nel and I are good friends, but mostly he hangs around with guys that are close to Gorfinkle, like Bill Jacobs and Hymie Stern. I got the impression from things Nel let drop that Gorfinkle was planning to announce the new committees tomorrow, and some of his appointments might be pretty raw from our point of view and from the point of view of a lot of members of the congregation."

"Like what?" demanded Edelstein.

"Like making Roger Epstein chairman of the Ritual Committee for openers," said Kallen.

"He wouldn't dare!" said Edelstein.

"Why wouldn't he dare? He's his best friend. The two families are so close they're—"

"But the Ritual Committee," insisted Edelstein. "The man doesn't know a word of Hebrew. If the rabbi didn't announce the page, he wouldn't know what prayer to say next. He'd never been in a temple before he came here. His folks were radicals, free thinkers. And his wife—she's Gentile."

"When she was converted, she became Jewish," Paff reminded him. "That's the law. But that's a can of worms we don't have to open. If Gorfinkle appoints Epstein, it's still a raw deal against the congregation. And I'm not saying that because it's me he's going to replace."

"All right," said Arons, "so as soon as he announces it, we make a stink."

"No." Paff was emphatic. "I got an idea. When Gorfinkle announces his committees at the meeting tomorrow, we don't say a damn word. We sit tight."

Everyone looked at him. "And what does that get us?"

"Just trust me. I tell you I got an idea. Sorry, boys, but I can't give it to you now. Let's just see what happens tomorrow and follow my lead. If I don't say anything, don't you say anything." He looked around the table. "Have I ever let you down?"

12

"But why the Ritual Committee?" asked Roger Epstein.

The Gorfinkles made a point of seeing their good friends, the Epsteins, at least once a week, usually on Saturday night. They would go to a movie together or have an evening of bridge or sometimes merely sit around and talk, as on this Saturday night. Roger Epstein had waited until the women had gone into the kitchen before speaking.

"What's the problem, Roger?" asked Ben Gorfinkle.

"Well, you know my background. What if the rabbi should raise an objection?"

Gorfinkle chuckled. "How can he when he won't even be at the meeting tomorrow?"

Epstein was a short, pudgy man, balding but with a tuft of hair in front, which he had a habit of pulling when disturbed. He pulled at it now. "So what? So he'll question it when he gets back. And he'll be right."

"He'll be wrong," said Gorfinkle flatly. "Appointment of committees and committee chairmen is purely an administrative function of the president."

"But this is the Ritual Committee. They supervise the order of the services. That makes it a concern of the rabbi, I would think. And what do I know about ritual? Besides, there's Samantha—"

"Look, Roger, you think you're required to be some sort of expert? You think Paff when he had the job was a specialist of the ritual? That's what the rabbi is there for. The way I see it, the Ritual Committee stands in relation to the congregation the way the School Committee here in town does to the citizens. You don't have to be a teacher or an educator to serve on the School Committee. We've got a superintendent of schools and principals and teachers for that. What you want on the School Committee is just somebody with common sense who has the welfare of all of us first and foremost in mind. Well, it's the same way with the Ritual Committee. There is a set order of prayers and it's shown in the prayer book. In case of any special question, there's the rabbi. As for the rest, I'd say that describes you to a T."

Epstein was still not convinced. "But why me?"

"Well, for one thing, the Ritual Committee parcels out the honors for the services, and especially for the holidays—that can be mighty important—and I want a man I can trust to head it up. For another thing, you're an artist—"

"Commercial artist," said Epstein with a deprecatory wave of the hand.

"An artist," his friend insisted. "There's a certain pageantry involved in religious services, and it takes an artist to sense it and bring it out."

"Well—"

From the kitchen, Samantha called out, "Coffee will be ready in a minute, boys." She came to the door. "How about some English muffins?" She was a good two inches taller than her husband; blonde and blue-eyed, with wide cheekbones, she looked like the daughter of a Viking.

"Just coffee for me, Sam," said her husband. "Too many calories."

"Aw c'mon, lover. You can indulge tonight. You've been a good boy all week."

"Well, all right. You twisted my arm."

"You'll have some, Ben, won't you?"

"You bet."

From upstairs, their daughter, Didi, called down. "You making coffee, Mum?"

A moment later she entered the room and waved to her parents' guests. She was a slim, elfin girl, whose hair was parted in the middle in two braids.

"You been here all evening?" asked Gorfinkle. "What have you been doing?"

"Telephoning, of course," her mother answered for her.

"Oh, Mummy," she protested, then turned to the Gorfinkles. "We're getting up a cookout on the beach for Monday evening. When's Stu coming home?"

"Probably around noon Sunday," said Gorfinkle.

"Gee, I hope he hasn't made any plans. We're having all the kids who'll be coming home from school. I guess whoever is coming will be home by tomorrow. That's why we figured on Monday."

"Where are you having it, dear?" asked her mother.

"Over on Tarlow's Point."

"Monday—that doesn't give you much time to prepare. Have you called everybody?"

"Some. Bill Jacobs, Sue Arons, Adam Sussman. But, then, a lot won't be in until late tonight or sometime tomorrow. The chances are I'll see most of them over at the rabbi's house tomorrow afternoon."

"Why?" asked Gorfinkle. "Is he holding some kind of a meeting?"

"Oh, all the kids from the post-confirmation class sort of drop in the first Sunday they get back for vacation. You know, it's like an open house. They just talk, tell how things are going at school."

"Hm—that's interesting." Gorfinkle *was* interested. "How come? I mean, how did this—this tradition start?"

"No tradition. Just that sometimes he held the confirmation class at his house, and we kind of got into the habit of going there—you know, every now and then."

"And he's popular with you kids? You all like him?"

She considered. The question struck her as requiring thought, not because she was unsure of her feelings, but because they were hard to frame in words. "He's not fun, exactly," she said tentatively, "and he doesn't try to be pally or even friendly. He doesn't try to be anything, I don't think, but—"

"Yes?"

"An equal, I guess," she said, finally finding the words. "When you're with him, you don't feel like a kid."

13

The rabbi phoned Wasserman as soon as he arrived home Sunday. He caught him just returning from the board meeting.

"Mr. Wasserman? Rabbi Small. I'm sorry I wasn't able to get back in time. They had arranged for a party for me at the college for Saturday night. I didn't know anything about it."

"*Nu*, it happens. If the party was for you, you had to go."

"Tell me, did anything happen at the meeting? Anything special?"

"Well, Gorfinkle announced the new committees, like I thought."

"Yes? And how are they?"

"Well, if he appointed they should do a job, I guess it's all right. After all, he didn't appoint idiots. But if what he wanted is to start a fight, the appointments are good for that, too."

"That bad, eh? And what did Paff say? Was he there?"

"Oh, he was there. And that's the only nice part of it, because he didn't say a word, not Paff, not Edelstein, not Kallen, none of them. So I guess they're giving in, and for a while we'll have a little peace. But how long it will keep up?"

But the rabbi was disturbed. "What do you mean, they didn't say a word? Did they have a chance to? Was there time for discussion?"

"Oh, time, there was plenty, but no objections, no discussion, not one word, I tell you."

The rabbi waited for Wasserman to say more, but nothing was forthcoming. "I don't like it," he said at last.

"Why not?" said Wasserman. "You remember I told you it was like a marriage. If an open break doesn't develop, it can be fixed up."

"Yes, but if they don't talk at all, if the husband insults the wife and she doesn't even bother to answer, then it can mean that she's already made up her mind and it doesn't make any difference anymore. It seems to me Paff should have reacted. And I don't like the fact the others remained silent too."

"You think they decided something already? Well, maybe. It's possible. After what happened Friday night at the Brotherhood service . . ."

14

"All right, Meyer," said Dr. Edelstein as Paff wove his way through the traffic. "We sat tight like you asked us to, and Gorfinkle went ahead and nominated Roger Epstein as chairman of the Ritual Committee and Ted Brennerman as Chairman of the Seating Committee. After his talk Friday night, that was really rubbing it in. So what's the big plan already?"

Right after the board meeting Paff had insisted he, Edelstein, Kallen, and Arons go for a ride in his car. "I promise to bring you back in half an hour, so you'll have plenty of time to drive on home for lunch. I got something to show you boys."

He put his foot on the brake and brought the car to a halt opposite Hillson House. All through the ride he had kept silent, refusing to be drawn, his only response to their questions a self-satisfied smirk. Now he said, "This is it, boys."

They looked at one another questioningly and then at him. "This is what, Meyer? Have you gone crazy or something?"

He looked at Edelstein and then turned to the back, where Kallen and Arons were sitting. "What you're looking at, gentlemen, is the site for the new temple. Prime shore front property. You said you'd pull out, Irving, and I told you there was no place else to go. Okay"—his hand swept out to encompass all before them—"here's a place."

No one said anything, but Paff seemed not in the least fazed by their silence, which made his deep rumble sound all the more booming. "All of us, we've all kicked in with big hunks of dough to the temple. Am I, are we going to let a bunch of Johnny-come-latelies push us around and tell us they're taking over and we should go peddle our papers someplace else?"

"You mean you want to start a new temple, here on the site of this old ark?" said Edelstein, finally managing to put what they all felt into words.

"I mean I want to use this old ark, as you put it, for the new temple. She's a hundred and fifty years old, but she's sound, because that's how they used to build in those days. Of course, it will cost some money to fix up—"

"Some money?" said Arons. "It'll cost a fortune."

"So what? I made my money too late to change my habits. My Laura is after me I should have my suits made to order. 'You've got it now; spend it.' But I can't. I can't get interested enough in clothes to bother. When I play poker, I play penny ante, and I notice that I get as much fun out of winning ninety cents as I would if it were ninety dollars. And Irving is just as sore at losing thirty-two cents."

"Thirty-seven cents."

"Right! Thirty-seven cents. See what I mean? None of us would ever think of gambling more than he could afford to lose, so it doesn't make any difference if it's pennies or dollars; we get the same kind of kick out of it. I used to trade my car every three or four years; now I trade every couple of years. Each time I come in to trade, Al Becker tries to get me to switch to a Lincoln. 'A man like you,' he says, 'should drive a big car.' What am I? A kid? A college boy? I got to ride around showing off in a big car to impress some dizzy little broad? For me, a car is just to get from one place to another, and I'm used to a small car. But the temple—that's something else. I helped build it. Jake Wasserman started it, but I was right there behind him plunking down hard cash when it was needed. So now when Gorfinkle and his boys steal the place out from under our noses, do we just sit quiet and keep handing over money to them so they can spend it the way they like? What are we, a bunch of lousy Arabs we should steal away in our tents? I say, let's give them a fight; let's give them some competition."

"But the money—"

"So what? If I'm not going to use my money for things I don't care about, and I'm not going to use it for things I do care about, what am I going to use it for?"

"Just what do you have in mind?" asked Edelstein.

"They're asking eighty thousand—"

"Eighty thousand? For an old ark?"

"Shore front, Irv, shore front. And there's a nice piece of land across the street that's part of the deal. That would make a nice parking lot. Believe me, it's a good investment even for a businessman."

"You mean you want us to buy it outright, just like that, with our own money?"

"Us and a few others I got in mind. We form a corporation and buy the place. Then we sell it to the new temple organization—at cost—and take back notes for our money. In the meantime it's a tax deduction. When the temple organization raises the money, they pay us off, and not only are we in the clear, but we've done a fine thing." He lowered his voice confidentially. "I'll tell you, I was thinking of it originally as a business deal."

"You mean you were planning to put up another bowling alley here?"

"You bet. But not just a bowling alley. I was going to combine it with a restaurant, maybe a dine and dance place, maybe billiards instead of bowling—it's getting big these days. And then while we were talking last night, I got to thinking what happened the day before, Friday—"

"You mean Ted's speech?"

"Believe me, that was just the climax. All day, from one town to another I got nothing but grief. You know, one of those days. So when we were talking last night, I thought to myself, What do I need another business enterprise for? At my age? Then I began thinking about this place as a temple. Lots of temples nowadays are converted homes—and a lot of them not half so fancy as this, let me tell you. We could set in some beams and pull out most of the interior walls on the first floor. That could be the sanctuary, and it would seat a couple of hundred people easy. We'd have to put in a new heating system and maybe the plumbing. But that's all. Structurally, it's sound. And then all the rooms on the second floor and the third floor could be used for a school."

"So you'd have an old ramshackle place," said Kallen, "with a bunch of little bedrooms you're going to try to make into classrooms and a sanctuary, which, no matter how you arrange it, will still look like a dining room and living room knocked together. Like that place in Salem that started with fifty members, and they've still got about fifty members. For the last ten years now they've been trying to raise money to build, and they still haven't been able to."

"That's right, Irv baby, but there's a difference. Ours would be a shore front property."

"So?"

"Let me show you." He led them down the path to the beach, talking all the while.

"So what do people join a temple for? Some, because maybe they want to be big shots, but the great majority, they don't want to be members of the board of directors. They know it costs money, that the members of the board are always being hit. Most of them just want a place to go for the High Holidays and a place where they can send their kids to a school. But once you get started, that isn't what keeps a temple going. The High Holidays are only three days in the year. And daily prayers—there isn't a temple in the entire area that can guarantee ten men for a minyan every single day of the year. As for Friday night services, how many are we drawing now? Fifty? Seventy-five? Now for all those things, our place would be big enough and more than big enough."

He stopped abruptly to let them fully take in the water view. "The thing that really pulls in the members are the facilities for the Bar Mitzvahs and the weddings—the parties, in other words. Now you just think of the vestry in our temple, which is all we have for parties. Compare that with what we can offer here in Hillson House." He led them to the sea wall. "Think of it during the summer when most weddings take place. Think of a patio out in front here with a view of the beach. Now you're going to have a wedding, and you're going to spend anywhere from three to ten thousand dollars, and your wife and daughter are determined that things are going to be just right. You may not care— You're just the guy that foots the bills. But they care. They take a look at the vestry in the basement in the present temple, and then they come down to us. We show them they can have their wedding in a beautiful old manison facing the ocean, and if the weather is warm, they can hold it outside, out of doors. You know, as a matter of fact, that's the Orthodox way to have a wedding, outdoors under the stars. Which would get the nod, the old temple or our place? You can bet that they would come to us. And we could afford to be exclusive. We wouldn't take just anybody. They'd have to petition for membership, and we wouldn't act on them right away. And if you don't think that would get them . . ."

"And what if the same thing happens again, Meyer?" asked Dr. Edelstein. "What if after a while the new members begin to outnumber us and try to take over?"

"I've thought of that," said Paff. "And I figure we can prevent it easy enough. We limit the number of members on the board, and then we write into the constitution that the founding members are permanent members. No sweat, believe me. And I'll tell you something else: I don't care if we don't pull so many the first couple of years. I'm a little sick of these shoe clerks and insurance agents and commission salesmen we got running things. That Gorfinkle crowd, they're a bunch of small-time guys, and I'd just as soon have the temple made up of our kind of people, who you run an affair you don't have to take them by the throat to squeeze the price of a couple of tickets out of them."

"When can we take a look at the place inside?" asked Kallen, and Paff knew he had sold them.

"Now you're talking," he said jovially. "Did you see that coach house in the front? That's part of the property. There's a son of a bitch of an old Yankee living there who is like a kind of caretaker. He's got a key." He led the way to the coach house door and rang the bell. "I've got ideas for this place, too," Paff went on. "How about this for a bride's dressing room? Maybe connected with the main building by a kind of covered walk. Or maybe better, extra classrooms for the school? Or even a clubhouse with ping pong tables and some gym stuff for the kids?"

"I guess he isn't in," said Arons after they had waited for several minutes.

"Tell you what," said Paff, "I'll get the key from the broker, and we can meet here tomorrow night. How about half past eight?"

"Okay with me."

"Suits me."

"Okay by me, too," said Arons. "But look, Meyer, you had this idea last night, right?"

"Right."

"So tell me, why were you so anxious we shouldn't say anything at the meeting this morning. Seems to me that if we had put up a fight, we would've got a lot of guys—"

Paff shook his head decisively. "You've got it wrong, Kerm. Years ago there was a little grocery store in Chelsea, where my mother, may she rest in peace, used to trade. It was run by two brothers, Moe and Abe Berg. Then they had a fight, and Abe moved out and started another store of his own down the street. But even though the new store was a couple of blocks nearer our house, my mother went right on trading with Moe. And carrying bundles that couple of blocks meant something. When my father, may he rest in peace, asked her why didn't she trade at the new store, she said, 'How can I? Everybody will think I'm going there because I think Moe was wrong and Abe was right. And I feel that Moe was right.' See, this way, we're not asking people to take sides. We're not asking them to decide who's right and who's wrong, because if they decide against us, they won't come over to us even if we offer them a better deal for their annual dues."

"I'll go along with that," said Kallen. "But I think it would help us if we could pull over some of the better respected members of the community. Now if Wasserman and Becker would come over—"

"Wasserman would never come over," said the doctor, shaking his head.

"I think I know what might bring him around," said Arons suddenly.

"Yeah?"

"If we got the rabbi to come over first."

They all looked at him and then turned to Paff. "I don't think the rabbi would come," said Paff. "And I'm not sure that we want him. He's pretty independent."

"He's popular with the kids," said Arons stubbornly. "They like him. And you know how kids are these days. They rule the roost. None of them really want to go to Hebrew school. Who can blame them? So if the rabbi were with us, and the kids liking him, their folks might come over, if only to make sure that the kids go to school."

"You've got a point," said Paff. "What bothers me is that I don't think I could sell him on the idea in the first place."

"I'll bet Wasserman could."

"But he wouldn't," said Paff. "Remember, you're trying to use the rabbi to sell Wasserman."

"How about Becker?" asked Kallen.

"I'll bet he'd go along. And he'd try to sell the rabbi on the idea. Then if we got the rabbi, we could get Wasserman."

"Now that's an idea," said Paff. "Tell you what, I'll drop in on Becker tomorrow." He winked. "It's getting to be trading time. This time maybe I'll be interested in a Lincoln."

15

Miriam opened the door of the rabbi's study to say that Mr. Carter had come.

"Mr. Carter?"

"Yes, David, the carpenter. He's come to fix the window cords and put up the screens."

Mr. Carter, a big, raw-boned man, stood framed in the doorway, with his heavy kit of carpenter's tools in one big gnarled hand showing no drag on his broad shoulders, like a businessman carrying a light attaché case. A lock of black hair fell across a slanting forehead; his face had the deep leathery tan of a man who spent much of his time outdoors.

"I arranged with the missus to come this morning," he said, "but when I got here, the house was closed and there was nobody home. I don't have much time today, but I can get started, and I'll finish up tomorrow or Tuesday."

"We were delayed and got back only an hour ago." The rabbi frowned. "Frankly, Mr. Carter, I don't like the idea of you working on Sunday, on your Sabbath. It doesn't look right."

"Oh, it's not my Sabbath, Rabbi, and most of the folks in town know it. So don't bother about what they might be thinking—"

"What do you mean? Are you the town atheist?" the rabbi asked with a smile as he led him inside to the windows that needed repair.

"No, I'm no atheist. I don't go to church, but I'm no atheist. I keep the Sabbath, but it's yours I keep, not Sundays."

"Seventh-Day Adventist?"

"No, although I hold with a lot they believe in. I keep the Sabbath because that's the day the Lord told me to keep."

"How do you mean the Lord told you?"

"Well, it's hard to explain—I mean just how He told me. You see it wasn't words, but if you translate it into words, it would be something like, 'Raphael, after spending six days in making the universe and everything in it, I rested, and that was a good thing. And what is good for Me is good for you, because I made you in My image. I want you to work six days in every week and then rest on the seventh. That's the right proportion. And one is as important as the other.'"

The rabbi looked at him doubtfully, wondering if he were pulling his leg, but Carter's face was open and without guile.

"And when did this happen?" asked the rabbi carefully, not knowing what sort of person he was dealing with.

"You mean when did the Lord give me that particular command?"

"I mean when did He talk to you?"

The carpenter laughed. "Bless you, Rabbi, it happens right along— real frequent. Sometimes more than at other times. Sometimes almost every day maybe for a week. And then weeks go by, and I don't hear a thing. The first time I had a lapse like that, I got real worried. I tried to make contact and I prayed. I said, 'Is there something Your servant has done that offends You?' And I didn't get any answer that day, but the very next day, He spoke to me again, and this time He told me not to worry about not hearing from Him—that He wouldn't be talking to me unless He had something definite He wanted to tell me. And that if I didn't hear from Him, it meant everything was going along all right. And thinking it over afterward, I had to admit that all that time things had been going along nicely for me—no trouble, no problems, just kind of humdrum, you might say."

Carter had already begun, and he continued as he talked. He cleaned all the old putty out of the sash and then scooped a handful of putty from a tin and began to roll it in his hands. He straightened up, and the rabbi was startled to see that although his complexion was swarthy, his eyes were a clear, piercing blue.

"It was right after I was married. Me and the wife had just got back from our honeymoon to Niagara Falls, and we were visiting around— you know, her folks—aunts, uncles, she showing me off, so to speak— and to my aunts and uncles so's I could show her off. It was kind of expected in those days. Well, we were visiting her Aunt Dorset and Uncle Abner. That was over by Lynnfield they lived. And there were other people there—cousins and such. And suddenly while we were all sitting in the parlor talking and Aunt Dorset was passing around some fruit, I heard a voice saying, 'Stand upon thy feet, and I will speak to you.' So, I got up and heard a voice talking, and it told me the first chapter of Genesis.

"Now, the point is that in all my life I had never read the Bible, but when I came to that day at Aunt Dorset's, I could repeat that first chapter of Genesis almost word for word."

"And what did your wife—and the rest of the company say?"

"They told me that I just stood there and didn't talk to anyone for some minutes. They thought I was under some kind of spell, maybe like a cataleptic, and I guess there was even some discussion about going for a doctor."

"And then?"

"And then the same thing happened the next day. I was on a job and working when it happened, and I was told another chapter. And I got a chapter or so every single day until I went right through the Pentateuch."

"And then?"

Carter shook his head. "After that I would get messages only when I needed them." He cut off a length of cord and ran it through the sash weight.

"How do you mean, when you needed them?"

He ran the weight up and down a couple of times to see if the pulley was moving freely. "Well, Rabbi, take the time the town voted on fluoridation. I was bothered about that. Myself, I didn't think it was a good idea. I don't believe much in chemicals—I mean taking them into your body. But the doctor who was taking care of my wife while she was having our last baby, I got to talking to him about it, and he was all for it. So I had doubts, you might say. Him being a fine man and respected. And then I got a message, and I knew I had been right in the first place." He swung the window in and then turned around and faced the rabbi. "Look at me, Rabbi. I'm fifty-eight and never been what you might call really sick a day in my life. I've got all my teeth, and I don't wear glasses. That's because I live right. I don't eat meat, and I don't eat candy. I don't drink tea or coffee or tonic."

"Was the injunction against meat one of the instructions you received? That's not quite the same as the dietary laws in the Pentateuch."

"Well, it is and it ain't, Rabbi. He expects you to use your intelligence." He snapped the edging of the window in place and screwed it down. "Now it says 'Thou shalt not kill.' And it also says that you can't eat part of a live animal. So that would seem to exclude the eating of flesh. Now I know it also says the kinds of animals you can eat—those with a cloven hoof and that chew the cud, but I figure that's for the mass of people who haven't got the strength of their own convictions. It's a kind of sop—for those who still hankered after the fleshpots of Egypt. Couldn't get it out of their systems, you might say. So He allowed them to eat certain kinds of animals. But you can see He'd like it better if they didn't eat any."

"I see."

"There was another time when I was really sort of perplexed, and I got a message from Him. That was the time my oldest boy—"

The rabbi asked how many children Mr. Carter had.

"I got five, three boys and two girls. Moses, he's my oldest. Maybe you heard of him. Moose Carter? They call him Moose, he's so big. He was quite a football player at the high school last year and year before. Last year they came that close to winning the state championship. My boy's picture was in the papers a lot. There was sixty-seven colleges, Rabbi, sixty-seven that was interested in having my boy go there."

The rabbi showed he was impressed. "Was he also a good student?"

"No, just a good football player. They sent people down to see him, some of them did. Coaches or scouts. And they offered all kinds of things. Why, one offered girls."

"Girls?"

"That's right. He said that they had a lot of co-eds that were pretty and rich and just aching to marry a great big handsome football hero. Then he says, and he winks, 'Or, you don't have to marry them.' I ordered him from the house. I didn't want my boy to go to any college and certainly not that one. I wanted him to get a job and go to work. But he finally did take one of those offers—a college in Alabama. I was all for putting my foot down and forbidding him, but his mother was mighty set on his going."

"And how did it work out?"

The carpenter shook his head dolefully. "He was there till Christmas, till after the football season, then they dropped him. He had hurt his knee, so he wasn't any use to them anymore, and besides, he was doing poor in his studies. So he came home. He's been home three months now and hasn't done a decent week's work. He works a couple of nights a week in a bowling alley in Lynn, and every now and then he gets an odd job to do, and that gives him a little spending money. I guess my wife gives him a few dollars now and then. She favors him —him being the oldest." He shook his head. "I've suggested to him that he come in with me and learn my trade, but he tells me there's no money in it, that all the money these days is in wheeling and dealing. Wants to be a promotor. I tell you, Rabbi, the college ruined that boy. If it weren't for my wife, I'd order him from the house."

He straightened up and looked about the room. "That's about all I have here, Rabbi. It took a little longer than I anticipated. I won't be able to finish today, but don't you worry. When I undertake a job, I finish it."

"It's just as well," said Rabbi Small, watching him carefully replace the tools in his kit. "I'm expecting a group of young people to be dropping over a little later in the afternoon."

"I'll come by tomorrow or Tuesday, depending how my work goes."

"Fine, Mr. Carter. Whenever you have the time."

16

"So then he says, 'I'm going to pass out copies of the new committees. I'll ask you to take these sheets home with you so that you can study them at your leisure, and then at the next meeting three weeks hence we can vote intelligently on confirmation.'" Malcolm Marks had been unconsciously mimicking the president. Now he resumed his normal tone. "And he passes out these mimeographed sheets, and I'm watching Meyer Paff. He's got his on the table in front of him, and he's reading the lists, sliding his finger on the page down the list and kind of making noises in his throat like he's pronouncing the names. And then he gets to Roger Epstein's name as chairman of the Ritual Committee, and I thought he was going to have a heart attack."

"But why should he be so upset?" asked his wife. "He must have known that Ben Gorfinkle wasn't going to reappoint him."

Marks made no attempt to hide his impatience. "Of course not. But Roger Epstein, for God's sake!"

The telephone rang. "I'll take it," called their daughter Betty from another room. And a moment later, "It's for me."

"Well, what's wrong with Roger Epstein?"

"With Roger Epstein as a person, maybe nothing. In fact, he's a very idealistic type who carries the whole world on his shoulders. But this is the Ritual Committee. You take the Building Fund Committee or the Membership Committee or even the High Holy Day Seating Committee, which all are important committees. Okay, Roger's fine and dandy. But strictly speaking, for the Ritual you should have not only a real pious type, I mean one who don't work on Saturdays and eats strictly kosher, but somebody who knows all about the rules of ritual. He's got to be practically a rabbi, strictly speaking. All right, we don't have too many like that. Maybe Jake Wasserman, but offhand I can't think of anybody else to speak of."

"So if nobody can do it, what's wrong with Roger Epstein?"

"Well, it's not exactly that nobody can do it. The point I'm making is that if you haven't got the type person who should be chairman of Ritual, you got to at least get somebody who, on the surface at least, seems okay. Now, Meyer Paff, maybe he doesn't know so much, but he keeps a kosher house—"

"Pooh! That's only because his mother-in-law lives with them, and she wouldn't eat there if they didn't have two sets of dishes. He couldn't let her starve to death, could he?"

"That's what I'm saying. It don't matter if he really believes in it, so long as he does it. That's what I mean by on the surface."

"All right. So what happened?" his wife asked.

"What do you mean?"

"When Paff saw that Roger Epstein was made chairman of the Ritual Committee. What happened already? What did he do? What did he say?"

"Nothing!" said her husband triumphantly.

She looked at him in amazement. "So what's the big *shpiel?* What's the excitement?"

"Don't you see? Paff has been the big wheel in the temple ever since it was built. He's never been president, but he's always been a power behind the throne. So Friday night Ted Brennerman gives him a ribbing right out in public. And don't tell me that Gorfinkle didn't know what Ted was planning. And from what I hear—we were down in the vestry at the time, so we missed it—Paff catches Ted up in the sanctuary, and he really lays him out in lavender. That's round one." He rotated a hand. "Mezzo, mezzo. Call it a draw; Paff gave it to Ted a lot harder than Ted gave it to him, but on the other hand, only a few people heard Paff, and everybody heard Ted. Yeah, I guess you could call it a draw.

"All right, round two. Gorfinkle doesn't let it lay; he comes out fighting. He says like, 'Make your play, Paff. Go for your gun. I'm not afraid of you. And I'm proving it by appointing my friend Roger Epstein to be chairman of Ritual, which not only you used to be chairman of and which, moreover, is a very special job that I wouldn't normally appoint Epstein to on account of his background, but I'm doing it right now, the first chance I got after Friday, just to show you who's boss. So put up or shut up.'"

"So he shut up."

"Not Meyer Paff. He don't give up that easy, and he don't back away from a fight. He just gets on his bicycle and goes in for a little fancy footwork to keep out of the way of Gorfinkle's reach so he can save his strength for the next round. The talk after the meeting was that he would line up his gang and either try to take over the town or burn it down."

"What do you mean burn it down? You mean he'd burn the temple?"

"Of course not. That's what they call a figure of speech," he said loftily. Then he lowered his voice. "Some people I talked to said they wouldn't be surprised if he pulled out of the temple and started one of his own."

"Over appointing Roger Epstein head of the Ritual Committee?"

"That and other things," said Marks defensively. "This thing has been building a long time."

She looked at him. "So where does that leave you?"

"That's just it. I'm like betwixt and between. I was appointed by Schwarz, and I got another year to go on my term. Ben Gorfinkle and Roger Epstein and the rest I'm kind of friendly with, but on the other hand, I'm friendly with Meyer Paff's gang, too. After all, if God forbid somebody needed an operation, we'd call Doc Edelstein, wouldn't we? So I can go either way. And my guess is both sides will be pulling for my vote."

Their daughter, Betty, sauntered into the room. She was short like both her parents. Her long blond hair was parted on one side and hung straight down over her shoulders, although one strand was looped over her ear with a barette and pushed forward to partially conceal her left eye. Where the hair was parted, one could see a trace of dark hair, suggesting it was time for another color rinse. Her innocent dark eyes were made knowing with eye shadow and a thin line of darker coloring that edged the lids. Her breasts pushed aggressively against her sweater, and her little rump rotated suggestively as she walked.

Her mother looked up in automatic question.

"A bunch of the kids are having a cookout tomorrow evening, at Tarlow's Point," she explained. "That was Didi Epstein. She wanted to know if I could make the scene."

Mr. Marks shot a significant glance at his wife, but she appeared not to notice. "Did you say you would go, dear?"

"I guess so. She said Stu Gorfinkle would pick me up—around five tomorrow."

"Did Didi say who else was going to be there?" asked her mother.

"Sue Arons and Gladys Shulman and Bill Jacobs and I think Adam Sussman—you know, the kids who have been away to college and are back for the vacation."

"It's a lovely idea," said her mother. "It'll be nice to see all your old friends again."

When she left the room, Mr. Marks said, "See, it's started already."

"What's started already?"

"Buttering us up. All the time she was in high school they never gave her a tumble—that Epstein girl and the Gorfinkle boy, they always acted as though she wasn't good enough for them."

"That's ridiculous. Didn't she go to Didi Epstein's for the after-prom breakfast last year?"

"Sure, the whole senior class was invited."

"Well, you're wrong. They started making up to her before that—when she was accepted at Connecticut College for Women. She got more brains in her little finger, let me tell you—and they know it. That Stu Gorfinkle was turned down by all the schools he applied to, and he had to go to his fallback, Mass State. And Didi ended up at an art school in Boston, for God's sake, and she was so sure she was going to Wellesley because her mother was an alma mater there. And that little Sussman pipsqueak. I remember his mother distinctly telling the girls at her table at a Sisterhood lunch that her son had applied to Harvard, Yale, and Columbia. So he ends up at a dinky little college out in Ohio that nobody ever heard of."

"All right, all right, but you mark my words—"

The telephone rang. "It's for you, Dad," Betty called out.

"Who is it?"

"Mr. Paff."

Mr. Marks favored his wife with a triumphant smirk and left the room to answer the phone.

17

Sunday night supper was usually a pickup meal in the Gorfinkle household, where dinner was served at midday. But with Stu home, Mrs. Gorfinkle felt guilty about not providing him with a hot meal. So when he came in and asked what was for supper, she answered, "How about some hamburgers? I've got buns and potato chips."

"Oh, sure, anything."

"Why, I'd like hamburgers for a change," said his father. "And a Coke."

"I'll take milk," said Stu.

"Milk with hamburgers?" questioned Mr. Gorfinkle.

"You suddenly kosher since you became president of the temple?" Stu asked sarcastically.

"No, but in my own house I don't like to see them eaten together."

"But in a restaurant you don't mind? That doesn't make sense to me," said his son.

Gorfinkle resented being challenged by his son, but he tried not to show it. "Tastes in food never make sense, Stu. That's just how I feel about it. Your mother never serves butter, for example, when she's serving meat. When I was a youngster, the thought of it turned my stomach. But I always expect butter for my bread when I'm eating in a restaurant."

He was even more annoyed when his wife brought a pitcher of milk to the table, and automatically—as always happened whenever he was angry or crossed—the corners of his mouth turned up in a frozen little smile that had no humor in it, as some of his subordinates at the plant had found to their cost.

"He's so thin," she said apologetically as she filled Stu's glass.

Gorfinkle looked away from her and said abruptly to his son, "Where were you all afternoon?"

"Oh, some of the kids dropped in to see the rabbi. He sort of expects it. I did it during Christmas vacation, too. It's a kind of open house."

"And what did he have to say?" He could not help adding, "I'm sure he didn't talk about the kashruth regulations."

"Oh no. We just talk about what we're doing at school. Didi Epstein kind of kidded him about what they were teaching her in art school— learning to make graven images, you know."

"That Didi," said Mrs. Gorfinkle. "I bet he thought she was fresh."

"I don't think so. He said he didn't mind as long as she doesn't worship them. So then she told him about this painting she's doing on Moses receiving the Law. And he said he'd like to see it. She promised to bring it over tomorrow." Stu chuckled. "He's a pretty free-minded guy. You should've heard him down at Binkerton at this party they gave for him."

"Oh?" his mother remarked.

"There was this Father Bennett who's head of the Newman Club— like the Hillel Club but for Catholics. He came over while I was sitting with him, and the rabbi kind of needled him about his religion. Very smooth, very cool. And then this priest comes right back and asks how he stands in the faith department. 'Do you believe?' So the rabbi kind of smiles and says, 'I guess I'm just like you; sometimes I do and sometimes I don't.' Pretty sharp."

"Well, I don't think that's the proper thing for a rabbi to say," said Mrs. Gorfinkle flatly.

"Why not?"

"Well, if he's a rabbi, it seems to me the least he could do is believe all the time."

"That's just exactly where you're wrong. Do you believe all the time? Does Dad?"

"Now, just a minute, just one minute," said his father sternly. "I don't, and I don't suppose your mother does, but, then, we're not rabbis. What your mother means is that as a rabbi, it's his duty to believe. I can see him talking that way with a priest when they're alone together. After all, they're both in the same profession. But I certainly don't think he should have said it in front of you or any of the other young people who were there."

"Why not?" demanded Stuart.

"Because you're not old enough or mature enough to—"

"And this business that's happening right here in the temple, I suppose I'm not old enough or mature enough to understand that either?"

"And what's happening here in the temple?" asked his father quietly.

"There's going to be a split," his son said hotly. "That's what's happening."

Gorfinkle's voice was tight, controlled. "Did the rabbi say that? Did he say there was going to be a split?"

"No, not exactly—but he didn't seem surprised when Sue Arons asked him about it."

"I see," said the elder Gorfinkle. "And what did he say?"

"Well, if you must know," said Stuart belligerently, "he said there was no reason for a split and that if one occurred, it would be as much the fault of one side as the other."

Gorfinkle drummed the table with his fingers. "I see. And did he indicate what his attitude would be in the event of this supposed—split?"

"Yeah. A plague on both your houses."

"A plague on—?"

"He didn't use those exact words, of course." Stu showed his exasperation with his father's literal-mindedness. "What he said was that if a split should take place, well, he wouldn't care to serve any longer."

The corners of Gorfinkle's mouth turned up now. "He shouldn't have said that, not to you kids."

Stu was aware that his father was angry, but he resented the implication that he and his friends were not concerned. "What do you mean, 'you kids'?"

"I mean that he was trying to influence you, and he has no right to."

"Isn't that what rabbis are supposed to do, influence people, especially kids?"

"There's legitimate influence, and there's influence that's strictly out of line," said his father. "When the rabbi gets up in the pulpit and explains about our religion and its traditions, that's legitimate. That's what he gets paid for. But the rabbi is not supposed to interfere in temple politics. If he prefers one side to another, he's supposed to keep it to himself. And when he urges his point of view on a bunch of kids who don't know what's involved, then he's out of line. And I think I'm just going to have a little conference with him and tell him so."

"Look here," said Stu, suddenly worried. "You can't do that."

"And why can't I?"

"Because he'll know it came from me."

"What do you suppose he told you for? If he didn't think it would get back to me—and to the other parents?"

"He did no such thing. He wouldn't, not the rabbi. He's straight."

"Straight? He's just a guy who's trying to keep a job."

Stu put down his half-eaten second bun and, pushing his chair back from the table, he rose, his face white with anger. "Yeah, you can go and wreck an organization, and that's all right, an organization that's just a sideline with you, a hobby that makes you feel like a big shot. You don't even care about it enough to keep kosher or anything like that, but if someone whose whole life is involved in it tries to preserve it, then you got to rub him out."

"Finish your meal, Stu," pleaded his mother.

"Sit down," ordered his father. "You don't know what you're talking about."

But the young man flung away from the table.

"Where are you going, Stu?" his mother called after him.

"Out!"

A moment later they heard the outer door bang.

"Why do you always fight with him?" asked Mrs. Gorfinkle plaintively.

"Because he's an idiot." He, too, rose from the table.

"Where are you going?"

"To make some telephone calls."

But the phone rang just as he reached for it. It was Ted Brennerman on the other end. "Ben? Ted. I got it via the grapevine that Paff and his gang are beginning to line up people."

"You mean to vote against my appointments? Naturally—"

"No, Ben, not to try to outvote us—to pull out and start another temple."

"Where'd you get that from?"

"Malcolm Marks. Paff called him."

"And I just found out that the rabbi has been shooting off his mouth to the kids to have them bring pressure on their parents. I think I'm beginning to understand. Look, we've got to have a meeting on this, and tonight. You got a list of the board members? Well, you know which ones are with us a hundred percent. Start calling them. You take the ones from A to M, and I'll take the rest. We'll meet here at my house, say around ten o'clock. That'll give everybody plenty of time."

18

From the bureau drawer Moose Carter selected a pair of Argyle socks. Though it was Monday and nearly noon, he still wasn't dressed. He sat on the edge of the bed as he drew them on absentmindedly while contemplating the immediate problem—money. In the room next door his sister Sharon, he knew, was lying on her bed reading. She was always reading.

"Hey, Sharon," he called through the wall, "got any scratch?"

"No." He had not expected anything else, but it was worth a try. He leaned close to the wall and spoke with great urgency. "You see, I've got this job lined up. The guy's in town, in Boston—" He heard the squeak of her bed and then a door slam closed. She had gone out.

"Bitch," he muttered.

He raised the edge of the mattress to remove the gray flannel slacks he had placed between the box spring and mattress the night before. As he drew them on he considered the possibilities offered by his brother Peter's room. The kid had a paper route and always had money. He wouldn't lend a nickel, though. He thought more of money than of his skin. But he wasn't home now. On the other hand, the kid was good at hiding it, and if Sharon heard him moving around in his room, she'd rat on him. His shoulders gave an involuntary twitch as he remembered the last time he had been caught borrowing from Peter's hoard; his father had showed his disapproval—with a half-inch dowel rod.

Still debating with himself the chances of a quick foray into Peter's room, he selected a yellow shirt from his meager supply. He heard the downstairs door open and close, signaling the return of his mother from her shopping. Hell, she'll give it to me, he thought and quickly finished dressing. The black tie, already knotted, needed only a quick jerk to tighten. He squirmed into his sport jacket, and with the aid of a forefinger, worried his feet into his loafers. Then he hurried down the stairs.

She was in the kitchen putting away the groceries. "You going to see a girl?" she asked sourly, seeing the way he was dressed.

He grinned at her, a wide infectious grin. "Girls is for nighttime, Ma, you know that. I'm going into town."

"Town?"

"Yuh, Boston. I gotta chance for a job. It's a special deal. I might be late getting home."

"Your father doesn't like it if you're not at the table at dinnertime."

"Well, gee, sure, I know, Ma, but I'll be hitchhiking back."

"You mean you haven't even got bus fare back?"

"I only have a dime. That's the truth. I had to get some stuff at the store for a job that I was doing for old man Begg, and he forgot to pay me back, and I forgot to ask him."

"Didn't he pay you for the job either?"

"Oh no, he never pays me until Friday, the end of the week."

"And that Mr. Paff at the bowling alley?"

"He'll pay me tonight."

"And how does it look that a boy like you should be thumbing rides," she demanded. "Why don't you get yourself a regular job?"

"Carpenter like Pa? No thanks. I've been able to manage since I got back, haven't I? Once in a while a fellow gets strapped. Well, that can happen to anyone. Now if this deal that I'm working on comes through, I'll be all set."

"What kind of a deal?" she asked.

"Oh, it's kind of promotion work. This fellow I knew—I met him in school when I was in Alabama—he's coming up North and he's building up an organization."

"And you're going to see him without a penny in your pocket?"

"Well, I'm not going to tell him that I'm broke," he said tartly.

"He'll see it in your face. He'll read it in your eyes," she said. "Like I do." She fumbled in her apron pocket and took out a coin purse. "Here, here's two dollars. That's all I can let you have, but you'll be able to get the bus both ways." She held the crumpled bills out to him. "Now you make sure you get home in time for dinner."

"Well, gee, Ma. I mean, I might have some business to talk over. He might ask me to have dinner with him. I can't just break away and say I've got to get home, my folks expect me home for dinner."

"Well, if you find that you're going to be delayed, you call up. Just excuse yourself and say you have a previous engagement you've got to cancel, and you call up and say you're going to be late. Now that's the proper way to do it. And if this man is any kind of businessman, he'll respect you for it."

"Okay, Ma. Guess you're right. Thanks for the money. You'll get it back no later than Friday."

From the hall closet he took his light-beige cotton raincoat, turned up the collar, and surveyed himself in the hall mirror. He was satisfied at what he saw—the young collegian, just like in *Playboy*. From the mirror he could see that his mother was watching him and that she was proud. He winked at his reflection and then with a gay, "Be seeing you," he left.

19

Didi cupped her hand over the mouthpiece of the telephone and whispered to her mother, "Remember that boy from school I told you about? Alan Jenkins? The colored boy? Well, he's in Lynn and wants to come over. What shall I tell him?"

"Ask him to come over, if you want," said Mrs. Epstein matter-of-factly. "Does he have a car?"

"He's got a motorcycle. But what about the cookout—"

"Invite him along if he wants to come."

"You think it will be all right?"

"I don't see why not. What's he like, anyway?"

"Oh, he's a little older than most of the freshmen; he was out working a couple of years. He's terribly talented. And he's easygoing and pleasant—I mean he's not surly or—you know—angry like some of them. I mean at school, it being an art school, well, it doesn't make any difference. I mean we don't think of him as being different, if you know what I mean."

"Then—" Mrs. Epstein shrugged her shoulders.

Didi uncupped the mouthpiece and said, "Oh, Alan? Sorry to keep you waiting. Look, some of the kids I went to school with—we're having a cookout on the beach. How would you like to make the scene? . . . About six or eight of us. . . . You can? Good— Oh, I just thought of something; I promised our rabbi I'd show him that painting I was working on at school—you know, Moses and the tables of the Law? So why don't you pick me up there? . . . No, we won't get hung up. . . . All right, here's what you do: Take the shore road out of Lynn and go along until the first set of traffic lights. . . ."

Alan gunned the motor and then let it die. Didi in white slacks climbed down from behind him, and he walked the bike up the driveway to the garage. "That rabbi seemed like a straight guy," he said. "Funny, I thought he'd be an old crock with a long beard. I thought all rabbis have beards."

Didi giggled. "No, just the kids at school. Come to think of it, though, I've never seen one with a beard."

"I figured he'd talk like a preacher—you know, about God and all that."

"Rabbis really aren't preachers; they're more like teachers," she explained. "Actually, according to our rabbi, his real job is interpreting and applying the law—like a lawyer or a judge."

Mrs. Epstein greeted them in the living room. "Your first time in Barnard's Crossing, Mr. Jenkins? Didi has told me so much about you." He was a nice-looking young man, of a deep coffee-brown. His lips, though bluish, were not overlarge. His nose, too, was high-bridged and well-formed. His hair was cut close to his head, and she was pleased to see no attempt had been made either to straighten or to smooth it down. He was of medium height but had a large chest and square shoulders, which seemed tensed at the moment.

"Yes, ma'am. I've been to the North Shore a couple of times—to Lynn. There's a guy—a man who sometimes sells some of my paintings for me there—"

"An art dealer? I didn't know there was an art store or gallery in Lynn," she said, offering him a chair.

"No, ma'am. He's got like a bookstore and greeting cards and some gift items—things like that. He hangs up some of my paintings when he's got the space, and when he sells one, he pays me."

"And do you sell many?" she asked.

He laughed, a fine, open laugh. "Not enough to retire on. I'm riding down to New York first thing tomorrow morning, and I was hoping he might have some loot for me." He shook his head. "Zilch—although he did say he had a couple of people interested in one picture."

"And what kind of pictures do you paint, Mr. Jenkins?"

"Oh, Alan does these marvelous abstracts—"

An auto horn sounded outside. "There's Stu now. Come on, Alan," said Didi.

"Take a sweater, dear. It can get chilly on the Point."

"Don't need one."

"Well, have a nice time, dear. Good-bye, Mr. Jenkins. And good luck on those paintings."

20

As Moose found himself picking his way between clumps of trash barrels and groups of squalling children, who spilled all over the street in the South End of Boston, he began to have misgivings. To be sure, the street must at one time have been very fine; it was divided in the middle by a broad grass plot, with wooden park benches set at regular intervals. But the grass even this early in the spring looked ill-cared for, and a litter of papers, tin cans, and bottles had piled up under the benches. Once grand brownstone-front town houses with short flights of granite stairs, each with its wrought-iron railing, were set back from the sidewalk. The ornate wooden doors, which no doubt had had massive brass knockers and brass doorknobs, showed years of wear and abuse; there was a hole in the door where the knocker had originally been, and instead of the doorknob only a round hole with a thong of greasy leather hanging from it to serve the purpose. Peeling, blistered paint showed layers of different colors on the door, flanking which were long, narrow windows suggesting high-ceilinged rooms inside. But most of the windows were cracked, and in one case the window had been shattered and replaced by a piece of weatherbeaten plywood. The sidewalks and sides of the houses were liberally sprinkled with chalk graffiti.

Moose found the number he was looking for and climbed the stairs. Finding no bell button (there was only a hole through which a couple of wires protruded), he rapped on the door. He waited a moment and, receiving no answer, pushed the door open. It was held closed by a coiled spring under considerable tension, so that the moment he released it the door slammed shut. At the noise a slatternly old woman poked her head into the vestibule and looked at him inquiringly.

"I'm looking for Mr. Wilcox," said Moose.

"Top floor, last bell," she said and closed her door.

Then Moose noticed a row of mailboxes, and he pushed the button under the name. Almost immediately there was an answering "Hello" through the speaking tube.

"I'm Moose Carter, Mr. Wilcox," he called into the tube. "I spoke to you on the phone."

"Come on up."

His initial misgivings were immediately allayed as he stepped inside. The room was large and well-furnished. There was an Oriental rug on the floor and oil paintings in heavy gold frames on the walls; large overstuffed chairs were scattered around the room, and facing a large window, from which could be seen the neighboring rooftops, was a massive sofa. Nearby was a marble-topped desk in carved mahogany and behind it a black-leather modern swivel chair set on a chrome pedestal.

Wilcox himself was not what Moose had expected. With his flannel slacks and tweed jacket, he reminded him of a youngish professor, like some of the ones he had known in college. His brown hair was cut close and showed signs of graying at the temples; his manner, easy and friendly.

"Some view you've got here," said Moose, approaching the window.

"I like it," said Wilcox. "I like to sit on that sofa there and just look out over the rooftops. Very relaxing."

"It's nice," said Moose. "I wouldn't have . . ." He stopped.

"Expected it? You mean from the appearance of the street? A lot of these houses are being bought and fixed up, like this one." He smiled, and it was a nice smile. "It's a sort of private slum reclamation project. This apartment here belonged to an artist friend of mine. He took a long-term lease and fixed it up as a studio, which accounts for the picture window. Then he decided to go to Europe. It's actually in a convenient part of the city here."

"This your office, Mr. Wilcox?"

The other eyed him speculatively and then said, "I do some business here." He motioned Moose to the sofa and then sat down at the other end, facing him. "You said you were interested in working with us."

"That's right, sir."

"Well, the stuff we deal in is not hard to get in the city, and there are plenty of people, retailers, who buy the stuff on their own from Tom, Dick, or Harry, and I guess maybe they make out all right. But we don't operate that way. We're an organization. Maybe at first it looks as though it might cost you a little bit more, but our people think it's worth it. When you buy from us, you can be sure the stuff is good. You don't have to worry whether it's mixed with oregano or catnip or worse, which could get you into a lot of trouble. You get any customers for other kinds of stuff we can supply them, but when we sell grass, grass is what you get. That's the way I like to operate.

"There are advantages to working with an organization," Wilcox went on. "We keep the competition down. Somebody comes in town and gets a supply, passes it on to his friends, or maybe sells it at his cost, we don't bother with that. But someone coming into your territory who is an operator, well—we take care of it. And then there are times when you get into trouble, and if it can be fixed, we'll fix it. Of course, one reason we'd like to have you with us is that the kids all know you and you can operate on a friendly basis with customers in your home-town, and that's a good thing."

Moose hesitated. "How about—"

Wilcox nodded. "Yes, the territory has been assigned already, but we're not entirely satisfied with the way it's been operated. Then you can argue that the territory has grown too big for one man." He reflected. "Maybe that would be the best angle. You need two to really work a good territory. So you can go and see him and tell him we said you're to come in with him. The arrangement will be a straight fifty-fifty split. Of course, he's paid for his present stock, so you could offer to work that off on a commission or a percentage basis. Say a quarter. I'd say that would be about right. A quarter on the old stock and a half on the new. We'll see how that goes for a while, and then maybe we'll make some changes."

"What kind of changes?"

Wilcox pursed his lips. "Well, if things go the way I'm hoping, there's no reason you couldn't handle it yourself some day. So we'd transfer him—that's right, we'd transfer him to another territory. That's kind of our regular policy. We transfer him to another territory." Wilcox opened a cigarette box on the coffee table and offered Moose a cigarette.

"When would I start?" asked Moose, lighting up.

"What's wrong with right away? Tomorrow, day after, tonight if you can arrange it."

"Well, when will you talk to him? I mean when are you going to let him know?"

Wilcox smiled. "I figured on you telling him."

"Me? But—but what if he doesn't believe me?"

"Well, I was counting on you to make him believe you. You might consider it a kind of test. Yes, that's what it is—a kind of test. You take an operation like ours, we don't have too much staff. Every man operates on his own. We can't have a man calling up the home office every time he runs into a little problem. So—you've got your instructions; you look like a persuasive lad"—he eyed Moose's size and smiled— "you'll know what to do. Of course, if he does contact us, we'll tell him what the situation is."

"Oh, sure, Mr. Wilcox, I understand. And I'd like you to know that I appreciate this chance, and I'll do my best—"

Wilcox smiled sardonically.

"I mean it, sir. I—"

Wilcox cut him off with a wave of the hand. "Everybody tries to knock a little off the top. We expect it. Just don't get greedy." He reached for his wallet. "You need a little expense money to tide you over?"

"I can manage."

Wilcox riffled through a sheaf of bills and then drew out two new twenties. "Well, call it an advance. Just a minute." He left the room but returned almost immediately with a plastic tobacco pouch, which he tossed to Moose. "There's an ounce package. You can consider this a kind of promotion package, uh—samples. There's no charge for this. But after this, everything is cash on the barrelhead. Get it?"

"Oh sure. And thanks."

Wilcox went over to the cigarette box and pressed a catch on the side. The top tray of cigarettes swiveled to one side, exposing another layer of cigarettes underneath—somewhat irregular in shape and obviously homemade. "Have a couple for yourself," he offered.

"Gee, that's neat."

Wilcox smiled. "A gimmick. Nothing to rely on if cops get around to actually looking." Moose picked up a cigarette from the box, rolled it in his fingers, and sniffed deeply.

"I don't think you'd better smoke it here. Take a few with you. You got a cigarette case? Wait a minute." He searched in the desk drawer and brought out a flat cigarette case of German silver. He slid a number of the cigarettes inside the elastic band of the case. "Here," he said. As Moose reached for it he had another thought. From the top tray of the cigarette box he took several ordinary cigarettes and slid them alongside the others. "Now you got an assortment," he said.

21

Much of the beach was rocky, and what sand there was was coarse and gravelly. But it was secluded. Principally that was because it was situated on a kind of peninsula, and when the tide was in—which would be shortly—it was surrounded by water on three sides. Broken branches from the stand of pines provided plenty of wood for a fire; and driftwood was plentiful, too, since the point jutted out into the current.

Bill Jacobs, who had been a camp counselor for the last two years, took command automatically. "Someone, put the beer and Cokes in the water to chill. You guys get some of these bigger rocks for a fireplace, and the chicks can gather the wood."

"Hey," said Adam Sussman, "remember when we had a cookout here some years ago—the Sea Scouts? Were you in that, Stu?"

"Yeah, I remember. There was some kind of stink about the fire. The beach isn't public; it belongs to the Hillson estate. We didn't have a permit, that was it. Say, Didi, did you get a permit for a fire for tonight?"

"We don't need one," said Didi, suddenly apprehensive. "I'm sure we don't. That's only during the summer."

"Well, all they can do is kick us off, I suppose," said Stu philosophically. And then he laughed, and Didi saw she was being ribbed and chucked a handful of sand at him. "You really had me going there—permit for a fire!"

"Well, let's at least wait until it gets dark," said Sue Arons. "That's when a fire is fun."

Everyone scattered to carry out his assigned task. Bill arranged the large rocks in a circle for the fireplace, and after the boys had finished, they helped the girls gather wood. After a while there was a big enough pile for Bill to call a halt. "Okay, you guys, I think we've got enough."

"I could use a beer right now," said Adam.

"Yeah, me too," said Stu. He looked at his watch. "Damn, I've got to cut out around six thirty to drive my folks over to Lynn."

"But we'll be doing our cooking around then," protested Didi. "You'll miss all the food."

"It was the only way I could get the car," he said. "But I'll be back in no time. Say, who's got the beer?"

"When are you going to light the fire, Bill?"

"I don't know. After it gets dark and we start getting hungry. Anyone in a hurry?"

"No, let's wait a little while."

The sea was calm, almost unnaturally so. They could hear the gentle swish of the waves as they struck against the sea wall. From the distance came the screeching of sea gulls. Otherwise the air was still, and there was something about the quiet that tended to restrict conversation. They had paired off now, and what talk there was tended to be between couples, and they kept their voices low. They sipped their drinks reflectively and waited for it to grow dark.

Adam Sussman rested his head on his girl's lap; encouraged by his example, the others began to maneuver into more intimate positions. Suddenly Sussman sat up and exclaimed in disgust, "Jee-sus."

"What's the matter?"

"We got company." He pointed at a lone figure coming toward them.

"Hey, it's Moose Carter," said Stu.

"God's gift to women," said Didi.

"Hiya, Moose." Bill Jacobs waved lazily at him.

"Hi, kids. H'lo Bill, Stuie. And Didi and little Sue. Betty baby, where you been?" Then he saw Jenkins. "Why shut my mouf if we haven't got us a genuwine integrated cookout."

"Take a can of beer and cool it," said Bill Jacobs shortly.

"Sho, sho, as we say down in Alabam. Don't mind if I do." He ripped open the top of a beer can and said, "Any of you ever seen this before?" He threw his head back and let the beer gurgle down his throat without a ripple of his Adam's apple.

"Alan Jenkins. Moose Carter."

Neither man offered his hand, but both said "Hi."

"Have another," suggested Jacobs.

"I guess I can use one. Maybe I'll sit down for this one." As he saw Stu move over to make room for him near Jenkins, he said, "I'll just sit over here with my old sweetheart Betty—in the front of the bus, if you don't mind, Stu."

Didi felt Stu's hand clench under hers. She peered at her watch. "It's half past six. If you have to go for your folks, you'd better leave now."

"Maybe I better stick around for a while," he muttered.

"No, go now," she whispered back. "It'll be all right."

It was only after Stu had been gone for some minutes that they felt the first drops of rain.

22

When it was his turn to lecture the executive trainees on personnel management, Ben Gorfinkle always ended with a short disquisition on the recalcitrant subordinate.

In dealing with a subordinate who has got out of line, even if you hold all the trumps and can fire him like that—a snap of the fingers— it's better to first give him a chance to shape up. Because if he's a good man and shapes up, then you're all set. But if you fire him, you have to get a replacement. And how do you know he won't be just as bad? It's a good idea to arrange for a conference.

As soon as he got home from the plant Monday, he called the rabbi. "I'd like to get together with you, Rabbi, for a little conference. We really haven't talked face to face since I became president, and I think there are a lot of things we ought to iron out."

"Any time at all."

Sometimes it's a good idea to arrange for the conference well in advance so that he can stew for a while. Other times, you may find it better to hold it right away, with no prior notice, so that he's kind of taken by surprise and is unprepared. It depends on the circumstances.

"How about this evening?"

"I go to the minyan at seven."

"I've got a dinner engagement at that time, but if we could get together a little before—"

"That would be all right."

"Stu has my car—"

"I can come over to your house," said the rabbi.

As the rabbi shook hands with Gorfinkle he could not help thinking that with each of the presidents of the temple, his relations had been different. With Jacob Wasserman, the first president who had originally selected him, there had been not only mutual respect, but a true friendship. In spite of the difference in their ages, they liked each other as people, and that first year at Barnard's Crossing the Wassermans had had them to dinner on any number of occasions, and the Smalls felt themselves free to drop in on them on a Sunday afternoon for a cup of tea and talk. He had needed a friend in the president then. Looking back, he realized that he had been incredibly young and inexperienced and that only the strong friendship of Wasserman and the respect with which the old man was held by the entire community had saved him from countless embarrassments, including the ultimate embarrassment of not having his contract renewed after his trial year.

With Al Becker, who had taken over after Wasserman, his relations were quite different. Originally Becker had been the leader of the opposition, and only by the sheer luck of being able to help him in a personal matter had the rabbi been able to win him over. Becker had felt guilty about his original opposition and became not only respectful but at times almost obsequious. Now he had no stauncher champion than Becker, but he never felt quite at ease with him.

Mortimer Schwarz, the third president and Gorfinkle's predecessor, had no such attitude toward the rabbi. He was friendly and sometimes even unbent enough to josh him about his little shortcomings, such as his chronic tardiness and his tendency to forget appointments that he didn't care to keep in the first place. But in Schwarz's mind, at least, this was strictly a one-way street, and when the rabbi occasionally answered in kind, he was sure he was considered presumptuous. However, he had grown in the years that he had been at Barnard's Crossing, and he had found the president's attitude amusing rather than annoying. The fact that he had been given a five-year contract may have had something to do with it.

Ben Gorfinkle was something else again. He knew something of his capacity from having sat on the board with him for several years, but he had had little chance to work with him. What few dealings they had had to date had been quite neutral, neither friendly nor hostile.

Start by putting him at ease. Establish a friendly atmosphere.

Gorfinkle led the way into the living room, and when they were both seated, he said, "You quite comfortable there, Rabbi? Would you prefer this chair?"

"No, this is fine."

Encourage discussion, but keep him on the defensive.

He smiled benignly. "I wish you'd tell me, Rabbi, what your idea is of the purpose and function of a temple and what you consider the rabbi's responsibility to the institution."

The rabbi recognized the gambit and declined it. He smiled. "I've spent the last half dozen years doing just that. Surely you didn't call me—so urgently and under pressure of a pending engagement—to hear me synopsize what I've been saying ever since I came here. I'm sure you have something to say to me."

Gorfinkle nodded in appreciation. He was silent for a minute and then he said, "You know, Rabbi, I don't think you understand what the temple is all about. I'm not sure that any rabbi ever does. They're too much involved in it; they have a professional interest."

"Indeed! Perhaps you can explain it to me."

In your part of the discussion, appear frank and open. Let him feel that you are not trying to conceal anything.

Gorfinkle disregarded the rabbi's irony. "You think of a temple as being started by a group of religious men, which once underway, draws other religious-minded people." He shook his head. "Maybe there's one man who is really religious, like perhaps Wasserman, but the rest are interested in it merely as an organization. And once the organization is successful—and it takes a lot of work—then the original group becomes a drag on the organization, and a different type of person has to take over. Sometimes originators get so puffed up with their success that there's no living with them. They act as though they own the place because they started it. It rubs the new people the wrong way. That's what happened here, and in a sense, that's how I happen to be president. But it goes even deeper than that: To start an enterprise calls for a different set of talents than those you need to keep it going. They're two kinds of people."

"They're both Jews," the rabbi observed.

"That's only incidental, Rabbi."

"Incidental? In a synagogue?"

Gorfinkle nodded. "That's right. You're aware that there are two factions in the temple, mine and the one led by Meyer Paff. Now Paff, for all his Orthodoxy, isn't terribly concerned about Judaism or religion in general. All these people who are involved with the temple, men and women both, do you think it's because they're religious? Or that religion is important to them?" He shook his head in violent negation. "No, Rabbi. Do you know what they're interested in? They're interested in the temple as an organization.

"Every man wants to be something, to be somebody. He wants a sense of achievement, of accomplishment. He's gone to school, and he's gone to college, and he dreamed of being somebody, of being important. Then he got himself a job or established a small business of some kind and thought at last he was on the road. And now at the age of thirty-five he realizes that he's not going to become the President of the United States or lead an army; he's not going to win a Nobel Prize; his wife is not a movie actress, and his children are not geniuses. He begins to realize that the business of getting up in the morning and going to work and coming home to go to sleep in order to get up in the morning to go to work—that is not going to change in any dramatic fashion. His whole life is going to be pretty much like that until he dies. And when he dies, his family will remember him, and that's all.

"That's a hard thing to swallow in a society like ours, where everybody starts out with the assumption that he can be President of the United States or at least a millionaire. So these people throw themselves into organization work so they can be somebody. It used to be lodges where they could wear a fancy uniform and have a fancy title. Well, lodges are a little out of fashion these days, and in a Yankee town like Barnard's Crossing it's not easy for newcomers, Jew or Gentile but especially Jewish newcomers, to have very much to do with the politics of the town. But here the temple is an organization that is theirs. They can do something and be somebody. There's the temple and the Brotherhood, and for the women there is the Sisterhood and Hadassah. All they have to do is do a little work, and sooner or later they become a somebody. They become chairman of a committee, or they become an officer. They get their names in the papers. And if you don't think that's important, you talk to some woman who folded napkins, say, for the Hadassah luncheon and didn't get her name mentioned along with the rest of the committee that was involved in setting it up.

"But to get back to Paff. All the time he was running things he was important. Now that he isn't running things, he's not important, and it irks him."

"If it were only that," said the rabbi mildly, "would he have contributed such large sums and done so much work and given so much time?"

Gorfinkle shrugged his shoulders. "What is a large sum to you, Rabbi, is not a large sum to Meyer Paff. You grow up to a certain standard of living. When you come into a lot of money, do you think you can change that standard very radically? You buy a bigger car, you buy an extra suit or two, and you pay a little more money for it; you have a few extra pairs of shoes, and you pay a little more money for them. It's still nothing. There's this vast sum of money coming in, and you're nowhere near being able to spend it. So what do you do with it? You use it for advertising. You move out of your thirty-thousand-dollar house into a hundred-thousand-dollar mansion. You buy paintings; you get an interior decorator. Why? Because you suddenly developed artistic sensibilities? No. You're successful, but you don't feel any different. So you do the things that prove to other people that you're successful. Their envy or respect make you feel like somebody. Some go in for display, and some let themselves be seen with expensive-looking women. Others, like Paff, give their money to various worthwhile institutions."

"And you?" asked the rabbi.

If challenged, don't hesitate to admit your own shortcomings. It makes for a better atmosphere.

Gorfinkle shrugged. "I'll admit it. I'm no different." He grinned. "You might even say I'm a classic example. I'm an electronics engineer. When I got through at MIT, the field was comparatively new at the time. I graduated high in my class, and I figured I'd be heading up a big electronics lab by the time I was thirty. But there was the war, for one thing, and that delayed me. Then when I did get started, I found that the promotions didn't always go to the most able man—not in big corporate industry, anyway. Being a Jew didn't help either. And then the Ph.D.'s began to appear on the scene—overeducated nincompoops. That didn't help the picture. So what do you do? If you're a married man with a child, you can't go back to school. You shift to another job that looks as though it might lead somewhere. And it doesn't, of course. You try again, and it doesn't pan out either. I even switched to a small outfit where there was talk about stock options—talk—but there would be a chance to grow with the company, and the company looked as though it might grow. I even took a small cut in salary, because I figured this was my last chance. In this business, you've got to make it when you're still in your thirties, or you don't make it at all.

"For a while it looked good. And then we sold out to a big outfit, one of the giants, and I was working for a big corporation again. So now, when I'm forty-five, I'm a section head, which means I'm middle management. And that's what I'll probably be until I retire. I admit that when I first threw myself into temple politics, it was because I felt I could do a better job. I still think that's part of it. But I don't kid myself. I know that a good part of it is just to be somebody, to have an influence on the people around me."

"Aren't you being overcynical and missing the main point, as cynicism usually does?" the rabbi asked.

"How do you mean?"

"Well, you say that some do it by building big houses or other kinds of ostentation, while still others do it by contributing to good causes. That's the major difference between people, isn't it? Nowadays we're all amateur psychologists and psychiatrists. We all presume to know the motives of men. But do we? In the last analysis, the only way you can judge by is results, and the man who uses his wealth for worthy causes, even ostentatiously, is better than the man who uses it only for ostentation. Yours is a very cynical view of the temple, if you don't mind my saying so, Mr. Gorfinkle. But cynicism is only disappointed idealism. We Jews speak of ourselves as a nation of priests, and it would follow that if we were completely true to our ideal, we would spend all our time in the temple in study and worship. We even tried it. In the small ghetto towns of Poland and Russia, there were those who did just that. But someone had to work, and it was usually the wives. I don't think I care for that. It's one of my objections to the monastery and the convent. I don't think the best way to live in the world is to avoid it. Ours is a practical religion, in which *parnossah*, making a living, is as important as prayer, and the world as important as the temple."

If he says something that you can show is similar to your position, point it out to him, even if you have to twist his words a little to make it fit. The psychology of that is that he's anxious to get off the hook, and you're giving him a face-saving out.

"Then why," Gorfinkle interposed swiftly, "have you consistently objected to our program, Rabbi? It's what we want, that the membership realize the temple is part of the world and has a role to play in the world."

"I don't object to your program as a program, although I think each individual should decide these things for himself. What concerns me is that it tends to antagonize the other party to the point where there is danger that they will actually leave the temple organization. I have seen signs of it for some time at the board meetings. In all fairness, the other side has been equally intemperate. There has been little or no discussion on the merits of issues these last few months. Rather, what your side has proposed the others have opposed, and when they made suggestions, they were similarly treated by your group and for the same reason. No organization can survive that kind of feuding. In the last few days, however, you have discarded what little propriety you have up till now maintained. Mr. Brennerman's sermon—"

"What about his sermon?"

"He had no right to abuse the privilege of the pulpit in that way."

"Just a minute, Rabbi. I heard that speech, and you didn't. Taking it

as a whole, I approved of it." Gorfinkle's lips turned up in his humor-
less smile.

"Then you are equally guilty, Mr. Gorfinkle."

"You forget that I am the president—"

"Of the temple organization, Mr. Gorfinkle. The pulpit belongs to
the rabbi."

"I didn't know that, Rabbi," said Gorfinkle mildly. "Is that Jewish
law?"

"It is the law of common courtesy! As rabbi, I am superintendent of
the religious school. Would I presume to take over a class from one
of the teachers without first asking his permission?"

It is sometimes worthwhile to yield a minor point.

"Well, maybe Ted did get a little out of line. He's enthusiastic and
gets carried away."

"And yesterday at the board meeting, you nominated Roger Epstein as chairman of the Ritual Committee."

"What's wrong with Roger Epstein?" Gorfinkle demanded indignantly.

"Nothing as a person. But he has had no temple background whatsoever and never attended one until coming here. The chairman of
the Ritual Committee approves the order of the services. Under the
circumstances, Mr. Paff's group, which tends toward Conservatism,
might consider it a deliberate affront."

"Now hold on, Rabbi. I picked Roger because the Ritual Committee
is the most important and he's my best friend. I'm not worried about
his ignorance of the order of the service. I figure you and the cantor
between you pretty much arrange that. But the chairman of the Ritual
Committee distributes the honors on the holidays. Our people set great
store by these honors and rightly so. I notice all the time Meyer Paff
was chairman of the Ritual Committee he made political hay out of it.
But while we're speaking of impropriety, Rabbi, how about the impropriety of getting a bunch of kids together, including my own son, and
lecturing them on these matters from the opposition point of view?
Isn't that abusing your privilege?"

"Kids? We accept the thirteen-year-old as a member of a minyan.
He can be called to the reading of the Torah, which is instruction to
the congregation. He can even lead the services. Can we say that bright
young college people of eighteen and nineteen are too immature to
understand what is going on in their temple community?"

"Look, Rabbi, I don't want any of your Talmudic runaround. I consider that politics, and I'm telling you I want it stopped."

The rabbi smiled. "You mean, you want me to stop talking to the young people?"

"I mean that you are not to talk to them about temple affairs. And I'm not asking you. I'm ordering you."

"You can't. *I* am the rabbi here, and it is for me to decide what I shall say to the members of the Jewish community."

There comes a point in your discussion when you realize there's no chance of an agreement or reconciliation. When you reach that point, don't pussyfoot. Lower the boom and lower it all the way.

Gorfinkle nodded. "You've said enough, Rabbi, to prove to me that you're part and parcel of Paff's apparatus. I'm not surprised. I suspected as much, as did the members of my group. We had a meeting last night, and I remind you that we represent a clear majority of the board. It was agreed that I was to talk to you and point out to you the impropriety of your behavior in the hope of bringing about a change. That's what this little conference is all about. But when I give them the gist of this conversation, along with your cavalier attitude toward religion in general, which has just recently come to my attention, I am sure they will vote to terminate your association with us.

"Of course, you can fight it, but you're a smart man, and I'm sure you realize that for a rabbi to fight for his job and lose is to jeopardize his chances of getting another. I can tell you now that you will lose and that after that meeting you won't be rabbi any longer." He rose to his feet in sign that the conference was over.

"I did not get my *smicha* from you," said the rabbi, also rising, "and you can't withdraw it. I am the rabbi of the Jewish community of Barnard's Crossing. The temple pays me, but I am not the creature of the temple, and I do not need a temple or synagogue to fulfill my function."

Outside there was the loud and persistent sound of an automobile horn.

Gorfinkle shrugged. "I'm sorry, Rabbi," he said smoothly. "That's Stu now, and I have to go."

23

Wilcox, his collar unbuttoned, his tie unknotted, the ends hanging loose, sat back in his armchair, his legs resting on a hassock, at peace with the world. He could tell from the way it started that this was going to be one of those all-the-time-in-the-world trips, where time slowed down to a deep, throbbing rhythm. He could hear the slow, steady movement of the gears inside his watch. And then, as if in accompaniment, he heard the pealing of the doorbell, a deep, insistent throbbing. He rose to his feet to answer. It was no simple motion, but a whole series of adventures in which each part of his body, each member, played some significant role, like a complicated army maneuver, or like a ballet in which his arms and legs, his hands, his fingers all had separate roles. All had to move at their appointed time. And although it seemed that the act of opening the door and admitting his visitor and then going back to his easy chair was a matter of hours, he had no feeling of exhaustion from this tremendous effort. The figure in the chair before him grew larger and larger, like an inflating balloon. And then smaller and smaller and then once again larger. And yet this shifting of outline was not alarming in any way. Amusing, rather, especially when he realized it was only the man's normal respiration he was watching. Thinking about it quite objectively he came to the conclusion that the man must have run up the stairs, because he seemed to be breathing heavily; there were beads of perspiration on his forehead that he could see individually course down from the hairline until they fell into and filled and overflowed a furrow on the man's brow and then spilled over to the next furrow, and the next, until finally they were dissipated in the hairy jungle of the man's eyebrow. The man was saying something that he could understand perfectly, but it seemed too utterly ridiculous to merit his attention. Something about having to park his car around the corner. Silly man. Why should that be of interest? And his difficulty in finding the apartment bell. Something about asking a woman which bell it was. What significance was there whether a woman knew which apartment it was or not. The man had a grievance. He understood it. He could understand it not merely in his mind, but it registered as waves of resentment on his very skin. And it was unpleasant. And he wanted an end to it. He spoke from a great distance, explaining for the silly creature. And it seemed that the other understood, for he rose from his chair. Not a bright person certainly. Not with man's intelligence. No. Nor the intelligence of a dog even. Or even of a much lower animal. Not even the intelligence of a worm. Perhaps a microbe, because instead of going toward the door as he was told he was coming toward him. Ah, he understood at last. The other was taking his leave formally. Should he rise? Should he offer his hand? But the man was reaching forward and taking not his hand, but both ends of his tie. Was this the way to take one's leave? Was this a new ceremony? And then he felt the stricture on his neck and then pain and pressure and pressure and pain.

And nothing.

24

Mr. Carter looked around the table slowly, and his eye came to rest on the empty place on his right. His wife at the foot of the table and his children ranged on either side, the two young boys on his right and the two girls on his left, all sat straight, their hands folded and resting on the edge of the table, waiting for him to say Grace.

"And where is Moses?" he asked.

"He hasn't come home yet," said his wife. "He went into Boston to apply for a job, and he may have stopped for a bite. He said he might be late."

"And didn't you tell him that I want him here for the evening meal? Doesn't he know it himself? And if he were detained, couldn't he call and tell us? Have we no telephone in the house?"

"Oh, Pa," said his wife, "what's the sense of fussing at the boy all the time. He might not have been handy to a telephone. Or he might have called and the line was busy. The way the girls use the phone, it's a wonder anyone can ever get through."

"I don't hold with members of a family coming in at any and all hours. This is a family, and it's going to stay a family. That's morality. When everyone flies off to wherever, and anyone eats anytime they've a mind to and wherever they happen to be, the family starts breaking up. The meal is a sacrament, and everyone who is part of this family is going to take part in it."

"He might have got caught in the storm," his wife suggested, "and waited until it ended. Most likely he saw he was going to be late and grabbed a bite somewhere and then went directly to the bowling alley. Come to think of it, I believe Moose said something about their wanting him to come in a little earlier Mondays."

"Enough," said her husband. "I will not wait any longer. I will now say Grace. If he comes in after, then he will not eat. I will not allow any member of my family to eat here who has not heard a decent benediction pronounced."

He looked around the table and saw that all heads were bowed. Then his hands clenched convulsively, and his eyes squeezed shut. For a full minute he was silent, his mind reaching out, out. Then he put his head back, directing his voice to the ceiling. "Dear Lord, we thank Thee for Thy mercy in giving us sustenance to strengthen our bodies so that we may do Thy work. We have observed Your commandments, and on our board there is no creature's flesh but only the fruits of Thy good earth. If we have sinned in Your eyes, it is because we are weak and lacking in understanding. Forgive us, O Lord, and deal kindly with us." Then he nodded and said, "I thank Thee, Lord, I am your servant, and I will obey."

He opened his eyes and looked around him. "Now we may eat."

The family ate in silence. No one wanted to hazard a remark that might set Mr. Carter off, and all were anxious to get away from the table as soon as possible. Mr. Carter himself sat in moody silence, his eyes focused on his plate. And when the meal was finished and the dishes cleared away, the young people eased out of the dining room quickly.

Mr. Carter continued to sit at his place at the dining room table while he was aware of the noises from the kitchen as his wife and the girls worked at washing the dishes. His wife came into the room.

"It's still raining pretty hard, Pa," she said. "I was wondering if Michael were to take the car and ride downtown and see if Moose is around—"

He looked at her, and she found it hard to meet his gaze. "I'll go out looking for him," he said.

"Oh, I'm just a worrying old woman. There's no need for anyone to go. He'll be along pretty soon—"

The phone rang, and Sharon hurried to answer it.

"That's Moose now," said Mrs. Carter.

But Sharon returned to report, "It was the bowling alley. They want to know where Moose is and why he isn't there."

But Mr. Carter had already got into his raincoat and was striding out of the house. He paused just long enough in the garage to select a length of dowel rod. He whipped it through the air once or twice and then took his place behind the wheel of his car and set the rod carefully on the seat beside him.

25

The rabbi wanted time to collect his thoughts before going home, to decide what he would tell Miriam or rather how he would tell her. It had started to rain almost as soon as he got into his car, and now as he drove aimlessly through the streets of the town it was coming down hard, striking against the windshield faster than the wipers could swish it away. Every now and then the skies suddenly grew daylight bright, with blinding flashes of lightning followed almost immediately by the crash of thunder. It was frightening and yet, because it suited his mood, exhilarating as well.

He wanted to talk the matter over with someone before seeing Miriam, but there was no one in town with whom he felt he could talk freely and openly unless it was—he could not help smiling—Hugh Lanigan, the pleasant, red-faced Irish chief of police. They had an honest, long-standing relationship, maybe, he thought wryly, because neither had anything to gain from the other. It struck him in a situation of this sort, where everyone in the congregation was on one side or the other, how isolated the rabbi was. Of course, there was Jacob Wasserman, who, as a sort of elder statesman of the congregation, tended to be above factions. They had always liked each other, and he respected the older man's judgment and understanding. Impulsively he drove to his house.

Mrs. Wasserman was a motherly woman, who, when she saw who it was, urged him—even taking him by the arm—to come in, come in.

"It's all right, Rabbi, so the rugs will get a little wet," she said, as he scraped his shoes against the cocomat.

"Who is it?" her husband called from inside. "The rabbi? Come in, Rabbi, come in. It must be a serious matter to bring you out on such a night. But I'm happy you came. Lately I haven't seen so much of you.

It's not so easy for me to get to the minyan these days. You know how it is. If the weather is not so good I stay in bed a little longer. Becker is here with me. He had supper here tonight. If it's private you want to talk, he can keep my wife company in the kitchen. I wouldn't be jealous. But if it's temple business, then maybe you'd like him to hear, too."

"Yes, I think it might be a good idea," said the rabbi.

The old man led him into the living room, and his wife followed them. "Look, Becker, I got another visitor," he called. Then to his wife, "So why don't you get the rabbi a cup of tea?"

"I have just seen Mr. Gorfinkle," said the rabbi and told them what had transpired. He expected the news to come, frankly, as something of a bombshell. Instead, the men were surprisingly unmoved.

"You mean he threatened not to renew your contract in the fall?" asked Becker, as if to make sure he had all the facts straight.

"No, that he would recommend it be terminated now."

"He can't do that; you've got a contract. Besides, that's something that the full board has to vote on."

"So they pay him the remaining money," said Wasserman with a shrug, "and if Gorfinkle has a majority, what difference does it make if it comes before the full board or not?"

The rabbi expected Becker to react belligerently. Instead, he looked at Wasserman and said, "Shall I tell him?"

Again the old man shrugged his shoulders. "What would be a better time?"

"In a way, Rabbi," began Becker, "it's funny you coming here tonight. You see, today Meyer Paff came to see me. It looks as if there's going to be a split in the temple. And Paff wanted me and Wasserman to join him."

"And did you agree?"

"For us it's easy, Rabbi. As past presidents, we are both permanent members of the board. And to join another temple is just a matter of paying an extra membership fee. It's like a donation. Even when I was president, I was a member of the synagogue in Lynn, and Jacob here is a member both in Lynn and Salem. But in the course of telling me what was on his mind, you came up for discussion. Paff asked me to approach you about coming over, on a long-term contract and at an increase in salary. That's what I was discussing with Jacob just before you came in."

The rabbi looked over at Wasserman, but the old man's face was impassive. "I didn't think I was so great a favorite of Mr. Paff's," he said to Becker.

"Look, Rabbi, I won't try to kid you. I'm sure that although Paff appreciates your work here, his main object in making the offer is that he expects it will pull members. But what do you care if you're bettering yourself?"

"And would I be bettering myself, Mr. Becker?"

"By three thousand dollars a year and a long-term contract. Even if this row with Gorfinkle hadn't occurred, you wouldn't be sure that your contract would be renewed. I guess that's bettering yourself. If you're not sure, ask Mrs. Small, who buys the groceries."

But the rabbi replied, "As things now stand, Mr. Becker, I am the rabbi of the Jews of Barnard's Crossing. I am the rabbi of the community and not merely the rabbi of a particular temple. And that is the way I think of my function. A rabbi is not part of the temple furniture."

"But the cantor—"

"The cantor is different. He needs a temple, or at least a congregation, in order to exercise his function. Can he sing to himself? But a rabbi does not. No doubt, if the community continues to grow, sooner or later a Reform temple will be established and a portion of our members will split away from us to join it. And no doubt, they will get a rabbi. But that break will be for ideological reasons and hence justified. Their rabbi will be the rabbi of the Reform Jews of Barnard's Crossing, while I remain the rabbi of its Conservative Jews."

"But congregations do split," Becker insisted.

"All too often, perhaps. When the split was not on ideological grounds, it was apt to be geographical. Jews would begin moving out of one area into another, and because it was considered a breach of the Sabbath to ride to services, another temple would be set up in order to have a place of worship within walking distance of the new area. That, too, would be reasonable.

"But the split that you plan is neither ideological nor geographical. You will have the same kind of Jews in the new temple as in the old, and the services will be virtually similar. In effect, you are setting up a competing temple, and you would like me to be its rabbi. No, thank you. Nor would I remain in my present job under those conditions. A temple is not a business enterprise in which competition is good for trade. But you will come to think of your temple in that way, and you will force the same kind of thinking on Gorfinkle and his group. Come join our temple—we have air conditioning, softer seats. Our cantor has a better voice, and our rabbi delivers shorter and snappier sermons. Hold your Bar Mitzvah or your wedding in our vestry. We give trading stamps."

"Now look here, Rabbi—"

"Mr. Paff doesn't need me. A temple doesn't need a rabbi, and a rabbi doesn't need a temple. The rabbi's functions in the temple—leading prayers and delivering sermons—are the most minor part of his duties. The first any thirteen-year-old boy can perform, and the second, isn't it for most a kind of relief to break the monotony and tedium of the service? No, Mr. Becker, I have no intention of being the extra added attraction of a new temple."

"But if Gorfinkle succeeds in voting you out—"

The rabbi looked at Wasserman in mute question.

The old man spread his hands. "In this world, Rabbi, you've got to make first a living. Here Paff offers you a job, at more money yet. All right, maybe the conditions aren't perfect. Where are they perfect? But it's a living; it's *parnossah.*"

The rabbi bit his lip in vexation. He had assumed that Wasserman at least would understand. "And is Barnard's Crossing the only place where I can make a living? No, Mr. Wasserman, if this split goes through, I will not accept a contract from either Mr. Paff's or Mr. Gorfinkle's group. I will leave Barnard's Crossing."

26

As Stuart Gorfinkle drove back to the cookout from Lynn, he felt a totally unreasonable resentment against his parents, especially his father. Why were there always strings attached when his father let him have the car? They were only going to his Aunt Edith's to eat; his uncle could have picked them up. He wondered uneasily if the kids had been able to find shelter somewhere when the rain really pelted down. And the lightning, had it been as bad at the beach as on the drive to Lynn?

The rain had let up and now was little more than a heavy mist. At Tarlow's Point he stopped his car and plunged down the path. When he came to the little grove of pine trees, he could see the beach and that no one was there. From the litter, the empty beer cans, the wet cellophane wrappers, he knew that they had left unexpectedly and in a hurry.

Then he saw the arrow on the log. Carefully he made his way to the house and up the back steps. He put his ear to the door and listened hard but heard nothing. He circled the house, went up to the front door, and again listened, then essayed a timid knock. He waited, listening, and this time he thought he heard something. He knocked harder and called, "It's me, Stu. You kids there?"

Instantly the door was thrown open, and his friends crowded around the doorway.

"Hey, you had me going there for a while."

"We thought you weren't coming back. We left an arrow with lipstick. Did you see it?"

"How'd you get in?" Stu asked. "Was the door open?"

"Nah, we climbed in through a window in back."

"Well, we better get going," said Stu. "The cruising car goes by here, and they check the unoccupied houses. They got a list."

They piled into the car, and Stu turned on the ignition. From in back Adam Sussman called, "Say, how about Moose?"

"What about him?" asked Stu.

"He's in there. He passed out, and we had to put him to bed."

"We'd better get him. We can't leave him in there like that."

"There's no room for him, especially the shape he's in."

"He wasn't invited to this party."

"Yeah, but he got us in out of the storm."

"I want to go home," wailed one of the girls. "My folks will be awfully worried."

"Get going, Stu," said Bill Jacobs. "We can swing back afterward and pick him up."

Stu and Bill Jacobs took Didi home last, and Alan Jenkins went along because his motorcycle was parked in the Epstein garage. The house was dark when they arrived, and on the kitchen table Didi found a note from her mother: "Gone to the movies—maybe somewhere for coffee afterward."

"You guys want some coffee?" she asked.

"Yeah, I could use something hot," said Jacobs.

"I should be starting back," said Jenkins, "but—okay, I'll have some too."

"But what about Moose?" asked Stu.

"He'll keep," said Jacobs. He laughed harshly. "He's good for hours."

"The way he poured that stuff down—" Stu shook his head. "Still, you wouldn't think beer would have that effect on him. At school I've seen guys who drink the stuff practically all night—"

"It wasn't the beer," Bill Jacobs explained, "although he had quite a few of those. As soon as we got into the house, he found himself a bottle of Scotch. He did the same trick with that—you know, tossing his head back and taking it down. He must've polished off half the bottle in a couple of swallows."

"Half a bottle?" said Stu, marveling. "And he passed out? Complete? Blotto? What'd you do, leave him lying on the floor?"

"On the floor?" Jacobs was indignant. "Hell no, on one of the beds."

"Well, like they say, on the floor he can't roll off," said Stu defensively.

Jenkins laughed, and Jacobs said grimly, "The way we laid him on the bed he won't roll anywhere."

"There was one of these plastic sheets," Jenkins explained, "and we wrapped him up real good."

"Just like you swaddle a baby in a blanket," Jacobs added with satisfaction.

Didi came in with coffee. They sipped it in silence, each immersed in his own thoughts for the moment.

Then Stu said suddenly, "Hey, how are we going to get back in? We're not going to have to go through the window, I hope? You shut the door."

"No sweat," said Bill Jacobs. "I left it on the latch."

Jenkins set his cup down and rose lazily to his feet. "I better be starting. Got to get up real early tomorrow."

"Hey," said Bill. "With Stu driving, I'm not sure I can handle Moose alone if he should start acting up. Can't you give us a hand?"

Jenkins smiled and shook his head. "You're asking the wrong party. Far as I'm concerned, he can stay there until he turns to green mold. If I was you cats, I'd forget about him."

As the roar of Jenkins' motorcycle died away, Stu said, "What was he so up tight about?"

Didi answered, "Moose was dumping on him most of the evening. Frankly, I don't blame Alan."

"Well, that leaves us in a bind," said Jacobs. He went to the window and looked out. "And it's started raining again."

They sat around and talked, waiting for the rain to let up. Every once in a while one of them would wander to the window to peer at the rain-lashed streets.

Suddenly a bolt of lightning flashed across the sky, followed immediately by a tremendous crash of thunder, and the room was plunged into darkness.

"That must have got a transformer," said Jacobs, looking down the darkened street. "Maybe the substation; it's dark all up and down the street."

"You got any candles, Didi?" asked Stu.

"I—I guess so." Didi's voice sounded frightened in the darkness, and then he felt her hand groping for his. He put his arm around her.

"Tell you what. Rather than sweat this out in darkness, why don't we all get in the car and drive over to pick up Moose now? The way it's coming down, it can't last long."

27

Mr. Morehead was apologetic. "Believe me, Mr. Paff, if I didn't have to meet my wife at the airport—"

"But I've arranged with the other men in the deal to meet them at the house. You could have let me know earlier."

"I didn't expect her until tomorrow, Mr. Paff. I just got a call from New York, from the airport. Look, you don't need me there anyway. You can get the key from—"

"Don't tell me to go to see that son of a bitch Begg again. He'll tell me he can't get away from his two-bit store and that he can't let me have the key because I might steal the furniture. Furniture! I've seen better at the Morgan Memorial. I'll drive up with a truck and load it with his goddam ratty furniture."

The other chuckled. "Begg is an old Yankee, all right. But look, how would it be if I left the key in Lynn?"

"Happens I've got to check something at the Lynn alley."

"Well, that's fine then. You know the drugstore on the corner where my building is? I'll leave the key there, and you can pick it up."

"Well, I guess that's all right. You just be sure that there's no slipup. Give them my name and tell them what I look like so there won't be any question when I come in for it."

"Nothing to worry about, Mr. Paff. And you look over the property as long as you like. Just be sure you turn out the lights and lock the door when you leave."

At the Lynn alley the manager greeted him with, "Your wife just called, Mr. Paff, and said for you to call a Mr. Kermit Arons."

Arons was remorseful. "Gee, Meyer, you'll never guess what I went and did. After I made this appointment with you for tonight I forgot all about my sister-in-law's wedding anniversary. She's throwing a big shindig, and if I don't go to it, well, I might just as well start discussing visitation rights to the children with my lawyer. So for tonight, I'm afraid you'll have to count me out."

"But we've got to act fast on this thing, Kerm. We can't futz around."

"So act. What do I know about buildings, anyway? If you guys say it's all right, then it's all right with me. I'll go along with whatever you decide."

As soon as he hung up, the manager bore down on him. "Look, Mr. Paff, Moose is late again. I called his house, and he wasn't home. I haven't eaten yet."

"Well, why don't you go out and grab a bite. I'll cover for you, and I'll get somebody for tonight. Frank over at the Malden Alley said he could work any night except Friday."

"Well, what if Moose comes in?"

"If he comes in while I'm here, I'll fire him. And if he doesn't show up, I'll tell him tomorrow he's through. Look, don't take too long; I've got an appointment."

"Sure, Mr. Paff, I'll just get a hamburger and a cup of coffee. Say, I know a young fellow who if you hire him, I know he'd be reliable and—"

"We'll talk about it. You go and eat now."

He started for the door, but Paff called after him, "Say, have the cops been in again since—"

"Oh, don't worry about them, Mr. Paff. I know how to handle *them*."

"Well, that's what I wanted to tell you. Lay off. Don't rile them. Understand?"

"Oh, sure, Mr. Paff."

"Don't act flip. Just cooperate."

While the other was gone, the phone rang. It was Dr. Edelstein. "Meyer? Your wife gave me this number, and said I might catch you here. I just got a call, and I got to go clear down to Lawrence for a consultation."

"But, Doc, Kermit Arons can't make it. He got to go to his sister-in-law's anniversary party, and now you—"

"It's a man's life, Meyer."

Parked under the streetlamp opposite Hillson House, Meyer Paff decided that he would wait just five more minutes for Irving Kallen and then leave. It was easier to get money out of his friends than work, he reflected bitterly. He was not merely annoyed; he was physically uncomfortable. Because of the rain he had to keep the car window up, and it was hot and sticky inside. He could have gone into the house—he had the key—but he remembered what Begg had said about vandals having broken in there on occasion, and he did not want to go in alone. Besides, half-hidden behind its overgrown hedge, the house now looked dark and forbidding. And the thunder and lightning didn't help things any.

He glanced at his watch and saw that he had been there almost half an hour. He looked uncertainly down the road and, seeing no car approaching, turned on the ignition and drove off.

28

". . . No ma'am, you notify the electric company. But I can tell you there's no need to call them either. They know about it. The power is out in all that part of town. The storm knocked out the substation."

Sergeant Hanks turned to Patrolman Smith, who had unbuttoned his tunic and was relaxing with a cup of coffee. "Boy, what a night! Must be a hundred people calling the electric company and then calling us when they can't get *them*."

Smith smiled sympathetically, but the sergeant was back at the phone again. "Barnard's Crossing Police Department, Sergeant Hanks speaking . . . Yes, Mr. Begg . . . Oh yes, that's one of the houses the cruising car checks regular . . . No sir, nothing was called in . . . You say it was lit up? . . . That's funny—all power in that part of town is out. You don't have lights, do you? . . . Oh, before . . . No, sir, I was not talking to my girl and not to my wife either . . . Well, I'm sorry about that, but people been calling in almost constantly for the last hour or so about the lights . . . Yes sir, I'll have the cruising car check. . . ."

He wheeled around in his swivel chair. "Son of a bitch!"

"Begg? No two opinions on him," said the patrolman. "Did I ever tell you about the time he—"

"I better call the cruising car," the sergeant interrupted. "It would be just like him to keep tabs on the time. Hear me, Bob? . . . Hanks . . . When did you pass Tarlow's Point? . . . Uh-huh . . . Well, take a run down there, will you? Old man Begg claims he saw a light there . . . No, just before the transformer blew . . . Okay."

29

They drove three in the front seat, Didi between the two boys. Stu turned the wipers to high speed to take care of the rain lashing against the windshield. "I sure don't envy that Jenkins riding a motorcycle in this kind of weather."

"Oh, he can always duck in someplace until it lets up," said Jacobs.

They parked in front of Hillson House, and Stu dug a flashlight out of the glove compartment and snapped on the beam.

"Hey," said Jacobs, "the door is open."

"Maybe Moose woke up and just walked out," said Stu hopefully.

"Could be, but we better take a look around. Here, let me have the flash." Bill mounted the stairs with Stu behind him. He pushed open the front door and cast the light around the room. Then he led the way down the hall to the study, where they had left Moose. He stopped at the threshold and focused the beam on the couch. What looked like a giant cocoon in silvery white plastic was resting on top of it.

Stu giggled nervously. "Geez, you sure wrapped him good. What did you put it over his head for?"

But Jacobs was already at the couch. "We didn't leave him like that. Help me!"

The figure was completely encased in the sheet, the top flap of which had been folded over the head and tucked tightly into the folds enwrapping the body.

Jacobs yanked at the flap frantically and then, with Stu's help, pulled the rest of the sheet from the body. The face was curiously white. Jacobs felt the forehead and cheeks. They were cold. He handed the flashlight to Stu and began to rub the hands of the figure on the couch. Then he dropped them in distaste.

"What's the matter?" Stu whispered.

"I think he's dead."

He thrust his hand underneath the shirt to see if he could feel a heartbeat.

"You can't tell that way," said Stu. "You got to hold something like a mirror up to his lips."

"I haven't got a mirror," said Bill savagely. "Put the lens of the flash to his mouth."

Stu offered the flashlight, but Bill said, "Let's get the hell out of here."

They started to walk out and then broke into a run. They clattered down the steps and then raced to the car. Stu pulled the car door open while Bill ran around the front to the other side.

"Where's Moose?" asked Didi as she moved over to let Stu get behind the wheel.

"Never mind." He turned on the ignition, but before he could shift to DRIVE a car zoomed toward them, veered over, and came to a stop immediately in front, its headlights on high beam shining in their eyes. Stu's door was pulled open by a policeman with a gun in his hand.

"Hold it," he commanded. "Now come out, all of you."

30

Harvey Kanter, Ben Gorfinkle's brother-in-law, was ten years his senior. Although in private he was radical, atheistic, and irreverent, in public, as the managing editor of the Lynn *Times-Herald*, he was Republican, conservative, and a staunch defender of the status quo. He wrote editorials supporting book censorship, prayers in the schools, law and order in the cities, and attacked student rioting, the coddling of criminals, and the hippie movement. He was a tall, rangy man, with a shock of iron-gray hair brushed back impatiently. Everything about him was impatient. He was nervous, fidgety; he could not sit still; he either got up and paced the floor, or if he remained seated, he would slide forward to rest on the end of his spine or pull a leg under him or slouch around if the chair permitted it so that his head was on one arm and his legs on the other.

His attitude toward Gorfinkle tended to be mocking and derisive, and his wife, Edith, was also apt to be somewhat patronizing to her younger sister, Mrs. Gorfinkle. Nevertheless, the Gorfinkles came to dinner when they were invited, partly as a matter of habit and partly because in a perverse kind of way Ben Gorfinkle enjoyed the discussions.

After dinner the two men lounged into the living room while the women cleared the table and proceeded to wash the dishes. Kanter bit off the end of a cigar, and as he held a match to the end he said, "I heard your rabbi the other day. Did I tell you?"

"No," said Gorfinkle cautiously. "When was that?"

"About a week ago. He was the speaker at the Chamber of Commerce meeting, save the mark."

"I didn't think you went to those."

"Hell, the paper has to be represented, and I drew the short straw. Your man wasn't bad."

"What did he talk about?"

"Oh, the usual—the place of the temple in the modern world. Seems to me I've heard a dozen priests and ministers and such godly folk at one affair or another in the last six months, and all they talk about is the place of the church, or in this case the synagogue, in the modern world. I figure if they talk about it so much, it's because it ain't so, but your guy seemed to make some sense."

"What did he say?"

"Oh, the point of his talk, as I remember it, was that the modern civilized world was finally coming around to the positions that the synagogue had been preaching for a couple of thousand years or more—social justice, civil rights, rights of women, importance of learning. His idea was that finally, after nearly two thousand years, the Jewish religion was coming into style."

"That's very interesting," said Gorfinkle. "I had a long talk with him —just before I came here, as a matter of fact. And it was about somewhat the same subject, but he took what I thought was the opposite point of view in his discussion with me. I guess there are some people who can take either side of a discussion, depending on how it suits them," he added.

"He didn't strike me as that type of man," said Kanter quietly. "What happened?"

"Well, you know, as in any organization, we have two parties—mine and what you might call the opposition, which is headed by Meyer Paff. You know him."

"Yeah, I know him."

"Well, we want the temple to get active in various movements that are current—like civil rights, for one. Paff's bunch want to keep it a place where—you know—you just come to pray on the High Holidays or on Friday nights. And I found out that the rabbi was carrying on some pretty active propaganda for the Paff group. So I had it out with him."

"And how did it end?"

"I told him in no uncertain terms that I wasn't going to stand for it and that the group that I represented—and we're a clear majority— weren't going to stand for it." He leaned forward in his chair. "You see, what he was doing was talking to the kids—telling them that we were in the wrong. He's kind of popular with the kids, and he was planning to use them to influence their parents."

"How did he take it?"

"Oh, he got on his high horse and said no one was going to tell him what to say, that he was the rabbi and he would decide what was proper for him to say and what wasn't."

"So?"

Gorfinkle was pleasantly conscious that he had captured his brother-in-law's interest and that, for once, what he was about to say would startle him out of his customary superciliousness. He smiled. "So I told him that I'd had a meeting with a majority of the board prior to our little talk and that we had decided that if he refused to go along, at the next meeting a motion would be offered—and passed—calling for his resignation."

"You fired him?"

He pursed his lips and canted his head to one side. "Just about."

"Nothing personal, of course."

"I flatter myself that I handled it pretty well," said Gorfinkle with a smirk.

Kanter got up from his chair and strode across the room. He turned and glared down his long nose at his brother-in-law. "By God, you nice respectable people can blunder into a situation and foul it up to make the angels weep. You get elected president, and before you have a chance to warm your arse on the chair you start firing people."

"An organization can't go in two directions at the same time," Gorfinkle protested. "If we're going to make any progress—"

"Progress? Why in hell do you have to make progress? Do you think everything has a balance sheet that has to be matched against the balance of the previous year to show you're going ahead? What the hell kind of progress does an institution that has lasted a couple of thousand years have to make?"

"If it's to be a living institution—"

"It's got to hop aboard the bandwagon, is that it? Civil rights, slum clearance, job opportunities—they're all in style now and respectable, so all the bleeding-heart liberals and social democrats try to get in on the act. Faugh! You guys make me sick. When did you get to be so goddam liberal? How many blacks have you hired at Hexatronics?"

"I don't do the hiring."

"But of course you picket the office of the one who does."

"I don't notice any great liberalism in the policy of the *Times-Herald*," said Gorfinkle drily, "and *you* run that."

"I run it for the owners. And I run it their way. Oh, I'm a prostitute, all right," he added cheerfully. "Most newspaper men have to be. But I don't fool myself. A prostitute yes, but no hypocrite."

"Well, I have reason to believe that Rabbi Small is, which had something to do with my decision," said Gorfinkle smugly.

"Doesn't wrap his phylacteries properly? Wears his prayer shawl inside out?"

"I had no idea you were so concerned about rabbis and things religious," said Gorfinkle.

"I'm not, and I hardly know your rabbi. I just don't like to see people hurt." He studied his brother-in-law for a moment. "And the effect on the congregation? Have you thought about that?"

Gorfinkle shrugged. "He really has no following, except maybe among the kids, and they don't count. As a matter of fact, it was the congregation I was thinking of when I had this talk with him. Fact is," he lowered his voice, "I was trying to prevent a serious split in the congregation. You see, there is this handful of dissidents—the old guard—who are opposed to every aspect of our program. Well, they'll either knuckle under or they'll get out. If they leave, it doesn't bother us too much; they're just a couple or three dozen of them. But if we let the rabbi continue, he might stir up enough opposition so that we could lose a hundred or more. That would be serious."

"So the strategy is to silence the opposition?"

"What's wrong with that? Why should we furnish the opposition with a rostrum?"

"Because it's democratic. The government does it."

They argued long and frequently loudly; and when, quite late, the Gorfinkles finally prepared to depart, neither man had convinced the other. They said their good-byes with formal politeness no different from the way any number of their discussions had ended in the past.

Five minutes after they had left, the phone rang and Harvey Kanter answered.

"Barnard's Crossing Police Department, Sergeant Hanks speaking. May I speak to Mr. Benjamin Gorfinkle?"

"He's just left."

"Is he on his way home, sir?"

"Sure, I guess so. What's this all about?"

"We'll get in touch with him there."

"Just a minute. I'm his brother-in-law, Harvey Kanter of the *Times-Herald*. Was there an accident? Was his place broken into?"

"No, Mr. Kanter, nothing like that." And the sergeant hung up, leaving Kanter wondering uneasily what he should do.

31

Sergeant Herder of the Boston Police Department was a man of infinite patience, and he found himself forced to use every bit of it as he dealt with the slattern before him. "Now, look, Madelaine, let's see if we can get a little cooperation. Remember what I told you: That man knows you saw him leave the Wilcox place, and he might get worried about it and try to do something drastic. Do you understand?"

The woman, her eyes fixed on him as though hypnotized, nodded her head rapidly.

"What do you understand?"

"He might try to do something."

"What?"

She shook her head. "I don't know."

Sergeant Herder got up and walked rapidly to the end of the room. He stood there for a moment, gazing at the wall. Then he came back slowly. "He might try to kill you, Madelaine, the way he did Wilcox. That's what he might try to do."

"Yes, sir."

"Yes, sir, what?"

"He might try to kill me."

"Fine. Just remember that. Just keep that in mind. So we've got to get him before he has the chance. And to get him, we have to know what he looks like. See?"

"I know what he looks like."

"I know you do, but we don't unless you tell us. Now what size man was he? Was he a big man or small?"

"Sort of middling."

"What color hair did he have?"

"He had his hat on."

"All right, what color hat was it?"

"Just a man's hat."

"Just a hat. Fine. Now Officer Donovan here is an artist, Madelaine. He draws pictures."

"I know what an artist is," she said with dignity.

"Sure you do. Now we're getting somewhere. Officer Donovan is going to show you some outlines of faces, and I want you to tell him which one looks most like the man's, the man we're talking about, the man you saw. Understand?"

She nodded.

"Show her one with a hat, Donovan."

She looked at the outline. "The hat was squashier," she said.

"How about the outline of the face?"

"Yeah, that could be it."

"Fine. Now we're getting somewhere."

"Just a minute," said Donovan. He sketched rapidly and presented another outline to her, quite different from the first. "How about this one?"

"Yeah, that could be it."

"Maybe you ought to try her on the mug shots again," suggested Donovan.

Herder shook his head in total frustration.

"I'm sure she'd know him if she saw him. She just can't describe him."

"By now, I'm not sure she even saw him."

"It was the same way with the other one, the football player, but she picked his picture out of the bunch we handed her."

"Yeah." He turned back to the woman. "Now, Madelaine, I'm going to show you a bunch of pictures and you tell me if you see him. All right?"

"Sure, Sergeant, anything you say."

32

When the telephone rang, Mrs. Carter was sure it was Moose. But there was a strange voice at the other end.

"Mr. Carter, please," it said.

"Mr. Carter isn't in just now," she replied. "Can I take a message?"

"This is the Barnard's Crossing Police Department calling. Can you tell me where we can reach Mr. Carter? When do you expect him?"

"He went out right after supper," she said. "Just a minute, I hear a car driving in. Maybe that's him now. Hold the line a minute."

She heard the door open and she called out, "Is that you, Raphael? You're wanted on the telephone."

He picked up the receiver. "Carter speaking," he said.

"This is the Barnard's Crossing Police Department. Lieutenant Jennings. Will you please wait for our Sergeant Hanks. He'll be right over."

"Police Department? What's this all about?"

"Sergeant Hanks will explain," said the voice at the other end, followed by a click as Lieutenant Jennings hung up.

33

"Damn funny, all your folks should be out for the evening," said Chief Lanigan. "What time are they expected back?"

Stu shrugged.

Didi said, "All I know is I found a note on the kitchen table saying they were going to a movie. They didn't say which one, but I know it wasn't the Seaside in Barnard's Crossing because they already saw that one. And then they might go on someplace for coffee."

"Well, I'll just have the sergeant keep calling every fifteen minutes or so until we get them. You kids wait right here and don't try anything funny."

And he left them sitting in his office, the two boys on a bench by the wall, Didi in an armchair near the window. She looked forlorn and puffy-eyed. The shock of hearing of the death of a boy she had seen only a few hours before, followed by her arrest, had unnerved her completely. She had control of her emotions now, however, and stared moodily out the window at the little grass plot in front of the station house.

Stu edged closer to Bill Jacobs and whispered, "You know, I don't think they're going to let us go without our folks coming down. Maybe I ought to tell them that they're at my Aunt Edith's, and that he can reach them there."

"You already told them you didn't know," Bill whispered back.

"No, I didn't. He asked us if we knew what time they are coming back, but he didn't ask us where they were."

"I think we should sit tight. Maybe when he calls and finds our folks are out, he'll let us go."

Stu sat back, unhappy, his fingers drumming nervously on the arm of the bench. He edged forward again. "You know what, Bill? I think we ought to tell them about Moose—I mean, about how we found him."

"Sure, why not? *You're* in the clear," said Bill bitterly. "It doesn't matter to you."

"What does that mean?"

"Well, you weren't in the house at all during the storm. And he was dead already when you showed up. But where does that leave me and Didi?"

"But they're going to find out sooner or later."

"How are they going to find out? From what I overheard the cops talking, they think he just died from an overdose of alcohol."

"Yeah, but that's just the cops. Once a doctor examines the body, he'll know he didn't die that way. He'll be able to tell whether a guy died of alcohol or from suffocation."

"I don't mean we shouldn't tell them," Bill temporized, "but I don't think we have to tell them anything without a lawyer. And they can't count it against us," he said with an assurance he did not feel. "That's the law."

"Maybe you're right. I wish my old man were here," said Stu unhappily. "He'd raise hell with me for getting involved, but he'd know what to do. He'd see that the cops treated us fair. Say, who do you think could have done it?"

Bill shook his head. "I left the door unlatched. Anybody could have come in."

"Hey, how about this Alan Jenkins? You all said Moose was leaning on him from the minute he laid eyes on him. These days they don't take that lying down."

"And he left Didi's house in plenty of time to swing back there."

"I know."

34

"What did you expect him to say, David? Mr. Wasserman is an old man; he's practical. I know how you feel, but sometimes you have to compromise. You yourself have said that *parnossah* is necessary for a good life, that you can't have a good life unless you're making a living." She had fussed over him like a mother hen, bringing him his slippers and pouring him a cup of hot tea liberally laced with whisky and lemon. "Drink it; it will ward off a cold."

"Making a living is a necessity," he said through her ministrations. "Making a good living is a luxury. I don't need luxury for a good life. I don't reject it, of course; I am not ascetic. But I don't need it."

"But wherever you go, except in small towns like Barnard's Crossing, there will be more than one temple. And that will mean competition."

He shook his head wearily. "You don't understand, Miriam. In the nature of things the rabbi is paid by a temple or synagogue because here in America it's the most practical way of compensating him for his work. But he is not the employee of the temple, just as a judge is compensated by the state but is still completely free to rule against it in an action. And if his courthouse burns down, it doesn't mean that he loses all function and responsibility and purpose. But here, if the temple should split, we would have an ugly situation. The rabbis of the two institutions would become bargaining points in the two campaigns for membership. And I want no part of it."

"But if, as you say, you insist on being the rabbi for the entire community, it means living in a small town."

"Well, I like small towns. Don't you?"

"Ye-es, but small towns mean small communities, and small communities mean small pay. Don't you have any personal ambition?"

He looked at her in surprise. "Of course. Why else would I spend so much time at my studies? But my ambition is to be a rabbi, not something else. I have no interest in using the rabbinate as a springboard to some other kind of work that pays more and carries greater prestige. I don't think I'd care to be a big rabbi with a big pulpit at some prestigious temple where I could never be found because I'd have speaking engagements all the time. I wouldn't like it, and"—he reached over and patted her hand reassuringly—"you wouldn't like it either. Maybe you'd be proud of me for a little while, seeing my name or my picture in the Jewish press. But after a while you'd get used to that, like everything else. Besides, I don't think I could do it, anyway."

"But you have to do some compromising, David, or—"

"Or what?"

"Or keep moving."

"We've been here almost six years. But you're right, we can't keep moving. It's not good for Jonathan, for one thing. And I've been thinking about it. Wherever I go, there will be other Gorfinkles and other Paffs."

"So what do you plan to do?" she asked quietly.

He shrugged. "Oh, one day this week I'll go down to New York and see Hanslick and tell him that I would like another position. I might look into the possibility of Hillel work—"

"David, is that why you are being so"—she was going to say stubborn, but decided on another word—"so resolute about this situation here?"

He gave her a sharp look and then smiled. "Catholics have their confessors," he said, "and Jews have their wives. I think I like our arrangement better."

"You're dodging me," she said but laughed in spite of herself.

"Am I? Yes, I suppose I am. Well, I think perhaps that is part of the reason. Didn't you like it—the two days in Binkerton? To tell the truth, dear, I'm tired of fighting. I've been doing it for almost six years, ever since I came here. I was prepared for a certain amount of it, but I thought that once it was established just who was the rabbi here, I'd be able to concentrate on my real job. But throughout my tenure, I've had to fight just to stay. I tell you I'm tired of it."

"You had an argument at Binkerton," she observed.

"That was different. That was a matter of principle. I don't know, maybe this is the wrong congregation for me. They're so—so contentious." He thrust his hands deep into his trouser pockets and strode the floor.

"Well, Jews have never been known as a passive people," Miriam said gently. "And what makes you think their sons and daughters in the colleges will be any different?"

"Perhaps not, but I'm hoping their disagreements would be over issues of greater moment than whether or not to have permanent seating arrangements, say. But it's more than that. A rabbi is primarily a student, a scholar. And for scholarship, a certain amount of leisure is necessary. In Hillel work, I'm hoping I would have the time—"

"But here you're doing things; in the college you'd only be reading about them."

"Well, I'd like a chance to do a little reading."

"Oh, you—" She controlled herself. "Your head is in the clouds, David. What about the immediate future? The community seder on Sunday, for instance. Will you be running it? Have you thought of that?"

"No, I haven't. But now that you mention it, I suppose that until I resign or am voted out I'm still the rabbi officially, and I would preside. Of course, Gorfinkle through his new Ritual Committee could decide to have the cantor run it, or Brooks, for that matter. It wouldn't bother me too much. As a lame-duck rabbi, I might find it embarrassing. Besides, the seder is not really a community affair. It's a family affair. The only reason we have a seder in the temple is because a lot of our members are either too lazy to run their own or feel that they can't."

"But if they did arrange for someone else to run it, what would you do?"

"Do? I'd stay home."

"But—"

The doorbell rang.

"Who can that be at this hour?" exclaimed the rabbi. "It's eleven o'clock."

Miriam hurried to the door. "Why, it's Mr. Carter. Come in, won't you."

He permitted himself to be led into the room and sat down on the chair that was drawn up for him. He sat on the edge, his back straight and not touching the chairback. "My son is dead," he announced.

A shocked glance passed between the rabbi and his wife.

"Oh, Mr. Carter, I'm so sorry," said Miriam.

"How did it happen?" asked the rabbi quietly. "Tell me about it. Is there anything I can do?"

"Maybe there is," said Carter. "They called me tonight. I was out, and they called just as I was coming in the house. Asked me to wait until some police sergeant got there. When he came, he wanted me to go down the station with him. I kept asking him what is the matter, and all he would say was that I'd find out when I got to the station house. The chief was there when I got there, and he told me. He wanted me to identify the body." He gave a short bitter laugh. "My boy's picture was in the paper practically every week last year. I'll bet that most people in town knew him better than the chairman of the Board of Selectmen. He was the guest of honor at the annual banquet of the Junior Chamber of Commerce at the end of the football season. But they needed me to identify him."

"That's just necessary formality, I believe," remarked the rabbi.

"Yuh, I guess so."

"Did they tell you how he had met his death?"

"They didn't say positive except that he had been drinking, that it looked like he had been drinking an awful lot. Well, that stuff is poison. He was intoxicated, that's what he was. That's a Latin word, and it means poison. Did you know that?"

The rabbi nodded.

"They took the body down to the police station," Carter went on, "in the police ambulance. They opened the door and there he was, with a blanket over him. The head was toward the front of the car, so I had to climb right in. Lanigan got in after me, and he pulled back the blanket. 'Is that your son?' he asks. And I says, 'Yes, that's my son.' So then they told me how they found him at Hillson House. He was lying on a couch there, and they could smell the whisky on him. Lanigan said how if you drink the stuff fast enough before the body has a chance to get rid of it, it can be very dangerous. So I guess that's what must have happened."

"You said you thought I could help," said the rabbi. "Did you want me to try to get further information on just how it happened?"

The carpenter shook his head, "No, I guess that's how it happened, the way Lanigan said. I knew that Moose drank even when he was in high school." He paused again and then went on. "Lanigan drove me home and left me to break the news to Mrs. Carter. She carried on something dreadful. Lanigan called a doctor, and he gave her something to quiet her. I didn't have the heart to prevent it, God forgive me."

"And how is she now?" asked Miriam gently.

"Well, right now she's asleep. My oldest girl is with her." He knuckled his eyes, as if to wipe the sleep out of them. "Then I went back to the station house—Lanigan had left earlier—to make arrangements to get the body so I could give it decent burial. And Lanigan told me that they might have to do an autopsy on him to find out for sure what the cause of death was."

"I suppose that's the law," said the rabbi.

"Well, I don't hold with it. I know the cause of death. Lanigan told me. So why do they have to cut him open?"

"I suppose they have to be sure."

"How much surer do they have to be than they are right now? The body is the temple of the spirit, Rabbi. Even if the spirit is gone, do you have a right to destroy the temple? I don't hold with it. It's against my religious beliefs." He fixed piercing eyes on the rabbi. "Now, I'm not looking for a fight with the police department or with the town, but if I have to fight, I will. But I've heard that you're friendly with Lanigan and have been almost since you came. I thought maybe you could speak to him about it for me."

"I have no legal standing in the matter," said the rabbi. "I mean, I'm not a lawyer, and I couldn't act as your legal representative. Have you thought of getting a lawyer?"

Carter shook his head. "It's not a fight I want right now, Rabbi. When it comes to going to court, I'll get a lawyer. Right now I'm thinking whether you could persuade him for my sake and my wife's sake."

"All right, I'll talk to him," said the rabbi. "But I wouldn't expect too much. Lanigan isn't the sort of man who would refuse a request of this kind unless he had a very good reason and saw it as a necessary duty. And if that is so, then I don't think I could persuade him. But I'll talk to him if you like."

"When?" asked Carter pointedly.

"Anytime you like."

"How about now? Tonight?"

35

"Did you make contact with the Hillsons?" asked Lanigan.

Lieutenant Jennings nodded. "Sort of contact," he amended. "I spoke to the housekeeper. A regular battle-ax. She said the girls—girls, the younger one is seventy-five!—anyway, they were asleep and she wasn't going to wake them, and I ought to be ashamed to be calling this time of the night, and she didn't care if I were the police or the United States Army."

"She said that? The United States Army?"

"Her words, Hugh. She even banged the receiver down once, but I called back"—he nodded in self-satisfaction—"and I told her that she better stay on the line until I got through with her, or I'd notify the local police to go out there and pick her up and bring her here. She must have believed me, because she didn't try it again. Then she wanted to know what had happened, and when I told her that I didn't have time to give her all the details, she said she was going to call the police, her police. Anyway, she finally told me that the house was up for sale and was in the hands of the Bellmore Realty Company of Lynn, who were the sole agents. Fortunately, I remembered that Bellmore was originally Bell and Morehead and that John Morehead lives here in town. So I called him and he told me that he was supposed to meet a group who were interested in buying the property at the house at half past eight, that he had given the key to one of them because something had come up and he wouldn't be able to meet them."

"Did he say who they were?"

"He didn't know, except the man he gave the key to. He was the only one he'd be dealing with, anyway."

"And who was that?"

"Meyer Paff. He's the—"

"Yeah, I know, the bowling alley man."

"Sure. He's got one in Lynn and Revere, all over the map, as far up as Gloucester."

Lanigan's eyes were shining. "And just the other day Kevin O'Connor called me to ask what I knew about him. The Lynn police have been watching that alley of his for pot."

"Hell, they watch every place where kids hang around, and kids hang around bowling alleys."

"Yes, but look here. We find pot on Moose, and he's dead. And we find there's a witness that can swear that earlier in the day he visited this guy Wilcox in Boston. And Wilcox was suspected of dealing in pot. And he's dead. And where do we find Moose? In Hillson House. And now here's Meyer Paff, who owns a place that the Lynn police suspect is a distribution point for pot. And Moose Carter works for Paff. And Meyer Paff has a key to Hillson House. And what's more, he had an appointment to meet some people there tonight."

"Yeah, but most of that is just coincidence."

"Sure, and it was just the coincidence of both having some connection with pot that led me to call the Boston police, which is how we found out that Moose had been to see this Wilcox earlier in the day. Have you called Paff yet?"

Through his pale-blue, watery eyes Lieutenant Jennings looked reproachfully at his chief. "I just finished talking to John Morehead, Hugh."

"All right. That's fine. Go dig him up."

"You mean tonight? Right now?"

"Sure. Bring him down and let him make a statement. He'll sleep better for it."

Jennings grinned. "Gotcha."

36

Chief Lanigan was startled when he saw his visitor. "You psychic or something, Rabbi?"

"What do you mean?"

Lanigan's broad red face relaxed in an easy smile. He ran a hand through his short white hair and eased back in his swivel chair. Although the smile remained on his face, his candid blue eyes were guarded. "Always happy to see you, you know that, but I'm sure you wouldn't come down to the station on a rainy Monday night just to say hello. Or were you passing by?"

"I'm here about Moose Carter. His father—"

"Don't tell me Carter is a member of your congregation," said Lanigan with a grin. "You know, you have no standing in the matter, Rabbi."

"I'm here at his request. Surely that gives me some position."

"Some, but not enough." His grin broadened.

The rabbi could not understand Lanigan's attitude, but he plunged ahead. "You told Carter that his son had died of alcohol poisoning. All right, he accepts your finding, and now all he wants is to give him proper burial. As I understand it, you refuse to surrender the body, and you hinted to him that you might order an autopsy. He has strong principles on the matter. His religious convictions are opposed to the idea."

"Religious convictions? Hell, the guy's a nut."

"He's not as crazy as you think. He would not oppose an autopsy if it meant finding out the cause of death, but here you know the cause of the death."

"And that's where you're wrong, Rabbi. I told him I thought it was alcohol poisoning, but I didn't say we were certain. There's an awful lot that needs explaining. Did you know the boy?"

The rabbi shook his head.

"He was a big boy, over two hundred pounds, and alcohol poisoning, you know, depends a good deal on body size. It takes more of the stuff to have the same effect on a big man than it would on a little man. The way it works—if you take enough of it and you take it fast enough before the body can get rid of it—the nerve controlling the breathing apparatus is paralyzed, and you're asphyxiated. And on the basis of the available evidence, it just doesn't look as if he had enough to kill him. And there are other angles. Come with me, and I'll show you something."

He led the way into a small room off the front entrance. From a filing cabinet he drew a large manila envelope and emptied its contents on a table. He held up a plastic tobacco pouch, unrolled it, and passed it to the rabbi. "What do you think of that?"

The rabbi sniffed at it and then took a pinch of the greenish flakes. Gingerly he touched it with the tip of his tongue.

"Careful, Rabbi, you're breaking the law."

"Then this is—"

"Grass, pot, Mary Jane, marihuana. We found that in Moose's trouser pocket. And here's his wallet." He held it by a corner and shook it in front of the rabbi's face. "It contains two crisp new twenty-dollar bills, Rabbi. Now ask me what makes them so interesting."

"All right, what makes them so interesting?"

"Because up until around noon today Moose Carter didn't have a dime. He was going into Boston, and he had to borrow a couple of dollars from his mother for bus fare."

"You mean he's been selling this stuff?"

"Maybe. But what makes it really interesting is that earlier today a man was murdered in Boston, in the South End, name of Wilcox. It came over the teletype. Boston narcotics squad had been suspicious of him for some time. Just before closing time, he had cashed a check at the local branch of his bank for five hundred dollars and got it in crisp new twenties. But when you get your money in new bills, the numbers run consecutively. So when we found the grass on Moose, I called the Boston police on the chance that there might be a connection. And that's when we found out about the money. Wilcox had four hundred and sixty dollars on him when he was found, and the two bills that Moose had were the next two numbers."

"You mean that Moose murdered this Wilcox?"

"No. As a matter of fact we know that he didn't, because Wilcox was alive after Moose was seen to leave."

"Then it is definite that Moose went there?"

"The two twenty-dollar bills pretty much prove that," said Lanigan drily. "That would be proof enough for me."

"And yet, he could have got them from whoever got them from Wilcox."

"Could have but didn't. Boston has an eyewitness that saw Moose going to visit Wilcox. So you can understand why I'm not releasing the body just yet."

The rabbi nodded slowly.

"All right." Once again Lanigan was grinning, "And now ask me how we found Moose in the first place."

"Go on." For some reason the rabbi was apprehensive.

"We got a call from the next door neighbor, man named Begg, who said he had seen a light in Hillson House. So we sent the cruising car around to check it out, and they got there just in time to catch a couple of young fellows coming out. They had a car parked in front of the house, and there was a young girl behind the wheel. Now *they* might interest you, Rabbi, because one of them is the son of the president of your temple, and the other two, William Jacobs and Diane Epstein, are also your people."

37

"You bothered about something, lover?" asked Samantha as she sipped her coffee.

"Troubled? No. Why?"

"Well, you've been pretty quiet all evening."

"Oh, I was just wondering how Ben made out with the rabbi," said Roger Epstein. "I thought he might call and tell me about it."

"Well, they were going to her sister's in Lynn. Sarah mentioned it the other night when they were over. I suppose he just explained to him what the new policy of the temple was and told him that he expected him to go along with it."

"That's just the point. From what I've seen of him, the rabbi isn't the sort of man you can just tell what to do."

Samantha looked up from her glass. "You mean he's stubborn?"

"No-o, not exactly stubborn. Maybe it's just that he knows just what he believes. Most people don't, you know. And he isn't the sort to do something that he believes wrong."

"But if Ben tells him—"

"All right, suppose he tells him and he refuses?"

"Well, gosh, doesn't he have to go along with Ben? Or is there some Jewish law about it? I mean, he isn't like a priest who is put in a parish by the bishop. You can ask him to leave, can't you?"

"Yes, we can. And that's what we agreed at the meeting. Ben was to spell it out for him, and if he refused to go along or if Ben decided that he wasn't going to go along—we left it up to Ben to use his judgment—why then, he was to tell him that a motion would be brought up before the board calling for his resignation." He ran his hand through his hair. "But I've been thinking about it, Sam, and I'm not so sure it was such a good idea. The way Ben explained it at the time, he could use the pulpit to help the opposition every chance he got—the Sabbath services, the community seder next week, there'll be a lot of people attending that, the holiday services the following week—besides all kinds of people who come calling on him or who he sees, like the kids yesterday, which precipitated the whole business. If we couldn't neutralize him, it would be better to fire him before he could do much damage. That was Ben's view, and we all went along with it."

"Well, it seems reasonable."

"Maybe it is, but I can't help feeling that maybe Ben exaggerated what the rabbi might do, and even more—" he hesitated.

"What?"

"I personally feel funny about it."

"How do you mean, lover?"

"Well, here I am—new to this whole game. I became a member of the temple only a few years ago, partly because Ben Gorfinkle urged me and partly because I thought, as an institution, I could use it to further the things that mean a lot to me—the Social Action Fund, for example. But I'm still only a new man. Before that, I never entered a temple from one year to the next. And here I am, one of the group who's laying down the law to the rabbi, even firing him maybe, and he's been in it all his life." He shook his head. "Well, I'm beginning to think it's damn presumptuous of me."

38

"All right, so it started to rain and you ran up to the house," said the rabbi, "and then what happened?"

"Well," said Bill Jacobs, "at first we tried to take shelter under the eaves—there was no porch—but it started to thunder and lightning, and the girls got frightened. It was awfully close. You can tell by how soon the thunder follows the lightning. You count—"

"I know how it's done."

"Yeah, well, so Moose suggested we go inside."

"It was Moose's suggestion? You're sure?"

"That's right," said Didi, "I remember one of the boys—I think it was Adam Sussman—asking how we were going to get in, and Moose in that very superior way of his said he'd show us. He puts the palms of his hands against the windowpane, and he sort of rotates it, and that causes the catch to loosen. Then with something thin and stiff—a little plastic ruler he had—you can stick it up between the window sashes and push it back." She demonstrated the technique.

"But weren't you worried about being seen?"

"Well, there's only this other house where this guy Begg lives, the one that notified the police, I understand," said Bill, "and Moose was sure he wouldn't bother us."

"Then one of you climbed in and let the others in—"

"Adam Sussman. He was the smallest and the lightest. The girls refused."

"You are talking about the window in the rear and the back door, right?"

"That's right."

"But you all went into the living room, which is in front of the house. Why was that?"

"We didn't want to put on a light, Rabbi, and that room got some illumination from the streetlamp across the way. Besides, I guess that was the one room that had plenty of chairs."

"And you all stayed together in that room?"

"More or less. There was some wandering around when we first came in, and a little later a couple of people went looking for the john, but mostly we just stayed in the living room, all except Moose, of course."

"Why do you say 'of course'?"

"Because he came back with this bottle of whisky. So I guess he'd done some exploring."

"How much was in it? I mean, was it a full bottle?"

"Oh, it was full all right. He had to take the seal off to open it. And he offered it around first, but none of us took any, so he drank it down same as he did the beer down at the beach—showing off."

"And then?"

"Then he started to act up."

"What do you mean by that, Bill?"

"Oh, he was sort of chasing after the girls, especially Betty Marks and Didi here."

"And what did the rest of you do?"

Jacobs reddened. "Well, he was pretty drunk. I mean, he couldn't catch them or anything like that, so I guess we thought it was funny. Once or twice we told him to cut it out and sit down, but most of the time we were laughing. You weren't bothered, were you, Didi?"

She shook her head.

"Then it suddenly hit him, and he got all red and just sat down. He was sweating, and he looked terrible. So I suggested he lie down for a while. I guess he thought it was a good idea, because he tried to get up. Then he just sat down again, so I helped him up, and me and Adam tried to walk him to this room I had noticed off the hall. But Moose is —was—I mean, Adam is pretty small, and Moose was a big guy. So I called to this guy Jenkins, the colored fellow, and the three of us got him into that room and laid him on the couch."

"I see."

"When we laid him down, he saw Jenkins and he started in on him again—you know, calling him names and saying things like he didn't need no help from no goddam nigger—that kind of thing. He was throwing himself around and trying to get up. The couch had this big sheet of plastic draped over it, like the rest of the furniture, so I suggested we wrap it around him. And almost immediately he fell off to sleep."

"How do you know he was asleep?" the rabbi demanded sharply.

"Because he was snoring."

"All right. Then you went back to the living room?"

"That's right. And then Stu came along."

"And then you came back to get Moose?"

"That's right," said Bill. "We went into the room where we had left him. I had the flashlight—" He paused and licked his lips. He looked questioningly at Stu and Didi.

"Go ahead," said Stu hoarsely. "Tell it all."

39

"Yes, I've got a key to Hillson House," said Meyer Paff guardedly.
"And you were there this evening?" asked Lieutenant Jennings.
"I was there, but I didn't go in. Say, what's this all about?"
"There was a little trouble, and we're just checking it over," said
Jennings easily. "Now, what time were you there?"
"Look, I was supposed to meet somebody at half past eight. I was a
little late, and it was raining so hard I thought this party might not
show. So when I got there and I saw that no one was around, I just
drove on."
"Didn't it occur to you that this party you were supposed to meet
might also be late? I'm surprised you didn't wait a while."
Paff shrugged. "Originally there were four of us supposed to meet.
So first one calls and tells me he can't make it. And then another calls,
and *he* can't make it. So I was bothered to begin with—you know, disgusted—and I half had the feeling that the third one would have begged
off if he could have reached me in time. So like I said, it was raining
and there was thunder and lightning, so I thought, What the hell, two
of them have disappointed me, so I'll disappoint a little on my end.
Good thing, too. It turns out when I got home and called him, he said he
thought he had a cold coming on and wasn't about to go out in that
kind of weather."
"Well, that's clear enough," said Jennings, closing his notebook. "However, just to get things all cleared up, I'd appreciate it if you'd come
down to the station house and make a statement."
"So what do you call this?"
"Oh, I mean a regular statement that a stenographer can take down
and you can sign."

"Well . . ."

"It won't take long, maybe half an hour or so," Jennings assured him.

"All right, I'll drop by in the morning—"

"I think the chief would like to have it tonight."

"You mean right now?"

"Why not? You're dressed. I can drive you down in ten minutes, and I'll bring you back afterward."

Paff was reluctant, but he could think of no reason to refuse. "Well, all right," he said, "I'll just tell my wife, and I'll put on a pair of shoes. I don't suppose I need to wear a tie," he added with feeble humor.

"Beauty," said Jennings appreciatively.

Paff headed for the door, then stopped. "Say, what happened down there? Was the place broken into, or—?"

"Why do you think that?" asked Jennings quickly.

"Well, I understand it happened once before."

Jennings nodded. "Yeah, it was broken into again, but this time it was a little more serious. Someone was found dead there. An employee of yours, as a matter of fact," he added placidly.

40

"I hate to say it to a man of the cloth . . ."

"I'm not a man of the cloth."

". . . but you've got an awful nerve, Rabbi. These kids tell me they find one of their friends murdered, and you ask me to let them go."

"Why not?"

Lanigan ticked off the points on his fingers. "First, because they're guilty of breaking and entering—"

"Not Stu Gorfinkle."

"He did the second time."

"The door was ajar."

"Let's not quibble, Rabbi. So it's illegal entry. Second, they were present in the same room with someone who had narcotics in his possession."

"They didn't know that."

"The law doesn't differentiate—not here in Massachusetts, it don't. Third, they were present in the same house where a man was murdered. Fourth, they could have committed the murder. And fifth, they did not report it to the proper authorities. And you ask me to release them!" Lanigan's face was red with indignation.

"Yes, I ask you to release them," he said soberly. "These are not vagabonds; they are respectable children of respectable parents, residents of this town. If you need them for questioning, they will be available. They are obviously guilty of the breaking and entering charge—they admit it, even though it's fully understandable in view of the storm. Still, if you should decide to prosecute them on that charge, they will appear. As for the narcotics charge, it is based on a law which obviously was never intended to be taken literally—would you arrest everyone on a streetcar, for example, if one passenger was carrying narcotics? No, it is intended to enable you to prosecute someone you have reason to believe is involved in narcotics, even though the actual possession may be with a companion. Are you suggesting that while they were waiting for transportation home they were smoking this drug?"

"And the murder?"

"That they didn't report it immediately—that was wrong of them but I think understandable. They're youngsters, and they were worried about what they should do. They were aware that suspicion could fall on them, and they wanted to discuss it among themselves—not whether to report it or not, but how. If you honestly think that one of them, or all of them, were actually involved in the murder, then again, they will be available for questioning." He smiled. "In the past, you have been receptive to suggestions that I have made that are based on Talmudic law—"

"You going to try to hornswoggle me with that pil—what do you call it?"

"Pilpul? No, but there is the principle of *miggo*."

"I don't think you ever tried that one on me before. How does it go?" asked Lanigan, interested in spite of himself.

"You might call it a principle of inferring credibility. The rabbi would use it when sitting in judgment. It is based on the general psychological principle that a man will not plead to a greater crime if a lesser or more advantageous plea is available to him, for 'the mouth that bound is the mouth that loosed.' "

"I don't get it."

"Let me give you a classic example. A marriageable woman coming from a distant land to a place where she is not known says that although she had been married, she is now divorced and free to marry again. She is to be believed both as to the marriage and the divorce, since she could easily have said that she had never been married at all and have no questions raised about her status."

"All right, and how does it apply here?"

"Once the youngsters unwrapped the body, there was no evidence that a murder had been committed. They could have remained silent, and you would have assumed that it was a natural death. After all, there were no marks visible on the body. But they made no attempt to conceal what they found. They told you, and so I say that under the principle of *miggo*, they are to be believed both on their testimony and on their innocence."

Lanigan rose from his chair and paced the floor while the rabbi maintained a watchful silence. Finally, he stepped in front of the rabbi and spread his hands in exasperation. "What do you want me to do, Rabbi? I called their parents and not one of them was home. The girl says her folks are at a movie; she doesn't even know which one. You want me to call all the local movie houses and have them paged? That Gorfinkle boy, he finally told me his folks were at his aunt's house, but when I called, they had left. And Mr. and Mrs. Jacobs—why, they're in Boston at some party. He doesn't know the name of the people—or he says he doesn't. You know I can't let them go until I get hold of their parents. They're minors."

"You'll be better off to let them go home. If you wait until their parents get here, this place will be a madhouse of hysterical parents and whatever lawyers they managed to bring along with them. There will be accusations and recriminations, and worst of all, the town will be full of rumors tomorrow morning that not only will do a great deal of harm to a lot of innocent people, but will make your investigation ten times as complicated and ten times as difficult."

Lanigan shook his head stubbornly. "If one of those kids turned out to be guilty and I let him get away when I had him right here in my own station house—" He broke off to ask a patrolman who had entered and was trying to catch his eye, "What is it, Tony?"

"Can I talk to you for a minute, Chief?" The two withdrew to a corner of the room, where the patrolman whispered to him earnestly for several minutes. The chief asked him a question and got a muttered reply. Then, with a "Thanks, Tony, that's a real help," he rejoined the rabbi.

"All right, Rabbi, I'll tell you what I'll do: I'll release them in your custody. You'll have to give me your word that they'll be available for questioning when I want them."

For a moment the rabbi hesitated. Then he nodded. "Very well, I guess I can do that."

41

They had been there almost an hour, and still there was no sign of agreement. Every now and then one of them would appeal to the rabbi —usually to support his position—but he was determined to be circumspect and refused to be drawn. When Lanigan first asked him to arrange for an informal meeting with all the youngsters who had been at the cookout, he had demurred. "I can't just ask them; their parents would have to agree to it."

"So ask the parents. Explain to them that all I want is information. I'm not trying to pin anything on anyone. No tricks. I just want to be sure I'm getting the complete story."

"They'll want their lawyers present," the rabbi warned.

"Nothing doing. I'm not going to have a bunch of wise guys raising objections every time I ask a question. If one didn't, another would."

"How about if they all agreed on one lawyer?"

"That would be the day. Besides, even if by some miracle they did, he'd feel he had to be extra careful, and he wouldn't let them volunteer anything."

The rabbi smiled. "Then I don't think you're going to get your meeting."

"Oh, I'll get it sooner or later," said Lanigan grimly. "I've got a clear case of breaking and entering against each and every one of those kids. I'll admit that there were extenuating circumstances and that probably no judge would sentence them. But in connection with the fact that they were all material witnesses to a murder—believe me, I'd have no trouble confining them to the jurisdiction. And when school starts again, they and their parents, too, are going to begin to chafe."

So, with great reluctance, the rabbi had agreed and called Mr. Jacobs to ask him to round up the others.

They met in his study, and after his preliminary remarks explaining the situation, he left the entire discussion to them. He sat teetering in his swivel chair behind his desk, following the argument as it shifted back and forth among the parents. Gorfinkle, for once, remained uncharacteristically silent, and the rabbi for his part tended to avoid looking in his direction.

"If he's going to accuse *my* child of being mixed up in the murder of this—this football player, then he's going to have to prove it," cried Betty Marks' mother. "The nerve of him to expect *me* to permit *him* to question *her* without a lawyer."

"I'm sure he doesn't suspect her, Mrs. Marks," said Roger Epstein. "He just wants to clear this business up as fast as he can. If we don't cooperate, he'll get nowhere, sure, but the case will not be solved."

"Well, that's his lookout," said Mrs. Marks.

"No, it's ours, too. If the case isn't solved and the murderer found, after a while suspicion may rest on our children, and that won't do any of them any good."

"Besides," said Mr. Schulman, "the kids did break into that house. No question about it. If we don't cooperate in this, he can bring a charge on the grounds of breaking and entering. Well, my Gladys has to get back to school; she has exams just as soon as she gets back. Am I going to let her kill a year just to be stubborn? Anyway, I trust my Gladys."

"Do you mean that I don't trust my Betty?"

"I'm sure you have every reason to, Mrs. Marks," said Epstein quickly.

"I think Bill should be able to handle himself," said Mr. Jacobs. "I'm willing to go along."

"Yes, but Bill was one of those who discovered the body," said Mr. Sussman. "His situation and your Stu's, Ben, they're different."

"I don't see that they're so different," said Gorfinkle. "After all, Stu never even entered the house until they went back for the other boy."

"You mean he's in the clear, and that's why you're so willing," Mr. Sussman pointed out.

"We'll be here all night if we keep on wrangling like this," said Mr. Arons. "What's it come down to? Chief Lanigan wants to question our kids all together on an informal basis. He's certainly got a right to question them, and we've got a right to have a lawyer present. So if he questions them individually, don't you think he'll get the answers to any questions he wants to ask even if there is a lawyer present? If he doesn't get it from one, he'll get it from another. You know, folks, I get the impression that this Lanigan is a sincere guy. I think he's on the level. I don't think he's trying to trap anybody."

"It just occurred to me," said Mr. Sussman. "If there's no lawyer present, then none of what is said can be used as evidence in court. So maybe we're better off without a lawyer."

"That's a good point," said Schulman.

"That's right. Maybe Lanigan outsmarted himself."

"I still think one of us ought to be present, though."

"I don't know how Lanigan would feel about that," said Jacobs. "Personally, I wouldn't care to be the one. I wouldn't care to be responsible to the rest of you for advising your kids. Suppose one of them said something damaging—"

"Suppose we got someone who is not involved, someone neutral," Epstein offered.

"Like who?"

"Perhaps"—Mr. Arons turned—"the rabbi here—"

42

Lieutenant Jennings glanced through the typed sheets and handed them over to his chief. "There's Paff's statement, Hugh. Nothing very interesting in it, although it struck me that he was kind of edgy."

"Everybody's edgy when they have to talk to the police," said Lanigan. "That's one of the troubles with being a cop." He read from the statement: "'QUESTION: What is your interest in Hillson House? ANSWER: I'm thinking of buying it; that is, a group of us are. QUESTION: For what purpose? ANSWER: It's a business venture.'" Lanigan looked up. "He never told you what it was?"

"No, Hugh, he acted pretty closed-mouthed about it, and I didn't feel I had the right to pry, especially when I couldn't see any connection. After all, if it's some special deal, he naturally wouldn't want it to get out before he was ready."

"Maybe you're right. But did he say who the group was?"

"Yeah, later on he mentions at least some of the names. There's a guy name of Arons who is the father of one of the kids, and there's Dr. Edelstein—you know him—and there's a man name of Kallen, Irving Kallen. He was supposed to meet them at the site, but none of them showed, so he drove off."

"That's a little funny," said Lanigan. "If he got there early, you'd think he'd wait. And if he got there late, he might assume that someone else could be late, and you'd think he'd wait for a few minutes anyway."

"Not if you read the statement, Hugh. Edelstein and Arons called earlier to tell him they wouldn't make it. It was raining so hard he figured Kallen wouldn't come out either." He leaned over and pointed to a paragraph on the typescript. "'I slowed down, saw that no one was there and the house was dark, and drove on.'"

"Hm—maybe. But still, there's the business of his bowling alleys—"

"Gosh, Hugh, bowling is respectable these days. Some alleys have these little tables where you have a bite, and there are even some where women can bring the kids and leave them with a baby-sitter while they bowl. Pool and billiard parlors, the same way. You know that one over at the shopping center? I dropped in there one evening while the missus was shopping in the supermarket, and there was this gal in a mini-skirt stretched out on that table making a shot for the corner pocket. You could see her whole whatsis. I tell you, I just had to get up and leave."

"I'll bet."

Jennings disregarded his chief's sarcasm. "Say, do you suppose that's the deal on Hillson House? He and his friends want to turn it into one of them fancy bowling alleys?"

"Could be. Still, it's funny about him."

"What's funny?"

"Well, there's that call from Kevin O'Connor. Kevin is an idiot, but he's also a cop. He wouldn't go asking me about Paff just to gossip. I take it that the Lynn police are really suspicious of that bowling alley of his. Anyway, it's a coincidence. And his having a key to Hillson House is another. And his driving by there that same night—that's still another. It's a lot of coincidences when you come to think of it."

"Yeah, but he's a big man in the community. What could the likes of him have to do with the likes of Moose Carter?"

"Well, for one thing, Moose worked for him."

"So?"

"So it's a connection. Suppose, just suppose," said Lanigan slowly, "Paff were distributing pot. Remember, a lot of kids come into his bowling alleys. Now suppose, just suppose, that after working there for a while, Moose tumbles onto it. You know the sort of kid he was. He wouldn't notify the police. Oh no, he'd tell Paff and make him cough up for it. All right, Paff goes to Hillson House for this special deal. When his friends don't show, he figures while he's there he might as well look the place over again. He goes from room to room, and then he sees Moose. Maybe so far the kid only hit him up for small change. Maybe for that package of pot we found on him. But he knows it's not going to stop there. It's going to get worse. And then he realizes that he can settle the whole business by just lifting up a corner of the sheet and tucking it in."

"You mean he'd kill him to avoid being blackmailed? Seems to me he'd be more apt to wait until the kid actually bore down on him."

"Maybe he did. Or look at it this way: Maybe he wouldn't go out of his way to do anything drastic, but here an opportunity presents itself. All he has to do is tuck in a fold of plastic and walk away."

"Beauty! But you've got to admit, Hugh, that it's pretty fanciful. I wouldn't want to put the arm on anybody on the basis of that kind of evidence."

"Oh, I'm keeping an open mind on the subject. I haven't written off those kids by a long shot. Remember, they all knew Moose. Any one of them could have done it, girls as well as boys. Maybe some of those girls were sweet on some of the boys and vice versa. And from what I can gather, Moose was cracking wise quite a bit. We know he fooled around with the girls, and maybe someone there didn't like it. So when he passed out—"

"All right, so now you've got the eight kids—no, seven, because the Gorfinkle boy wasn't there. Are you sure you can't get him involved?"

Lanigan disregarded Jennings' sarcasm. "No, I can't come up with anything for him. I'd say he was in the clear."

"Then I'll give you one. How about old man Carter?"

"Carter, the boy's father?"

"Stepfather, Hugh."

"That's right. I forgot about that. What difference does it make, though? He adopted him, I suppose. Anyway he brought him up as his own. Who *was* the boy's father?"

Jennings grinned. "He was born over the left. He wasn't Carter's boy, that's for sure. And the old man could never forget it. Whenever he had trouble with him, and there was trouble with the police once or twice, he blamed it on the boy's birth. He told me once when Moose was involved on a matter of vandalism that it was because he was a child of sin and came of bad seed."

"Pretty rotten that."

"Oh, it's what you'd expect from these religious types. Well, now, that night Carter wasn't home. When we called, he was just coming in."

"I suppose it might be worthwhile knowing where he was," Lanigan admitted with no great interest. "Anyone else?"

"There's the colored fellow, of course."

"Well, naturally. He's probably the one. Still, no harm in checking over the possibles."

43

The manager of the Lynn alleys greeted Paff with, "Tough about the kid, huh?"

Paff shook his head regretfully. "It certainly is. A young fellow like that, a good-looking boy, an athlete—"

"You know, I called his house like you told me, to see why he hadn't showed, and I spoke to his Ma. When I think that he was probably dead at the time—you know, it kind of gives you the shivers—I mean asking her what time she expects him back and all."

"Yeah."

"You got somebody else lined up to take his place, Mr. Paff? Because life got to go on, like they say, and I don't mind working overtime a couple of nights to help you out, but—"

"I'll get somebody to relieve you—tomorrow night for sure."

"If you're having trouble getting somebody, there's this kid that lives right next door to me. He's smart, knows how to handle himself."

"Yeah? What's he doing now?"

"Well, right now, he's not doing much of anything, just sort of looking around."

"Well—"

"I could have him come down tomorrow evening, and you could talk to him."

"Right now, I've got things pretty well lined up."

A customer tapped impatiently on the counter with a coin, and the manager hurried over to wait on him. As he came back he fished in his pocket and brought forth a bit of paper. "Say, I almost forgot. Did a Mr. Kallen get in touch with you the other night? He called right after you left. He said he was supposed to meet you"—he referred to the paper—

"at Hillson House. He said he wouldn't be able to make it. Say, wasn't that the place that—"

"Yeah, I spoke to him. Look, er—" he nodded him down to the other end of the counter. "The other night I was kind of upset. I had a tough day, understand?"

"Sure, Mr. Paff. We all have them."

"Well, in case anybody comes down to make inquiries—not likely to, you understand, but just in case—I'd rather you wouldn't mention I was planning to fire the kid. They might get the wrong impression." He laughed—a deep bass burble. "Hell, I wouldn't have fired him, not a kid from my hometown."

"Sure, Mr. Paff. What they don't know won't hurt them."

"I want you to cooperate with them, understand? Tell them every-thing, but there's no need to tell them anything unimportant. Now if they should ask when I left here, you remember it was sometime after eight o'clock—"

"Oh, no, Mr. Paff, it was quite a bit before—"

"No, it was after, almost quarter past. This friend of yours—you think he'd work out?"

"Oh, he's smart, Mr. Paff."

"All right, I guess you're a pretty good judge of character. Tell him to come down tomorrow night, and I'll put him on."

"Gee, thanks, Mr. Paff. You leave him to me, and I'll show him the ropes. You won't be sorry."

44

Chief Lanigan knew that the youngsters in his living room were there by coercion and that if he tried to appear friendly, they would only mistrust him more. So he tried candor.

"I won't ask you to make yourselves comfortable because I know you can't until this business is cleared up. That would be asking a lot. But there's coffee here and some cookies and for those who want something cold, Coke. Help yourselves."

"I'll have a cup of coffee," said Adam Sussman.

"So will I," said Bill Jacobs.

"I'd like a Coke, please," said Betty Marks.

Chief Lanigan, with the rabbi helping, passed out drinks and cookies. Then, when they were settled, he began again. "All of you participated in a cookout on the beach at Tarlow's Point last Monday evening—"

"Just a minute," said Jacobs. "There was someone else."

"You're referring to Alan Jenkins?"

"That's right."

"I asked the Boston police to contact him for us. He lives in a boarding house, and his landlady said he had gone off to New York. We have also contacted the New York police and asked them to look him up for us. In the meantime I'm afraid we'll have to do without him. Now, sometime during the evening you were joined by Moose Carter. And a little while later Gorfinkle here had to leave to pick up his folks, thus leaving you without transportation when the storm started. You ran for cover to Hillson House, forced a window, and took shelter inside."

"Just a minute," said Adam Sussman. "I'm not admitting anything."

Lanigan sighed. "Let's get one thing straight, Sussman: I'm not trying to trap you. Everything I have said and everything I'm going to say I can prove easily. I'm just trying to find out what happened. The point I was trying to make is that you were all guilty of breaking and entering. Under the circumstances, your behavior has some justification. That was a pretty frightening storm. What's more, it seems that you did nothing but take shelter. There is no evidence of vandalism, and as far as we can make out, nothing was taken. But it was breaking and entering, and I can hold you for it." He looked around at them pointedly.

"That's blackmail, isn't it?" said Jacobs.

"Yes," said Lanigan pleasantly.

"So what do you want to know?"

"Let's start from the beginning."

"All right, so you, Jacobs, and Sussman marched him into the study," said Lanigan. "Just a minute." He went to the hall closet and came back with a package. "I stopped off at the hardware store earlier and got one of those plastic drop cloths. It's just about the size of the plastic dust cover in the study at Hillson House." He unfolded it and spread it on the floor. "Now, Gorfinkle, suppose you lie down on that, and Jacobs can show us how he wrapped Moose."

Stu lay down on the sheet as everyone craned forward to watch. But Bill Jacobs shook his head. "The sheet was draped sort of catty-cornered on the couch, so that Moose was lying on the diagonal. Move your carcass around, Stu. That's right." Suiting the action to the words, he proceeded to demonstrate. "First, we picked up this corner and covered his feet. Then we picked up this corner and wrapped it tight around his body and kind of tucked it in. Then we picked up the opposite corner and wrapped it over that and tucked it under him, like this."

"And was anything said at the time, or had Moose passed out?"

"No, he was swearing, mostly at Jenkins."

"And Jenkins, did he say anything?"

"Not that I remember, except when we finished wrapping him up and he fell asleep, Jenkins said—but it was just in fun—"

"What did he say?"

"Oh, something about we ought to put it over his flippin' head." And then Jacobs added quickly, "But he was just joking."

"Of course," said Lanigan easily. "Now, when you came back to Hillson House, how did you find Moose? Any change in the way he was wrapped?"

"Well, this top corner had been pulled over and tucked in where the folds of the plastic met."

"Show me."

"Hey!" from Stu.

"Don't worry, Gorfinkle, we won't leave you there," Lanigan reassured him.

Bill Jacobs lifted the upper corner of the sheet and folded it over Stu's head and tucked it in.

Sue Arons shrieked. "Take it off," she cried hysterically, "take it off!"

45

In company Pearl Jacobs was gay, almost giddy, but in the privacy of her home, with her family, she could be sober and shrewd. When her husband had finished describing the meeting of the parents at the rabbi's study, she said, "I don't understand why the rabbi called you. I should think it would be Gorfinkle he'd call. He's the president."

"He said it was because our Bill was the only one who had been involved with the affair from beginning to end, but of course, his real reason was that he was probably embarrassed about calling Ben Gorfinkle after he had threatened to give him the ax."

"I'll bet Ben wouldn't be elected now if he were to run."

"Why? Because he ticked off the rabbi? You think *he's* so popular?"

"No. I mean, I don't know how popular the rabbi is. I know he doesn't have a special following. And some of those parents may feel sore at him for getting the kids to tell the police what they knew."

"You think so?"

She nodded. "I felt that way myself when I first heard of it, but then I realized it was bound to come out sooner or later. Besides, I didn't like the idea of a murderer running around loose and—"

"What's that got to do with Ben Gorfinkle?" said her husband patiently.

She looked at him in surprise. "Simply that a lot of the girls feel that this fight in the congregation he started is not such a good idea."

"Yes, but the girls don't vote."

"Maybe not," she said, "but a lot of them can influence those who do vote. And in Reform congregations they do vote, and I think it's a good idea. Anyway, a lot of the women I talked to, they don't like the idea of building an organization like this and then breaking it in two over a silly business of who is to sit where."

"Look, Pearl, I hope you don't talk that way outside. We weren't trying to split the organization. And it isn't over the seating business;
that's just incidental. We have a program and a damn good program,
and at every step of the way we were blocked by Paff and his group.
Since we can't get them to agree, wouldn't it be better if the two views,
the two philosophies, should each have their own machinery for doing
what they consider important, instead of each preventing the other
from doing anything?"

"Isn't that just like a man?" She shook her head. "You say we don't
want to split; we just want to do the things that cause a split. And that
satisfies your conscience. Well, let me tell you that women are a lot more
realistic. You're like a bunch of kids who think if you don't give it a
name, it doesn't exist. But you know what a split does? It isn't just that
you get two temples where you only had one before. It means that you
get two groups that tend to keep away from each other. The people of
one temple tend to stay away from the people of the other temple. It
doesn't make so much difference to the men—they're away all day, and
most evenings they're too tired to do anything. But the women are
around here all day long. Take me and Marjie Arons; we're both
in Women's League. And we're close. All right, the temple splits, and
I'm in one temple and Marjie is in the other. Don't you think that will
put up a wall between us?"

"But we don't see them socially, anyway," he protested.

"We don't as a couple see them as a couple, because you don't like
him, and I'm not crazy about him either. But Marjie and I see each
other. And how about the kids?"

"What about them?" he asked.

"Well, if there are two temples, there will be different affairs, and
the kids from one temple will feel funny about going to affairs from
the other place. Here's Bill out in this dinky little college in a town in
Minnesota that nobody has ever heard of. From what he tells me, there
are less than a dozen Jewish families in the whole town and practically
no eligible Jewish girls. Do you think that doesn't worry me? But at least
when he comes home for his vacations here, there are plenty of Jewish
girls. He can play the field. And you now want to cut off half of them.
Do you want your son to marry a Gentile, God forbid?"

"Come on, Pearl, you're making a big deal—do you think if Bill
wants to take a girl out, he's going to bother about what temple
her folks go to?"

"No," she said, "but he'll have less chance of meeting them."

"Well, a temple is not a matrimonial bureau."

"There are lots worse things that it could be, especially in a Yankee town like Barnard's Crossing. Why do you suppose the Sisterhood works so hard to make a go of it? You think it's so that you men can go there two or three times a year to mumble your prayers? We put on bazaars, and we put on shows. We have luncheons and brunches and whatnot. We have a big educational program. And at the end of the year, we hand the temple organization a whopping big check. We do it, I suppose, because some of it is fun and keeps us busy. But Marjie Arons does it partly to increase the chances of her Sue marrying a Jewish boy, and I do it to help insure that Bill marries a Jewish girl."

"The rabbi—"

"He doesn't know any more about it than you do. He's a man, too. I'll bet the *rebbitzin* understands though."

"I see," Jacobs said with a laugh. "And how long have you girls been plotting? When do you plan to take over?"

"Who needs it? You men want to run things? Go ahead. Big shots! You're like kids with a toy. You play with it, and then you get tired of it and leave it lying around or break it. You go ahead and plan and appoint committees, take votes, pass resolutions, make—what did Ben Gorfinkle call it?—'an active voice for social reform in the community' or what the rabbi is always talking about, 'a house of study and prayer'—but don't break it. Because it isn't only for you; it's for us—and for the kids."

"I see, so the kids are in on it, too?" he asked sarcastically.

"Don't run down the kids. Sometimes they show more sense than their parents. Our Bill is no fool. He was talking to me about it. He was concerned that the rabbi might leave. Now the kids like him and respect him. That's why Bill told the police—because the rabbi said he ought to, and Bill trusted him."

"Does Mrs. Paff think the way you do?"

"She has no children, so she doesn't feel about these things the way I do, I suppose. But Paff himself—if I were in his business that depends so much on kids, I wouldn't go out of my way to antagonize them."

46

"Well, what do you think?" asked Lanigan.

"I don't think you learned too much, did you?" the rabbi countered. "Still, there were a number of points brought out that I thought interesting. They seemed quite unanimously agreed that it was the Carter boy who first suggested that they invade Hillson House and who assured them that they would not be seen."

Lanigan grinned. "Sure, it was safe to blame him; he can't answer back."

"There is that, of course—"

"I found that little dig by the Epstein girl about the Marks girl having dated Moose quite a bit last year interesting."

"You attribute any significance to that? You didn't pursue it at the time."

"I thought it would be more profitable to inquire about it later on."

"Really? I regarded it as normal female cattiness," observed the rabbi. "About the only other bit of evidence I found worthwhile was the matter of the front door."

"What was that?"

"Bill Jacobs saying that he remembered fixing the latch on the front door so that they could come back and get Moose."

"Oh yes," said Lanigan. "Why do you regard that as especially important?"

"Because it means that after they left, anyone could have got in."

"If they had known," Lanigan interjected swiftly. "But it wouldn't have made any difference to someone with a key."

"Like who?"

"Like a man named Paff. Know him? He's a member of your temple."

"Meyer Paff?"

"That's right. He had a key to the place and was around there that night at about the right time."

Rabbi Small did not answer immediately. "Look here," he said at last, "obviously there's much about this case I don't know. There's no reason for me to know it. It's police business. But if it concerns members of my congregation and you want me to cooperate—"

"Keep your shirt on, Rabbi. I was planning to give it all to you." He went to the hall closet and returned with an attaché case. "Here's a copy of Paff's statement."

The rabbi read it through and then looked up and said mildly, "It seems straightforward enough."

"Oh, it is," said Lanigan hastily. "And yet, there are some interesting aspects to the very fact that he was there. For one thing, he knew the boy. Moose worked for him."

"Mr. Paff is an active member of the Boosters Club here in town and knows most of the high school athletes. He would certainly know Moose Carter."

"It's just a little detail. Here's another: The Lynn bowling alley has been under the surveillance of the Lynn police. They suspect it of being a distribution point for pot. Paff owns it, and that was where Moose used to work evenings as an assistant manager."

"Are you suggesting that Moose did the distributing and that Paff killed him for it?"

"That's a possibility," said Lanigan judiciously.

"Almost anything is," said the rabbi with a shrug. "But I doubt if you're really serious about Mr. Paff—"

"No, and why not?"

"Well, for one thing, I don't think you would have gone to the trouble of rounding up these youngsters and questioning them all evening."

"That's for sure," he grinned. "But unlike you, Rabbi, I found this meeting with the kids very enlightening."

"Indeed!"

"In fact, it practically proved what I've suspected all along, but I had to have this meeting to confirm it. A definite pattern developed— and it all points unmistakably to Jenkins."

"Oh?"

"Yes, it started when Moose first joined the group. He began to ride Jenkins, and there is no doubt from what the kids said that the colored fellow was burning about it. They were all in agreement on that."

"But Jenkins didn't do anything about it. None of them reported him as saying anything," the rabbi observed.

"No, and he didn't come out swinging at any time either. Maybe it would have been better if he had. That kind of thing builds up. He doesn't say anything until Moose is being wrapped up in the sheet. Then he cracks they ought to put it over his head. The Jacobs boy said he was joking, but you know that a lot of jokes—things that just pop out—are meant seriously."

"Go on."

"Next point: Jacobs leaves the door off the latch. Now who knows that? Why, only Jacobs. You remember I questioned him on that rather closely. He was the last one out, and he set the latch. Now later, when they were in the Epstein house and were planning to go back for Moose, Gorfinkle asked how they were going to get in and it was *then* that Jacobs told the others that he had set the latch so that it wouldn't lock. It's the usual front-door lock with two buttons. One releases the latch, and the other locks it. And notice, that's when Jenkins said he had to be getting right home because he was setting out for New York the next morning early."

"And you think he rode off and on the way to Boston stopped off at Hillson House."

"I'm damn sure of it. He had the opportunity; that is, he had transportation—his motorbike. And he had the motive. He's the only one we know definitely had a motive."

"Because young Carter made fun of him? Did it ever occur to you that Jenkins might be used to this kind of embarrassment? That this incident probably was merely another of a long series of similar incidents he has had to suffer all his life?"

"You mean you can get used to it. Sure, but it can also build up. And this could have been the last straw. You can argue these things either way. I should think you'd be happy over the turn of events."

"Happy? Happy that a young man who has visited in my house however briefly is suspected of murder?"

"Come on, Rabbi. Let's be practical. Moose Carter was murdered, and that means that somebody murdered him. Now who are the suspects? Well, up till now it has been the kids from your congregation and Meyer Paff, another of your people. I should think that you'd be happy that it's not them, that it's not somebody you're closely associated with, that it's somebody from out of town, a stranger."

"Ah, the stranger. Thank God for the stranger."

The rabbi rose from his chair and began striding back and forth across the room. "We Jews celebrate the Passover in a couple of days.

In many respects it's a most unique holiday, and we celebrate it in a unique way. We begin by cleaning the house of all foods and even all utensils that we use during the year, and during the week of the festival we not only buy special foods, but prepare them in special utensils and eat them from special dishes with special silverware that are used for just that week. Then on the eve of the holiday we have a feast, which is repeated the following night. And in each case the feast is preceded by an elaborate ritual in which the youngest person present asks the meaning of the feast, of the unusual foods that we eat, and the unusual manner of eating them. And then we, the rest of the company, explain how we were slaves in Egypt and were oppressed and how God responded to our suffering by bringing us forth with a mighty hand from our slavery and oppression."

"Yes, Rabbi, I know the reason for the holiday. But what's the point?"

"The point is that Passover is not merely a holiday of thanksgiving or rejoicing. We have several such holidays, but this is the only one that has a very elaborate and specific ritual and involves the use of a special set of instructions, the Haggadah, to make sure we follow it exactly right. Why?"

"Tell me."

"To engrave the lessons it teaches on our minds," said the rabbi. "It's a mnemonic, a string around the finger, a way of forcing on our consciousness and memory what people would rather not think of or would easily forget."

"Once a year the Pope washes and kisses the feet of beggars," Lanigan said.

"Precisely. And no doubt he profits by the lesson in humility that it teaches him," said the rabbi primly. Then he added as an afterthought, "It's a pity it isn't required of all members of your faith."

Lanigan laughed. "All right, Rabbi. Now what is it that your holiday teaches?"

"It is associated with a specific commandment that is central in our law: 'And if a stranger sojourn with thee in your land, ye shall not do him wrong . . . he shall be as the home-born among you; for ye were strangers in the land of Egypt.'"

"You saying that I'm being unfair to Jenkins because he's colored and from out of town?"

"Do you have him in custody, and has he confessed?"

"We haven't got him yet, Rabbi, but we'll get him. It's that motorbike of his—it's not like a car. You can wheel one of those over the sidewalk into a hallway or even a cellar, and how is it to be found? But I have alerted the New York police, and they'll find him."

"But you don't have any real evidence against him—only what you consider his motive and the opportunity."

"Oh, we've got the evidence, all right," said Lanigan. "We had it that first night, which is why I let your young people go home. As soon as the youngsters told us what they found and we knew it was murder, I sent some of my men scouring around Hillson House to see what they could pick up. And right off the bat, we got it. There's a tall, thick hedge in front of the house, and behind it, in the soft earth where it would be hidden from the street, we found a perfect motorbike tire mark."

47

The carpenter entered diffidently, awkwardly doffed his old-fashioned, wide-brimmed felt hat, and in response to the rabbi's invitation, sat down on the edge of the chair. "My wife thought I ought to change," he said in explanation of the black suit he was wearing, the highly polished black shoes, the white shirt, its collar uncomfortably tight, the wide florid necktie. "Out of respect, you know."

The rabbi nodded, not because he understood, but as a sign for him to go on.

"Lanigan called me this morning to tell me to come down to make arrangements for the burial. He said they had decided that they didn't need an autopsy."

"I see."

"So after I made the arrangements, I thought I'd stop off and thank you."

"I did nothing, Mr. Carter. Nothing."

"Well, I figure if you hadn't gone down Monday night—"

"No, Mr. Carter," said the rabbi firmly, "that really had nothing to do with it. Chief Lanigan quite properly refused to release the body then because he had doubts about the cause of death. Quite rightly, as it turned out. When he discovered that the death was by asphyxiation, he consulted with the Medical Examiner, who told him that an autopsy was unnecessary and that they would learn nothing by it. As I understand it, acute alcohol poisoning results in a paralysis of the nerve that controls breathing, so that the effect on the organs is the same as asphyxiation."

"I still think that if you hadn't gone down there they might have gone through with it anyway. Doctors have been known to do it, you know, just for practice," he added darkly.

"You've made plans for the funeral?" asked the rabbi to get him off the subject.

Carter nodded. "We're having a private affair—just the family. We didn't want a crowd, so it's just the family and a preacher friend of mine that I worked with on the fluoridation campaign. He'll say a few words."

"I think that's best."

"You know, Rabbi, I might have saved that boy." Carter clenched his fists. "I wouldn't say it to my wife, but I'm telling you."

"How do you mean?"

"I didn't listen, Rabbi. The Lord spoke to me, and I didn't listen."

The rabbi looked up with interest. "Oh?"

"I went out looking for him that night. I looked downtown and looked in the taverns, because that's where I thought I might find him. And when he wasn't there, I just rode around, up one street and down the other, aimless-like. I rode up by Tarlow's Point. Now why did I go up there if the Lord wasn't directing me? I even slowed down as I passed Hillson House. Was the Lord directing my footsteps or wasn't He?" he demanded. "But I was angry with the lad, and it blocked out the voice of the Lord. If I had been receptive, He would have spoken to me and told me where to look. But my mind was blocked, Rabbi, and the voice couldn't come through."

"You mustn't think that way, Mr. Carter."

"I feel better for having unburdened myself, Rabbi. I had to say it to someone, and I just couldn't say it to my wife. Oh, I know the Lord moves in mysterious ways, and it's part of some great plan that's beyond the capacity of my mind or else it's punishment on me or maybe even on my wife for sins committed in the past. But I want you to know that my own faith hasn't wavered—not for a moment. And if my anger blocked out the voice, maybe that was part of the divine plan, too. Or maybe it was to teach me that my anger was a wickedness."

"Are you suggesting the Lord would take your son's life just to teach you to control your anger?" asked the rabbi sharply.

"I don't know, but it is the duty of His servants to try to understand Him. And why else did the thought come to my head?"

"Not all the thoughts that come to a man's head, Mr. Carter, are put there by God. And not all the things that happen are God's work. If you see His hand in everything that happens, after a while you'll begin blaming Him for unpleasant and wicked things that happen. Some things are the results of our own mistakes, and some things just happen by accident."

Carter rose. "I don't like to hear you say that, Rabbi. It seems to me that it shows a lack of faith, and I didn't expect it of you. But maybe you're just saying it to make me feel better." He rose and went to the door. He seemed hurt.

"You'll find, Rabbi," he said, and he patted him on the arm, "that if you have faith, everything comes out right in the end." He brightened and his face even relaxed in a grin. "By the by, they've caught that colored fellow that took my boy's life. They were bringing him in when I was down the station."

Carter left, and the rabbi turned to Miriam. "Where's my coat?" he said, "I'm going down to the station house."

48

Ben Gorfinkle had called up in midmorning to say that he was coming home for lunch. "I want to talk to Stu. He hasn't gone out, has he?"

"He's still in bed, Ben," said his wife.

"It's eleven o'clock. Do you think perhaps he might condescend to get up by noon so that I can have a few words with him?"

"Well, you kept him up so late last night quizzing him about the meeting."

"I stayed up just as late, didn't I? It didn't prevent me from getting up at a reasonable hour."

"Well, he's a young boy, and they need more sleep. Is anything the matter?"

"I just want to talk to him. You just make sure that he stays there until I get home."

He had finished his Spartan lunch of a sandwich and coffee by the time Stu, yawning and gaping, appeared in pajamas and bathrobe.

"What's up, Dad?"

"If you'd been up, you might have got the news on the radio. This Jenkins fellow—he's been taken into custody."

"Oh yeah? So?"

"I've talked to one of our lawyers down at the plant. He thinks it was a mistake on our part to let Lanigan quiz you without the protection of a lawyer present."

"Well, natch, he's a lawyer. What else is he going to say?"

The elder Gorfinkle gave his son a mental mark for shrewdness. "Anyway, he agreed with me that your case is entirely different from that of the others, and if you play your cards right, you don't have to get involved at all." Seeing his son was about to object, he plunged on.

"Now, listen to me, will you? There are just three things, three hurdles that we've got to get over. First, there's the business of holding the picnic on Tarlow's Point. If that's a private beach, then you were trespassing. As far as I can make out, you had nothing to do with deciding to hold the cookout there, but on the other hand, you did the driving. Then again, as I understand it, even the town council isn't sure whether that's a private beach or not. It's my opinion that you're perfectly safe in admitting that you knew you were going to the Point. You just say that you thought it was a public beach because there have been cookouts there before."

"Well, sure—"

"Just listen, will you! All right. You left before the storm, and you had nothing to do with breaking into Hillson House. Right? And when you came back—the first time, I mean—you didn't go in, did you?"

Stu shook his head, wondering what his father was getting at.

"You heard them inside, and so you called out that you had come back, and they opened the door. Right?"

"Well, I knocked—"

"But you heard them in there. That's why you knocked. To let them know you had come back. And you yourself didn't go in. That's right, isn't it? You didn't go in."

"Yeah, they came out."

"All right. So far, you're in the clear. You were just like a bus driver or a cab driver who delivers a bunch of people to a party and then comes back for them. Now, when you returned to get that boy, Moose, that's when you made a mistake, because you had no right to enter that house. One thing in your favor, of course, is that the door was open, so it was not breaking and entering. And get this. All the time you were thinking that there was this friend of yours lying sick, maybe seriously sick, in that house there—"

"You mean Moose? He was no friend of mine."

"He was a classmate, wasn't he? You never had a fight with him, did you? All right, so he was a friend of yours. And he was sick—"

"He was drunk."

"You didn't know that. All you knew was that they told you he had passed out. That's like fainted. That's serious. You had a car, so naturally you felt you had to go help him." He glared at his son as though daring him to object to his interpretation.

And when his son remained silent, he leaned forward and said, "Now, this is important, and I want you to pay strict attention. You didn't know what was wrong with Moose when you saw him. After all, you're not a doctor. All you know is that he was lying there still. So your idea was to get out of there fast and get some help, call the police or a doctor. The idea that he might have been murdered never entered your head. All you know is that he didn't look right—"

"But it had to be murder, because somebody put that sheet over his head."

"You didn't see how they wrapped him in the first place, did you?"

"No, but—"

"Look, what I'm trying to tell you is that you were not involved with any of this. You didn't pick the place; you didn't break into the house; you went back to get Moose only because he was sick and you had a car; and finally, when you saw he was very sick, your one thought was to get help for him."

"But Didi and Bill said—"

"You wouldn't be likely to remember what they said. All you remember was there was some talk about Moose and how they put him to bed. The details, you just don't remember. You weren't there; you didn't see anything; you don't know anything."

"Yeah, I just pussyfoot."

"That's it," said his father eagerly.

Stu rose. "And afterward, when it's all over, what do I do? Get myself a new set of friends or move to another town? And what do I do about living with myself? I'm just a dumb kid, and you're a smart big-time executive. Well, maybe you're too smart. Nobody, certainly not Lanigan, is going to believe that all I had were noble thoughts. If I'm not involved, then I'm damn sure Lanigan's not going to get me involved. Besides, I don't think you're worried about me, anyway." He went to the door, and from the threshold he said, "It's you, your reputation, you're worried about."

Mrs. Gorfinkle came in. "Oh—where's Stu? Have you finished with him?"

"Yes, I've finished with him," her husband said between clenched teeth.

"What's the matter? Did you quarrel again?"

"You work and sweat and slave"—but Gorfinkle was talking to himself—"for what if not for your children? And what thanks do you get? To them you're a hypocrite. You're just thinking of yourself."

49

Jenkins looked curiously from the rabbi to Lanigan. "Here's this guy been dumping on me all evening, and you wonder why I don't want to help get him home so his daddy won't know he'd been drinking? The way I felt it would have been better than a hootnanny to see his old man skin him alive. I don't believe this turn the other cheek business you religious types go in for, Rabbi."

"Neither do we. That's Christian doctrine. We regard it as condoning sin."

"Oh yeah?" He nodded. "That's interesting."

"You preferred to get back at him?" Lanigan suggested.

The Negro shrugged his shoulders. "I didn't give it no thought if you want to know. I just wanted to split. These were kids—most of them nice kids—but kids."

"You only wanted to get home," the rabbi offered.

"That's right. It'd been a pretty dreary evening. It wasn't the kids' fault, but on the other hand, they didn't help any. I just wanted out. So I picked up my bike at Didi's and took off. Well, I hadn't gone far when it started to rain. I could've gone back to Didi's, I suppose, but then I thought of that Hillson House, and I knew the door was open."

"Which was nearer, Hillson House or Didi's?" asked the rabbi.

Jenkins shrugged. "What difference? Hillson House was on the way. Didi's meant going back."

"And you weren't thinking about Moose lying there all nicely tied up and helpless?" asked Lanigan sarcastically.

"Not until after I got in," said Jenkins cheerfully.

"Yet you were careful to wheel your bike across the sidewalk and hide it behind the bushes."

"Why sure, man, I had no right to be in there for all the door was open." He looked from one to the other to see if they understood. "So I went in and put the latch on the door."

"Why did you do that?"

"They said the police come by and sometimes try the door. Then I looked out, and I see this car coming along. When he gets near the house, he slows down and just crawls by like he's trying to look in, maybe. But he rides on."

"Paff," said Lanigan in an aside to the rabbi. The rabbi nodded.

"That kind of frightened me," Jenkins went on, "so I pulled the shades down. I had a flashlight with me, but then I noticed I could still see some of the light from the streetlamp through the shades, so maybe somebody outside could see in. So I unhooked these heavy lined velvet drapes until it was pitch dark, and then I figured I was safe to use my flash."

"Did you go in the little room to see Moose? Was he all right?"

"I didn't have to see him; I could hear him snoring away. I peeked through the drapes, and this time I see this car parked right under the streetlamp, with a guy sitting at the wheel like he's got nothing but time."

"The same car?" asked Lanigan.

Jenkins shook his head. "I don't know. I just got a glimpse of the car the first time—mostly his headlights, but at the time I don't think it was the same one, because I started worrying about the third car."

"The third car?"

"Sure. I see one car, and he passes slow. I see another, and he stops and waits. You know the drill. Trouble comes in threes. And the third car that comes along, the guy is bound to come in." He looked at his questioners, satisfied that his logic was unassailable and that they would understand.

"And all this time you never once thought about Moose?" Lanigan's voice showed disbelief.

"Sure, I thought about him," said Jenkins. "I thought about him lying there, as you say, nice and helpless."

"Ah." Lanigan hitched his chair forward.

"I thought I ought to get some of my own back. Some stupid kid trick, but just something to make me feel better. If I'd had my paints with me, I would have painted his face black, maybe. That cracked me up— the thought of seeing his look when the kids found him like that. I thought of giving him a haircut maybe, something special, like trimming my initials in that whiffle of his, or maybe just pinching his shoes and hiding them on him. But, of course, that would have meant unwrapping him, and I didn't want to do that."

"Naturally," said Lanigan drily.

"You think I was afraid of him?"

"The thought had crossed my mind," said Lanigan.

Jenkins shook his head. "I wouldn't fight him fair and square. Why should I? He had fifty pounds on me. But if we'd been alone together down the beach and he'd started to crack wise, I would have gone after him with a rock. I couldn't with the kids there. They'd have stopped it."

"But they weren't there now."

"That's right. And I started to get mad. There I had this wonderful chance, and there was nothing I could do. So then I remembered about his cigarette case, and I decided to take it so it shouldn't be a total loss."

"You took his cigarette case?"

"Yeah, I'd noticed it earlier in the evening. One side had cigarettes and one side had sticks."

"Sticks?" asked the rabbi.

"That's right, pot."

"He was smoking those during the evening?" asked Lanigan.

"Oh no, he smoked the regulars, but I'd spotted the others. I was going down to New York the next morning, and I figured they'd come in handy. The case was in his shirt pocket, and I just slid it out. And when I came back in the living room and peeked through the curtains again, I see the car is gone. Believe me, I didn't wait. I lit right out of there."

"You unlatched the door for Gorfinkle and Jacobs, of course," suggested the rabbi.

Jenkins smiled and shook his head. "What would I do that for? No, I left it locked. They were just coming to rescue this Moose. Why make it easy for them?"

50

The young man was indignant. "I see him bring the prisoner in, and I try to get a pic, and this Lieutenant Jennings blocks me. Then I ask the chief for a statement, and he says, 'No statement now.' So I figure I'll hang around and speak to him when things quiet down a little. So then—now get this: A guy that one of the cops tells me is the rabbi of the local synagogue comes in and goes into Lanigan's office. And pretty soon Lanigan and this rabbi come out, and the two of them go down to the cellblock to question the prisoner. I try to go along, and Lanigan shuts the door in my face. If a rabbi can be present while the prisoner is being questioned—and he's not Jewish, because he's colored, so he can't be his spiritual adviser, that's for sure—why can't a reporter?"

"All right. Let it go." Harvey Kanter dismissed the young man and reached for the telephone. "Hello, Hugh? Harvey Kanter. How are you?"

"Okay, and you?"

"Never better. And the missus?"

"She's fine."

"What do you hear from the boy?"

"Turning the West Coast upside down according to his last letter."

"Good. Hey, what are you doing Sunday night?"

"Nothing that I know of."

"Well, Edith is planning a regular seafood dinner—clam chowder, steamers, lobsters—the works. How about you and the missus coming over?"

"Sounds good, but isn't it your holiday?"

"Come to think of it." He chuckled. "I got a brother-in-law who's president of a synagogue, and I got to call a Catholic to tell me it's the seder. But I haven't kept it for so long I wouldn't know how to start. I'll scrounge around and find a skullcap for you if it'll make you feel any better. Is it a date?"

"Oh, sure, but I'll have to check with Gladys—"

"Edith will call her. Say, while I've got you on the line, what is this I hear you been doing to my boy? He tells me you won't give him the right time."

"He's pushy, Harvey. Why don't you teach him some manners down there?"

Kanter chuckled. "We don't teach them anything these days. They come from a school of journalism, and they know it all. He's a good kid, but he's been watching *The Front Page* on the late-night movie, and he thinks he's Hildy Johnson. He tells me you've got Jenkins. Did he talk?"

"Oh, he talked, all right . . ."

Kanter reached for a pencil and a pad of paper.

51

"He's lying. I just don't buy the idea of him going out to Hillson House to get in out of the rain and then sitting around in the living room doing nothing except peer out into the street every now and then to see if the car has gone, entirely content with having scored on Moose because he's pinched his cigarette case. If that's all he was planning to do, why all this business of latching the door—?"

"The police might—"

"All right, I'll let that go, but why pull down the shades and then draw the drapes? No, Rabbi, I've got a different idea of how he spent those twenty minutes. It's my feeling that he came in there the way he says, all right, but he took all these elaborate precautions with the drapes and all because he was planning to be there for some time. He went into the room where Moose was, pinched his cigarette case, and then put that plastic sheet over his head—as he'd been thinking all along—and then came back to the living room to wait."

"For whom?"

"Not for whom, Rabbi, for what. He came back to wait until Moose stopped breathing. Motive, opportunity, method—he had them all. And what's more, that remark he made to Jacobs about covering his head when they swaddled him up in the first place—that's going to prove premeditation. I put it to you, isn't it damn funny that this Jenkins, who wouldn't have anything to do with helping Moose get home, was ready to help put him to bed there at Hillson House? Why didn't he say then, 'To hell with him. Let him lie on the floor'? We didn't inquire into it, but I'll bet when we start preparing this case, we'll find it was Jenkins who suggested swaddling him up in the first place."

"Yes, I suppose you will," said the rabbi sadly. "I'm sure that, without meaning to be unfair and with no thought that you're in fact being unfair, you'll suggest it to Jacobs, and he'll come to believe that it's true."

"You're saying that it's easy to believe what you'd like to believe. All right," said Lanigan. "I'll admit it's possible. It's a normal human failing. But it cuts both ways. It's just as wrong to refuse to see evidence because it points to someone you feel sorry for. In any case, it's a minor point. You haven't shown me what's wrong with my reasoning."

"What's wrong? The boys, Gorfinkle and Jacobs, found the door unlatched and ajar. Jenkins said he set the latch so it would lock. He wouldn't lie about something like that. It would be pointless."

"Sometimes the lock doesn't catch. The wind could have blown it open."

"All right. The boys said they found the body with the head covered. That's how they knew it was murder. If Jenkins did it and waited to make sure Moose was dead, why didn't he then remove that part of the sheet once the boy had smothered? That would be the obvious thing to do. Then it would have looked like an accidental death. To leave it over his head was to leave proof that it was murder. He's a bright lad; he'd realize he would be likely to get involved."

Lanigan shrugged his shoulders. "He might have panicked."

"After he calmly sat around for twenty minutes or so?"

"How do you know it was calmly? He may have been in a panic all along. How do we know he did stay there for twenty minutes? Moose would have used up the available oxygen in that plastic sheet in a lot less time than that. And this car that he said he saw parked in front of the house— I don't believe it. What would anyone be doing there at that time of night and on such a night? If it were a couple who stopped to do a little necking, they wouldn't have parked underneath the street-lamp. I think he put that in to suggest to us that someone entered Hillson House after he left."

Lanigan shook his head. "No, Rabbi, stick to the essentials. He was sore because Moose—what's the term the kids use? Dumped, that's it—dumped on him. The idea of covering his head was in his mind, because he made the remark. Remember, he didn't deny making it. He wanted to get even with Moose. He admits that. He even admits going into the room where Moose was lying. And while he was looking down on him, he thought of the things Moose had said, and he picked up that last fold of the sheet and pulled it over his head and tucked it in. And if you don't think it happened that way, you've got to come up with some mysterious stranger who somehow knows that Moose is there, who can get into the house, who knows that Moose is conveniently tied up and then covers his head." He paused an impressive moment. "The only ones who fit that set of particulars, Rabbi, are your two young friends, Gorfinkle and Jacobs."

52

They were not hostile to the idea; they were just not enthusiastic. And it bothered Roger Epstein. "I don't understand," he said, "we're supposed to be all for social action." He turned to Brennerman. "You said that you wanted to see the temple involved. And you, Ben, social action is supposed to be the key to your whole program. Are you interested only when it's at a distance, someplace down South?"

"No, of course not, Roger," said Gorfinkle easily. "It's just that the key word is justice. Now you heard the news broadcast; what's more, I called my brother-in-law to check on that report, and he said it was accurate. He got it himself from Lanigan. Now, maybe I'm wrong, but my impression is that this colored fellow—what's his name? Jenkins— my impression is that Jenkins is guilty as all hell. You get a bunch of red-necks down in some Southern town framing some boy because he's colored, and I'm prepared to go all out. But this fellow was caught dead to rights."

"That's the way I feel," said Brennerman.

"Me too," said Jacobs.

"I don't see how you can be so sure," Epstein began.

"Aw, come," said Gorfinkle. "You don't believe, you don't really believe, that he'd go back there just to steal a handful of cigarettes, do you?"

"And remember," Jacobs pointed out, "our own kids are involved in this, Roger—your Didi as well as my Bill and Ben's boy, Stu."

"Sure, and what if one of them found himself in the position of this boy?" demanded Epstein. "I don't care whether he did it or not; he still has the right to a fair trial."

"He'll get one, won't he? This is Massachusetts. There won't be any funny stuff here, no lynch mob—"

"What kind of a fair trial can he get when he doesn't even have a lawyer?" demanded Epstein.

"If that's what's worrying you, forget it," said Gorfinkle. "As far as I know, he hasn't been formally charged yet. When he is, the court will appoint a lawyer if he doesn't have one or if he can't afford one."

"Sure, I understand there's a fixed fee for that kind of legal service, something like five hundred dollars. And you know what kind of lawyer he'll get—some kid just out of law school who maybe hasn't tried a case yet."

"What do you want us to do, Roger?"

"I want us to show that we mean what we say and have the courage of our convictions. Jenkins has the right to a good lawyer, a good trial lawyer, someone like Warren Donohue, say. I'd like for us to start a Jenkins Defense Committee to raise funds so we could get him. You mark my words, before this is over a lot of the more liberal churches are going to get involved in this. So why can't we be the first, instead of tagging along after the others?"

Gorfinkle pursed his lips and considered. "Well, you know, you might just have something there. But Donohue's fee comes high."

"So what?" Brennerman was excited now.

"And can we get him?"

"If we can raise his fee," said Jacobs, "why not? Our money's as good as the next guy's."

"And if we set up a Defense Committee, we can raise his fee," said Brennerman, "if we go about it right."

"We could solicit funds from the entire community," said Epstein, "but it would have to be a temple project, not just something we as individuals are sponsoring."

"And that ties right into our program!" exclaimed Brennerman.

"Now that presents problems," said Gorfinkle, "because if we offer it as a temple project, the rabbi is going to have something to say about it. And right now, my stock isn't exactly soaring with our rabbi. As a matter of fact, so far as he knows he's on his way out at the next board meeting."

"Yeah, I'm afraid you jumped the gun, Ben," said Brennerman gloomily. "You shouldn't have fired him—"

"I didn't fire him," said Gorfinkle, "I just warned him. And if this whole business hadn't come up, I still think it was the right thing to do."

"We all agreed to it, remember," said Jacobs, "so don't go blaming Ben."

"Well, mind you, I'm not blaming you, Ben," said Epstein, "but I'm inclined to think that regardless of the present situation, we acted too fast. I for one feel funny about it."

To Gorfinkle this was criticism from an unexpected source. "What is it you feel funny about, Roger?" he asked quietly.

"I feel funny about the whole deal. I feel funny about me, a new man at this temple business, firing the rabbi, who's been involved with it all his life. I feel funny about being chairman of the Ritual Committee. In a way, that's what set the whole business off, but I certainly never thought it would split the congregation. If I had, I wouldn't have let you talk me into it. Well, maybe it's not too late to repair the damage. I'm bowing out as of right now."

"Bowing out of what?" demanded Jacobs.

"I'm declining the nomination for chairman of the Ritual Committee. And I'm not waiting for you to announce it at the next board meeting. I think, considering what the nomination resulted in, I ought to tell the rabbi myself. It would be a good chance to get him behind this Defense Committee, and maybe he'll figure a way to speak to Paff and his group and pull the pieces together."

"You mean you think I ought to keep Paff as chairman? Is that your idea, Roger?" asked Gorfinkle.

"No, but I don't see why you can't get someone else, someone who's neutral. How about Wasserman?"

"Yeah, how about Wasserman?" said Brennerman.

"Well . . ."

53

They were playing halfheartedly, their minds not on the game. Quite early in the evening Irving Kallen pushed his chair back. "I've had enough," he said. "I just can't seem to get interested."

"Once around?" asked Paff.

"If you want."

Dr. Edelstein pushed back from the table, too. "What's the point, Meyer? Personally, I'd rather have a cup of coffee."

"That's easy enough," said Paff. He tilted back in his chair and called out to his wife in another room, "How about some coffee for the boys, Laura?" He gathered in the cards that were lying on the table and riffled them. "I was in Chelsea yesterday, and I bumped into this fellow I know—his brother is a rabbi, a real Orthodox type—and I happened to mention about somebody dying in a place that was going to be used for a synagogue. According to him, he didn't think that ruled it out. He said he'd ask his brother, though."

"Forget it, Meyer," said Kermit Arons. "Hillson House is out. Remember, it wasn't just somebody dying. After all, in our own temple, you remember Arthur Barron had a heart attack—was it two years ago?"

"Three years ago," said Doc Edelstein. "But he didn't die in the sanctuary. We took him to the hospital, and I pronounced him dead there."

"It doesn't make any difference. The point is that he just died. Here, you had a murder. It wouldn't make any difference if the entire Board of Rabbis pronounced it okay. For years to come that house will be known as the place where somebody was murdered. Who'll you get to join that kind of a temple? To tell the truth, I'd feel funny myself, wondering if my seat was where the kid got it."

"So where does it leave us?" asked Paff.

"I guess right back where we started from," said Kallen. He brightened. "You know, you didn't plan it that way, Meyer, I mean that we should sit tight at the last meeting, but when you come right down to it, it was a smart move. If we had actually kicked up a fuss when Gorfinkle announced the new committees, we'd have to eat crow now."

"I don't see that there's any real problem," Edelstein offered. "Irv is right. We're right back where we started from. We never made any official announcement about any new temple; we didn't walk out when the new committees were announced. We sat tight, and we can continue to sit tight."

"That's right."

"What the hell—"

"You want I should sit by and let those guys do just as they please?" demanded Paff.

"We'll still be able to oppose them on the board," said Edelstein.

"Yeah, fat lot of good that will do us where they've got a clear majority."

"You mean they're going to go ahead with calling for the rabbi's resignation at the next meeting?" asked Edelstein. "Frankly, I think that's pretty rotten after all the work he did for the kids, and—"

"What work?" asked Arons. "He got young Gorfinkle and young Jacobs to give their story to the cops. I personally think it was the right thing to do, but a lot of the parents of the other kids were pretty sore about it. I certainly don't think Gorfinkle or Jacobs were too pleased. Fortunately, they got this colored guy, but if it hadn't been for that—"

"Then you think they will go ahead with the resignation?" asked Edelstein.

"No-o," said Arons. "I'm inclined to think they'll let it rest for the time being. You see, where the case isn't settled yet and the rabbi is such good friends with the police chief, it would be kind of foolish to let him go. My guess is that they'll just wait until his contract runs out and then won't renew."

"By God, we'll make them renew!" said Paff.

"Since when are you so keen on the rabbi?" asked Arons.

"I'm not," snapped Paff. "Never was and never will be. But you're missing the point."

"What point? They're going to drop him."

"They're going to try to drop him, you mean," Paff amended.

"But they got a clear majority on the board."

"Yes," said Paff, "and there we can't beat them. But the question of dropping a rabbi who has served the congregation for six years already, who has the respect of the Gentile community—that doesn't have to be kept a strictly board matter. That's something that the whole membership is interested in. Now, I don't know how popular the rabbi is, but I know it's a lot harder to fire somebody than it is to let him stay on. Nobody likes to fire."

"So?"

"So that gives us an issue that we got a chance to win on. And if we win and the rabbi remains, we've evened up the odds, because when we oppose them, they just outvote us, but when he opposes them, he usually makes it a matter of ritual law or Jewish principle, and he sticks to it until they knuckle under."

Edelstein smiled. Kallen considered the proposition and then nodded his agreement. Arons said, "It's an idea, Meyer; it's an idea."

54

All week long the Small household had been busy with the cleaning and scrubbing and lining of shelves and cupboards that were normal preparation for the Passover week. The rabbi helped as much as possible, bringing up the rickety ladder from the basement and handing down to Miriam the stacks of Passover dishes and utensils that were kept on the topmost shelf of the cupboard for use only during the Passover week. The brunt of the work naturally fell on Miriam, and this year it was even more difficult, because Jonathan was old enough to follow her around and get in the way and continually demand attention. But finally, Saturday night, they had finished. While Miriam luxuriated on the living room couch the rabbi, followed step by step by his young son, had gone about the ritual symbolic search for the *chometz*, the crumbs of leaven left lying around on purpose to be found by candlelight, and with a feather swept onto a wooden spoon, which would be burned the next morning.

"Do you want me to take Jonathan off your hands, David?" Miriam called to him, with no real thought her offer would be accepted.

"Oh no. I always helped my father search for the *chometz* when I was a youngster. Kids like it. Do you remember where I put the candle and the—never mind, I've got them." He recited the benediction. "Blessed art Thou, O Lord . . . Who commanded us to remove the leaven," and then as his small son watched wide-eyed, by the flickering light of his candle he swept the leaven from the shelf where it had been previously placed and wrapped it in a bit of cloth and put it aside. He recited the ancient formula: "All manner of leaven that is in my possession which I have not seen or removed shall be null and accounted as the dust of the earth."

"Tomorrow," he said to Jonathan, "you can watch us burn it." And he called to his wife and asked her to get him ready for bed. Mr. Epstein was due any moment.

The rabbi shook his head. "I'm sorry, Mr. Epstein. I know you mean well, but I think you're making a serious mistake—"

"I don't understand, Rabbi. We've got to help Alan Jenkins the best way we can. We're involved. My Didi invited him, and all the kids there were our kids."

"Then why don't you force the jail?"

"That's ridiculous, Rabbi."

"Precisely. And yet that would really help him. What I'm saying is that not all well-meaning actions necessarily result in the greatest good. You tell me that you have engaged this Donohue to act for him. I've heard of him; who hasn't? And now you tell me he's going to demand a change of venue on the grounds that the young man can't get a fair trial in this community? Well, I don't want the Jewish community to go on record as doubting the good faith of the town. We have been here for some years now, and there has never been anything to suggest that. But I'll tell you what your action does suggest. It suggests that you're pretty sure that Jenkins is guilty. If he is, he should be convicted, but until all the evidence is in, I for one intend to keep an open mind."

"But this change of venue—that's just a standard tactic."

"Yes, but what you consider a standard tactic someone else might regard as an unfair tactic. That's what's wrong with your whole social action concept, if I may say so. You're not satisfied with doing what you can; you must have everyone else in the temple doing it, too. Our religion has an ethical code, a guideline for conduct, Mr. Epstein, but it is the individual who implements it according to the dictates of his conscience and his own intelligence. One person may join a picket line and another no less interested in the same cause may feel better results are to be gained through the courts or private negotiations or by making contributions. It is a matter for the individual to decide. Even in our services we pray as individuals rather than in a chorus. You can mount a campaign and make a plea for funds, but so long as a single member of the congregation opposes, you have no right to make it in the name of the temple, regardless of how big a majority you can muster on the board of directors."

"I don't understand you, David." Miriam pressed her fist against her mouth, as though to stifle harsh words of reproof. "He came to make amends. He was trying so hard to effect a reconciliation. And he's a good man."

"Of course, he's a good man. And so are Gorfinkle and the rest of them. They're all good men, or they wouldn't be so concerned about what may happen to a poor Negro that stumbled into a mess of trouble. But goodness is not enough. The people who took part in the religious wars were good men, but they killed and maimed in the tens of thousands nevertheless."

"Oh, David, you're so—so inflexible. Can't you bend a little?"

He looked at her in surprise. "I bend when I have to, and I can. But I've got to be careful not to bend so far that I'll fall over."

55

On Sundays the minyan was held at nine instead of seven thirty, as it was on weekday mornings. Although it was a lovely day and he had plenty of time to walk, the rabbi took his car. He did not go directly to the temple, but drove along the shore, stopping once or twice along the way to enjoy the sight of the waves breaking against the rocks and the gulls swooping down low over the water.

The road hugged the shore and then fell away, and he looked ahead and realized that he was approaching Hillson House. He slowed down as he came abreast of it and for a moment thought of stopping to look around. But he saw a man standing at the window of the adjoining house, talking into a telephone, so he drove on.

He arrived just in time for the service. Sundays always drew a larger crowd, because many fathers who brought their children to the Sunday school attended the minyan for lack of anything better to do while waiting to take them home. Today the short service was followed by a collation, given by one of the regular members in honor of his daughter's engagement.

They stood around, sipping their tea or coffee, munching cake and cookies, unleavened, of course, in keeping with the Passover regulation, since the holiday began that evening. Arthur Nussbaum was there, still pushing his pet project. "Look, fellows, I tell you it makes no sense to keep all that dough just sitting in a bank—"

"It's earning interest, isn't it?"

"So every year costs go up twice as much. Sooner or later, everybody knows we're going to change those seats. If we had gone ahead when the money was first left to us, we could have done half the sanctuary, right up to the center aisle. This year the money probably wouldn't cover more than a third."

"Yeah, fat chance of having some seats of one kind and the rest another. It will look terrible. The women will raise Cain."

"Let 'em. Don't you see," Nussbaum urged, "if they think it looks funny, they'll work all the harder to get the rest put in."

"Yeah? Well, if you think there was a stink about permanent seating, just wait till the first third of the sanctuary is fancied up with one kind of seat—"

The rabbi, who was standing nearby, murmured, "So why does it have to be the first third? Why not start replacing the seats from the rear?" He spotted Paff leaving the chapel and excused himself.

Nussbaum overheard the remark and repeated it to the others.

"Is he kidding?"

"That would be even worse. That would guarantee getting everyone sore."

"Not as sore as our present seats," said Dr. Edelstein. "You put padded seats in back, and you can put me down for one right now."

Irving Kallen nodded. "You may have something at that, Doc. For me I don't care. I'm well-padded, but my old man, I'd bet he'd really appreciate it."

"When you come down to it," said Nussbaum slowly, "it's only fair."

Brennerman, who was standing by, pursed his lips, then suddenly broke into a delighted roar of laughter. "By God, Nussbaum, you're right. The rabbi's come up with the perfect solution!"

They all looked at him.

"Don't you see it, boys? Front row *yicchus*, back row *tuchus*. Suit yourself!" Laughing loudly, he spotted Gorfinkle and hurried over to tell him what had happened.

The rabbi hailed Paff and led him to a side corridor. When they were a safe distance from the others, he said, "I read your statement to the police, Mr. Paff. Judging from the names of those people you listed as partners in your business deal, I suspect you were interested in Hillson House as a possible new temple."

Paff grinned. "That's right, Rabbi, but of course, it's out of the question now. We're letting the whole matter drop for the time being." He thought of something. "I was going to tell you, of course, but Becker reported that you weren't interested anyway."

"That's all right," the rabbi hastened to assure him. "I wasn't, and I'm not. My reason for questioning you is that I wanted to clarify some things in my own mind with respect to this case. You told the police that you slowed down as you approached Hillson House and then drove on. Is that correct?"

"Yes?"

"You didn't stop?"

Paff considered. "I may have stopped for a moment."

"You're quite sure you didn't stop for much longer than a moment?"

"What are you getting at, Rabbi?"

"I'm suggesting that you stopped for quite a while, perhaps fifteen or twenty minutes or even longer."

"Why do you say that?"

"Because as it stands your statement doesn't ring true. I passed Hillson House on my way over to the temple this morning. That's a straight stretch of road, no turn, nothing blocking your vision. Even in a rainstorm, long before you reached Hillson House by whichever direction you approached, you could see whether someone was waiting there or not. So there was no need for you to slow down. And since you expected to meet someone there, I suggest that you would have waited for fifteen minutes anyway."

"All right, suppose I did?"

"Then the police might wonder why you didn't bother to go inside in all that time."

"I didn't. I swear I didn't, Rabbi."

"Why not?"

His face showed resignation. "I don't really know. I've been by there any number of times, but I guess it was during the daytime, and it always looked bright and cheerful. And this night it was all dark, and it was raining, and I just didn't like the idea of going in alone."

"Then why didn't you tell the police the truth?"

"You know how it is, Rabbi. I heard that Moose had been found in there. Well, he worked for me, and I knew him. If I said I had been waiting around there for half an hour or so, they'd begin to ask me questions: Did I hear anything? Did I see anything? Why didn't I go in? No, I just didn't want to get involved."

"Well, I'd say you were involved now. If I were you, I'd go down to the police and tell them you'd like to change your statement."

"But that would mean that I was lying, and that would look suspicious."

"It will look a lot more suspicious when they find out the truth."

Paff sighed. "I suppose you're right, Rabbi."

56

When he arrived home, he found Lanigan waiting for him.

"I thought those morning prayer services of yours only last about half an hour," the chief of police complained.

"There was a collation afterward," said the rabbi, "and then I had to perform an errand of mercy; I went to visit the sick. Sorry you had to wait. Is it business or purely social?"

Lanigan grinned. "I guess it's always a little bit of both when I come visiting. I understand, Rabbi, that there's a movement afoot to set up a Jenkins Defense Committee. You know anything about it?"

"Yes, as a matter of fact, I do. Why, do you object to it?"

"Well, of course, every man has a right—yes, I object to it!" said Lanigan. "I know this man Donohue. He'll stir up a lot of trouble and maybe create an atmosphere in this town that we might be years getting over. And none of it will do Jenkins any good. It will just be a lot of propaganda about social justice and the rights of the underprivileged and Lord knows what all. And it won't have any bearing on this case, because Jenkins is going to get a fair trial, and it's got nothing to do with whether he's black, white, or green with yellow polka dots."

"I'm not sure. Are you giving him a fair shake? It seems to me that you've made up your mind that he's guilty—"

"I don't decide whether he's guilty or not. That's up to a judge and jury. But naturally I have an opinion. I've dealt fairly with him throughout. You were present when I questioned him. Did I browbeat him? I practically begged him to get a lawyer. He didn't want one."

"But when he told his story, didn't you automatically assume those parts that indicated he was guilty were true and those that suggested he might be innocent a pack of lies?"

"You've always got to choose from the available material what you'll believe and what you won't. You know that. Take Jenkins' statement that there was somebody parked right across the street for about twenty minutes—"

"That's true."

"How do you mean?"

The rabbi told of his conversation with Paff.

Lanigan strode around the room as he thought aloud. "That means Paff might have seen Jenkins enter the house and waited there to see what would happen. When Jenkins doesn't come out, he rides off? So that leaves him on the scene with transportation to return and no real alibi—" He shook his head vigorously. "No, I don't believe it, Rabbi. You wouldn't throw a member of your congregation to the wolves just like that. You must have something else in mind."

"I'm merely suggesting that there are other possibilities. You yourself suggested Gorfinkle and Jacobs. The point is that Jenkins is not the only one whose actions are suspect; besides, your case against him is full of holes."

"Like what?"

"How about the death of that man in Boston? How does Jenkins fit into that?"

"I don't say he had anything to do with that. His death and the connection with Moose—that's pure coincidence."

"Coincidences happen, but not often. But the big objection to your case against Jenkins is that the next door neighbor, this—"

"Mr. Begg?"

"Yes, Mr. Begg. He saw a light. That's what led him to call the police."

Lanigan looked puzzled for a moment, and then his face cleared. "Oh, I see what you're getting at—that someone came to the house after Jenkins left, that *he* put on the light, and that *he* presumably killed Moose—maybe your Mr. Paff. It's a good effort, Rabbi, but here's where I demolish it. Jenkins said that he drew the shades and the drapes before he put on a light. Right?"

"Right."

"And there was no reason for him to lie about something like that."

"Agreed."

"So if someone, Paff or a mysterious stranger, had put on a light, it would not have shown."

"Precisely. Then how could Begg have seen a light?"

"Huh?"

"The youngsters were all agreed that they did not put on a light.

Jenkins used a flashlight but only after he had drawn the drapes—"

"Then how could Begg have seen a light in the house?"

"That was my question," said the rabbi pointedly. "But I can suggest an answer. The only way he could have seen a light with all the windows blocked off was by having himself been in the house and put them on."

"You saying—"

"I'm saying that he entered the house after Jenkins left. Since as the caretaker he must have had a key, the locked door presented no problem. He snapped on the light on entering and then went through each of the rooms. I'm suggesting that he put the plastic sheet over the boy's head, and then, leaving the lights on as an excuse to call the police, he hurried back to his own house, where there was a phone."

"And forgot to close the front door?"

"No, left it ajar purposely, I imagine, either on the chance of the crusing car spotting it—in which case, he would not be involved even as informer—or perhaps so as not to raise any immediate question of how the murderer had got in."

Lanigan massaged his square chin with a big red hand as he checked back over the rabbi's reasoning. Then he grinned. "You had me going there for a minute, Rabbi. It all sounds plausible except"—he held up an admonishing forefinger—"that he called from his own house. On the way back, he would have noticed that there was no light coming through the windows of Hillson House, because the blinds were drawn."

The rabbi nodded. "Yes, and the phone is in a room which overlooks Hillson House. I drove by this morning and saw him at the window, phone in hand. So standing there, talking to the police, he'd certainly notice that there was no light coming from the windows of Hillson House. And the explanation is that there is where a real coincidence occurred."

"What coincidence?"

"That while he was still inside Hillson House, or just as he left, all the lights in that part of town went out."

"You mean the transformer blowing?"

"M-hm. That was the only coincidence."

"How about his happening to go over there?"

"That was no coincidence. He went right after Jenkins left *because* Jenkins left. I mean he may have seen Jenkins leave or heard him starting up his motorcycle, right next door so to speak, so he hurried over to investigate. It looked all right; the door was locked and it was dark. But, of course, he had to make sure. He had a key and went in. Naturally, he put on the lights. Maybe he listened for a moment or called out.

Then he went for a look around and found Moose. Since he wanted the body found immediately, that very night—"

"Why did it have to be that night?"

"Because if he waited a day or two, he himself would have to find the body—he was the caretaker. This way, it would be the police who would find the body, and if they came that night, they would see fresh evidence of someone having been there—cigarette butts, beer cans."

Lanigan smiled. "Nice work, Rabbi. I'll add Begg to my list of Jenkins, Paff, Carter, and seven assorted kids. While chewing the fat with Eban Jennings, my lieutenant, I made as good a case against each of those others. But, of course, they all have flaws. For instance, Begg couldn't have known that Moose was in Hillson House, now could he?"

The rabbi shook his head.

"So if he had some reason for killing Moose, which you haven't bothered to mention, by the way, how would he have known to go in there? The normal thing, if he thought someone had broken into the place, was to call the police and ask them to check."

"I suppose because he had to go there. Before calling the police, he had to make sure that nothing had been taken."

"Like what?"

"Like marihuana. He'd be more likely to cache it there than keep it in his own house."

"But Mr. Begg? A pusher? Oh, that's impossible, Rabbi." His face showed utter incredulity. "He's an old-time resident of the town, a crusty Yankee."

The rabbi's grin was derisive. "And former teacher and former selectman who couldn't do anything wrong. It must be an outsider, a stranger."

"All right, I suppose I deserve that," said Lanigan, "but what I really meant is that—that he's a cantankerous sort of man who's always in our hair. If he were engaged in something like pot peddling, he wouldn't be calling attention to himself."

The rabbi shrugged off the argument. "Protective coloration. It evidently worked better than to try to be unobtrusive, especially in a small town like this. He always had the reputation of being a crank, so he went on being one when he began selling this stuff. It was safer than suddenly changing his image."

Lanigan was silent, then he said quietly, "What made you think of him? Did you work this out by this Talmudic pil—whatever it is?"

"Pilpul? Not at all. I thought of Begg because he was the most obvious suspect. You would have seen it, too, if you weren't conditioned to focus first and foremost on the outsider, the stranger, Alan Jenkins, who was not only from outside the town, but also colored."

"But Begg is a kind of outsider. He's a kind of recluse and a nut."

"Not at all. He's eccentric but well within the acceptable. He's even traditional—the hard-headed, cantankerous Yankee who sticks up for his rights."

"But what did he do that made you suspect him?"

"For one thing, he runs a place where youngsters hang out. He sells soda and some school supplies and lets them play the pinball machines. You've seen the place. What is there in that that makes it possible for him to even pay the rent? For another, Moose came from his house. He had to, because the tide was in and he couldn't have come from farther along the beach. And then when the youngsters were breaking into the house and they were worried that they might be seen by someone next door, remember it was Moose who assured them that Begg wouldn't bother them. Begg, a known crank and buttinsky. How could he possibly know that? Only if he knew Begg was going to leave. They probably left at the same time. And finally, I began thinking of Begg because it seemed odd that he should call to report he had seen a light. Unless he were a timid man, I would have assumed that he would first have investigated himself or at least reconnoitered."

"Then, according to you, there's a cache of marihuana in Hillson House."

The rabbi shook his head. "There was. I assume he removed it before calling the police. That's why he had to go there. And by this time, he wouldn't have it in his own house either."

"You realize, of course," said Lanigan, "that there isn't a particle of evidence against him. If we find his fingerprints in Hillson House, he says he's been there many times as caretaker."

"You might ask him about seeing the light."

Once again Lanigan got up to stride around the room. "That's not evidence. He has only to insist that he either saw it or thought he saw it. No jury would convict a man for saying he saw a light that he couldn't have seen. They'd assume a natural mistake, the headlight of a car, the reflection of a streetlamp. No, it's a pity we can't introduce this pilpul of yours as legal evidence."

"We could try."

Lanigan hitched his chair up and said eagerly, "For instance?"

"Well, this man in Boston who was murdered the same day. We might think about him for a while to good effect."

"Wilcox?"

"Yes, Wilcox. We know Moose went to see him because of the two twenty-dollar bills."

"And the marihuana."

"Marihuana he could have got from any number of sources, but two twenty-dollar bills whose serial numbers ran consecutive with those Wilcox had—those could have come only from Wilcox."

"All right."

"How did Moose get them?" asked the rabbi.

"What do you mean?"

"He could have taken them, or they could have been given to him."

"Oh, I see. Well, obviously they were given to him, because if he had taken them, why stop at just two?"

"Precisely. Now why were they given to him? Two of them, mind you."

"We can't know that, Rabbi."

"Let me put it another way. Suppose in the course of conversation Moose had mentioned that he was broke. Conceivably, Wilcox might have been willing to lend him some to tide him over. Normally, that would mean a dollar or two, or five dollars, or even ten. But if he had nothing smaller on him at the time than twenties, he might have given him one of those. But he gave him two twenties—forty dollars. What does that suggest?"

Lanigan shook his head. "I pass."

"It suggests payment for something. But since Moose was broke and had nothing Wilcox could want, it suggests some sort of payment in advance."

"For what?"

"We can't be certain, of course, but didn't you say this Wilcox was connected with the drug traffic?"

"The Boston police are sure he was a dealer."

"All right, and since you also found a rather sizable quantity of the marihuana on Moose, and Jenkins admits having taken ten cigarettes from him, I suggest this was either an advance on salary or on commissions on sales. Mrs. Carter said that Moose had gone to Boston for a job. I think he got it."

"Yeah, could be. Could be he was setting him up in business. All right, I'll buy that. What's the connection with his death? And with Begg?"

"We haven't finished with Moose's activities," said the rabbi reproachfully.

"Why, what did he do then?"

"He came back to Barnard's Crossing and went directly to see Mr. Begg."

"Any more on Moose?"

The rabbi shook his head. "I didn't know the young man. I can only speculate that the description of his behavior at the cookout, his drinking and carrying on there and again at the Hillson House, suggests he was euphoric. And when you add in the fact he neglected to go home to dinner, which was a serious offense in the Carter household, it indicates he no longer had reason to fear his father."

"And Begg?" Lanigan asked sarcastically. "Do you know what he did? Where he went after he left Moose?"

"I'm afraid it would be pure speculation," said the rabbi primly.

"I see. Well, why stop now? Go ahead and speculate."

"Very well, I imagine he went to see Wilcox. The fact that Moose came to see Begg directly after leaving a narcotics dealer who had just set him up in business suggests that Begg was another agent of Wilcox, or a partner. If he were an agent, he certainly would have objected to anyone sharing the territory, Moose particularly. And if he were a partner, he may have gone to protest an injudicious appointment."

Lanigan sat back and stared at the rabbi in silence. Finally he said, "I don't suppose you'd care to amplify that with a fact or two, would you? Or did you mention something I happened to overlook?"

The rabbi grinned good-naturedly. "I said it was pure speculation, but if we consider it from the other end, it may seem more reasonable. For example, it gives us the first real motive for killing Moose. When Begg left his house, Moose knew where Begg was going, and when he heard of the death of Wilcox, he would know who did it."

Lanigan stared at the rabbi in silence. Finally he said, "So now you've got Begg killing Wilcox, too."

"It adds up."

"And proof?"

"Perhaps fingerprints, Begg's, in Wilcox's apartment?"

Lanigan shook his head. "Not after a week, with cops all over the place."

"Just a minute. Didn't you say some woman had seen him?"

"Madelaine Spinney. The Boston police thought they had something when she recognized Moose from a photograph they got from the files of the Boston papers. It's a different size than rogue's gallery pictures. That's probably why she picked it; it was different. From what they say, I doubt if she'd be able to identify your man. She's not very bright."

"Maybe he would identify her," suggested the rabbi.

57

"His car is in the driveway? . . . Good, then he's home."

"Now, how do you want us to work it, Chief?" asked the Boston detective.

"Just drive along, and when you come to the house, stop," said Lanigan. "Keep your motor running, just as you would if you stopped to ask someone for directions. Madelaine will get out. The house will be on her side. Keep your coat buttoned and push the collar up, Madelaine. That's fine. Put your head down a little. That's right. Then you just go up and ring the bell. When the door opens and he answers, you let him get a good look at you and ask how to get onto the road to Boston. Nothing to be afraid of. The worst he can do is slam the door in your face." He turned to the policeman. "You just sit tight unless you see something unusual."

"Like what?"

"Like anything different from the way a man normally would behave if somebody asked him directions. We'll be behind you, but we'll keep out of sight. If we see you get out of the car, we'll come a-running. All right?"

"Check."

The two cars began to move, Madelaine Spinney and the policeman from Boston in one, Lanigan and Jennings in the other. When they reached Tarlow's Point, the woman got out and walked up to Begg's house. She rang the bell, and a moment later the door was thrown open. "Yes?"

As instructed, she raised her head from her coat collar. The two stared at each other.

"You!"

The policeman moved rapidly toward the house.

58

It was late in the afternoon, and Miriam watched with some concern as her husband paced the floor. Every now and then, he would pick up a book and try to read, only to put it aside and resume his pacing.

"Don't you think you ought to go over to the temple, David, just to see if everything is all right?"

"No, I'm staying home until I hear from Lanigan. Somebody will be there to check, the cantor or Brooks or maybe Mr. Wasserman."

Whenever the phone rang, he ran to it. Most of the calls were indeed for him, but he answered as briefly as possible, fearful that Lanigan might be trying to reach him. Finally, when it was almost time to go to the temple to begin the seder, Lanigan called. The rabbi listened for a moment and then smiled. "Thank you," he said, "and thank you for calling me."

"Is it all right?" Miriam asked when he hung up. "Can we go now?"

"Yes, we can go now."

The baby-sitter had been there for half an hour, waiting for them to leave so that she could turn on the TV. Miriam gave her some last-minute instructions and went out to the car. When the rabbi came out a minute later, she saw that he was carrying the tape recorder he used to dictate letters, presumably so that he could tape the proceedings. She was mildly amused at his sudden sentimentality.

When they arrived at the temple, the members were still milling around, looking for place cards, talking, trying to shift from the table they had been assigned to another where their friends were. The tables looked festive, with snowy white tablecloths and gleaming silver, and the long head table had a magnificent floral centerpiece. Drawn up to

the head table were armchairs, each with a pillow to lean on in
accordance with the prescribed ritual, and beside each armchair, ordinary chairs for the wives. In front of the rabbi's place were the required
three matsoth covered with a napkin and the seder plate, with its egg,
shank bone, bitter herbs, green herbs, and its two little dishes, one for
horseradish and the other for the mixture of chopped nuts and apple.

Those at the head table were already seated, and before taking his
place, the rabbi went to each one for the customary greeting and handshake.

"In good voice, Cantor?"

"Fine, Rabbi."

Mr. Wasserman looked old and frail swallowed up in the huge armchair reserved for the chairman of the Ritual Committee. He clasped
the rabbi's hand with both of his.

"Always I like to have the seder in my own house, but this year my
children couldn't come. And besides, sometimes for the good of everybody . . ."

Gorfinkle had been covertly watching the rabbi's progress down the
line. When he approached him, he rose and formally offered his hand.

"Stu planning to go back to school tomorrow?"

Gorfinkle shrugged. "He was hoping to, but I haven't heard from
Lanigan yet. Maybe he'll call tonight."

"It's all right. He can go."

"And the others?" asked Gorfinkle eagerly.

"They too."

Emotion welled up into Gorfinkle's eyes. "That's wonderful, Rabbi,
just wonderful. I don't know how we can ever thank you."

The rabbi circled the table and took his seat. He looked out across
the crowded room and waited for the last person to find his seat.

When he saw that the waiters had filled all the wineglasses, he
nodded to the cantor, who rose and, holding his glass high, began to
chant the benediction over the wine.

The men at the head table left the room for the ritual washing of
hands, and when they returned, the rabbi dipped a sprig of parsley in
a dish of salt water and recited the benediction over the fruits of the
earth.

He uncovered the matzoh and, removing the egg and the shank bone
from the plate, passed it to Mr. Wasserman, who recited the *Holach-
manya*, "Lo! this is the bread of affliction which our ancestors ate in the
land of Egypt; let all those who are hungry enter and eat thereof; and
all who are in need come and celebrate the Passover . . ."

Once again the wineglasses were filled, and the rabbi nodded to the principal, who was seated at one of the round tables with the family of the youngster who was to ask the Four Questions. Morton Brooks whispered to the child, who stood up and in a childish treble began to recite: "*Ma nishtana halayla hazzeh* . . ."

When the child finished, the rabbi placed on the table in front of him the tape recorder he had kept on the floor beside his chair. "The English translation was to have been given by Arlene Feldberg," he announced, "but unfortunately, Arlene came down with the measles. However, we wouldn't want her to miss her portion." He pressed the switch—but it was his own voice that came through the machine, saying, "Sincerely yours. Make an extra copy, will you, Miriam?" This was followed immediately by the thin, reedy voice of the little girl: "Wherefore is this night distinguished from all other nights?" Weeks of coaching by the principal were reflected in the slow, stilted reading of the lines. "All other nights we may eat either leavened or unleavened bread, but tonight only unleavened."

The rabbi looked down at Miriam. "You see," he whispered, "I *can* bend a little."

"And it works," she whispered back.

"Why may we eat only bitter herbs . . . dip our food twice . . . eat while leaning?" Mr. Wasserman plucked at the rabbi's sleeve, and he leaned over to hear what the old man was saying. The tape recorder whirred on. ". . . beg off from that dinner, will you, Miriam. Fib a little if you have to." It was the rabbi's voice.

There was a roar of laughter from the assembled company, and Miriam hastily reached forward and shut off the machine. The rabbi blushed and said, "We will now read in unison . . ."

Dinner was served, a traditional festive meal, beginning with gefillte fish and chicken soup. As soon as it was over, a number left, pleading that their children were tired and falling asleep at the table, but most stayed on for the rest of the service with its prayers, benedictions and ceremonial songs. At last the fourth cup of wine was drunk, and the president announced, "The order of the Passover is now accomplished and prescribed according to all its laws and customs . . ." and then all called out in loud and joyous voices the traditional fervent hope expressed for centuries by Jews all over the world at the end of the Passover service: "Next year in Jerusalem."

The rabbi leaned over and whispered to Miriam, "Why not?"

"What?"

"The way things look, we'll be free next year. Why not spend it in Jerusalem?"

59

"You've heard the minutes of the previous meeting. Any corrections or additions? Chair recognizes Mr. Sokolow."

"Seems to me we spent most of the meeting arguing about a new contract for the rabbi, but there wasn't a word of it in the minutes."

"You left early, Harry," said Gorfinkle. "It was decided not to mention it in the minutes for obvious reasons. What if the rabbi were here today? It might be embarrassing."

"Well, so how do I know what happened?"

"I appointed a committee with Al Becker as chairman—maybe you'd like to fill him in, Al."

"Sure," Becker got up and walked to the head of the table. "We discussed mostly the terms of the contract. Some of the guys thought we ought to just make it for another five years, with a raise, of course. But there was a lot of sentiment for a lifetime contract, too. For that we'd have to discuss it with the rabbi himself."

"So how'd you make out with the rabbi?" asked Harry Sokolow.

"Well, we decided not to speak to him just yet," said Becker. "See, something came up that I think we ought to hash out first." He cleared his throat. "At the end of this year, as many around this table may not realize, the rabbi will be rounding out his sixth year with us. So the new contract will be starting the seventh year. Well, a lot of congregations give their rabbi the seventh year as a sabbatical. So we on the committee didn't want to get caught short if the rabbi raises that question without knowing beforehand the pleasure of this board. Speaking for myself, I'm all for offering it to him even before he asks."

Immediately there was a storm of discussion.

"Plenty of temples don't give sabbaticals."

"In my brother's place they gave their rabbi a sabbatical last year, sure, but he had been there twenty years already."

"Teachers get them."

"Yeah, but only if they're going to do some special study."

"My wife tells me she heard the *rebbitzin* say they wanted to go to Israel. That seems a reasonable project for a sabbatical for a rabbi."

"What does he need it for? After all, he gets the whole summer off. I should be so lucky."

Mr. Wasserman was recognized. "The seventh year is a special time. It's like the Sabbath year. What is the Sabbath? It's something we invented, no? Six days you work, and on the seventh day you rest. Used to be people worked the whole seven days. So it's ours—an invention. And the whole world accepted it—you should take one day in the week a rest. The only one who doesn't get a rest one day in seven is the rabbi. On the Sabbath, when we get off, he works. And on the days we work he works, too. He's a scholar, our rabbi, so that every day he's at his studies. And when he's not studying, he's called different places to speak, or he goes to committees. And all the time, seven days a week, he's still got the congregation. One day a Bar Mitzvah, the next day a wedding or, God forbid, a funeral. So the only way he can have a rest is if he goes away from the congregation and the community for a while where he won't have to give sermons or be on committees or have to answer all kinds of questions. So I say, we should offer him this Sabbath if he asks for it, because I tell you the rabbi needs a rest sometimes from his congregation."

No one said anything, and then Paff muttered something in his deep bass to Doc Edelstein.

"What's that?" Gorfinkle looked up. "Did you say something, Mr. Paff?"

Paff raised his big voice and said, "All I said was that goes double—sometimes the congregation needs a rest from the rabbi."

Brennerman laughed. Edelstein chuckled. Jacobs guffawed. Then they all laughed and kept on laughing. And Gorfinkle said, "You may have something there, Meyer. By God, I think this time you really hit the nail on the head."